WHEREVER
SHE GOES

WHEREVER

SHE

GOES

K.L. ARMSTRONG

DOUBLEDAY CANADA

Doubleday Canada and colophon are registered trademarks of Penguin Random House Canada Limited

Library and Archives Canada Cataloguing in Publication data is avaailable upon request

ISBN 978-0-385-69364-6 (softcover)
ISBN 978-0-385-69365-3 (EPUB)
ISBN 978-0-385-69468-1 (HC)

This book is a work of fiction. Names, characters, places and incidents are products of the author's imagination or are used fictitiously. Any resemblance to actual events or locales or persons, living or dead, is entirely coincidental.

Cover design: Terri Nimmo
Cover art: playground © Dragasanu/ Shutterstock; © Karina Vegas/Arcangel

Printed and bound in Canada

Published in Canada by Doubleday Canada,
a division of Penguin Random House Canada Limited

www.penguinrandomhouse.ca

10 9 8 7 6 5 4 3 2 1

Penguin
Random House
DOUBLEDAY CANADA

For Jeff

ONE

I have made mistakes in my life. Mistakes that should loom over this one like skyscrapers. But this one feels the biggest.

This one hurts the most.

I lie in bed, massaging the old bullet wound in my shoulder as I try not to think of what used to happen when I woke in pain. One of those tiny things that seemed such an ordinary part of an ordinary life, and now I realize that it hadn't been ordinary at all.

I used to wake like this, my shoulder aching, heart racing from nightmare, huddled in bed, trying to be quiet so I didn't wake Paul. He'd still stir, as if he sensed me waking. He'd reach for me with one hand, his glasses with the other, and I'd hear the clatter of them on the nightstand, never quite where he expected them to be.

"Aubrey? You okay?"

"Just a nightmare."

"The car accident?"

I'd murmur something as guilt stabbed through me. The car accident. Yet another lie I'd told.

"Do you want to talk about it?"

"No, I'm fine."

The memory flutters off in his sigh, and I want to chase it. Go back there.

No, I want to go back to the beginning, before "Will you take this man," before Charlotte. Back to the first time a nightmare woke me beside Paul, and he asked if I wanted to talk about it, and this time I will say, "Yes. I need to tell you the truth."

It's too late for that.

It'd been too late from the first moment I dodged a question, hinted at a falsehood; I placed my foot on a path from which I could not turn back. Those lies, though, hadn't ended our marriage. I almost wished they had—that I had confessed my past and our marriage had imploded in spectacular fashion.

The truth was much simpler: water wearing down rock, the insidious erosion of secrets untold. All the things I should have said from the start, but the longer it went on, the more I *couldn't* say them. A vicious cycle that pushed us further apart with each revolution.

Pushed us apart? No, that implies action and forethought. In the end, I'd felt like we were on rafts in a lazy river, Paul drifting away, me madly paddling to stay close, telling myself he just didn't realize he was floating away from me and then . . .

Well, there comes a moment when you can't keep pretending that your partner doesn't notice the drift. It had gone on too long, my floundering too obvious, his unhappiness too obvious.

I'm going to take Charlie to the company ball game. Give us some daddy-daughter time while you enjoy an afternoon alone.

I can't go away this weekend after all. I'm in court Monday, and I need to prep. We'll do it another time. Maybe in the fall.

I think we should stop trying to have another baby, Bree.

Even the ending had been so . . . empty. I told Paul that I

could tell he wasn't happy, and it was better for Charlotte if we realized our mistake now. I said the words, and I waited for him to wake up. To snap out of it and say, "What are you talking about? I *am* happy."

He did not say that. He just nodded. He just agreed.

So I set Paul free. I took nothing from him. It was all his, and I left it behind. He asked only one thing of me—that I leave Charlotte, too. Temporarily. Leave her in her home, in the life she knew. We would co-parent, but she would live with him until I was settled and we could agree on a long-term arrangement.

I agreed.

The mature and responsible decision.

The naive and unbelievably stupid decision.

TWO

As I hang from the exercise rings, two women turn to stare. I could tell myself they're wowed by my enviable upper-body strength, but their expressions are far less complimentary. That may have something to do with the fact that the rings are in a playground, and I'm dangling from them, knees pulled up so I don't scrape the ground.

It's Sunday. The end of my weekend with Charlotte. It's been six months since Paul and I split, and he's still not ready to discuss joint custody. I've begun to realize he never will be ready. I'm going to have to push him—with divorce proceedings and a custody battle. I'm not ready for that fight yet. But I'm getting there.

As I dangle from the rings, Charlotte hangs in front of me. "Ten, eight, nine, seven . . ."

"You keep going," I say.

"No! Mommy stay! Three, two—"

I drop onto my butt, and Charlotte lets out a squeal of laughter, her chubby legs kicking so hard one sneaker flies off.

Then she lets go. I catch her, and she giggles, wrenches out of my arms and tears off.

"Charlie, wait!"

As I race after her, scooping up her abandoned shoe, I hear the women behind me.

"Recapturing her lost childhood?"

"I'm not sure she ever left it. Look at her."

I let Charlotte braid my hair this morning, the result being exactly what you expect from a three-year-old, complete with crooked plastic barrettes. She also picked out my shirt, a ragged Minnie Mouse tee I only keep because she loves it. I brought a jacket for camouflage, but I'd discarded that when the blazing sun heated up a cool May day, with only a hint of Chicago's legendary winds blowing into our suburban city.

As I'm trying to remember where I left my jacket, Charlotte runs for the slide. I take off after her, and I help her onto the rungs. Then I climb behind her, mostly because it's the only way I can ensure she doesn't fall off the top or slide down backward. I sense eyes on me, I see bemused head shakes, and I feel the prickle of embarrassment.

I don't know how other parents do it. I honestly do not. They sit. They chat. They answer emails. They read books. And somehow, their children survive.

Motherhood does not come naturally to me. My own mother died when I was very young, and my father never remarried. I grew up on a string of army bases, cared for by whoever happened to be available. So when Paul and I decided to have a baby, I knew I needed to prepare. I did—with endless classes and books. Then Charlotte came along, and I felt as if I'd walked into a math exam after cramming for history.

When I used to confess my fears to Paul, he'd hug me and say, "You're doing awesome, Bree. Your daughter is bright and happy and healthy. What more could you want?"

What more could I want? To feel like *I'd* achieved that. Not like Charlotte managed to be all that in spite of me. Because of Paul.

Now I'm damned sure that when it comes time for a court to decide custody, Paul is not going to tell the judge that I'm "doing awesome."

So no more floundering. No more muddling through. No more being the "quirky" parent. I must be the most normal mom possible. That means I need to learn how.

Observe and assimilate.

When we head to the swings, I try to just stand behind Charlotte and push her, like other parents. That isn't what she wants, though. She wants me to swing beside her and see who can go highest.

Paul doesn't swing with Charlotte or climb the slide or hang from the rings. The very image makes me smile. Nor, however, would he be on a bench reading the paper or checking his phone. He stands close, keeping a watchful eye, ready to jump in if she needs him. And that's fine with Charlotte, who never asks or expects him to join in. Joining in is for Mommy.

I remember when I'd bring her back from the park with grass-stained knees and dirt-streaked face and hair that looked as if she stepped out of a wind tunnel.

"Someone had fun today," Paul would say.

"She skinned her knee again. I'm sorry. I don't know how that happens."

He laughs. "Because she's a little cyclone when she's with you. She knows Daddy can't keep up." He swings her into his arms. "Did you have fun, sweetheart?" he asks, as they walk away, Charlotte babbling a mile a minute.

If I fretted later, he'd say, "She had fun. That's what matters, Bree. Skinned knees heal. It's good to see her active."

Does he still think that? Or does he remember those skinned knees and see them as a sign that I hadn't watched our daughter closely enough?

"Mommy, jump!"

I react without thinking, swinging high and then jumping. I hit the ground in a crouch, and as I bounce to my feet, her gales of laughter ring out.

"Mommy, catch!"

Again, I turn on autopilot, my arms fly up as Charlotte launches herself from the swing.

I do catch her.

I always do.

Always, always, always.

This is what I want to be for you, baby. The mother who will always catch you. The mother who knows what dangers you face, and will be there to stop them. To fix the problems, even when I cause them myself.

"Is it time for tea?" I ask as I set her on the ground.

"Yes!"

As we drink our apple juice and munch cookies, I watch the parents in the playground, analyzing how far they let their kids run without giving chase, what they allow their children to do without interfering.

I gaze longingly at the groups of chatting parents. As much as I love playing with my child, I feel like I should be *there,* getting the support and answers I need. I've done all the things that parenting blogs recommend for meeting others—*join mom-tot groups, hang around at the playground, just put yourself out there!*—but I always feel like I used to when I switched schools midterm. The cliques had already formed, those doors slammed shut.

When I first had Charlotte, I tried joining the suburban mommies in our neighborhood, but their life experience was a million miles from mine. They seemed to sense my "otherness," like a bevy of swans with a goose intent on sneaking into their ranks. As invitations to playdates dried up—and my own were refused—I saw myself condemning Charlotte to the same kind of life. An outsider by association.

That changed after I left. Apparently, the mommies who

didn't have time for me had plenty of it for my poor abandoned child and her doting single daddy.

As I gaze across the playground, I notice another woman by herself. She's with a little boy near a patch of forest, maybe twenty feet away. They're playing a hiding game, where one of them tucks away a small object and the other finds it.

At first, I think the woman must be a sitter or older sister. I'm thirty, and she looks nearly a decade younger, the boy maybe five. But then he gives a delighted shriek, saying, "Found it, Mama! That was a good spot."

They both seem to be enjoying the game, and I take note. Charlotte would love it, and it's definitely a more dignified way of playing with my child.

Speaking of dignity, when we finish our tea, Charlotte wants to do cartwheels. I try to just help her, but she insists I demonstrate. I do a double, ending up by the woods, and as I thump down, the little boy says, "Whoa, did you see that, Mama?"

"Very cool," his mother says, with a careful smile. "You must have been a cheerleader."

I laugh. "Not exactly. But thanks."

"Can you do that, Mama?" her son asks.

Now it's her turn to laugh, relaxing as she squeezes his shoulder. "I could when I was your age. Not since then, though. I was *definitely* not a cheerleader."

She passes me a smile, and there's a spark of connection as we both look over at a gaggle of suburban mommies, as if to say *they* were probably cheerleaders, but not us. Never us.

She isn't much older than I first thought. Maybe twenty-three. Slender with a blond ponytail and no makeup except for thick black eyeliner. Is that eyeliner a remnant of another life? She wears long sleeves, but one is pushed up, showing what looks like the ghosts of old track marks. Dark circles underscore her eyes, and there's a strained, distant look in them, as if she's exhausted by the stresses of what might be single motherhood, given the lack of a wedding band.

"You do car-wheel," Charlotte says to the woman. "Mommy show."

The woman smiles. "Not me, hon. My body doesn't do that anymore."

"Can I try?" her son asks.

"I show!" Charlotte says.

We stand and watch Charlotte try to instruct the boy in a proper cartwheel while I give pointers. I tread a fine line here. I don't want to seem like the new girl at school, puppy-eager for attention, even if that's how I feel. I glance at the other woman, and then I look at the poised suburban mommies on the benches, and it doesn't matter if I'd been one of them six months ago. I'm not anymore and, really, I never was, even when I wore the title.

I see this young woman, with her old needle scars and her worn jeans and her shabby sneakers and the way her face glows every time her gaze lights on her son, and she's the mother I connect to.

Still I am careful. Years of new-kid-in-class life has taught me how to tread this line. Snatches of conversation mixed with quips and laughs as I show her son how to do a cartwheel.

I'm holding up his legs when her phone rings. She looks down at the screen and blanches. Then she murmurs, "Sorry, I have to get this."

She steps away to take the call. I can't tell what she's saying—she isn't speaking English—but her tone tells me enough, rising from anger to alarm.

She keeps moving away, lowering her voice while keeping her gaze on her son.

Finally I bend in front of the boy and say, "We should go, so your mom can finish her call. Tell her we said goodbye. It was very nice meeting you, and I hope to see you both again."

When I extend a hand, his thin face lights up in a smile. He shakes my hand vigorously, with a mature "Nice meeting you, too."

Charlotte shakes his hand as she giggles a goodbye. Then we quickly gather our things and leave.

THREE

Two days later, I'm taking my usual lunchtime jog in the park where I played with Charlotte on Sunday. After a couple of laps, I slow near the playground and circle to a forlorn bench, too far from the equipment to be of any use to watchful parents.

I put up my leg and begin stretching. As I do, I tug out my earbuds so I can listen to three mothers sitting nearby.

Eavesdrop. Spy. Learn.

As I stretch, a middle-aged jogger pulls over to do the same, sharing my bench. I keep my attention on the lesson unfolding ahead.

I contemplate the trio of moms. They don't seem to be watching their children at all, engrossed as they are in the scandal of another parent who let her child play with an iPad. Is that a problem? I have several educational apps on my phone, and Charlotte and I play them together. I *thought* that was a good thing, but—

A child shrieks. I wheel to see two kids fighting over the slide. As I peer around for the parents, the kids work it out on their own, and I suppose that's the way to handle it—watch and see if they can resolve it before interfering.

The war for the slide ends, but it calls my attention to a boy swinging by himself. It looks like the boy from Sunday, the one we'd shown how to do cartwheels. I squint. Yes, that's definitely him. His mom is nowhere in sight.

The boy jumps off the swing and starts gazing around. Then he heads for the path. Leaving the safety of the playground. I look around anxiously, hoping Mom will notice.

"You're doing your quadriceps stretches wrong."

I jump and glance over to see the middle-aged guy who took up stretching at my bench.

"You want to do them like this," he says, and proceeds to demonstrate . . . with a hamstring stretch.

I know better than to point out his mistake, so I murmur a thank-you and glance back at the boy.

He's still walking. Getting farther from the equipment, with no sign of anyone giving chase. So I do.

I stay at a slow jog, no panic, just keeping an eye on the child. Mom will notice. Mom will come after him, and she doesn't need me making her feel like she's failed her parental duties. So I stay back, subtly watchful.

"You hit the ground a little hard."

The middle-aged guy jogs up beside me.

"You have really good form," he says, "but you're hitting the ground too hard. You'll injure your knees. I've seen you before—we run at about the same time—and I thought I should mention it."

Don't get distracted. Remember the boy.

I turn my attention back. The child's gone.

Damn it, *no.* Where—

He appears, walking out from behind a trash can. That's a relief. The not-such-a-relief part? He's heading straight for the parking lot.

Where *is* his mother?

It doesn't matter. As much as I hate to embarrass another parent, that's a busy lot with an even busier thoroughfare beside it.

I kick my jog up to a run.

"You could just say no thanks," the guy shouts after me, and then mutters, "Bitch," under his breath.

Aubrey Finch, making friends wherever she goes.

Forget him. The important thing is the boy, and in that moment of distraction, I've lost sight of him again.

Tires screech, and my chest seizes as I look about wildly. A vehicle has slammed on its brakes in the parking lot, and I can just make out a roof rack over the sea of parked vehicles.

I spot the boy. He's still at the edge of the lot, standing on his tiptoes, as if looking for the source of the screeching tires.

A voice calls from the direction of the vehicle. It's a single word, but I can't make it out. The boy hears, though, and starts running toward it.

Seeing him dash into that jammed parking lot, I cringe and have to chomp down on a shout of warning. Fortunately, the lot is silent except for the rumble of what I can now see is a big SUV.

Mom must have gone to fetch the car, unable to find a spot in the lot. She's told him he could swing for a few more minutes while she brought the car around. Not the choice I'd make but—

A sharp boyish yelp of surprise. Then, "No!"

I burst into a run as a man's low voice says, "Get in," and "Stop that."

The boy shouts, "No! Let me go!" Then he screams "Mama!" at the top of his lungs as I run full out.

A door slams shut, muffling the boy's cries.

An engine revs.

I grit my teeth and will my body to go faster, just a little faster, damn it.

The SUV takes off, speeding through the lot, and all I see is that damned roof rack.

Faster! Harder! I hear my father's bark. *Dig deeper. Work harder. You can do better, Bree.*

You can always do better.

The SUV has stopped at the roadway, engine idling as it waits for a break in the heavy traffic. If I can just get past the next row of cars, I'll be able to get a plate number.

I jog across the lane. A solid flow of traffic still blocks the exit. I can do this. Twenty feet more, and I'll have a clear sight line to the SUV, and there is no way it can pull away before that.

Get my phone out to snap pictures. Even if I can't see the license plate, I can enhance the photo.

The SUV is just ahead. I lift my phone while fumbling to turn on the camera. It's fine. Steady traffic. I have time. I—

A horn blasts. A long, solid blast.

Tires squeal.

The SUV cuts into traffic and roars off.

I race toward the road. No time for a photo. Just get a look at the license. The SUV is pulling away, the rear bumper visible, the license . . .

The license plate is mud-splattered and unreadable.

The vehicle then. Stop squinting at the plate, and get the vehicle make and model—

The SUV cuts into the next lane before I can see the emblem. It's a large SUV. Dark blue . . . or black . . .

Not good enough. Not good enough at all.

I keep going, but the SUV is already at the next light, turning left and . . .

And it's gone.

I inhale and look down, feeling the weight of the cell phone in my hand.

Uh, yes. Cell phone?

I hit numbers as I head back toward the park.

"Nine-one-one, what's your emergency?"

"Kidnap—" I struggle for breath, like I've run a marathon. "Kidnapping. I witnessed a kidnapping."

"Slow down, ma'am, and repeat that please?"

"I just witnessed a kidnapping. I saw a boy pulled into a car—an SUV. A dark-colored SUV on . . ." *Street. What is the street?* "On Cliff View. Near Grant Park. The children's playground. There's a parking lot off Cliff View into Grant Park, right next to the playground. It happened there. Just now."

"You witnessed a young man—"

"Boy, child, maybe four or five years old."

"A child being pulled into a dark SUV in the parking lot . . ."

The dispatcher continues rhyming off the information, and I want to shout, *Yes, yes to all of that, now just get someone here.*

When the woman finishes, I say, calmly, "Yes, that's right. Please hurry. They just left."

"I've already dispatched a car, ma'am. Can you remain on the scene, please?"

"I'll be here. In the playground. I know what his mom looks like. I'm going to find her. You can reach me at this number or just tell the officers I'm wearing a gray sweat suit, and I have a dark brown ponytail. My name is Aubrey Finch."

The dispatcher signs off, and I'm on the move again.

I pass two mothers leaving with children and I can't help wishing they could have been five minutes sooner, extra witnesses who might have seen more.

Someone *must* have seen more. There will be a CCTV camera or a street passerby or maybe even that guy who pestered me about my "form"—he can't have gone far.

Someone will have seen something.

I reach the playground and scan it for the boy's mother, expecting to see her anxiously searching. She must have turned her back, maybe talking to another parent or engrossed in a book.

It only takes a moment.

Just last month, in the mall, I let go of Charlotte's hand to adjust my shopping bag, and she disappeared. It only took two seconds to spot her dark curls bobbing toward the pet shop, but even as I raced toward her, I imagined showing up at Paul's doorstep and saying, "I lost her."

I lost our baby.

Now I am about to inflict that hell on another woman.

I saw your baby get taken. I know, you only looked away for a moment.

But it only takes a moment.

I can't see the boy's mother. The playground is even busier now. I spot a blond woman reading a book and take a step her way, only to have her look up and reveal the face of a grandmother.

Another blond woman stands at the side, but she has a baby carriage.

Another blonde, heavyset and tending to a girl Charlotte's age.

I spin, skimming faces as they blur before me.

"Are you okay?" a voice asks.

I look into the concerned face of a young dad. I nod and walk away, searching the crowd.

Then I spot her. Off to the far side by that patch of forest, a woman with a blond ponytail hurries from tree to tree as she calls for a child.

As I jog over, I rehearse what I'll say.

Should I be the one to do it? The police will be here any second.

No, I'm a fellow mom, and we've met, if briefly. The news should come from me.

I take a deep breath and walk up behind the increasingly frantic woman. I open my mouth and—

"Found me!" a little girl squeals as she launches herself from behind a bush.

The woman scoops her up. "Don't *ever* take off on me like that, Amber."

"I was hiding."

"You need to *tell* me you're going to hide. You can't—"

The woman nearly crashes into me. I murmur, "Excuse me," and she continues past, still scolding the child.

"Ms. Finch?" a voice says.

I turn to see a uniformed officer. He's nearing retirement age. Bulldog-faced, his eyes and jowls and belly drooping, like someone who's been pulling double shifts all his life and has resigned himself to permanent exhaustion. His nameplate reads COOPER.

Three younger officers follow—two men and a woman—but they stay back as Cooper approaches me.

"Oh, thank God," I say. "I can't find the boy's mother anywhere."

"It's okay, ma'am. We're here now. You said you saw a boy taken from the playground?"

"No, the parking lot." I point. "He was on the swings and wandered that way."

I explain. Slow and relaxed and careful. Step by step, despite the voice in my head screaming that they need to find that SUV, find it now.

This is how they *will* find it. By me staying calm and explaining.

When I finish, Cooper says, "So you saw him here with his mother, and she didn't follow him when he walked off."

"No, I only saw *her* on Sunday, when I spoke to them both."

Cooper's brows shoot up. "You were jogging through the park Sunday and saw them then, too?"

"I was here with my daughter on Sunday. I jog on my lunch hours. I work nearby."

"Describe the boy, please," he says to me. "In as much detail as possible. We'll ask around, see who saw him, figure out where his mom is."

"He's school age, but just barely. About this tall." I motion. "Thin. White. Short blond hair."

He pauses. When I don't continue, he says, "Anything more *specific*?" He points to another boy, fair haired, about the same age. "How would he be different from that kid? Taller? Thinner? Hair darker, lighter, shorter, longer?"

"Thinner in the face. Maybe a bit taller."

Cooper points to another child, who also looks similar. In this neighborhood, towheaded white kids are as common as German-built cars. As I struggle to remember distinguishing features, my heart hammers. What if it *wasn't* the boy from Sunday? I only saw him from a distance today, and several of the kids Cooper points out do look like him.

That doesn't matter. A child is still missing. Just limit my description to what I remember of the boy I saw *today*.

"What's he wearing?" Cooper asks.

I pull up a mental picture, and . . . it's blank.

Stop that. I saw him. I *chased* him. Surely I can remember—

"Jeans," I blurt. "Jeans and sneakers and a T-shirt."

Cooper casts a pointed look at the playground, where nearly every child is in jeans and sneakers, and at least half are in tees.

"The shirt was blue. A medium shade. Like that." I point to a woman's blouse.

"And his mother?"

"Young, early twenties. She's blond and wears her hair in a ponytail. Well, she did Sunday and . . . ." Deep breath. "Just focus on the boy, please. Even if it's not the same child, I did see a child get pulled into an SUV."

Cooper nods. "Okay." He turns to the officers. "Don't let anyone leave before speaking to you."

As they walk toward the playground, he says, "You mentioned being on a lunch break. Are you late for work?"

"Yes, but I can stay—"

"We have this. I'll take your contact information and be in touch."

"I just work over at the library. It's a few blocks away. If you need to stop by, I'm there until five."

"A phone number and home address will be fine, Ms. Finch. Thank you for your help. We'll take it from here."

FOUR

The police don't show up or call during my shift. I have to grab a few groceries on the way home, but I keep it quick, in case they stop by. As I enter my building, I'm well aware of how it will look to Officer Cooper. My apartment is affordable. Very affordable. I could do better, even with my part-time job, but I want a down payment on a condo before I fight for Charlotte, so I took a cheap downtown apartment while squirreling away the extra.

I do have money, from before, but I can't access much of that. Not without raising questions I don't dare answer.

I've lived in worse places, and I'm comfortable here. There are a few veterans on disability that I run errands for, while cursing the system that put them into this situation.

Once inside, I tidy my apartment. It's never bad—I grew up fixing my bed the moment I rolled out of it. But I want to make the best impression possible, overcoming any negative one left by the old building itself.

I'm washing the breakfast dishes when a knock comes at the door.

I open it to find Officer Cooper and the female coworker

who was with him earlier. I invite them in and offer refreshments. They don't accept the latter. We sit in the living room, and Cooper looks around.

"Is your daughter here?" he asks.

"She lives with her dad."

I catch their reactions and wince. I need to stop saying that. I really do. *She's with her dad today.* That's the way to phrase it. Otherwise, I get this—both of them looking up sharply, like I've just confessed to armed robbery.

Cooper's brow furrows, as if the concept of a three-year-old living with her father confuses him. The younger officer—Jackson—compresses her lips.

When Jackson's gaze scans the apartment again, I say, "Yes, this isn't the sort of place I want my daughter full-time which is why she's with her dad on weekdays. It's a recent separation. I'm saving up for something better."

Her expression judges me for my decision. I bristle at that. Kids *do* live in this building. Sometimes you don't have a choice.

I do, though. I live here—and bring my daughter here—voluntarily.

"Have you found the boy?" I ask.

"No one is missing a child," Jackson says.

"What?" I say.

"Some parents said they saw boys matching your description," Cooper says. "They just didn't see one wander off."

"Because it was busy. A packed playground with plenty of kids who look like him."

Jackson opens her mouth, but a look from Cooper stops her.

"I know what I saw," I say.

"A boy pulled into an SUV," Cooper says.

I relax. "Yes."

"You heard someone call to the boy from an SUV. He ran to it. *Willingly* ran to it. Yes?"

"Right, but then he freaked out. He shouted 'no' and began screaming for his mom as a man dragged him into the vehicle."

"Is it possible . . . ?" He shifts on the sofa. "You have a little girl. I'm sure you've needed to carry her to the car once or twice, when she's overtired, overstimulated, kicking and screaming bloody murder."

"That's not—"

"Kids love the playground. They hate to leave it. There can be screaming. A good parent doesn't drag their kid into the car like that. Unfortunately, questionable parenting isn't illegal."

"That's not what it looked like at all. Are you sure no one saw *anything*?"

"A couple of parents saw *you*," says Jackson. "They noticed you jog past. With a man."

"What? Oh, right. I wasn't *with* him. He was just . . ."

"Just what?" Jackson says when I trail off.

Hitting on me. That's what I was going to say. Then I realize how it sounds. *Yeah, so this guy told me I was stretching wrong and running wrong, but I'm sure he was just coming on to me. Really.*

These officers already think I'm delusional. *That* won't help.

"He was talking about stretches," I say. "I was busy watching the little boy, so he took off." I stop and look at Cooper. "He would have seen the boy. He must have. He said he jogs through the park at lunchtime, too. I could—"

"Parents said they see *you* there quite often," Jackson cuts in. "Hanging around the benches, watching them, watching their kids."

That throws me, and it takes me a second to recover and say, "Yes, like I said, I work nearby, and I jog through the park. I do my stretches near the playground. At the benches."

"There are other benches in the park, Ms. Finch."

I cut off a snippy reply and say, evenly, "I used to be a

stay-at-home mom, and I miss being with my daughter all day. Stretching in the playground helps me cope."

I'm baring more of myself here than I like . . . and it doesn't cut me one iota of slack with Jackson, as her eyes narrow.

"You make some of the other parents uncomfortable," she says.

"What?" I've misheard her. I must have.

"How would you feel, if you took your kid to the playground, and you kept seeing this woman there, hanging around, with no child in tow."

My cheeks blaze. "It's not like that. I stretch near the playground sometimes. That's all."

"And you watch the kids."

"I . . . I guess I do. While I stretch. I just . . . I enjoy seeing kids play."

"Do you know how often we hear that, Ms. Finch? Every time we question a pedophile for hanging around a playground."

My heart slams into my throat. "Wh-what? No. I have never—"

"No one's accusing you of that." Cooper glares at his young partner. "We're just pointing out how it could look."

"And that if you were a man, this would be a very different conversation," Jackson says. "Personally, I don't think gender should play a role in how we handle these complaints."

"There was a *complaint*?" My voice squeaks.

"No," Cooper says. "A couple of people mentioned it, but we all know parents can be overly cautious. You might want to run somewhere else, though, in future."

Humiliation swallows my voice, and it takes a moment for me to say, "Yes, of course."

Cooper continues, but I don't hear it over the blood pounding in my ears. I always figured I was invisible, just a jogger stretching at a bench. It never occurred to me that anyone would notice, let alone remember me from one day to the next.

I made other parents nervous.

They saw me as a threat.

Did they talk about me? Whisper warnings to each other?

Have you seen that woman with the dark ponytail? She comes by every lunch and pretends to be stretching, but she's watching us. Eavesdropping on our conversations. Staring at our children.

I'll never be able to set foot in that park again.

"Ms. Finch?"

I struggle to refocus. This is about the boy, not me. Remember that.

"I know what I saw," I say. "And it wasn't an angry dad hauling his kid into a car."

Jackson gives Cooper a look, as if waiting for him to respond. When he doesn't, she opens her mouth, but he cuts in with, "Either way, we are taking it seriously, Ms. Finch. We put an alert out for the SUV."

"An AMBER Alert?"

"Without a parent reporting a child missing, we cannot do that. We need to know who we would be looking for."

"It's been five hours," Jackson says. "It's not as if Mom left the park by herself, forgetting she brought a kid."

"We *are* investigating, Ms. Finch," Cooper says. "We wouldn't ignore something like this." He pushes to his feet. "If a child is reported missing, we'll let you know."

FIVE

After they leave, I sink into the sofa, ignoring the broken spring that pokes back. Did I make a mistake? My gut insists that I know what I saw. And what I saw was a child being dragged, screaming, into an SUV. A young child who'd been wandering alone in the park. That isn't normal.

Not normal, yes. But maybe like Officer Cooper said, it was just bad parenting. Charlotte has had tantrums. She's three—it happens. Once, when she got overtired, she threw a fit in a restaurant, deciding the world was a cruel and unfair place if they didn't have sprinkles for her ice cream. I carried her to the car while Paul quickly paid the bill. I remember hurrying through the restaurant, dodging glares. Then I got outside and heard her gasp and discovered that in trying to quiet her, I'd been pressing her face into my shoulder. Forcibly silencing her.

When I realized what I'd done, I nearly threw up in the parking lot. It took everything I had to wait for Paul to reach the car before I blurted my confession.

He laughs softly and hugs me. "Charlie's fine. Everyone's just tired. And hey, it did make her stop crying, right?"

On top of the guilt came the shame. What if someone saw

me and thought I was intentionally smothering my child to keep her quiet?

I remember another time, when Charlotte smacked a kid in the playroom at McDonald's. Horrified, I'd hauled her out while apologizing to the boy's grandfather. After we got home, I found a red circle around her wrist. Not only had I been hurting her as I marched her along, but she hadn't complained. Had it seemed as if I was dragging Charlotte from the playroom? Had that grandfather watched me, and shaken his head, thinking, *Well, I know where that poor child gets it from*?

What if *that* was all I saw this morning? A frustrated dad forcibly putting his protesting son into their vehicle.

That could be what I saw.

But it doesn't feel like it.

It just doesn't.

An hour later, I get a call from Paul. He has a client emergency.

"Is there any way you can take Charlotte for the evening?"

"You don't ever have to ask," I say. "Even if I was working, I'd find a way to swing it."

"Thank you."

I tense hearing that. It's genuine gratitude, which is the problem. He knows I'm eager to take Charlotte any chance I get, but he still acts as if each extremely rare circumstance is some great favor. I want a casual "Thanks, Bree," perfunctory and offhand. I don't want to keep score.

"She can stay the night," I say. "I'll drop her off at daycare tomorrow."

Silence.

"Unless that's a problem . . ." I say.

"No, no. That would be great. Saves me worrying about how late I get back tonight."

I'm waiting downstairs when Paul arrives. He sees me out front and motions he'll pull into the lot. He insists on that, as if dropping her at the curb smacks of abandonment. Also, there is a clear No Stopping sign in front of the building, and Paul always obeys the law. Which is one reason I never told him about my past.

I don't wait indoors, because Paul has only ever seen my building from the outside, where it looks like a stately old apartment complex in the city core. Oxford began life as a small town before exploding into a bedroom community. What remains of that original town is well-preserved old buildings—like the library where I work—and shabbier ones like this. Paul grew up and works in Chicago, which means he doesn't know Oxford well enough to tell the good areas from the . . . less good. He parks his Mercedes across the lot from my decade-old Corolla. I think he does that on purpose, so no one will see the disparity and judge him for it. They shouldn't. The Mercedes used to be mine. He bought it when Charlotte was born, wanting a newer, safer car for us. When I left, I took his Corolla instead. That was fair. That was right. Which didn't keep him from acting like I'd thrown the keys in his face.

"I bought that car for you, Bree."

"You bought it for Charlie. Since you have her now, you keep the car."

He hung up on me after that. Didn't slam the phone down. Didn't curse. Just disconnected and never said another word about it.

I open the door to get Charlotte as quickly as I can, so I don't waste a moment of our time together. I remember when I used to fist-pump every time she went down for a nap, as giddy as a kid granted an unexpected recess. Now, when she naps, I sit in the room, reading with one eye, watching her with the other, waiting for her to wake up again.

As I open the door, Paul comes around the car. He looks . . . like Paul. Nothing new. Nothing different. Every time I see him, there's a moment when I forget we're separated, and I only see the face I woke up to every morning. Familiar and comfortable. Then I remember that I'm not his wife anymore. Not his wife, not his friend, not even an ally in raising our child.

I'm the woman who could take Charlotte from him.

I'm the enemy.

He looks tired. He always does these days, and guilt stabs me. Anger chases the guilt, though. I'm here, anytime he needs me, eager to take our daughter and give him a break.

I go to lift Charlotte out, but he waves me away. When he pulls her out of her seat, I see his expression, and I slingshot back to those times he came home from work a little irritable, a little distant, and my first thought had always been *He knows.*

He knows about me.

Which was ridiculous, of course. If my past ever did reach Paul, he wouldn't be coming home "a little irritable," and telling me, "It's nothing, just work." He'd be scooping up Charlotte and making a beeline for the nearest hotel.

Now, when I see that expression, there is only a split second of the old fear. Then I realize the far more likely truth.

Someone told him about the boy in the park.

Someone at the police department recognized my name and knew my husband was a defense attorney and contacted him. Told him that I reported a kidnapped child . . . where, evidently, no child has been kidnapped.

And I am okay with that. I see him, see the set of his mouth, and all I can think is *Good*. If Paul knows, he can help. He's a lawyer. He has contacts. I will explain what I saw, and even if he doesn't quite believe me, it'll be in his best interests to prove his ex isn't delusional.

"Is everything okay?" I ask carefully.

He spots something on the passenger seat and heaves a sigh of relief. It's Matt, Charlotte's beloved stuffed rat. I made the mistake of watching *The Princess Bride* with her last year, and she's obsessed, both with the movie and the ROUSes—rodents of unusual size. Other kids have teddy bears and puppies; mine has a stuffed rat.

"I thought I forgot him," Paul says. "That would have been a crisis."

He slides me a smile, and when he does . . . God, I hate that smile. I hate how it makes me feel. I hate *that* it makes me feel. The first time we met, I will fully admit that I dismissed Paul. He was just a very average guy, the sort I never really noticed. Then he smiled, and I saw more. I paid attention, and I never stopped paying attention; even now, when he smiles at me, I stop and I stare, and I feel.

I feel so much.

He hefts Charlotte and glances at me. "Are you sure this is okay? Dropping her off?"

"Absolutely. Go save the world. I've got this."

I find myself leaning forward to kiss his cheek. At the last second, I manage to divert and shut the car door instead, as if that's what I'd been leaning in to do. How long does it take for this to stop? For the neural pathways of my brain to reroute. To see Paul and hear his voice and smell his aftershave and not tumble back in time, ready to kiss his cheek or lean my head on his shoulder or tell him all my troubles.

Well, not all my troubles. Never all of them.

He lifts Charlotte and kisses her cheek before passing her to me. "What time do you work in the morning?"

"Nine. Like I said, I can get her to daycare."

He passes over Charlie's bag. "Why don't we meet up for breakfast first. Charlie would like that. And we can . . ." He shrugs. "Talk."

Does that mean he *has* heard about the incident today? Or does he really just want to talk? I would love that. I really would, and I should be able to look at his expression and tell whether this is a "we have a problem" talk or just an invitation to breakfast. But we never developed that bond, the kind where couples finish each other's sentences. I loved him. Still do. Yet there had been a surface quality to our marriage. My monsters lurk in the depths, so I swim in shallow waters, and if I insisted on staying there, I couldn't dive deeper *with* him.

I do want to talk to him about the boy. I want his advice so badly. Yet if he doesn't know, should I tell him? What if he uses it against me in the custody battle, as proof that I'm not quite stable?

I cannot take that chance. The boy is important, but my daughter is more important. I will not jeopardize my future with her to enlist Paul's help.

"I take it that's a no?" he says as his smile fades.

"I—"

His phone rings. He glances at it. "My client. Probably wondering where I am. I should go."

I open my mouth to say breakfast would be fine, and yes, let's do that. But he's already saying goodbye to Charlotte and then walking around the car, without another word to me.

SIX

I circle the daycare lot, waiting for a spot. Two have cleared so far, only to have other drivers whip in while I was figuring out which of us had been there first. Evidently, not me.

I check the car clock. Five minutes to drop Charlotte off, twenty to drive to work, five to get at my post. Exactly enough time . . . if I find a parking spot in the next ten seconds.

"Mommy? I has cough. See?" Charlotte gives two quick— and obviously fake—hacks. "I stay home with you?"

I wish you could, baby. I really wish you could.

"Mommy works now, remember, Charlie?"

There! A spot. I start turning in . . . just as a toddler darts from between parked cars. I hit the brakes so hard I slam into the seat belt. The car stops twenty feet from the child, but I still squeeze my eyes shut, catching my breath as my heart pounds.

Careful. Always be careful.

It only takes a moment.

Another car ducks into the empty spot.

"Damn it," I mutter.

"Dammit," Charlotte chirps. "Dammit!"

"No, baby. That's not a good word. Mommy—"

Spot!

I snag it. Out of the car in two seconds. Two more, and Charlotte is on my hip as I sprint for the door.

An exiting father holds it open. I race through with thanks.

I couldn't sleep last night. I'd been stressed over the missing boy. After a night of tossing and turning, I'd woken early to go online, hoping for news that a child . . .

Hoping for news that a child was missing? That sounds horrible. Of course I hope to see he's been found. That's the ideal situation. A boy was temporarily missing, but now he's home. Yet if that wasn't the case, then yes, I hoped for proof that an investigation had been launched.

When I didn't find it, I kept searching, digging deeper, calling on skills I hadn't used in so many years, cursing my crappy computer as I hunted.

No, no, Paul, I don't need a fancy laptop. I can barely use email.

Liar, liar, pants on fire.

I searched online until the last possible moment before getting Charlotte up. I managed to get her outside with just enough time to drop her off and get to work. Then, as I buckled Charlotte into her gazillion-point car seat . . . I realized she'd dropped Matt in the apartment hall.

For one moment, I had wondered if I could just go grab it. Leave her locked in the car and run back inside. The impulse only lasted a second, shut down by a wave of horror, but the memory still shames me.

I jog down the daycare hallway, ignoring the looks from other parents. Someone has jacked up the building's heat. Sweat beads on my forehead, and the smell of a loaded diaper makes my stomach regret that wolfed-down breakfast muffin.

As I run, Charlotte giggles on my hip. When I plunk her onto the floor, though, her giggles evaporate.

"I has cough." Big brown eyes look up into mine. Two more fake hacks.

"You shouldn't bring her if she's sick," a mother says as she walks by.

"She's not really—"

The other woman is gone, judgment rendered.

Charlotte's hand reaches for mine. "No go, Mommy. Please."

A dart of frustration, quickly squelched. If I'm running late, that's on me.

I bend. "Charlie, if you really are sick, then I *will* stay home. But I'll have to cancel our princess tea tomorrow, and we'll do it another time, just to be safe."

She straightens. "All better."

I ruffle her hair. "Excellent. Then we shall have tea tomorrow. Mommy and Charlie in their new princess dresses."

I take her hand. Then I spin and say, "Oh, wait! You don't *have* a princess dress."

"Yes!" Charlotte squeals. "Blue like Princess Buttercup. We buy."

"Are you sure? I don't remember buying a blue dress. Now, there was a pink one . . ."

"Pink? Nooo." Her face screws up.

"Oh, I'm sure it was pink. Bright, bright pink."

I continue teasing Charlotte as I lead her inside. The distraction works right up to the moment where I hug her goodbye and her arms death-grip my neck, soft face pressed against my cheek.

I swallow. *Don't feel guilty. The moment you leave, she's fine. You know that.*

"Tomorrow," I say, as the daycare worker takes Charlotte's hand. "I'll pick you up tomorrow for the princess tea. Daddy said you can wear your dress all day."

Charlotte nods and lets the worker lead her away. With each step, she glances over her shoulder, puppy eyes finding me.

She *will* be fine. I remember the first time I brought her, when she clung and cried. I got as far as the door before guilt forced me back. I think that might have been the one thing that could have sent me back to Paul, begging for reconciliation. I'd wanted to be a stay-at-home mom until Charlotte was in school. If she suffered because I left, it'd have been a reason to go home.

No, let's be honest. It'd have been an *excuse*. A chance to say I made a mistake and beg Paul for another chance.

That first day, I'd run back into the daycare, ready to scoop her up and take her home . . . and instead found her happily playing with a little boy, already chattering away.

So I know now she will be fine. That doesn't mean I can turn and walk away while she's in sight. Every time I bring her, I stand here, and I suffer those sad eyes, and I remind myself that this was my choice.

I wait until she's gone. Then I hurry back into the hall.

SEVEN

I'm at work, in the central library, a gorgeous period building where every whisper echoes under the domed ceiling. When my phone vibrates with an incoming text, I swear people in the stacks jump and spin, as if a swarm of bees is launching an attack from the circulation desk.

The text is from Paul. I don't check it, just tuck the phone away. My supervisor, Ingrid, looks over, her long face drooping with disapproval.

"Sorry," I say, and continue checking in returned books.

With a sniff, she swoops from behind the library desk and trills, "Can I help you find something?" to a hovering patron.

I texted Ingrid to say I'd be a few minutes late. Texted from the first red light . . . and then glanced up to see a cruiser right beside me, the officer staring my way. I dropped the phone so fast it fell between the seats, and I spent three extra minutes in the library parking lot fishing it out.

I did not, however, get a ticket, thank God. That would have been the capper to my morning. Let's just say it wouldn't be my first traffic violation. That's actually how I met Paul. I'd worked in the ground-floor bookstore of his law firm's offices, and he'd seen me get a ticket out front. He'd suggested I fight it. It became a cute "how we met" story.

He's a lawyer . . . and I needed one. Ha-ha.

As it turned out, that's also the story of our marriage. The competent professional and his screwup bride.

My running-late text hasn't cut me any slack with Ingrid. Nothing does, ever since she found out I'm a noncustodial parent.

"How does a mother lose custody of her child?" I heard her whisper to Nancy, another librarian. "Everyone knows the courts favor the mom, no matter what."

There hasn't *been* a court hearing. I don't explain that to Ingrid. It would only lead to a bigger question: *What kind of mom voluntarily gives up her daughter?*

A good mother, I thought. Mature and fair.

Or stupid. Naive and unbelievably stupid.

My phone vibrates, reminding me of that waiting text.

Ten feet away, Ingrid still hears it. Before I can apologize, she waves in annoyance.

"Take your break," she says. "And leave *that* in the staff room."

As I close the door to the tiny staff room, the smell of stale leftovers envelops me. I make a coffee to cover the stink as I check the text from Paul. It's nothing more than a check-in, making sure all went well this morning.

I send back a thumbs-up. Then I pause. Pause. Deep breath as I send another text.

Me: Breakfast would have been OK. Just caught me off guard. Sorry if it sounded like I was hesitating.

He sends his own thumbs-up, and I spend way too long staring at that, trying to interpret it. Paul is not an emoji guy. I'm actually surprised he knows where to find them on his phone. Is he saying it's fine, and he understands, or . . .

I rub my eyes. *Stop, Aubrey. It's an emoji, not the Enigma code. Just stop.*

I set a timer on my phone, so I won't linger past my break. Then I get to work on the old staff room computer, my fingers flying over the keyboard as I run a few lines of machine code to cover my virtual footprints.

I'm hacking the police department's internal email system.

I glance at my phone and imagine saying that to Paul. Imagine the look on his face. There would be, of course, a moment of horror that I'd suggest such a clearly criminal action. But that would last only a moment before he'd laugh, certain I was joking. Hacking? His *wife*, who had to ask him to install security updates on her laptop?

Liar, liar . . .

It hasn't been easy, pretending I barely know how to operate a computer. That's part of the price I pay, though, for my choices straight from the *How to Disappear* handbook. Distance yourself from all aspects of your former life, particularly those you excelled in.

The first thing I ever hacked was a radio. It started with my dad bringing home a couple of walkie-talkies. Surplus from base.

"They don't work that well, but I know a guy who can fix them up, give you and your friends something to play with."

Which was great, except that Dad wasn't always quick to fulfill promises. He got busy and remembering to get the radios fixed wasn't a high priority.

So I did it myself. I wrangled schematics from an indulgent engineer on base, and I opened up the radios. At first, Dad was as amused as that engineer. Sure, let the kid take a shot at it—curiosity is good. Then I not only fixed them, but made them as good as new. As for using them to hack into a secure military frequency, well, that came later.

Once Dad realized I had a talent for electronics, he brought me things to fix, things to take apart. And the guy who wouldn't stop working long enough to play cards with me would watch me tinker for hours. He'd give me a look, like he couldn't quite figure out where this little girl came from. For the first time in my life, I was a revelation to him. The more fascinated he was by my talent, the harder I worked to improve it.

I still remember the day he brought me my first computer. I came home from school, and it was there, and he waved at it, much like one might wave at a troll crouching in the corner.

"You know how to use these things?" he asks.

I laugh. "It's a computer, Dad. We have them in school."

Let's just say that my father is the reason I'm able to impersonate a technophobe so well.

Computers, as I discovered, were for much more than just typing up an assignment. I could control them. Bend them to my will in a way I couldn't—or wouldn't—with people. I could open them up, like a radio, and manipulate them there. Or I could go in through code and use them to achieve my goal that way. Which sometimes meant hacking.

When I was young, hacking was a challenge. Nothing more. I didn't do anything with my skills. Not until my world fell apart, and a tech career in the army was the absolute last thing I wanted, and I was angry, so damned angry, and it was just the right time in my life for someone to suggest I use those skills in a very different way.

I don't get access to the police email system over my lunch break. My skills are far too rusty for that. Instead, I accomplish step one: finding the server and poking at it a bit, seeing how hard it'll be to hack.

Hack in and find out what's going on with my case. What Officer Cooper really thinks of my story.

Find out whether that boy has a hope of ever being found.

And if the answer is no?

I'm not sure what I'll do about that. Not sure what I can do.

No, that's a lie. I know what I *can* do. I'm just not sure that I will.

EIGHT

I get an early start the next morning . . . and my car does not. It won't start at all. I open the hood to find a broken fan belt. An easy fix, and I mentally calculate the time it'll take me to jog to the hardware store.

No, I can't risk showing up at work late again. So I catch a cab. Not really in my budget, but if I lose my job, I won't have an income *to* budget.

I arrive at the library twenty minutes early. Not that it does any good—my coworker Nancy doesn't show up with the keys until mere seconds before her shift begins.

I put my things away, head straight to the book-return bin, and focus on my task. I'm still distracted, fretting about yesterday, and I cannot afford to make any mistakes.

I like my job. Being a librarian isn't just shelving and checking out books. There's so much else—from helping a senior citizen send an email to helping a student find research material. A combination of public service and problem-solving that I love.

I'd love it even more if I could throw my tech skills into the mix, but that would lead to questions I can't answer. Like how

I got those skills when there's no postsecondary education or tech job on my résumé.

I do use those skills on my break. I try hacking into the police system. It's been thirty-six hours since Officer Cooper came to my apartment, and I haven't heard a peep from him since. Nor have I found any mention of the case online. So I'm determined to get into the departmental email and see what they're doing about it.

That takes both coffee breaks and my lunch hour, which would have been embarrassing five years ago. This isn't the Chicago Police Department. It's a suburban force with outdated cybersecurity. I've been out of the game so long, though, that even "outdated" means it's newer than most systems I've hacked. By the time I succeed, my last break is over. I'll need to postpone actually searching emails until tomorrow.

There's something bugging me, too—a growing sense that I'm forgetting something. I keep running through the scenario in the park, both when I first met the boy with his mom, and later, when I saw the boy taken. Am I missing something?

The more I fret, the harder I need to concentrate on work. I count the minutes until my shift ends. Then Ingrid asks me to stay an extra hour—to make up for my double tardiness yesterday—and that sense that I'm forgetting something surges.

I finally get off work, and I'm walking to the parking lot when my phone buzzes. Thinking it's the police, I scramble to yank it from my pocket.

Bright Horizons Daycare.

I wince. There's only one reason they ever call me: if Charlotte is sick. Paul can't dash in from the city, obviously, so this is the one responsibility he allows me to take.

Maybe Charlotte *wasn't* faking her cough yesterday.

I answer quickly with, "Aubrey Finch."

"Ms. Finch? Your husband said you were picking Charlotte up today."

Today? Why would I pick Charlotte up on a Wednesday—

The princess tea. *That's* what I forgot.

"Yes, I'm getting her today," I say as calmly as I can. "Thank you for checking. I'll be there in a half hour."

A pause. "We closed five minutes ago, Ms. Finch."

What? No. I get off at five and . . .

I stayed an extra hour. It's past six.

"I'm so sorry," I say as I run for the parking lot. "I was asked to work late and totally lost track of time. I'll be there in . . ."

I look around the lot. Where is my—?

Oh, no . . . I don't have my car.

"In a few minutes," I say as I race back to the road, frantically searching for a cab. "I'll pay the late fee myself. Please don't charge Paul. This is on me, and I'm so sorry. I'll be *right* there."

I jump out of the cab. As I run across the empty daycare lot, the side door opens, and Charlotte walks out . . . clutching the hand of a stranger.

For two seconds, reality snaps, and all I can think is *I'm losing my mind.*

That's the only explanation as I watch my daughter being led away by a stranger, two days after I saw a boy snatched. This is not possible.

"Mommy!" Charlotte shouts.

She breaks away from the stranger and starts to run. The woman hurries after her and catches her hand. Then they walk toward me.

"You must be Aubrey," the woman says.

She isn't a daycare worker. Not dressed like this—sensible but stylish, from her heels to her dress to her hairstyle, short and smart.

Sophisticated. That's the word that comes to mind. Stylish and sophisticated.

She's in her late thirties. Not beautiful, but striking and self-possessed. The kind of woman I visualize for my future, when I've overcome all the bumps and gotten my act together.

The woman extends her free hand, the other one still holding Charlotte's.

"Gayle Lansing," she says.

Gayle . . .

Oh, no.

I shake her hand and babble something about being pleased to meet her. It is, quite possibly, the biggest lie I've told in a long time, and that's saying something.

Gayle Lansing is Paul's new girlfriend.

When he told me a few weeks ago that he was seeing someone—doing the right thing and warning me that there was a new face in Charlotte's life—he said she worked in his office, and I thought, *Really? He's dating some cute young assistant? Figures.*

Except that it didn't figure at all, and deep down, I knew that. So I looked Gayle up . . . and promptly began wishing Paul really *were* dating a twenty-something assistant.

Gayle Lansing. Thirty-nine, the same age as Paul. A lawyer at his firm. A new *partner* at his firm. As I've learned since, Gayle is divorced, with custody of her two children, who attend a private school, win tons of awards, and are shining examples of parenting perfection.

Naturally.

I look at her, and my memory kaleidoscopes through scenes from every social function I attended as Paul's wife. At first, they'd seemed endless—the firm dinners, the charity banquets.

At every one, I'd looked at wives like Gayle, poised and professional, and it didn't matter how conservatively I dressed or intelligently I spoke, I felt like the stripper Paul met in Vegas and married after too many free drinks at the casino.

I tried to tell myself I was imagining it—being self-conscious again—but eventually we stopped going to those functions, and when I asked Paul, he shrugged it off and said he didn't need to do that, now that he'd made partner. Which was a lie. The truth was that having me at those functions hurt his career more than not attending.

Having someone like this woman on his arm, though? That would be an entirely different matter.

"I am so, so sorry," I say. "My supervisor asked me to work late, and I completely forgot why I *couldn't*. I was just about to call the daycare when they phoned me. I guess I'm not the only number they dialed."

"They notified Paul, but he's in court, and I was already heading home, so he asked me to come by."

"Again, I'm sorry. I know this looks terrible."

She smiles. It isn't exactly a bright and friendly smile, but it's not fake either. Just restrained.

"Work emergencies happen," she says. "I tried daycare when mine were young. I had to switch to a nanny because they threatened to kick my kids out if I was late one more time."

I relax a little. "I *am* sorry they called Paul. I'll—"

"Mommy?" Charlotte cut in. "Where princess dress?"

I smile down at her. "Don't worry. It's—"

In my car. I'd put it in there last night, so I wouldn't forget it.

"It's in my car," I say. "Which broke down this morning, and I completely forgot to grab my outfit. We'll head there now. I'll call the princess tea shop and tell them we'll be a little late for our reservation."

"Late?" Charlotte's eyes widen.

"Or I could just go like this." I force a smile. "Ever heard of a librarian princess?"

She looks me up and down, and her lower lip quivers.

"Let's decide on the way," I say as I boost her up. "We don't want to be *too* late, and I'm sure Ms. Lansing has to get home to her kids." I turn to Gayle. "Thank you, and again, I cannot apologize enough."

I got two steps when Gayle says, "Aubrey?"

"Hmm?"

"Did you come by cab?"

I nod. "I have an app. I can get one here in a few minutes."

"And Charlotte?"

I pause.

"Her car seat?"

I only mouth a curse, but Gayle winces as if I shouted the word.

I look around. "The cab company might have . . ."

"Let me drive you," she says. "My youngest is seven, not quite out of a seat yet, so I have a booster in my car."

"I . . ."

I want to die. Right now. Just let the pavement open and swallow me.

"Mommy need dress," Charlotte says. "Princess dress."

"I . . . I know."

"No be late." She shakes her head, curls bouncing.

"I could take her," Gayle says softly.

My head jerks up.

"I don't mean to interfere," she says. "I know you two had this planned for weeks, but you do have a reservation, and you're already . . ." She clears her throat. "A little late. You can rebook, and I'll take her today." She waves down at her outfit. "It's not exactly a princess dress, but . . ."

But it's a whole lot closer to it than my outfit: a blouse, dress pants, and flats.

I want to say no. Hell, no. You've been dating my husband for three weeks. That doesn't give you the right to take my daughter to tea. *Our* tea.

Step off, bitch.

As soon as I think that, I am ashamed. This isn't a smooth play to win my daughter's affections. It's a sensible woman offering a sensible solution.

I bend in front of Charlotte.

"Ms. Lansing is going to be your fellow princess today, okay, baby? I don't want you to miss tea. I know how much you were looking forward to it."

That lip quivers even more. "Mommy not come?"

"Mommy will come next time." I hug her as tight as I can. "Two princess teas with two princess friends. How lucky are you?"

She nods, saying nothing.

"You look so pretty in your dress," I say.

"Blue like Buttercup's," she whispered, gaze down, words almost too soft to hear.

"Blue like Buttercup's. And do you know what else is blue?" I take off my necklace, a turquoise pendant my dad gave me when I got accepted to MIT. "Mommy's special necklace." I fasten it around her neck.

"The perfect finishing touch," Gayle says.

I get a tiny smile from Charlotte.

"Be sure to get pictures for me, okay? Now hurry, you don't want to be late."

Gayle says, "At least let me drop you off somewhere, Aubrey."

I don't want her kindness. I want snide remarks and rolled eyes. Because this feels like pity, and it only makes the humiliation that much worse. Even my husband's new girlfriend doesn't feel threatened by me.

"I've got this," I say. "I'll probably . . . walk a bit and grab a coffee, steal a few minutes to do some work. Thank you again. I really do appreciate it."

I accompany them to Gayle's car. Like her, it's nothing showy. A solid, dependable sedan . . . with a price tag triple my annual salary.

I put Charlotte into the booster. Secure it. Double-check. Kiss her cheek. Then I go around the car and fumble for my wallet so I can pay for the tea. Instead, I endure the fresh humiliation of Gayle's sympathetic smile and assurances that she has it covered.

Don't even think of paying, Aubrey. You very clearly need that money more than I do.

I thank Gayle again. As the car pulls away, I wave and smile. Then, the moment it turns the corner, I run.

I run as hard and as fast as I can.

NINE

I don't drink. That was my father's crutch, and after his death . . .

No, his *suicide*. Call it what it was. He got back from Iraq, and I was off at college, too caught up in my life to realize he was in trouble, and no one else gave a damn—suck it up, buttercup—and by the time I realized how bad it'd gotten . . .

Gun to head. Bullet through brain. A note left on the counter. *I love you, Bree.*

Didn't love me enough to hang on, did you?

I squeeze my eyes shut. That's how I felt then. I know better now. I understand that in his depression, he didn't see me, *couldn't* see me. And I didn't see him. I was busy, and the damned army certainly didn't help—

I don't blame him now. Don't even blame them as much as I used to. But at the time, God, I'd been furious. At myself mostly, but I couldn't handle that so I blamed the world. Dropped out of MIT. Abandoned any thought of enlisting—vomited just thinking about it. And then . . .

Hey, Bree. Got a proposition for you. Use those magic fingers to put some cash in your pocket.

I shove that aside. The point was that no matter how bad life got, I didn't drink. I won't take meds for my shoulder either. I refuse to engage in any activity that could provide a false sense of relief.

But that day, after Gayle leaves with Charlotte, I walk into a grocery store and stare at the glittering rows of bottles.

Just this once. Please just this once.

I tear myself away and wander the aisles, looking for something to cheer me up. I stand in the ice cream aisle and gaze at the Ben & Jerry's. That's the cliché, isn't it? Drown your sorrows in ice cream?

If only I liked ice cream.

I walk to the cookie aisle. Again, not really my thing, but I select a small bag for Charlotte as a treat. She won't get the whole bag, obviously. One cookie, and maybe even a milky cup of decaffeinated tea. Our own princess tea, to hold her over until I can have a new reservation. I try not to think of the fact that it took me two months to get today's.

I've already left a message at the tea shop, and when my phone rings, I yank it out. It's a spam text, offering me work as a mystery shopper. At this point, if I thought it was legit, I might take it. God knows, I could use the money.

I console myself by opening my photo album to find the pictures of Charlotte trying on her princess dress. The first photograph I see is one I don't recognize. I'm not even sure what it is.

A mis-hit shutter button, it seems—the kind where you get a shot of your leg while taking out your phone. Except it isn't my leg. It's the back end of a vehicle.

The back of a dark SUV, its license plate smeared with mud.

It's *the* SUV. The one that took the boy. I had been lifting my phone, fumbling to set up the camera, and I must have snapped the shutter without realizing it.

It's a crappy shot. Off-center and blurred, the camera in motion. But the full plate is there, and I can make out enough of the vehicle emblem—

"*Excuse* me." A glowering senior waves me aside brusquely. "You are blocking the biscuits."

I pay for the cookies and hurry from the store. When I spot a coffee shop, I veer toward it. I'm tempted to bypass the counter. Sit and pretend I'm waiting for someone while I get a better look at the photo. But I squelch the urge, treat myself to a caramel latte and a blondie, and then take a seat buoyed by the righteousness of having paid to occupy it.

I import the photo into an app and refine it. I don't have proper graphics programs these days, but basic apps will do a decent job. The first thing I notice starts my heart pounding.

This isn't mud splatter from a dirt road. The dirt has been deliberately applied. I have a three-year-old; I know the pattern finger painting leaves. I can see the marks where fingers smeared on the mud. The rest of the car is spotless.

I reach for my phone. Then I stop.

A child is missing. And while I pray it's only a custody issue, it could be more. It could be worse. I need all the ammunition I can get before I place this call.

I can see part of the SUV emblem and the first two letters of the vehicle name. *TA*. I'm no good at recognizing car logos, so I search on my phone browser and get a page of images.

It's a Chevrolet. And while my mind immediately fills in the rest of the name as "Tahoe," I search for all Chevrolet SUV and crossover names. Three start with *T*: Tahoe, Trax, and Traverse. It's possible that the second letter is an *R* instead, but I'm definitely looking at a big SUV, not a crossover.

A Chevrolet Tahoe with a deliberately mud-smeared license plate. I can get access to better enhancement software and try making out the plate, but that takes time. The police need this information now.

I pick up my phone and dial Officer Cooper's number. Voice mail answers.

I call the station's main number instead and say I need to speak to Officer Cooper urgently, concerning a case.

I'm finished with my latte and my blondie before he phones back, and even then, when I answer, he greets me with a weary, "Yes, Ms. Finch," as if I've been calling him hourly.

"I have a photo. Of the vehicle."

A pause long enough that I wonder if he's hung up. Then a slow, "Photo?"

"I wanted to take one of the SUV, but it pulled away while I was getting my camera ready. Apparently, I still snapped a shot. It's not great, but I can identify the vehicle as a Chevrolet Tahoe. A dark blue Chevy Tahoe."

A sigh vibrates along the line. "I appreciate you letting me know, Ms. Finch, but we still have no report of a missing child. Without any evidence of a crime, I can't chase down a vehicle based on a make, model, and color."

"The license plate was deliberately smeared with mud."

"What?"

I try to keep the lilt of satisfaction out of my voice. Calm and steady. "I have a shot of the plate, which you may be able to analyze for the actual number, but right now, I can tell you that it isn't accidentally splattered with mud. It's been smeared on. I can see finger marks."

Silence.

"There is no mud on the rest of the vehicle, sir," I say. "Just the plate, where the number has been disguised."

"You can tell that the plate has been deliberately smeared with mud."

"I have a three-year-old, sir. I know what smearing looks like. Paint, food, dirt, you name it, I've seen it smeared. The whorl pattern is there, and the lines—"

"I . . . appreciate your . . . diligence in this matter, Ms. Finch. You have gone . . . above and beyond."

That tone in his voice isn't admiration. I hear the hesitation, as if he's struggling not to tell me I'm crazy. I open my mouth, but he continues.

"There isn't a missing child," he says. "It comes down to that. Few crimes are reported as quickly as a snatched kid. Even then, kidnapped children are exceedingly rare. I know you've probably seen a hundred movies with children grabbed on the street, but I've been on the force thirty years and never worked a single stranger-grab case. It just doesn't happen."

"Because it's usually custody based. The noncustodial parent takes their child. There's no reason that isn't what we have here, sir."

"Yes, there is, Ms. Finch. There is the lack of a reported missing child. You're a single mom with a little girl. Imagine if your ex lost custody and grabbed her at the playground."

He wouldn't. First, Paul is too good a parent to ever lose custody altogether. Second, he'd never take her. He will fight like hell, but he would never resort to kidnapping.

Would I?

My gut seizes at the question. I don't want to consider it. I certainly don't want to answer it.

Cooper continues. "How long would it take you to report her missing, Ms. Finch? Not two days, I bet."

"Maybe the mom is trying to resolve this on her own. Maybe the father is threatening their son, and she's afraid to call the—"

"Again, you are falling into dangerous speculative territory, Ms. Finch."

"Okay, but—"

"It remains an open case. I am still investigating. I can assure you of that. Now, I'm afraid I'm going to have to let you go, but I do appreciate your diligence in this matter. Thank you."

He disconnects before I can say anything else.

Cooper has a point. Without a missing-child report, there isn't a case. The situation fully supports his theory—that I witnessed a parent-child dispute—and in light of that, I can see where my "I can tell the mud was smeared" revelation seemed like something from a civilian who watches too much *CSI*.

When my phone rings, I've been on the internet for hours, hunting for other cases that might explain why this disappearance wasn't reported.

I reach over and answer, engrossed in an article and not checking caller ID.

"You actually picked up," Paul says. "That's a first."

His tone tells me I shouldn't have.

"Hey," I say.

"So, it's almost eleven at night, and I've been telling myself you'll call. Of course you'll call. Well, no, you never call. You text. Sometimes email. But you will make contact and explain yourself."

"Explain myself?" I bristle. "If you're talking about Gayle and the princess tea—"

"Is there another fiasco I should know about?"

I grit my teeth and count to three.

"You're right," I say. "I should have told you. I got . . . caught up in something. I did ask Gayle to pass on my apologies to you."

"She shouldn't have to."

"Fair enough. I'm sorry, Paul. I really am. I'm sorry you got called when you were in court, and I'm even more sorry that Gayle had to clean up my mess."

Silence.

Not the calm response you were expecting? I have other things on my mind right now. More important things.

"I'd like to call Gayle," I say. "To apologize again. If you could give me her number—"

He snorts. "No, I'm not giving you her number. God only knows what you'd do with it."

"Excuse me? I would use it to apologize and thank her. If you think I have any issue with you dating again, I don't. I'm glad you are. She seems—"

"This isn't about Gayle. It's about our daughter, who has been looking forward to this for weeks. To having tea with her mother. Her mother who *forgot*. Completely forgot, and then made up some story about working late and car trouble and—"

"Made up?" My calm teeters, ready to shatter. "Seriously, Paul? When I make mistakes, I *own* them. This is no one's fault but mine. Yes, there was a moment where I forgot, because I have a lot on my mind. But I *did* work late, and my car belt *is* broken." I head for the apartment door. "Here, let me send you a photo of the engine."

"You don't have to do that, Aubrey." His voice lowers. "You're right. That was uncalled for. I'm sure your car—"

"Oh, hell, no. I'm sending you the proof. Just like I'll send you a photo of my time card. You aren't going to question me and then not give me the chance to defend myself, Counselor."

"Don't pull that. I am not a lawyer here, Aubrey. I'm your— the father of your child, who is calling about that child."

I keep walking, stocking-footed, into the building hall. "And I disappointed her. Do you think I don't realize that? Do you think I'm not completely ashamed and humiliated?"

"You don't need to be. It was . . ." He sighs. "It was a mistake. I understand that. If you need money to fix your car—"

"No."

I swear he inhales, as if fighting an argument, before he says, calmly, "You are entitled to alimony, Aubrey. You took three years off to raise our child while I worked. My income was *our* income."

"I'm fine."

"No, you're stubborn. Stubborn and impulsive and absolutely impossible to deal—" He bites off the rest. A moment's silence as I walk into the parking lot. Then he says, his voice softer, "What's going on, Bree?"

"I'm having a really crappy week."

"Maybe, but it's more than that. Something has that busy brain of yours whirring."

"Just . . . work. And I meant it about conveying my thanks again to Gayle."

"I will. She has photos for me to send. And she got you reservations for tea a week from Sunday. Does that work?"

It does. I originally wanted a Sunday reservation, and was told they were booked up for the next six months. So how did Gayle manage it?

Because she's the kind of woman who knows how to do things like that, skills I will never possess.

"That's perfect. Thank you. And yes"—I pop the hood—"I'm sending you a photo of my engine, Paul, because I *am* stubborn, and if you call me on it, I have to defend myself."

"You realize I wouldn't know a broken fan belt from a loose wire, right?" He pauses. "And since when do you know how to fix a car?"

Damn it. I really am distracted.

"I don't," I say. "But I can Google the symptoms and narrow down the issue, and apparently, it's a broken belt. I know Charlie's in bed, but tomorrow, please give her a kiss for me, and we'll Skype after dinner."

"All right. Good night, Aubrey."

Back in the apartment, I find an online florist and send a small thank-you arrangement to Gayle, at the law firm.

I do appreciate what she's done, even if it makes me uncomfortable. I should be happy Paul's new girlfriend isn't an evil bitch, but somehow, it might have been easier if she were. When he first told me he was seeing someone, I was genuinely happy for him. What I hadn't realized was that it raised the potential of a scenario I never considered.

A stepmom for Charlotte.

If there ever is such a thing—and there will be, Paul isn't going to leave that void unfilled—then I want her to be everything Gayle seems to be. Kind, intelligent, and responsible. The perfect partner for Paul. The ideal role model for our daughter.

But where does that leave me?

TEN

I've turned off my alarm—I don't work Thursdays. My internal drill instructor still wakes me at seven and berates me for sleeping the day away.

While I lie in bed for another twenty minutes, it's obvious sleep isn't an option. I decide to make sure my floral delivery for Gayle went through okay. Leaving Paul also meant leaving our joint credit cards. That had turned into a weird game of Mastercard hot potato.

I'd left my card on my nightstand after we had "the talk." Then two weeks passed, and maybe that was how long it took him to realize I wasn't coming back. After those two weeks, he mailed the card to me. No note. Just the card.

I returned it, also by mail. He put it into Charlotte's weekend bag. I *left* it in Charlotte's weekend bag. He put it on my passenger seat while I was strapping Charlotte in. I gave up and shredded it. The whole time, we didn't exchange a single word about the card—just kept silently passing it back and forth.

I have my own card now, but with my lack of credit history, the limit is embarrassingly low, and even a small arrangement of flowers isn't cheap, so I'm worried the charge might not have gone through. I check, and then I pay off enough to buy a fan belt and try not to reminisce about the days of a platinum Mastercard with a limit that would have paid for a whole new car.

Even back then, though, I only used the card for necessities. Paul used to fret about that. He'd get the statement and say, "You can spend more, Bree."

"I don't need to."

"The card isn't just for household expenses. We're sharing a salary. You can buy things you'd like."

"I'm good."

His lips would tighten at that, and I'd tease that he should be *glad* I wasn't blowing up the card at Lululemon. He'd mutter and walk away, and I never figured out what I'd done wrong.

That had been in our last few months together, when it seemed like nothing I did made him happy. When I felt like an intruder in his house, in his life.

I inhale and flip to the local news. Today's top headline?

UNIDENTIFIED WOMAN'S BODY FOUND IN PARK.

I scroll past that to see if there's any more useful news . . . like a missing child. Yet I can't help skim-reading the article as I scroll. A woman in her early twenties. Found in Harris Park. Shot in the head, execution style. No ID, but CCTV cameras picked her up just outside the park on Tuesday morning—

I stop scrolling.

I turn up the brightness on my phone and enlarge the CCTV photo. It's been enhanced, but it's still blurry around the edges. At the moment of the freeze frame, though, she was turned toward the camera, giving a near-perfect head shot of a young woman with a blond ponytail.

It's the woman from Sunday. The one with the boy.

I stare at the photo. She's grim-faced, but I remember her smiles—the hesitant one for me and the joyful one for her son.

Her son.

I scramble up and start hitting 911. Then I stop and go into my recent calls and redial Cooper's number instead.

When I get his voice mail, I hang up and try the main line I used yesterday.

"I'm calling about the murdered woman," I say. "The one you're trying to identify."

"Do you recognize her?"

"Yes, I—"

"Let me connect you."

A click. Another click. Two rings. Then a message, telling me that the line is in use, but my call is important and please hold.

Please hold.

Yep, keep holding.

As I wait, I look back at the photo.

Do you recognize the woman?

Yes, I met her.

You know her then?

Well, no, I mean, I don't know her name or . . . anything about her actually, but I spoke to her briefly in the park.

The park where she was killed?

No, two blocks over, in Grant Park.

You saw her in Grant Park the day of her murder?

No, I saw her two days before. On the day of her murder, I saw her son being kidnapped . . .

Yeah, that conversation is not going to end well. I need to speak to someone who knows about my initial report.

I need to speak to Officer Cooper.

ELEVEN

I catch a cab to the police station, well aware that I'm now spending more on taxi fares than I would on a damned fan belt. This, however, is urgent.

I get into the station and ask to speak to Officer Cooper. He's out. I explain that it's about the murdered woman, and that just gets confusing. Cooper isn't involved with that case, and the woman on the desk isn't aware of any kidnapping.

I'm about to try explaining better when an officer crosses behind the desk. She's about my age, with dark skin, close-cropped curls, and high cheekbones. She wears a tailored blouse with a pencil skirt, but I recognize her even out of uniform.

Officer Jackson.

I hesitate. She's not exactly my biggest cheerleader, but I brush off the misgivings—when she hears what I have to say, her opinion will change. It has to.

I leave the desk and take off after her, catching up near the entrance.

"Officer Jackson," I say. "Aubrey Finch. I'm not sure if you remember me—"

"Yes, ma'am, I do." Her lips tighten, and I swear her gaze shunts toward the door, as if measuring the distance.

"It's about the murdered woman, the one whose body was found in the park. She's connected to the kidnapping."

"There is no kidnapping, Ms. Finch." She speaks slowly—clearly I'm having trouble processing this concept. "No child has been reported missing."

"Because his mother is dead. That's the woman you found. I recognized her the moment I saw her photo."

"I see . . ." Another glance toward the entrance, now filled with people coming in, talking fast among themselves. "If you believe you have information, I suggest you speak to the front desk. I really need to—"

"I'm telling you why that boy hasn't been reported missing. His mother is *dead*. She was murdered only two blocks from where I saw him taken. That's why he was in the park. That's why she didn't report his disappearance. She's *dead*."

Her gaze rises over my shoulder. "Ms. Finch, why don't you—"

"Are you listening to me? Look at my report. The woman in that photo matches my description. She was murdered two blocks from where I saw her child kidnapped—on the *day* she was murdered. Her son was wandering around the park alone, and then he was grabbed into an SUV, probably by the guy who just shot his mom."

"Excuse me," a voice says behind me. "Ms. . . . . Finch you said?"

"Aubrey Finch," I say as I turn to see a man in a suit and overcoat. A detective. Thank God.

"You said you saw the dead woman?" he continues. "With a child?"

"Yes, a little boy who was kidnapped by a man in an SUV—"

That's when I spot the camera. Right over the shoulder of

the man in the overcoat. A video camera with the local news call letters emblazoned on the side.

I see that camera with the recording light on, and I see myself reflected in the lens, my eyes wide, my hair shoved into a ponytail, my collar half tucked under.

I flip out my collar as I turn away from the man and the camera.

"The press conference is being held in room 1-B," Jackson says as she shuttles me off down a side hall. She opens a door and bustles me inside.

"I'm sorry," I say. "I thought that was a detective."

"I don't know what your deal is, Ms. Finch—"

"My *deal* is that I witnessed a kidnapping, and I understand that without a reported disappearance, there's no case. But this woman's death explains it. She was murdered, and her son ran to the playground. Her killer came for him. He knew the boy's name and when he called it, the boy ran over. Then he saw a stranger and freaked out. Her killer took him."

"There is *no* sign of a child with the woman on that CCTV footage. Which was taken two blocks away . . . and almost an hour *after* you reported the supposed kidnapping."

"Then . . ." I struggle for an explanation. "Then they grabbed the boy first."

She crosses her arms. "So why wasn't he with his mom? Why wasn't she in the park with him?"

"I . . . I don't know, but there must be an explanation. What I do know is that this is, beyond any doubt, the woman I saw Sunday afternoon."

"Sure, okay, this woman matches the description you provided. The very, very vague description."

"I can give you more. On Sunday, she wore no makeup except thick black eyeliner. She had what looked like track marks on her arms. Old ones."

Her brows shoot up. "You know what track marks look like, Ms. Finch?"

"I have seen them before. Now, when I was talking to her on Sunday, she took a call. She sounded very upset. She was speaking in another language. I don't know exactly, but I'm guessing Slavic."

"And your linguistic experience comes from . . . ?"

I walk farther into the room, taking a moment to relax. Don't get my temper up. Don't take offense.

"I'm not claiming any expertise, Officer. They may have been pockmarks, not track marks. She may have been speaking Portuguese. I'm taking wild guesses, the upshot being that this woman has marks on her arms and speaks a second language."

"You may say you're not positioning yourself as an expert, Ms. Finch, but there is a name for what you *are* doing. It's called attention seeking. Officer Cooper believes you did see a boy pulled into an SUV. I'm not so sure, and I think this proves I'm right. You invented a kidnapping story, and when that failed, you jumped on this tragedy to insinuate yourself into a real investigation."

"I don't want to insinuate myself into anything. I just want you to take my information and do your damned job."

Her eyes flash. "We are *trying* to do our job, Ms. Finch. That job right now is solving a murder. Please do not make that any more difficult than it already is."

She opens the door for me to leave.

"I'd like to speak to Officer Cooper, please," I say, with as much dignity as I can muster.

"You've wasted enough of his time."

I straighten and walk out, head high. I get three steps when a woman says, "Ms. Finch?"

I turn too eagerly, as if in the last three seconds Jackson has realized her mistake. Instead, I'm facing a woman with a microphone, a cameraman behind her.

"Ms. Finch? Aubrey Finch? Is that right?"

I look at the camera. I see that recording light on again. I see the call letters again, too, with two words I'd missed: Live News.

LIVE.

The reporter continues, "Did you say you know the woman whose body was found in Harris Park this morning?"

Live. I am on live TV.

My face. My name. On the news.

I back away slowly. "No, I'm sorry. I need to—"

"You said her son was kidnapped? You saw him taken the same day she was murdered?"

My face is on live television.

That's all I can process, her words barely penetrating.

"N-no. I'm sorry. It—it was a mistake."

I try to stop the babbling denials. I should not retract my words. I *know* the dead woman is the young mom. I know her son was taken.

I want to say yes. State my case. If the police aren't paying attention, well, maybe they will when I explain the situation on live television, and they're flooded with calls demanding that they investigate.

That is what I want to do. The heroic thing.

Instead I babble something unintelligible, and then hurry off down the hall. I take the coward's path, but it is already too late.

My name is in the news. My face is on television, connected to a major crime case.

What have I done?

TWELVE

I spend the rest of the morning obsessively watching the footage of me on the local news channel. It's there before I get back to my apartment. I stand at my laptop, newly bought fan belt abandoned on the counter as I watch and rewatch the video.

I could remove the segment. I know how. But that's as pointless as pulling a risqué photo uploaded by a pissed-off ex. Believe me—I know *that* from experience. The guy has the original, and by removing the copy, you only show him that it's upsetting you, which is the point. If I remove this, the news station will just replace the video and then wonder what made it hackworthy.

My footage is short. Mercifully so. I tell myself I don't look that bad in it. Yes, I appear to have just rolled out of bed, but I don't look crazy.

Is that what it's come to? I don't look *crazy*?

I don't *sound* crazy either. That's even more important. On the way home, I kept replaying those moments, and with each iteration, I imagined myself falling deeper into raving-maniac territory. But what I see is just a harried-looking woman explaining an admittedly wild theory.

My five seconds of infamy is buried in a longer clip of raw footage shot as they'd been coming into the station and caught me trying to talk to Officer Jackson. There's already a polished version of the live broadcast, which I have been left out of. Discarded on the editing room floor.

I should be grateful for that. This raw footage will be removed soon, and I will disappear. That's what I want. Let me fade back into anonymity again. My fear is not that the police will come after me. The statute of limitations has already run out on my crimes. But if my past catches up, it'll give Paul so much ammunition that I might as well sign Charlotte over to him now.

I'm glad that I've been cut from the official news clip. The problem is it means my claim is being ignored. There's even a brief note under the raw footage, reassuring the viewer that no child is missing.

No child is missing.

Not even "no child has been *reported* missing." My claim has been red-stamped with the absolute certainty of a veto.

Please ignore this woman. No child was harmed in the making of this murder.

I don't need to hack into the police department email server now. I know what they've decided. No child has been reported missing, and so my claim is being ignored. Understandably ignored. I must admit that. This isn't a case of incompetent policing. Officer Cooper, at least, has been fair and patient with me. The fact remains, though, that three days have passed with no evidence of a missing child.

Because his mother is dead.

That makes perfect sense to me, but I can see how it sounded to Officer Jackson, considering that she already thought I was attention-seeking. There's nothing to tie this boy to the dead woman.

Over and over, I refresh the news page and pray that I will

see more. An update. That the woman has been identified, and the police have discovered she *did* have a child, who is now missing. Once that's out, the authorities will throw all their resources into the hunt, and the child will be found, frightened but safe, the killer caught, the young mother avenged.

And they all lived happily ever after.

Except they don't, do they?

His mother is still dead. And her son will live with that forever.

I know what that will be like. I know exactly what it will be like.

I tell people my mother died when I was "just a baby." I'm parroting the words I heard growing up. People often presume that means she died in childbirth, and I don't correct them. The truth . . .

The truth is the sickening crunch of metal. The world spinning, flipping upside down. Me, screaming, wordlessly screaming in absolute terror. Then my mother's voice, weak and whispery.

"Bree?"

Her fingers finding my arm. Clutching it. Her hand wet and sticky.

"It's going to be okay, Bree. Someone will come."

Someone will come.

Night fell, and the car went dark. My mother told me she loved me. Over and over, she told me. And then, after a while, everything went quiet.

Once I admitted to my father what I remember.

"Stop that."

"But I—"

"You couldn't remember that. You were just a baby."

Except I *wasn't* a baby, not in any more than the colloquial sense. I'd been two years old, and I do remember. I remember waiting for someone to come and save us. I remember hearing cars passing on the country highway. I remember that no one stopped, not until the next day, morning sun glinting off the car, and by then it was too late.

People saw the car. They must have. Whoever hit us knew what they did, and they just kept going, driving away as fast as they could. Then others passed, and they saw a damaged vehicle in the field, and they told themselves there was no one in it. Just a crashed car waiting for a tow truck. Or kids abandoning a wreck after a joy ride.

I'm sure no one's in it, and really, I don't have time to stop and check.

My mom died when I was a baby.

I was not a baby. I was old enough to have toddled to that road and gotten help.

"Stop that, Bree. You were trapped in a car seat."

"Maybe if—"

"You were a baby."

I was not a baby.

My phone rings. I jump. It isn't a number I recognize, so I wait to see if they'll leave a message. When they don't, I stare at my list of received calls, and see Paul's number, from yesterday.

I've thought of calling him. Twice, I've gotten as far as pulling up his number, my finger hovering over the Call icon.

Hey, Paul. Sorry to bother you at work, but I, uh, need to tell you something. So there's this news clip . . .

Is that really necessary?

This is the question that stops me. The video clip will probably be removed. My name doesn't appear in the article. Paul is the kind of guy who flips through his headline feed once a day and assimilates the data based on that. UNIDENTIFIED WOMAN MURDERED IN GRANT PARK. Check. CITY HALL ARGUING OVER INFRASTRUCTURE BUDGET. Check. TENSIONS RISE IN MIDDLE EAST. Check.

There, I have a basic idea of what's going on in the world, now let's get back to work.

When we were dating, I learned that if I mentioned current events I'd get a long pause followed by him saying, "Tell me more about that." He was happy to get the information; he just felt no need to seek it out on his own. If I wanted that kind of conversation with Paul, I was far better off delving into the background of the news. Let's talk about the issues surrounding murdered women. Let's talk about the city's infrastructure problems. Let's talk about the history of the conflict in the Middle East. *That's* what interested him, and I remember how exciting it was to be able to talk to someone who wanted a conversation deeper than news bites, a guy who knew the history *behind* those news bites, who actually enjoyed talking about it, having a *real* conversation.

Except, for us, that's what passed for real conversation. An in-depth discussion of Middle Eastern politics.

Paul, I need to talk to you. There are things I need to explain. Things about me . . .

I put my phone aside. I'm going to roll these dice and play the odds and wager on Paul never seeing the video clip. If he does, I can explain it.

As for who else might view it, I won't worry about that either. It's five seconds in an unedited segment from a suburban news station. No one outside of Oxford will see it, and very few inside will.

I'm safe.

Which is more than I can say for that little boy.

It's six o'clock Thursday evening. I've been out for a couple of hours, getting groceries after replacing the fan belt in my car. It doesn't take me that long to shop for myself, but before I go, I always check on a few less-mobile neighbors to "see if they need anything from the store."

In truth, I didn't need *anything* myself today. I was conducting a test. If I go out in public, will anyone recognize me? While I caught a few looks, no one said anything, and I suspect I was just being paranoid about those looks. I will presume that if anyone saw me on the news this morning, they didn't recognize me. Given how I looked in that video, I'd hope they wouldn't recognize me.

I return to my building, drop off bags for my neighbors, and bask in a few moments of Zen calm. There's been no fallout from the video clip, and now I have done good deeds. I have made people smile. I feel good about myself.

Then I climb the stairs to my floor and hear someone banging at a door. I pause, groceries in hand, and I consider withdrawing.

I consider fleeing.

Because I hear someone knocking at a door? It's probably not even mine.

I glance around the corner to see someone standing in front of my door, hand rising to knock again.

Paul.

I pull back and ponder sneaking down the stairs, tossing the groceries in my car, and going for coffee. Wait it out.

That would be cowardly. Also, pointless. If Paul wants to talk to me, he's going to find a way, even if it involves skywriting "Pick up the damned phone, Bree."

I step from the stairwell. He turns, and I expect he'll wait there, not saying a word until we're safely ensconced in the privacy of my apartment.

Instead, he bears down on me, and on his face there's an expression I don't think I've ever seen. Barely contained rage.

"What the hell is this?" He waves around the hall. "I didn't even have to ring up. There's no damned lock on the front door."

"There is. It's broken."

And has been since I moved in.

"This place reeks of pot," he says.

I stare at him. "Are you accusing me of smoking pot, Paul?"

"Well, that might explain a few things."

He knows about the news clip.

I fix him with a level stare. "You know I don't drink. I certainly don't do drugs. If you are accusing me of that, I will take a test. Just say the word."

"I'm not accusing you of anything, Aubrey. I'm saying people here are smoking pot."

I sputter a laugh. "If you think you can find any building—uptown or downtown—that doesn't have at least one resident smoking pot, you need a reality check, Counselor."

"Don't—" He bites it off and advances on me, voice lowering. "This is about embarrassing me, isn't it? I keep offering you money, but you've made it clear that you're fine. And then I see this."

I pass him to open my door. I step inside and hold it open. He follows.

"My apartment isn't fancy—" I begin.

"It's a dump."

"The fact that you can even say that proves you need to get out of midtown Chicago a little more often. Go see how people live when they aren't born with an Ivy League education fund. This isn't skid row. It's working-class America, and I'm fine with it, and I think it's fine for our daughter to see a little bit of it, too. Broaden her horizons."

"My daughter's horizons don't include walking past that junkie parked on the front step."

I wheel on him. "That is a military veteran who lost his damned leg. Show a little respect."

He steps back. Rubs his hands over his face. "All right. I'm sorry. That was uncalled for. But I don't understand what you're doing here, Aubrey."

"Not trying to embarrass you or punish you."

"Punish yourself, then." He meets my gaze. "That's it. This is about punishing yourself. You had an affair, didn't you?"

"*What?*"

He walks into the apartment, still talking, his back to me. "That was the first thing I thought when you left. You'd met someone. I expected you'd wait a few weeks after leaving and then drop the bomb. When you didn't, I thought that must not be the answer. But it was, wasn't it? Not that you left me for another man. That you met someone and had an affair. A fling. Then you left out of guilt, and now you won't take anything from me because you're punishing yourself."

I laugh. I can't help it. The sound startles him, and he turns.

"Seriously, Paul? I was home with a toddler. How the hell would I find time to meet someone, let alone have an affair?" I walk into the kitchen. "Now, if you'd like coffee—"

"I saw the video clips," he says. "Someone spotted you on the news and told me. I watched it and . . . and I don't know what to say."

I stop. Then I turn to face him. "I'm sorry. I should have warned you. If this causes you any embarrassment—"

"Christ, Bree. No. I'm worried about *you*. You saw something in the park."

"I didn't see 'something.' I saw a boy get taken. Kidnapped."

"Putting aside what you think you saw—"

"What I *think* I saw? A boy was taken, and now his mother is dead, and the police are ignoring me."

He goes quiet. Then he says, carefully, "I know you wanted more children—"

"*What?*"

He runs a hand through his hair. "You said that had nothing to do with you leaving, but you left shortly after I told you I wanted to wait."

"What does this have to do with me seeing a child abducted?"

"You want more kids, so when you thought you saw a child in danger—"

"You think I'm hallucinating a kidnapped kid because, what? I feel like my future babies have been stolen from me? That is the most messed-up amateur psychobabble I have ever heard."

His lips compress. "Don't mock me, Aubrey. I'm trying to help."

"You know what help sounds like, Paul? 'Aubrey, I saw that clip on the news, and I can't believe the police are brushing you off. Let me see what I can do—I have contacts in the department.'"

He opens his mouth.

"No," I say. "Those aren't the words coming out of your mouth, so I don't want to hear the ones that are. Get out."

"I just want—"

"And I don't give a damn. You want to know the real reason why I don't take money from you? Because paying for this place means it's mine. All mine. So if I tell you to get your ass out, you are going to turn around and do it. *Now.*"

He hesitates. Then he stalks out, the door slapping shut behind him.

Now I'm angry. No, I am furious, in a way I haven't been for years. A way I haven't allowed myself to be. At last, I have a target for my bottled-up rage.

Paul.

He didn't give me hell for being on the news. Didn't storm over here to accuse me of publicly humiliating him. I think that might be better. Then I could have snarled back that this wasn't about him.

What he did is worse. It's condescending crap. It's Paul thinking his wife has lost her mind. Poor, poor Aubrey. She's hallucinating missing children because she's sad that she doesn't have another baby yet.

Screw you, Paul. I saw a boy kidnapped. Any doubt I had evaporated the moment I saw his mother's photo. That is the woman. He was the boy. He was taken.

And I'm going to prove it.

THIRTEEN

I have the photo. The one the police are very clearly not interested in. So it's time to show them what I can do with it. I'm going to get numbers on that plate, and then I'm going to find that SUV, if it means hacking into the damned DMV to do it.

Yeah . . .

That doesn't turn out quite as well as I hope. I can't get any characters from the plate even when I download an illegal copy of the best enhancement software I know. Whoever obscured that plate knew what they were doing, and the mud is caked on thick enough that all I can make out is a few straight lines.

It's a setback, but not a dead end. I'm too pissed off to let it be a dead end.

I met the dead woman. However shallow our conversation might have been, there is a clue there. I'm sure of it. So I meditate, clearing my mind to focus on our conversation, tugging wispy threads from memory and writing them down. Then I return to meditating and teasing out more threads.

It takes two hours to recall our brief chat, one that wasn't even a conversation, but simply a series of exchanges punctuating a lesson on cartwheels.

"A librarian," she laughs when I tell her what I do for a living. "I did not picture you as a librarian. But I suppose that proves it's been a long time since I set foot in a library. I really should take my son sometime."

"You should. We have great early-reader programs."

"That'd be good. I've been reading with him at night."

My son. Him. She never gave me a name. Not for the boy, not for herself.

"Do they have morning programs?" she asks. "I work at a pizza place. We don't open until noon so I never work mornings."

A pizza place. That's all I have. She works at a pizza place that opens at noon.

There are thirteen pizza parlors in Oxford. Only five open at noon, and two are chains. If she worked at one of those, I'd think she'd say, "I work at Domino's."

I'll start with non-chain pizza parlors.

I rise from my laptop . . . and see the clock on the microwave. It's after eleven at night, and I won't get far questioning sleepy employees.

This can wait until tomorrow.

It has to.

I wake the next morning to a voice mail from Paul.

"Aubrey, it's, uh, me."

As if I couldn't tell by the phone number.

"I realize how my remarks yesterday could have been misconstrued."

Yeah, pretty sure you knew exactly what you were saying.

"I don't doubt that you saw a child pulled into a van."

You just think, like Officer Cooper, that I overreacted to a frustrated parent hauling their kid from the playground.

"I'd like to discuss this. If there's any possibility that the police are in error here, I will help you get through to them."

Sure, you'll help . . . if I'm actually right, which you seriously doubt. Let's talk, and you can convince me that I've made a mistake.

"Call me, Bree. Please."

I hit Delete and get ready for work.

Ingrid knows about the video clip. So does Nancy, the other librarian on duty. One of them saw the live coverage and told the other. They don't say a word about it to me. Which means I'm robbed of the opportunity to explain. They just keep sneaking looks my way.

Those looks aren't disapproving. Again, like with Paul, I almost wish that they were. I can deal with disapproval. Instead, their looks ooze trepidation. Like Paul, they question my mental stability.

By eleven, I'm ready to confront Ingrid. March her into the staff room and have it out.

I know you saw that news clip. Let me give my side of the story.

Let me show you I am fine.

I'm considering how to do that without being confrontational, when a voice says, "Aubrey?"

I turn with my "How may I help you?" smile. I don't recognize the guy. He's about my age, good-looking in a ten-years-post-frat way. Really not my taste in men, but he fixes me with a blazing smile that says he's pretty damned sure he's *every* woman's taste in men.

"Hey there," he says.

"May I help you?"

Another toothy grin. "I certainly hope so."

Not today, asshole. Come back tomorrow, and maybe I'll be ready for your crap, with an empty smile and then, "Oh, I think you want to speak to Nancy about that."

Nancy is nearing retirement age, and on my first day, she said that if I ever had a customer being too friendly, I could pass him off to her. I'd laughed at the time, certain that no one hits on librarians. I'd been wrong. I have appreciated Nancy's kindness and help in the past, which makes her wary looks today so much harder to handle.

Right now, though, I am in no mood for this. The old Aubrey rises as I stand, stone-faced, waiting for the guy to say something productive.

"Has anyone ever told you that you don't look like a librarian?" he says.

"I'm sure every librarian has been told—repeatedly—that she does not look like a librarian. Or, at least, not like the image of a librarian held by people who don't frequent libraries."

His smile falters at that. He opens his mouth. Shuts it. Straightens. And I think he's actually going to abort course. But after a moment, he leans over the counter.

"You're the girl from the news, right?"

"I stopped being a 'girl' about ten years ago. But if you're asking whether I was briefly on the news yesterday, yes, I was. I didn't realize I was talking to a reporter. I was just there to make a statement."

"You don't like reporters?"

He smiles when he says it, casual, overly charming, gaze never leaving mine. But the problem with trying to flirt while holding eye contact? You give yourself away in little things. Eyelids lowering or rising. Pupils dilating or contracting, just for a second.

"I like reporters just fine," I say. "Except when they're trying to get a story by pretending they aren't reporters." I lean in to whisper, "Don't you *hate* that?"

He blinks.

"Go away," I say. "There's no story here."

I walk toward the other side of the circulation desk. The guy skirts the exterior, following me.

"Can't blame a guy for trying, right?" He winks, sliding back into frat-boy mode. "You said you were trying to give a statement. The police weren't listening. That doesn't seem fair. You're obviously a smart woman. Look where you work." He waves around the library. "And you saw right through my patter. I don't think anyone has ever—"

"Cut the crap," I say.

Ingrid looks over fast enough to inflict whiplash.

"I made my statement to the police," I say. "I trust that they will handle it. I don't want to impede their investigation, so I have nothing more to say on the matter."

"They're ignoring you. You do know that, right?"

"Their priority is identifying a murdered woman. As soon as they do, they'll discover she has a child, who is missing."

"Can I quote you on that?"

"No, but you can quote me on this."

I start to raise my middle finger. I stop myself, but Ingrid still lets out a chirp of alarm and scampers over.

"I am so sorry, sir. Ms. Finch has been under a great deal of stress."

"He's a reporter," I say. "One who doesn't understand that I am at work."

"What time do you get off?" he says. "We can grab coffee. Maybe a drink."

I snort.

"*Aubrey*," Ingrid whispers. To the reporter, she warbles something about stress again as she shunts me off to the staff room.

"You cannot speak like that in front of patrons," she says as she closes the door.

"I'm sorry," I say.

She hovers, as if waiting for an argument.

When I don't give it, she nods slowly and says, "I'm concerned. That's not like you, Aubrey."

Actually, it's totally like me. It's the me I abandoned when I met Paul. I'm not saying I miss that girl. In some ways, I feel like her older sister, rolling her eyes and saying, "Seriously?" Yet the other part of that girl, the part that had no problem telling a reporter where to shove his shtick? Yeah, I kinda miss her.

"You're right," I say. "I'm under a lot of stress. About the news clip, I'd like to explain—"

"No need."

"I'd really like—"

"Why don't you take the rest of the day off? It's slow today." She pats my shoulder, but there's a hesitancy to it, like patting a Rottweiler.

"I'm fine," I say. "I—"

"Really. I insist. Take the day off and rest. We'll see you tomorrow."

I have an unexpected half day off. I'm trying not to freak out about that. In fact, I'm trying to tell myself it's exactly what I need. The more time I have to investigate, the faster I can vindicate myself.

Of course, the first thing I do is go online, in hopes I've already been vindicated. But there's no update on the case, nothing to indicate the murdered woman has been identified.

Time to get to work. When I left this morning, I took care with my outfit. Dress pants, a white blouse, a dark blazer. Hair pulled back in a sleek ponytail. Minimal makeup. I leave my contacts out and wear my black-rimmed glasses.

Does the mirror show a woman who could pass for a police detective or federal agent? Yes, and that's no accident. I won't tell anyone I'm a cop, but if they draw that conclusion, it isn't my fault. Or so I tell myself. The truth is that I'm no longer the pissed-at-the-world twenty-year-old who pulls crap like that and doesn't give a damn. I know better.

It's 12:10 when I reach the first pizza place on my list. No one there has seen the woman in the photo. On to the next one. I hesitate in the parking lot. Pop's Pizzeria is a hole-in-the-wall. A tiny take-out parlor in a tiny strip mall. The sign actually reads POPS PIZZERIA. It's that kind of sign, the sort you get done by a friend who has a buzz saw and a few cans of paint and a C in grade school English. It's either going to have the most amazing pizza ever . . . or the worst. From the lack of cars out front, I'm betting the latter.

I go inside. The counter area is empty, of both customers and staff. When I call "Hello?" I hear voices in the back, speaking Italian. I call again. A door opens and a woman emerges, wiping flour-covered hands on an apron. A mix of yeast and tomato and oregano wafts out, and it smells amazing.

"Five minutes," she says in heavily accented English. "It is ready in five minutes."

"I'm not picking up an order," I say.

"You make order?"

I smile. "I wasn't planning to, but judging from that smell, I might." I extend my hand. "Bree Minor. I'm trying to find a missing woman."

I'm straddling a line, using my maiden name and not calling myself a police officer. I'm still nervous. Still not sure I can pull this off. But for the missing woman and her son, I'm going to try.

I continue. "We have reason to believe she worked at a pizza—"

"Kim." Before I can speak, she opens the door into the back room and calls out in urgent, rapid-fire Italian.

A man walks out. He's younger, maybe my age.

"Is Kim okay?" he asks.

I hesitate. I have no idea what police protocol would be in an actual murder investigation. But these people aren't going to know either, and I'll have better luck getting details if I admit there's been a crime.

"I'm sorry," I say. "I'm investigating a murder."

I pause a moment, respect for the dead; then I open a manila folder and hold out the printed photo.

The man takes it, and his eyes shut for a second before he nods. "Yes, that's Kim. She didn't come in to work yesterday, and I've been calling. That isn't like her. Mamma was worried. I said I'd stop by her place later."

He bends in front of his mother and talks to her in Italian. She crosses herself and then folds her hands in her lap, her gaze down.

"I'm very sorry," I say. "But I do thank you for identifying her. I also need to ask about her son."

The man frowns. "Kim had a son?"

My heart thuds. "Evidently."

"She never mentioned any kids. Did he live with his father?"

No. Please, no.

"I only know she had a little boy," I say. "Four or five years old."

The man frowns, turns to his mother, and says something. Her eyes widen, and she shakes her head vehemently.

"Kim did not have any children," the woman says in English. "I would always tease her, saying she needed to find a nice young man and have babies. Perhaps this woman is not her."

"That's Kim, Mamma," her son says softly.

"When was her last shift?" I ask.

"Monday. She works Fridays, Saturdays, and Mondays. Can I ask when she . . . ?"

"Tuesday."

"And it was in the news?" He curses under his breath, and his mother berates him in Italian. He apologizes for the profanity and says, "I haven't been paying attention to the news lately." He gestures at the shop. "We only opened a few months ago, and Kim is—was—our only employee. I've been putting in twelve-hour shifts every day."

"I understand. Would I be able to see her employment record? I need her current address."

"Sure." He starts heading for the back and then slows. When he turns, he stammers. "I–I'm not sure I have her record. Here, I mean. Like I said, we're new, and we haven't quite caught up on paperwork."

"I'm not with the IRS, sir. Whatever arrangement you had with Kim, I'm sure she planned to pay her income taxes."

He nods. "Right. Yes. It was just . . . informal."

"While a Social Security number would be useful, I'll take anything. My only interest is in catching her killer."

"Give the girl whatever you have, Francis," the woman says.

"Of course, Mamma."

FOURTEEN

Kim *must* be the dead woman. Her employers both ID'd the photo, and they haven't heard from her since before the murder. But Kim doesn't have a child.

So how can she be the young mother I met in the park?

Is there a chance the dead woman isn't the person I met?

No. The young woman I met said she worked in a pizza parlor that opened at noon. Two people just identified the murdered woman as an employee in their pizza parlor, which opens at noon.

I must pursue this until either I solve this puzzle or I am somehow proven wrong. Even thinking that last part sets my heart racing, my breath coming short.

If I am wrong . . .

If I am wrong, I've given Paul what he needs to paint me as an unstable mother. First, I start hallucinating kidnapped kids. Now, I'm pursuing my delusion even after I've learned that the dead woman didn't seem to *have* a child.

I am risking the one thing that is most important to me—custody of my daughter—and for what? Even if I am right, is it worth the risk to help a stranger?

I should have stopped as soon as Cooper told me there was no missing child. That's what other people would do. Normal people. If they even took the time to *report* what looked like an abduction, they'd have dropped it there. Duty done, let the police handle the rest. It's none of their business.

I did report the kidnapping. I reported that the dead woman was the boy's mother. Now I've learned that the dead woman wasn't *anyone's* mother. So drop it. Drop it and step away before I get into more trouble.

I should do that. But I can't. I will always be that little girl trapped in a car with her dying mother, the girl who grew up knowing she might still have a mother if someone had stopped, if someone had even taken a moment to report seeing a wrecked car. I will always be the eighteen-year-old rushing home to help her father when no one else would, arriving too late to stop him from taking his life.

No one helped my mother. No one helped my father. No one wanted to get involved. I cannot be that person. Ever. If there is any chance that a boy is out there, in trouble, and no one is searching for him, then I must *be* that one person. The person who cares. The person who gets involved.

Whatever the cost.

Kim's employers gave me her address. Before I check it out, I place a call to the police station tip line.

"Hi, I'm phoning about the young woman found in the park. I'm sure I've seen her working at Pop's Pizzeria over on the west side. I think her name's Kimberly."

It's not perfect, but at this point, calling in under my own name is a surefire way to make sure no one follows up.

The address leads to an apartment building. A nicer one than mine, though hardly upscale. At least it has a controlled entry. That would work better if I didn't just need to stand outside fumbling in my purse for my "key" until a resident came out. He even held the door for me.

I head straight up. Kim's apartment is at the end of the hall, which is perfect. I slip out through the stairwell, make sure no one's around, and walk to her door.

I should just go get the super. Make up a story, like I did with the pizza places. That *should* be my only option here, confronted with a locked door.

It is not my only option.

Hacking isn't the extent of my skills. It isn't the extent of my crimes.

I bend to check the lock. Old building; simple security. I can open it.

I'll get inside and find evidence of a child. That's all I need. Just the reassurance that a child exists, and then I will back off and wait for the police to ID Kim and figure it out for themselves.

I'm about to start on the lock when I hear a noise inside. I put my ear to the door and pick up a radio or TV.

Maybe she left it on when she went out.

That's reasonable, but still . . .

I rap on the door. Ten seconds later, it swings open. A woman stands there, late twenties, tiny build, brown skin, her hair swept into the kind of style I know well: grab an elastic at 5 A.M. when the baby wakes, shove your hair up, and leave it like that until you collapse in bed at night and maybe, just maybe, remember to take it out. Sure enough, bright-colored wooden blocks litter the hall floor, and through the open door I spot a high chair in the kitchen.

The woman stage-whispers, "Yes?"

"Baby napping?"

A tired smile and a nod. "She just went down."

I gesture to ask if she'd rather speak in the hall. She nods again and steps out, while keeping the door cracked open.

"I'm looking for Kim Mason," I say.

Her brows knit. "Kim . . ."

"Mason. Her employer gave me this address."

The frown deepens. I tell her the address, and she says, "That's this apartment, but I don't know a Kim."

"How long have you lived here?"

"My husband and I moved in after we got married. Two . . . no, two and a half years ago."

Long before the pizza place even opened, meaning Kim didn't move recently and forget to update her address with her employer.

I take out the photo. "Have you seen this woman before?"

Her eyes widen. "That's the girl on the news. The one who was murdered."

"Have you ever seen her anywhere else?"

She shakes her head. "If I had, I'd have called it in." She looks up at me. "You're with the police."

"I'm helping with the investigation." *True enough.*

Her gaze returns to the photo. Then she looks at me. "This is exactly why we left the city. My parents said that since my husband had a good job, we should move someplace safe to raise our babies."

No place is safe. Because every place has people, and the threat isn't always the gangbanger on the corner. It can be the woman next door. Or the guy lying in bed beside you.

Which isn't what she wants to hear.

I remember Paul last night, giving me crap about my building's broken front door. When we picked our house, he'd looked around and declared it a good neighborhood. A "safe" one. The sort of place he felt comfortable leaving his new wife and raising his future kids, and I wanted to gape at him and say, "You're a *lawyer*. You should know better."

It was like mistaking our white picket fence for ten feet of electrical barbed wire. But he couldn't see that. Which I suppose explains how he ended up with me. He saw what he wanted. He accepted the image I presented, of a woman who had never done anything worse than rack up traffic tickets. A bit scattered and quirky but totally harmless. That's the package he bought. What he got . . .

What he got was very different. He'd finally sensed that and backed away.

I ask the young woman a few more questions. It's clear, though, that she'd never seen Kim before her photo appeared on the news.

Outside, I walk around. There's only one other apartment building on this street, and it's five stories tall. Kim gave a seventh-floor address.

Which means she gave a *false* one.

FIFTEEN

I am at home, tracking down Kim Mason. Or the woman pretending to be Kim Mason. It's a fake identity, too, as I quickly discover. Working under the table. Giving her employer a false address. Hiding the fact she has a child. Those are not the actions of a young woman who's just a little cagey with her personal info.

A fake ID takes this to a whole other level, especially if she had documentation to back it up. There was a time when I toyed with that option. It didn't last long, but I learned what building a false identity entails, and despite what we see on television, there isn't some guy in the shady part of town who'll set you up with an ironclad birth certificate for ten grand.

What you *can* get from that dude in the shady neighborhood, though, is fake ID cards, and for a whole lot less than ten grand. Those cards will get you into a bar before you hit twenty-one. They will not get you past a police check.

If Kim Mason was working under the table, that suggests she's only using fake ID, not an actual false identity complete with Social Security number. She's living under a false name the cheap way.

Why would she do that? Tons of reasons, as I well know, most of them involving mistakes made, a fresh start needed. But her situation adds a wrinkle. A hidden son.

But I need to prove there *was* a son. That a child has been taken. And I am no closer to accomplishing that goal than I was when the police first turned me away.

So I am home, utilizing skills left rusty for years. I'm hacking my way to Kim Mason.

I know that's a fake name. Her address, and likely 99 percent of everything she gave her employer, is also fake. But there will be that 1 percent. The single piece of information she provided that needed to be genuine.

A phone number.

Her boss said that he'd used that number in the past, and she answered. So it is correct.

I quickly establish that it's a prepaid. Which is what I expect. Someone like this won't have a legitimate credit card, much less be paying a monthly cell phone bill with it.

What I need are her call lists. That could take serious work. Tech companies update their security constantly. Or they do . . . if they're not selling cheap prepaids, which is ironic really. People buy prepaids because they provide anonymity, and yet hacking into those records isn't nearly as tough as it would be with a regular phone.

I download an encrypted version of her call records for my laptop and run it through a simple decryption program. Then I write out the last dozen numbers of calls made and received and dial her last call placed. That number goes to a take-out place. The next is her work. The third just rings, no voice mail. The fourth tells me the number is no longer in service, which means I put a big red circle around it for later. It's the fifth-oldest call that actually gives me a response. When a man answers, I say, "Hi, I just found this phone on the sidewalk, and I'm trying to track down the owner. All I have is a first name. Do you know anyone named Kim?"

"Kim Lyons?"

"Maybe?"

"I've got a girl, rents a place of mine, named Kim Lyons."

"Is her phone number . . . ?" I read it out.

He checks and says, "Yeah, that's Kim."

"Great! I'll drop this off for her. Where does she live?"

I don't expect him to actually tell me, but I guess that just goes to prove that the world is full of people far more trusting than me. People who hear a friendly female voice on the phone, a Good Samaritan trying to return a lost phone, and they don't even consider nefarious possibilities.

He rattles off an address and then says, "That's really nice of you, you know that? Most people would just walk right past a phone on the ground. Or swipe it. Kim's a good kid. She'll appreciate that."

"It's the least I can do. I know how tough it is, being a single mom."

He pauses. "Single mom?"

"Bad guess?" I laugh. "Sorry. Apparently, I suck at this amateur detective stuff. I was trying to figure out whose phone it was, and I saw a photo of a little boy. I thought it might be hers."

"Nah, Kim's just a kid herself. No little ones yet. But she'll be thrilled to get her phone back. So thanks for doing that."

"Happy to help."

Kim Mason—or whoever she is—has rented a house on the outskirts of Oxford. It's no country manor. There *are* no country manors in that area, too close to the city's waste disposal, too close to the railroad tracks. The house is much bigger than any apartment, but in a secluded area, away from public transport and city amenities.

A secluded place.

A private place.

That's the first word that comes to mind when I see the property: "privacy." It's on a dirt road, and the house itself is surrounded by trees and set a couple hundred feet back. There's a rear yard where a child would never be spotted. The nearest neighbors are a half mile away. A child could play unseen *and* unheard, even at preschooler decibels.

Could I hide Charlotte in a place like this? Yes. Room for the two of us to walk and play, and a driveway that loops around the rear, so I could get her out into a waiting vehicle and take her into the city, where I'd be just another woman with a child.

I break in the back door. It's easy work—simple locks and no chance of a passerby spotting me behind the house. Once I get the door open, though, I see that it shouldn't have been so easy to break in. There are two dead bolts. *Good* dead bolts, plus a basic security system. But the dead bolts weren't fastened and the security system isn't on.

I head straight for the kitchen. This is where I'll find evidence of the boy. When Charlotte isn't staying over, I put away her toys and store her booster seat, and take her special pillow from the bed we share, and she disappears . . . until you open my fridge.

I am not a mass consumer of juice boxes or string cheese or tiny yogurt containers covered in cartoon animals. Even without that, you'll find signs of Charlotte in my cutlery drawer, two child-size sets with plastic handles. There's more plastic in the china cupboard—cups and plates and bowls. A five-year-old might have graduated to silver cutlery, but I know there will be signs of him in that kitchen.

There are not.

I check every cupboard, and all I find is glassware and china. There's food in the fridge and the pantry, but nothing particularly child-friendly. Not even a box of Cheerios.

I open every drawer and door, and I see only what I'd expect in the house of a twenty-three-year-old. The basics. That's it.

He is here.

He must be here.

And what if he's not?

I won't think of that. I can't. There is a child, and I will find evidence of him in this house, proof I can take to the police.

The living room is empty. Yes, there's furniture, but only the sort that comes with a rented house—not so much as a magazine or a blanket added. In the bathroom, I find only women's toiletries. No tear-free shampoo. No superhero-shaped bottle of bubble bath. No tiny toothbrush alongside hers.

I grip the counter, looking at myself in the mirror.

Have I made a mistake?

What have I done? What have I risked?

Keep looking.

I head into the bedrooms. There are three. Two have nothing but bare beds and empty dressers. The third is Kim's room. There's not much, but it's clearly occupied, and again, it's all hers. Women's clothing. Women's shoes. Women's accessories. Nothing more.

I walk into the bedroom right beside Kim's. That's the one I'd pick for Charlotte, keeping her close. But then I hear a truck rattle past and realize the window overlooks the front yard. While I can't see the road through the trees, if I was being paranoid, I wouldn't want light visible from more than one bedroom at night.

I search the third bedroom, with a rear-facing window. I open every drawer. I pull them all the way out and check underneath. I open the closet, pat the shelves and then bring in a kitchen chair to examine them closer. I don't even find a piece of LEGO.

It is only when I peer beneath the bed that I spot something. I crawl under it, and my hand closes around the familiar shape of a juice box.

Gripping it, I start backing out, and my other hand brushes something smooth and slick. When I pull that out with me, I find myself holding a book.

Where the Wild Things Are.

I smile, as I crack open the cover. I know every word of this book. It's one of Charlotte's favorites. I flip through, and I remember the woman's words.

"I've been reading with him."

I hold the book up to the light. There's no dust on the cover, meaning it hasn't been under there since the last tenants.

I flip through again, and there, written on the inside cover in shaky block letters . . .

BRANDON.

I examine the empty drink box. It's a child-sized one, grape juice, with a purple mouse on the front. Also no sign of dust. When I turn the box upside down, a drop of purple liquid falls.

As I watch that drop fall, a thought forms. I toss the book and box onto the bed and race around the house, checking the garbage cans.

Every one is empty.

Completely empty.

There is not one item of trash inside. And no bags outside.

You erased him. You knew something was coming—someone was coming—and you erased every trace of him.

I go back into the bedroom, and I pick up the box and the book.

Found you, Brandon.

No, I've found proof of him. Proof that I cannot take to the police, because it'll be like when I told Officer Cooper about the mud-smeared license plate.

"*See this juice box? This book? Here's the proof.*"

"*A . . . juice box. And a . . . book. Left under a bed.*"

"*Right, but—*"

"*Tell me again how you happened to find these things, Ms. Finch?*"

I would admit to breaking in—even to hacking—if it would convince the police that a child is missing. It will not.

I found *evidence* of you, Brandon.

And now I need to find *you*.

SIXTEEN

When I leave Kim's rental, I head to Chicago, for a rental locker I have not visited since the day I married Paul. No, that isn't true. I did come here three years ago. To the locker I rent under a fake name, from the kind of company that doesn't ask questions if you pay in cash.

The last time I visited was a week after Charlotte was born. And I removed a gun. For six months, I kept that between the mattress and box spring of our bed, until Charlotte started to crawl, and the day she did I brought it back to this locker.

Paul never knew about the gun. Aubrey Finch isn't the kind of woman who'd even know how to hold one. She certainly wouldn't want one in the house. Not with a child, I agree, yet when Charlotte was born, all my old fears ignited.

They are irrational fears. I know that. It isn't as if I have a million bucks, stolen from my partners, stashed in this locker. No one is going to come after me. When I first left home, I'd slept with a gun under my pillow for a year before realizing I was safe. After Charlotte, though, nightmares plagued every bit of post-baby sleep I got—nightmares of someone coming for her, taking her, hurting her. Those, too, eventually died down, and I was fine returning the gun.

Now, though, I am again worried. I'm digging into something dangerous. Kim is dead. Her son is missing. It is my earliest fears with Charlotte come to life. Someone from Kim's past came for her. I'm certain of it. If that person finds out I'm digging into Brandon's disappearance? Into Kim's death?

Time to visit the storage locker.

The space is barely closet sized. My possessions would actually fit into a box. But I can't exactly stick a box in a sketchy storage locker without the risk of someone prying open the door and knowing they've hit the jackpot.

I've scattered my treasures among thrift store furniture. Taped under each drawer of a dresser is twenty thousand dollars. None of it is stolen. When Ruben first came to me with his hacking offer, it'd been a get-rich-quick scheme. Such things always are, aren't they? The problem is that most thieves don't funnel their ill-gotten gains into a 401K. They stuff it into a needle or spend it on a blackjack table. Not me. Of the money I made, I kept one-third to live on. One-third I donated to charity for veterans suffering from PTSD. The final third I gifted, anonymously, to people in need. That doesn't make me Robin Hood. I *did* keep the one-third, and I enjoyed "sticking it to the man" a little too much.

This hidden money, though, comes from my father. It is my inheritance. When I walked away from my criminal life and reinvented myself, I knew better than to throw around money, even if it was legally mine. I lived the life I'd created for myself—a girl with a high-school education, working sales jobs. Then I met Paul, and I couldn't exactly produce a hundred grand in cash without raising questions. So the money stays here until I have a condo and joint custody of Charlotte. Then I can begin slipping it out to pay off my mortgage.

I'm storing memories here, too. My mother's photo album. Her rings. My father's medals. His watch. A locket he gave me when I turned sixteen. Thumb drives, too, of digital documents and photos. My past takes up so little space. Less even than the money.

The gun is taped under a nightstand. As I pull it out, I remember the first time I held one. On my twelfth birthday, I asked my father to take me to the range. He refused. Continued to refuse until he caught me in a field, target shooting with friends.

At the time, I thought he refused because I was a girl. I know now that he didn't want me following him down his path into service. He never said that, but I see proof in my memories, of every time I raised the subject and he'd start talking about good civilian tech jobs and I'd get so angry, certain he just didn't think I could handle army life.

I'd been determined to prove him wrong. I practiced shooting until my shoulder ached. I ran until I collapsed from exhaustion. I lifted weights until I tore muscles. And still he talked about that damned desk job, tossing around visions of Silicon Valley like it was Disney World. Which it had been, to him—the dream of a safe and successful life for his daughter.

I'm sorry, Dad. I didn't understand.

I heft the gun—a Glock 19—and I remember the day Ruben tried to hand me a Ruger LC9. Until then, I'd worked from my laptop, hacking security systems so his group could break in. That day, two members were out sick, right before a massive job.

"We just need eyes on the ground," Ruben said. "The same thing you do from your computer, except IRL."

He actually said "IRL" as if we "tech geeks" spoke in text acronyms.

"You'll get your cut, plus one of theirs," he said.

"I want both of theirs."

He laughed. "You can't do the job of two—"

"If I can, you'll pay me both their shares?"

He agreed . . . and he paid out. After that, I was no longer sitting on my laptop. I learned how to wield a set of lock picks. I learned how to case a property. I learned how to steal . . . IRL, as he'd put it.

Yet when he'd tried to hand me the Ruger, I refused.

He rolled his eyes. "Let me guess. Army Girl needs a bigger gun."

"No, 'Army Girl' doesn't carry a gun. That escalates a situation."

"That's the idea, kid."

We argued. I won, and never once did I regret being unarmed. Not even after the last job, when the guy who was playing "eyes on the ground" screwed up, and the returning homeowner shot me in the shoulder. Afterward, Ruben said, "I bet you wish you'd had a gun for that."

No, I was glad I hadn't, or I might have returned fire, and a guy defending his property did not deserve that. I *did* deserve what I got, and that awareness proved I was no longer the angry kid who signed on with Ruben.

It was the proverbial wake-up call, not even the shot itself so much as what followed—the realization that I couldn't check into a hospital. Not with a gunshot wound. Ruben knew people. Doctors, or those who passed for doctors, because honestly, someone who takes cash for off-the-books medical care has probably lost his license, and not through a tragic miscarriage of justice. So I pay the price, with the pain in my shoulder as a constant reminder of a choice I made.

I put the gun into my purse, and my phone rings, making me jump. I look to see an unfamiliar number. I answer.

"Aubrey?" a woman's voice asks.

"Yes?"

"It's Gayle. Gayle Lansing. I wanted to thank you for the flowers."

It takes a minute to realize what she's talking about. Hell, it takes a minute to remember who she is. Standing here with a gun, among the ghosts of my storage locker, I am someone else. I am the Aubrey who's never had a husband, never imagined she would have one, certainly not a woman who envisioned she'd someday have an ex-husband with a girlfriend.

I cover my hesitation with a babble of "Oh, you're welcome" and "Thank you again for taking Charlie." That goes on for a few exchanges—her with "I was happy to" and me thanking her again and her assuring me it's all good.

Then she says, "I wanted to ask you a favor. About this weekend. Is there any chance Paul can keep Charlie for Saturday?"

"Keep her?"

"I know he brings her over first thing Saturday morning, but it's my daughter's birthday, and we were going horseback riding. Charlie would love it."

My hackles rise. I force them down. Gayle isn't inventing special treats to woo my daughter. She's taking her daughter for her birthday and asking Charlotte to join.

Still, I can't resist saying, "I don't think she's old enough for horses."

Gayle laughs. "Oh, of course, she isn't going to ride by herself. She'll be with Paul. And I haven't mentioned it to her, so if you would rather not, I completely understand. Libby would *love* to have her along, though, and we could bring Charlie to you first thing Sunday morning."

"Why not Saturday night?"

There's a pause. Then, "The horseback riding is in Wisconsin, so it's a bit of a drive. I know you had Charlie this week for an extra night, so I thought you might like the evening to your-self. We'll bring her first thing."

She's being reasonable. Perfectly reasonable. Which only makes some childish part of me dig in her heels and want to be *unreasonable*. That extra night had been a bonus, not a chore, and I will take every one with my daughter that I can. Also why the hell didn't she ask this sooner? It's Friday night, for God's sake. I might have had our weekend planned.

Except I didn't, and the reason she's asking now is because she's met me. We have exchanged our peace offerings—she got me the princess tea reservation and I sent flowers. She has to have been worried about me, what kind of person I'd be, how I'd treat her, and now all is fine, so she's taking a chance on asking for Charlotte to come to her daughter's party.

Yet even as I calm myself down, there's a part of me that can-not help but wonder whether I'm misreading this entirely.

Could this be Paul's idea? He thinks I'm a wee bit unstable right now. Did he confess his fears to Gayle?

"I . . . just don't want Charlie going over this weekend."

"Wait. I have an idea, Paul."

Have they conspired to undermine my parental rights?

Or am I being a paranoid bitch even considering that?

I shift my weight, and as I do, I feel the extra heft of the gun in my purse.

Charlotte.

I forgot about Charlotte.

I didn't forget she was coming for the weekend, of course, but I failed to put the pieces together. I was retrieving a gun to take home . . . when Charlotte will be there.

If I am so concerned about safety that I'm getting a gun, should I even have Charlotte over?

No, I'm overreacting on the threat. Charlotte is not in danger.

I do not *need* a gun. I could put it back and insist on taking Charlotte tomorrow. Still . . .

I make it clear to Gayle that I don't require an extra night off and that I'm more than happy to take Charlotte anytime Paul needs it. However, I don't want to interfere with their plans. Bringing her Sunday morning is fine.

We make arrangements. After I sign off, I tuck the gun back into its hiding place. If I need it, I'll come back—after Charlotte's gone.

SEVENTEEN

Gayle's call caught me off guard. The more I think about it, though, the more suspicious I become. The drive home from Chicago, in Friday-night traffic, gives me plenty of time to think. Too much time.

After that call, part of my brain whirls in a cyclone of paranoia. A little homunculus inside my head runs in circles shouting "Doom! Doom! Doom!" like a cartoon character. That is the worst side of me. The most childlike side. The most guilty side. The part that is somehow convinced I have gotten off far too easy in life, considering my crimes, and the hammer of karma hangs over my head, waiting for the absolute worst way to punish me.

You are a thief, Aubrey. You stole from people, and you were not caught, and that ache in your shoulder doesn't repay your crimes.

You think you can run from all that? Fall in love and marry a great guy and have an amazing child and a perfect life? You think that a marriage breakup is the worst thing that can happen? Think again.

The worst thing that can happen is that I lose my daughter. Not through a court of law, but through a foe I cannot fight. Through Charlotte herself. She lives in the only home she's known. Sleeps in the only bedroom she's known. She lives there with her perfect daddy, and the only thing missing is her mommy. But what if another mommy comes along? A mommy who'll take her to princess teas when her own mother forgets. A mommy who'll whisk her off on surprise horseback rides and birthday parties. A mommy who brings a cool older sister and brother. A mommy who could slide into that house and take her mother's place, and everything will be the way it was. No, everything will be *better.*

I want to scream at that version of Gayle, the one who knows exactly what she's doing, the one who wants to steal my daughter, steal my place. Steal my husband? I can say I'm happy for Paul, but is there a tiny part that hoped for some fantasy reunion? Yes. Yes, there is. And it *isn't* tiny. Not at all.

Yet Gayle isn't that monster. She's just a woman who's gone through her own divorce and has now met a wonderful guy . . . a guy I gave up. While part of me wishes she would move a little slower—*does Charlotte really need to go to your daughter's party already?*—that might just be my own fears speaking. The fears that know this is one step along a road I don't want to see them take.

Whatever Gayle's intent, Paul is up to something. It's too co-incidental otherwise. We parted on bad terms yesterday. Could this be his revenge? That's not the man I know, but I *have* hurt him—I know that—and maybe he's finally lashing out.

Whatever the answer, he should have been the one to call me. That's what I realize during that drive home, what I'd missed earlier, in my confusion. Paul wanted a day of my time with our daughter. Time that we had agreed upon. We allow for exceptions, of course. We were determined never to put our own needs above our child's. We've negotiated these exceptions with no actual negotiation required. The one who said "I'd like her for *x*" was the one who also said "I know that isn't our arrangement, so here's how I suggest making up for it."

His requests are always reasonable, and so I am reasonable in return. Even this one—for Gayle's daughter—is logical. So he should have called me.

Having Gayle phone only makes me more suspicious. Makes me wonder whether adding Charlotte to the outing seems last minute because it *is* last minute.

"*I . . . just don't want Charlie going over to Aubrey's this weekend.*"

"*Wait. I have an idea, Paul. Why don't we invite Charlie to Libby's party?*"

"*I would love that. I'm just . . . I'm not sure Aubrey will go for it. She knows I'm upset. She might see through this.*"

"*Here, let me handle it.*"

I'm in Oxford when my phone rings. I go to grab it. I'd never talk on my cell with Charlotte in the car, but she's not here, and I'm certain it's Gayle calling again or maybe Paul this time.

"*On second thought, I think we should keep Charlie for the whole weekend. She'll be so tired Sunday.*"

I snatch up the phone, only to see a private number. I pull over and let it ring to voice mail. Then I retrieve the message.

"Ms. Finch? It's Laila Jackson from the Oxford PD. Please call me back." She rhymes off a number.

I sit there, holding the phone. If it were Officer Cooper, I'd be hitting those digits as fast as I could, certain he was calling to say they'd finally realized I was right—their dead woman had a son, who is now missing.

But it's his partner, the woman who really doesn't like me, which means this almost certainly isn't a you-were-right call. Still, I cling to that hope and replay it a couple of times, as I listen to her tone. It's crisp, sharp even. Laila Jackson does not sound like a woman calling to tell me she's made a horrible mistake.

She knows I'm the one who left that anonymous tip about Kim. I'm sure of it. I was careful. I found a pay phone, which isn't easy to do these days. I made sure it wasn't near my home or work. I left nothing that could identify me. I even pitched my voice lower, and there'd been enough traffic in the background to add to the distortion.

It doesn't matter. A woman called in that tip, and Jackson is convinced I'm an attention-seeker. She'll know it was me.

Does that mean they're ignoring the tip? Has she said "Oh, I know who that is" and told the department she'll handle it?

Just ignore her. She's a bit of a nutjob.

My fingers hover over the keys. I need to set her straight. I need to make sure the police investigate. Finding this boy isn't my job, damn it. I'm not that person anymore. Not someone who puts her own safety in danger, breaking laws to help strangers. Certainly not someone who'll endanger her daughter to do that.

I need the police to pay attention.

Which means I need more evidence. If Jackson has convinced the police to ignore me, I have to dig deeper. I need Kim's real identity, and then I need to send it to someone they'll listen to.

Paul.

My gut rejects that the moment I think of it. Paul isn't exactly my ally here. Yet as angry as I am with him, I still trust him to do the right thing.

Without Charlotte coming over, I have all of tomorrow to track Kim down online. Find her name. Talk to Paul Sunday morning. Prove that I'm not losing my mind and ask him to take my information to the police.

"Here's her real name. The dead woman's. The boy's mother."

"Her real . . . ? The police don't even have this, Bree. How did you find it?"

Cross that bridge when I come to it. For now, I have a goal.

Paul phones at eight the next morning. He leaves a message not unlike Jackson's—call me back. Nothing more. I consider doing that, just as I considered answering when I saw his number. What if he's changed his mind, and he wants to bring Charlotte over?

Then he'd say so in his message. He doesn't, which means I cannot afford to place that call. I'm afraid he's found an excuse to keep Charlotte all weekend. He won't leave that on a message. And if I don't return his call, then he has to carry through on his promise to drop her off in the morning.

Last night, before I left the storage locker, I'd taken some money. This morning, I drive back to Chicago and pay cash for a better laptop. Then I plot out a map of coffee shops, all within walking distance of each other. Each of these shops offers free Wi-Fi, and that's the attraction, far more than the fancy drinks.

I still get one of those drinks at each shop. An overpriced coffee and a pastry, which buys me ninety minutes in a Saturday-busy café. That's how long I figure it'll take before anyone realizes I'm camped out in the corner. I could probably go longer—I'm a thirty-year-old white woman on a new Apple laptop, hardly attention-getting—but I want to play it safe.

Step one: analyze the call logs from Kim's phone. There's the number that's no longer in service. That's important. I know it is. Same as the one that goes unanswered. Judging from the time stamp, that's the call that came in while we were in the park. I don't start there, though. I need more data.

I pull the call logs for the past month. One entry stands out. Every week, like clockwork, Kim calls a number with an area code I don't recognize. I look it up. South Dakota. It's a landline number, and when I do a reverse check, it's registered to a Thom Milano. I consider my options, and as tempted as I am to go deep, I know I don't have to here. With an uncommon name like that, hacking probably isn't required.

I head over to Facebook. I have a name. I have a vicinity. Two minutes later, I have a personal page. Thom Milano, thirty-five, married, two kids. Owns a construction company, which sets off alarm bells—construction is a good cover for illegitimate business interests. But a quick search reveals that it's just a small, local company. Milano and his crew build homes in Sioux Falls, South Dakota.

He's posted a few photo updates this week—his daughter at her softball game, his men working on a house, a candid shot of his wife laughing at home. That's where I stop. I'm looking for signs that Milano is Brandon's father, and instead I get a picture of Ellie Milano . . . who is the spitting image of Kim Lyons.

On closer inspection, I realize that's not actually true. Ellie is older, close to my age, and she's heavier than Kim, but in a healthy way, with no sign of a hard-spent youth. In this picture, I see Kim a decade from now. If she kept her life on track. If she'd settled into the kind of life I had once. Healthy, happy, and carefree.

This is the person Kim has been calling. Not Thom Milano, but his wife. A relative of Kim's. A *close* relative. I would guess sister, but I won't jump to that conclusion.

I find Ellie's profile easily—Thom's links to it. Neither has theirs set to private. They aren't that sort of people. A very average middle-class couple, raising their family in a flyover state, posting pics of softball games. Maybe that should make them boring. It doesn't. I read their profiles and skim their pages, and envy stabs so sharp it physically hurts.

This isn't just a couple putting their best face forward on social media—there is such genuineness in their smiles, in their posts, that I do not for one moment doubt their happiness. When I envy them, I feel guilty, too. Guilty for thinking of myself, how once upon a time, I had this. Had it. Lost it. The guilt comes because I should be thinking of Kim. This is about her, and if I feel anything, it should be sorrow for this reflection of a life *she* might have had.

Forget all that. Focus on Ellie.

Thirty years old. Married since she was twenty-one. Two kids quickly followed. Ellie grew up in Cedar Rapids, Iowa. Maiden name: Mikhailov. I search on the name. It's Russian. I remember Kim on the phone. I remember telling Officer Jackson about it.

"She sounded very upset. She was speaking in another language. I don't know exactly, but I'm guessing Slavic."

Russian had actually been my guess, but I'd been wary of saying that. I didn't want to sound too certain.

Had Kim been talking to her sister?

I jump to Ellie's profile section for languages spoken. "English. Some Russian, but really only enough to curse out people who cut me off in traffic :)"

Kim hadn't been talking to Ellie on the phone then. It was, however, a family mother tongue. So maybe they were cousins rather than sisters—Kim coming from a branch of the family that maintained their native language more.

That's when I get to the section for family. Ellie lists a sister. Seven years younger. And her name? Kimmy.

I mine Ellie's profile for every mention of this younger sister. There's no link to a Facebook profile for her. There are photos, though untagged. Ellie has posted old photos of herself and sometimes she's with her little sister. In those photos, Kim grows from a baby to a fifteen-year-old. There's a final picture, for Kim's fifteenth birthday. And then she's gone.

Fifteen.

Is that when Kim had Brandon? Ejected from her family for a teen pregnancy? No. I'm sure Brandon was no older than five, and according to this timeline, Kim would have been twenty-three when she died, meaning she'd had Brandon when she was closer to seventeen.

While I don't find more recent photos of Kim on Ellie's page, I do find references to her. Old friends periodically ask how Kim's doing, and Ellie replies that she's fine, living her own life, but they're in contact and she's doing great. Sometimes she'll say she visited with "Kimmy" last month or that she just talked to her.

Still, there are no recent photos of them together. No updates saying that Ellie was going to visit her sister or that Kim was coming over. If I hadn't seen those phone records, I might think these claims of contact were fake. But they did talk, weekly, often for an hour or more. That isn't two sisters who've drifted apart and only exchange cards at Christmas.

There are a couple of instances where someone asks "Where's Kimmy living these days?" . . . and Ellie doesn't reply, as if she missed the question. In another one, a guy from Cedar Rapids asks if he can get in touch with Kimmy, and Ellie answers that her sister isn't on Facebook. When he asks for an email address, she pretends not to see the question.

There are also no mentions of Brandon. No suggestion that Kim has a child. And that, I am sure, is not accidental.

Ellie is guarding her sister's privacy. Because her sister is in hiding. Using a fake name. Concealing her child from the world. Staying in close contact with her sister, but otherwise cutting all ties with her former life.

I imagine a world where I had someone I could keep in touch with. A sister or a brother or even a cousin I couldn't bear to cut from my life when I went on the run. I tell myself it's better this way—beholden to no one, endangering no one—but that's a lie. I envy Kim for having Ellie in her life.

That's when I realize Ellie is out there, going about her Saturday in South Dakota, with no idea what's happened to her sister. No idea her sister is dead.

I have Ellie's phone number. I could call. But that'd be wrong. As hard as it will be to hear this news from the police, it wouldn't be any easier from a stranger. Let Ellie continue her weekend unaware. Let her enjoy it. The news will come soon enough now that I have Kim's real name.

EIGHTEEN

I do not stop with that name. I can't. I feel like I'm catching snippets of Kim's life, just enough that my analytical brain cannot help filling in the gaps and making educated guesses. It's like catching a glimpse of an elegant security system and think *I wonder if I can hack that.*

I can't walk away now. I need to know, to satisfy my curiosity. What I'm doing here is perfectly safe and legal. I'm sitting in coffee shop number three, drinking a decaf latte, and browsing the Web, like half the other people here. I expected to spend the day with Charlotte, so I have no other plans. I can continue working this puzzle.

Girl from Cedar Rapids seems to drop out of family life at fifteen. She has a child two years later. A child she hides from the world, as she lives in a Chicago suburb under an assumed name. Yet she maintains contact with her older sister, who keeps her secrets for her.

There are patterns in life. Old stories, often told. Personal tragedies rendered almost banal by their very commonness. I see one of those in Kim's story, and I want to chide myself for being so unimaginative. The truth is, though, that I am very good at recognizing patterns, at predicting cause and effect. I remember in high school, we'd done some aptitude test measuring our intellectual strengths. Mine was logical reasoning, and when my guidance counselor saw the results, she actually double-checked to be sure she was reading them right. This is what makes me so good with computers. I can analyze, and I can foresee outcomes, and it's hard for me to understand why others cannot.

When I took that bullet to my shoulder, I didn't for one moment think *Why me?* I wasn't shocked. Not even surprised. This was one of the potential outcomes. So was jail. Or betrayal. Or death. The others had been outraged on my behalf. I'd laughed at them.

After I split with Paul, I'd gone to a group for newly separated women. I could say I was seeking support, but really, I just wanted information. I wanted to learn from their experiences. I remember one woman who'd been shell-shocked by her separation . . . which she instigated. She'd given her husband an ultimatum, and he chose divorce. Somehow, that surprised her. She'd only wanted him to know she was serious, and threatening divorce seemed the way to do it.

That baffled me. When I told Paul our marriage didn't seem to be working, of course I wanted it to be the wake-up call that would save us. But I knew it might also be the excuse he needed to jump in and say "I agree." Which is exactly what he did, and as much as that hurt, I would rather know how he felt and set him free to be happy. I love him. I'm not going to trap him in an empty marriage.

So in Kim's story, I see a pattern. There's more to it. I have noticed that while Ellie talks about going home to see her mother, there's no mention of her father. According to condolences in her timeline, he died three years ago, yet she never mentioned the death, responding to those messages with a simple "Thank you."

My dad and I had our differences—blow-out fights, the front door slammed, me spending the night at friends'—but I loved him like I loved no one else before Paul came along. When my father died, I was inconsolable with grief and rage. The chill I see on Ellie's page speaks to more than a strained relationship. Death heals those wounds. This one did not.

I study the last photos of Kim. At her fifteenth birthday celebration, it is obvious she's putting on a good face for her big sister—home from South Dakota and very pregnant—but I do not miss the look in Kim's eyes, the one that says she has already, in her mind, hit the road, putting as much distance as she can between her and a bad home life.

I know I might be wrong. I might be carelessly stuffing Kim into a convenient box. Girl with harsh home life flees and ends up in an even worse place, addicted to drugs, hooking up with the wrong guy, pregnant at seventeen. Then she has a maternal-instinct wake-up call, takes the kid, and flees, living under a false name with a child hidden from his daddy.

Old story, often told.

So I take Kim's real name and what few details I can glean, and I set about trying to prove myself wrong. Find the piece of evidence that says I'm full of crap, seen too many movies, read too many novels.

There are traces of Kim Mikhailov online. Nothing since she was fifteen, but I expect that. I skim through those bits and pieces—high school website archives, abandoned social media footprints—and put them aside for later. I'm looking for . . .

I find what I'm looking for in a newspaper article dated two months after Kim turned fifteen. LOCAL TEEN MISSING. The article has been written with obvious reluctance by a journalist who's convinced he's dealing with a teen runaway, but has been persuaded to mention it briefly and make the family happy.

Kimberly Mikhailov disappeared one night after an argument with her father. Her mother admitted this wasn't the first time she'd left but said she always returned the next day. This time, she didn't. After two weeks, the family was desperate for any word from her. Mom and sister, Ellie, pleaded for news, any news.

I see no mention of her dad.

I find another scrap online, dated two years later. The passing mention of a divorce case, nothing newsworthy, just a tidbit in a list of court proceedings. The dissolution of a marriage between Kim and Ellie's parents. I find her father's obituary, too, asking for donations to be made to the American Liver Foundation and AL-ANON. An alcoholic's death.

Old story. Often told.

After that I begin to reconstruct Kim's missing past. Which sounds like I'm some kind of detective prodigy. *Give me an hour on the Web, and I'll give you the bio of a woman who's been in hiding for ten years!* It's not like that. I'm chasing threads, vapors really, of the trail she's left. A comment here. A mention there. Spot the faintest whorl of smoke and follow it for miles, only to find a long-dead campfire at the end, the stories told around it evaporated. I am running through the internet pathways for hours, popping pain meds when my shoulder screams for mercy, setting timers on my watch so I don't overstay my welcome, moving from shop to shop.

I know how to use this piece of metal to my advantage, how to stalk the Web for my prey with every tool at my disposal. Image recognition is my best friend today. Here is this picture of a fifteen-year-old girl. Find me more like it.

The tool I'm using isn't a free Web service either. A couple of years ago, I saw a news piece about a "suburban housewife" who'd been exposed as a former drug mule by a partner in crime stumbling over her photo online. That sparked a fresh wave of my paranoia, and I'd gone through a period of obsessively checking for my photo online, untagging it on Facebook and so on. I found the best photo-recognition software available, and I still have access to it.

Even that entails wading through photos of blond girls until I have to make a pit stop at a pharmacy for eye drops. There is something about Kim's face that sets it apart, though, things I hadn't fully processed when I first met her. Wide-spaced eyes. A widow's peak. A nose that's just a little crooked, as if it's been reset. A tooth chipped and never repaired.

I excavate the mountain of near hits and find Kim Mikhailov at the bottom, in an advertisement for "barely-legal exotic dancers" in LA. At the time, she'd been sixteen, wearing enough makeup that men could tell themselves she was older, but they'd know better.

I then find her in another photo, dated six months later, when she'd have just turned seventeen. She's under the arm of a guy who looks about twenty. She's dressed in a sheath dress that barely covers her top or bottom, and the photo catches her tugging down the back. I see marks on her arm now, but there's no drugged-out vacancy behind those eyes. Instead, there's a wide-eyed . . . Not innocence. I didn't see that in her even at sixteen.

This look is one that's staring wide-eyed at the world, feeling it stare back and not enjoying the sensation. She's ducked down into the man's arm, taking shelter there. He's well-dressed, sleek-haired, looking very pleased with himself.

The photo appears on an old Facebook page for a defunct club. There's no name attached to either Kim or her date. It's just part of a series of photos taken at the opening celebrations.

But when I search on the guy's face, I get an exact copy of this photo on a personal Facebook page, a private one that I have to hack to access. There the same photo has a caption: "The boss & his girl, looking fine."

Dig, dig, dig. Find the connection. Endlessly chase those connections.

The guy who owns this page once worked for the young man with Kim, and the fact that he called her the boss's "girl" suggests she was more than a casual date.

I find the answer with less work than I would have expected . . . because the guy who owns the Facebook profile once worked for the club where Kim danced. That club had been owned by two guys. One of them died years ago of a drug overdose. The other's name is Denis Zima. He's the one in the photo with Kim.

It doesn't take much research to learn that Zima wasn't just an entrepreneurial nineteen-year-old with the cash to open a strip club. He's the son of a guy with links to the Russian mob. He started the club with a friend from high school—the one who died of an overdose. That club, where Kim worked, closed a year later, and Zima started a chain of nightclubs without the strippers and underage girls.

I'm not sure this gets me anywhere new. Yes, Denis Zima seems to have been Kim's boyfriend at the right time to make him a candidate for Brandon's daddy. And he's definitely a shady character. But that's for the police to investigate.

I'm about to close my browser when I see the results of my last search, looking for more information on Denis Zima and his clubs. My gaze catches on the third listing from the top, the search engine picking up my current location and highlighting results that might interest me most.

It's an advertisement announcing the opening of Zima's fifth club, Zodiac Five. Right here in Chicago. While it's been operating for the past week, it hasn't had an official grand opening. That's tonight.

I do not make plans to go to the Zodiac Five grand opening. That would be crazy. I am not—I am *rarely* crazy.

The point is that, according to the article, Zima is in town for the opening. Coincidence that he's here around the same time his ex was murdered? I have no idea. I'll leave that to the police. I'll let them know about Zima when I give them Kim's name. That doesn't stop me from periodically pausing my searches to look for any progress on the murder case, hoping that I'll see something new. That I'll find proof the police have followed my lead and identified the murdered woman, at least as Kim Mason. When I don't, I'm frustrated, and it only furthers my fear that Officer Jackson blocked my tip.

It doesn't help that Jackson has left two more increasingly terse "Call me back" messages. Before I leave Chicago, though, I make a call of my own, after hunting down a pay phone. I dial the Oxford Police Department tip line. This time, I don't bother with the preamble.

"Your dead woman is Kimberly Mikhailov," I say. "She's been living here as Kim Mason. She's originally from Cedar Rapids, and she has a son named—"

"Please hold."

"What? No. You don't understand. I know the identity of the woman shot in Harris Park this week. Her name—"

The phone is ringing, my words unheard. I wait, seething. I understand Oxford is a small city, but putting a tipster on hold is unbelievably—

"Laila Jackson," a woman's voice says.

I freeze.

"You have the identity of the woman murdered in Harris Park?" she prompts.

"Yes . . ." I say, dropping my voice an octave.

"Is this Aubrey Finch?"

I hang up. Then I stand and stare at the pay phone.

This can't be happening. It's like something out of a B-grade thriller, the kind I'd watch and roll my eyes at, saying, "Real cops wouldn't do that."

Or would they? Yes, from my point of view, I'm being blocked from giving the police a vital clue toward solving a crime. To Officer Jackson, though, I'm an attention-seeking nutjob, and she is not going to let me waste one moment of the department's time.

There *are* people like the ones she's pegged me for. People who fixate on the police and fancy themselves thwarted law officers. Or those who want their fifteen minutes of fame.

How do I convince Jackson that isn't me? I keep thinking I have the evidence to do that . . . only to be stopped from delivering it.

Paul.

There's no pretending anymore. I really need Paul's help.

Except that asking for his help risks exposing my secrets. If he found out about my past, that would endanger my chances of joint custody.

I won't give up my daughter. I'm sorry, Kim. I'm sorry, Brandon. I just won't.

I will, however, keep trying to solve this dilemma. I spend the ride home coming up with scenarios. My best bet is Officer Cooper. I must find a way to get to him . . . circumventing his pit bull partner, Laila Jackson.

Email. That's the answer. Find Cooper's personal email and send him everything. Include photos and screenshots. Send him evidence that, once seen, he cannot unsee, cannot deny.

I return to my apartment. It's after eight, and I need dinner—my stomach is complaining from the nonstop coffee and pastries. I'll pop in here and then go hang out in a local coffee shop, buy something relatively healthy and send that email.

There, that's my night sorted. Afterward maybe I'll even rent a movie and try to distract—

I'm stepping out of the stairwell when I spot a figure at my apartment door. I flash back to Thursday and think it's Paul again.

It's not.

It's Officer Jackson.

She's in civilian clothes—jeans, heeled ankle boots, and a stylish leather jacket—and she's standing outside my door, browsing on her phone. Killing time. Waiting for her quarry to return.

I back up fast, ease open the stairwell door, and retreat as quietly as I can. I go straight for my car, and I don't pause to think until I'm a few blocks from home. Then I pull into a strip mall, park, and sit there, hands on the steering wheel as I stare out the windshield.

I can't make an end run around Jackson to get to Cooper. She won't let me. For whatever reason, Laila Jackson has made "stop Aubrey Finch" her mission, and she's locked fast to it until I back off.

I will not back off.

So what do I do now? Check into a hotel for the night to avoid her? Paul will be bringing Charlotte to my apartment in the morning.

That's fine—she won't still be there come morning. I just need to find something to do for a few hours, something that will help bolster my case.

Like what? I have Kim's *name*. I have her bio details. I even know who might be the father of her child. What more can I get?

I keep thinking of the club's grand opening tonight. Which is, again, crazy. What do I hope to gain there? Get a look at Denis Zima and confirm he's Brandon's father? A visual scan is hardly a DNA test. So what would I gain from going to that club tonight? I have no idea. I just know that I'm frustrated and restless, and there's a police officer staking outside my apartment door, and I have time to kill and . . .

And I know none of that is a reason. Excuses, that's all I have. The truth, I suspect, is that I've been fighting this urge ever since I saw that ad. I have no idea what I expect to accomplish at Zima's club, but I'm going.

Which is crazy.

And, right now, I don't care.

NINETEEN

Being unable to get into my apartment means I can't get ready there. Not that it matters much. Nothing in my closet these days is clubworthy. I did have a few dresses, back when I met Paul, and my coworkers could occasionally drag me to a club. That isn't Paul's scene, though.

I remember a couple of weeks after we'd begun dating, he suggested a club, which shocked the hell out of me. I'd pulled on my little black dress, and we spent exactly twenty awkward minutes in the club, before I confessed it really wasn't my thing, and I swear he melted in relief. Instead, we'd bought a bottle of champagne and checked into a hotel, and he showed me that, while clubs themselves weren't for him, he *did* appreciate my clubwear.

Even if I had those dresses, they wouldn't fit anymore. I put on fifteen pounds with Charlotte, and I decided to keep most of it. I was in good shape, and I kind of liked the extra weight— it made me feel more like my image of a mother, whatever that might be. So I needed to do some shopping.

Fortunately, I'd taken out more money than I needed for the laptop. I bought a dress, heels, undergarments . . . I left my fancier underthings behind when I split with Paul—not much use for them in my current celibate life. While I won't be showing off my panties tonight—definitely *not* on my agenda— the new ones make me *feel* like a single girl going to a club.

Buy clothing. Buy makeup. Buy pins and styling products for my hair. Find a mall restroom and transform from suburban mommy into . . . well, suburban-mommy-goes-clubbing. That's still what I see when I look in the mirror. At least all the component parts are there—the hair, makeup, short dress, and heels—and if I look like a young single mommy on the make, oh well. I'm sure I won't be the only one there tonight.

I arrive at the club just after eleven, which I seem to recall is a good time, not too early but not hard-partier late. What I've forgotten after three years of stay-at-home-mommy life is that you don't just show up to a club and walk in. There's a line. A massive one that isn't moving because, duh, it's the grand opening.

I also realize, as I'm getting out of the cab, that I'm alone. Of course I am—I'm on a mission. But I have enough ego to be very aware of how I look, a thirty-year-old going to a club by herself. So as I'm trying to figure out my next move, I stand at the head of the line, pretending to scan it for my friends.

"Hey, Blue Dress," someone behind me says.

I keep searching the line, wondering what my chances are of sneaking in a back entrance, when the guy calls again, and I realize *I'm* wearing a blue dress.

I turn to see one of the bouncers waving me over. He's mid-forties, bald, steroid-pumped. I wonder what I'm doing wrong, maybe breaking some rule about hanging out too close to the doors.

"You look like you know your way around a gym," he says, as I walk over.

"Uh . . . yes . . ."

"You should try Bart's."

"I . . . don't think I know that one."

"It's very exclusive. Here." He takes a Sharpie from his co-bouncer's pocket and motions for my hand. I give it to him. He writes "Bart," and then what I think is an address, but when I look, I realize it's a phone number. It actually takes about five seconds for me to realize *he's* Bart, and this is his cell, and there is no gym.

Yes, I've been married for a while.

"I might . . . check that out," I manage to say, as my brain struggles to ignite my rusty flirting skills and use them to get into this bar. "Thank you."

"No problem. And your friends? They're inside. They said to watch for you." He winks. "Hot brunette with a blue dress and biceps. That's gotta be you, right?"

"Yes . . . Yes, it is. Thank you."

He opens the door. Again, it takes a few seconds for me to realize I don't coincidentally fit the description of an actual "friend" someone's waiting for. He's letting me in ahead of the line, in hopes I might actually call his number. If not, well, a party can always use more single women. Maybe I *don't* look as mom-ish as I feel. Or maybe the bouncer just decided to shake things up for variety.

Inside, the club is packed, as one might expect from that line. If I felt old walking up, I feel ancient now. It's loud. So freaking loud. And it stinks—perfume and aftershave and BO mingling together. Then there are the lights, colored strobes and mirror balls.

I stare at the mirror balls before remembering that's the theme of Zima's clubs: faux seventies. Mirror balls. Caged go-go dancers. Disco songs that have been remixed because the illusion of the seventies is all well and fine, but please don't make us listen to the music.

Outside, I'd been worried about how I'd fit in without friends. Now I laugh at that. Even if I had friends in here, I'd lose them in three seconds. No one's going to notice that I'm alone.

I make my way to the bar. When I get past the mob hanging out there, I lean over the bar and say, "Dark and stormy, please."

The bartender hesitates.

"It's rum and—" I begin.

"Oh, believe me, I know how to make it. I've made so many that I'm out of ginger beer."

I must look surprised, because he chuckles, "Haven't been clubbing in a while, huh?"

"Evidently not. I guess it was just a matter of time before my drink actually became popular. Now I'll have to find a new one."

"Hipster," he says, and I laugh at that, and he promises to make me "something special."

We chat a bit. Nothing flirtatious. He's wearing a wedding band and seems happy to spend a few moments talking to someone who isn't checking him out.

When I go to pay, a guy behind me leans over and says, "I'll pay . . ."

He stops as he gets a look at me. Apparently, I look younger from the back. Or hotter. When he sees me, he withdraws the twenty in his hand and mumbles something as he turns to talk to his friends.

"Asshole," the bartender says. "This one's on me."

I shake my head and give him a twenty and a "keep the change." Then I slide away, smiling to myself. I'll admit to an ego bump when the bouncer let me in, and apparently the universe decided that needed straightening out, with the put-down at the bar. The thought puts me in a better mood than it should, and I'm wandering, sipping my drink, lost in my thoughts when I spot Denis Zima.

That's no coincidence. Zima is there to be seen, as much as those caged go-go dancers. Along one side of the room there are box seats, like those you find in old theaters, except these are raised just enough that the plebes on the dance floor can't stumble into them. In the biggest box seat, Zima sits in an over-sized throne-like chair, surveying his club while others in his box try—and fail—to catch his attention.

According to my research, Zima is only twenty-seven. He looks older, though. There's no uncertainty in his gaze, no hesitation. He's the king of his pride, surveying the watering hole while his lionesses and hyenas all jockey for his attention.

Seeing him up close does not answer the question of whether or not he's Brandon's father. Brandon takes after his mother, and Zima looks like the photo I saw—good-looking white guy with dark blond hair and blue eyes. Brandon is also white, blond, and blue-eyed. So is—was—Kim.

But this is still Denis Zima. The reason I'm here. Now what?

I have no idea. I don't know what I was hoping for—that I'd see him and notice some secret mark that proved he was Brandon's father? Hell, I hadn't seen such a mark on the boy, so how would I find the same one on Zima?

I didn't know why I came here. Now I don't know why I'm staying here. Desperation, I guess. Desperation and frustration, and the sense that this was the next logical step and that if I showed up here tonight, all would be revealed to me.

Forget what I hoped to find. What *can* I find, now that I'm here? What am I looking for?

Brandon.

I am following a trail to Brandon. To a lost boy that no one else knows is lost.

Kim Mikhailov is dead. After years of hiding her son from the world, she has been murdered, her son gone. And the boy's potential father just happens to be in Chicago at the same time. That must mean something.

I slip into a back hall. I'm looking for an office. Looking for a computer. There's bound to be one, and there's unlikely to be anyone working on it at this time of night.

Find an office computer and search it for anything useful. I'd love to find emails or documents telling me where Zima is staying—and might be keeping Brandon—but I'll settle for any useful tidbits. A computer always has those.

I establish the layout of the building quickly. That's one thing Ruben taught me. When breaking into a place, don't go straight for the goods, even if you know where they are. Look around and get a mental map. Note exits. Note hiding spots. Note areas that might contain unexpected treasure . . . or dangers.

The first floor is the club itself. There's also a small kitchen. Nothing huge—this is a place that serves food because it doesn't want you leaving if you get peckish, not because it wants you coming for dinner. There's a basement. I'm going to guess that's storage. There's also a second story, with stairs around the back. That's the most likely spot to find an office.

I don't just walk around opening doors. There are people here, staff zipping up and down the corridors. Staff who will be quick to point me back to the dance floor. Still, I do know how to do this. These skills don't come from Ruben. We only ever broke into empty houses. I learned this part from, well, from playing video games.

I've always been fond of first-person shooters, and I'm not the kind of player who blasts her way through to a goal. I approach the task with care, favoring stealth over force. Games like that offer an endless array of almost-empty buildings with the quest target hidden in the middle, requiring the player to pass umpteen guards who are, apparently, assigned to patrol one hall and only one hall. Which means that I'm very good at scoping out an area, finding every hiding spot, and then leapfrogging from one to the next while avoiding that gun-toting commando . . . or eagle-eyed server.

I make it upstairs without being spotted. It's not a full level—the club takes up part with its high ceiling. From the top of the stairs, it's dark, and I see and hear nothing.

I check doors as I walk. There's a lounge area. An empty room with construction equipment. And then a locked door. It's a simple lock, intended to keep people from accidentally wandering in. I open it with a credit card.

Right inside the door, a dead bolt waits on the floor, along with a cordless screwdriver. That makes me chuckle. It seems that someone did foresee the need for more security . . . they just haven't quite gotten to it yet.

This is indeed the office. Filing cabinets. Two desks. One desktop computer. I check the cabinets first. Empty. Then I flip through a stack of papers on the desk. Purchase orders and work orders. On to the computer.

It's password-protected, which would take time to crack, if I didn't check under the keyboard and find the password there. Hey, it's a new office, new computer . . . it's easy to forget these things. To their credit, they've used a complex password, one of random letters and numbers. Good for security; lousy for re-membering.

I enter the password. The desktop opens, and I go straight to the contact list. I find an entry for Zima. I make note of his cell phone number and email address. That's when I remember the two unidentified numbers on Kim's phone record, the one with no answer and the one out of service. I pull those up on my cell and punch them into the desktop computer for full file-system search. No match.

I zip through email, but the computer belongs to whoever is

playing office manager, and it's clean. Clean in the sense that there's nothing incriminating. It's all business.

I type in Kim's names, real and fake. A global document search brings up nothing.

I try "Brandon." I do get matches, but only because that's the surname of a contractor.

Next I go into the trash—the computer's trash bin, that is. Nothing.

If the office manager plays any role in Zima's less-than-legal business, it's not here. I don't even know that Zima *has* less-than-legal business. I'm—

Footsteps sound on the stairs. I dart into the supply closet. I pull the door shut behind me and duck behind a stack of boxes.

The footsteps echo through the empty upper floor. Then the office door opens and the footsteps enter.

"What do you mean we don't have the security cameras up and running?" a man's voice asks.

There's a pause, as if he's on the phone. Then, "Dummy cameras? Well, guess who's telling Denis that. Hint? It's not me."

A creak, as if the guy sat on the edge of the desk. "Right now, he's busy looking for the chick from the news. He thinks she's here tonight."

I freeze in a moment of sheer panic before I almost laugh aloud. Chick from the news? At a grand opening? Obviously, he means that Zima is hoping he's spotted media coverage.

The man continues. "Yeah, well, if those cameras aren't working, I'd suggest you get all eyes on the floor. You saw her in the news?"

A moment of silence. Then a frustrated growl. "Pay attention, asshole. Didn't you get the memo?"

Pause.

"No, it wasn't an *actual* memo. No wonder you're a security guard. You aren't even bright enough to be a beat cop, and that's saying something. Yeah, yeah, stop sputtering. The chick's about my age. Dark hair. Bright blue dress. That's the clincher—the dress."

I look down at my dress.

It's bright blue.

He means me? Zima saw *me* on the news? Saw me downstairs?

The man continues, "Between you and me, I think Denis is seeing things. He's all worked up about the kid."

The kid. My heart slams into my ribs.

Stop panicking and get your phone out. Start recording this conversation.

I'm fumbling in my purse as the guy says, "Yeah, I don't know why she'd be here. She's some chick from the suburbs, says she met Kimmy in the park. And now she's clubbing in the city? Doesn't make sense. But you know Denis. We've got to make it look good. Find every dark-haired chick in a blue dress, and tell her she's . . . won free drinks or something. Specially selected to come speak to the boss."

I finally find my phone.

"Yeah, I know it's a pain in the ass. But it's your goddamned job."

Where's the app to record? I've never used it before.

Damn it!

The guy's talking again. "Hey, asshole, watch your mouth. I might think Denis is wrong about the chick, but I don't blame him. Not one bit. Put yourself in his place."

There. Found the app. I open it and click Record as the man continues.

"Imagine your girl takes off. Disappears from the face of the earth. Then, five years later, you see this chick on the news, talking about your girl having a little boy. A little boy who's *five years old*. Suddenly you know why your girl left. Not only did she leave, but she took something of yours, something you never realized you had. A son."

My head shoots up.

Did he say Zima didn't know about Brandon?

No. I've misheard. Please let me have misheard.

"Yeah, that's what I thought," the guy says. "Denis might be hallucinating this chick being at the club tonight, but he's not hallucinating the fact he's got a little boy. A kid who's disappeared."

A pause.

"No, dumbass. The boy didn't randomly get kidnapped the same day Kimmy dies. Someone has him. Someone's taking care of him. Someone who is not his daddy. That's a problem. One Denis is going to fix."

TWENTY

The guy has been gone for at least three minutes, and I'm still in that closet, paralyzed, barely able to gasp breath.

What have I done?

Oh God, what have I done?

Zima never knew he had a son . . . until he saw me on the television, telling the world I'd seen his dead ex with a five-year-old child.

Kim must have run from Zima before he knew she was pregnant. She hid Brandon so Zima would never find out he had a child. When she realized she was in danger she must have made arrangements for Brandon. That's what this guy obviously thinks, and from the way he's talking, he knew Kim.

She found a safe place for Brandon, put him in that park and told him to wait for someone to come get him. His rescuer comes. Brandon hears his name, and he runs over. He sees a stranger. He's confused. He panics. The man quickly bundles him into the SUV and spirits him off to safety.

Kim has protected her son again. Her final *act* was protecting him. She got him to safety before Zima found out he exists.

And then I came along and ruined everything.

As I make my way down the hall, I focus on how I will fix this. Get my audio recording to the police. Let them stop Zima. I've made a terrible mistake, but I can still fix it. I *will* fix it.

That resolve lets me concentrate on my escape. There's no one upstairs again, so I get to the first level easily. I leapfrog from hiding place to hiding place. I remember an exit door partway down the back hall. I'll use that.

I get to the door and find it emblazoned with a huge sign warning that opening it will set off an alarm.

I do not want an alarm. But the alternative is to go back through the club, while every employee is looking for a dark-haired woman in a bright blue dress.

I remember the conversation between Zima's employee/friend and the head of security. If the cameras aren't operating yet, and the dead bolt isn't on the office door, that suggests the security team wasn't fully prepared for tonight's opening. Is it possible, then, that this door *isn't* armed?

Even if an alarm does sound, I can run. It's not like I have to worry about security cameras.

I tug off my heels. Then I press down on the bar handle and carefully push the door . . .

It doesn't budge. I depress the handle harder. Still nothing.

They've locked the damn emergency exit.

Shoes slap the concrete. I duck into a hiding spot. A guy hurries past. Once he's gone, I make my way toward the club. The entrance to the dance floor is just up ahead. I'll cut a beeline through it to the exit, sticking to groups of people and avoiding that box where Zima sits. I'll just—

There's a security guard outside the women's restroom. He's stationed there, and he's watching every woman who walks in.

I dart back to my last hiding spot and duck in. As I do, I hear footfalls. It's the employee who passed me earlier. He's returning with a crate of bottles.

Once he passes, I retrace his steps to the basement door. It's unlocked. I open it and use my phone flashlight to guide me down the dark steps. At the bottom, I see closed doors. The ones at the end have key locks. At this end are two doors with regular knobs marked with makeshift stick figures of a man and a woman. I push open the door with the skirted figure and find the women's staff room.

I quickly open lockers. Most have jeans or sweats. A couple, though, contain dresses. I check tags. There's a black one in my size. I quickly change and wad up the blue dress into my purse. Then I take out a hundred bucks and slide it into the employee's bag.

Out the staff room. Listen for footsteps. Scamper up the stairs. Down the hall and . . .

I still need to pass that security guard, who'll notice I've come from the wrong direction.

I'm tucked into a side hall, considering my options, when I hear him talking. I poke my head out to see a dark-haired girl in a blue dress.

He's turned away, talking to her. I slip off my heels again and creep into the restroom behind his back. A moment later, as I'm putting my shoes on, the girl comes in. The guard must have dismissed her, realizing her dress isn't *bright* blue and she's barely drinking age.

I walk right past him. I make my way through the club. I'm trying not to rush—I don't want to call attention to myself. I'm weaving toward the exit when I catch a glimpse of what looks like a familiar face. A face that stops me short.

It's Laila Jackson.

No, that isn't possible. I'm seeing another thirty-year-old, short-haired black woman and making a horribly stereotyped mistake. Except I'm not. At my apartment, she was dressed in skinny jeans, high-heeled boots, and a cropped leather jacket. This woman is wearing skinny jeans, high-heeled boots, and a cropped leather jacket.

Laila Jackson followed me to the club.

What is wrong with this woman? What have I done to piss her off so much that she's trailing me in her off time?

No, I shouldn't think of it that way. Not "What have I done to this woman?" but "What have I done to this police officer?" I haven't personally pissed her off. This is business.

Something is up here. There's no way she's tracked me to a club to warn me, yet again, to back off.

I feel the weight of my cell phone in my purse. The cell phone with that recording, proving Kim had a child. Whatever Jackson's beef, I could end it here by triumphantly presenting her with proof that Aubrey Finch is not a crazed attention-seeker.

But do I trust her?

No. Her behavior is suspicious, and I must be extra cautious here. A child's life is at stake.

I'm turning toward the exit when Jackson's head swivels my way. She spots me. I pick up speed, weaving through the few people between me and the exit. I hurry outside, past the bouncers, and the one from earlier thankfully doesn't notice me in the black dress.

I move at a fast walk to the alley beside the club. Then I dart in, tug off my heels, and break into a run.

"Aubrey!" Jackson's voice shouts behind me.

I keep going. There are trash bins ahead, and I race around them like an obstacle course. A wooden fence blocks the alley. I grab the top and swing my legs up, ignoring the pain stabbing through my shoulder. I crouch on top to get a quick look at where I'll be jumping down. Onto trash bins. Great.

"Aubrey Finch!"

I grip the edge, ready to leap, hoping I can clear the bins—

"Aubrey Stapleton!"

I stop.

Run, just run.

That's what I want to do. What my gut screams for me to do. But my head knows better. My head analyzes the scenario and calculates possible outcomes in an eyeblink.

The chance that I can swing down, escape, and then pretend it was never me . . . and Jackson will buy it? Next to zero.

The chance that I'll only make things worse by running? Next to perfect.

I turn. Jackson walks toward me. She says nothing until she's right below. Then she looks up at me, crouched on the fence, and she shakes her head.

"You really need to work on your suburban-mommy librarian routine, you know that?"

"It's not a routine. I am a librarian. I am a mother. I live in the suburbs."

Another shake of her head. "Get down. Put your shoes on. We need to talk."

"If you're arresting me—"

"This isn't how I arrest people, Aubrey. We're going for coffee. Now come on."

TWENTY-ONE

We're in the coffee shop. Jackson pulls out her chair and sits. "So, Aubrey Stapleton . . ."

I say nothing. This hammer has been poised over my head for ten years now. The laws of probability say it will fall at some point.

The statute of limitations has passed on my crimes. That no longer matters. The problem is that I have a daughter, and if I am discovered, I will lose her. That is a fate worse than jail.

It's also a fate I've earned.

I can argue the whole "robbed from the rich and gave to the poor" thing, but I'm not Robin Hood. I can say I was only a kid. But I knew what I was doing.

Now my past has caught me. If I'm calm about it, that isn't indifference. I'm dying inside, numb and exhausted. Officer Jackson sits there, smiling like the proverbial cat that caught the canary, and I feel no urge to wipe that smirk off her face. This isn't about her.

"Aubrey Stapleton," she repeats. "Mother died in an accident when you were two. Dad when you were eighteen. PTSD."

She doesn't say suicide, and I'll grant her a point for that.

PTSD is what killed my father. A life spent in service without the resources to help him deal with that. Without the resources to let him know it was okay to *need* to deal with that.

"You dropped out of college when he died. Dropped out of *MIT,* where you were in the top ten percent of your computer engineering class."

She's done her homework, and she's proud of it. Fine. Let her show off and get this over with.

She continues, "You rattled around for a bit after that with part-time jobs. Then you disappeared. Took off and dropped out. Stopped using your name."

"I used Minor. That's my mother's maiden name, and it's my second middle name. As long as I paid my taxes, I wasn't breaking any laws."

"By paying your taxes under a false name? I think the IRS would have something to say about that."

Yes, what I did isn't exactly legal, but I suspect the IRS's biggest concern is that they got their money, and I was meticulous about that.

"You married under a false—" she begins.

"No, I didn't. On the marriage license, I'm Aubrey Rose Minor. On my birth certificate, I'm Aubrey Rose Minor Stapleton."

She gives me a hard look, and my gut flip-flops. I've always told myself that what I did wouldn't negate my marriage. But did I ever investigate that to be one hundred percent sure? No, I didn't.

"I'm not asking for alimony or even an equal distribution of marital assets," I say. "I didn't deceive my husband."

Liar, liar, pants on fire.

I realize then that she's skipped something. Something vital. The part that I expected to be at the heart of her accusation.

My criminal past.

She's saving it for last. The sucker punch. *Go on, Officer Jackson. Just get it over with.*

"I saw you on that fence," she says. "You're no suburban-mommy librarian."

I tense but force a calm response. "Yes, I am. That's who I've chosen to be, like you've chosen to be a police officer. I may have been faking a few things, but not my job, not my daughter. And there'd be a lot of suburbanites and mothers and librarians who wouldn't appreciate you suggesting that they can't climb a fence."

"*Vault* onto a fence. In a dress and heels."

"In heels? That'd be crazy. I took those off."

She leans over the table. "You can leap that fence because your dad was a career soldier. You planned to join the army. You stay in shape as if you're *still* planning to."

"I stay in shape because I need to keep up with a three-year-old."

I get a small smile for that, and she eases back in her seat.

"The point is that you're in excellent shape, with skills that the average suburb—*person* doesn't have. Then there's the tech. You have a gift. One most people would take full advantage of. And you don't."

"That's my choice."

"Is it? I don't know what happened after your dad died. I can understand you deciding not to go into the army after that. As for the tech stuff, maybe you quit out of misplaced guilt, because you were in college when he died. I'm not going to play amateur shrink here. You have physical and technological skills that you choose not to use, having reinvented yourself for whatever reason, which is none of my business. *My* business is how you're using those skills now."

My mouth opens. Then it shuts, as I realize what she's said.

That she doesn't know why I cut ties with my old life. She suspects it's my father's suicide, and that's good enough for her.

She has no idea what I did after his death.

And she doesn't seem to care.

She continues, "Just because you have some special skills, Aubrey, does not make you a detective."

"You're right, and I have no desire to become one." I meet her gaze. "I'm stuck doing this because the police are not. And you aren't a detective either."

She flinches at that. I didn't mean it as an insult, but she clearly takes it as one.

"I only joined the force three years ago, and I have every intention of becoming a detective."

"That wasn't a challenge," I say.

"Then don't make it sound like one."

"Then stop talking to me like I'm the scatterbrained suburbanite you thought I was last week."

I wait for the rejoinder. Instead, she pulls back. Considers. Then she nods. "Fair enough. My mistake. My stereotyping. So I apologize. But you are doing a job you are not qualified to do. A job you are not allowed to do."

"Yes, actually, I am allowed to do it. As long as I don't break any laws or misrepresent myself—"

"The owners of that pizza parlor seem to think you were a police officer."

"I said nothing of the sort. If they inferred that?" I shrug. "Clearly a misunderstanding because I never said it."

She allows a small smile. Before she can speak, I say, "So you've been to that pizza parlor. Did they tell you about Kim?"

"Kim Mason. Also known as Kim Lyons. That's our dead woman."

I must look surprised, because she says, "I *have* been listening to you, Aubrey. I've been getting those messages, and I've been passing them on to the detectives-in-charge, and we've been investigating. That's what I've been trying to tell you. Thank you for the information, but stop. Please stop. Let us do our jobs."

"I haven't seen anything in the paper saying she's been identified."

"Because she *hasn't* been. We're still tracking down her real identity."

"Kim Mikhailov," I say. "Born in Cedar Rapids. Ran away at the age of fifteen. Dancing in a strip club by the time she was sixteen. A strip club owned by a guy she ended up dating. Denis Zima. Who also owns—"

"Zodiac Five. The club you just left." She shakes her head. "I wondered what you were doing there. Okay, so you suspect Kim Mason is this Kim Mikhailov."

"Not suspect. *Know.* Kim was calling a woman named Ellie Milano weekly. Ellie's Facebook page mentions a younger sister, Kim. It includes photos of Kim as a teen. She is undeniably your dead woman."

"How the hell did you figure out all that?"

"I'm good with computers."

"Okay, you *would* make a good detective. But you're not one. I want to be one, and I'm using your tips, Aubrey, because they'll help me get my shield. So thank you. However, I truly need you to stop. For your own safety."

"Yes."

She eyes me. "I mean that. Don't blow me off—"

"You're not the one who's been blown off. I never wanted to play detective. Trying to get you to listen cost me a weekend with my daughter. All I want—all I *ever* wanted—was for you to take me seriously."

"Well, I am. I appreciate the ID on our dead woman *and* the link to Denis Zima. With him involved, though, you definitely don't want to be chasing this lead."

"Because his dad is a Russian mobster."

She makes a face. "That sounds very Hollywood. Let's just say his family has been under investigation for years, which is public record. I have no idea how Denis fits in, but I'll dig for more."

"He doesn't have the boy."

She looks up sharply.

"Brandon," I say. "That's Kim's son. The boy I saw taken."

She sighs. Deeply.

"You still don't believe I saw a child taken?" I say. "You just said you misjudged me."

"You saw a kid get pulled into a car. I do not doubt that. You didn't intentionally misreport—"

"I didn't misreport *anything*. Kim had a son named Brandon. She was hiding him from Zima, who now realizes he has a son, thanks to me. I have the proof right here." I pull out my phone. As I flip to the recorder, I say, "I taped one of his men talking about it."

I hit Play. The man's voice is muffled. Too muffled to make out.

"No, no, no." I jack up the volume, but it only increases the sound of my breathing. "Damn it, no. I was in a closet. You can enhance the quality, though."

"You taped one of Zima's men from a closet? You were *hiding* in a closet?"

"I was checking the office computer when he came upstairs."

She gives another of those deep sighs. "Aubrey . . ."

"Forget the tape for now." I put my phone down. "You can enhance the recording, and you'll hear the guy say that Denis is looking for his son. For Kim's boy. He thinks Brandon is someplace safe—that Kim got him to safety. He's not safe now, though, because Denis is after him."

"This guy randomly started talking about all this while you were in the closet?"

"Well, no. He was telling the head of security that Denis thought he spotted me at the club."

"*What?*"

"Denis saw me on TV the other day. That's how he knew he had a son."

Jackson closes her eyes and shakes her head.

"Yes," I say. "This is my fault. I accept that. If it wasn't for me, Denis wouldn't know about Brandon. He'd be safe with whoever Kim trusted to care for him."

"That's not why I'm shaking my head, Aubrey. First, having Denis Zima looking for you is like painting a target on your back. Do you even realize that?"

"He thinks he saw me in the club. Even his people believe he was imagining it. The security cameras aren't functional, and I changed my dress to sneak out. The only reason he'd be concerned about me is if he has proof I came snooping around. Otherwise, I'm just the crazy lady on the television."

"Fair enough. But I was also shaking my head because this doesn't prove there's a child. Denis believes there's a child because *you* said so. That's all he's going on."

"I found the house where she'd been staying. There was a drink box and a children's book there. A book with the name Brandon in it."

"You broke in—"

"I went in through an open window. Kim was in a hurry to leave and forgot to close it. That's still trespassing, but I was desperate. She'd cleared away every sign of a child being there. I found the drink box and book, though."

"That's . . . No. Just no, Aubrey. That isn't proof, and you know it, which is why you didn't report it."

"You *still* don't believe me?" I straighten. "Fine. It doesn't matter anymore. Talk to Kim's sister. She'll know there was a child. Just ask her."

"I will."

TWENTY-TWO

I don't know how much I trust Laila Jackson. I'm too eager for an ally, and she was clearly not one a few days ago. Yet I do believe, once she knows Brandon exists, she'll want to find him. She's also aiming for detective, and if she can use my information to get there, that's fine by me. Because she's right about one thing: I'm not a private investigator. I don't want to be. I just want justice for Kim and safety for Brandon. We seem to be on that track now.

I go home and get some sleep. Laila has promised to call as soon as she's made contact with Ellie. Yes, I think of her as "Laila" now. "Officer Jackson" seems oddly formal. Thinking of her as more than a cop also, ironically, *keeps me* from jumping to claim her as an ally. She's not an unbiased representative of the law. She's a fully rounded person, with her own agenda and her own ambitions.

I'm up at eight thirty, expecting Charlotte at nine. At 8:55, a knock sounds at my door. I throw it open to see Paul standing there . . . alone.

"Charlie's not with me," he says.

"Is everything okay?" My heart pounds. My first thought is

that he's keeping her from me, that he's here to challenge me on custody. My second is that something's happened to her, that she fell off the horse or—

"She's fine," he says. "Gayle has her while I speak to you."

I step back to let him in. "It's . . . awfully early for her to be at Gayle's, Paul. It's none of my business if you're spending the night, but if Charlie's going to be there, too, I think we need to discuss that."

"What?" He seems confused. "No. Of course not. I dropped her off. I just . . . I want to talk, and I'd rather not do that with Charlie here."

"Okay. Can I get you a coffee?"

I expect him to say no, and I'm relieved when he nods, but it's an absent one, as if he's barely listening.

I go in the kitchen and pour a cup. "Just brewed, so it's still fresh."

"I'm sorry about keeping Charlie yesterday," he says.

It honestly takes a moment to realize what he's talking about. When I do, I answer with care. My fury from Friday night has blown over, and I don't want to fight about this. Nor, however, do I want to brush it aside.

"I completely understand Gayle's daughter wanting Charlie at her party," I say. "I'd have liked more notice, but I know it was a last-minute decision. Next time, I would really appreciate it if *you* called. I don't have an issue talking to Gayle. This isn't me versus her."

He seems to flinch at that, and I'm not sure why. This should be what he wants to hear, right?

I hand him his coffee. "I don't know how serious you two are—"

He opens his mouth, as if to answer, and then shuts it.

"Even if you're serious," I say, "I just met her. A call to change our arrangement should come from you."

"I didn't know." He blurts the words and then hesitates, as if ready to pull them back. Instead, he sits at my tiny dinette table. "Gayle called you without asking me."

I pour a cup of coffee for myself and sit across from him.

"Her daughter asked, and Gayle . . . She wants . . ." He rubs his chin and shakes his head.

"She wants . . . ?" I prompt.

Another shake of his head, gaze down. "She's just . . . moving faster than . . ." He straightens and shrugs it off with a roll of his shoulders. "She overstepped her boundaries, and I've said so, as nicely as possible. She didn't see the harm in calling you herself. She thought, that way, it'd be clear it was her idea, and you wouldn't be upset with me."

"I wouldn't ever be—"

"I've told her that. You and I don't have that kind of . . ." Another roll of his shoulders, and he makes a face. "She didn't mean any harm. I've been clear—clearer—that you and I have a very cordial relationship."

Cordial.

That hurts. Cordial is the relationship you have with a cousin you don't share anything in common with beyond blood. It's the ex you don't share anything in common with beyond a child.

It used to be more.

So much more.

And now it's just "cordial" and I almost wonder if "hostile" wouldn't be better, if it wouldn't be easier.

For me, maybe. But not easier for our daughter, and that's what counts.

"Okay," I say. "Thank you for explaining. I thought you didn't call yourself because you were still upset with me after Thursday night."

"No, not at all." He pauses. "About that. You said you could use my help. I want to offer it. If you're having trouble getting the police to listen . . ."

"They're listening," I say. "Well, they aren't convinced there's a missing child, but I helped them ID the murdered woman, so they know I'm not a complete nutjob."

As I say that, I realize that I'm taking this conversation in a direction it shouldn't go. The one that will have him furrowing his brow and asking *how* I helped ID a dead woman. Instead, he just nods and says, "Well, that's good."

He's still distracted, obviously. I should drop it here. Don't go filling in any blanks that can stay blank. Just hope Paul doesn't look back on this conversation later, when he's less distracted, and say, "Wait a second . . ."

But as I think that, I realize I can't drop it. Laila Jackson knows I'm not who I claim to be. She wields that power over me, and I don't know her well enough to entrust her with that secret.

"Paul . . ."

"Hmm?" He sips his coffee, his gaze distant.

"I . . . I need to talk to you about something," I say. "Something that came up with the police."

He puts the mug down. "All right."

"I . . ." My heart thuds so hard I can barely form words. "Before I met you . . ."

His gaze lifts to mine and the words dry up.

I swallow. "Before I met you . . . things happened, and I . . . I haven't been entirely"—*entirely?*—"honest with you about my past and . . ."

"And now you want to be, not because you've had an epiphany, but because you're in trouble."

His voice is cold. Colder than I've ever heard it, and those blue eyes turn just as icy. My insides freeze, and I'm seized by this overwhelming urge to hide, just hide.

"Do not ask me to get you out of this, Aubrey," he says.

"I-I'd never—"

"Good. I think I've done enough. My only advice is not to let the police bully you into a confession. The statute of limitations for theft in California is three years. You are well past that."

I stare at him. I just stare. Then my mouth opens, and all I can manage is a strangled noise.

His hands tighten on his mug. "Nine months before you left, I received a call from a man named Ruben Dubrand. He tried to extort money from me, threatening to expose you."

"Ruben extorted *money*—"

"Tried." Paul gives me a hard look. "I'm a defense attorney. I know the law. I set him straight, uncovered his own identity and threatened to use that against him if he ever came at my family again."

I can't speak. I just can't even process this. I must still be asleep, caught in a nightmare where Paul tells me he knows what I've done. That he's known for . . .

Nine months before we split.

That would be our last Christmas together. Exactly the time when I started noticing rifts in our marriage. It'd been the holidays, and he'd found excuses to skip parties, given me a perfunctory gift, taken Charlotte to his mother's alone "because I know you two don't get along, and you can use a post-holiday break."

That's when he decided we should stop trying for a second child.

I always presumed that I first noticed the trouble at Christmas only because holidays are stressful, and so that's when the schism became obvious. That isn't true. The schism started there. After Ruben contacted him.

I have spent the last year trying to figure out where our marriage went wrong, how we drifted apart, how I failed him.

Now I know.

"I-I . . ." It's all I can say, all I can manage.

"You were someone else before you met me. I haven't dug into your past. I don't want to know. All Dubrand told me was that you'd committed robberies—break-and-enters—as part of a group. At first, I didn't believe him. Then he told me about your shoulder. On your last job, the homeowner shot you there, and you didn't get proper medical attention for it."

"Yes," I say, and when the word comes, it's an exhale of something like relief. "It's . . . it's a long story but—"

"I don't want to hear it."

My head jerks up, eyes meeting his. I hadn't been about to explain. I didn't want to hide behind excuses. But that cold rejection makes my hackles rise. I force them down again before I speak.

"I was about to say that it's a long story, but I'm not going to make excuses. Yes, I broke into homes and robbed them. I got shot. I got out. I started using my mother's maiden name and eventually wound up in Chicago, where you met me."

"Convenient, wasn't it?"

I frown. "Convenient?"

He pushes back his chair. "Before I met you, I was in serious danger of becoming one of those men who whines about how nice guys always finish last, how women don't want a nice guy. I had a couple of women break it off with the 'you're such a great guy, but you're just not for me' crap. The kiss-off that tells me I'm boring as hell. I stopped dating and started complaining. My friends sat me down for an intervention. They challenged me to try again. To take a real chance. Was there a woman I'd love to ask out, but was sure she'd turn me down? I said yes: you."

"Me?"

"I saw you when I'd go into the bookstore café. I'd hear you laughing. I'd see you goofing around with coworkers. I'd see you being kind to patrons. I noticed you, and I knew I was not the kind of guy you'd ever go out with. But that night with my friends, I'd had a few drinks, and they convinced me to go for it. Two days later, as I was trying to work up the nerve . . ."

"You saw me get a traffic ticket right outside the building. You said I should fight it."

"Perfect timing, wasn't it?" he says.

I think he means the ticket. I've forgotten he's angry, and I'm about to smile and say, yes, that ticket came at the perfect time. Then I see his expression.

"A boring, ordinary guy," he says. "Who fell so hard for you he never once questioned what you saw in him."

I blink. "What?"

"Plus he's a criminal defense attorney," he says. "It didn't get any better than that."

"What are you talking about?"

"You used me, Bree. I realize that now. When Dubrand first contacted me and I began to have doubts about our marriage, I tried to tell myself I was wrong. Okay, not *wrong*. I understood that you were on the run, and you needed to hide, and I was your cover."

"*What?* No, I *never*—"

"I pursued you. So it wasn't as if you targeted me. But you saw an opportunity."

"*No.*"

"Maybe it wasn't that Machiavellian. I don't actually think it was. You just . . . settled. It was an arranged marriage of sorts. I just didn't realize it."

"Paul, *no.* I did not—"

"That's why I never confronted you. I loved you. Forget *why* you were with me. You were with me. By choice. Maybe I'd even won you over, however it started. And then you said it wasn't working, and I knew what that meant. I'd served my purpose."

"That was *not*—"

"At first, I thought you found someone. Eventually I realized that wasn't the case. Maybe you got tired of me. Maybe you just got tired of the lies. I go back and forth, Aubrey. When I'm feeling sorry for myself, I'm certain you used me. Used me and left me. Then I see you with Charlotte, and I must give you the benefit of the doubt. There was a time when I even wondered if you had Charlotte to trap me. Something to threaten me with, if I tried to expose you. Or if I wouldn't pay you off."

"I have not taken one red *dime*—"

"I know." His hands fold around his mug again. "You can stop pretending now, though. Bring out your money. I presume that's why you didn't take mine. You still have the money you stole."

"I gave that away."

His gaze lifts to mine. "What?"

"But I *do* have money. An inheritance, which means, yes, I don't need yours. I did not use you, Paul. I swear I did not. But I did lie to you. I misled you. Which is why I don't want any of our marital estate. All I care about is joint custody of Charlotte."

He looks at me. For at least a minute, he looks at me. Then he says, slowly, "Would a half-million dollars convince you to give up that claim?"

I stiffen. "I will *never*—"

"You can still see her. Still be part of her life."

I speak slowly, enunciating each word. "I would give you every penny I have for joint custody. Not full custody, because I would never take Charlie away from you. I don't have a half million. Maybe a fifth of that. But it's yours if you agree to joint custody."

He shakes his head. "I'd never take your money. And I'd never try to take her from you, either. I was just . . ."

"Checking. In case I'm faking maternal affection."

"I'm sorry."

"I did not do what you think, Paul. I fell for you. I fell in love—"

"Don't."

"I'm—"

"Don't. Please." He gets to his feet. "You need to say that. I know your secret, so you'll never risk hurting my feelings by admitting that you married me to be safe. I understand that you love Charlotte. I understand that you aren't going to take anything from me, including her. I want . . ." He exhales "I want a civil relationship, for her sake." A pause. "I'll go get her."

I shake my head. "I can't . . . Not today. If you had plans, if you need me to take her . . ."

"I don't."

"Then I'll wait until next weekend."

He nods, and he leaves. That's it. He just leaves.

TWENTY-THREE

I spend the rest of the morning in bed. Laila calls at ten, and I don't answer. Right now, I don't care about anyone else's problems.

Paul knew about my past. He's known for months, and that is what ended our marriage. My lies.

This was a possibility I never foresaw, and now that I do, I realize what a monumental mistake I made in not telling him from the start. If I'd done that, he'd know that marrying him wasn't about hiding or seeking sanctuary. But he's right that nothing I say now will matter. I never stopped to see it from his point of view. Even if I had, I'm not sure I could have anticipated how he'd feel.

Yes, he wasn't the sort of guy I usually dated. Yes, we didn't seem to have a lot in common. And, yes, God help me, I never noticed him coming into the bookstore café, because he wasn't the kind of man I noticed.

Guys like Paul didn't usually end up with girls like me, and that's no insult to him. We move in different spheres, and there was no point noticing a guy like him because he wasn't going to notice me back. He'd look for a woman like Gayle. A stable, competent fellow professional. Maybe, if I'd finished college and found a career in tech, it'd be different, but I'd been a twenty-five-year-old with a high school education, working in a bookstore. I had not been wife material for a man like Paul. And yet he married me, had a child with me, and I'd felt blessed.

I have hurt a man I loved. A man I still love.

I've deeply hurt him. Dealt a blow to his pride and his self-confidence but worse, I betrayed him. Betrayed his trust.

Whenever I've grieved over the loss of my marriage, I've fortified myself with the knowledge that Paul had been unhappy, so ending it was the right and noble thing for me to do. He had indeed been unhappy . . . because he thought his wife married him as a safe haven, a security blanket. When I suggested it wasn't working, his quick agreement had stung to the core. Surprised me, too, because I didn't honestly believe he was divorce-level miserable. Just less happy than I wanted him to be. To him, though, my leaving only proved his point. He'd done the same thing I had—he set me free.

I spend the first two hours that afternoon writing him letters. Write. Rewrite. Rewrite again. I cannot find the words to prove that he's wrong. I don't know how, and when I try to put my feelings on paper, it sounds like the worst kind of fakery, over-the-top sentimentality worthy of a cheap greeting card.

I try to tell him my past, but that sounds like excuses. He's a defense attorney—he's heard truly tragic life stories, and mine seems weak in comparison.

Your mommy died when you were little. Your daddy killed himself when you were eighteen. Boo-hoo. It happens. They raised you well, with everything you needed for a decent life. If you threw that away, Aubrey, then you're not a tragic heroine—you're a spoiled little brat.

My father dies, and I fly into a tantrum, turning to crime to repay the world for its unkindness? That's worse than a cheap greeting card sentiment. It's the lamest villain backstory ever.

I write. I rewrite. I send nothing.

Midafternoon, I pull on sweats to go for a jog. I'm swinging out the front door and nearly bash into a woman coming in. I murmur an apology and start past her.

"Aubrey?" the woman says.

I look, and it's Laila Jackson. She's dressed in a uniform, but not a police one. It's a softball uniform, one that used to be white, but it's faded to gray with use, the knees brown from slides into base. There's dirt on her cheek, and any makeup she'd worn has sweated away. Her eyes gleam with a look I know well—the afterglow of adrenaline from a good workout.

"Did you win?" I say.

"I did," she says. "Two home runs, and three runs batted in. Problem is the rest of my damned team."

I laugh softly. "Come on up, and I'll get you a soda."

She shakes her head. "Better keep me outside. Showers weren't working at the field. I was heading home, and then realized I was driving through downtown, and maybe I should stop and see why you aren't taking my calls. In case you got yourself into trouble and were lying in a pool of blood somewhere. Crazy thought, I know. You're such a nice, quiet librarian."

"You aren't going to let up on the librarian thing, are you?"

"Nope." She waves to the road. "Let's walk."

I glance over at her as we move onto the sidewalk. "What position do you play?"

"Right field. You got a team?"

I shake my head. "Organized sports aren't really my thing. Sports in general aren't my thing these days, not with my schedule. I'm trying to fit something in. Maybe a class."

"Let me guess. Hot yoga or SoulCycle?"

"Sword fighting."

Her perfectly sculpted brows shoot up. "Fencing?"

"No, swords. Real swords. I saw this notice come through on the interlibrary system for classes at a branch in Chicago. All-women sword fighting."

"That sounds . . ." She purses her lips. "I'm torn between weird and cool."

"Weirdly cool. Totally up my alley."

She chuckles. "I'm shocked, really. So, sword-fighting classes for women, at a library. That's just odd enough that I might actually ask you to send me a link."

"I'll do that."

We go three more steps before she says, "Ellie Milano says Kim didn't have a son."

I stop walking. My jaw works. I look at her. "What?"

She says it again, slower. I can't read her expression, and that only pisses me off more. Ten seconds ago, we're chatting about sword fighting, and I'm finally relaxing, feeling like I've made a connection, and now I get this impenetrable stare, these words, spoken with no preamble, no buffer.

"All right," I say. "Clearly I have made a horrible mistake, and I hallucinated the fact that I spoke to this woman and her son in Grant Park last week. My daughter hallucinated it, too. It must be hereditary."

"I don't doubt that you spoke to someone who looked like Kim Mikhailov."

"Yep, wasn't her, though. Which is weird. I mean, this woman and I talked about her job, and she said she worked at a pizza place, and that's how I found Kim. Oh, and I heard that woman talking Russian on the phone, and both Kim and Denis come from Russian families, but hey, just a coincidence."

"You got the pizza parlor lead from the woman in the park?"

"No, I pulled it out of my ass. How else would I have known the dead woman worked at a pizza place?"

No change in her expression, as if my sarcasm bounces right off her. She just looks at me. After a moment she says, "Then you did speak to Kim."

"Kinda said that."

"Which means the boy who was with her must not have been her son."

"He called her mama. Why the hell is it so difficult for you people to believe she had a son? A son she was hiding—which is why no one knows about him. You just keep explaining away everything I say—" I cut myself short. "No, never mind. I don't care. There's a boy, and he's safe, and that's all that matters. Now if you guys can stop Denis Zima, my imaginary boy will stay safe. I have more important things to do than bash my head against this wall."

I turn and stalk back to my apartment building. Laila Jackson doesn't follow.

I try to forget about Brandon and Kim. I really do. But thinking about them has temporarily distracted me from the crash-and-burn of my life. When I try to return to composing that letter for Paul, I keep feeling Brandon's tug.

There *is* a child. I can entertain doubt, when I get pushback from Laila Jackson, but it only takes a hard reality check to realize there is no other explanation for what I've seen and experienced. So why is Laila pushing back?

Is she lying about Ellie Milano?

Why would she?

She would if she's covering something up. If she's complicit in all this. If she's on the payroll of Denis Zima or his father.

Oh my God. Did I really just think that? I sound like exactly what the police have accused me of being: a lady who watches way too much crime TV. I don't, actually. Sure, I can enjoy a classic or modern mystery novel, but I know that fiction isn't reality. Ruben didn't run an international ring of superthieves, able to break through the highest security to steal world-class art. The fact that he employed a hacker meant he was, for his field, very high-tech. Yet we were still breaking into houses with cheap security systems, stealing valuables left lying in drawers and closets. Easy pickings. Ruben selected his targets with care, too, and most times they never even called the cops, because if they did that, they'd invite more scrutiny into their income than they wanted.

When I suspect Laila of being in the Zima family's pocket, I feel like that layperson who watches too many police dramas. I also know, from living with Paul, that corruption happens. Police, politicians, lawyers . . . Most are good people, but if there's a way to make a little extra in *any* profession, someone will.

I want to call Ellie Milano myself and be sure she told Laila she doesn't have a nephew. I know I shouldn't. If Ellie calls the Oxford PD to complain, Laila will know it was me. Since there is no missing child, though, I can't be interfering with the investigation into a missing child, right?

It's not just idle curiosity that compels me to call. If Ellie is hiding Brandon for Kim, then she needs to know about Zima.

I have Ellie's number from Kim's phone records. She answers on the third ring.

"I'm a friend of Kim's," I say. "I'm calling about Brandon."

There's a pause. Such a long pause. Then a cautious "Brandon?"

"Her son."

No response. I swear I hear her breathing across the line. Swear I hear that breathing pick up speed.

She says nothing. She just waits, and this tells me what I need to know. There is a Brandon.

An oddly muffled voice speaks in the background. I hear other sounds, too, as if she's in a busy place.

"I met Kim in Oxford," I say. "I know she was hiding her son—"

"My sister didn't have a son."

"I met Brandon. He's about five. Blond hair—"

"I'm sorry, but you're mistaken. I understand there was a woman on the news who said she saw my sister with a son. She was wrong. Kim didn't have a child."

"I'm that woman. I know Kim had—"

"Stop. Please. I just lost my sister. I'm going to hang up now."

"Denis Zima," I blurt.

Silence. Then, "I don't know that name."

"He's Brandon's father. Or he thinks he is."

"I'm hanging up and phoning the police."

"Denis knows about Brandon. He's looking for him. He thinks Kim put Brandon someplace safe. I realize now that I saw a rescue, not a kidnapping. If you have any way to warn the people who have Brandon, please do. Denis Zima is looking for his son. If Kim didn't want Denis finding him, then I know you don't either."

The line disconnects. But she heard me. I know she did.

I'm finishing dinner when Paul texts.

Charlie would like to Skype with you.

She wants to tell you about yesterday.

I stare at the texts and draw a blank. Yesterday? What . . .

The party. The horseback riding. The fact that my daughter was supposed to be here with me today, and I canceled, and I never even said, "Hey, I'd like to talk to her."

I text back quickly and ask him to have Charlotte call whenever she wants. I'll have my laptop ready.

I've barely got Skype open when she connects, and guilt churns my stomach. My daughter has been waiting, eager to talk to me, and I've been caught up in my own concerns.

I forgot her last week for the princess tea. Now I've done it again.

"Hey, baby," I say when she appears. She's someplace I don't recognize, with people passing behind her. "Where are you?"

"Train house," she says.

An announcement sounds in the background. She's in the Chicago train station. My gut goes cold with a sudden image flashing of Paul bustling her onto a train, out of my life forever.

I push back the panic. Paul would never do that. Even if he tried, seized by a sudden fit of madness, he would hardly have Charlotte call me from the station.

"What are you doing there?" I ask, as casually as I can.

Paul's voice comes from the background. He doesn't lean in to the camera, as he usually does. He remains a disembodied voice.

"Gayle's daughter is going on a school trip," he says. "We were dropping her off."

"Ah, did she catch her train okay?"

He doesn't answer. I'm asking a polite but meaningless question, and he's not going to bother responding. This is where we stand.

"How Mummy tummy?" Charlotte asks.

"My . . . ?"

"Daddy say Mommy sick."

I exhale. *Thank you, Paul.* I'd wondered what excuse he'd given. The easy one would be to say I was busy, and I'd really hoped he hadn't—I'd never want Charlotte to think I was too busy for her. But he did the right thing, as always. No matter how upset he was with me, he rose above it.

I assure her that I feel much better—probably something I ate—and then I ask about the party. As she regales me with her day of excitement, another announcement blares, and it pokes at my brain. Then I remember the background noise on my call with Ellie. That muffled voice had been an announcement.

She'd been in a train station. Or an airline terminal.

Was she traveling to see Brandon? To take him back from whoever had him?

"Mommy?"

I scramble to remember what Charlotte said. I'm replaying her words when Paul leans down, just for a second, to be sure I'm still there.

"Sorry," I say. "It's a bad connection. What did you say, sweetheart?"

She repeats it, and I respond appropriately. I push aside thoughts of Ellie.

Repeat after me, Bree. This is what matters—your daughter. Let Ellie take care of Brandon. If she's going to fetch him, that's a good thing.

Charlotte keeps talking, and I corral my thoughts. It's a struggle, and that gnaws at me. I lost my weekend with Charlotte, and now I can't afford fifteen minutes to listen to her talk about her day?

I focus until Paul says it's time to go. This is the point where, normally, he'd come on for a quick exchange of parental information, like telling me she has a dental appointment or that she's really enjoying a certain book. Today, Charlotte says good-bye . . . and he disconnects the line.

I text him: I can have her next weekend, right?

He replies: Of course.

And that's it. Conversation over.

TWENTY-FOUR

I need to get Kim and Brandon out of my head. They aren't my concern, and they're interfering with things that are. After that Skype call, I plan my next weekend with Charlotte. We have tea reservations for Sunday. I'll get her a new dress. We'll do that on Saturday. Maybe I'll ask Paul if I can have her Friday to make up for my last weekend.

No, not maybe. I will. In fact, I'm going to do that right now. At the very least, it'll help me gauge how dire this situation with him is.

I send the text. Then I spend the next twenty minutes freaking out because he's not replying.

Things *have* changed. He might have found out the truth over a year ago, but this has brought it all back. Maybe he was holding out hope that I had another explanation.

Robbery? Is that what Ruben said? Not at all. He's a guy I knew back home. Yes, that shoulder injury is a bullet. It was a stupid thing— me and some friends—and I didn't want you to get the wrong idea, think you married a redneck. Ruben's just being a jerk.

He hoped for an explanation. I didn't give one. So now he must accept that he married a thief. A woman who robbed homes and got shot and went on the run and hooked up with him to reinvent herself.

He's going to take Charlotte away.

I'm not the person he wants raising his daughter.

He hasn't quite decided that yet, but the idea is forming. He has the ammunition he needs to take her. As for depriving her of a mother, well, Gayle is a much better role model.

Stop that, Bree. Just stop.

He's slow in responding because he's considering my request. I had Charlotte for an extra night this week, and it was my choice not to have her today, so he's thinking he doesn't owe me Friday. He just doesn't want to refuse and sound pissy.

I need to tell him that I have something planned. That ups the ante. If he still refuses me then, I'll know something's wrong.

As I pull up the calendar of local events, I remember there's a pizza party at the library.

Pizza. Maybe Kim's employers know—

I thrust the thought aside and compose the text to Paul.

Me: My library is having a pizza-and-jammies evening Friday. I'd love to sign Charlie up, if that's okay with you.

Hit Send. Wait five minutes, counting it on the clock. Then I send another.

Me: I could give up Sunday night if it's a problem. I'd drop her off after our princess tea.

Giving her up early Sunday defeats the purpose of having extra time with her. This is another test, though. Is he not answering because I'm asking for extra time? Or is he going to start blocking me when I request off-schedule hours with Charlotte, even for something special?

Five more minutes. Send another text.

Me: I understand if you already have plans.

Two minutes. I'm going to call at the five-minute mark. I'll—

My phone buzzes as a text comes in.

Paul: Just got back from city.

Paul: Let me put Charlie to bed and check the calendar.

I curse myself. Of course it'd taken him a while to text back. He'd been at the train station in Chicago when I talked to Charlotte.

I make myself a tea and try not to obsessively watch the clock. It takes about fifteen minutes to settle Charlotte in. More if he gives her a bath, but it's almost nine, so he'll probably skip—

The text comes in at fourteen minutes.

Paul: Friday's fine.

Paul: Sunday is your call.

I send back that I'd love to keep her until Monday, dropping her at daycare as we usually do. I just didn't want to cut into his time. He replies that Friday through Monday is fine—he had her this weekend.

I want to say more. I want to tell him that I spent the afternoon composing letters. I want to tell him he's wrong, so wrong. I want to tell him my version of the day we met, that yes, I might not have noticed him before, but when he smiled at me, I noticed, and I never stopped noticing. When he asked me out, I did think it was a mistake, but only because guys like him never asked girls like me, and if they did, maybe it's because they were expecting something he wasn't going to get from me on a first date. When he continued asking me out, I kept waiting for the other shoe to fall, kept looking for *his* angle.

I want to tell him all that.

I start composing texts, and I don't get past a few words.

Finally, before he can put his phone away, conversation over, I text.

Me: I'm sorry.

He doesn't reply. He's already gone.

He's been gone for a very long time.

———

I go for a run after that. Laila Jackson's visit had aborted my earlier attempt, and I *really* want that jog now. I need to clear my head, run until my legs wobble and my lungs burn and I can no longer think about Paul or Charlotte or Kim or Brandon. Run until it takes every ounce of mental energy just to drag myself back to my apartment and collapse into dreamless sleep.

I've barely gone a couple of blocks when a voice at my shoulder says, "Where's the fire?"

I give a start and look over to see that another jogger has joined me. His voice sounds familiar, and I think immediately of the guy in the park, the fellow jogger who pestered me the day Brandon disappeared. It's not him, though—this guy is about my age. But that reminds me that I never did try to find that guy, get him to corroborate my story about Brandon.

Stop that.

No new evidence will make the police believe me now, and what difference would it make if they did? Brandon is safe unless Zima catches up with him. Zima, though, is going to be the police's top suspect in Kim's murder, so he won't have time to look for his son.

Brandon is safe. The only thing to be gained by proving he existed is repairing my public reputation.

See, I was right. I'm not a delusional attention-seeker.

Clear my name . . . and put Brandon in more danger. As it stands right now, Zima only thinks Brandon exists because I said so. If everyone believes I'm wrong, then while that hurts my pride, it's better for the child.

"I asked, where's the fire," the guy says, and it takes me a moment to mentally snap back to him.

He's smiling at me, friendly. A little too friendly? Maybe. It happens. It's like sitting in a public place, trying to read a book. Some guys take that as a hint that you really need something better to do with your time. Headphones help, but in my rush to get out tonight, I left mine at home.

"Fire?" I say.

"You're running like there's someone on your tail. Or are you just trying to get done before dark?"

He jerks his chin up, and I see that the streetlights have come on. It's almost nine, and dusk is falling fast.

I glance at him. He's smiling at me again, and I don't like the smile. No more than I like him pointing out that it's getting dark.

I laugh. "No, I'm not afraid of the dark. Just trying to burn off a big Sunday dinner."

I cross at the light, veering off my usual course to make a sharp left. He follows.

"You shouldn't be out after dark in this neighborhood," he says. "That's just asking for trouble."

"It's never been a problem before," I say.

I kick it up a notch. He does, too.

"I keep thinking I've seen you somewhere," he says.

"I work downtown here."

"No, it's . . . Wait. I know. The news. You're the one who said you saw the boy. That murdered chick's kid."

The way he says "murdered chick" makes my hackles rise. It also nudges a memory, but it flits by before I can catch it.

I take the next right, heading back. That seems to be the only way I'll lose this guy. Except I don't want to lead him to my front door.

Damn.

Where can I go . . . ?

Coffee. That's the first idea that springs to mind, not surprisingly, given that I spent most of yesterday in coffee shops. There's a twenty-four-hour diner a block from my place. I've been there often enough that I know most of the servers. If this guy follows me in, they'll see my "problem" and help me shake him.

"So you think she had a kid?" he says.

I start to say yes. Then I remember what I was just thinking. Squelch my pride. Protect the boy.

"No, I made a mistake," I say. "The woman who died didn't have any kids."

"How do you know that? The cops haven't ID'd her."

My gut freezes. Then I shrug. "That's what they told me."

"So the police *have* ID'd her?"

"They never said that. They just told me there wasn't a boy. I was mistaken."

I cross the road. He keeps pace.

"You're sure?" he continues.

"Yes, I'm . . ." I trail off as I look at the guy. As I *really* look at him.

He's not a jogger. He's wearing sweatpants and sneakers, but they're leisure pants and designer high-tops, both meant for style, not running. There's a bulge in his waistband. The bulge of a handgun.

That's when I remember thinking his voice sounded familiar. It *is* familiar. I heard it just last night, through a closet door. He's the guy from Zodiac Five. Denis Zima's friend.

Stay calm. Just stay calm.

I look over at him. "Are you a reporter?"

His surprise is almost comical. "Hell, no. I just remember seeing that on the news, and thinking it was a helluva thing. That chick getting bumped off for her kid. That's what it seemed like—some sicko killed her for her little boy. Some pervert. But when I looked it up later, seeing if they found the kid, I find out the police didn't believe you. That pissed me off. They do that sometimes, with women. They don't believe them."

"Well, in this case, they were correct. I was mistaken."

"Are you sure?"

I glance at him. "What difference does it make?"

"I'm curious, okay," he says, and there's a faint growl to his voice, one that warns he's just about done playing nice.

"I saw a woman with a boy," I say. "It wasn't the same woman. She just had a similar look—young, blond, slender."

"And she had a son?"

"Maybe? She was with a kid. About eight or nine."

"Eight or nine?"

I shrug. "Maybe older? I don't have kids, so I can never tell."

"What were they doing?"

"Hmm?"

"The chick and her kid. What were they doing when you saw them?"

I'm about to say they were on the swings—just make something up. But when I see his expression, I realize I don't want to give anything away.

"Look," I say. "I get it. You don't want me to know you're a reporter. But it's obvious you are. No one else asks me these kind of questions."

"Except the police."

"Yes."

"So the police asked you?"

I turn another corner. The diner is a block ahead. I only have to get that far.

"The police didn't ask me much of anything," I say. "Because they didn't believe there was a child, and it turns out they were right. I made a mistake. An embarrassing mistake. Now, if you'll just leave me alone please—"

He elbows me. It's so fast and sharp that I never see it coming. His elbow strikes my bad shoulder and I stagger with a gasp. Then he grabs that same shoulder and shoves me hard into a narrow passage between two buildings.

"What the hell?" I say as I recover. "This is not the way to get a story."

His hand goes to my throat. Again, I don't see it coming. I don't expect it. He may have knocked me into this alley, but that was just a fit of temper, and he'll see he's made a mistake and cover it up.

Did I bump your shoulder? I'm so sorry.

That's what I expect. Just stand firm, and he'll back down and regroup. Instead, there's a hand at my throat, and then he's slamming me into the wall, my feet barely touching the ground.

"Let's try this again," he says. "I want to know everything about that kid. Understand?"

I glower at him, and he lifts me by the neck until I'm on tiptoes . . . and his T-shirt rises up over his waistband.

I wheeze for breath and nod frantically.

"Good," he says.

As he lowers me down again, I grab the gun. Grab it and jab the barrel into his stomach. He grunts in shock and jerks back, like I've sucker punched him. Then he sees the gun.

"What the—?" he begins.

"Did I mention that I'm not worried about running at night? I can take care of myself. Now step away."

He grabs for the gun. I *do* hit him in the stomach then. A hard jab to the solar plexus that has him bent over, gasping.

"You said you thought that boy was grabbed by a pedophile," I say. "Well, maybe that's because you know all about them."

"Wh-what?" he manages between gasps.

"You're taking way too much interest in a missing kid." I start backing out of the alley, gun still aimed at him. "I think maybe I should call the police. Have them find out why you're so interested in little boys."

He makes a run at me, but the gun—or the look in my eyes—stops him.

"There is no little boy," I say. "I made a mistake. I don't know what your problem is, but you need to stay away from me, or I *will* make that call."

I keep backing from the alley. When I reach the sidewalk, he makes another run for me. A car comes around the corner just then. My back's to it—the driver can't see the gun—but he does see Zima's thug. He hits the brakes. The thug stops short. I continue backing toward the car. When I hear it coming my way, I lower the gun and hide it.

The whir of a window rolling down.

"You okay, ma'am?"

It's a teenager wearing a fast-food-restaurant uniform.

"Someone's following me," I say. "Would you mind giving me a lift for a block or two?"

"Uh, sure. Hop in."

He shoves a backpack off the passenger seat. I climb in, never turning my back on Zima's man, who stands there, watching and seething.

I shut the door. "Drive past him, please."

The kid nods and does that. Zima's man stays on the sidewalk and watches us go.

"You okay?" the kid asks.

"I was out jogging, and that guy decided he wanted to run alongside me. I wasn't looking for company. He really wasn't taking the hint."

"Jerk."

"If you could just turn right at the next intersection. I'll get out there."

He does and then insists on driving another block before pulling over. I thank him and try to give him twenty bucks. When he refuses, I start getting out and tuck the money under the seat. Then I thank him again and take off.

TWENTY-FIVE

I head to my apartment building. I keep an eye out, but there's no sign of Zima's thug. I hover inside the door to be sure no one has followed. Then I zip up the stairs and to my apartment and . . .

Someone has tried forcing open my door, but I installed a double-cylinder jimmy-proof dead bolt. I used to rob homes; I know how to secure one. The intruder couldn't break that. Still, I open it with care, and when I move inside, I have the thug's gun in my hand.

My apartment is empty.

I secure it behind me. As soon as I step in, though, I don't feel like I usually do, the dead bolt turned, the world shut out, me safe behind the door. I feel vulnerable, as if I've trapped my-self by locking that door, and any minute now, whoever tried to break in will return with someone more capable.

There's a moment where I wonder how they found my apart-ment. I'm still in shock from what happened in the alley. Having one of Zima's thugs pump me for information while pretend-ing to be a fellow jogger is reasonable. Having that same guy toss me into an alley and slam me against a wall is not. So I'm still reeling from that, which explains why I don't see the obvious right away.

How did they find my apartment? Well, I'm pretty sure that thug didn't just happen to be wandering around my neighborhood when he spotted me. I gave my name on TV, and they've tracked me to my apartment. That thug wasn't just pumping me for information—he was distracting me while others broke in.

I pack an overnight bag. Then I clear my apartment of every sign that I have a daughter. I told the thug that I don't have kids, and he didn't argue, which suggests they haven't dug that deep. So I hide evidence of Charlotte, and I take everything that suggests I was investigating Brandon's disappearance. Then I climb into the car, and I drive.

I intended to go to a hotel.

This is not a hotel.

I'm sitting in a driveway, staring at a house that used to be mine. I see a car in the drive that used to be mine. And inside that home is a family that used to be mine.

I sit in that drive, and I cry. I can't help it. I slump over the steering wheel, forehead against it, and I cry.

I think of all the times I pulled into this drive and took it for granted. Pulled in and just wanted to get Charlotte out of the car, because she was fussing, and it'd been a long day of errands. Wanted to get her out and put her down for a nap and rest, just rest.

I loved my life, but I'd be lying if I said there weren't times I wanted to escape it, too. Times when I longed for Charlotte to sleep so I'd have a few moments to myself. Times when I'd be making dinner and wish someone would cook it for me, wish

I'd be the one coming home from work. Times when I even thought, *Dear God, what have I done?*

But that despair and regret never lasted long. The pressures and, yes, the loneliness of being a stay-at-home mom piled up, and I caved under it for an hour or two. Felt sorry for myself. Envied other lives. Far more often, though, I'd be in the yard with Charlotte, and I'd see other mothers hurrying to work, herding kids into the car, and I'd be so glad that wasn't me. I'd be in the park with her, see the snarl of the morning commute, and I'd count my blessings. Staying home wasn't for every parent, but it'd been what I wanted. Just give me a few years with my daughter—with all my kids, including those yet to come—and then I'd happily return to the workforce and find satisfaction there.

I had that. And I didn't lose it. I gave it up. Now I sit in the car and look at that house, and I cry.

I came here to warn Paul. Tell him what's going on and make sure he realizes the danger.

That's it.

No, that's not it. I came here for sanctuary. To tell Paul of the danger, yes, but then hope he'll ask me to stay. Hope he'll *let* me stay, just for the night.

I am afraid, and this is my home, and I desperately want to be here, where it's safe. With Paul, where it's safe. With Charlotte, where I know she's safe, where I can watch out for her.

Too bad.

I can't put this on Paul. I do need to warn him, but that can be accomplished with a phone call.

As I put the car into reverse, the front door opens. Paul steps out. His shirt is half-buttoned, his feet are bare, and his state of undress reminds me what he'd been doing earlier. Taking Gayle's daughter to the train station. Presumably with Gayle, who might be in the house right now.

I start to back out. He raises his hand for me to stop. I put down the passenger window as he walks over.

"I'm sorry," I say. "I wanted to talk to you, but I should have just called."

He leans down to the open window. "Come inside."

I shake my head. "I don't want to interrupt your evening."

"I'm working, Bree. Interruptions are welcome."

"Gayle isn't here?"

His brows knit.

"You looked . . . I thought Gayle might be here."

He glances down at himself, and it takes a moment for him to realize what I mean. "No, Aubrey, you didn't 'interrupt' any-thing. Charlie's in the house. I got comfortable because the office is stuffy. The air conditioner isn't working right again."

"You need to clear the weeds from the unit. They choke the fan. Here, let me do that, and then I'll go."

I turn off the car. When I get out and head for the backyard, Paul steps into my path.

"You aren't here to fix the air conditioner, Bree. Come in-side and talk."

"I'll explain while I fix it."

He sighs but follows me into the yard. I'm glad for the dark-ness. It hides the play set and the sandbox and everything that will remind me of Charlotte and our life here. As I'm making my way to the air-conditioning unit, I smack into something in my path. It's a hammock. My hammock, still stretched be-tween two trees.

Paul bought it for me to read on while Charlotte played. I remember laughing at the thought that I could laze out here, reading, instead of chasing her. I did use it, though, when she was napping. I'd read and relax with the baby monitor beside me.

I remember Paul reading outside in a chair, and I'd tried to convince him to use the hammock.

"That takes far more motor skill than I possess," he'd said.

Yet it's still here. As if I never left it. As if I could grab a book and settle in—

I push past the hammock as Paul flips on the deck lights. Sure enough, vines choke the AC unit. As I pull them off, Paul says, "I can do that."

"Got it."

I keep tugging.

"Bree?" he says.

I don't look up.

"I know you came here to explain," he says, "and you know I don't want to hear it."

I'm about to say no, that's not it, but he continues.

"I really don't," he says. "I need some time. But if you're worried that I'll keep Charlie from you, don't be. Please. I already said I wouldn't and . . ."

He exhales and leans against the deck railing, as I untangle vines below.

"I know who you are," he says. "Who you were."

I try not to tense.

"I don't just mean what you did," he continues. "When we talked this morning, you said you gave away the money."

"Not all—"

He continues as if he didn't hear me. "That made me dig where I told myself I wasn't going to dig. Into your life. Who you were. You didn't get that shoulder scar from an accident that killed your parents. But they are gone. Both of them."

I go still.

"You didn't lie," he says. "Not entirely. Your mother died in a car accident when you were two. You were found in the car a day later. I think of Charlotte and try to imagine—" He inhales. "I *can't* imagine. I only know that something that . . . horrific . . . would have an impact. A huge one."

"It's not an excuse—"

"You grew up on army bases. No siblings. Your dad never remarried, and he was often deployed. I remember all the times you'd fly into a panic, worrying that you weren't a good parent, that you didn't know how to be, and I never understood why you'd get so worked up. Now I do."

"It wasn't that bad," I say. "I'd stay with good people when he deployed. I wasn't neglected or abused. My dad loved me. We were close."

"Until he took his life."

I stiffen.

"I'm sorry," Paul says quickly. "That sounded harsh."

"It was harsh. There's no nice way to put it. I was away at college, and he came home from deployment, and he was worse than usual. I kept telling myself talking to him on the phone was enough, that I'd get him help when I got home on break and then—"

I snap a vine so hard it slices into my finger. Blood wells. I wipe it off before Paul notices.

"That's when it happened, isn't it?" Paul says. "You dropped out of college, and Ruben took advantage—"

"No." I meet his gaze. "There aren't excuses, Paul. I wasn't tricked into what I did. I chose it. I was angry, and I was stupid, and I chose it."

"Who'd you give the money to?"

I flail, hands flapping, before I quickly return to the vines. "It doesn't—"

"Bree?"

"I kept a third."

"And the rest?"

I hesitate. Then I say, "One-third to a PTSD group. The rest was anonymous gifts to people who needed it, mostly around the base."

"Rob from the rich, give to the veterans?"

He smiles, but I shake my head vehemently, my eyes filling with tears.

"Don't," I say. "I was young. I was angry. I was stupid. I didn't do it for others. That's just how I used the money, because it wasn't about the money. Young. Angry. Stupid. That's all."

He nods. "Okay."

I resume pulling vines. "I knew the statute of limitations had run out before I married you, Paul. No one suspected me. I wasn't fleeing anything but my own mistakes." I look up at him. "I wasn't looking for safe haven."

He shifts, as uncomfortable as I was discussing the money. He opens his mouth, and I know he's going to tell me not to pursue this, so I quickly say, "I left because I thought you were unhappy. We were drifting apart, and that's a lousy reason for ending a marriage, but I didn't want it to get worse. I thought if I mentioned the problem, and you agreed that it wasn't fixable, then I'd leave. I took the risk that you'd agree. I felt like I had to. For you and for Charlie. Now I know *why* you weren't happy, and I wish to God I could go back to the day we met and tell you the truth, but I can't."

I rip off another vine, my attention back on that.

"You couldn't," he says after a moment. "Not when you'd first met me. It was too soon. But I wish you had, at some point. At any point."

"I know. I just . . . The further it went, the more afraid I got. The easier it seemed to just *become* someone else."

"Were you?" he asks softly. "Were you actually someone else, Bree? Or were you just pretending to be?"

"Was I pretending to be your wife? Charlie's mommy? No." I look at him. "Pretending to be happy? No. But the person you fell in love with, the one you married, you had a child with, that wasn't the whole me, and I'm sorry."

He says nothing. I bend and snake out a last bit of vine.

"So, MIT, huh?" he says, and when I look over, he's smiling. It's not his usual smile—it's a little sad, a little confused—so I just nod.

"When you're done with the AC, my desktop has been acting up," he says. "Think you can fix that, too?"

I find a half smile for him. "Probably." I straighten. "Let's see if this works."

"It should." A long pause. "Will you stay for coffee?"

"I will, but only because all this isn't what I came to talk to you about. Let's go inside."

TWENTY-SIX

We sit at the kitchen table, and I tell him everything, as succinctly as I can. I explain how I identified Kim Mikhailov, linked her to Denis Zima, went to Zima's club and overheard that conversation . . . and then had Zima's thug menace me on my jog tonight.

"So, my concern is . . ." I begin, and then I trail off as I catch his expression and realize he's no longer hearing me. He's just staring.

"I'm okay," I say carefully.

"I can see that." He pulls back and rubs his hands over his face.

"Paul?" I say. "Are *you* okay?"

"My wife just told me how she identified a dead woman, staked out a Russian mobster's nightclub, taped a covert conversation from the closet, and then overpowered one of his thugs."

"I didn't exactly overpower—"

"You took a *gun* from a man who wouldn't hesitate to use it on you."

"It was in his waistband. He hadn't pulled it. I knew what I was doing."

"Yes, Aubrey, that would be my point. You knew what you were doing. With all of it."

"Oh."

Earlier I said the woman he married wasn't the whole me, and now I see the truth of that in his expression. He's known I'm a thief, a tech whiz, but it hasn't penetrated until this moment. He's looking at me the way he'd look at a stranger. Because he's realized that's what I am.

A stranger he married. A stranger who bore his child, who is now helping raise his child.

I take a deep breath. "Yes, I grew up knowing how to fight back. I learned some martial arts, some marksmanship. Part of that was because I planned to go into the army, but part was because my father knew that as a woman I might need those skills outside a battlefield. You're wondering now how much of that I've passed on to our daughter. You've seen our pretend sword fighting, our roughhousing. I haven't initiated any of that. Maybe whatever makes me crave exercise is what makes her love physical play, too. I'm not trying to turn her into me, Paul. I wouldn't do that."

"That's not—" He shakes his head. "Your father was right. Harnessing that physicality to defend yourself was a good idea. I hope to God that Charlie is never pulled into an alley, but if she is, I want her to be able to do what you did. To fight back. To escape. I just . . . You're not . . ."

"The woman you thought you married."

A long silence.

I put my mug down with a clack. "I'll leave in a minute, Paul. I just wanted you to know what happened. I offhandedly mentioned that I didn't have kids, and Zima's thug didn't bat an eye, so I'm hoping that means they don't know about Charlie. I hid everything of hers in my apartment, so if they finish breaking in, they won't find it."

"*Finish* breaking in?"

"Someone tried while the thug distracted me. That's why I left. I'm going to a hotel, but I wanted you to know what happened, in case you think that endangers you or Charlie."

He shakes his head. "I don't. You said this thug didn't even believe you saw Kim with a child. That's what he said on the phone. He must have tracked you down to see what you'd say in person. When you brushed him off, he snapped. Men like him aren't accustomed to that sort of treatment. You supported his conviction that there's no child, though. That's what he'll take back to Zima—even *you* have retracted your story. The boy is safe somewhere, and his aunt is probably on her way to get him."

"Yes, but be careful, please. Lock the doors. Arm the security system. I'd offer to look after Charlie tomorrow, but that's not a good idea. Is there anyone else who can take her, so she's not at daycare?"

"I'd stay home, but I have trial. Gayle's taking a few days off. Maybe I could ask . . ." He doesn't finish.

"That's fine with me."

He nods, but it's absent, his gaze distant.

I rise. "If anything else happens, I'll let you know."

He gets to his feet before I can leave. "You should stay here tonight."

"I'll be fine. I'll get a hotel—"

"No, stay. That's safer, and Charlie will like to see you."

I hesitate. "I don't want to confuse her. Having me here . . ."

"We'll tell her that you stopped by for breakfast because you didn't get to see her on the weekend."

I nod slowly. "Okay, I'll take the futon in your study."

"I'll take the futon. You have the bed."

I think of that. Of sleeping in my old bed. Of waking in the night, thinking I'm home. Waking in the morning, thinking I never left, and these six months have been a bad dream. And then realizing the truth.

"No," I say. "Please. I don't . . . I'd rather take the futon."

He nods and goes to find bedding for it.

I still wake in the night. Wake smelling my home. Then I remember what woke me. I'd dreamed of Charlotte finding me on the futon, and seeing my purse, and going to check whether I brought her anything and pulling out the thug's gun—

I inhale so sharply it hurts. Then I scramble for my purse, only to remember that I left the gun in the car. I put it under the seat.

Did I lock the car doors? I'm sure I did but . . .

I slip outside. The car *is* locked, but I open it and move the gun into the glove box. Then I lock that. Lock the car next. Go back inside, lock *those* doors and rearm the security system. I hear a noise overhead, the creak of a footstep. Paul appears at the top of the stairs.

"Aubrey?" he says, and there's a note in his voice as if I'm not the only one who is confused, finding me here. Then he shakes off sleep and comes down the steps. "Is everything okay?"

"I had a nightmare about the gun," I say. "I was just making sure it was secured."

He nods, and that sleepy confusion lingers in his eyes. He gives my arm a squeeze and leans over to kiss the top of my head. Then he stops, as if realizing what he's doing, simple reflex.

I squeeze his arm in return and murmur something as I slip back to his office to sleep.

———

I wake on that futon and . . . God, this is hard. Harder than I would have ever imagined. I haven't been back to this house since I left, and I didn't think that was intentional, but I realize now that it was. I stayed away even when I had reasons to come there, when I'd need something for Charlotte on the weekend and Paul wouldn't be home, and he'd say, "Just go grab it. The key's in the usual place." I went without rather than set foot in this house.

I remember once, as a child, we got a home off base. Dad didn't care much for the base housing options, and there were good places to rent elsewhere. I had a house with a yard and a pool and a purple bedroom with sunflower curtains. I made friends with a girl next door and a boy down the street, my first non-military friendships. We spent the summer exploring the ravine and forest behind our house. When Dad got transferred, I ran away. After we left, I cried every night. He painted my new room purple. He bought me sunflower curtains. And I hated them, because I'd wake up and think I was back there.

That's what this felt like, only ten times worse. I'd been happy in that other house, but I'd never been an *un*happy child. I'd just found something special there. In this home, with Paul and Charlotte, I'd been unbelievably happy. Now I wake on the futon, and I want to grab my overnight bag and run, still wearing my nighttime sweats.

I don't, of course. That's as childish as running away from my father, and I'm no longer a child. I suck it up, and I slip into the kitchen, and I make coffee. I notice Paul has bought one of those K-Cup brewers, and I have to smile at that. He never could make proper coffee, and he'd happily given up his K-Cup bachelor machine when we moved in together. Now the old brew pot is shoved back on the counter, dusty and unused. I find coffee in the freezer, right where I kept it. The *same* coffee I left there. I push back pangs of grief, and I brew a pot. I open the cupboard, and I reach for his cup and . . .

It's gone.

We had a set of *Lady and the Tramp* coffee mugs, ones we bought at Disney World. When you pushed them together, the handle cutouts formed a heart. Couple mugs. Tossed out, I presume, until I spot them at the back of the cupboard. I take out two generic ones. Fill them. Feel another pang as I add his cream, never pausing for a second to remember how much he takes. I fix his coffee by motor memory.

When I lived here, I'd get up early to make coffee and wake him with his mug. Once I have this one ready, I'm halfway up the stairs before I remember this is no longer my place. Our bedroom is *definitely* not my place. It's the one spot in this house I shouldn't enter. I'm heading back down when I hear his footsteps in the hall. Then, "Bree?"

I hold up the mug. He comes down. He's pulled on sweatpants, but that's it, and I notice he's lost weight. That thickening through his middle is gone, the early stages of a spare tire reversed, and I feel a stab of pain even at that. It's a sign he'd made a conscious effort to lose that extra weight in preparation for dating.

Can't blame him for that, can I?

He takes the coffee, and I'm about to head down to the kitchen when he says, "Do you want to wake Charlie?"

I frown, thinking it's too early. Normally I'd get him up and off to work and then relax with a second coffee until Charlotte wakes around eight, maybe even nine if I'm lucky.

That's how we did things when Mommy stayed home. Mommy no longer stays home, and Daddy needs to drop Charlotte off on his way to work.

I nod and slip past him. I climb the steps to my daughter's

room, for the first time in six months. I open the door, and I see her sleeping and . . . The crib is gone. She's in a bed. Her own bed. My baby sleeping in a regular bed. My baby growing up . . . without me.

I've been so careful, stifling the pangs of grief, feeling my eyes well, allowing no more than a single tear to slide down my cheek. Now that self-restraint snaps. It starts with a burst of tears, and then I'm sobbing.

"Bree?"

It's Paul. He's right behind me. He must have been there the whole time, and when I turn, he quickly puts his coffee mug on the bannister.

I close Charlotte's door. "I-I can't," I manage between heaving breaths. "I-I'm sorry. I need . . . I need to go."

I bolt for the stairs, tears blinding me. I hit his coffee mug, and I hear it crash. I let out a gasp and a frantic apology. Paul's arms go around me. I think he's just keeping me from tumbling half-blind down the stairs. Then he pulls me against him.

At first I resist. I smell the faint scent of night sweat, and I feel his skin against my cheek, and I hear his heartbeat, and my brain screams that this isn't mine, not anymore. It's like seeing Charlotte in her new bed. I want to flee while I still can. But Paul pulls me into a tight embrace, and he whispers in my ear that it's okay. I collapse against him. He pats my back with one hand and holds me with the other, and he tells me it's okay, and I hear permission to break down, to fall apart. So I do.

I sob against his chest until the pressure finally eases, until I can lift my head to say I'm all right. I look up and . . . he kisses me. His mouth goes to mine, and there isn't a moment of surprise in that, not a moment of hesitation either. He's kissing me, and my arms go around his neck, and I'm kissing him back and oh God, I've missed this. I've missed him so much. Time blurs as I pour that longing and need into my kiss. I forget where I am.

I forget whatever I should be doing. I certainly forget that I should not be doing this. Or maybe I do remember that last part . . . and I just don't care.

It's a deep, desperate kiss, and the next thing I know, I'm in our bedroom. He lowers me onto the bed. Or maybe I pull him down onto it. I have no idea who does what—I only know that neither one needs to prod the other. I'm on the bed, and he's over me, and we're still kissing. He has my shirt up, and I'm tugging down his sweatpants, and it comes as naturally as fixing his coffee. Motor memory, the hungry kiss, and then both of us falling into bed and—

His phone buzzes. I glance over to see it standing on the charger. Paul puts his hands to my face, getting my attention and ignoring his phone, but when I see the name that flashes, I pull away. He glances at the phone. He sees the name—he must—but it doesn't seem to register. He only lowers his mouth to mine again. I pull back and scramble from under him.

"Gayle," I say.

There's still no reaction. Or if there is, it's confusion, like I'm speaking an unfamiliar name.

I wave at the ringing phone as I clamber off the bed. "We can't. I'm sorry. I shouldn't have— That's not right. You have . . . Gayle."

He gives a soft—and uncharacteristic—curse and hits the Ignore button. By then, I'm at the door. He doesn't come after me. He just sits on the edge of the bed, face in his hands.

"I'm sorry," I say again. "I shouldn't have—"

"It wasn't you."

"It's . . ." I inhale. "Habit, right? Being here. It's just habit. I'm sorry. I'd never— I know you have . . . someone . . . and I wouldn't try to do that. It's disrespectful."

"Disrespectful." He gives a short laugh and shakes his head.

"I'll go," I say. "I shouldn't have been here. I'm sorry."

As I turn, he says, "No," and rises to his feet. His hand lands on my shoulder. "Charlie would love to see you. If you'd rather I wake her, I'll do that."

"No, I can. It was just . . ." I twist to look back at him. "I see you got her a real bed." I smile when I'm saying it, but that starts the tears again, my eyes filling. I wipe them away. "Sorry, it's just . . ."

I'm missing her life. I'm missing so much of it.

Missing you, too. Missing both of you.

He gives me a one-armed hug, more careful now. "I know. You go get her up, then, and I'll shower and dress. There's cereal and bagels. She goes back and forth between them."

"Do you have eggs?" I ask.

He hesitates, and when he forces a smile, it's a little awkward, a little sad. "That would require me knowing how to cook them."

I nod. Then I murmur that I'll figure out something and slip from the room. As I go, I hear him pick up his phone to call Gayle back.

TWENTY-SEVEN

I hold it together for Charlotte. That's easier than I feared. She's thrilled to see me, even though I'm quick to explain that I just stopped by. It doesn't matter. She wakes with a bounce, as always, and there's no time to grieve for what I've lost. I get a taste of it this morning, and I'll take that as a gift and make the most of it.

I find bacon in the freezer—bacon I'd put there. I thaw it and whip up pancakes, also from my legacy baking ingredients. Paul comes down, and we eat, and the awkwardness disappears with Charlotte there, talking a mile a minute.

"So you're taking her to Gayle's today?" I ask.

He stops with the fork halfway to his mouth. Then he shakes his head. "I changed my mind. Gayle will have brought work home, and Charlie is a full-time job."

"I has job?" Charlotte says, following our conversation.

"Yes," Paul says. "A very special job, but it might be too hard. I need you"—he leans toward her—"to be good for Mrs. Mueller. You're going to stay with her today."

"And Becky and Pete?"

"Yes, you're staying with Mrs. Mueller, and her son Pete and her cat Becky."

Charlotte squeals. "Noooo. Becky is girl. Pete is dog."

Paul frowns. "Are you sure? Becky kind of looks like a little girl, but I'm pretty sure Pete is a rat. A huge rat, like Matt."

"Pete is dog!"

"Chihuahua," Paul murmurs to me.

"Ah," I say. "Well, I can see where you'd get confused." I turn to Charlotte. "I bet Pete loves Matt."

Charlotte shakes her head, curls bouncing. "No. Pete scared of Matt. Becky like Matt."

"The Muellers moved in down the road," Paul says. "Becky's four. Her mom has offered to take Charlie anytime daycare doesn't work out, so I called this morning. I also let the day-care know she'd be away."

"Thank you."

He's about to speak again when his phone rings. He checks the screen. Hits Ignore.

"I'd like to talk to you later," he says. "More about what's going on. And I would rather you didn't go back to your apart-ment without me. Well, without *someone,* but I'd prefer it to be someone who knows what's going on, and I'm guessing that's just me?"

"It is."

"We'll discuss—" His phone buzzes with a text. He flicks it to vibrate without checking the message. "We'll discuss . . . nighttime arrangements then. If you'd be okay coming back here for dinner . . ."

"Yes!" Charlotte says. "Mommy come dinner."

"I will," I say, then add quickly for Charlotte, "this one time."

"Good, Charlie can watch a movie while we talk. What time are you done—?" Paul says.

His phone vibrates.

"I think someone's trying to get hold of you," I say.

"Just work. I'll call back in the car."

"Over Bluetooth, I hope."

His eyes crease in a smile. "Yes, over Bluetooth. Now, if you wouldn't mind getting Charlie ready, I'll tidy up here."

Charlotte's dressed and only needs to brush her teeth. so when I come back, he's still clearing the breakfast dishes.

"I'll tackle those," I say. "You go on to work."

I'm brushing past him to clear the table when his phone vibrates again. I see that it's Gayle. He stuffs it into his pocket. I hesitate, debating. Then I say, "I would like you to let Gayle know that I was here last night."

His brows rise.

I put the mugs into the dishwasher. "I'd rather you told her and explained than have her find out later. I don't want to cause trouble for you."

"You're not—"

"Please? Humor me? I just . . . I want you to be happy."

He nods abruptly and mumbles something. Then he calls for Charlotte to grab Matt and tells me he'll see me tonight, and they're gone.

I'm at work, and I'm happy. Happier than I've been in a long time. More at peace than I've been in a very long time. Paul knows my secrets. All of them. And we have moved past it. Not to marital reconciliation. I'd be lying if I said I don't still hold out hope for that. This morning, when we'd been in bed together and I realized who was calling, yes, I hoped he might say it didn't matter . . . and let us finish what we started. I'd entertained the fantasy of him admitting it was over with Gayle, and he wanted to try again with me. That only lasted a moment. If it did happen, I'd have worried it was temporary, lust clouding his judgment. If there's any hope of reconciliation, it won't come today or even tomorrow. I can't push either. He is the wronged party, and that choice must be his.

I am happy because we've achieved something less life-changing but even more important. Personal reconciliation. He knows my secrets, and yes, they have hurt him. Yet that hasn't marked the beginning of an icy-cold post-separation wasteland, where I can no longer reach him, no longer talk to him, no longer co-parent with him. We're returning to equilibrium, and if that's the best I can hope for, then I'll take it.

I think Paul was right. Zima's goon was testing me last night. Menacing me in hopes of proving—or disproving—my story about a missing child. No one wants there to be a missing child. It's inconvenient. If I'm the only person who says there was one, and I've retracted my claim, then the thug can go back to Denis Zima and say, "That chick was wrong."

You don't have a son, Denis. There's nothing to see here. Let's move along.

We're short-staffed at the library today, so I'm doing mom-and-tot story time, which I love. I'm good at it, too—I do all the voices, and I'm definitely not afraid to be silly. I'm hoping that if I impress Ingrid, I'll get to do more programming, especially with little ones. Now that Paul knows about my past, there's nothing to stop me from going back to school part-time. Get a degree in library science. I'd also like to throw my tech skills into the mix. Play to my strengths and my interests, after so many years of hiding them.

God, that feels good. I don't know if I ever truly realized the weight of those secrets. Once it's lifted, the possibilities roll out before me like a red carpet. I can get my degree and a proper librarian job. I can use my inheritance money to buy a condo. I can openly negotiate child custody with Paul, now that I don't have to worry about him digging into my past.

I can breathe again. That's what it feels like. I can finally breathe.

I'm helping the little ones check out their post-story-time books when my phone buzzes. It's under the counter, and I glance at it while the screen is lit up. It's an incoming text from a number I don't recognize. I'll admit to a jolt of fear when I see that, as a million horrible scenarios run through my mind. Life is going too well this morning, and the universe will surely stomp out my joy with a text from Zima or his goon.

I whip through the checkouts. Then I surreptitiously unlock my phone. The text is a video with a still of Charlotte climbing a slide. I smile. Paul must have given Mrs. Mueller my number.

I'm about to text back a "Thanks!" when Ingrid appears from the stacks. I slide my phone under the counter, and I head out to shelve books. As I'm leaving the desk, a mother stops to gush about my story-time skills . . . just as Ingrid is passing to overhear. When I come back from shelving, she tells me several of the parents commented, and Nancy has been talking about giving up story time, and maybe I could take it over. It is the icing on my cupcake-perfect morning. Ingrid and I talk, too, really talk. At break time I grab my phone to continue the delicious sweetness of my day by watching my daughter play.

I sit in the staff room with a fresh cup of coffee and a doughnut dropped off by a patron. I hit Play on the video. I watch Charlotte and a preschooler tear through the tiny playground in their neighborhood. I smile as I enjoy the video and my doughnut. Then I see a woman holding a Chihuahua on a leash. She's close to the girls, keeping an eye on them. This must be the neighbor—Mrs. Mueller.

I think that . . . and then I pause. If that's Mrs. Mueller, who's taking the video?

Maybe her spouse works from home. Or has the day off. That makes sense. Except, when I start thinking about that, I notice another oddity. No one turns to the camera. No one waves at it. No one smiles over at it.

If this videographer is with Mrs. Mueller, then the kids know they're being filmed. There isn't a chance in hell that two pre-schoolers wouldn't look over at least once.

A chill slides between my shoulder blades.

I flip to the text message and send back: Who is this?

A response comes within seconds: Are you sure you don't know anything about that little boy, Aubrey? Maybe my video jogged your memory?

My fingers tremble as I hit Call to dial the number. No one answers. I send back a text: I told you there isn't a little boy. I made a mistake.

The response: I don't think you did.

Then: You have such a pretty little girl.

My heart slams against my ribs. I start to compose a response, but I can't untangle my fingers to write anything coherent. I dial Paul's number instead. It goes straight to voice mail. I pull up his office number from my contacts, and I call. He has a new admin assistant, but when I tell her who I am, she says Paul's in court, and she'll take a message. She'll make sure he gets it on his next break. I leave a message. *Call me back. It's urgent.* She promises to get it to him as soon as she can.

Next my fingers hover over Laila Jackson's number, but it'll take too long to explain. I go to directory assistance and begin searching for the Muellers' number. I have the name and the street. They only moved in recently, though, so I don't know if there's much chance . . .

Yes! They have a home number, and it's listed.

I call. No one answers. I leave a message saying who I am and that I'm worried about Charlotte and could they call me back right away.

"Aubrey?" Ingrid appears. "I'm going to need you to end your break early. The desk is swamped."

"Actually, I have to go," I say.

"What?"

I'm about to lie. Say I'm sick. But I stop myself—no more lies, not when the truth is a perfectly valid excuse.

"My daughter is in trouble, and her dad's in court today. I need to leave."

"All right, come help me with this, and we'll call someone in to cover for you."

"No, it's urgent." I hold out my phone. "Someone just texted me a video of her as a threat."

"What?" Her face screws up, not in horror but confusion.

"It's connected to that missing boy. I–I'll explain later." I grab my purse. "I can't reach the sitter, so I need to go check on her."

"If your daughter really is in danger, call the police."

I don't miss the way she says "if."

"I will," I say. "On my way there. I just need to be sure Charlotte's okay. I'll be back in thirty minutes."

"No." Ingrid steps into my path. "I need you up front, Aubrey, and I've had enough of this nonsense. If you are legitimately concerned, call the police. Then do your job until I get someone to cover your shift."

I fight the panic coiled in my gut. That video came in nearly twenty minutes ago. Whoever sent it is toying with me, and the longer I argue with Ingrid, the later it'll be before I can leave.

"I'll help you with the desk," I say. "Five minutes. I'll check people through and then—"

"I said no, Aubrey. You will stay until—"

I swing past her and break into a jog.

"If you leave this building, do not come back," she calls after me. "I have had enough of your . . ."

I don't hear the rest. I'm already flying out the door.

TWENTY-EIGHT

On the drive, I call Laila Jackson . . . and get her voice mail. I don't leave a message. Not yet. First I want to be sure Charlotte is okay. When a call comes in moments later, I glance at the screen, hoping it's Paul. It's Ellie Milano. I let it go to voice mail—whatever she has to say, I don't need the distraction right now. She doesn't leave a message.

I drive straight to the park. It's nearly empty, and I can tell in a sweep that Charlotte isn't there. I spot one of the moms I knew from before. I pull over, jog to her, and ask if she's seen Charlotte.

She gives me this look, her eyes narrowing, and then she says carefully, "No, I haven't."

I wonder why I'm getting that look. Then it hits. She knows I'm not the custodial parent.

"There's a problem," I say. "Paul's in court. I'm just wondering if you've seen her."

She says no, but I can't tell if she's still suspicious. I hop back in my car. I have the Muellers' address from the phone listing. It's a half dozen doors down from Paul's place. I pull into the drive and race to the front door.

I ring the bell. Then I knock. There's no response to either. I call, and I hear the phone ringing inside.

The car is in the drive, and they aren't at the park. Where—?

A child's laugh echoes from the backyard. I heave a sigh of relief and race to the gate. It's a chain-link fence, and I can see Mrs. Mueller through it. The dog—Pete—races at the heels of a little girl who is not my daughter. There's no sign of Charlotte.

He's taken her. Whoever sent those photos took her.

How could I have let a stranger care for Charlotte today? Anyone could walk up and say Paul sent them to fetch Charlotte.

Mrs. Mueller sees me running to her fence, and she looks over in alarm with a called "Hello?"

I resist the urge to leap into her yard. "I'm Aubrey Finch," I call back. "I'm Charlotte's mom. Where is she?"

There's a long pause, as my heart hammers. I know what's coming. She sees my face. She realizes there's a problem, realizes she shouldn't have trusted that person who said he'd come for Charlotte.

Then she walks to the fence, and I see the same look I got from the neighbor at the park. Suspicion.

"I'm afraid I don't know your custody arrangement—" she begins.

"I just need to know where she is. Someone sent me a threatening video. I called. I left a message. Please, just tell me what happened."

"Charlie's napping."

I exhale and take a few deep breaths. "Okay. Thank you. Paul's in court, and I can't get hold of him. I raced over from work."

She nods. A slow nod, still wary.

"Can you wake Charlie up, please?" I say. "I'm sorry. She

just . . . She shouldn't be alone. I don't know how much Paul told you about the situation . . ."

"Only that she couldn't go to care today, and to let no one except him pick her up. He said there was a situation. I thought it was custody-related."

"What? No." Another deep breath. "Not at all, but I didn't come to take her. I totally respect your concern, and I thank you for being careful. The problem is that I've found myself caught up in a police investigation, and there had been threats. Not against Charlotte, but Paul and I were still cautious. I just received a video that clearly targets her." I hold out my phone. "It's one of you with her in the park."

She takes the phone, brows knitted. She presses Play and her eyes widen.

"Mommy?" The little girl runs over, dog tumbling along behind. Mrs. Mueller motions for her to come closer and says, "We're going to get Charlie up. I think she's napped long enough." She opens the gate. "Come and sit on the deck. We'll be back in a moment."

"Thank you."

Charlotte is awake, and Paul is on his way. His admin assistant got the message to him as soon as court ended. He called, and I said everything was fine, but he wanted to come get us.

I sit outside with Mrs. Mueller for a very awkward hour before Paul arrives. The first thing he does is apologize to her. He shouldn't have put her in this position, and he wouldn't have if he'd had any idea this might happen. He's also quick to say I warned him. I appreciate that, so it doesn't sound as if I'm the one who underplayed the danger.

We drive to his house. I check the locks before we go in, but there's no sign anyone tampered with them. He tells Charlotte to go brush her teeth, and we'll all go for ice cream.

"You're telling her to brush her teeth *before* ice cream?" I say as she races off.

He screws up his face. "Okay, that makes no sense. I'm not thinking straight."

He looks exhausted, as if he ran all the way from Chicago. I resist the urge to give him a hug, and I offer a smile instead, saying, "I'm teasing. You know that."

He nods. "I do. I'm just . . ." He looks at me. "I'm sorry, Bree. You were worried about that guy, and I blew you off."

"You didn't blow—"

"Some thug came at you with a gun last night. Obviously, he was serious. I just thought . . ." He throws up his hands. "I don't know what I thought. Men like that often have guns, and he didn't pull it, so I presumed he was just trying to intimidate you."

"If I thought Charlie was in actual danger, I'd have said so. Sending her to a sitter made sense."

Charlotte races in, saying, "Ice cream! Ice cream!"

Paul looks at me. "I thought we'd go to Elsa's Castle. She can play while we talk. Is that all right or do you need to get back to work?"

I had called Ingrid as soon as I got off the phone with Paul. I said Charlotte was fine, and I was just staying with her until he arrived. She coldly informed me that there was no need to come in today. Nor any need to come in tomorrow.

"I have the day off," I say.

We sit outside at the ice cream parlor and watch Charlotte on the play equipment while we talk. She ate half her ice cream and then wanted Mommy to come play, but as soon as Paul said he needed to speak to me, she zoomed off.

"That was easy," I say. "The last time I tried to get her to play alone, you'd have thought I was sentencing her to a year of solitary confinement."

"She's just happy to see us . . ." He shrugs.

"Together." I glance over at her, and she's climbing while smiling at us like a grown-up watching her kid on a date. "Do you think we're giving her . . . I don't want to . . ."

"She's fine, Bree. Now tell me what happened."

I do, leaving out the part about Ingrid.

"I thought it was the sitter sending the video," I say, "or I'd have looked at it sooner."

"Honestly, that's what I thought, too, when I first saw it."

When I blink, he makes a face. "Sorry, did I mention I'm not running on all cylinders?" He takes out his phone. "I got the same video."

"What?"

He shows me. It was sent a few minutes after mine, while he'd been in court. He didn't see it until after he got my message. The text accompanying his reads: **Your ex is sticking her nose where it doesn't belong. Tell her to stay out of our business, and we'll stay out of yours.**

My gut twists. "I'm sorry, Paul. I'm so—"

"Stop. You did nothing wrong, Aubrey. You were trying to help a little boy, and I don't know what Zima's problem with you is."

"He thinks I know more. Somehow he's found out I'm investigating, and he isn't buying my story that I made a mistake about Brandon."

"Did you report the video?"

"I wanted to. I called my police contact but got her voice mail. Now I'm wondering if my contact is the one who's telling

Zima that I know more. She's the only person who *realizes* I know more." I exhale. "And I'm being paranoid thinking that, aren't I? Suspecting a cop of being in a mobster's pocket."

"It wouldn't be the first time, unfortunately. It's rare, but yes, if you give me a name, I'll run a few discreet checks."

I give him Laila's name and everything I know about her. Then we discuss the video itself. I'd asked the sitter if she'd seen anyone videotaping in the park. She hadn't.

"From what I can tell," I say, "it was taken from the east end of the park. There's new construction there, so I'm wondering if whoever filmed it was tucked in there, out of sight—"

My phone rings. It's Ellie Milano again. I motion to Paul that I'm going to take it, and he nods and then heads over to watch Charlotte.

"It's Ellie Milano," she says when I answer. "You called me yesterday about Brandon."

She said his name. She actually said his name. Please tell me that means she knows he exists—and she's not parroting back the name I used.

"Who are you?" she asks.

Now I hesitate. Two days ago, I'd have given my name, address and whatever else would convince her that I wasn't some crank. That's changed. I glance at my daughter, running to jump into Paul's arms. That *has* to change.

"I'd rather not say," I say. "I'm sorry, but getting involved in this has caused trouble for my own family. I'm going to ask you to call the Oxford Police Department. I reported seeing Brandon to them. They have no evidence to corroborate my story, so they aren't looking for him, and the fact that you told them he doesn't exist really didn't help."

"Wait!" she says, as if expecting me to hang up. "I'm sorry. I'm just protecting my nephew. That's what Kimmy wanted. It was"—her voice catches—"the only thing she wanted, the only thing she cared about."

That catch reminds me this is a woman in mourning, and my tone softens as I say, "I'm sorry."

She takes a deep breath. "You were trying to help. I didn't dare admit you were right, but I should have been polite about it."

"You were thinking about Brandon. His situation. Kim was afraid for him."

"*Terrified* for him."

"Terrified of his father. Denis Zima."

"Is that his name?"

"She never gave it?"

"She refused," Ellie says. "She said it was a guy she'd been with in LA, and his family was into crime." A harsh laugh. "God, that sounds like being into fashion or the music industry. They were criminals. That's all I know. She left him when she got pregnant, and her plan was to hide Brandon until he was school age. By then, she figured it'd be safe. He was going to school this fall, and she was so excited." Her voice hitches in a soft sob.

"But he will go to school now," I say. "He's safe with whoever she gave him to—"

"No, he's not."

"What?"

She takes a deep breath, as if calming herself to speak. "Kimmy always told me as little as possible, for my own safety. I knew about Brandon. I've visited them, but my kids don't even know they have a cousin. She was *so* careful. She said, if anything ever happened to her, she had arranged for someone to take Brandon. I said no, I wanted him. He should be with family. I convinced her I was right, and I think she was relieved. That's what she wanted. Brandon to be with me. She just didn't want to assume I'd be okay with it."

"So you were supposed to take him from whoever had him."

"Right. She gave me an address in Chicago. If anything happened to her, I'd get a call, and then I should go to this address. It wouldn't be safe to give me the address over the phone, so I needed it in advance. The day before she . . . before she was murdered, she called to see if I still had the address. I asked if anything was wrong. She laughed. Said she'd had a nightmare that I'd lost the address, so she was checking. She did things like that, so I never questioned it. I should . . . Oh God, I should have questioned."

"She didn't want to put you in danger."

"I know." Another deep breath. "Then the police phoned about Kimmy, and I flew into a panic because no one had called about Brandon. You did, and I thought for a second *that* was the call . . ."

"But it wasn't."

"No, and I was already on my way to Chicago. I thought maybe his caregivers couldn't get through or they'd lost my phone number. I told myself everything was fine, Brandon was fine. But then I got to the address where he was supposed to be . . ."

"And he wasn't there."

"*No* one was there. It's an empty house. I freaked out. I searched it for any sign that he'd been there, and there was nothing. Now I'm in Chicago, and my husband thinks I'm making arrangements to bring Kimmy's—to bring her home—but I haven't even spoken to the police yet. I just keep waiting for that call, and circling back to the address, in case I missed them and . . . And I don't even know what to do."

I open my mouth to say I'll be right there. It's the first thing that comes. Then I see Paul, lifting Charlotte onto the play structure.

I can't do this. For the sake of my family, I cannot do this.

Yet I can't say that either. There's a woman in crisis on the other end of this line. A woman whose sister has been murdered. Whose nephew is missing. I will not say "I can't help you" and hang up.

"My husband is a lawyer," I say. "A criminal attorney. He's right here. He knows what's been going on. May I get his advice and call you back?"

There's a pause, and I'm not sure if she's hesitating about me explaining to Paul or she just doesn't want to let me go. When she gives a reluctant yes, I promise to call ASAP and disconnect.

Paul catches my eye, and I only nod, letting him know I'm off the phone. He's playing with Charlotte, and I don't want to interrupt him. After a moment, he comes over and says, "Is everything okay?"

I tell him what's happened. When I finish, he pushes his glasses up his nose and pinches the bridge, his eyes shut. It's a gesture I know well, the one he'd make if I came to him with a problem after a long day of work. It means he's too exhausted to deal with this, but he won't say that. He never says that.

"I'm sorry," I say. "You don't need this—"

"Aubrey?" He meets my gaze. "Don't."

"I just—"

"You're trying to help this woman. I want to help you. I'm just thinking that it's a mess. An unfortunate and tragic mess, and I'm not even sure what to tell you. I know what you need to tell *her,* though. Call the police."

"Go to them, not me. I should stay out of it."

"I'm not saying that either. Charlotte is fine. I'm taking her to my mother's for a few days. If you want to help this woman, then I will do what you needed me to do from the start—support your decision. But at this moment, she needs to tell the police everything. Not this Officer Jackson. Let me check her out first. Have Ellie contact the detective in charge of Kim Mikhailov's murder and tell them about her son. Tell them what's happened."

I nod. Then I make the call.

TWENTY-NINE

Ellie won't contact the police. Kim didn't trust them, so she doesn't either. I can't do it myself, not when she's adamantly opposed. So I'm stuck. I tell myself that's a good thing. I cannot get involved. I have already endangered my child getting involved. Ellie needs to handle this, and with any luck, she'll realize that the best way to do that is to involve the police.

I will not feel guilty about telling her I can't help.

I won't.

I do, of course. But I've made the right choice, and I need to let it go.

We're driving to the house. Paul is taking Charlotte to his mother's tonight, and he'd like me to come with them for the drive.

I shake my head. "I've never been your mom's favorite person. Apparently, she had good instincts."

Paul's hands tighten on the steering wheel. "I'd like to put that aside for now. Please."

I glance back at Charlotte, asleep in her seat. "I'm not trying to start a fight."

"I know. But I need to set it aside. I'm here to help you. I'd like . . . I'd like us to get past this, which means at some point, yes, we need to hash it out. Under the circumstances, though, it's counterproductive. I'm not over it, but I'm not as angry as I was. I'd like to put the rest on pause."

"Okay."

"As for my mother, I don't think I ever dated anyone who lived up to her expectations. You were too young for me. Too different from me. She thought you were after a husband with a good job, and then you'd leave and take half my money."

"A gold digger."

"A gold digger with very modest aspirations."

I laugh at that.

"Obviously, she was wrong," he says, "though it did make me more sensitive to the issue of why you married me when I found out—" He stops short. "And that's not dropping the subject, is it?"

"No, but I understand."

He sighs and leans back against the headrest. "I say I want to put it aside, but that's cowardice. I want to forget it. I want to pretend . . ."

"It never happened. Because when you remember it did, you question whether I should be here, whether you should be helping me."

He makes a face. "Not like that. I accept that you didn't marry me as a shield to hide behind. But you *did* lie, and you did deceive me, and I do feel betrayed. I do feel like I married a stranger. I'm just . . ." His fingers tighten on the wheel again. "I'm hurt."

"If I could start over, I'd do it differently. But I understand that there's no undoing that now. There's no making up for it. Which means I appreciate this all the more, Paul. I really do."

He nods. There's silence, then. So much silence, before he says, "If you won't come to my mother's, will you at least stay at the house?"

I hesitate.

"I'd like you to stay there, Aubrey," he says. "With the security system and . . ." He glances to make sure Charlotte's asleep, but still lowers his voice. "That gun. Just stay there, safe, until I return. Please."

"All right."

I've been at Paul's place for about two hours when he calls. That's what I must think of it as. Paul's place. Not ours. Not even "my old house." That's a dangerous path. He bought it. I left it. Now it is his.

Paul calls about Laila Jackson. His contacts have gotten back to him, and the word is that while she can be "difficult" and "ambitious," there's never been any hint of corruption.

"As my one contact said," Paul says, "she's more likely to be the person reporting corruption. In hopes it'll free up a job, he says. Which isn't fair. She's a woman of color, and she's ambitious, and that doesn't always play well with the good old boys. But someone like that isn't going to risk her career for a quick payday from the mob. Even those who don't care for Laila Jackson say she's good at her job."

"Should I report the video directly to her, then?"

"I would. You know her, and that's more useful than placing a call to the switchboard. I could give you a contact of mine if you'd prefer . . ."

"No, I'm okay with Laila. She's not my biggest fan, but some-times that's helpful. She'll be straight with me. I'll tell her about my encounter Sunday night and the video today. I won't men-tion Ellie Milano."

"Unless it means lying," Paul says. "If she asks you any-thing where you'd need to lie to protect Ellie's privacy, I would strongly suggest you don't. Just avoid volunteering information."

"Got it. Oh, if Laila wants to speak to me in person, should I go to the station?"

He pauses. "I'd rather she came to the house. I'd like her take on this—how much danger you might be in personally—before you go out alone. She'll bring her partner to take the report, and I'll be home in about ninety minutes."

"Great. Thank you."

I call Laila. She's out on patrol, but when I ask if I should re-port this to another officer, she's quick to say no. Less than an hour later, she's on the doorstep. And she's alone.

"Where's Officer Cooper?" I ask.

"Buried in paperwork. He said I can handle this."

I hesitate in the doorway, not moving aside to let her in. "I thought police were supposed to work in pairs."

"Technically, yes, but I know you, and this is part of an on-going case. A case he'd rather not bother with."

When I still don't move, she arches her brows. Then she laughs. "Ah, you think this is suspect, me showing up alone."

She holds out her phone. On it is a text string between her and Cooper, where she tells him "that Finch woman" wants to report an incident, and he grumbles. She says she'll take it.

"Yes," she says as she puts her phone away. "I was dismissive, because I *wanted* to talk to you alone. Coop is . . ." She seems to check herself and says, carefully, "Let's just say that I'm sure you thought he was the one taking you seriously about the boy, and I was the one blowing you off, but that's not the way it worked. While I was suspicious, I still investigated. Mostly alone. Whatever you say to me tonight will go into an official report, and you can call the station later to verify that."

I back up. "Sorry. I'm just a little suspicious myself right now."

"I see that."

As she walks in, her gaze moves through the hall, taking the measure of this house.

"It was my choice," I say.

"Hmm?"

"Before you draw any conclusions about why I'm in that crappy apartment while my husband lives here, it was my choice."

"Ah."

She's still looking as she walks through. Then she stops at a photo. It's the three of us—Paul, Charlotte, and me—at the beach.

"Wandered a bit, did you?" she says.

"What?"

She shrugs. "I don't blame you. I think I'd go nuts in a place like this. Especially with a toddler. You got bored and wandered."

"If you're asking whether I cheated on my husband, the answer is no. I'm not living in a lousy apartment out of guilt. Our marriage didn't work out, and Paul was the one who bought this house, so I left him with it. That seemed fair. As long as he was staying, our daughter should, too, at least until we straighten out the divorce. Also fair."

She studies me. Then she nods. "Okay, I can understand that."

"So, if you're done questioning my life choices . . ."

"Hey, you're suspicious. I am, too. We both want to know who we're dealing with. Why don't we sit, and you can give me your statement."

THIRTY

I tell Laila what happened with Zima's thug. By the time I finish, we don't need a functioning air conditioner to chill the room—her look does it just fine.

"This happened last night?" she says. "And you didn't contact me?"

"I handled it."

Her face hardens, eyes flashing. "You are not *supposed* to *handle* armed stalkers, Aubrey. You are supposed to call us."

"Somehow I didn't think he'd wait while I dialed 911."

"You know what I mean. As soon as you got away, you should have called me. This is connected to the case. It's not a matter of whether or not you can handle it yourself. I needed to know."

"And I needed to know you could be trusted with that information."

"Are you questioning my competency as an officer."

"No, I'm saying that you and I got off on the wrong footing, and I wasn't ready to trust you. Now I am. Which is why you're here."

"This is a police investigation. You don't get to decide—"

"I handled it the best I could. I was very, very clear to this thug that I thought I'd misunderstood the situation and didn't actually see a boy. There was no way I'd let Denis Zima think he has a son out there. I said I made a mistake. That I *definitely* made a mistake. He didn't like that answer."

Laila chews this over, and I can tell she's debating whether or not to pursue our disagreement. After a moment, she says, "Did he seem to think you were lying?"

"I'm not sure. It's the same guy I taped on the phone. I'm sure of that. That night, he told whoever was on the line that he thought I was wrong. That there was no kid. So he might have just been pushing me around, making sure I stuck to my story. That's what Paul thinks, and I'd tend to agree."

"Can you describe the man?"

"I can do better than that. I have a name. Hugh Orbec."

She looks up at me.

I shrug. "I had some time to kill. The man I heard on the phone knew Kim, so he dated back that far in Denis Zima's life. Social media is a wonderful thing for tracking friends. That's what Orbec is. He's three years older than Zima. Worked for Zima Senior, who lent him to Denis for the LA clubs. They apparently became close, and when Denis quit the underage-strip-joint racket, Orbec followed him. He's head of operations for the Zodiac chain."

Laila's quiet, and I feel the temperature drop again.

I sigh. "Now what have I done?"

Her gaze meets mine, hard as steel. "Potentially ruined our case against the man, that's all. If a defense attorney found out that you'd positively identified your attacker as Hugh Orbec *before* you gave your statement, he can claim your recollection is based on Orbec, not the man in the alley."

"It doesn't matter. I'm not filing a complaint about what

happened in the alley. There's no point. I'm not injured. He didn't pull his gun. He probably even has a permit for carrying it. If I complain, I'll only make a dangerous enemy. My complaint is about what happened next."

I tell her about the video. Then I show it to her, along with the text.

"I'm not claiming *this* is Orbec," I say. "When I spoke to him, I offhandedly said I didn't have kids, and he never questioned that. If he sent the video, I'd think he'd reference that. Say something like 'I see you *do* have a kid.'"

"Maybe. But that's hardly proof that it wasn't him." She takes my phone and rereads the texts.

"It also doesn't quite fit with Orbec," I say. "Why keep pushing if you *want* me to stick to my story? To say there was no kid? What reason would I have to lie about being wrong . . . after he threw me into a wall?"

"But you did."

"To protect my family and Brandon. As far as Orbec knows, though, I'm just some lady from the suburbs claiming that a dead woman had a kid. To him, I don't know who Kim is. I don't know Denis Zima's connection. I've done nothing more than witness something . . . and then retract my statement. Why keep harassing me?"

"Because someone realizes you're more than you seem, Aubrey. Someone knows you're involved. Someone knows you've been digging."

Which is the answer I don't want. Of course I realize that's the most obvious explanation. I just want her to give me one that means these people will leave my family alone.

I'm about to ask her advice when Paul gets home. He greets Laila—handshake, introduction, civil but not overly warm. He feels the chill in the air. I know he does—he keeps sneaking glances at me, gauging the situation.

When she asks to see his video and texts, he gives them to her. She forwards them to herself at the station, as she did mine.

"We'll be investigating." She turns to me. "By *we,* I mean the Oxford Police Department. Not you, Aubrey. You are to stay out of this. Understand?"

I can barely unhinge my jaw to answer. "I understand."

So, once again, I'm on my own. If I had any hope of an alliance with Laila, it evaporated in that conversation. She's a cop, and I'm not, and that is a line she's not letting me cross, no matter how helpful I've been.

I don't know if I'll dig deeper. No, that's a lie. I will dig. I must. I just won't be out there, sneaking into clubs and playing spy anymore. Or jogging at nightfall in my neighborhood.

Paul and I talk after that. He orders dinner in, and we spend the evening talking and polishing off a bottle of wine. He knows I'll investigate the phone number and video. He doesn't even ask about that—just proceeds as if it's a given. Which proves that while he may not have known the particulars of my life, he does know me.

I consider making sure he tells Gayle that I'll be staying over again. I might say I'm protecting their relationship, but I'm really protecting ours. I don't want to be the cause of their breakup, something he can later resent me for. Nor do I want to give her any reason to peg me as the evil ex wriggling back into his life.

I don't say anything, though. I did this morning and to keep harping on it is interfering. He knows Gayle. He'll know whether he needs to keep her apprised of the ongoing situation.

So we drink, and we talk. Mostly about the case. A little about Charlotte. Nothing about us. When it's time to retire, I take the futon and he heads upstairs to bed.

———

I am in the car where my mother died. I see her reach for me. Feel her hand wrapping around mine. Hear her tell me it'll be all right, that someone will come.

I know no one will come. I see her smiling at me, and I know she will die if I don't help. I know I could wriggle out of my seat. I've done it before. I'm not supposed to, but I could. Yet I don't.

I don't escape and go for help. I don't scream for someone to come. I don't scream for someone to save my mother. I just sit there . . . and I watch her die.

The nightmare stutters to a stop. Rewinds. Starts over.

This time she begs for help. This time she undoes my seat so I can get free. This time the car door lolls open, giving me no excuse, and she's begging, *begging,* me to go for help.

I ignore her. I pick up a toy, and I play with it, and I ignore her.

Inside my head, I'm screaming at myself to do something. Screaming so loud. But all I do is play with that damned toy, and I want to knock it from my hands and—

"Aubrey? *Aubrey.*"

A hand grips my shoulder, and I think someone's there. Someone's come to save my mother.

Someone has finally come.

The hand squeezes, and my eyes fly open, and it's Paul. He's crouched beside the futon, his hand on my shoulder.

I scramble up, looking around, blood rushing in my ears and drowning out his words.

Nightmare. He's telling me I was having a nightmare.

I know that. But it doesn't matter. I'm still shaking and gasping for breath.

"I'm okay," I say. I'm not, but I say it anyway.

"You were calling for your mother," he says. "For someone to help your mother." He wipes a finger over my cheek, and I realize it's hot and wet with tears. "It was about the accident, wasn't it?"

"I didn't get help. She unbuckled me and told me to go get help and . . ." I squeeze my eyes shut. "No, that's not how it happened. Or, I don't think that's . . ."

"It isn't," he says. "I read the police report. You were buckled in your seat, which was jammed shut by the accident."

"I could have wiggled out. I could have—"

"Bree?" He puts a hand on each shoulder, turning me to look at him. "You couldn't have. Your mother would have never expected you to. You were barely two."

"No one came," I say. "She was there all night. She was alive all night. They could see the car in the field. And no one stopped."

His arms go around me, and I collapse into them, sobbing.

THIRTY-ONE

Over breakfast, Paul asks whether I've heard from Ellie.

I shake my head. "She never called back. I hope that means she contacted the police and doesn't need my help. She only reached out once, in hopes . . ." I shake my head, gaze on my plate, and I don't finish.

"She reached out in hope," he says.

I nod, and I sip my coffee.

"You want to help her," he says. "You feel bad about refusing."

I shrug and keep drinking.

"That's what the nightmare was about," he says. "No one stopped for your mother. No one helped. And now you feel like you're doing that with Brandon."

I take a deep breath. "Rationally, I know better. He's not lost in a field, with no one looking for him. Ellie knows he's gone. She's his aunt. It's her responsibility to call the police."

He eats quietly for a moment. Then he says, "If you want to contact her, that wouldn't be a bad idea. Try to convince her she can trust Officer Jackson. If she still won't . . ." He takes a deep breath. "I need to work at the office this morning, but I'm taking the afternoon off. Whatever you do about Ellie, please don't physically investigate until I'm here. I know you can look after yourself, but I can watch your back. I'd like to watch your back."

I agree.

Before Paul leaves, he tells me I should take a nap.

"I know you won't," he says. "But you had a rough night, so I'm going to suggest it anyway. If you're calling Ellie, maybe wait a bit. Give her time to wake up and realize she needs to contact the police."

"I'll do that."

"You gave Officer Jackson Orbec's gun, right?" he asks.

I nod.

"Then since you have the day off, I'll ask you to stay in with the security system set. Obviously, you can tell me where to stick my advice . . ."

I smile. "I'd never do that. But yes, I know it's just a suggestion. A wise one. I'm going to spend the morning online. I won't hack anything from the home Wi-Fi, though."

"Hack?"

"Er, sorry. I meant—"

He presses a finger to my lips. "You meant hack. I get it. Maybe someday you'll explain *that* part, but for now, as long as you don't 'hack' government security, I'm not too worried about it. We have an open Wi-Fi channel. If anyone reports hacking, I'll blame it on Mrs. McDonnell next door."

"Eighty-year-old invalid Mrs. McDonnell?"

"She needs a way to spend her time."

I laugh. "Okay. I'll be careful, though. I'll mask the IP."

He shakes his head. "I'm not even going to ask what that means. I'll be home by one, and I'll bring lunch. Be safe."

He leans forward to give me a goodbye kiss, as he did every morning of our marriage. Then he stops and pulls back, mumbling something.

I kiss his cheek, a quick peck. "Old habit, I know. If this gets too cozy for you, just say the word. I can stay in a hotel."

He gives me an awkward, one-arm hug. "It's fine. I'll rest better with you here."

"You know I appreciate it."

"I do. Now arm the system as soon as I leave."

"Yes, sir."

I don't nap, of course. I couldn't sleep even if I wanted to. I have a job to do, which will keep me from fretting about many things . . . including the fact that I may not have an *actual* job. I told Paul that I have the day off. That's true. It's just not a scheduled one.

I called Ingrid last night to tell her that I'd reported the video incident, and I gave her Laila's number to follow up on that. She said that was fine . . . but that my job was under review for "other reasons," and I should stay home until they decided the future of my employment with the Oxford Central Library.

I pull up the video from yesterday's threat. I keep feeling like I should be able to get something from it. That's not my area of expertise, though. I analyze the metadata, but there's nothing useful there. I already knew the date and the location and there was little more I could gather from the data. On to the video itself then. It's less than three minutes long, which makes it easy to parse and view frame by frame.

I hope for some secret in those frames. I don't know what. A reflection of the videographer in a window? A glimpse of his shadow, with some distinctive hair or headgear? Ridiculous, I know, but I still look. The problem is that it's a distance shot, with nothing in the videographer's immediate surroundings.

I see Charlotte and Mrs. Mueller and Becky and the dog. At one point, another woman and her child join, and I think I recognize her. I can ask Paul if he does and find out whether she saw anything untoward. Otherwise, it's just a video of the park, with a house in the background and two cars parked on the street.

One of the cars catches my eye. I zoom in. The playground doesn't have a parking lot—people walk to it or they park on the street. There are two cars clearly in the video. The one that grabbed my attention is farther down, and the video only includes the back end.

I've seen that car before. I can't make out the make or model, but the rear bumper tweaks a memory. It's a luxury sedan in a neighborhood full of luxury sedans. I must recognize it because I've seen it around before.

Still, I screenshot the image for later, along with one of the neighbor and her son, for Paul to follow up on.

Next comes the phone number. For that, I do need to hack. It turns out to belong to a prepaid—surprise! I trace back to the call records. It was activated yesterday morning, and it has sent two videos—one to me and Paul—and four texts, all to us. That's it. No calls. No other texts.

I stare at that meager call log . . . and it reminds me about something. The calls on Kim's phone. I'd traced a few, including Ellie's, but there's the one that came in while I was with her in the park and a couple of times before that.

Time for more hacking. This one's easier than I expected, and I kick myself for not digging deeper before now. When a simple search hadn't returned an owner, I presumed it was prepaid. Yet when I dig, I come up with an actual account . . . one owned by Hugh Orbec. I look for the call I heard him make Saturday night, when I was in the closet at Zodiac Five, but it's not there. That suggests two phones: personal and business.

Why would Hugh Orbec be so careless, using his personal phone to call Kim?

Or had someone else used it? Denis Zima could probably get access to Orbec's cell phone. Was he setting up his old friend? I don't know. But I do make note of other numbers that called and texted with Orbec's phone. I'm doing that when my alarm goes off, telling me it's 11 A.M. Time to phone Ellie, having given her plenty of time to wake up and realize she needs to get the police involved.

That's how I greet her. Not with "Hello" or "Good morning," but "It's Aubrey. Have you called the police yet?"

She hasn't. She's absolutely convinced that if she involves them, Brandon will suffer. I try to talk her into contacting Laila Jackson. It doesn't work.

"If they didn't believe you, they won't believe me," she says. "You're a librarian. I'm a stay-at-home mom from South Dakota."

"You're Brandon's aunt. You know him. The police can't say you hallucinated a nephew."

"And then what? Where will they go from there? Whoever has Brandon murdered Kim. They'll kill him too if the cops rush in."

"So what are you going to do?" I ask. "Just hope they'll take good care of him?"

"Of course not. I'm hiring a private investigator. I've found someone. I just need to figure out how to cover his retainer. It's . . . more than I expected. But I can do it."

I struggle to keep the impatience from my voice. "Any PI worth his salt would tell you to contact the police. Private investigators are a last resort, when the police won't get in-volved. If he's not telling you that, he just wants your money. How much is the retainer?"

"Five thousand."

"What? No. That's crazy."

"How much would you charge?"

"Me?" I sputter. "I'm not a private investigator. I'm a librarian, like you said—"

"Which means you're smart. Detective work might not be your job, but you're really good at it. You identified Kim. You found out who Brandon's dad is, and even I didn't know that. You are—"

"—not a private eye."

"But I'd pay you."

"I don't need money."

Silence.

I should wish her luck and sign off. *Let me know how it goes! I'll cross my fingers for you!*

I can't do that. Physically cannot.

I take a deep breath. "Can I get that address? The one Kim gave you?"

She gives it.

"Let me do some digging," I say. "I'll get back to you. If you decide to contact Officer Jackson, please do that and let me know. But hold off on hiring a PI and spending five grand you don't have. Please."

Not surprisingly, there's no public listing for the owner of that house. Still, obtaining the owner of record is easy enough through property taxes. But that requires doing exactly what Paul asked me not to—hacking into government servers. I'll wait for Paul on that. In the meantime, this triggers another thought. Kim must have been in contact with whomever she asked to take Brandon.

A scan of her prepaid call record identifies the most likely number. It's one she dialed twice in the days before her death. One call was made on the Friday, and then one shortly after she spoke to Hugh Orbec—or whoever used his phone. The initial one was short, as if she was reaching out.

I may be in trouble. I may need your help.

The second is longer, as if it was the planning call. Orbec had made contact, presumably threatening Kim, given what I'd heard of the exchange. She realizes then that she must enact her plan with Brandon, and she places the second call.

I try to trace that phone number, but I have no luck.

Paul gets home shortly after that. He's brought lunch and a sympathetic ear as I vent my frustration. First, he takes what action he can, by asking his assistant to investigate the tax situation on that house. Then he just listens.

"I don't know what to do," I say.

"What do you want to do?"

I shake my head. "That doesn't matter. I already endangered Charlie doing what I wanted to do."

"No, some thug *threatened* Charlie to scare you off. Whoever these people are, Aubrey, they're not going to kidnap your daughter. It was empty posturing. But, in the event that it wasn't, we've removed our daughter from the equation. She's safe."

I nod, but I don't say anything.

"You're right about the private eye," Paul continues. "He's scamming Ellie. You're also right to keep pushing her toward Officer Jackson. Eventually, she will have to make that call. If, in the meantime, you want to keep digging, I don't see any problem with that. As long as 'digging' doesn't mean marching to that club to confront Denis Zima."

I chuckle. "I'm not that stupid."

He takes another plate of pad Thai. "On that note, I also had my clerk dig into the Zimas. It's an interesting situation, and I'm not sure what to make of it. Denis's father definitely has ties to organized crime. It's the kind of scenario where everyone knows he's breaking the law, and no one can prove it. They even tried doing an Al Capone by going after him for tax evasion. He's very, very careful. He has good connections to the Russian mob through his wife's family. So Denis grew up right in the heart of that. There are all kinds of rumors about his old strip club in LA. The most pervasive was that it wasn't just selling underage strippers, but underage girls themselves."

"Prostitution?"

"More like sex slavery."

"Do you think Kim was part of that?"

He takes a bite of his food before answering. "On the surface, that makes sense. Teenage girl starts dancing in his club and then gets together with him. It seems very . . . suspect."

"Uh-huh."

"But I'm not sure it's as cut-and-dried as it seems. Kim stayed with Zima after he closed the club. And he's the one who closed it. The rumor is that he had a falling-out with his parents and decided to go straight."

"He closed the strip club and started the Zodiacs."

"It's more than that. Apparently, he started to cut a deal with the feds, turning on his parents. He told the feds that he had information. He asked for witness protection for himself and Kim. She was using another name at the time, but it was clearly her. They were brokering a deal with him when he backed out. He said he'd made a mistake, and he didn't have anything for them."

"Was it grandstanding? He wanted something from his parents so he threatened to expose them?"

"Possibly. That's a dangerous way to get a bigger allowance, though. It's more likely that he realized the danger. Either way, it looks as if Brandon was born about ten months later."

"Which probably means he didn't go straight after all. Kim ran and hid her baby for five years. She knew Zima was dangerous."

"I'd agree. Throughout all that, Hugh Orbec was at his side. He's definitely Zima's right-hand man . . . whatever business Zima is into these days."

We talk some more. I pull up the still images from the video of Charlie. He recognizes the mother and boy, and he says he'll talk to them, see whether they noticed anyone hanging around the park or videotaping nearby. When I show him the photo of the car, he chuckles at first, and says, "Lots of those around here. Probably a lot in Denis Zima's world, too. I could try to find out what he and Orbec drive. Do you have a better shot of it? I can't see much from this angle."

"No, this is it."

I zoom in. "Do you recognize it?" I say.

He pauses, lips pressed. "Possibly? I'm not sure. Leave it with me."

I'm making coffee when Paul's law clerk gets back to him. The house is a secondary address owned by a Chicago woman named Elizabeth Kenner.

I look up Kenner. She's a retired social worker, active in several youth organizations. She's been living in Chicago for seven years. And before that? She's from Cedar Rapids, Iowa. Where Kim and Ellie grew up.

I call Ellie. When I tell her the name, she's quiet for a moment. Then she says, "Yes! Of course. Beth. She was Kimmy's outreach worker. Before Kimmy left, she had some problems. Our dad . . ."

"There were problems," I say when she trails off. "Between him and Kim."

"Him and all of us, but Kimmy got the worst of it. She was tough, and the tougher she got, the harder he . . ." She inhales sharply. "It was bad. I didn't realize *how* bad because I moved out when she was still a kid. Anyway, Kimmy got into trouble, and she was assigned a youth outreach worker. That was Beth. I met her a bunch of times in hopes I could help."

She describes the woman she remembers, and it matches the photographs of Elizabeth Kenner.

"That makes sense, doesn't it?" Ellie says. "My sister trusted Beth. When she needed help, she might have contacted her. Kimmy might even have moved to Chicago because of her."

"It does make sense," I say.

"Then we need to speak to Beth. Do you have an address?"

"I do, but I really think the police—"

"No," she says firmly. "I need to know what went wrong. Why Brandon isn't with Beth. If we call in the police, we might spook Beth. Especially if she knows what kind of person Brandon's father is. If you can't come with me, I understand. Just give me her address."

I tell Ellie I'll get back to her. Then I hang up and go into the study, where Paul is working. I tell him everything.

"If you're comfortable going with her, that's probably a good idea," he says. "It would help to have a witness to whatever this woman says. I don't see any danger. This is the person Kim trusted with her child." He gets to his feet. "And I know you'd like to hear the answers firsthand."

"I would."

"I'll go with you and wait in the car."

I shake my head. "This is just an interview. I can handle it."

He hesitates. Then he nods. "All right. I do kind of wish you'd kept the gun, though. I'm not a fan of firearms, but this is one time when I can see the appeal."

"I do actually have one, in a storage locker in the city. It's even registered. But I don't have a concealed carry permit."

"Right now, I don't care. If you're already heading to Chicago, I'd like you to swing by and grab it." He pauses. "I'll drive into the city with you. I forgot a few files at the office."

THIRTY-TWO

Paul and I drive to Chicago in our own cars. I told Paul that he could follow me to the locker, if he wanted, and he does. There's no reason for him to come along. No practical reason, that is. The invitation is symbolic—this locker is what remains of my old life, the repository of my secrets. If he'd like to see that, he's welcome to. I'm not hiding anything. Not anymore.

When I open my locker, I see him looking about.

"Yes, it's kinda sleazy," I say. "This is what you get when you pay cash."

"Actually, I was thinking it's very small. This is everything you have?"

I nod and turn on the light. He walks to a rickety dresser.

"This is . . . a family piece, I'm guessing?"

I smile. "No. It's just junk. I bought the furniture to hide what's inside it, in case of a break-in."

I take out the gun and place it on the dresser. He leans in to examine the firearm without touching it, and I struggle not to laugh at that.

"You can poke around if you like," I say. "There's money.

That's my inheritance, not my ill-gotten gains." I pause. "Though, considering I was living off the stolen money while saving this, I'm splitting hairs."

"It's not actual stolen cash, which is the main thing." He takes out a bundle. "If it's an inheritance, then you've already paid taxes on it. There's no reason to hide it."

"I was saving it for a condo. Then we got married, and I couldn't bring it out without raising questions, so . . ."

"So you've been living in a crappy apartment rather than use this?"

"I didn't want—" I clear my throat. "I was concerned about the custody implications."

He seems confused for a moment. Then he says, "You thought if you suddenly had money, I could unearth your past and use that to get full custody of Charlie."

I nod.

He sets the money down. "No matter how angry I got, I never considered stealing her from you, Aubrey. You are free to bring out this money and put a down payment on a house or a condo or whatever you want. If you need help making the mortgage payments, I'll pitch in. I've said before that you gave up your earning potential to care for our child. You are *owed* money for that."

"I don't want—"

"Yes, I know. You feel guilty, and you want to be fair. *This* is fair."

"I have enough for a good down payment, and once I get a new job, I'll be able to cover the mortgage."

"New job?" He pauses. "Ah, one that uses your tech skills. Good. I was going to suggest that." He catches my expression and says, "Which isn't what you meant at all, is it?"

"I'll be fine. Now, I've got my gun so—"

"What's happened with your job?" He pauses. "This better not have anything to do with you rushing off after Charlie on Monday."

I don't need to answer. Again, he sees it in my face.

"They can't terminate you for that," he says. "Legally—"

"I don't want to work someplace that doesn't want me. Legal termination or not. If they fire me, I'll wave around the threat of a lawsuit, but only to negotiate a decent reference. I appreciate the outrage, but I've got this. Now, if you're ready to go . . ."

He looks around. "Money and a gun. Is that everything you have here?"

I shrug. "There are a few mementos."

"May I see them? If you have time?"

"I do."

I've spoken to Ellie by phone, and I've seen her on Facebook, so it's hard to remember that we haven't actually met. She is what I saw online—an older, more full-figured version of her sister. I meet her in her hotel lobby, and we head out.

Chicago is the third-largest city in the U.S., and I'd be lying if I said I got to know it well in my few years there, before I moved to Oxford with Paul. I got to know my apartment neighborhood and my work neighborhood. That's normal for me, after a life spent moving around army bases. I focus on my narrow sphere. It's only in Oxford that I feel I "know" the city.

So I set my GPS for Beth Kenner's address, without knowing where it'll lead. As it turns out, it takes me to a neighborhood that was probably a former suburb. Winding streets. Massive trees. Post–World War II houses that look mass-produced from two basic molds.

We park around the corner from Beth's place. I know there's

no danger here, but I'm being careful. I can't help it. The address leads us to a cute bungalow with a steep roof and massive front picture window. There's a car in the drive, which I hope means she's home.

When I knock, I hear sounds within, but no one answers. I put my ear to the door. It's gone quiet.

I knock again. Ellie leans to look through the picture window, and I reach to pull her back.

"Careful," I whisper. "I don't like the sounds of—"

Footsteps patter across the floor inside. A lock turns. Then another. A small, white-haired woman throws open the door with, "Ellie!"

She opens the screen and ushers us in. "I was out back reading. Then I heard the bell and saw your friend through the peephole. I thought she was selling something. Come in, come in."

She keeps prodding us until we're in the living room. Then she hugs Ellie.

"It is so good to see you," she says. "Are you here visiting Kimmy?"

Ellie looks at me. I wince. The older woman looks from me to Ellie.

"Is something wrong?" she asks, her words slow, her back tightening.

"When did you last hear from Kim?" I ask.

She settles onto the sofa, her hands fluttering. "Oh, I'm not even sure. We get together now and then. But it's been a few weeks. Is she all right?"

"She . . ." I look at Ellie, but she's frozen. "I'm sorry, but she's been killed. That's why Ellie's here. We thought you knew."

Beth stares at us. "Killed? An . . . accident?" Her voice rises in a way that says she hopes that's what I mean, but she knows better.

"She was murdered," I say. "It was in the news."

She looks at me blankly, and I remember we're in Chicago, not Oxford. I'm sure Kim's death made the news here, but not the way it had at home. Kim hasn't been identified officially either. There's no reason Beth *would* know.

"I'm sorry," I say. "So you haven't heard from her in weeks?"

She nods, but even if I didn't know better, I'd see the lie in her expression.

"I know that's not true," I say gently. "I have phone records. I know she spoke to you twice before her death. Once on the Friday before she died and once the Sunday before."

I can't prove the number was Beth's. Not yet. But I must sound convincing, because she goes still.

"It was about Brandon, wasn't it?" I say. "You were supposed to take him."

She glances at Ellie.

"I know about the house," I say. "Your country place. That's the address Kim gave Ellie for picking up Brandon if anything happened to her."

Beth exhales. "Yes," she says. A moment of silence then, again, "Yes. I was supposed to take Brandon in an emergency. Kim called me two weeks ago. She was worried, and she wanted to make sure I was around, in case she needed me to take Brandon. Then she called back a few days later and said she'd found another way. She said everything was okay, but she was taking Brandon away for a while, just until . . . his father left town."

"His father was *in* town to open a new club."

She nods and seems relieved that I know who Brandon's dad is. "She was worried with Denis being in Chicago, but she found a solution. She said she had something Denis wanted, and if she gave it to him, everything would be fine. She'd do that and then take Brandon on vacation until Denis left Chicago, just to be safe. That's the last I heard from her."

———

Beth offers coffee after that, but neither of us is in the mood to socialize . . . and I don't think she is either. Ellie tells Beth that she'll let her know about funeral arrangements.

Beth has no idea who might have Brandon. We're all holding out hope that Kim really did make alternate arrangements. Better and safer ones that she didn't dare tell Beth, for fear even that would endanger Brandon.

That is our hope. That he is with someone, and that person has Ellie's number but has chosen not to contact her until they know what's going on with Kim's murder. Solve that first. Put Denis Zima behind bars. Then Brandon will be safe.

Yet, according to Beth Kenner, Kim thought she already had a way to keep him safe. She said that Zima wanted something from her, something that was presumably not Brandon himself. If she handed that over, Zima would stop pursuing.

I've presumed that Kim was on the run all these years to hide Brandon from his father. What if, instead, she was in danger because she took something else when she left.

When I broke ties with Ruben, I'd considered preventative measures against future blackmailing. Hack his own computer. Tape an incriminating conversation. Gather some intelligence I could use if he ever came after me . . . as he eventually did with Paul. I'd decided against it because that is a dangerous game. I already knew things I could threaten Ruben with. Gathering extra would only make him all the more determined *not* to let me walk away.

What if Kim took out her own insurance policy? Her getting pregnant was like me getting shot—a wake-up call, probably fueled by a generous dose of panic. We needed to escape. Immediately. Yet neither of us was a wide-eyed naïf. We knew who we'd gotten mixed up with, and we knew our past could come back to destroy us. So we went into hiding. But I'd left knowing I had a small insurance policy against Ruben and deciding against a larger one. What if Kim—being younger and more desperate—grabbed the big insurance policy before she left . . . only to realize later that having it further endangered her child.

If Kim took something incriminating, she thought it'd be insurance. What she would have discovered is that Denis Zima would happily kidnap his own son and use him to get what she stole. Then he'd keep the boy *and* kill Kim.

That means whoever is holding Brandon might want the same thing: Kim's insurance policy. And if they don't get it? We're not talking about a father taking his child. We're talking about a bargaining chip that will lose its value once no payoff appears.

This must go to Laila Jackson and the police. Once I get away from here, I'm pulling over and calling her. I'm thinking this as I climb in the car, having not said a word to Ellie since we left Beth Kenner's. I'm about to tell her when I'm idling at a four-way stop and see the driver in the vehicle across from us.

It's the man who accosted me Sunday night.

Hugh Orbec.

There's a moment, of course, where I think I'm wrong. I catch a glimpse of a man who resembles him, driving a Dodge Charger, and I think I'm mistaken. Then he looks over—not at me, just a casual glance toward my vehicle as I pass—and there is no question.

That's Hugh Orbec . . . and he's heading in the direction I just came.

Toward Beth Kenner's house.

At first, I'm sure he's followed me. But that makes no sense considering he drove right past. Even if he knows what I drive, this isn't my car—Paul insisted we switch vehicles after the storage locker, giving me an extra layer of privacy.

If I've led Orbec to Beth Kenner, it's not physically, but in another way—he's following my virtual footsteps or tapping my phones or he's arrived at the same conclusion independent of me. He's been doing amateur detective work of his own, and he thinks Brandon is with Beth.

How Orbec got here doesn't matter. The important thing is where he's going—to the home of a retired woman who lives alone, who tried to help a young woman in need, and is now going to suffer for it. If Orbec thinks Beth has Brandon, he's not going to take "Sorry, you're mistaken" for an answer.

I watch as Orbec turns the corner behind me. Then I stop at the curb and throw open my door, startling Ellie from her own thoughts.

"Take the car," I say. "Drive to . . . to a coffee shop. The first one you see. Text me the address."

"What—?"

"I just saw one of Denis's men heading for Beth's. They think she has Brandon."

Ellie's mouth opens in an O, her eyes widening. "Shouldn't I come with you?"

I shake my head. "I've got this. You get someplace safe." I want to tell her to call Laila. Call Paul. Call someone and tell them where I am. But I don't have time to explain. I have my phone. I can text her as soon as I get a second. And if I don't get one? Ellie knows where I went and why. Good enough.

THIRTY-THREE

I call Beth. She gave us her number but warned she no longer carries her cell phone around, now that she's retired. It rings three times. Then her cheerful voice invites me to leave a message. As I ask her to call back, I remember she'd been reading on the back deck when we arrived, and I curse under my breath.

I remind myself that she hadn't been quick to open the door for us. She only did so when she saw Ellie. This *isn't* a naive senior citizen—she was a social worker, and she knows to be cautious. That won't help, though, if Orbec forces his way in. Or if he surprises her in the rear yard.

I zip to the street behind hers. I can't see her yard from there, not with privacy fences and hedges everywhere.

I sprint down three houses. The driveway behind Beth's is empty, the house dark. I race into the yard. There's a six-foot fence between that yard and Beth's. I hop onto the lower rail and peek over.

She's not on her deck.

I'm about to hop the fence when my phone rings. It's Beth. I jump into her yard and then spot her at the kitchen window, phone to her ear. I answer as I cross the yard.

"One of Denis Zima's men is here," I say.

"Here?"

"I think so. Is your front door locked?"

"Of course."

She spots me as I hop onto her deck. She opens the door for me and starts stepping out, but I wave her back inside and follow. I go straight to the front door and double-check it. Both the dead bolt and key lock are engaged.

"We can leave out the back," I say. "I'll call Ellie and have her pick us up."

"If you're suggesting I hop that fence, I'm not your age," she says. "I don't even think I could climb it." She looks around. "Do we need to leave? I'd feel better staying here and dealing with it."

"This isn't the sort of person you can deal with."

She smiles at me, the kind of smile you give a very sweet but misguided child. "I was a social worker for forty years. I've talked drug dealers into putting down their guns. I've talked homicidal fathers into handing me their children. I can get rid of him, dear. He'll walk away and rethink his strategy, and while he does that, we'll contact the police."

"Okay. But we can't let him see me. Can you pull the front blinds?"

"That'll seem suspicious, won't it?" She looks around. "Why don't you wait in the bedroom . . . no, those blinds are open. Maybe the back—" Footsteps sound on the front steps.

As she looks around again, Orbec rings the bell. Beth spins me toward a door off the kitchen. "The basement. Go down there and wait for me."

"I'd rather—"

"I can handle this."

I let her prod me onto the steps.

"There's a TV room at the bottom," she says. "Wait there."

The door closes behind me as the bell rings again. As soon as her footsteps retreat, I creep back to the top step and crack open the door.

Orbec is knocking now. The dead bolt clanks. Then the front door squeaks open.

I have my gun in hand.

"Miz Kenner?" Orbec says. "Elizabeth Kenner?"

"Yes, that's me, and whatever you're selling—"

"I'm a friend of Kim's." Orbec goes on to weave a story about how he knows Kim and Brandon, and he was told that if anything ever happened to Kim, he's to come to this house and ask for Elizabeth Kenner.

As he drones on, I relax. Beth was right. He's not going to force his way in at gunpoint. It's broad daylight in a residential neighborhood. He's playing it cool with a plausible story. When that fails, he'll retreat to formulate a new strategy.

That's exactly what he does. Beth insists she has no idea what or who he's talking about, and when she asks him to leave, he does.

The door closes. The house goes quiet, as if she's watching him leave. Then I hear her voice, low, murmured. Something about . . .

A basement?

Did she just say something about a basement?

Is she on the phone to the police?

Why would she tell the police I'm in the basement?

She wouldn't, and she hasn't been on that phone long enough to explain the situation. She's barely had time to place a call . . .

She *hasn't* placed a call. Because she left her phone on the kitchen counter. She put it down before answering the door and never returned to the kitchen.

Which means . . .

I figure out what it means one second before I hear the murmur of another voice.

Hugh Orbec.

Beth just told *him* I'm in the basement. There's no other explanation.

There's no way I can get to the back door without them seeing me. I quickly shut the basement door and hightail it down the stairs. I race into the TV room. Turn on the light. Shut the door. Sprint down the hall. Open another door to find a laundry room with a window.

I shut that door and leave the light off. The window is right over the washing machine. I climb up onto it. It gives a creak, and I freeze, but the sound is covered by the thump of feet on the stairs.

The window is fixed, no way to open it. I grab a towel from the top of the dryer; then, with one eye on the door, I wrap the towel around my gun and force myself to wait.

The TV room door opens. As Beth calls "Aubrey?" I smash the window with the towel-wrapped gun. I wince at the noise but I clear the sill as fast as I can. Beth calls my name again, casual, not having heard the window break. I toss the gun out and hoist myself up and . . . Damn it, this is one time I wish I hadn't kept those extra pounds.

My hips stick in the window. Beth calls again, but Orbec has already figured it out. He lets out a curse. I'm wiggling as hard as I can, pushing hard, trying—

My hips pop through just as the laundry door slaps open.

"You—" Orbec begins.

I don't hear the rest. I'm sure he's not complimenting me on my ingenuity.

As Orbec snarls curses, I spring to my feet and run. He comes after me, but for him, that means going through the basement, up the stairs, past Beth—who I'm sure will demand an explanation—and out the back door. By that time, I've vaulted over the fence and reached the street. From his footsteps, he presumes I've gone the way he saw me run—for the back fence. Instead, I've climbed the front one, and I'm already jogging down Beth's road.

My gun's put away, and I have my cell phone in hand instead, my fingers poised over the emergency button. If I hear anyone running behind me, I'll push it. I take every turn I come to until I reach a small market.

The shop reminds me of the one in my old neighborhood, the kind that sells overpriced organic staples for those who can't bother driving into the city. Which means it's *not* like the corner stores in my new neighborhood, where Orbec could barrel in, grab me by the hair, and haul me out, and the clerks would busy themselves checking the cigarette stock.

Before I walk inside, I fix my ponytail, straighten my shirt, and then check for blood and dirt. There is some of both. I hadn't done a perfect job clearing that windowsill, and I cut my bare arm. My hands and knees are filthy from crawling out into Beth's garden. Fortunately, this is also the sort of shop that has a dog tap outside for thirsty pooches. I quickly clean my hands and knock dirt from my jeans. Then I go inside and call for a taxi.

Maybe I should be phoning the police, but honestly, I expect the taxi will come faster. I feel safe enough now, and the Chicago police would require a full explanation. If I gave it, they'd probably figure I was high on meth or oxy. So a taxi it is. As I wait I pick out a snack I won't eat—gourmet soda and veggie chips—and then chat with the cashier until my cab pulls up.

I call Ellie next. According to the text she'd sent, she's only a few blocks away, but I can't risk leading Orbec to her. I tell her to take my car back to her hotel and stay there until I can get in touch again.

"Is Beth all right?" she asks.

It takes me a moment to remember that I'd gone back to "save" Beth. I stifle a snort at that. I haven't even processed what Beth has done. I haven't had time.

"Beth is fine," I say. "But she's working with Denis."

"*What?*"

"That's why Denis's thug was there. Remember how long it took Beth to get to the door when we arrived? I think she was calling him. That's why she didn't want us leaving so soon."

"Oh my God." A pause. "Are you sure?"

"Am I sure she called him? No. Am I sure she's in on it all? No. But she told me to go in the basement while she got rid of him. She pretended to do that. He pretended to leave. Then she told him I was in the basement. I escaped out a basement window."

"Oh my God." She inhales. "I keep saying that. I'm sorry. It's just . . . Kimmy was so afraid, and I kept telling her she was overreacting. We'd fight about it. I told her she was ruining her life and damaging Brandon's out of pure paranoia. Once, I even suggested she see a therapist. Kimmy didn't always make the best choices, but I could not imagine she fell in love with any guy who frightened her that much. She'd never talk about him, though. She'd shut me down and say it didn't matter, that Brandon was in danger. Serious danger. And I didn't believe her."

Her voice breaks. I tell her the important thing is that she's here for Brandon now. That she believes Kim now. And, understanding the danger, she'll stay in that hotel room, right?

"I will. I absolutely will."

"Good. Put the keys under the car mat, please. I'm going to

swing by and take it. I'm also getting the police involved. I know that's not what you wanted, and if you insist, I'll leave you out of it . . ."

"No, you were right. This is a matter for the police. Tell them everything."

"Okay. For now, get to your hotel. Park. Don't contact me again. I'll find the car. You stay safe."

THIRTY-FOUR

I have the taxi circle, so I can be sure Ellie parks and leaves before I arrive at the hotel. I find the car easily enough—at midafternoon the lot is almost empty. I drive straight to Paul's office. I want him with me when I contact Laila. At this point, I'm starting to feel like legal representation might be wise. No, that's an excuse. I just want to be with Paul. I'm holding it together and faking calm, but inside, I'm freaking out.

Part of me doesn't even want to speculate on what's going on here. Just shove aside any need to interpret and take the facts to Laila. But I can't help trying to figure it out. Trying to make sense of it.

Beth Kenner is working with Hugh Orbec, which means she's working with Zima. If Kim had handed over Brandon, as planned, Ellie still wouldn't have gotten that call to come get the boy. He'd have gone straight to Denis.

But now Denis is looking for Brandon, which means he doesn't have him. Kim didn't give Brandon to Beth. Did she figure out that the one person she trusted in Chicago wasn't trustworthy at all? Was Beth telling the truth about that—Kim called and pretended everything was fine, said she didn't need Beth's help after all? I think so. Something tipped her off, and she changed her plans.

But what did she change them *to*? Did she find someone else to take Brandon? Or did she turn over her insurance policy . . . and then pay for that mistake with her life?

I want to believe she found someone else, and Brandon is safe, and as soon as Denis is arrested for Kim's murder, Brandon's caretaker will decide to contact Ellie. Everyone lives happily ever after.

Thinking back to that day when Brandon was taken, I can find evidence to support my theory. Kim must have told Brandon to play for a while and then gave him a time to meet his guardian in the parking lot.

Then why did he fight it? He ran over, as if expecting to see someone he knew. Yet the man who came out of that SUV was a stranger, and Brandon fought.

Maybe in her haste to make new arrangements, Kim forgot to tell Brandon it wouldn't be Beth picking him up. Or maybe Brandon just expected a woman.

It doesn't matter who has the boy. He's safe. I'll take what I have to Laila, and the police will pick up the investigation from there.

I call Paul to let him know I'm coming. His cell goes to voice mail. I try his office instead.

"He's not here, Mrs. Finch," his admin assistant says.

"It's Aubrey, please. He stepped out?"

"No, he's gone for the day. He said if you called or stopped by, I should let you know he'd left and tell you to call his cell."

I'd expected he'd wait for me to be done. Which is silly. As far as we knew, I was on a completely safe mission to interview a friend of Kim's. No need for him to stay in Chicago, and if

I'm disappointed, that's personal. I wanted him to be waiting for me. He isn't. Too bad.

"All right," I say. "He's not answering his cell, but I'll leave a message. Did he say he was heading home?"

"He . . ." She goes quiet, and then says quickly, "He was looking for Ms. Lansing."

"Gayle?"

"Yes. He came in looking for her, but she'd just left. She was planning to work from home for the afternoon. He went after her."

"Ah, okay. Thanks."

I disconnect and idle at a green light until someone lays on the horn behind me.

Paul lied to me. He said he was picking up files. Instead, he was looking for Gayle. When I asked how Gayle felt about him helping me, he said she was fine with it . . . and then changed the subject.

Gayle must not be fine with it, and he went to the office to speak to her. Now he's followed her home. That's okay. It's time for me to tackle this on my own and not screw up his new life any more than I have.

I'll call Laila before I get to Oxford and meet her at the police station, where I'll tell her and Cooper the whole story. I don't need Paul to hold my hand for that.

I do call him, though. Just a quick one to say I have everything under control. The phone only rings once. Then someone answers. Only it's not Paul.

"Hello, Aubrey." The woman's voice is ice cold.

"Gayle?"

"Yes."

"Is Paul there?" I hurry on with, "This will only take a moment."

"Haven't you taken up enough of his time?"

I should wince. I should apologize. I'd just been thinking that very thing. But it's not as if I strong-armed Paul into helping me. Or sobbed on his shoulder, begging for his assistance.

"Yes," I say, injecting an equal dose of ice into my voice. "Paul comes with some baggage, and that baggage is me. But if you know him—at all—then you understand that this is how he is. I'm having a problem that affects our daughter, and he is helping me resolve it. I am very sorry if that has upset or inconvenienced you, but it is almost over. Just let me—"

"It's over *now,* Aubrey."

"Where's Paul?"

"Here. He's asked me to handle this."

I snort a laugh. "Uh, no. He hasn't. Let me guess, he's temporarily out of the room, and you grabbed his phone."

Her silence tells me I'm right. In that silence, I hear the ticking of a grandfather clock. The one at our—Paul's—house. So they've gone there, and he's stepped into the bathroom, and she's seen me call and answered.

"Paul wants me to tell you—" she begins.

"Like hell. Paul is a nice guy. A good guy. A guy who doesn't particularly like confrontations, but he's not a coward. If he has something to say to me, he'll say it himself. Just like he would have asked me about horseback riding last Saturday. I thought that seemed odd. Turns out you lied to me, which—by the way—I haven't told him. Now hand the damned phone to Paul."

"Gayle?" Paul's voice sounds in the background, underscored by the smack of his loafers along the hall. "I thought I asked you to leave—"

Gayle hangs up.

You bitch.

You royal bitch.

I start to call back. Then I stop myself. I'm not getting into a tug-of-war between them. I don't know what's happened, but Paul's tone and his words tell me they've had an argument. If it's about me, then I'm sorry for that, but I've done nothing wrong.

I know Paul's at home. I'll be there in twenty minutes, and I'll talk to him in person. By then, Gayle will be gone.

I call Laila and leave a message saying I'm coming to the station to speak to her. I'll be there in an hour.

Whatever's happening with Beth, it's not an urgent situation. No more urgent than it has been since Kim's death. I lost Orbec back at Beth's place, and I've seen no sign of him or his car since then. I've been watching for them. Back when I walked away from Ruben's operation, I educated myself on Fugitive Life 101—everything I needed to rest assured that no one was after me. So I know how to spot a tail. I don't have one.

As I round the corner to Paul's house, I see Gayle's car in the drive. I let out a curse, and I slow.

If they're still arguing, I don't want to walk into that. And if they're making up, I *definitely* don't want to walk into that.

I will admit that it takes some effort to decide I'm not going into that house. I know it's the right stance—the selfless choice I should make if I care about Paul. If Gayle makes him happy, he should be with Gayle. But that's me making a conscious effort to do the right thing. There's still a little part of me—okay, not *too* little—that wants to barrel in there and have it out with her and let Paul know what she did on the phone.

I love him. I would love to have him back. I'm not denying that. I just need to keep my distance until he figures out what he wants. I owe him that much.

As I pass the house, I slow. I'm looking at Gayle's car, and something's prickling the back of my mind, pushing through the warring voices of "stay out of this" and "get in there and fight for him." Those voices are loud enough that the niggling really has to push hard to break through. But it does, and I realize what I'm seeing.

The car from the playground video.

I squeeze my eyes shut and give my head a sharp shake. I'm angry at Gayle. Outraged and fighting the overwhelming urge to show her why messing with my family is a very bad idea. In that state of mind, I'm jumping to ridiculous conclusions that paint her as something far worse than a woman who wants my ex-husband.

I take out my phone and find the still image of that car. I enlarge it. I compare the two.

It's definitely Gayle's. There's a scrape on the rear bumper that matches. I saw her car at the daycare and thought it looked like the vehicle of a woman who belonged with Paul. That's why it stuck in my mind.

I remember Paul seeing this picture. I remember him hesitating. This is why he wanted to stop by the office. Not to pick up files. According to his admin assistant, Paul went there to see Gayle. True. He went to confront her about this.

The fact that Gayle's car is in the video is not proof that she sent it. A court would see it as circumstantial evidence. But there is no other logical reason for Gayle's car to be near that park. She doesn't even live in Oxford.

Paul said she was working from home Monday. He'd considered sending Charlotte there and then changed his mind and left her with the neighbor instead. Had he told Gayle that? If so, she'd know exactly where to find Charlotte. It would be easy to follow them to the playground and shoot the video.

Shoot a video of our daughter and send it from a prepaid phone with threatening texts? Why the hell would Gayle do that?

I don't care. I'm not going to sit at this curb and ponder her motivation. This woman scared the life out of me and cost me my job. She also scared the life out of Paul—a man she supposedly cares for.

I march to the house.

I glance at her car as I pass. I even run my finger down that scrape, to be sure I'm not hallucinating it. I'm not. This is the car in the video.

The rear gate is ajar, and I swing it open and continue through onto the deck. The back sliding door is also not quite shut, as if someone strode through this way, too angry to close gates and doors behind them. I'm reaching for the sliding door handle when I see something smeared across the glass.

That smear gives me pause. Paul might have a three-year-old, but he also has a housekeeper three days a week. He'd be quick to clean it himself, too.

It looks like jam or candy. A light smear of red . . .

Red.

Blood. There's a smear of blood on our back door. I grab the handle and have to forcibly stop myself.

I take out my phone to dial 911. Then I reconsider, pocket the phone, and pull my gun instead. I slide the door as carefully as I can.

Inside, it's cool and dark. Quiet, too. Completely quiet. My heart thuds faster.

What have I done?

What the *hell* have I done?

Led Orbec to Paul, that's what I've done. I traipsed off after my escape at Beth Kenner's, and I'd been so pleased with myself. No need to rush and call Paul. No need to rush and call the police. The situation is under control.

I take a deep breath. Plenty of time for self-recriminations later. Right now, I need to focus.

Ahead, I see a lamp on the floor, the shade knocked off. Signs of a struggle.

Don't run. Just keep moving. Be careful and keep moving.

I continue into the living room. And there is Gayle, sprawled on the carpet. I race to her. There's no sign of blood. No sign of injury either. She's breathing fine, sound asleep.

I grab Gayle by the shoulder. She wakes, flailing, her eyes wide.

"Where's Paul?" I say.

She looks around, as if expecting to see him standing there.

"Where is Paul?" I repeat.

She blinks. "He-he took him. The man. The one who broke . . ." She seems to lose her train of thought and rubs at her temple, wincing.

"Where is he now?"

"I have no idea," she snaps. "You're the one who brought that man into his house."

"What man? Describe him."

She describes Hugh Orbec. Then she goes on to say that Orbec broke in and knocked her out, and the last thing she remembers, he was telling Paul to come along. Orbec was taking him hostage. That's when she lost consciousness.

As she's telling me this, I search for a note. If Orbec took Paul, he's left a note.

As I hunt, Gayle follows me, still talking. "I don't know what kind of hold you have over Paul, but he cannot break free of it. God knows, I've tried. It took months to even get him on a date, and then he's dragging his feet every step of the way."

"And you didn't take a hint?" I say as I check the kitchen counters.

She glares at me. "I knew what he needed. I knew what Charlotte needed. I just had to make him realize it. I finally start seeing progress, and then you slam back into his life like a tornado. All of a sudden, I can't do anything right. I fix your mess with the princess tea, and he tells me I handled it wrong, that I should have encouraged you to go despite not being dressed for it. I invite Charlotte to my daughter's party, and he accuses me of planning it at the last minute."

I'm barely listening, too focused on finding that note. If Orbec took Paul hostage, he must have left something for me. A threat. A warning. An ultimatum.

Gayle keeps talking. "Sunday evening, he calls to say you're in trouble and staying here for the night. He asks if I can take Charlotte the next day. I'm not happy about you sleeping over, but I suck it up. I figured I'd deal with that later. The next morning, he calls and ends it. Breaks it off. No explanation. Just 'it's not working out.'"

"And that's why you sent the video?"

She looks at me.

"I know you sent it," I say. "I saw your car in it. Paul did, too. He confronted you. Didn't he?"

She chews on that for a moment, deciding which angle to play here. Then she spits, "Yes. All right? I sent it to protect Paul from his crazy ex. To show him how dangerous you are. What kind of danger you pose to his daughter."

I spin on her. "Danger I pose? The only threat against our daughter was that video. Which *you* made. You call me craz—" I bite it off and head for the back door. "If Paul dumped you, that's on you. I can tell you one thing, though. Now that he knows who sent that video, you don't have a hope in hell of getting him back."

"And you'll make sure of that?"

"I won't need to," I say as I head out the back door.

THIRTY-FIVE

I'm in Paul's car, trying to decide my next move, fighting against absolute panic, when Orbec calls.

"I believe I have something of yours," he says when I answer.

"Do you really think this is going to work?" I say. "I know who you are. All I have to do—"

"—is call the police? Do you really think *that* is going to work? Leave the cops out of this, and I won't hurt your husband, Aubrey."

"You already have. I saw the blood."

A short laugh. "That would be mine. He punched me in the nose. I have no interest in you or him. What I want is that data."

"What data?"

"Don't play coy. You're a friend of Kimmy's. You know exactly what's going on here."

"*Friend*? I met her once, for ten minutes, in a park—"

"Do you honestly expect me to believe that? The police didn't, did they? They thought you were a whackjob. I know better. You're a friend of Kimmy's, and you know what's going on, and you're trying to help her and the boy. It's too late for her, but I'm going to tell you how you can help Brandon—and your husband."

"I'm telling you, I don't know Kim—"

"So you did all this for a stranger? A woman you met, as you say, for ten minutes? No one does that. Stop prolonging this conversation. I will call again in an hour. You will have the data. We will trade. You'll get your husband and something else you've been looking for."

"Brandon? Are you telling me you have—?"

He hangs up.

Hugh Orbec thinks I'm a friend of Kim's. He thinks I'm involved in this, that I know her and I've been pretending to be a stranger caught up in it to help her and Brandon. Because that's the obvious answer. If I wasn't so freaked out, I'd laugh. This is what I get for playing Good Samaritan. For being the person who stops to help. It's so far outside Orbec's experience that he's rejected the possibility. I must know Kim. I must know about her situation with Denis Zima. I must know about the "data"— whatever the hell that is.

No, wait, I do know what it is. Kim's insurance policy. That must be it. Now I'm supposed to find this "data" and hand it over? Mission impossible.

I'm barely off the phone when Laila Jackson calls. I want to answer that call. I want to answer it so badly. *Ten minutes earlier, Laila, and I could have told you everything.* Now I don't dare. She leaves a message. I don't even retrieve it.

I call the number Kim had for Orbec. He doesn't answer. I consider pleading my case, my ignorance, but I know that'll do no good. Worse, he might punish Paul for it.

I try Beth Kenner next. Yes, she's part of all this, but she was a social worker. There must be a streak of goodness in her that I can appeal to, more than I could with Orbec. At least I can ask her what he's looking for exactly.

I call the number. The line is disconnected.

I could go there. Confront her . . . if she's home, which I doubt. She knows I might come back.

That leaves one option. The riskiest of all. Stop playing with the hired help, and go straight to the top of the food chain.

Earlier, I told Paul I wouldn't do anything as crazy as confront Denis Zima. Now I'm convinced that's exactly what I need to do.

Finding Zima is easy. Men like him don't hide.

To locate him, I make a few calls. Tell a few lies. Concoct a few stories. And soon learn that Zima is at Zodiac Five, working for the day.

So he's working, maybe clearing some paperwork . . . while his thug menaces me and kidnaps my husband. Just another day at the office for Denis Zima.

When I return to the club, I see that I missed a potential escape route Saturday night. There's a fire escape with a second-floor emergency exit. I get up onto that and pick the door lock. It's easy enough—it seems Zima's security team still hasn't brought the place up to the boss's standards.

I'm stepping into the hall when Laila calls again. My phone vibrates loud enough that I quickly back onto the fire escape and shut it off.

I reenter the club. The upper hall is dark, the only light coming from under the office door. I creep to it, gun in hand. Then I put my ear to the wood. I hear the clackity-clack of someone striking a keyboard with typewriter force. It's fast spurts, patter-patter-patter, pause, patter-patter-patter, pause. At that speed, I'm wondering if it's someone else. Denis Zima doesn't strike me as the kind of guy who took keyboarding in high school.

A phone rings, and whoever's in the office lets out a curse. He answers. I've never heard Denis Zima speak, but this does seem to be him—he's telling someone in security that if the work isn't done this week, they're out of a job. He hangs up and grumbles under his breath. Then back to typing.

If there were anyone else in the room, I'd expect some conversation after that call. The silence tells me he's alone. Still, I only crack the door a half inch, enough to peer through. Zima sits at the desk, intent on whatever he's typing on a laptop. There's no sign of anyone else.

Zima pauses. Thinking through his next words. When he attacks the keyboard with fresh ferocity, I use the clatter of those keys to push open the door. He never even notices. When he pauses, though, he goes still. He doesn't look my way, but I know he senses someone there. I expect him to reach for a holstered gun. Instead his hand slides toward a closed drawer.

"Stop," I say.

His chin jerks up, as if he's surprised by my voice. Surprised by the gender of it, I presume. Then he looks over, and his eyes widen before his brow furrows. As he stares at me, I lock the door behind my back.

"You're . . . the woman from the video?" His voice inflects, as if he must be wrong.

"Surprised I actually showed up? You have my husband. I'm not going to cry in a corner, hoping you'll be nice and give him back."

His face screws up. "What?"

I move forward, gun pointed at his forehead. "If you're stalling in hope of rescue, I'd strongly advise you to reconsider. You have my husband. I can't get you what you want in exchange. So I'm a little short on options. If I hear footsteps outside that door, this turns into a hostage situation with a woman too desperate to control her trigger finger."

"I'm not stalling, Ms. . . ." He struggles, as if to remember. "Finch, right? Ms. Finch? If I'm acting confused, it's because I am. I don't have your husband. I have no idea—"

"Hugh Orbec."

He stops. "Sure, I know Hugh. He works for me. He's a friend."

"He's also your hired gun. He broke into my house two hours ago and took my husband. He left a witness who described Orbec perfectly. I'd know, because I've met the man. First when he slammed me into a wall while I was out jogging Sunday night. Then today, when he tried to corner me at Elizabeth Kenner's house."

"Elizabeth Kenner?"

I tell myself he's faking his confusion. He must be, even if it doesn't seem like it.

I push on. "The woman Kim trusted to take Brandon . . . well, until she didn't trust her. For good reason it seems."

"Brandon?" Something sparks in his eyes. "My . . . you mean my son? That's his name?"

That spark hits me square in the gut. There's no way to fake that look, that glimmer, the way he perks up, as if that's all he heard, the rest only white noise.

I take a split second to regroup. Then I plow forward again, because it's all I can do. Don't hang everything on a look. Acknowledge it and keep going.

"Hugh Orbec kidnapped my husband. He called me an hour ago and said if I gave him the data, he'd return Paul."

"Data?"

"Kim's insurance policy."

When he still looks confused, I say, "Whatever she took when she left you."

He pauses. Then his eyes go wide, and he lets out a string of curses. Again, his surprise doesn't seem faked. Not unless he's an Oscar-caliber actor playing a two-bit mobster.

My gut twists. What if I'm wrong? What if I've miscalculated completely?

Keep going. That's all I can do. Just keep going.

I say, "The problem is that I don't know where to find this insurance policy. I don't even know *what* it is. I only know Kim took something from you because Beth Kenner said so."

"Beth . . . ?"

His confusion still seems real. All his reactions seem real, and I want to tell myself they aren't, but my gut says that Denis Zima hasn't the faintest clue what I'm talking about.

If he doesn't know about Paul's kidnapping, though, that means Orbec isn't acting on his boss's orders. So what the hell is going on here?

Keep going. Let this play through and hope I can figure it out.

"Beth is Elizabeth Kenner," I say. "Kim's former social worker. She'd retired and moved to Chicago. I think that's why Kim moved here. Because she trusted Beth. Wrongly, as it turns out. But the point is that Kim took something of yours and Orbec wants it back, and I have no idea what he's talking about, so I'm kind of screwed."

"The thumb drive," he murmurs, as if to himself.

"Thumb . . ."

"USB drive. One of those—"

"I know what a thumb drive is. I'm just confirming that's what you said. So when Kim left you, she took a thumb drive full of evidence that could send you to jail."

"Not me. My—" He stops short and straightens. "It was my

drive. I took the data from someone else. I'd been planning to use it but . . ."

I remember what Paul said. "It's the evidence against your family."

His head shoots up.

I go on. "I've done my homework. Six years ago, you offered evidence to the feds. Evidence against your family. Then you changed your mind. I'm guessing that was a tactic to spook your father, to get something you wanted."

He shakes his head. "No, it was a tactic to get the hell away from my family, once and for all. Only it backfired. They threatened Kimmy. So I changed my mind. Then when Kimmy left, she took the drive. For insurance, I guess. I couldn't blame her. I just . . . The thought that she might have been pregnant? That she left because she was scared of my family?" He runs his hand through his hair. Then he throws it off and straightens again. "Does Hugh have my son?"

"Don't know. Right now, don't care. He has my husband, and that's my primary concern. So there's a USB drive that contains incriminating data you compiled after you got tired of working in the family business."

"I *never* worked in the family business." His voice is sharp, emphatic, eyes bright with anger.

"You ran an underage strip club—"

"I was young. I was stupid. I believed the girls when they said they were eighteen. Yeah, young and stupid, okay? A strip club with eighteen-year-olds isn't exactly a business to be proud of, but in my family, that bar's set pretty damned low. To me, that *was* going legit. It was also an enterprise my parents supported. They helped me set it up. Then I found out they were using it as a front for—" Again, he cuts himself off. "I found out my club wasn't as legal as I thought. So I closed it down and started the Zodiacs. Which *are* legit. Or they damned well better be. If Hugh . . ."

He gives his head a shake, that anger surging again. "What the hell am I saying? Of course my parents have their fingers in the Zodiacs. I was a damned fool. *Again*."

He takes a deep breath and looks at me. "Hugh was my parents' employee. They gave him to me for the strip clubs. We became friends. He comes from the same place I do, just lower on the totem pole. He wanted out, too. Or so he said. So when I broke it off with my parents, Hugh came with me. I *trusted* him."

I'm still struggling to keep up here, to work it out, so I say, "You think he's been working for your parents all along. *They're* the ones who want the USB drive back, and they're using him to get it. He's doing this for them, not for you."

"Definitely not for me, that son of a bitch. I only wanted him to find my son. I thought he—Brandon—was out there somewhere, maybe taken by whoever killed Kimmy."

Zima pushes to his feet. I jump forward with "Uh-uh," gun still raised, and he seems to struggle to focus on it, as if he's distracted, forgetting the whole held-at-gunpoint situation.

When he realizes it, he waves me off. "You don't need that. I'm going to handle this. I'll call—"

I stop him as he reaches for his phone. "Explain first."

"The main thing right now is getting your husband and Brandon back. I'm going to call Hugh. He might be my parents' man, but I've got enough dirt on him to make him give back whoever he has."

I nod. "Go ahead, but I'm listening."

"I know." He hits speed dial. Listens. Then curses and hangs up. Tries again. Curses again.

"Not answering, is he?" I say.

"No, and I won't even bother leaving a message. That was his one and only chance to straighten this out. Now I go to my parents."

"They're in Chicago?"

He nods. "They came to celebrate the opening. Or I *thought* that's why they were here."

I'm putting it all together. "Hugh saw Kim in Chicago. He called your father, who had her killed."

Zima goes still. His hand reaches blindly, finding and gripping the desktop. He looks as if he's going to be sick, and I realize he hadn't connected the dots that far. He closes his eyes and takes a deep breath, composing himself.

When he speaks again his voice is low and controlled but strumming with anger. "I will handle this."

"I really don't have any idea where that drive is. Hugh is convinced I knew Kim, and that she told me about it. But I only met her once. I just got caught up in this."

He nods but doesn't seem to hear me, still lost in his thoughts, in his grief and anger.

"I don't care about the drive," he says. "This is about my son."

"And my husband."

He nods, but again, it's distracted. "I'll get him back for you. Everything will be fine. My father will listen to me. I'll straighten this out."

He walks away before I can say another word.

THIRTY-SIX

I go after Zima . . . at least to make sure we exchange numbers. Then he's gone, hell-bent on his mission.

I don't trust him.

But I do believe him when he says he had nothing to do with killing Kim or kidnapping Paul. His confusion and anger and grief were genuine. His story is true. The part I don't trust is him saying he'll get Paul back for me. Oh, he'll try, but that's not his priority. Brandon is. Zima's family is his responsibility, and my family is mine.

Orbec calls as I reach the car. Again I try reasoning with him. Try telling him I don't know anything about this "data." He won't even hear me out. I have one more hour to find it. One more hour until he calls. Then I'm out of time.

I need that USB drive. I have no damned idea where it is. I can't imagine Kim stashing it in the farmhouse. She'd find a safe place where they'd never look. . . .

I flash back to that first day in the park, when I met Kim. She'd been playing a hiding game with Brandon, and I'd noticed, thinking it'd be a fine game to play with Charlotte. I'd watched her hiding a small object . . . an object the size of a USB drive.

She'd been trying to find just the right spot for the drive. One Brandon couldn't easily figure out . . . meaning no one would accidentally see it. But also, I think, letting Brandon know where it was, in case it came to this, a situation where his life might depend on being able to find that drive. She made it an absolute last resort. If something happened to her and he was taken into safe custody, then he was better off not knowing about the drive. But if he was taken hostage and questioned properly—*do you remember Mommy hiding something about this size*—he'd think of the park.

It was an imperfect plan. So imperfect that clearly it'd gone wrong. Either his captors weren't asking Brandon the right questions or he wasn't around to—

No, I wouldn't think of that.

Get the data. That was my goal. Pray that I wasn't making wild and desperate connections. Pray that USB drive was where I thought it would be.

I'm in the park. I've driven back to Oxford, watching to be sure I'm not tailed. Laila has called twice. I haven't heard from Zima. I doubt I will. I suspect that even if he manages to get Paul away from Orbec, I'll hear from Paul instead, Zima too concerned with finding his son and settling a score with his parents.

I saw Kim play her hiding game in a small patch of forest. On the drive here, I mentally move past the "finding the USB" part and on to planning my next move. That's how easy I expected this search to be. It's a quarter acre of forest. I know what I'm looking for. It's a simple matter of retrieving the drive.

It is not a simple matter. A quarter acre seems tiny when

you're playing with a child. I remember once walking through this "forest" with Charlotte and laughing as she darted from tree to tree, hoping to spot a deer or fox. I remember thinking I really needed to get my daughter out of the city more often if this was her idea of wilderness.

Yes, this patch wouldn't hide a herd of deer, but it's more than a few trees. It's dozens of them, plus fallen logs and piles of dead leaves and pockets of brush. After ten minutes of wild searching—under this log, in this knothole—I stop and force myself to proceed methodically. Check every tree for knotholes. Lift every log and fallen branch. Forget the leaf piles for now—if I were Kim, I'd pick a spot he'd remember, and a random leaf pile wasn't good enough.

I'm still searching when my phone rings. I think it'll be Laila again, and I'm ready to ignore it when I see that it's Orbec. I check the clock. It's been fifty-five minutes.

"You said an hour," I say when I answer.

He gives a chuckle. It sounds strained, but it's probably just the connection. "If you don't have it by now, you won't have it in the next five minutes, Aubrey. Did I make a mistake taking your *estranged* husband? Are you hoping I'll kill him? Save you the hassle of a divorce?"

"If that's a joke, it's not funny."

"Good. I read the situation correctly. You want him back, which means you have the drive—"

"I don't have your drive, asshole. I met Kim *once*. Maybe you can't imagine a stranger getting involved in this, but take a closer look at your life and consider the possibility that's just you."

"No, I'm quite certain it's not. If you're stalling—"

"Yes." I check yet another knothole. "Yes, I *am* stalling. Because I'm hunting for this damned drive. I have a good idea where it is. That's detective work, not insider information. I'm searching for it right now."

"I don't believe you."

I let out a string of profanity that makes him chuckle again.

"You have quite the mouth on you, Aubrey. Not exactly the nice little librarian you pretend to be."

"Give me another half hour."

"I'm not giving you another half minute—"

I let out a grunt of pain that stops him short. I've stubbed my toe, walking with my gaze on the trees. I look down to see a rock. A rock beside a depression. A rock that has been moved.

While Orbec blusters, I bend and move the rock. There, under it, is a small black box. My hands shake as I take it out. I open it to see . . .

"I found it!" I say. "I have the drive."

I swear I hear Orbec exhale in relief. Apparently, I'm not the only one who needs this data. If he doesn't get it, he'll be in deep trouble with his boss . . . a guy who solves problems with bullets.

"Describe it," he says.

"Thumb drive. Silver swing top. Blue base. There's lettering . . . Zima Auto Body."

He definitely exhales now. "That's it. Bring—"

"I want to speak to my husband."

"You'll *see* him soon."

"I don't trust you. Let me speak to him, or I turn this over to the feds."

A growl of frustration. Footsteps. A door creaks.

"Mr. Finch, please tell your wife you are fine."

"Aubrey?" Paul's voice comes from the distance. "Call the police. I don't care what he's told you. Just call—"

The door slams shut. Orbec walks away, and Paul's muffled voice falls to silence.

"I trust you will not take his advice," Orbec says.

"Not unless I have to," I say. "But I'll be ready to. You give me the slightest reason to think you're going to screw me over, and I have the cops on speed dial."

I expect him to threaten me, but he only says, "Fine. I'm not going to cheat you, Aubrey. Like you said, you know who I am. This is a dangerous game we're both playing, and we just want it over with. I'm going to give you an address and exactly enough time to get there. You'll give me the drive. I'll give you your husband. If you don't do anything stupid, this will be painless. You have my word on that."

I try not to snort. Then I say, "And Brandon?"

"We'll discuss that."

"Do you have Brandon?"

"He's fine. Now, meet me—"

"If it's a back alley in Chicago, the answer is no."

"This isn't a gangster movie, Aubrey. I have nothing to gain by hurting you or your husband. I just want the drive. Give me that, and everyone's life gets a whole lot easier. Mine included. We're going to meet in a park. You seem to like parks."

I say nothing.

He tells me which park and which visitor lot, and then says, "It's a public enough place. I'm not driving up with your hubby in a gag and cuffs. He'll be riding shotgun. I'll park. You'll pull in beside me. We'll do the exchange there, and for all anyone will know, it's just a guy switching cars. No cloak-and-dagger crap. Okay?"

"Okay."

I drive straight to the park. When I enter the visitors' lot, I see Orbec's Charger pull into a spot, as if he timed my arrival. He's down at the end, under a huge oak, away from the other cars. There's one couple tugging a jogging stroller from their SUV.

Otherwise, while the lot is dotted with cars, there are no people. Relatively public, like he promised.

I pull in beside his car. Paul's in the passenger seat. He tries to smile for me. It's strained, but he looks fine.

Orbec lowers the passenger window. "See? He's okay. Now, he's going to reach out, and you're going to put the drive in his hand. He passes it to me. Then he gets out."

I look at Paul. He finds that weak smile again and mouths, "It's okay."

"Where's Brandon?" I ask.

Orbec sighs. "You just don't give up, do you? Brandon is fine. Hubby here has seen him, yes?"

Paul nods.

Orbec continues. "I have the number for his aunt Ellie, from Beth. As soon as I've verified the data on this drive, I'll place that call, and Ellie can come and get him."

"Not good enough."

His brows arch. "Excuse me?"

"I don't trust you, so here's the new plan. I give you the drive, and you let Paul go. He leaves with this car. I go with you to verify the drive, and then I take Brandon for Ellie."

Paul's mouth opens, and I brace for him to object. But then he meets my gaze, and he nods. He knows I need to do this, and he will not interfere, and God, I love him for that.

Orbec is muttering under his breath. Uncomplimentary things, I'm sure, but he doesn't object either. He just glares at me and says, "If you *aren't* a friend of Kim's, then you're a crazy bitch, you know that?"

"No, I'm a mom. And since Brandon's mother can't help him get home, I will."

He goes quiet at that and then nods. A moment of silence, before he sighs and looks past Paul to me. His voice is softer when he says, "Look, I know how this seems, but it's not like that. You don't need to come with me. I'll get Brandon to his auntie. All I need is that USB drive, and everyone will be safe."

"I don't care. I can't trust you."

"Fine. Paul, get that drive from your wife, and then you two swap places."

Paul shakes his head. "If Aubrey goes, I go."

"*What?*" Orbec says.

"You heard me. If Aubrey goes with you, so do I."

"Oh, hell, you two make a great pair. So I get the USB and an *extra* hostage? You do understand that's not how ransom works, right?"

"If Paul stays, that's his choice," I say. "But I'm not handing over the drive. I'm getting into your backseat with it. You'll take me to Brandon, where I will verify integrity of the drive while you watch. Then I walk away with Brandon."

Orbec throws up his hands. "Fine. You're both nuts, but fine. Let's do this."

THIRTY-SEVEN

Paul insists on sitting in the backseat with me. He holds my hand, and I try to apologize, but he stops me.

"I'm all right," he says, our voices quiet, muffled by the rumble of the car. "Everything's all right. Brandon's fine. I've seen him. Whatever's going on here, he's not in danger. He's a bargaining chip. That's all."

"Gayle's okay, too," I say, whispering so Orbec doesn't overhear.

He makes a face, like he's about to say he doesn't care before he stops himself.

"I know what she did," I say, "with the video."

He leans in to whisper back. "I should have told you when I thought I recognized her car. I just couldn't believe it. I had to confront her." He shakes his head and continues, his voice still low. "Gayle wasn't . . . I'm not even sure what she was. She pursued me, and I gave in, and I hope part of it wasn't me trying to make you jealous, but I honestly don't know."

"I think, to be jealous, I'd have to feel like I could compete. She seemed perfect for you. After what I did to you, I wanted to make amends, and if that meant forcing myself to be happy that you were with someone who made *you* happy . . ."

"She didn't."

His hand tightens again, holding mine tighter now. Am I hoping for more? A declaration? Of course I am. But what I have is this—that he's coming with me, staying at my side, holding my hand. That's enough for now.

We take a convoluted route to our destination. I'm watching the position of the sun, and I can tell the car loops back on its route a few times. I try not to worry about that—it makes sense that Orbec wouldn't follow a straight path.

We leave the city and eventually arrive at a farmhouse not unlike the one where Kim had been living. It's a ramshackle two-story home surrounded by forest and field. Paul nods to me, confirming this is where he'd been before. Orbec takes us inside without preamble. He steps in and calls, "Lynn?"

A young woman opens a door and peeks out warily.

"Bring the boy," he says.

She retreats and returns with Brandon. He looks wan, with dark circles under his eyes, but he's obviously been cared for, his clothing new, his hair and face clean. When he sees Paul, he smiles and runs over. Then he spots me and skids to a stop. He blinks.

"You're . . . you're the mom from the park," he says. "You did cartwheels."

I nod. "I am."

The smile fades as he eyes me.

"This is my wife, Aubrey," Paul says. "She's here to get you back to your aunt Ellie."

Brandon perks up. "Aunt Ellie's here?"

"She's in the city," I say. "First, though . . . Before you saw me in the park, had you ever met me before, Brandon?"

His face scrunches in confusion. "No . . ."

I shoot a glare at Orbec, who only shrugs. Then Orbec says, "Go back with Lynn, Brandon. The grown-ups need to talk, and then Paul and Aubrey can take you home."

"I'll stay with him," Paul says. "I believe we have a game of Chutes and Ladders to finish."

Brandon lights up and takes Paul's hand, leading him to the other room. The young woman follows and starts to close the door behind them.

"Leave it open," I say.

She looks at Orbec, who nods. Once she's gone, I say, "Okay, get me a computer. I'll open the drive and confirm its integrity."

"Integrity?"

"Make sure the drive and the files aren't corrupted."

I can tell he still has no idea what I'm talking about, but he nods as if he does. Which tells me that if I do find problems, I don't need to let *him* know.

He brings out a laptop. I plug in the USB and confirm there are files on the drive. I run a quick disk scan. Everything comes up clean, and I show him the results.

"The drive is undamaged," I say. "Now open a few files to be sure it's the right one. I'll turn around. I don't even want to *see* what's on those."

I turn. After a few clicks, he says, "Yeah, it's the data."

"Good, so I get Brandon and you can deliver the drive to your boss."

He snorts. "My boss is the guy who made this damned drive. Denis. The idiot. Six years ago, I tried to tell him it was a stupid idea, but did he listen to me? Hell, no."

"I mean you can give it to your real boss. Denis's father."

"My *boss* is Denis Zima, Ms. Finch. I work for him, not his old man."

I look over sharply. "So Denis *was* behind this? *He* wants this drive?"

"He might, but it's going to his parents. Denis is my friend, and I look after my friends."

"I can see that. Was killing Kim and kidnapping Brandon for his own good, too? With friends like you, Denis Zima sure as hell doesn't need enemies."

Orbec glares at me. "You think you've got it all figured out, don't you? I'm the thug here. I'm the bad guy. The one who murders innocent girls and kidnaps their babies. You look at me, and you think you know all about me."

He steps toward me. "I don't work for Denis's parents. I didn't kill Kimmy. I didn't want to take her little boy. You tell me you got caught up in this, stuck in the middle of someone else's problem? Well, maybe you aren't the only one."

He eases back. "Papa Zima found out Kimmy was living near Chicago. I still have friends in his organization, and they warned me. I tried to warn her. I offered to help, but no, she had her own plans. She didn't trust me. I knew whatever plans Kimmy had, they weren't good enough. So I used her phone records to track down Beth Kenner. When I couldn't make *her* see reason either, I intercepted their plans for Brandon. Beth was supposed to pick him up at the park, but I beat her to it. Beth started listening to me then . . . or she did after those bastards got to Kimmy."

"So you and Beth Kenner have been working together to hold Brandon in protective custody. Until when? What was your end game?"

He waves the drive. "This, obviously. Find the data. Give it to Papa Zima. Back him off. Then call Kimmy's sister and give her the boy, preferably without Denis ever knowing he had a son. Which is a lousy thing to do to a friend, but it was for the kid's own good. Denis's, too. Denis's parents would hold the kid over his head, leverage to get Denis back into the fold."

"And now that Denis knows about Brandon?"

"We'll figure that one out. For now, I have this." He raises the drive. "And you can have the boy. I'll give you a lift back to the city."

"Thanks, but no. I think we'll take it from here."

He shrugs. "Suit yourself. Brandon? Come on out. It's time to go home."

We have Brandon. Orbec offers again to drive us to the city, but he doesn't seem surprised when we refuse. Whatever his motivations, he is still the one who took Paul and threatened me, and now that I have what I came for, I'm getting the hell out. Paul agrees.

We walk onto the front porch.

"At the end of the drive, turn left," Orbec says as he steps onto the porch with us. "It's about a mile to a gas station. You can get a cab to pick you up there. Don't get any ideas about calling the cops. Please. That'll just make this a lot more complicated than it needs to be."

"I have what I wanted," I say.

"Good. Then get going—"

"Yes," says a voice behind me. "You and your husband should go. The boy stays with me."

Paul and I both wheel to see a woman walking from the forest. She's about fifty, tall and sturdy . . . and flanked by two men with guns. Two more men appear around the other side of the house.

"Don't, Hugh," she says. "You know that's a very bad idea."

Orbec goes still, hand poised over his gun. He slowly withdraws it.

"Mama Zima," Orbec says. "I was just about to come see you and Papa. I have something you want."

He holds up the USB drive.

"Excellent," she says. "But you actually have *two* things I want. I'll take the drive . . . and I'll take my grandson."

Orbec shakes his head. "He's not your grandson, Mama. He's just Kimmy's kid. She got knocked up after she left Denis. I took him, in hopes she'd turn over the drive in exchange, but someone else got to her first. Luckily, these two cared enough about the brat to make the trade."

"So this isn't my son's boy?"

"If Denis got Kimmy knocked up, she'd have ridden that train to the end. Sunk her hooks even deeper into Denis and never let go. Nah, this is just some brat—"

"Liar."

I don't see the gun in Mama Zima's hand until that hand rises, that gun firing. I wheel toward Paul and Brandon. Paul's lunging to shield me, but the shot whizzes past. Orbec falls. I scoop up Brandon, who's frozen. Paul shoves us both back through the still-open door. I'm running for cover when I realize Paul isn't behind me. I wheel, nearly dropping Brandon. Paul's there, slamming shut the dead bolt.

Outside, Mama Zima laughs. "Do you really think that's going to help? Give me my grandson, and I'll let you leave, but if I have to come in there after you . . ."

She doesn't bother finishing the threat. I give Brandon to Paul and take out my gun as I yank open an interior door. Behind it, Lynn stumbles back through what looks like a living room. She has her hands raised.

"Pl-please, don't—" she begins.

I shush her and whisper, "Where's the basement?"

She points. So do I . . . with the gun, aiming it at her.

"Where *exactly*?" I say.

She tells me.

I shove her toward the sofa. "Hide there. Don't come out."

I race into the hall, where Paul's waiting. Outside, Mama Zima is ordering her men to surround the house.

"Basement," I call to Paul, then I shut the living room door . . . and hustle them to the stairs leading up instead.

Paul has Brandon in his arms. The boy hasn't said a word. He's spent his lifetime hiding, and he only peeks at me over Paul's shoulder, and then buries his face in it as Paul whispers reassurances.

We get up the stairs just as the front door opens. Paul glances back at me, but I only motion for him to move farther down the hall. Then I stop him and start checking rooms. Below, I hear someone say, "It's me."

Lynn comes out from her hiding place and starts talking quickly to Mama Zima, telling her we're in the basement. Is she ratting us out in hopes of winning her freedom? Or is she the one who *brought* Denis's mother here? Either is equally likely, and I'm not the least bit surprised to hear her.

The third door opens to another staircase, ascending into a dark attic. I wave Paul over.

"Take him up there," I whisper. "I'll handle this."

"I'll find him a place to hide," Paul says. "Then I'm coming to help you."

I shake my head. He opens his mouth to protest, but I grip his arm.

"I have a gun," I say. "You do not. I need you to stay with Brandon. Please. Call the police and stay with him."

He still hesitates, and I know he wants to argue, but he also knows this is the right plan. Finally, he gives an abrupt nod and says, "Don't engage. Just stall."

I nod and start to go.

He grips my arm. "Be careful."

I lean in to kiss his cheek. "I will."

THIRTY-EIGHT

Below, Mama Zima is telling someone to check downstairs. Two sets of heavy footfalls retreat. That means two men are in the house and two are patrolling outside. Mama herself stays on the main level. Once the footsteps retreat down the steps, she says to Lynn, "Go outside. Wait in the car."

Lynn's footsteps head toward the front door. A shot fires. A body thuds to the floor, and I close my eyes, forcing my hammering heart to slow.

Mama Zima shot Orbec. Killed him without warning. Now she's killed a girl who helped her, a girl who'd probably been on her payroll the whole time.

She will not hesitate to shoot me.

Shoot me. Then go after Paul and Brandon, and if she does that, I have no doubt of what will happen to Paul. Another loose end to be clipped off. That's all he is to her. All we are.

What the hell have I done? What have I gotten my family into?

I thought I had this under control. I thought Hugh Orbec was the worst thing I had to deal with, and he was the sort of person I'd dealt with before. A thug. A man who would use force to get his way, but a man who could be reasoned with, a man who had no justification for killing me and therefore would not.

That isn't what I'm dealing with now.

I have never encountered anything like what I'm dealing with now.

I am not prepared for it. I don't know how to prepare for it. I don't know—

Breathe. Just breathe.

Two options here.

Retreat upstairs and hope Paul managed to contact the police, and they are on their way and will arrive before Mama Zima's thugs find us.

Or confront the problem.

I'm not a fool. I know I can't take on five armed criminals. The police are my best bet, and the only question is how I'll stall. Whether my best hope for stalling is defense or offense.

Offense.

I don't really have a choice here. To retreat puts Paul at risk. To confront means putting myself at risk, and praying that will buy enough time for the police to arrive. If that costs me my life, well, it's better than costing us both ours. Better than robbing our daughter of both her parents.

Distract. Stall.

Pray.

I start my descent. The problem with coming down a set of stairs? Mama Zima below will see my feet long before I spot *her*. So I try to angle myself away from the bannister, and with every step, I duck to get a look. I also listen. I can hear the men downstairs. I don't know how big the basement is, but there's a limited amount of time they'll spend down there before realizing they've been duped.

What I don't hear is Mama Zima. I take another two steps and then spot her shadow stretching across the floor. She's right around the corner. As soon as I come down, she'll see me.

So much for the element of surprise.

I'll need to go big. Hope to startle her and dodge and keep dodging.

While she shoots at me? While the sound of my running feet brings the thugs racing upstairs?

This isn't going to work. It cannot—

Deep breath.

I take out my phone. I need to text Paul. Make sure he's summoned the police and maybe find out how long—

There's no cell signal.

My phone has no signal.

No.

Oh God, no.

Either there's no signal here or they've blocked it.

Of course they've blocked it, you idiot. Otherwise they wouldn't be taking their time searching. They'd know we would call for help.

Movement flickers below. It's Mama Zima's shadow . . . moving away.

I close my eyes and strain to listen. For a big woman, she walks with very little noise, but she's definitely moving in the opposite direction.

Maybe if she continues into another room—

No maybes. No hopes. No prayers.

No waiting for the perfect opportunity.

I fly down the stairs as fast as I can. I'm leaping off the bottom step when she hears me. She starts to turn. I'm halfway to her, only a few feet left to go, but she's spinning, gun going up—

I slam into her. It's like hitting a brick wall, and all I can think is *You're a fool, Aubrey Finch. A stupid, senseless fool.* I've played my ace, throwing my entire body into hers, and she's barely stumbling.

Except she still does stumble. It's only a slight stagger, but I've caught her as she was turning, and her feet twist, and it's enough. I've knocked her off-balance. I slam into her again, and we go down with a crash.

Her gun flies up. I hit her arm and the gun snaps backward, but she doesn't drop it. I strike again, and this time, I'm off-target. I barely hit her. But her hand opens, eyes widening, and I realize I've struck her ulnar nerve.

The gun falls.

It clacks to the hardwood floor, but I only dimly hear it over the footsteps thundering up the stairs. The thugs have heard us fall, and they're coming.

I knock her gun away and yank out my own. Beneath me, she's struggling, bucking with formidable strength. But I have her pinned. Then I have the gun, pointed at her forehead, just as the basement door flies open.

"Stop!" I shout. "Guns down, or I pull this trigger."

The first man through the door hesitates. I press the gun into Mama Zima's head. She glowers at me and doesn't even flinch. But the thug notices. He sees my expression. And he holsters his gun.

"No," I say. "You're going to drop that. Then you'll go outside. Get your comrades. They'll toss their guns through the front door. Then you'll let us leave. All three of us."

"Do you really think they'll let you leave?" Mama Zima says.

"They will if I take you with me," I say.

"Then you'll need to deal with *me*."

"I guess I will." I look at the man. "Outside. Now."

He goes, and the other thug follows. Neither looks over at

Mama Zima, who's shooting them death glares and cursing in Russian.

"Hey, they're saving your life," I say.

"If they think so, they are mistaken." She raises her voice so they can hear. "You see that girl on the floor? That will be you."

"Maybe," I say. "But this gives them a chance to plead their case with your husband. Otherwise, if you don't survive this, I suspect they'll have more to worry about than a bullet in the back of the head."

"My husband is not the Zima they should worry about. They should know that. I am the one here for my grandson. You understand that. You are here with me, and I see no sign of *your* husband."

"Maybe so," I say as the door closes behind the two men, "but apparently, they don't dare go home without you. Now, you're going to roll over and put your hands—"

She bucks. I'm ready for it—I've been ready the whole time she's been talking—but when I go to shove her down, she kicks up instead, and that *does* catch me off-guard. When I teeter, she goes for the gun. I swing it against the side of her skull. It hits with a thwack, her head snapping sideways, but she only snarls and grabs my ponytail.

She yanks my head back. I let out a gasp and try to jerk free, but she's got my hair wrapped around her hand. Her other hand goes for the gun. I swing it up, out of her reach. At the last second, her hand chops downward instead, smacking me in the ribs.

I fall to the side. I'm focused on keeping the gun. That's all I care about. She never goes for it, though. She rolls from under me and lunges for her gun, lying on the floor.

I hear the thud of footsteps. I glance over just in time to see Paul running for her. He's going for the gun, to kick it away, but he's not close enough. Her fingers wrap around it, and she swings it up, barrel heading his way. I throw myself on her. The gun fires. With both hands, I grab her gun arm and wrench it back, thudding into the floor.

Mama Zima fights with everything she has, kicking and scratching. Paul has the gun, and he's staying far from the barrel as he pries her fingers away. She fires again. The shot goes wild, but the sound startles Paul. He relaxes his hold just enough for her to turn the gun his way—

I slam her arm into the floor. Paul wrenches the gun from her hand. Outside, there's a commotion. Shouting. Running footfalls. I scramble for my dropped gun, and I swing it up just as the door opens—

"Police!" Laila Jackson shouts. "Drop your weapons."

More officers push in behind her, and I still hear more outside, handling the thugs. I lift my hands and drop to my knees as the police rush in.

THIRTY-NINE

Laila gets Paul and me away from our guns. Then she focuses on Mama Zima and the thugs, letting us slip off to the side.

"Don't go *anywhere*," she says.

I nod. When I turn to Paul, I say, "You *did* call them."

"Actually, no." His voice wavers. He takes a deep breath and shakes it off. "I couldn't. When I realized I didn't have cell service, I found a spot to hide Brandon and snuck to the steps to make sure you were okay. You weren't, so I came down armed with . . ." He points at a broken chair leg, dropped by the fight scene, and gives me a wry smile.

"Thank you." I put my arms around his neck and kiss him. Then I pull back fast. "Sorry. I—"

He cuts me off with a deep kiss. A moment later, a throat clears behind us. We turn to see Laila.

"Mind if I interrupt?" she says.

"Yes," I say.

She gives me a hard look and waves for us to follow her.

"Brandon," Paul says. "He's hiding in the attic. May we get him? With an officer escort, of course."

Laila agrees and sends Paul to do it. I'm not going anywhere, apparently. Once he's gone, she leads me outside. Paramedics are loading Hugh Orbec into an ambulance.

"Is he . . . ?" I begin.

"Alive. For now." She turns her back on the paramedics and faces me. "Before you ask, it was Ellie Milano. She finally contacted me, and only because she was worried about you. Took me a while to get permission to track your cell to its last location. I'd like to say you're lucky we showed up but . . ." She glances back at the house and then says, grudgingly, "You seemed to be doing okay."

"No, trust me, I'm still glad you showed up."

"I could have helped a whole lot sooner," she says. "And I'd love to give you hell for that, but . . ." She sighs as she scans the yard, the officers taking the thugs into custody. "We got off to a bad start. I just didn't want you getting caught up in something dangerous. Glad to see *that* didn't happen."

"I'm sorry."

She shakes her head and keeps surveying the situation. "Helluva mess. Didn't know what you got yourself into, did you?"

"Nope, but I'm guessing you didn't either. No one's ever really prepared for gun-toting, mobster grannies."

She snorts at that. "I've heard stories about Mama Zima, but I'd almost be impressed . . . if she wasn't such a cold-blooded bitch."

Laila's about to speak again when Brandon appears at the doorway, clutching Paul's hand.

"And there's the cause of all this commotion," she says. "Looks pretty good for an imaginary boy. Poor kid. His aunt should be here—"

A police car rolls into the drive, the passenger door opening before it even stops. Ellie leaps out, and Laila says, "Perfect timing."

Paul lets go of Brandon, and he runs for his aunt, who scoops him up in a bear hug. As we watch, another car appears, this one a BMW roaring into the drive. Laila swears. Before she can move, Cooper appears at a jog, shouting orders. Officers train their weapons on the vehicle as Cooper yells for the driver to get out of it. He already is, and seeing him, Laila curses again.

It's Denis Zima. He has his hands on his head, but he's stepping away from the car. Cooper shouts for him to stop.

"He's okay," I say. "Or I think he is. Oh, hell, at this point, I'm not even sure."

"I just want to see my—" Zima begins. Then he spots Brandon. He stops and stares, and he wobbles, just a little. There's a moment of absolute silence. Then he turns to Cooper. "I was speaking to my father. He had no idea what I was talking about. That's when I realized he wasn't the one behind this."

Zima's gaze shoots to the front door as it opens, his mother coming out in handcuffs. Zima surges forward, fists clenched, but Cooper gets in his path. Zima rocks back. Then his gaze goes to Brandon.

"May I see . . . ?" he begins.

Ellie picks Brandon up again and heads toward Zima. I turn away and glance at Paul, who passes me a smile and starts for me.

"Go on," Laila says, jerking her chin toward Brandon. "Join the reunion. You're the one who made it possible."

I shake my head. "I'm done. This part's for them."

I walk to Paul instead, and he takes my hand as I collapse against his shoulder.

We don't just get to walk away after this. We have to give statements at the station, and it's hours before I'm released.

As I'm leaving, Laila comes jogging after me.

"You still owe me," she says.

I turn. "What?"

"You owe me a link to that sword-fighting class. You probably also owe me a lift to it. The least you can do, really, since I saved your ass."

"You saved my ass about as much as I solved your case, which is, I believe, about fifty-fifty of each. We're taking turns driving to class."

She gives me her personal email address, and we talk for another minute, and as I walk away, I think back to that moment in the park with Kim, when I thought she was someone I could talk to, someone I could relate to. I may have actually found that, just not in the place I expected.

I walk out to find Paul waiting. He says nothing, just takes my hand, fingers interlocking with mine, and leads me to the parking lot, where the officers let us bring our car earlier.

"How are you doing?" he asks when we reach the car.

"I'm glad it worked out but . . ." I shake my head and climb in the passenger side.

When he's in, I say, "I'm sorry. Yes, it all worked out, but I could have gotten you killed. I was in over my head. Way over my head."

He manages a smile. "Seems like you were swimming just fine. You didn't drag me in, Bree. We both underestimated the situation, but neither of us went in with our eyes closed. I'm a lawyer. I knew I was getting involved in something potentially dangerous, and I chose to do so."

I nod and say nothing, just turn to stare out the window.

He backs the car out. "I'm fine. Charlie's fine. You're fine. And so is Brandon."

I nod again.

He drives from the lot. A couple of minutes pass, and then he starts to say something, but I'm already speaking, saying, "Does this change anything?"

His fingers tighten on the wheel.

"I don't mean with us," I say. "You stuck by me, and you can't imagine how much I appreciated that, but I know it doesn't mean things have changed. I'm talking about Charlie. You knew what I was . . . and now you've seen what I can be. What I'm capable of. Does that change anything with her? With the custody? I know that after what's happened, you might not think I'm the most responsible parent, but I swear, I would never have done any of this with her around."

He nods. That's all he does. He nods, and my heart hammers. "Paul—"

"We'll discuss that later." He makes a sharp right. "First, I want to show you something."

As we ride in silence, I can barely breathe. When I asked if this changed his opinion of me as a mother, I was hoping he'd say of course not, that he'd acknowledge that I'd looked after Charlotte first, that he'd say he knows I'm a good mother. Instead, he's made that sharp—angry?—turn and ended the conversation.

He takes us to a new subdivision on the edge of Oxford. It's one I've never seen before. He drives onto a street of duplexes, a few inhabited, some still under construction. He pulls into the drive of a finished one with darkened windows. Then he gets out.

When I don't follow, he waves for me. I carefully climb from the car.

"What do you think?" he says.

It takes me a moment to realize he's talking about the duplex.

"It's . . . nice?" I say. "Is this . . . ? Do you mean as a possible place for me?"

He nods. I just keep looking from him to the duplex. Is this his way of saying he still wants to support me? Or is he changing the subject, distracting me from talk of custody?

"I . . . I'm not sure I could afford it," I say. "I have the down payment, but I should wait until I have a new job. I'll get a full-time one. I should—since I don't have Charlie to look after."

"Do you want Charlie to look after?"

My heart leaps, but I keep my expression neutral.

"In an ideal world, Bree, what would you want?" he says. "No pressure. No judgment. Full-time job? Full-time parent? Part-time both? Go back to school?"

"I . . ."

"Perfect world. Just tell me."

"I loved being home full-time but . . ."

"No judgment."

I take a deep breath. "In a perfect world, I'd stay home with Charlie and go back to school part-time. I'd let her go to day-care a couple of days a week because I think it's been good for her."

"Then that's what you'll do."

I nod. "Okay, I'll find a better apartment—"

"I'd like you to live here, Aubrey. The left-hand unit has a nice sunroom you can use as a study. The right-hand one is better for me—the office has a lousy view, which will keep me from getting distracted."

I turn to look at him.

"This is for us," he says. He steps toward me. "You're concerned that I don't want you parenting our daughter anymore. This is my answer. I found it yesterday, and I haven't changed my mind. I would like to change the custody arrangement. To this." He nods at the duplex. "Extreme co-parenting. If you'd be interested."

Tears prickle my eyelids. "I would absolutely be interested."

He shoves his hands into his pockets. "I'd love to just ask you to move back into the house, so we can try again, but even if you want to try again—"

"I do."

"Then I think we need to get to know each other first. Start over, and let me meet the real Aubrey." He looks up at the house. "Which will be a lot easier like this."

"I get to date the boy next door?"

He smiles. "Yes, I guess you do. And if it works . . ." He shrugs. "The neighborhood is a work in progress. It's a good investment. Easy to sell if we want closer quarters. I just don't want to rush. I'm sorry. I know that's not the most romantic solution—"

I throw my arms around his neck. "It's the perfect solution. Thank you."

He kisses me, a long and passionate kiss. When he pulls back, he says, "Will you come with me to get Charlie?"

"That depends. Think we can find a hotel along the way?"

His brows arch.

I grin. "Well, you did say you want to get to know me again. Not to rush or anything . . ."

"That doesn't sound like rushing at all. Perfectly logical." He puts his arm around my waist and leads me back to the car. "I'll tell my mother to expect us first thing in the morning."

DATE DUE

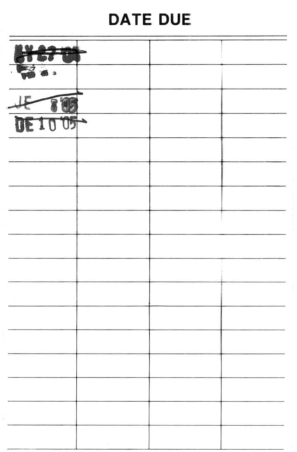

The American Social Experience Series
GENERAL EDITOR: JAMES KIRBY MARTIN
EDITORS: PAULA S. FASS, STEVEN H. MINTZ,
CARL PRINCE, JAMES W. REED & PETER N. STEARNS

MEDICAL MALPRACTICE IN NINETEENTH-CENTURY AMERICA

Origins and Legacy

KENNETH ALLEN DE VILLE

NEW YORK UNIVERSITY PRESS
NEW YORK AND LONDON
1990

Library of Congress Cataloging-in-Publication Data
De Ville, Kenneth Allen, 1955–
Medical malpractice in nineteenth-century America : origins and
legacy / Kenneth Allen De Ville.
    p.   cm. — (The American social experience series ; v. 19)
Includes bibliographical references.
ISBN 0-8147-1832-9 (alk. paper)
1. Physicians—Malpractice—United States—History—19th century.
I. Title.   II. Series.
[DNLM: 1. History of Medicine, 19th Cent.—United States.
2. Malpractice—history—United States.   WZ 70 AA1 D4m]
KF2905.3.D4   1990
346.7303'32'09034—dc20
[347.30633209034]
DLC
for Library of Congress   90-5823
                                    CIP

New York University Press books are printed on acid-free paper,
and their binding materials are chosen for strength and durability.

Book design by Ken Venezio

Contents

CONTENTS

Illustrations

Preface

A nineteenth-century physician commenting on malpractice law suits observed that "[t]he remedy of these evils in the profession involves many and grave problems in sociology which I cannot now stop to consider."[1] The writer was correct. The malpractice phenomenon, like other legal issues, was and is a reflection of social, cultural, and professional trends that have yet to be identified and explained. Neither nineteenth-century observers nor modern scholars in legal, medical, or social history have attempted to document and interpret the development of medical malpractice in America. Instead, scholars have made only passing reference to the issue and have failed to exploit a rich and multidimensional topic.

The short tradition of malpractice history began with Hubert Winston Smith's lengthy 1941 study in the *Journal of the American Medical Association*.[2] Smith explained basic legal doctrine to his readers and traced the genealogy of a twentieth-century American malpractice decision to its English common law ancestors. Smith's most valuable contribution to the discussion was his tabulation of all the American malpractice appellate cases between 1793 and 1940. Other writers have followed Smith's approach and used state appellate court decisions to understand the history of malpractice.[3]

But appellate decisions tell only part of the story. The majority of trial cases never reach an appellate court. Although useful, the information gleaned from these higher court decisions is uneven. Appellate courts deal primarily with legal doctrine and seldom provide detailed information about the mechanics of the trial or the life of the litigants. Moreover, the writers who have used these materials have tended to treat law and legal development as an entity divorced from the cultural contexts of specific times. Strictly linear tracing of cases often results in important omissions and limited insight into the causes and development of malpractice suits.

Although a few writers have begun to study twentieth-century malpractice, professional historians have virtually ignored it.[4] In 1969, Chester Burns recognized the research potential of the topic, identified the 1840s as the first outbreak of malpractice suits, and implicitly called for an investigation into its nineteenth-century roots.[5] Unfortunately, no one has expanded on Burns's work. General medical and legal historians occasionally mention increased malpractice litigation in the nineteenth century, and they have provided clues to its origins. William Rothstein, for example, explained that nineteenth-century malpractice rates increased as scientific advancements made objective evaluations of physicians possible.[6]

For the most part, however, lack of resources, both primary and secondary, has handicapped attempts to understand fully the history of medical malpractice. There are no studies that consider trial court decisions or local peculiarities. Quantitative approaches to the problem are restricted by the nature of trial court activity. Nineteenth-century trial records have sometimes disappeared, while the surviving ones are often inaccessible and seldom in good condition. A systematic tabulation of trial court cases would require a search of hundreds, if not thousands of locations and would be, according to one writer, "practically speaking, impossible."[7] Ultimately, smaller scale studies of individual states may be warranted but they will never provide a completely accurate report of the number of cases in nineteenth-century America.

Until recently, the secondary literature in several fields was not sufficiently developed to support a viable study of the issues surrounding the topic. Malpractice is neither solely a medical issue nor a legal one. It also has social, political, and religious components. Before the 1970s medical historians (with some notable exceptions) concentrated on great doctors, major diseases, or specific events. While their work was competent and valuable, they generally did not explore the ways in which medical practice and thought interacted with the cultural and political environment.[8] Similarly, traditional legal historians tended to emphasize "great cases" and major constitutional changes while ignoring the law's relationship with society, the market, and contemporary intellectual developments.

In the past two decades, however, both legal and medical historians, using fresh approaches, have explored new areas of research. They have examined law and medicine not as self-contained disciplines but as part of the society in which they exist. These new works help provide a perspective from which to view malpractice litigation. In addition, the enormous growth in social history and anthropological studies has enhanced understanding of the nineteenth-century world and provided important new insights. Because of this prodigious increase in secondary literature in a wide range of fields, a synthetic study of the origins of medical malpractice is now feasible.

Problems remain, but many can be overcome. When malpractice became a perceptible problem in the 1840s, medical journals published accounts and editorials on scores of malpractice suits. Some of these articles contained portions of trial transcripts, detailed descriptions of the treatment involved, and contemporary commentary. Sometimes physicians or disgruntled patients published pamphlets containing partial or full accounts of trials. Nineteenth-century physicians often discussed malpractice in their memoirs, and state medical societies regularly appointed committees to study the problem. By midcentury, medical and legal writers produced entire treatises and compendia on the subject. And, despite their deficiencies, appellate court decisions are a crucial source of information.

I do not intend to provide a comprehensive history of medical malpractice in the nineteenth century. The issues are so numerous and rich and the country so large and diverse that a full history is far beyond the reach of any single book. I do, however, hope to offer a historical discussion of the origins of modern medical malpractice. I am interested in presenting close-up pictures of medical and legal life, but I am equally concerned with identifying, and at least partially illuminating, the fundamental and topical causes of the phenomenon in America.

Acknowledgments

I have always considered myself lucky. In completing this book I have been fortunate enough to incur a wide range of debts, which I take great pleasure in recognizing.

Rice University history department provided consistent intellectual and financial support for this project and my general academic development. I am sincerely grateful. Vali, Michelle, and Douglas in the Rice University Fondren Library interlibrary loan department performed remarkable feats in acquiring often obscure materials. Inci Bowman of the University of Texas Medical Branch at Galveston and Elizabeth White and Linda Davenport of the University of Texas Health Science Center at Houston also helped me gather research and illustrations.

Many individuals have offered various types of help at different points of the project. Randy Sparks, Matt Taylor, and Bill Warren provided regular and essential encouragement. John Boles, Albert Van Helden, and Mary Winkler contributed valuable insights on many of the issues discussed in chapter 5. Members of the 1988–1989 Rice University Legal History Seminar, including Brian Dirck, Randall Jamail, Charles Robinson, James Schmidt, Patricia Tidwell, and Charles Zelden, read each chapter as it was completed; their comments were both helpful and charitable. Baruch Brody, Chester Burns, Elizabeth Heitman, James Kirby Martin, Steven Mintz, Mark Steiner, Albert Van Helden, and Martin Wiener all read various complete versions of the manuscript. They provided enormous editorial and intellectual aid.

My deepest gratitude and most profound respect are reserved for Harold M. Hyman. Harold played an integral role in the conception and completion of this project. More importantly, he guided and shaped my general academic and professional development. His example and tutelage have convinced me that opportunity, hard work, and discipline can yield undreamed of results and satisfaction.

Finally, I want to thank Chris Moore De Ville (who clearly had better things to do) for her unremitting support and saintly patience.

CHAPTER I

Before the Flood,
1790–1835

In March 1829 Dr. Asabel Humphrey instructed his student to vaccinate Harriet Landon for smallpox. The physician had been hired by the town of Salisbury, Connecticut, to vaccinate its citizens Humphrey's student made two punctures just above Landon's elbow joint. After the treatment Landon found that her lower arm was almost paralyzed. When her condition did not improve, she sued Humphrey for malpractice. After several witnesses, including a medical school professor, testified that the vaccination punctures were in a "very unusual place" and had caused irreparable injury, the jury awarded Landon $500 in damages. In reporting the case for the *Boston Medical and Surgical Journal*, an editorialist "confess[ed]" that he was "somewhat incredulous as to the justice of the decision" and declared that the case should "excite the astonishment of every medical man."[1]

By the mid–nineteenth century commentators in medical literature rarely expressed incredulity or astonishment when a patient sued a physician. They had begun to view the malpractice suit as a ubiquitous and possibly permanent fixture of medical practice. Before the late 1830s and early 1840s, however, malpractice cases had been rare in the United States, and physicians did not consider lawsuits a significant threat to their income or status. The social, political, legal, technological, and professional transformations that would eventually incite and sustain the malpractice phenomenon were underway, but they had not yet created the environment conducive to widespread prosecutions. The years from 1790 to 1835 were a period of relative judicial safety for the physician, and only isolated cases presaged the menace on the horizon.

"Not a Very Commendable Sight Anymore Than a Very Customary Sight"

While there is no accurate way to calculate the absolute number of malpractice suits in this or any other period, certain legal records, medical literature, and contemporary responses clearly illustrate the relative frequency or infrequency of the litigation. Soon after the American Revolution, individual compilers began publishing reports of all the cases decided in the appellate courts of the respective states.[2] Appellate reports did not record cases decided at the trial level but provided state supreme court rulings on lower court judgments. Appellate decisions were accepted elaborations and, occasionally, alterations of the common law and could be used as precedents in subsequent trial and appellate court cases. Therefore, appellate decisions are valuable sources of legal theory and doctrine.

Unfortunately, they are less useful for determining the exact number of malpractice cases at the trial level. A variety of legal, social, financial, and historical factors contributed to the decision to appeal a trial court ruling, and only a small percentage of trial judgments terminated in appellate court rulings. One writer developed a formula that suggested there were nine malpractice charges filed at the trial level for each reported appellate decision. Another study estimated that the proportion was 100:1.[3] The 9:1 ratio is an unreasonably low conjecture.[4] The 100:1 figure corresponds with some known nineteenth- and twentieth-century rates and is probably a better estimate. For example, an 1860 Ohio medical commentator on malpractice reported that there had been over 200 malpractice cases in the state while the Ohio supreme court had reported only two appellate court decisions regarding malpractice.[5] Still, the vagaries of appellate jurisprudence rob even the 100:1 figure of much of its certitude and utility.

Nevertheless, reported appellate decisions serve as a broad measure of the frequency of malpractice litigation. There were 216 appellate malpractice cases reported between 1790 and 1900. Out of the 216 total, only 5 cases, or 2.3 percent, were reported before 1835.[6] Despite the uncertainty involved in correlating appellate decisions to trial court judgments, the insignificant number of malpractice cases in the first third of the century contrasts sharply with the acceleration of reported decisions after 1840. Although the rate of increase intensified in the course of the nineteenth century and continued to soar in the twentieth, the initial increase in the late 1830s and early 1840s represented a fundamental break with the past. In the early part of the century malpractice suits were virtually nonexistent; after 1840 they became a prominent feature of the medical world.

The contrast between malpractice rates before and after the first third of the century is even more striking when these rates are compared to population increases. Between 1790 and 1840 the United States population grew 334 percent, from 3,929,214 to 17,069,453. During this period, the number of appellate malpractice decisions remained almost constant: 7 appellate decisions were scattered over fifty years. However, between 1840 and 1880 the population increased 194 percent, from 17,069,453 to 50,155,783, but the total number of appellate malpractice decisions jumped 1228 percent, from 7 cases as of 1840 to 93 cases by 1880.[7] While the rate of appellate malpractice decisions was seemingly unaffected by a 334 percent population increase between 1790 and 1840, the rate of reported cases far outstripped population growth over the next forty years.

TABLE I [8]

Appellate Court Malpractice Decisions, 1790–1950

Years	# of Decisions	% Increase in Cases	% Increase in Population
1790–1830	2	—	227
1830–1860	21	950	144
1860–1890	117	457	100
1890–1920	485	308	68
1920–1950	1,143	136	43

In fact, the interval between 1790 and 1840 has been the only period in American history in which the proliferation of appellate malpractice decisions failed to surpass the growth rate of the population (see table 1). These observations suggest that the increase in reported suits in the last two-thirds of the nineteenth century was not directly related to population increases, and they reinforce the conclusion that the late 1830s represented a critical turning point in the history of American medical malpractice litigation.

The low frequency of reports of malpractice in early nineteenth-century medical journals corroborates the rarity of suits before 1835. Physicians developed their views about malpractice suits in medical publications, where they communicated their attitudes to other doctors. Detailed malpractice reports helped physicians gauge the frequency of litigation, speculate on the causes of the suits, and suggest possible remedies. These commentaries, while virtually absent from early journals, were published at a furious rate beginning in the late 1830s. For example, between 1812 and 1835 the *New England Journal of Medicine and Surgery* and its successor, the *Boston Medical and Surgical Journal*, reported on only three malpractice cases. These three cases included one suit each from France, England, and the United States.[9] In contrast, between 1835 and 1865 the *Boston Medical and Surgical Journal* published forty-eight reports and editorials on malpractice.[10] Other journals exhibited a similar disparity between the number of suits reported before and after 1840. In New York (the state considered the center of the new malpractice phenomenon in the 1840s) the medical society reported on only one malpractice incident before 1835 in its *Transactions*—and that involved an illegal abortion, not a lawsuit.[11] Similarly, the *Medical Examiner*, founded in the 1830s, did not report a single malpractice case until the next decade. Publishers did not attempt to provide a comprehensive list of suits, but the scores of malpractice reports between 1835 and 1865 reflected the general trend of litigation and the level of professional concern. While these later articles were filled with the medical community's concerns regarding the frequency of malpractice suits, the few existing reports in the *Boston Medical and Surgical Journal* and other publications from the years 1790–1835 reflected little anxiety and treated the cases as regrettable, but isolated incidents.[12]

Although the field of medical jurisprudence blossomed in the early nineteenth century, legal scholars seldom, if ever, addressed the issue of malpractice before 1835.[13] Two of the most widely circulated works in America were Theodoric Beck's *Elements of Medical Jurisprudence* (1823) and Joseph Chitty's *A Practical Treatise on Medical Jurisprudence* (1834). Neither Chitty, a lawyer, nor Beck, a New York physician, contributed a word of advice or information on malpractice.[14] When R. E. Griffith added an American chapter to Michael Ryan's work on medical jurisprudence in 1832, he merely noted that there were three types of malpractice: willful, negligent, and ignorant. He did not cite any cases or suggest that such litigation was prevalent.[15] Timothy Walker, a professor of law at Cincinnati College, published an extensive *First Book for Students* in 1837. Walker described *malpractice* as the attempt to produce an abortion. He did not include the incompetent practice of physicians that resulted in permanent injuries to patients in his definition.[16] When physicians and lawyers discussed malpractice in the first third of the century, they were most likely referring to nonlicensed practice, ethical violations, or criminal abortion. Civil lawsuits for damages after treatment received scant attention and generated no concern.

The Law

When late eighteenth- and early nineteenth-century American lawyers brought malpractice suits against physicians, they were able to refer to a slowly expanding body of legal literature for guidance, but no specialized works. Lawyers at the time of the American Revolution read William Blackstone's or Edward Coke's commentaries, referred to scattered English court decisions, and learned from assisting their preceptors. After Independence Americans published their own law journals, case reports, treatises, and legal handbooks.[17] Despite this relative outpouring of reference material, the essential mechanics of malpractice prosecutions remained relatively unchanged.

American lawyers eagerly bought Blackstone's *Commentaries* when they first became available in 1765. The first American edition printed in 1771–1772, and St. George Tucker's annotated version published in 1803, made the commentaries accessible to virtually every lawyer in the country. In fact, for those lawyers who trained in the late 1700s and practiced into the mid-1830s Blackstone was the most important legal resource.[18] Blackstone categorized *mala practice* not under *contract* or *mercantile law*, but under the heading of *private wrongs*. He defined *malpractice* as an injury or damage to a person's "vigor or constitution" sustained as a result of "the neglect or unskillful management of [a] physician, surgeon, or apothecary." Blackstone declared that malpractice was an offense because "it breaks the trust which the party placed in his physician." The injured patient possessed a remedy for damages with the special legal action, or *writ*, of "trespass on the case."[19]

The trespass on the case writ was the technical name of the action in a malpractice suit.[20] This writ served as the common law remedy for all cases in which one person purportedly caused another an injury without the use of force. The scope of trespass on the case included damages sustained as the result of breach of duty, negligence, or carelessness. An attorney had to convince the judge and jury that the accused physician had failed to live up to the common law definition of professional responsibility and that this lapse had resulted in an injury to the defendant. Judges and lawyers drew on English precedents to form the American standard for malpractice. While the law did not demand that physicians implicitly guarantee effective treatment, it required that they exercise "ordinary diligence, care, and skill."[21] Although the precise wording of the requirement varied and was occasionally qualified in significant ways, the essential standard remained. Doctors were expected to possess and apply an ordinary and reasonable degree of care, skill, and diligence in their work with patients. Individual physicians' performance would be measured against the therapeutic conventions, or standards of "ordinary" or average members of the profession.

The common law reserved an important role for the jury in malpractice cases. While trial judges articulated the legal standards by which juries were required to assess physicians, jurors were asked to determine "questions of fact" such as what constituted carelessness and the standards of the profession at large. Although expert medical testimony was required to guide the jury's deliberations, laymen were entrusted with the tremendous power to designate the boundaries of acceptable medical behavior. Since juries made these decisions on a case-by-case basis, acceptable standards of care, skill, and diligence were highly sensitive to popular conceptions of the medical profession and medical practice.[22] Similarly, the use of physicians as medical witnesses provided an official inlet for the personal or professional prejudices of rival medical practitioners. These provisions, contained in the common law, would play a role in the multiplication of suits in the 1840s and 1850s.

The Cases

Malpractice suits were such an uncommon occurrence before 1835 that it is difficult to draw many confident generalizations. Still, some trends do appear. The lawsuit was neither a common nor a completely acceptable response to personal misfortune. Generally, only in cases of severe injury or death did individuals overcome tradition and sue physicians. Patients and their families rarely won in court. Although malpractice suits of all kinds were infrequent before 1835, cases that did not involve death or amputation were especially rare. Fractures that did not result in amputations—which would become the most common source of suits after 1835—were seldom the source of litigation.

For example, in 1767 a physician was accused, but not charged, of malpractice when a patient died as a result of a blood-letting procedure.[23] The earliest reported American appellate decision, *Cross* v. *Guthery*, was decided in 1794.[24] Cross, a Connecticut physician, amputated one of Mrs. Guthery's breasts; she died three hours later. Her husband sued the physician, asking £1,000 for "his costs and expense, and deprivation of the service and company of his wife." Although the jury ruled in favor of Guthery, they awarded him only £40 in damages.[25] In 1825, Michael O'Neil accused Dr. Gerard Bancker of infecting his four-year-old son with a fatal dose of smallpox during a vaccination and sued for $5,000. A New York City jury refused to award the father any damages.[26] A third case from this period that resulted in death occurred in Ohio in the early 1830s. A physician, using a knife and hook to remove a fetus, injured the mother, who subsequently died. The patient's husband sued the physician for malpractice, but the trial court judge dismissed the case as a nonsuit.[27]

In addition to cases involving deaths, patients also sued physicians in this early period when they believed that improper treatment had resulted in an amputation or a severe deformity. Another obstetric case in the first decade of the century involved a man who, having been a merchant, a grocer, a dancing instructor, and a fencing master, claimed proficiency in medicine, surgery, and midwifery. During a difficult delivery he violently used a pair of scissors and his hands to remove a fetus, presumably to save the mother's life. In doing so, he produced an "irreparable injury to the internal parts of the mother" and caused her "great and unnecessary pain." The prosecution presented evidence to show that the defendant had received no form of organized medical training. Several physicians testified that the defendant's procedure was unusual and unwarrantable, and a Connecticut jury found him guilty of malpractice.[28] The defendant appealed the verdict to the state supreme court, claiming that the prosecution had no right to introduce evidence concerning his previous occupations and lack of training. In 1812 the state supreme court noted that any "attempt to practice in cases of this sort, without the necessary previous qualifications, clearly manifests extreme depravity, and evinces a general hostility towards the human race," and it upheld the verdict.[29] In a Pennsylvania suit in the late 1820s, a patient accused a physician of improperly treating his broken leg. The limb remained swollen and inflamed for twelve months after the injury until amputation was the only remedy. Although the patient won his case at the trial level, the Pennsylvania state supreme court overturned the judgment.[30] As a final example of the character of these early, rare suits, in the 1832 case of *Landon* v. *Humphrey* there was confrontation between a physician and a woman who reportedly suffered a paralyzed arm after an improper vaccination procedure.[31]

The narrow range of cases prosecuted in the early nineteenth century provides a clue to, and a preview of, the subsequent increases in malpractice suits. The suits before 1835 generally involved obstetrical or vaccination cases or profound deformities such as amputations, and it is notable that at this time the public viewed obstetrics and vaccination procedures as having a mechanical certitude. For example, a judge in 1827 noted that a "physician may mistake the symptoms of a patient;

or may misjudge as to the nature of his disease; and even as to the powers of a medicine; and yet his error may be of that pardonable kind, that will do him no essential prejudice." But, the judge observed, while a physician often was part of a profession "beset by great difficulties, the employment of a man midwife and surgeon for the most part, is merely mechanical, and therefore held to a higher standard of performance."[32]

By the 1820s and 1830s smallpox vaccination was widely considered a predictable, almost routine, procedure. Statistics from European countries convinced Americans of the value of vaccination, and several state legislatures required counties to provide the procedure for all citizens.[33] These attitudes toward particular medical treatments engendered a false sense of certitude and confidence. Both obstetrics and vaccination were still uncertain fields subject to the vagaries of individual patients and practitioners. But public perception was more important than reality: If a physician did not perform a seemingly mechanistic, simple procedure with success, then the public often assumed that he must have been guilty of a lapse in care or skill.

The image of the body as a machine and the physician as a mechanic grew out of the triumph of Cartesian thought in the eighteenth century. The mechanistic view of the body and of certain medical practices did not have a major impact on the frequency of malpractice litigation until advancements in medical technology created a reasonable, yet illusory, expectation of success.[34] More important, however, the complex of social and professioinal factors necessary for widespread litigation had not entirely coalesced in the first third of the nineteenth century. An early suit in Maine illustrates the social, medical, and legal environment of this period and suggests some of the reasons for the increase in malpractice suits after the first third of the century.

Lowell v. Hawks and Faxon

In September 1821, Charles Lowell, 30, was riding in the country near the village of Lubec, Maine. Lowell's "young and restive" horse threw him from the saddle and then fell across his legs. Lowell's companions carried him home and called for Dr. John Faxon. Although Faxon, according to Lowell, was "not a thorough bred physician," he was the only doctor in town and had treated Lowell's family for several years. Faxon examined Lowell and discovered that the man's left hip was dislocated and that the left leg was twisted at a forty-five degree angle from the right leg. Using a ball made of a large sheet as a fulcrum and the dislocated limb as a lever, Faxon attempted to force the hip bone back into the socket. He could not correct the injury, so he sent a messenger to the nearby village of Eastport to bring Dr. Micajah Hawks.[35]

During the three-mile journey from Eastport, Hawks told the messenger that Faxon "was not fit to doctor a sheep or a hog, much less a human being." However, when Hawks reached Lowell's house, he was courteous and allowed Faxon to assist him. Hawks directed several men to pull on Lowell's good leg, others to pull at his arms, and ordered Faxon and three additional men to manipulate the injured leg. Without anesthesia this was a profoundly painful procedure that Lowell referred to as "torture." Witnesses heard "a kind of grating," and Hawks declared that the hip was in its proper position. Hawks tied a handkerchief around Lowell's knees and told him to lie still for fourteen days. Hawks said that he would not come back but that he would tell Faxon how to proceed. Hawks spent a total of fifteen minutes with Lowell.[36]

Lowell repeatedly sent messages to Hawks asking to see him. Hawks refused to visit. Neither Hawks or Faxon were concerned when Lowell discovered a mysterious indentation near his hip joint. Hawks visited Lowell in late October 1821, and, though Lowell had reported that the injured leg was very painful and three inches shorter than the other one, the physician refused to examine it. Hawks finally told Lowell that he had "gotten to be a cripple for life and all through Faxon's ignorance and quackery." Even though Lowell had been in bed with his legs bound together, Hawks claimed that Faxon had allowed the patient to reinjure the hip. Now Lowell was in constant pain and was unable to walk without crutches.[37]

In December 1821, about four months after the accident, Lowell traveled 250 miles to Boston aboard a cargo ship to meet with Dr. John Collins Warren, easily the most distinguished physician in the country. Warren had studied at schools and hospitals in London, Edinburgh, and Paris. He was an accomplished surgeon, held the chair of anatomy and surgery at Harvard medical school, and had helped found Massachusetts General Hospital and the *New England Journal of Medicine*. Warren examined Lowell first in a public coffee house in Boston. The physician informed Lowell that he had suffered a simple hip dislocation, but that because the injury had been left untreated for such a long time, nothing could be done to remedy the deformity. He declared that it "was nonsense for Hawks to say he ever reduced the dislocation and that [Lowell had] displaced the bone again lying in

LETTER

TO THE

HON. ISAAC PARKER.

CHIEF JUSTICE OF THE SUPREME COURT OF THE STATE OF
MASSACHUSETTS,

CONTAINING REMARKS

ON THE

DISLOCATION OF THE HIP JOINT,

OCCASIONED

BY THE PUBLICATION OF A TRIAL

WHICH

TOOK PLACE AT MACHIAS, IN THE STATE OF MAINE, JUNE, 1824.

BY JOHN C. WARREN, M. D.

PROFESSOR OF ANATOMY AND SURGERY IN HARVARD UNIVERSITY, AND ACTING
SURGEON IN THE MASSACHUSETTS GENERAL HOSPITAL.

WITH AN APPENDIX

OF

DOCUMENTS FROM THE TRIAL NECESSARY TO ILLUSTRATE

THE

HISTORY OF THE CASE.

CAMBRIDGE:

PRINTED BY HILLIARD AND METCALF

1826

Title page from John Warren's 142-page pamphlet explaining his role in the Lowell malpractice case (1826). (Courtesy of the Truman G. Blocker, Jr., History of Medicine Collections, Moody Medical Library, Galveston, Texas.)

bed." Warren consulted four other physicians from the hospital, and they all agreed that Lowell's deformity and handicap were the result of an untreated simple dislocation. Although Warren said that nothing could be done to repair the limb, Lowell begged the physician to intervene, explaining that he depended on his leg for a living. Lowell announced that he was "prepared in mind and body for the pain of [an] operation," had a family to support, and convinced Warren and his associates to try and treat the leg.[38]

Since the coffee house did not contain the necessary equipment for the procedure, Warren had Lowell taken to Massachusetts General Hospital. The physician consulted a medical text written by the English surgical pioneer Astley Cooper, who specialized in fractures and dislocations. Following Cooper's direction, Warren began. He provided tartar emetics to induce vomiting, "that deadly sickness, which relaxes the whole muscular system." Warren's associates placed Lowell in a hot water bath "at as high a temperature as he could bear" for an hour. Warren employed a series of pulleys, bandages, and cords suggested by Cooper's work, in an attempt to force Lowell's leg back into its proper position. Medical assistants tied Lowell to a table. A band of leather was placed around his thigh and attached to a pulley, another around his leg and above his knee. Warren placed additional bands around each thigh and attached them to the walls of the operating theater. The pulley on the upper thigh would draw the leg away from the body; the pulley above the knee would wrench it from its frozen position. Immediately before the procedure, according to Warren, "a vein was opened in the arm, and blood drawn as rapidly, and in as large quantities, as the faintness of the patient would allow." Then Warren ordered several men to pull simultaneously on the ropes attached to the various pulleys.[39]

He conducted the operation with the pulley device between one and two hours in front of one hundred students and physicians but could not improve the condition of the leg. According to Warren, Lowell submitted to the painful ordeal "most courageously, and never uttered a complaint."[40] Lowell consulted one or two other Boston physicians before returning to Maine but all the doctors told him that there was little they could do to restore his injured limb. Returning to his hometown, crippled and bitter, Lowell declared, "I am aware of the necessity of kissing the rod, and him who hath anointed it; and were it purely an act of God, I would accept it without a murmur." But after leaving Boston, he "was satisfied that [his] ruin had been brought on by ignorance, stupidity, and unpardonable neglect."[41]

Lowell sued Faxon and Hawks for malpractice and asked for $10,000 in damages. In March 1823 a jury for the Court of Common Pleas found Faxon and Hawks guilty of malpractice and awarded Lowell $1,962, an extraordinary sum in the early nineteenth century. The physicians appealed the case and won the opportunity for a retrial. The jury in the second trial could not decide on a verdict and passed the case to the trial judge, who awarded Lowell only $100. The defendants appealed this verdict too, which led to a third trial.[42]

In the third trial, as in the earlier hearings, John Warren and his associates from Massachusetts General supplied the most damaging evidence against the defendants. The physicians gave sworn depositions in Boston that were presented to the Maine court. Warren disagreed with the primary physician on the specific type of injury Lowell had suffered. He repeated his assertion that Lowell's injury was a simple dislocation, downward and backward, that could have been corrected with prompt treatment. He said that a physician of "ordinary skill" ought to know that a limb that was three inches shorter than the other was dislocated. Warren also agreed with Lowell's attorney that "common and ordinary attention" would lead to regular examinations, comparisons of the lengths of the patient's legs, and concern over any chronic pain. Warren also contended that if "naked hand force" was not sufficient to reset the dislocation, then it was improper treatment to neglect the use of some mechanical means such as pulleys. Warren concluded by stating that he believed that physicians of high standing would agree with his diagnosis and treatment in the case. Several other doctors testified that dislocations were easy to diagnose and treat.[43]

Faxon and Hawks' attorneys countered Warren's testimony by introducing Dr. Nathan Smith, a well-known New England physician and the founder of Dartmouth and Yale medical schools. Warren's father had been instrumental in the establishment of Harvard's medical program, which may have generated rivalry between the two men. When Smith heard Warren's deposition, he called the Boston doctors "a pack of old grannies." Smith blamed the near unanimity of the evidence against the defendants on Warren. "I suppose Warren said

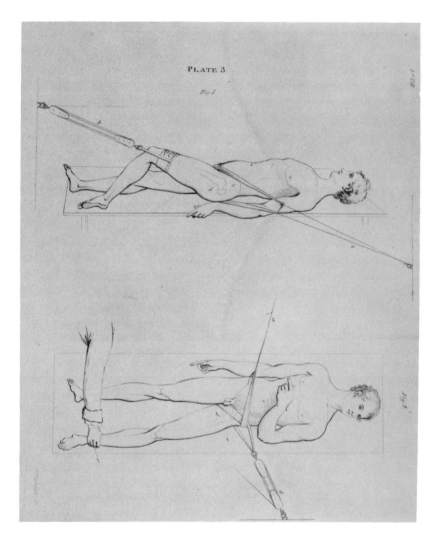

Apparatus to relocate dislocated hips. From Astley Cooper, Surgical Essays *(1821). (Courtesy of the Historical Research Center, Houston Academy of Medicine, Texas Medical Center Library, Houston, Texas.)*

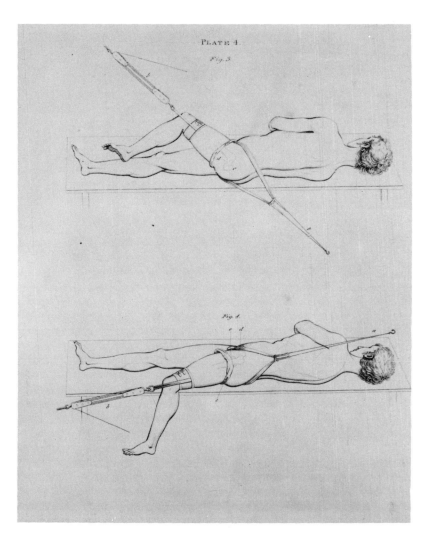

PLATE 4.

Fig. 3

Fig. 4

so, and all the rest fell in with his opinions." Smith had examined Lowell's leg in June of 1822. He testified that Lowell did not have a dislocation but had broken the bones of the joint in his fall from the horse. In such a situation, Smith argued, nothing could have been done to cure the injury. Smith declared that pulleys such as Warren used were not necessary and that they had often been injurious. When Lowell's lawyers cross-examined Smith, the physician admitted that he knew Hawks and that he had once told Lowell that "he had better drop his action [malpractice suit] and try and get well, which would be better than to try to get damages out of the doctors."[44]

In his short closing statement Lowell's attorney declared that it was a "known principle of law" that he "who undertakes any business for another shall conduct that business with ordinary skill." Nothing would be more just, he continued, than "that one man should not suffer of the carelessness of another." According to Lowell and his lawyer, Hawks was negligent because he left a patient in the care of Faxon, a man he did not consider fit to treat a "sheep or a hog." Hawks had been hasty in his treatment of Lowell, careless in not noticing the shortened leg, and negligent in allowing Faxon to treat patients. The lawyer asked the jury to award Lowell enough damages to support the injured man for life.[45]

John Davies' closing argument for the defendants filled over fifty pages of text. Davies portrayed Hawks as a modest but committed physician. Hawks did not claim the highest powers and honors of his profession but he had used the best means at hand to reduce a difficult dislocation. According to Davies, Hawks did not expect to cure Lowell completely because he was always "satisfied that there was some interior injury which his art could not reach and which he thought best to be trusted to the healing power of nature." Davies noted that malpractice cases were rare and difficult to adjudicate because "[t]he work of a physician is all tentative and experimental . . . [n]ew observations and discoveries are continually enlarging the field and changing the instruments of professional power." Therefore, Davies reasoned, "The same degree of skill cannot be expected in all places nor exacted of all persons. A young physician cannot be equal to an old one, nor a village apothecary set up to rival a college professor."[46]

After arguing that physicians' skills should be judged on the standard of care in their locality, Davies tried to persuade the jury that the quality of medical care in rural Maine was probably preferable to the scientific advances of Boston. According to the lawyer, Hawks and Faxon did not try to adjust Lowell's leg further because they believed that he was beyond help and did not wish to subject him to more pain. Davies' sarcastic tone throughout the closing argument was designed to create resentment in the small-town jury against the pretensions of big city medicine. Davies told the jurors that John Warren and the "learned faculty of that eminent institution [Massachusetts General]" came together to examine "the case of an unfortunate victim of village quackery." Davies described the Boston doctors as "[c]radled in the love and honor of our society, nursed in the laps of ease, enjoying the patronage of power and opulence, having walked perhaps one after another the hospitals of Europe . . . a Boston jury would hardly permit the winds of Heaven to visit them too roughly." In contrast, Davies contended, Hawks's "opportunities" were more limited.[47]

While "persons of loftier standing" than Hawks might be "a little more adventurous," "it behoove[d] such humble individuals as himself to be cautious and circumspect in their conduct . . . [and] not to perform experiments at random." In Boston, Davies declared, they were less cautious. Warren and his colleagues had argued that Hawks and Faxon should have used mechanical means to treat the dislocation. Davies lampooned the scene in Boston as Warren prepared to treat Lowell. "The rising usefulness of this grand institution [Massachusetts General] was about to be attested by a decisive achievement—and a day of glory was about to dawn upon Massachusetts General Hospital." Davies described how Warren had administered powerful cathartics and nauseating doses of antimony and had bled Lowell as freely as possible.[48]

Davies compared Warren's use of a pulley on Lowell to seventeenth-century torture. He quoted medical books that discouraged the use of mechanical devices and declared that the treatment was so painful and dangerous that "[t]he wonder is not that the operation was unsuccessful but that the patient survived." Yet, Davies reminded the jury, Hawks and Faxon were being persecuted because they had not used the dread pulley device. Finally, Davies asked the jurors to consider the impact of a guilty verdict on the community since Hawks and Faxon were the only physicians in their respective villages, demanding, "What is the consequence of a limb like Lowell's . . . compared with the usefulness of such a physician as Dr. Hawks, entirely lost to the present scene from his practice?"[49]

After Davies finished his argument, Judge Nathan Weston instructed the jury on the applicable law. Accepting Davies' description of the legal responsibilities of surgeons, Weston declared:

> It is not to be expected of a Surgeon or a Physician in a country or obscure village, that he will possess the skill of a surgeon in the city of London, or any large city—this would be unreasonable to expect . . . all that is required is ordinary skill according to the general state of medical science in the section of the country in which he lives.

Judge Weston was clearly partisan. He said that he did not think the leg had ever been dislocated. While he believed the Boston physicians "spoke with too much certainty," he knew of no reason why the jurors should not believe the witnesses for the defense. The Boston physicians had testified that Hawks and Faxon should have used a pulley. Weston followed the defense attorney's lead and suggested that mechanical devices might be dangerous. But, according to Weston, even if the pulleys were the most appropriate treatment, "it did not appear that anything of the kind could be had" in Lubec.[50]

The jury could not decide on a verdict, and Judge Weston convinced Lowell to drop the malpractice charge permanently. Lowell later felt that he had been coerced and published a twenty-nine-page pamphlet exposing "the official conduct of Judge Weston and the candor and intelligence of the Jurors of this county." In addition a 117-page account by a friend of the accused physician and a 142-page report by Warren were published.[51] The volume of literature on this case far exceeded the literature published on any other suit in the century and underlines the rarity of the litigation in this period. Lowell claimed that Weston had "instructed the jury in the most novel and extraordinary way" and that the public "excitement and prejudice was so great that there would be no probability of getting an impartial trial." He forsook any further legal action and lamented that "[the trials] doomed me to a miserable existence, through the residue of my mortal life for every step I take, I am reminded of my now irreparable misfortune."[52]

The Lowell drama generated intense national interest and haunted the central characters for years. The series of trials reportedly cost Lowell $2,000 and left him in financial ruin. Dr. Hawks spent between $2,000 and $3,000 on his defense and labored for years to overcome his debt. Ironically, a postmortem examination of Lowell's injury revealed that all the diagnoses offered at the trial had been wrong. Lowell had indeed suffered a dislocation, but of a character not anticipated by his physicians or Warren and Smith, two of the best medical minds in America.[53]

The suits and their aftermath generated unwanted public attention for Warren and Massachusetts General Hospital. Soon after the publication of the first two pamphlets on the case in 1825 and 1826, Dr. Hawks's hometown newspaper carried a lengthy attack on Warren and the Boston institution. The author speculated that patients of the hospital must be in the "most deplorable of any situation that I can imagine" and added that Warren "must take a high rank among the detestable class of men who pretend to[o] much and know but little."[54]

In response to the pamphlets and the subsequent attacks, Warren followed with his own account in 1826. Although his testimony seemed unequivocally to favor Lowell's contention that Hawks and Faxon had acted incompetently, Warren claimed that his evidence and actions thoughout the trial had been badly misconstrued. He complained that the publications had brought discredit and ridicule upon himself, his colleagues, and his institution. One of the pamphlets contained the defense attorney's mocking description of the hospital and Warren's treatment. After praising the credentials of the institution and its physicians, Warren asked: "Are the names of such persons proper subjects for the jeers of a lawyer, to be thrown out in a court of justice, and afterwards distributed through the community?"[55] While some observers had accused Warren of causing the suit, he argued that "nothing could be further from the truth." From the beginning, he explained, he had informed Lowell that it was a difficult injury. He recalled telling Lowell that the first physicians had done the best they could and that there were many aspects of medical practice that laymen did not understand. Warren claimed that he had discouraged the suit, told Lowell that a victory in court was unlikely, and then refused to testify. He ultimately had provided a deposition only because he believed that the law required his testimony. Finally, Warren explained that many of his more damaging statements against the defendants had been made before he realized that a suit was underway and were later added to his official statement.[56]

The *Lowell* case was an anomaly for its time, but it foreshadowed the imminent onslaught of suits and helps illustrate some of the factors that would instigate future litigation. By 1824 the social, religious, and political assumptions of colonial society were well on their way to being destroyed. Early America had been characterized by the existence of organic communities in which individuals were bound together by common interests and dependency relationships. The good of the community was often placed above the good of the individual, and stability and consensus were the order of the day. Most communities were small, and emigration was relatively rare. Local issues remained local. Since relationships among citizens were intimate, mediation of disputes through community opinion was both possible and necessary. Stability and order were maintained by a network of hierarchical and familial relationships that emphasized deference and compromise over conflict. These orderly, closed, communal relationships began to break down under the stresses of economic development, emigration, and the growth of egalitarian ideas, especially after 1776.

Although social upheaval and fragmentation of communal structures continued unabated after the American Revolution, a decisive break with colonial structures did not occur until the second third of the nineteenth century.[57] Therefore, remnants of many colonial assumptions, though dramatically undermined, persisted into the period embracing the 1824 *Lowell* lawsuit. Several factors in this unusual and transitional case anticipated the foundations of increased malpractice prosecutions later in the century.

Judge Weston had charged the *Lowell* jury that a physician practicing in an "obscure village" was not required to possess the same degree of medical knowledge as a practitioner in a large city. The jury was asked to compute a physician's acceptable degree of skill according to the state of local medical practice. This doctrine, which became known as the *locality rule* in the latter part of the century, reflected the condition of both the medical profession and the nation in the first part of the nineteenth century.[58] Rural practitioners were usually isolated from urban centers of medical progress, and in 1824 there were few medical schools and journals to disseminate knowledge on a national scale. When juries judged physicians by local standards, they expressed the more general commitment to localism and antiurbanism of the period. Davies, Hawks's attorney, manipulated this strain of local pride in his description of the elite Boston physicians who testified for the prosecution. He also argued that malpractice suits were difficult and uncommon partially because "the work of the physician is all tentative and experimental; it is all as it were underwater."[59] Unfortunately, these sentiments could also work against medical advancement and proper care by putting a low premium on superior skill, protecting incompetent physicians, and discouraging suits. The arguments and result of the Lowell case reflected the country's diverse medical culture and were an explicit legal toleration of lower medical standards.

Three decades later, at midcentury, both the country and the medical profession looked quite different. The assumptions of the judge, defense attorney, and jury were no longer as obviously applicable. Much of the public was willing to hold physicians to a higher standard of accountability after 1835. Physicians' performances were seldom measured against only the standard of care in their own community. Thus, in 1860 Stephen Smith, one of the patriarchs of nineteenth-century American medicine, argued that while it may have once been proper to gauge the amount of skill required by physicians by the locality in which they lived, it would be "manifestly dangerous" to accept the practice. It was ludicrous, Smith declared, for a physician to plead ignorance of generally recognized knowledge "in our time when communication is so rapid, and books and periodicals are abundant and cheap."[60] Reality, however, did not match perception. While medical care had improved nearly everywhere by midcentury, it had not developed uniformly. Physicians' and patients' inflated expectations in the wake of medical advancements between 1820 and 1840 contributed to dissatisfaction with medical treatment and undermined the development of realistic standards of care.

The defense attorney also warned the jury that a guilty verdict would hurt more than just the physician. Medical practitioners were crucial members of society. "The consequences [of a verdict] extend therefore to the community, which is hardly less interested in the result." The attorney urged the jury to consider "What is the consequence of a limb like Lowell's . . . compared with the usefulness of such a physician as Dr. Hawks, entirely lost to the present scene from his practice?" He argued that though their natural sympathy may be with the injured parties, the physician's importance should also be weighed. The lawyer exhorted the jury to "[r]ise then above the influence of prejudice, and restore him [the physician] to society."[61]

Both Hawks and Faxon were the only physicians in their respective communities, and the prospect of their loss following a successful malpractice prosecution undoubtedly influenced the jury's decision. Lowell, in fact, had charged that jurors from Hawks's community had consistently protected him. Lowell lived in Lubec, Hawks in Eastport. The towns were in the same county, and jurors were drawn from both communities. At the first trial the one Eastport juror held out eight hours after the other eleven men had decided in Lowell's favor. In the second trial three Eastport men held out against the others and forced the trial judge to decide the case. He awarded Lowell the much reduced sum of $100. Lowell and his attorney claimed that community leaders from Eastport had talked to the jurors from that town and convinced them to vote in favor of their sole local physician.[62] In the early years of the nineteenth century physicians were scarce in rural areas.[63] As physicians became significantly more plentiful later in the century, however, patients, juries, and judges could afford to charge and convict malpractice defendants without the fear that the community would be left without a medical man.

Finally, the *Lowell* case illustrated that the decision to sue a physician also depended on complex cultural preconditions. Lowell's terse apologia affirming the religious necessity of accepting adversity by "kissing the rod and him who hath anointed it" suggests that much of society still believed that misfortune emanated from the hand of God rather than from the irresponsible actions of humans.[64] The proper response to an act of God was humble acceptance, not a lawsuit. As religious beliefs concerning divine providence evolved, victims of misfortune were freed to search for temporal causes and blame human actors.[65] Hawks's attorney had observed, "It is not a very commendable sight anymore than very customary sight to see a patient prosecuting his physician. It is rather doubtful whether the intensity of moral obligation can be increased in such a case by legal action."⁶⁶ Davies contended, rather, that "public judgment" was the "proper tribunal to regulate this species of responsibility."

In the closed, parochial communities of the late eighteenth and early nineteenth centuries Davies was probably correct. For example, Ephraim McDowell became legendary for performing the first ovariotomy in 1809. His small, backwoods community of Danville, Kentucky, however, vehemently opposed the historic operation. Local physicians, including his nephew and partner, questioned McDowell's judgment and morality. Ministers attacked him from their pulpits. While Mc-Dowell operated, an angry mob waited outside, not with lawyers and writs, but with a rope swung over a tree. At one point the indignant crowd attempted to burst into the patient's home to stop the surgery.⁶⁷ This type of communal enforcement was common in the small, cohesive settlements of early America. Citizens often relied on extralegal remedies, coercion, group action, and moral suasion in various areas of public life. Davies, Hawks's attorney, appealed to this tradition when he declared that "legal action" was not appropriate "in such a case." These attitudes may have limited the public acceptance of suing physicians well into the 1830s, and even later in some areas of the country. As social, economic, and geographic mobility began to destroy the basis of communal "public judgment," however, disgruntled patients were more likely to turn to courts for satisfaction.

By the 1840s episodes like the *Lowell* case were common, and medical men felt they were in the midst of an unprecedented malpractice epidemic. Suits disrupted professional relations, injured individual reputations, and burdened physicians with legal fees and damage awards. The unorganized medical profession of the first half of the nineteenth century was unable to devise an appropriate response to this new threat. Malpractice law was in a state of flux and sensitive to various social pressures. Judges and lawyers relied on English precedents with minor alterations, but the resulting changes in legal doctrine were not responsible for the sudden outbreak of suits.

American patients began to sue their physicians on a wide scale because of specific social, medical, and technological developments in the first half of the nineteenth century. The antistatus, antiprofessional sentiment of the Jacksonian period increasingly turned the lay public against orthodox, trained practitioners. In addition, Americans, with a long tradition of self-cure, home remedy, and folk healing, had little patience with doctors who demanded deference and privilege but offered few cures. Physicians' authority and public respect also declined as a parade of alternative medical practitioners offered their services to antebellum Americans. Physicians exacerbated their own descent in esteem and contributed to the litigious trend. As medical men of all types became more plentiful in the 1830s and 1840s, intraprofessional competition generated conflict, and many medical men incited suits against fellow practitioners. Dramatic advances in several areas of medicine created unrealistic expectations in both physicians and patients and blurred standards of care.

These immediate causes, however, would not have engendered widespread suits without concurrent fundamental cultural changes. Many Americans decisively changed their views on divine providence in the first half of the nineteenth century. This transformation allowed individuals to seek earthly causes for their misfortunes, assign blame, and demand compensation. At the same time, a variety of forces combined to make Americans dramatically more concerned with physical well-being and significantly more confident that they could do something about it. Finally, the erosion of traditional community customs inhibiting litigation and a transformation in individualism allowed patients to attack their physicians in court more frequently. These changes in the larger culture did not cause malpractice suits, but without them widespread litigation would not have been possible.

The patterns set in the first half of the century continued through 1900. Many of the inciting causes of the 1840s disappeared, but new technological, social, professional, and legal factors arose to take their place. More importantly, the underlying cultural trends that made the suits possible continued to develop and provided an increasingly hospitable social environment for malpractice suits.

CHAPTER 2

The Deluge,
1835–1865

In 1844 a writer for the *Boston Medical and Surgical Journal* warned that qualified physicians were "constantly liable to vexatious suits instituted by ignorant and unprincipled persons."[1] In 1853 the *Western Journal of Medical and Physical Sciences* reported that malpractice suits "occur almost every month in the year and everywhere in our country."[2] These writers were not exaggerating, and their suspicions and fears were well-founded. They and their contemporaries were witnessing the first symptoms of a professional disease that would plague the medical community for the next 150 years.

Although medical malpractice suits were virtually nonexistent between 1790 and 1835, thereafter patients suddenly began to sue their physicians at an increasing and unprecedented rate. As early as the 1840s the frequency of suits in some parts of the country had filled doctors with a mixture of anger, panic, and confusion. The suits and the alarm increased as the decades passed. Frank Hamilton, a New York physician, claimed that between 1833 and 1856 "suits for malpractice were so very frequent in the Northern states" that many men "abandoned the practice of surgery, leaving it to those who, with less skill and experience, had less reputation and property to lose."[3] By 1860 John Elwell, a physician and a lawyer who wrote a book on the subject, could claim that "[t]here can hardly be found a place in the country, where the oldest physicians in it have not, at some periods in their lives, been actually sued or annoyingly threatened."[4]

The rate of prosecutions in this period was probably not as great as in comparable periods later in the century, and certainly not as intense as in the twentieth century, but the initial explosion of litigation in the 1840s represented a basic, fateful, and irrevocable shift in attitudes toward the practice. While a variety of technological, intraprofessional, economic, and social changes would push litigation rates to soaring heights over the next century and a half, the profession and the country crossed over the critical threshold in the 1840s and 1850s.

"An Incubus upon the Profession"

Every available indicator suggested that the doctor-patient relationship was entering a dramatic new phase. Of the 216 reported appellate malpractice decisions in the nineteenth century, only 5 had occurred before 1835. In contrast, state supreme courts ruled on 42 malpractice cases between 1835 and 1870, 45 cases from 1870 to 1880, and 47 cases from 1880 to 1890.[5] The period between 1835 and 1870 also marked the first time that the increase in appellate malpractice decisions outran the increase in the nation's population. State supreme courts continued to rule on malpractice cases at a rate faster than that of the growth of the population through the twentieth century. Although the numbers of appellate cases represented only a small fraction of the total number of actual prosecutions, they underscore the sudden prevalence of the practice after 1835.

Similarly, medical journals printed hundreds of accounts and comments on malpractice cases between 1835 and 1865. The editorials, rare in the first third of the century, reflected the novelty and intensity of the phenomenon. As Alden March, a prominent New York physician, reported in an 1847 issue of the *Boston Medical and Surgical Journal*, "Legal prosecutions for mal-practice occur so often that even a respectable surgeon may well fear the results of his surgical practice."[6] A writer for the *Medical Examiner* in 1851 lamented that "[m]ischievous prosecutions for some years have alarmed medical gentlemen in various parts of the country to such a degree that many have concluded to let all surgical patients go unassisted in their afflictions."[7] Worthington Hooker, the Connecticut doctor who wrote the influential *Physician and*

Patient in the 1840s, declared that "the professional reputation of medical men seems to be considered by common consent as fair game for the shafts of all, whether high or low, learned or unlearned. Although the charge of mal-practice is a serious charge . . . it is exceedingly common to hear this charge put forth without any hesitation."[8]

Observers believed that the new and dangerous trend began in western New York in the late 1830s and early 1840s and quickly spread both east and west. A writer for the *Boston Medical and Surgical Journal* noted in 1847 that the malpractice "fever" first became popular in western New York "a few years since," and then spread through other eastern states, into Vermont, and even into Canada.[9] Frank Hamilton told the 1843 graduating class of Geneva Medical College that he knew of over twenty malpractice prosecutions against "respectable and eminent" New York state surgeons in 1840 and 1841 alone.[10]

These commentators were probably correct. New York accounted for the lion's share of the publicized cases in the 1840s. One 1839 New York case gained national attention and opened a widespread debate in the pages of the major medical journals. When one of the medical witnesses in the trial was subjected to a retaliatory suit two years later, a commentator warned that western New York was the country's hotbed of medical malpractice.[11] In 1844 Dr. James White of Erie County, New York, treated William Tims, who had suffered an oblique fracture of his thigh bone after falling from the roof of a railway depot. When Tims's limb healed, it was crooked and had a bony protuberance at the point of the injury. He sued White for malpractice but the jury refused to reach a verdict. Tims sued White again the next year with the same result. Finally, in 1848 a jury decided the case in favor of the physician. During the trial, Dr. Trowbridge of Buffalo, who served as one of the medical witnesses, testified that while he had never been sued, the frequency of malpractice prosecutions in the state had driven him from practice. The editor of the *Buffalo Medical Journal* congratulated Trowbridge for his "timely and judicious course in laying down the scalpel" and reported that "in this city [Buffalo] there are but a few surgeons of years or reputation in the profession, who have not latterly crowned with the accompanying honors of a public prosecution for malpractice."[12]

When Adolphus Gates, a German laborer in Buffalo, was awarded $600 after his fractured wrist healed in a frozen position, an editorialist in the same journal wrote in the early 1850s that "the whole system of trials for malpractice is so radically wrong that the defendant must be mulcted in every case where he is not sustained by the entire professional evidence." According to the author:

evidence of a single man, contradicting all surgical experience, and evidently based on an egregious error in diagnosis, outweighed the opinions of older and better surgeons, and subjected a poor, hard-working and intelligent practitioner to a judgment and costs heavy enough to sweep away the greater portion of the small earnings of many years.[13]

New York physicians became more preoccupied by the phenomenon as the suits multiplied. In 1853 a reviewer for the *New York Journal of Medicine* barely mentioned the two books he was ostensibly reviewing and used the occasion to rail against malpractice litigation in the state. "The disposition to institute legal proceedings against the surgeon for the treatment of fractures has become so strong, that prosecutions have been made where there was not the slightest ground for complaint." "And," he observed, "this spirit of persecution is stimulated and more widely disseminated on every repetition of these trials."[14] In less than fifteen years, from 1839 to 1853, malpractice suits in New York went from being rare and unimportant to being common and a major concern to all New York physicians.[15]

New York may have been the apparent source of the malpractice "fever" in the 1840s, but the disease did not spread to other states by imitation alone. While patients and physicians in other regions may have been aware of the growing malpractice epidemic in 1840s New York, the practice could not have spread to other states unless the complex of social and professional factors that favored its existence were already present.[16] Intraprofessional rivalry, numerous medical sects, and low public esteem fueled by particularly strong Jacksonian sentiment made doctors in New York somewhat more vulnerable than their colleagues in other states. These factors and others, albeit in slightly diminished intensity, quickly provided the environment necessary for the more frequent prosecution of physicians in other states.

By 1850 suits began to appear at an increasing rate in western states such as Ohio. Several malpractice cases surfaced in the state in the

1830s but the prosecutions did not alarm the profession unti midcentury.[17] The appearance of suits in some counties for the first time in the late 1840s heightened physicians' fear. Washington Coun-y, Ohio, reported its first malpractice case in 1849, when a patient asked for $10,000 in damages after his thigh fracture resulted in a shortened limb (he received only $200). According to the *Western Lancet*, Meigs County, Ohio, suffered its first malpractice suit in 1850.[18] During one week in 1855, four cases were tried in four separate Ohio counties. The same year, the Ohio Medical Society created a committee to investigate the sudden onslaught of suits in the state. The committee published accounts of seven cases and called the phenomenon "a standing and cumulative evil bearing with the weight of an incubus upon the profession."[19] The *Ohio Medical and Surgical Journal* published numerous such accounts between 1850 and 1865, and as in New York, doctors reportedly left the profession because of the frequency of lawsuits. One editorialist claimed in 1861 that "from first to last there have been over 200 prosecutions in Ohio."[20] While many counties in the state had recorded their first suits as late as 1850, lawsuits were common enough to be considered a major threat as early as a decade later.

Within ten years of the first outbreak of malpractice suits in 1840s New York, other eastern physicians began to complain of the malady. William Wood, a Pennsylvania physician, warned in 1849 that "the principles of law, intended for the protection of the community, are perverted into powerful instruments of wrong and injustice." Echoing the claims of observers in New York and Ohio, Wood reported that "[s]ome of the most competent young men are driven off, and such as remain refuse to take the responsibility of surgical cases." To illustrate the situation in Pennsylvania, Wood chronicled the plight of Charles Brandes, a young German physician who set up practice in the late 1840s. Almost immediately he was plagued by malpractice suits and threats of suits. He was charged twice for the improper vaccination of patients and once for the unskillful treatment of a thigh fracture.[21] Like those in Ohio, local Pennsylvania medical societies established committees to investigate this new threat to the profession.[22] The malpractice litigation phenomenon reached even such isolated states as New Hampshire and Vermont. Dixi Crosby, a prominent Vermont physician, was sued for $5,000 after offering advice to another physician on a thigh fracture in 1853. After the jury awarded the patient $800 in damages, a judge exclaimed that in Vermont "a man had better be in any other profession than in the medical."[23]

The experience of physicians in Massachusetts more than anywhere else demonstrates the timing, rapidity, and amplitude of the initial increase in malpractice litigation. A medical writer commenting on an 1842 Vermont malpractice case regretted that the defendant "could not have had a hearing before an enlightened jury of Massachusetts, where his high attainments in medicine and surgery would have been appreciated."[24] This writer believed that Massachusetts was not fruitful ground for the widespread prosecution of physicians. Through most of the 1840s this judgment appeared sound, and there were few lawsuits. As late as 1847, the *Boston Medical and Surgical Journal* could confidently assert: "Here in Massachusetts the trick has been attempted on a small scale two or three times, but the result has not been sufficiently encouraging to induce many to embark on it." The writer believed that "there happens to be too much intelligence here, for such depradators to succeed."[25]

The medical journalist's optimistic certainty that Massachusetts was immune to the "mania" that was sweeping the Northeast was unfounded and short-lived. By 1853 the tone of the Massachusetts medical commentators had changed from sympathy for their colleagues in other states to concern for their own professional safety. After a spate of cases in the state, the *Boston Medical and Surgical Journal* warned that "[e]very surgeon in the community is liable to a lawsuit for damages." Even more ominously, the journal observed that "[j]uries appear to have been particularly sympathizing with plaintiffs."[26] In 1853 another writer declared: "A fresh disposition to prosecute physicians for alledged [sic] malpractice is manifest in Massachusetts. It is becoming a hazardous enterprise to give surgical assistance in this ancient Commonwealth. It is even worse in some respects, than in western New York or Vermont."[27] A flood of suits struck the state as suddenly and dramatically as it had in other areas of the country. Between 1850 and 1856, for example, there were five malpractice suits in Middlesex County alone.[28]

By the mid-1850s Massachusetts physicians, like those in New

TABLE 2
Sample Malpractice Cases, 1835–1865

Type	Example
fracture	*BufMJMR* 4 (August 1848):131–54
hernia	*StLMSJ* 3 (May 1846):529–63
amputation	28 Me. 97 (1847)
laceration	*NWMSJ* 5 (1848–1849):536–46
abandonment	*MNL* 6 (May 1848):60
obstetric	*OMSJ* 2 (September 1849):6–10
dislocation	*WL* 11 (1850):763–68
vaccination	*AJMS* 22 (July 1851):43–50
calomel	*WJMPS* 24 (1851):168–70
aneurism	*BMSJ* 35 (12 August 1846):43–45
patent medicine	OMSJ 6 (November 1853):182
death	12 *Howard* 323 (1855)
bleeding	Elwell, *Treatise*, (1857), 142–62
misdiagnosis	21 *Tx.* 111 (1858)
chloroform	Smith, *Doctor in Medicine* (ca. 1860), 277–78
ocular	*BMSJ* 32 (2 April 1845):185
tonsils	*BMSJ* 28 (15 February 1843):29–33

York, Ohio, Pennsylvania, Vermont, and New Hampshire, were being sued in all parts of the state. In fact, malpractice charges had become a recognizable and urgent problem throughout the North, even though they remained rare in the South.[29] The actual number of lawsuits between 1835 and 1865 is impossible to determine without a court-house-to-courthouse search of every state. It is clear, however, from appellate court reports, medical journals, and contemporary commentaries that these years represented a fundamentally new era in the history of medical malpractice.

The types of treatment that engendered lawsuits between 1835 and 1865 also broke with the patterns of the past. As noted earlier, in the first third of the nineteenth century malpractice cases typically involved severe deformity, vaccination, or obstetrics; less severe injuries seldom led to lawsuits. After 1840, however, patients began to charge physicians for malpractice involving a wider range of treatments (see table 2).

In addition, patients regularly sued physicians for less severe injuries than they had before 1835. For example, in 1839 a New York man sued his physicians when his badly fractured leg healed, but was $1\frac{1}{4}$ inches shorter than his other limb.[30] In an 1843 case, John Basset of Independence, New York, injured his thigh when his wagon overturned and crushed his leg. Two weeks after the accident, doctors John Collins and Anthony Barney examined Basset and after noting his shortened leg and out-turned toes, decided that the injury was a dislocated hip. They used ropes and pulleys to adjust the hip to its proper position. When the physicians heard the characteristic "pop" that generally accompanied the relocation of bones and the leg was restored to its natural length, they dismissed Basset as cured. Within a year his leg was shortened $1\frac{1}{2}$ inches, and he charged the physicians with malpractice. After two trials and four years a jury decided in favor of Collins and Barney.[31] Dixi Crosby was sued and fined $800 for providing consultation in a fracture case in which the patient's injured leg lost a quarter of an inch in length.[32] Although these disfigurements may have been traumatic for the individuals involved, the cases were significantly less serious than the typical case in the first third of the century.

The increased variety in the types of cases brought to trial after 1835 and patients' marked tendency to sue for significantly less severe injuries were both products of a transformed attitude toward malpractice. The increased willingness of individuals to sue and society's accompanying acceptance of the practice encouraged litigation of all types. Unrealistic public and professional expectations, born of technical advancement, particularly in fracture treatment, helped fuel the trend.[33] Before 1835, when personal and public reservations concerning malpractice prosecutions dampened the flow of cases through the courts, injuries and complaints generally had to be serious enough to overcome traditional doubts about the practice. Therefore, death and amputation cases dominate the small sample of early suits. As personal doubt and public disapprobation regarding the litigation dissipated, patients felt justified in suing physicians for injuries that resulted in minor deformities, pain, or even inconveniences.

After 1835 deformities following fractures and dislocations suddenly became the major source of malpractice prosecutions. In his

1860 *Treatise on Medical Malpractice* John Elwell claimed that "nine-tenths of all the cases of malpractice that come before the courts for adjudication arise either from the treatment of amputations, fractures, or dislocations."[34] Although Elwell was correct in noting the precom-inance of fracture-dislocation cases, his estimated proportion was prob-ably inflated. The wide variety of suits prosecuted after 1835 made it unlikely that fracture-dislocation-amputation cases could account for 90 percent of the total. Elwell also misled his audience by combining amputation cases with fractures and dislocations. Suits involving am-putations were rare after 1835, and lumping them together with other orthopedic injuries masked their insignificant contribution to the total number of cases. Stephen Smith, also writing in 1860, countered Elwell's claim by using statistics that he had gathered from "several hundred suits for malpractice." He argued that 142, or a "little over two-thirds" of the cases he studied, grew out of amputations, fractures, and dislocations. Of these 142 suits, only 8, or about 4 percent of the approximately 213 in his study originated from amputations, while 102 suits grew out of fractures, and 32 suits stemmed from disloca-tions.[35]

Smith's figures are in general agreement with the distribution of suits and the rate at which they were reported in contemporary medi-cal literature. Fracture-dislocation cases accounted for about two-thirds of the malpractice cases between 1835 and 1865, with the rest of the suits represented by the causes listed in table 2. While fracture-dislo-cation cases did not account for 90 percent of the litigation as Elwell had claimed, they did constitute a majority of the suits in the nine-teenth century. The particular propensity to sue physicians for the maltreatment of fractures and dislocations aggravated an atmosphere that was already conducive to widespread litigation and played a role in making the initial increase in suits more profound. Suits were, for a variety of reasons, becoming more socially and morally acceptable by the middle of the century. Because individuals did not feel the same compulsion to justify their actions to themselves and their community, they were freer to demand monetary remuneration even when their injuries were relatively minor, as in the type of results that often followed fracture treatment. Therefore, the general tendency to sue physicians after 1835 and the new found inclination to sue for fracture type-injuries interacted and pushed the climbing malpractice rates higher.[36]

"Shocking Outrage[s] on Professional Humanity"

Most patients, of course, chose not to sue their physicians. At the same time, many incompetent doctors escaped guilty verdicts and even prosecution. While innocent physicians were sometimes sued for minor or fabricated injuries during the first half of the century, a variety of legal rules and procedures protected ignorant and careless medical men from the grasp of justice. John Ordronaux, a frequent midcentury commentator on medical-legal issues, confirmed that "strange as it may seem, one might, through unskillfulness, sacrifice a human life with more impunity than he could mutilate or deform a toe or a finger."[37]

When patients died, it was particularly difficult to sustain a suit against the offending physician. The wronged patient could not present himself or herself to the jury as was possible in fractures and other visible injuries. Rarely was the actual cause of death readily apparent or easily demonstrable. And, as Ordronaux explained, "who would presume to say, in the case of a patient's death, that he had not naturally reached that 'last illness' foreordained to all men and of which the physician's unsuccessful treatment is the only official testimony?"[38]

Medical journals commonly chronicled egregious episodes of medical incompetence. In 1850 the parents of a young girl who was suffering from a tumor on her arm sought the advice of the most distinguished physicians available. The physicians agreed that the growth was malignant and, because it intertwined with major blood vessels, could not be removed without amputating the limb. The parents consulted a less respected, less experienced physician, who agreed to excise the tumor and save the arm. During the operation, performed in a dimly lit room, no tourniquet was employed and no pressure applied to stop the flow of blood. The doctor clumsily cut into the growth instead of removing it whole. To stop the "frightful" bleeding, the physician tied off the main artery and large veins and "bandage[d] the arm tightly from the fingers up." According to one editorialist,

"This extraordinary and unheard of proceeding, was well calculated to insure [sic] the fatal result that followed." Despite breaking several rules of established practice, the surgeon apparently escaped legal action.[39]

Physicians at respected institutions also committed "shocking outrage[s] on professional humanity." In the mid-1850s doctors at the New York Academy of Medicine and Bellevue Hospital experimented with the injection of silver nitrate into the trachea and lungs to cure bronchitis, tubercular symptoms, and other pulmonary maladies. The treatment, performed primarily on charity patients, resulted in suffering and death within a few days. *Scalpel*, a New York medical journal, alerted the district attorney to the "utterly absurd, and highly reprehensible" procedures, and pleaded with its readers to "forever guard our public charities against such cruel experiments."[40]

One of the most grotesque episodes of medical incompetence occurred in the late 1860s. A physician struggling with a difficult birth prescribed ergot to a woman to induce contractions and the expulsion of her child. The drug did not help, and during the protracted labor the woman's uterus ruptured. The physician dissected the fetus to save the patient's life, but the severed head escaped the uterus into the abdominal cavity. The doctor frantically removed the fetus and afterbirth to relieve the patient. The attending midwife suddenly noticed adult intestines intertwined with the removed placenta and infant body parts. When the physician realized his error, he told the patient that "if she had anything to say she had better say it." She asked for her minister and died several hours later. Despite the gross incompetence of the physician, he never faced a malpractice jury. The woman's husband accepted $300 in lieu of litigation.[41]

The nineteenth-century common law doctrine and statutes governing wrongful death made it difficult to convict a physician for the death of a patient. When a person died under a physician's care, the doctor might theoretically be charged under criminal or civil law. *Criminal charges* generally refer to offenses against the public, while *civil charges* pertain to private wrongs. Criminal charges were nearly impossible to sustain against physicians. The patient's consent to the fatal treatment virtually eliminated the chance of a murder or manslaughter conviction.

The most important precedent for manslaughter charges against a physician was the 1809 Massachusetts case of *Commonwealth* v. *Samuel Thomson*. Thomson, the founder of the immensely popular Thomsonian medical sect, was called to the home of Ezra Lovett, a young man who had been confined to his bed for several days with a severe cold. Thomson wrapped Lovett in hot blankets and gave him dose after dose of powerful emetics, which induced violent vomiting. In addition, Thomson supplied his patient with a concoction that induced profuse sweating. Thomson prescribed dozens of emetic and sweating procedures over several days. When the emetics ceased to work, Thomson administered a cathartic (laxative) concoction, and Lovett went into convulsions—at which point Thomson's assistants held the thrashing Lovett so that Thomson could administer yet another emetic dose. After three days of almost constant convulsions, Lovett died.

Acting on reports that several of Thomson's patients had died after severe treatments, the Massachusetts attorney general brought murder charges against the practitioner. The chief judge of the state supreme court acknowledged that it was clear that Lovett had died as a result of Thomson's treatment, but he explained that that charge of murder required that "the killing must have been done with malice, either express or implied." He held that there was no evidence that suggested that Thomson intended to kill or injure his patient. The judges on the court also ruled that Thomson could be convicted of manslaughter only if the death had been the result of an unlawful act or "gross negligence." If a physician "acted with the honest intention and expectation of curing the deceased," he could not be found guilty of manslaughter. *Commonwealth* v. *Thomson* served as the shield that protected even ignorant physicians from criminal prosecution for much of the century. Defense attorneys could argue that almost any form of treatment was performed with the honest intention of curing.[42]

Similarly, the nineteenth-century doctrine of *wrongful death*, a civil offense, also tended to benefit medical men whose treatment resulted in the death of their patients. In the English common law of the seventeenth century, under the doctrine of *acti personalis moritur cum persona*, a claim for personal injury could not survive the death of the victim. In other words, the deceased's family could not sue for damages inflicted while the victim was still alive. When a person died as a result of injuries, it was considered a felony, and the family of the victim received a proportion of the perpetrator's property. Since the criminal law provided an award for the victim's family, the common law allowed no other remedy for wrongful death. Death was a public, not a private wrong. This doctrine forbade noncriminal awards for wrongful death long after the practice of confiscating the convicted felon's property was abolished. Even though the original justification for the rule had disappeared, an English court in *Baker* v. *Bolton* (1808) reaffirmed the doctrine that the death of a human being was not grounds for legal action for monetary damages.[43]

In several early decisions it appeared as if American courts would not accept the English rule.[44] Even after the 1808 *Baker* v. *Bolton* decision, which explicitly overruled wrongful death actions, some American courts in the early nineteenth century allowed nonfelon suits for wrongful death damages. American judges argued that the original justification for the doctrine was superannuated and had no place in American law.[45] The new environment and an informal sense of justice temporarily prevailed over formal doctrine.

In the first half of the nineteenth century the industrial revolution swept across the eastern seaboard, leaving a wide variety of unnatural deaths in its wake. Innovations in manufacturing and transportation generated a revolution in the scale and gruesomeness of accidental injury. Fatal railroad and steamboat accidents were common. The development of these industries would be severely hampered by frequent and costly wrongful death claims. State judges who in effect favored the expansion of industrial capitalism devised a variety of doctrinal innovations and adjustments that limited the personal injury liability of these enterprises. For example, between 1842 and 1850 Massachusetts Chief Justice Lemuel Shaw transformed the nature of legal liability by championing the *fellow servant rule, contributory negligence,* and *assumption of risk.* In addition he shifted the notion of legal responsibility from strict liability to no liability without fault. These modifications benefitted venture capitalism and decreased the likelihood of personal awards by requiring a higher degree of proof from injured parties.[46]

In the same spirit, Shaw's court in the landmark *Carey* v. *Berkshire R.R.* (1848) ignored three decades of American precedent, cited the

English *Baker* v. *Bolton* case, and ruled that there was not, and never had been, a common law action for wrongful death. Appellate courts after 1848 followed the *Carey* decision's lead and began to deny families of accident victims the right to sue for damages. In railroad law, it was cheaper to kill than to injure. To remedy this omission, from 1840 to 1887, numerous state legislatures passed laws allowing wrongful death actions against common carriers such as railroads and steamboats. Although these statutes in many cases were written to remedy the specific problem of railroad death, many contained wording that seemed to support other kinds of death actions.[47]

In cases involving physicians, trial court judges sometimes allowed juries to use the new statutes to award damages to the families of dead patients. In June 1863 Albert Braunberger was working at a tannery in Pittsburgh, Pennsylvania. His leg "came into contact" with the machine he was working on and an exposed piston shaft about two inches in diameter crushed the limb below the knee. Braunberger crawled twenty feet from the engine to the door and called for a fellow workman. Dr. George Cleis examined Braunberger at home, declared that the injury was "only a flesh wound," sewed up the gash, and told the man's family that he would soon be back to work. Braunberger maintained that his leg was badly broken.

After seven days Braunberger developed a severe fever, his abdomen became distended, and his leg began to swell and discharge profuse and offensive matter from the wound. The injured man asked for another physician. When the second doctor arrived, the odor in the room forced him to cover his face with a handkerchief. He removed the stitches and surveyed the injury. The muscles below the knee were "lacerated and broken," those of the thigh separated from the bone. The bones of the knee and lower leg, according to his account, "were not simply broken, they were absolutely ground." The physician declared that the rule of practice of "every intelligent civil and military surgeon" would have been to amputate the leg immediately after the accident and not sew up the wound. A team of physicians attempted to nurse Braunberger back to health and to amputate his mangled leg, but he died nine days after the accident.[48]

Braunberger's wife sued Cleis for wrongful death for ignorantly sewing up the wound, misdiagnosing the obvious injury, and failing to amputate the leg at the proper and customary time. Her attorney argued that these actions had led to Braunberger's death. The trial court judge explained to the jury that the law required physicians to exercise a "reasonable degree of care and skill in the treatment of this patient." He held that though there had been no common law action for wrongful death, the Pennsylvania legislature had passed a statute declaring that when death was caused by "unlawful violence or negligence," the survivor of the deceased could sue and recover damages for the death. The physician's attorney admitted that the treatment may have constituted malpractice, but argued that "mere malpractice" was not "unlawful violence or negligence as [was] contemplated by the act." Therefore, there should be no award granted for wrongful death. The local trial judge and jury, however, believed that the statute applied to medically induced deaths and awarded Mrs. Braunberger $3,250.[49]

Wrongful death awards for incompetent medical treatment often depended on how trial court judges and juries interpreted the new statutes. In flagrant instances of medical ineptitude or carelessness, local courts sometimes relied on the statutes and a subjective sense of justice to award the victim's family compensation. When defendants appealed to state supreme courts, however, appellate judges, insulated from local pressures, sometimes applied a narrower, more formal interpretation of the statutes and relied on the general notion that there could be no recovery after death, even in the face of flagrant incompetence. Though Cleis apparently did not appeal the verdict, the Michigan case of *Hyatt* v. *Adams* illustrated the unsettled nature of wrongful death law.[50]

In 1865 Lucinda Adams visited Dr. Loften Hyatt complaining of pain in her abdomen. Hyatt diagnosed the pain as a uterine tumor and assured Adams that he could safely remove the growth in half an hour. Hyatt performed the operation in the presence of three women, in the bedroom of the Adams' farmhouse. Using morphine and chloroform, Hyatt struggled for an hour with his hands and forceps to pull the tumor free. Hyatt abandoned the forceps and told the witnesses that he needed some instrument "bent like a fishhook." After in fact attempting to use a large fishhook, the physician bent a large knitting needle into the desired shape and sharpened the end on a grindstone. The futile attempts to remove the tumor lasted several hours over two days. Adams' husband later said that he could hear her screams several acres away. Hyatt declared that he had shredded the tumor sufficiently so that it would pass naturally, but Mrs. Adams died the following day.[51]

Adams sued Hyatt for *loss of consortium*, or the loss of the service, comfort, and society of his wife. He also claimed damages for his and his wife's mental suffering. During the trial, Mrs. Adams' body was exhumed, and an examination revealed that despite the energetic attempts of the physician, the tumor had not been touched. Instead, the operation had injured the woman's pelvic cavity and had resulted in infection, shock, and death. Several physicians testified against Hyatt and his mode of treatment. The Michigan jury deliberated only a short time before granting Adams an award of $2,000 plus $159 in costs.[52]

Hyatt and his lawyers appealed the case to the Michigan supreme court. While the jury was supposed to award Adams damages only for his loss of consortium, it had granted what amounted to death damages. The physician's attorney argued that "at common law the death of a human being cannot be made the ground for legal action." The lawyer concluded that defendants could be held liable only for damages incurred in the interval between injury and death. In this instance, Mrs. Adams lived three days after the initial surgical procedure.[53]

Chief Judge Christiancy, who wrote the majority decision in *Hyatt v. Adams*, observed that while "total want of skill" and a high degree of carelessness could have made Hyatt guilty of manslaughter, he was charged only with depriving Adams of his wife's services and companionship. Any claim that Mrs. Adams had against the physician died when she did. Citing the 1848 *Carey v. Berkshire R.R.* case, Christiancy declared that it "is admitted on all hands, and can not be denied" that at common law there was no civil action for the death of a human being "or for any damages suffered by any person in consequence of such death."[54] The Michigan judge, like other appellate jurists after the *Carey* case ignored the early American decisions that suggested that there was a common law wrongful death action.

Christiancy discusssed at length why he believed that there was no civil law death remedy. Conventional wisdom held that there was no action because under the old common law, relatives were provided for by felony confiscation rules. Christiancy offered a more fundamental explanation. The judge declared that there was a "natural and almost universal repugnance among enlightened nations to setting a price on human life." He argued that Christian people found the notion of compensating loss of life with money revolting. Christiancy admitted that Michigan had passed a wrongful death statute (almost identical to the one in Pennsylvania), but he implied that it was necessary only to meet the demands of "the new modes of travel and business" and could not apply to all forms of death. He believed that it was the role of the appellate courts "to prevent the best and most benevolent feelings of our nature from clouding the judgment of jurors and prompting them to intemperate verdicts in the vain endeavor to give money compensation for that which, in its very nature, is incapable of valuation by any such standard." He warned that the idea of pecuniary compensation for human life would tend to render it less sacred in the public estimation.[55]

Finally, Christiancy condemned the concept of mental anguish of the husband as indeterminate. If a husband could recover for mental suffering, then why not a mother, a friend, or a neighbor? In concluding, Christiancy agreed with Hyatt's attorney and ruled that there could be no award for the death, or for the husband's mental suffering. Adams, however, did deserve to be compensated for the loss of his wife's services and companionship for the three days from the initial surgery to her death. The court determined her service at $.50 day and calculated Hyatt's total legal liability at $1.50.[56]

Suits for the wrongful death of patients were legally and substantively different from other forms of malpractice litigation. These factors undermined attempts to sue physicians in fatal cases through the first two-thirds of the century. Consequently, death suits did not play a significant role in the initial increase of suits against physicians, and many of the worst cases of medical incompetence probably went unpunished.

Dissatisfied Patients
and the "Noble Sister Profession"

When patients received permanent injuries after treatment for fractures or other maladies, different factors precipitated the initial decision to hire a lawyer and begin a lawsuit. Often patients acted on their own without any apparent prodding from friends, lawyers, or other physicians. For example, in the mid-1850s, after an Ohio man suffered a compound fracture of his lower leg, his family summoned a physician who set and wrapped the victim's seriously injured leg. Within days the leg became inflamed and swollen, so the physician removed all the wrappings from the limb. The family, believing that the physician was neglecting the fracture, dismissed the doctor after two weeks. The patient suffered in bed for almost a year. His first action upon leaving his bed on crutches was to visit, and hire, an attorney.[57] In a similar case in 1856, Nathan Varner was riding his sleigh, drunk, about two miles from his home in Zanesville, Ohio. Varner lost control of the horse, fell from the sleigh, and broke his lower leg. When Dr. Thaddeus Reamy was treating the injury, he told Varner that there was almost always shortening after these types of injuries and asked his patient if he was going to sue if the leg did not heal perfectly. Reamy replied that he would be "damned if he wouldn't" and warned that he would make the physician "pay like hell." Varner believed that his patient was joking. He was not, and when his injured leg healed 1⅛ inch shorter than normal, Reamy found a lawyer and sued the physician for $3,000.[58]

Although there were many instances in which patients began litigation on their own initiative, outside parties and the physician himself often played important roles in the decision to file malpractice charges. When a young New York man's fractured elbow mended but froze in a rigid position in 1845, his friends convinced him to sue for damages; he won an award of $450.[59] In the late 1830s in another New York case members of the community began a subscription drive to raise money to help an injured man sue his doctors.[60]

Some malpractice suits arose out of cross-complaints after a physician sued his patient for fees. Other patients used the threat of malpractice to intimidate physicians into dropping their claims for fees.[61] Patients who were sued by their physicians for nonpayment of fees could effectively use a cross-suit of malpractice because of the loosening of traditional legal pleading rules in the late eighteenth and early nineteenth centuries and the civil procedure reforms of the late 1840s and early 1850s.[62] In 1850 a Kentucky patient refused to pay his medical bill, claiming that the physician had infected his family with smallpox while treating them for typhus. The physician sued for fees, and the patient, on a cross-complaint, sued for malpractice damages.[63] In the 1850s Dr. William Gautier sued Texas slaveholder William Graham for $187.57 in fees for treating ten slaves who died. Gautier had treated the slaves for cholera. Graham, however, claimed that the physician had wrongly diagnosed the slaves and caused their deaths and demanded $10,700 for the costs of the slaves.[64]

Even though disputes over fees surfaced regularly in malpractice cases, reluctance of patients to pay medical bills alone cannot explain the sudden appearance of numerous suits in the 1840s. Patients would have been able to file cross-suits well before 1840. Suits for delinquent medical bills did indeed reflect the general popular antipathy that formed part of the environment responsible for engendering malpractice prosecutions. But disputes over fees provided only the precipitating incident of an occasional suit rather than the cause of the dramatic increase of litigation.

Medical fees became an important issue in the nineteenth-century malpractice debate because they helped characterize the type of patient whom physicians most distrusted. Because so many malpractice plaintiffs had not paid their bills, physicians began to believe that their poorer patients were the most likely to sue. Undoubtedly, many patients refused to pay because they were dissatisfied with their treatment. But, these plaintiffs' poverty was substantiated by the fact that in many cases they could not pay their court costs either. Physicians regularly observed that a disproportionate number of malpractice plaintiffs could afford neither the doctor's bill nor the legal costs of the suits. This "class of persons," physicians argued, constituted the profession's biggest malpractice risk.[65] An 1878 survey of malpractice in Maine discovered that the vast majority of malpractice plaintiffs could not pay court costs.[66] Even if indigent patients constituted a majority of malpractice plaintiffs, they were not the "cause" of the malpractice phenomenon. Physicians treated poor patients before the outbreak of malpractice fever, and the inability to pay bills did not spark lawsuits on a broad scale.

In contrast to many twentieth-century physicians' claims that lawyers incite malpractice suits either directly or indirectly, mid–nineteenth-century doctors believed that attorneys were mostly honorable and more guilty of misunderstanding than malevolence. Stephen Smith was convinced:

Could the capable and the conscientious legal adviser clearly understand and be thoroughly impressed with the inherent difficulties in the practice of medicine, he would be slow to counsel prosecutions of medical men; and had the court the same knowledge, we believe that a nonsuit would be the summary termination of many a trial for alleged malpractice.[67]

Frank Hamilton, a respected New York surgeon and a perpetual expert witness, maintained that while there may have been a few who undertook malpractice suits, "honorable and intelligent lawyers seldom countenance these prosecutions."[68] Joshua Spencer, a New York attorney, explained in 1855 that while he had frequently served as counsel for physicians in malpractice cases, he had never worked for the plaintiff/patient. "My brethren," he noted, "generally, look upon the complaints with suspicion and refuse to meddle with them."[69]

Physicians acknowledged that lawyers regularly refused to represent undeserving clients and often withdrew from cases when they discovered the true nature of the injury involved. One physician in 1856 exhorted his colleagues, "[L]et us be thankful that the poor and unenlightened will often find counsellors actuated by higher motives than the paltry profits of a suit, and so honest as to use the influence which they possess over their clients to prevent rather than forward so ill-judged an action."[70] Samuel Parkman, a surgeon at Massachusetts General Hospital, examined the physician's relation to the law at midcentury and concluded that "the practitioner of medicine has no cause of complaint against the law or its ministers."[71] Most accounts seemed to confirm this judgment. A report on malpractice in Ohio recounted suits in which "some difficulty was experienced in finding a lawyer to undertake the case."[72] The *Boston Medical and Surgical Journal* reported an incident in 1860 in which a New York man searched his county for a lawyer to sue his son's physician. Despite the physician's treatment for a degenerative hip disease, the boy's hip had frozen in one position. "To the honor of the legal profession," the journal observed, "no attorney in the County could be induced to engage in the suit." However, "[a]n obscure 'limb of the law' was found in an adjoining county" to handle the case.[73]

Elwell argued in his *Treatise on Medical Malpractice* that lawyers were hampered by the lack of relevant medical and legal materials on the topic. "[T]he attorney," he explained, "experiences the greatest difficulty, doubt, and perplexity, in preparing cases involving the question of Malpractice."[74] Through the 1860s law journals rarely contained articles or commentary on malpractice, and lawyers had to rely on their own scant knowledge of medical issues and on legal authorities scattered, undigested, through appellate law reports. Many writers seemed to believe sincerely that most lawyers would decline or drop illegitimate cases once they were apprised of the intricacies and uncertainties of the medical world. One Worcester, Massachusetts, lawyer helped a patient sue a physician whose supposedly inept treatment had resulted in a withered and deformed arm after what was allegedly a simple fracture. After listening to several medical witnesses, the attorney rose in court and declared that the case would proceed no further. He had mistakenly believed that the injury was a simple fracture, but the evidence had demonstrated that the injury had been compound and was very difficult to treat. He "handsomely" and "honorabl[y]," according to one medical journal, praised the physician's treatment and abandoned the suit.[75]

Despite the general era of good feeling between the professions, some writers foreshadowed the more negative attitude that became prevalent in the late nineteenth and early twentieth centuries. In 1854 Dr. T. J. Pray observed that in trials for malpractice, "it seems to be the great forte of legal gentlemen to make an abusive tirade upon the medical profession at large." He warned that "*Braying* and *sound argument* are two different kinds of action, and originate generally not from the same species of animals . . . A man may put on a lion's skin, but too often certain long appendages will peep out from under their concealment, and betray the wearer."[76] Pray's observations, however, did not reflect the majority position among physicians. Admittedly, lawyers served as an essential tool of the malpractice plaintiff. But the lowering standards for entry into the profession had only slightly increased the number of attorneys in practice. Some lawyers used contingency fee arrangements, but physicians did not directly attack the practice as an evil incitement to litigation.

Although change was already underway, physicians and lawyers often came from the same social class and held similar interests. In addition, lawyers were commonly believed to exert a restraining influence on the antielite, antiprofessional sentiments of the period. Alexis de Tocqueville reported that Jacksonian lawyers provided "the strongest barrier against the faults of democracy." When the common people "let themselves get intoxicated by their ideas," de Tocqueville explained, "the lawyers apply an almost invisible brake which slows them down and halts them."[77] Lawyers and physicians, along with the clergy, constituted the "liberal professions," which, in the eyes of members of these groups, provided enlightenment, order, and cohesion to American society.[78] Consequently, between 1835 and 1865 physicians did not believe that lawyers were unredeemable villains but felt instead that they constituted a misguided, underinformed, but "noble sister profession."[79]

Physicians usually laid most of the blame for inciting suits on other heads. Many physicians believed that other doctors played a central role in convincing patients to sue. During the nineteenth century *allopaths*, or *regular* doctors, were joined by a variety of alternative healers, or *irregular* practitioners, such as *Thomsonians, homeopaths,* and *hydropaths,* who followed radically different treatment regimes. Occasionally irregular practitioners encouraged patients to sue regular physicians. Most observers agreed, however, that regular physicians stirred up more suits than their irregular counterparts. Regular physicians frequently incited suits against their own kind. They competed bitterly with their colleagues and purposefully advised patients to sue rivals in order to ruin their reputations and gain patients.[80]

An "Ordinary Standard of Care, Skill, and Diligence"

No matter how a patient made the initial decision to sue his physician, through friends, a lawyer, a rival practitioner, or his own initiative, the path afterward followed a fairly standard pattern. True, legal rules of evidence and procedure varied from state to state and from decade to decade. Nevertheless a model of a typical case may be imagined.

Most malpractice plaintiffs were men; when women were the victims of supposed medical malpractice, their husbands or fathers generally sued the physician. After an injured patient, usually with a fractured or dislocated limb, decided to sue his physician, he hired a lawyer. Sometimes lawyers made contingency arrangements and prosecuted a case for a percentage of the anticipated damage award. In other cases, attorneys merely deferred payment until after the trial or were paid at the time of their employment.

With rare exceptions, malpractice cases were heard by a jury in a county court house. Although physicians occasionally favored the use of arbitrators to decide malpractice complaints, by the 1840s it was an uncommon practice.[81] Jury trials were the almost unalterable rule. Until the late 1840s the lawyer and his client filed a writ of *trespass on the case* or *action on the case*.[82] After the late 1840s various states abolished the writ system, and thereafter all civil offenses, including malpractice, fell under the rubric of a catch-all civil action writ. Law reformers had hoped that this civil procedure reform would simplify the complex, traditional pleading requirements. However, with the exception of abolishing the category of specific writs, most of the pleading requirements remained, and the reforms did not significantly alter the broad outlines of malpractice procedure.[83]

The common law required that the plaintiff prove that a doctor-patient relationship had existed between him and the physician/defendant. This point was seldom in dispute. Physicians usually admitted to treating the patient, and treatment was enough evidence to establish that a *duty-filled* relationship existed. After confirming the existence of a doctor-patient relationship, the court would examine whether the physician was legally liable for the permanent injuries or pain of the patient. The physician was always held legally responsible for everything that he explicitly promised to do. For example, if a physician claimed that he could save a patient's badly crushed leg and "make it as good as new" yet was unable to fulfill his promise, the injured man would have a strong case against the practitioner.

However, such simple situations constituted a very small proportion of the suits against physicians in the nineteenth century. Physicians rarely guaranteed their work, and if they did so orally, the existence of such a promise would be very difficult to prove in court. In fact, liability based on a promise to cure constituted an entirely different type of case from the typical medical malpractice charge. Responsibility based on promises to cure involved an explicit, conscious agreement between doctor and patient, an ordinary contract. The theoretical and doctrinal source of most malpractice liability was more ambiguous.[84]

The more common situation did not involve a physician's promise to cure patients. In such situations the common law did not require a complete cure. In 1833 an Ohio man tried to bring charges against a physician under a writ of assumpsit, or breach of promise, for failing to deliver safely the plaintiff's baby. The trial court judge dismissed the case because "the law does not raise from the fact of employment, an implied undertaking to cure."[85]

The element of explicit contract to cure aside, when trial court judges held or even implied that physicians guaranteed cures, appellate courts consistently overturned the decisions and granted physician/ defendants new trials. For example, an Ohio man who charged a physician with malpractice in the 1830s declared to the court that he had retained the physician to "manage, take care of, and *cure*" (original emphasis) his fractured leg. Although the physician "promised" to set and *cure* his leg, the plaintiff insisted that he had lost his limb to amputation because of the doctor's failure. The physician asked the trial court judge to tell the jury that the law required proof of the existence of an explicit promise to cure. The judge, however, explained to the jury that because the defendant had held himself out to the world as a physician, there was no need to prove an explicit promise to cure; the law assumed the existence of that duty. The jury found the physician guilty of malpractice. The Ohio supreme court summarily reversed the decision, ruling that physicians did not implicitly promise to cure every case and they would not be held responsible for such a promise.[86]

Few trial court judges ignored the clear common law precedents regarding implied promises to cure, but when they did, state appellate courts invariably reversed the decisions. In 1853 one rogue Pennsylvania trial judge went so far as to tell a jury that the defendant/physician was required to use the skill necessary "to set the leg so as to make it straight and of equal length with the other." The judge even suggested that "if suits were more frequently brought, we would have perhaps fewer practitioners of medicine and surgery not possessing the requisite professional skill and knowledge." Although the trial jury ruled against the physician, the state supreme court overturned the decision and reiterated the common law precedent that "the implied contract of a physician is not to cure—to restore a fractured limb to its natural perfectness—but to treat the case with care, diligence, and skill."[37]

The bulk of the legal arguments, evidence, and testimony centered not on promises and guarantees to cure, but rather on the meaning and requirements of the terms ordinary *care, diligence*, and *skill*. Before malpractice juries retired to make their decisions, trial court judges would instruct them on the common law rules. Judges across the country drew on virtually the same precedents, and their essential requirements varied little from state to state. In 1833 a trial court judge told a Connecticut jury that "if there was either carelessness, or a want of ordinary diligence, care, and skill, then the plaintiff was entitled to recover."[88] The Maine supreme court declared in 1848 that "[t]he [malpractice] defendant is not liable for a want of the highest degree of skill, but for ordinary skill. And of course only for the want of ordinary care and judgment."[89] The Illinois supreme court enunciated one of the clearest and most enduring renderings of the doctrine in an 1860 case in which Abraham Lincoln was an attorney for the patient. Justice Walker wrote:

The principle is plain and of uniform application, that when a person assumes the profession of physician and surgeon, he must, in its exercise, be held to employ a reasonable amount of care and skill. For any thing short of that degree of skill in his practice, the law will hold him responsible for any injury that may result from its absence. While he is not required to possess the highest order of qualification, to which some men may attain, still he must possess and exercise that degree of skill which is ordinarily possessed by members of the profession.[90]

The first American treatise on tort law, published by Francis Hillard in 1859, reinforced the essential permanence of the ordinary skill and care doctrine, as did Amasa Redfield's important *Treatise on the Law of Negligence* in 1870.[91]

Although the formal legal definitions of standard of care over the first half of the nineteenth century were similar and fairly consistent, in actual operation the principles of malpractice liability were anything but "plain" and of "uniform application."[92] The unornamented simplicity of the maxim "ordinary diligence, care, and skill" engendered ambiguity. In addition, the requirements of the trial process and the prerogatives of trial judges complicated the ostensibly simple "ordinary" care standard.

The "Glorious Uncertainty of Legal Justice and Medical Testimony"

The plaintiff/patient was required to present expert witnesses to prove that his physician had not exercised "ordinary" skill and care. In rebuttal, the defendant/physician could offer testimony from his own expert witnesses. Witnesses testified to both fact and opinion. However, an expert was not allowed to make a judgment on whether the treatment constituted malpractice. Expert witnesses were required to give their opinion on whether the plaintiff's injury was permanent and whether the treatment provided by the defendant was standard. They were also asked whether the type and the degree of the plaintiff's permanent injury would have occurred after competent medical care. The first question rarely generated much controversy. Permanent injuries were usually readily apparent and not disputed by the defendant. Most of the disagreement among witnesses, and, indeed, the central issue in most malpractice cases, derived from problems in determining what constituted ordinary care in each instance. Precedents applied only to legal doctrine and not to technical information. Medical practice was evolving. Every injury was ostensibly unique. Therefore, this phase of the trial was unpredictable.

Expert witnesses complicated the determination of what constituted an ordinary degree of skill and acceptable results. Since medical licensure was mostly a dead letter by the late 1830s, courts allowed any practicing physician, licensed or unlicensed, educated or not, to serve as an expert witness. According to one text, "Extra knowledge on questions of science, skill, trade, business or other matters requiring special knowledge, qualifi[ed] the person thus informed to give opinions in courts of justice."[93]

Practitioners from different schools of medicine, regular physicians, homeopaths, hydropaths, and Thomsonians were allowed to testify interchangeably at each other's trials. This practice was remarkable because therapeutically, competitively, and socially, the various schools of medicine were generally at odds with one another. Complicating the matter further, even though a variety of types of practitioners could testify at a trial, the defendant was required to exercise ordinary skill only according to the standards of his own school of practice.

For example, in the late 1840s an Iowa man sued a Thomsonian physician because he had caused the man's wife pain and injury during and after the delivery of a child. The Thomsonian had failed to remove the placenta following the birth, and the mother suffered a massive loss of blood and great pain. The afterbirth was finally removed by a regular physician, who testified at the malpractice trial. He explained that it was standard practice to remove the placenta at a much earlier period and that a delay was injurious and created the risk of puerperal fever. Several other regular physicians concurred and testified against the defendant.[94]

The Thomsonian physician attempted to prove that his school of medicine considered it improper to remove the placenta until it was expelled by nature. The trial judge, however, refused to allow the introduction of the evidence, and the jury found the Thomsonian guilty. He appealed the judgment to the Iowa supreme court, which overturned the decision. Writing for the majority of the court, the chief judge explained that because there "is no particular system of medicine established or favored by the laws of Iowa, . . . [t]he people are free to select from the various classes of medical men." "While a regular physician is expected to follow the rules of the old school in the art of curing, the botanic physician must be equally expected to adhere to his adopted method."[95]

Paradoxes multiplied. Courts strictly followed the doctrine that physicians were accountable for injuries resulting from the failure to supply ordinary skill and care only according to their respective systems of treating diseases. Yet, through the first half of the century judges continued to accept any practicing physician as an expert witness. Not until the early 1860s did state legislatures and appellate courts begin making changes in the rules of evidence so that physicians from different schools could not testify against one another. Regular practitioners appeared to suffer much more from this practice than their irregular counterparts. While irregular practitioners were rarely sued, regular practitioners bore the brunt of the majority of the suits and routinely had to face their hostile counterparts in court.[96] For example, in 1849 a young doctor was sued after he failed to save a patient's life following a difficult fracture and amputation. While two regular physicians testified on his behalf, a homeopath and a Thomsonian were aligned against him as expert witnesses for the prosecution.[97]

Although testimony from rival schools of medical practice contributed to the confusion and antipathy in the witness-box, evidence presented by regular physicians against regular physicians constituted the majority of the proof in malpractice trials. The same features that characterized irregular practitioners' testimony applied equally to regular physicians' testimony in court. The competition among regular physicians was nearly as vigorous as that between regulars and irregulars. Often this contention among regulars carried over into court, and physicians found their rivals testifying against them.[98]

In addition, medical evidence on appropriate treatment for injuries or illnesses was not always consistent, even when all the witnesses were regular physicians. Many times the expert witnesses came from radically different regions of the country; sometimes expert witnesses practiced in areas quite different from those of the defendant/physician. Elwell recounted the episode of a rural Ohio man who had lost his leg to amputation after crushing it while building a log cabin in a new settlement. Several years later, the man and some friends recovered the bone, cleaned it, and used it as the basis of a suit against the physician who performed the operation. The bone was shipped to Philadelphia, New York, and Washington, D.C., where physicians examined it and provided depositions. Another trial, for the mistreatment of an eye ailment in Cleveland, elicited expert opinions from physicians who practiced in Boston and New York.[99] Although the physicians won the several trials related to these cases, the incidents demonstrate how witnesses were sometimes drawn from diverse community and medical surroundings and asked to judge the competency of a medical defendant. Often, however, defendants had more to fear from local colleagues. Keen competition for patients or personal animosity could influence the testimony of local practitioners.

Even when expert witnesses were not competing with the defendant for patients or practicing in a center of medical excellence, their testimony seldom clearly delineated the acceptable standards of the profession. The unspecific nature of the malpractice doctrine allowed even disinterested medical witnesses to disagree on what constituted ordinary care. The state of medicine between 1835 and 1865 also contributed to the frequent dissension among medical witnesses. The difficulty in defining standard practice once a case was taken to court was aggravated by attacks from irregular practitioners, the growth of statistical scrutiny of procedures, and universal recognition of the considerable uncertainty in medicine. As John Elwell noted in 1860:

While the uncertainty of medicine is readily admitted, the reasons of this uncertainty, and the unsolved state of the science, are far from being understood; and not being understood, more blame is often thrown upon the physician or surgeon than if there existed an intelligent knowledge of the real inherent difficulties of his profession.[100]

Even in the treatment of fractures, where significant progress had been made in the first third of the century, competing theories and expectations were more prevalent than many practitioners realized.[101] A single trial often yielded several opinions on the correct procedure for setting a broken leg.

Similarly, obstetric treatment, where physicians claimed to possess scientific advantage over midwives, was far from standardized. In 1864 a Pennsylvania man sued a physician for injuring a child during its delivery. Six years earlier the plaintiff's wife had suffered a difficult labor. She bled profusely and lay for nearly eight hours with only the arm of the baby protruding from the birth canal. The woman pleaded with the physician to "take away the child and save her [the mother's] life." Finally, the doctor amputated the arm claiming that he believed the baby was dead and that he feared for the life of the mother. Immediately after the amputation, however, the woman delivered an otherwise healthy girl. During the trial, at which the six-year-old girl was present, medical witnesses presented greatly divergent views on the case. One physician criticized the defendant saying that the practice of amputation in such cases had been long abandoned. He also contended that ether, then available, could have been used to ease delivery and turn the child so that a natural birth would have ensued. Other witnesses testified that the amputation did nothing to ease delivery and that other methods would have been preferable. Still other physicians favored the use of morphine or other relaxants. The witnesses who testified for the defendant, however, opposed the use of anesthesia in such cases, praised the doctor's treatment, and claimed that both mother and child would have died in any other circumstances. After hearing the wide range of medical opinions, the plaintiff's attorney informed the judge that he wished to drop charges against the physician.[102]

Conflicting expert testimony did not always work in favor of the defendant. Both malicious and innocent disagreements of medical witnesses extended the already wide latitude of discretion left to the jury. A medical editorialist in 1847 condemned the "glorious uncertainty of legal justice and of medical testimony" and warned that conflicting testimony "bewildered" lay juries.[103] Jurors were not bound to accept the evidence of expert testimony even when it was unanimous; disagreement among medical witnesses gave jurors even freer rein. As one irate New York doctor reported in 1854, "A single dissenting voice among the surgeons on the stand is enough to turn the scale in favor of the plaintiff, toward whom the sympathies of the jury invariably run."[104]

Juries frequently found against the defendant even when the bulk and quality of the expert testimony supported the physician. The jury's social beliefs and attitudes toward the profession surfaced in many ways. If a juror harbored a general antipathy toward the medical profession at large, as much of society did in the period, he might vote against the physician regardless of the evidence to the contrary. If a juror used the service of an irregular practitioner, he might have been more likely to believe a homeopathic witness for example, or less likely to rule against a Thomsonian defendant in a malpractice case.

The Locality Rule

The nature and development of national medical practice further complicated the determination of what constituted an "ordinary" standard of care. In the 1824 *Lowell* v. *Faxon & Hawks* case, the trial judge instructed the jury that a physician in an "obscure village" was not required to possess the same degree of skill as his urban counterpart.[105] Instead, he need only possess and exercise the degree of skill that was ordinarily possessed and exercised by other rural practitioners in similar communities. This notion, which became known as the *locality rule* in the late nineteenth century, was a recognition of the decentralized nature of the medical profession and the nation. The locality rule was unknown in English common law and until the 1870s, unsupported by any state appellate court decision. In the first third of the century some judges instructed juries to abide by its formula. Other juries, because they understood and sympathized with the plight of the rural practitioner, probably often applied an informal version of the locality rule when they considered the "ordinary" care requirement.

The locality rule, however, did not become a general feature of malpractice law until the last third of the nineteenth century. Between 1835 and 1865, national medical journals multiplied, and transportation and communication improved. As Stephen Smith argued, it was "manifestly dangerous" to accept the locality rule in 1860 because every physician now had the opportunity and the duty to keep abreast of medical advancement.[106] Much had changed since the first part of the century. Judges only irregularly instructed juries to calculate the required medical competency by community standards. Jurors, with less general sympathy for physicians and under the mistaken impression that the American medical world was becoming homogeneous, were more willing to hold parochial physicians to the standards of their better educated and more practiced cosmopolitan counterparts. Plaintiffs would summon medical experts from larger cities, other communities, and even other states without regard to the relative standards of practice. In the case of small communities, urban physicians usually served as witnesses to the detriment of the defendant/ physician.

Medical practice in America, however, had not become homogeneous. Despite the proliferation of medical journals and schools and the increased interconnectedness of the rest of society and the economy, physicians' skill in different geographic locations and social surroundings varied greatly. Hospital-based physicians with thriving urban practices, for example, were exposed to a wider range and greater number of injuries and illnesses. Some writers and jurists recognized the still decentralized and uneven nature of American medicine and the need for adjusted standards of care. One observer argued in 1849 that there was only one remedy for the wave of malpractice prosecutions. He demanded, "Let judges make themselves acquainted with what should be the qualifications required of medical men, according to the *standard justified by their location*, and charge juries definitely and clearly upon that point."[107] Elwell agreed that it was sometimes difficult to define *ordinary* degree of skill:

> It may vary in the same state or country. There are many neighborhoods, in the West especially, where medical aid is of little attainment; yet cases of disease and surgery are constantly occurring, and they must, of necessity fall into the hands of those who have given the subject but little if any thought.[108]

Therefore, Elwell believed that the locality rule, or *community standard doctrine*, should be applied in all malpractice cases.

Only a few trial and appellate court judges invoked the locality rule between 1835 and 1865, and when they did, it was not in forums that would set doctrinal precedent. In 1857 a patient sued two Ohio oculists for malpractice after treatment that left him in bed for two months and unable to read for two years. The oculists had bled the patient and dosed him with cathartics for several weeks. The trial court judge instructed the jury that "[a]n absolute necessity requires that the wants of the community be supplied with the best medical knowledge its means and location will command."[109] The jury was unable to reach a verdict. In a similar instance, a patient sued his physician in Massachusetts for a deformity following a severe hip injury. Although the medical witnesses for the defense and the prosecution both agreed that the results of the treatment were the best that could be expected, the jury returned a verdict against the physician for $365. The physician appealed the decision to the state supreme court, which overturned the verdict for being against the weight of the evidence. In writing the opinion for the court, the eminent chief justice of Massachusetts, Lemuel Shaw, noted that the defendant/physician had "shown a degree of skill beyond what is usually expected of surgeons residing in the country."[110] Since Shaw's comment did not clearly articulate the principle, and was incidental to the decision in the case, it was probably considered *obiter dictum* and therefore not binding as precedent. At any rate, the decision was ignored by other courts and had no impact on the law of malpractice.

Elwell's comment and the Massachusetts and Ohio cases are important as points of contrast. Most judges and the majority of society were not inclined to measure physicians only against community standards even though geographic location and professional atmosphere could have a profound impact on the intellectual and technical development of individual practitioners. The failure of the locality rule to take hold between 1835 and 1865 was the result of two developments. First, the public and most judges misunderstood and overestimated the degree of change in the medical profession in the first half of the century. Despite the substantial development of a more integrated national economy, the establishment of a national medical organization for regular physicians in 1846, and increased communication among national medical practitioners, the profession could still best be characterized as a diffuse collection of small groups of doctors of varying knowledge and skill.

Second, the acceptance of the locality, or community standard, rule would have been out of harmony with developments in other areas of American law. Between 1780 and 1860 state and federal judges transformed many aspects of the traditional common law in ways that reflected and encouraged the growth of national economic development. For example, Joseph Story, in his career as a treatise writer and Supreme Court justice (1811–1843), devoted much of his time to creating and fostering a uniform federal common law to neutralize the pluralistic tendency of the states. He attempted to formulate a uniform national commercial law and worked on schemes to adjudicate conflicts of laws among states.[111] The John Marshall court (1801–1836), of which Story was a member, and the subsequent Roger Taney court, made numerous "nationalizing" decisions calculated to facilitate economic integration by extending federal oversight.[112] In one of them, *Swift* v. *Tyson* (1842), the Taney court ruled that federal courts were bound to follow state court commercial law decisions only in strictly state matters. Other economic issues could be decided by federal courts on the basis of general principles of commercial law.[113] The intent of the ruling was to open the door to national commercial uniformity. Changes in such areas of the law as contract also reflected the same nationalizing tendencies. For example, in the late eighteenth and early nineteenth centuries courts began to scrutinize contracts less by community standards of fairness and more according to the explicit terms of the agreement. This new view of contractual liability was designed to facilitate long-distance, future-oriented agreements with strangers rather than immediate exchanges between individuals in parochial communities.[114]

Story wrote in 1837, "I am myself no friend to the almost indiscriminate habit . . . of setting up particular usages or customs in almost all kinds of business and trade, to control, vary or annul the general liabilities of parties under the common law."[115] The application of the locality rule in malpractice cases was incompatible with this sentiment and with the general context of jurisprudential thought in antebellum America. The locality rule stressed diversity while economic development and law were bolstering national uniformity.

Unfortunately for malpractice defendants, the nationalizing tendency in law arrived long before the medical community could deliver a consistent level of care nationwide. Physicians in isolated communities could not acquire the same training, education, and experience as physicians in thriving urban centers. The failure of judges and the public to understand or to admit this fact did not cause the wave of malpractice suits in the 1840s and 1850s, but it clearly aggravated an already complicated situation. The use of the locality rule between 1835 and 1865 could have softened the blow of the initial increase in suits. Instead, judges continued to allow expert witness from centers of medical excellence to testify at the trials of rural practitioners without instructing juries to consider their relative theaters of practice. The confusion that resulted from admitting testimony from a variety of witnesses with differing standards of practice played a role in enhancing the discretion of the jury.[116]

Disgrace, Vexation, and Ruin

It appeared to many physicians that they had little chance in a courtroom once they were sued for malpractice. As one physician noted,

"[T]he defendant must be mulcted in every case where he is not sustained by the entire professional evidence."[117] Other writers, however, actually believed that there was no escape from conviction even if all the witnesses supported the defendant. "The fact is," reported an editorialist in 1855, "that sometimes surgeons have been mulcted in damages simply because the jury believed from the united character of the medical testimony that it was a conspiracy and the more conclusive the testimony, the more certain with some jurors is the defendant to suffer."[118] These two varying viewpoints both reflected the prevalent belief among medical practitioners that the "sympathy of a jury of citizens is not generally with the doctor, but rather on the side of the poor, ill-advised, unfortunate victim of incurable injury."[119]

These writers exaggerated juries' inclination to rule against physicians. In the majority of medical malpractice trials reported in the medical literature, juries ruled in favor of the defendant/physician. Although many patients were more willing to sue physicians, it is not clear that all of society approved of the practice in these early years. Thus, when suits did come to court, juries could have demonstrated their disapproval by finding for the defendant. Jurors, some already skeptical about the propriety of suing physicians, would be especially hesitant to penalize a defendant where the plaintiff had received only a relatively minor deformity, like those from unsuccessful fracture treatments. Some contemporary estimates of acquittal rates are remarkably high. An Ohio physician in 1859 estimated that while the tendency to prosecute physicians was increasing, "[t]his certainly has not originated from the success connected with these prosecutions. In not one instance in twenty as far as my observation extends—have they been successful."[120] While the Ohio writer's estimate was unrealistically optimistic, it provided a counter to the gloomy predictions of other physicians. Even when physicians lost their cases in the initial trials, they often received favorable verdicts in retrials or at the appellate level. Appellate ruling victories in the nineteenth century were fairly evenly split between physicians and patients.[121] State appellate courts overturned trial verdicts against physicians when the trial judge had improperly instructed the jury on the "ordinary" care requirement, when juries awarded excess damages, and when evidence was improp-

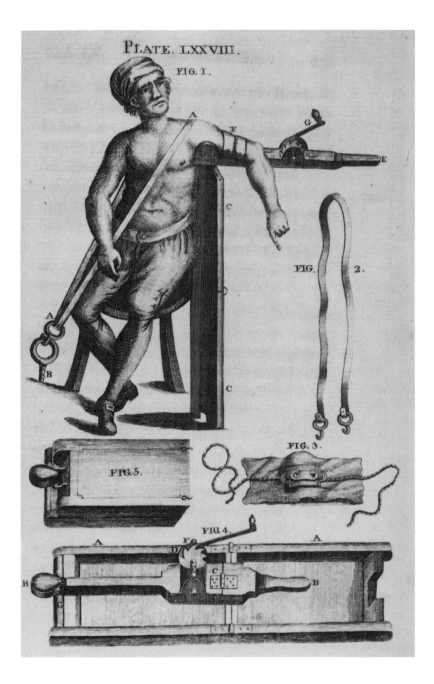

erly admitted or rejected. Including acquittal verdicts gained by malpractice defendants in retrials and on appeals, physicians probably prevailed in well over half the malpractice suits of 1835–1865.[122] Yet, these successes were small consolation to a profession that felt deluged by prosecutions and believed, as did John Elwell, that "[v]ictory in these cases is in one sense, defeat because the disgrace. vexations, and cost are generally ruinous."[123]

When judges incorrectly or prejudicially instructed juries or juries flagrantly ignored evidence, physicians could either ask the trial judge for a new trial or appeal their case to a higher state court. Indeed, the typical legal battle between a patient and his physician consisted of multiple trials involving numerous witnesses and covering several years. For example, when Lorenzo Slack first accused Dixi Crosby of malpractice in the spring of 1851, it had been nearly six years (two days before the statutory limit) since Crosby had treated the man's broken leg. The first trial, in which Slack asked for $5,000 in damages, was delayed until 1853. The jury awarded Slack $800 plus $300 in costs. A second trial yielded similar results, and it was not until nine years after the incident that a third trial jury acquitted Crosby.[124] Another fracture case in New Hampshire began in 1850 and was not concluded until 1855, after a long procession of trials, hearings, and negotiations. At the first trial the patient was awarded $1,500 plus court costs. A jury at the second trial awarded him only $525 plus costs. The physician appealed the decision to the New Hampshire supreme court, which overturned the decision on the basis of the trial court judge's instructions to the jury. A third jury again ruled against the physician in 1854, but the state supreme court overruled this verdict because some of the jurors had shared some brandy the night before they reported their decision. Finally, the patient and the physician settled the dispute out of court for an undisclosed sum of money.[125]

These two cases were the rule, not the exception. The number and length of the trials growing out of each malpractice charge were significant because the litigation subjected the physician to more anxiety,

Device to relocate dislocated shoulder. From Benjamin Bell, A System of Surgery *(1788). (Courtesy of the Historical Research Center, Houston Academy of Medicine, Texas Medical Center Library, Houston, Texas.)*

cost, and publicity. The trials of the New Hampshire physician lasted several days each and played to regularly packed courthouses. One trial employed sixty witnesses. Although the legal costs and attorneys' fees undoubtedly varied greatly, five trials in Massachusetts in the mid-1850s generated $10,000 in trial costs and fees. One of the defendants reportedly paid $2,000 of that total, an enormous sum in the mid–nineteenth century.[126] This figure was abnormally high, but costs often approached the amount of damages awarded to the patients.

When a jury found a defendant guilty of malpractice, it was asked to calculate the monetary value of the damages to the plaintiff. The injured patient could receive money for all the consequences of the injury, past and future. In addition, the jury was authorized to take into account the effects of the injury, including pain, personal inconvenience, and decreased income capacity. The award, however, could not exceed the amount claimed by the plaintiff at the beginning of the trial.

Patients invariably asked for damage awards of $5,000, $10,000, $20,000, and $25,000. Juries' awards, however, never approached the damage claims of the patients. While there were several awards between 1835 and 1865 in the $1,000 to $3,000 range, the typical malpractice damage judgments fell between $200 and $800 (see appendix A).[127] If an appellate court believed that an award was excessive, it could overturn the judgment, as did the Maine supreme court in 1848. A patient had accused a physician of malpractice because he failed to amputate the plaintiff's leg high enough. Consequently, the man required two more operations to remove progressively more of the stump of the leg. A jury returned a verdict for the plaintiff in the amount of $2,025. The physician appealed the verdict, claiming that it was excessive and against the weight of the evidence. The state supreme court demanded that the patient agree to remit $500 of the judgment because "surgeons should not be deterred from the pursuit of their profession by intemperate and extravagant verdicts." If the patient refused to accept $1,525, the court threatened to grant the physician a new trial. The court justified its decision by explaining that "[t]he compensation to surgeons in the country is small, . . . and an error of judgment is visited with a severe penalty, which takes from one a large share of the surplus earnings of a long life."[128] On the low end of the awards scale, a Pennsylvania jury in 1847 granted a black man only $50 for a permanent injury to his shoulder.[129]

These awards seem almost insignificant by mid– and late–twentieth century standards. But they shocked nineteenth-century physicians. Eight hundred dollars was no inconsequential sum in 1850, even for a physician. Wages were low, and the majority of physicians had to pursue sideline occupations to support their families. While a handful of physicians might have earned as much as $6,000–$8,000 per year, the *Boston Medical and Surgical Journal* considered $500 normal for an established, full-time doctor in 1833. Expenses could have depleted that figure to as low as $350. Many rural doctors earned less, and a portion of their income usually included payment-in-kind rather than money.[130] Second, nineteenth-century physicians were not shielded from malpractice claims by any form of insurance. Malpractice insurance and group defense schemes did not surface until the last decade of the nineteenth century and were not an established feature of medical life until the early twentieth century.[131] Before then, physicians had to fend and pay for themselves.

Finally, the dollar amount of early damage awards was of secondary importance to both antebellum physicians and to the overall development of medical malpractice in America. When a physician was charged with malpractice, he felt as if his professional future had been put in jeopardy even if the damage award against him was small, or even if he won his case. Many malpractice suits were highly visible local events. After an Ohio suit in 1849 in which the courthouse had been crowded for four days, one observer declared that "there has been no case [of any kind] tried within the county during the last ten years which has elicited so much attention."[132] Members of the community could sit and listen to a parade of witnesses testify that the accused physician was unskillful, incompetent, or careless. Members of the patient's family, rival or more accomplished physicians, and the prosecuting attorney could all join in the attack.

In the highly competitive medical environment of the mid–nineteenth century, an era when public trust of regular physicians was tenuous at best, attacks on a doctor's competency could have significant fallout. A writer for the *Ohio Medical and Surgical Journal* in 1861 affirmed that a malpractice suit was a "grave matter" to both the accused physician and the profession. As he explained, "The reputation of the physician is his stock in trade. He cherishes it beyond all price." A physician could bear the loss of property, arduous labors, obscurity, and poverty, but the "formal and public attack on his reputation, and the concurrence of twelve disinterested members of the community," struck at the core of his, and his colleagues', professional respectability. "It is not very difficult to see that the event, from its very inception casts a long shadow upon the future, pregnant with fears, uncertainties, apprehensions, and future forbodings."[133]

The writer's prophetic statement expressed the profession's well-justified impression that the sudden and dramatic appearance of widespread and frequent malpractice suits was an augur of things to come and a fundamental threat to the medical community at large. As he predicted, "The public knowledge of a verdict for the prosecution will beget a brood of new cases, in which, quite as likely as otherwise, the most skillful and diligent of the profession will be the victims."[134]

While damage awards were smaller than in later years, they were not inconsequential. In addition, it is important to remember that most patients did not sue their physicians. Those who did, however, broke decisively with the past. But a focus on the amount of the awards or the percentage of patients involved obscures the more important contemporary and historical issues. The first malpractice "crisis" of 1835–1865 was the genesis of a modern professional epidemic, the first step over a threshold into a new era of American medicine. Many nineteenth-century physicians saw it as such and desperately tried to unravel the twisted social and professional motives behind the suits. The questions of the size of the damage awards or who won the majority of the cases are important; but they are dwarfed by the need to explain why the suits originated in the first place and how the phenomenon's origins continued to generate suits for the next 150 years.

CHAPTER 3

Schools for Scandal

The increase in malpractice suits and threats of suits in the early 1840s was sudden and dramatic. Contemporaries identified several factors as the underlying cause of the phenomenon. Medical society committees on malpractice in Pennsylvania in 1850, Kentucky in 1853, Massachusetts in 1854, and Ohio in 1855, plus scores of individual physicians, agreed that the status of the profession was deteriorating.[1] However ill defined, a view prevailed that the increase in malpractice suits was inextricably related to this decline in public confidence. In addition, physicians contended that the specific agents of the decline, aspects of medical treatment, competition, and antiprofessional sentiment were also the specific causes of the litigation crisis.

These perceptive commentators accurately explained physicians' low status. But they were unable to recognize and interpret the long-term cultural trends that created the environment conducive to widespread litigation. Instead, observers in the mid–nineteenth century mistook important topical factors for fundamental causes. These immediate factors may have incited suits in the 1840s and 1850s, but they cannot explain why the number of suits continued to increase into the twentieth century. Indeed, frequent malpractice litigation persisted long after the so-called causes identified by mid–nineteenth-century physicians had disappeared.

The immediate causes of the increased incidence of malpractice prosecution were usually apparent to contemporary observers. Although their social standing in America had never been high, most doctors were painfully aware of the medical profession's abysmal status in the first half of the nineteenth century. At a meeting of the American Medical Association in 1848 Nathan Chapman noted that the "once revered" and "venerated profession has become corrupt, and degenerative to the forfeiture of its social position."[2] In 1858 a physician confirmed that the medical profession had "been losing its hold on the respect and confidence of the people" for fifty years. Since the early part of the century, the physician lamented, the profession had lost its favored position, when children had been "taught to raise their caps, if boys; and drop and curtsey, if girls, in token of respect, when they met their family physician on the street . . . even when that physician was under the influence of intoxicating drink."[3]

Alexander Garnett, writing for the *Medical and Surgical Reporter*, outlined the causes of the profession's meager social standing. According to Garnett, by 1854 doctors were held in low public esteem because of "defective medical acquirements," the "want of union and harmony among physicians," and "the radical and progressive proclivities of the present age."[4] Garnett's three factors deserve closer analysis for they explain physicians' low status, accurately characterize the medical environment of the first half of the nineteenth century, and provide insight into the source of many malpractice suits.

"Defective Medical Acquirements"

In the late eighteenth century American physicians attempted to introduce the English institutions that bestowed a unique, elevated social status on physicians. They organized medical schools, founded professional societies, and convinced state legislatures to pass licensure laws. But despite these temporary successes, American physicians were unable to inspire widespread confidence and respect and gain a monopoly over medical practice.[5]

Physicians' inability to demonstrate the superiority of their methods of treatment was one of the central components of this failure. Americans had a long tradition of domestic medicine. Although full-time physicians existed, much of the medical practice in the eighteenth and early nineteenth century was dispensed by part-time practitioners and lay persons.[6] Since the family served as the center of economic and social activity, it was not surprising that medical care was often dispensed by a mother, a grandmother, or an aunt. In addition, self-care reflected the geographic isolation of families living in rural areas and on the frontier as well as the shortage of trained physicians in the eighteenth century. Before the proliferation of medical schools in the first half of the nineteenth century, a single physician might serve several communities. Even in large cities physicians' time was divided among a large clientele and charitable service in almshouses and dispensaries. The periodic, and sometimes regular, unavailability of a family physician forced many sick to look for help within their own families. Often, even when a trained physician was obtainable, poor immigrants or farmers could not afford his services. Armed with folk remedies and widely available patent medicines, many people served as their own doctors. Lay practitioners could also refer to the nearly ubiquitous handbooks on home health care. William Buchan's *Domestic Medicine*, for example, was reprinted in 142 editions between 1769 and 1871.[7] Since many families had supplied their own medical care for generations, much of the public had little respect for pretentious physicians who offered what were recognized as ineffective, unpleasant, and sometimes dangerous therapies.

Conventional medical theory in the late eighteenth and early nineteenth centuries was dominated by the *heroic* treatments popularized by Benjamin Rush. Rush contended that all disease and illness was the result of "morbid excitement" of the capillaries and vascular tissue. He advocated the copious use of emetics and cathartics to induce vomiting and evacuation and advised the massive bleeding of patients to ease this capillary tension.[8] Although the centuries-old system of humoral pathology included bleeding and employed agents that induced vomiting, diarrhea, and perspiration, heroic practitioners, under Rush's inspiration, disregarded traditional restraints and employed active agents in immense quantities. Physicians removed blood using small cuts, or *scarification*, and suction cups. In other instances they resorted to leaches placed, internally and externally, on literally every part of the body. For larger volumes, doctors opened major blood vessels with a small-bladed knife, or *lancet*. Often, patients were bled until they fainted. Rush suggested that in some cases four-fifths of all the blood in the body might be removed. He epitomized the typical physicians' commitment to heroic bleeding when he declared: "I would sooner die with my Lancet in my hand . . . than to give it up while I had Breath to maintain it or a hand to use it."[9]

Physicians applied similarly enormous doses of cathartics and emetics. As one nineteenth-century doctor recalled, "If vomited, they did not come up in gentle puffs and gusts, but the action was cyclonic. If perchance, the stomach was passed the expulsion would be by the rectum and anus, and this would be equal to a regular oil-well gusher."[10] Calomel, a mercury-based cathartic, was often prescribed until the gums bled (a sign of mercury poisoning). Patients lost hair, teeth, tongues, palates, and in some cases sections of their jaw bones as a result of over zealously prescribed mercury-based remedies. As one disgruntled patient complained in 1832, "I was in the first place bled 3 times & Physicked almost to deth." He acknowledged that "the Doctors have got an idea into their heads that they must give calomel for evry complaint[;] they have fed me so much on it since I been hir that I have lost all my hair from my head and a good share of my teeth."[11] Blistering served as another weapon in the heroic armory. Physicians used caustic substances and heat to raise blisters on various parts of the body, in theory to draw poisons from the patient through the expulsion of pus. Similarly, they purposely incited infection in some cases by inserting foreign substances in open wounds.[12]

Heroic therapy won converts in wide circles, but it was also the object of considerable derision and one of the main sources of public antipathy toward the profession. A physician in 1835 claimed that the injudicious use of heroic treatments "has produced, does continue, and will perpetuate (unless obviated), the fear, jealousy, and suspicion that exists between . . . the community, and the profession at large."[13] Physicians also weakened public confidence by their conflicting and inconsistent diagnoses and therapies. Doctors not only employed depletive therapies like bleeding in varying degrees, but prescribed drugs and tonics such as opium, quinine, antimony, and arsenic in a fickle and unsystematized fashion. Because they did not understand the pharmacological working of their "remedies" and possessed no diagnostic tools except their senses, physicians favored drugs and doses that induced visible results.[14] Because the same remedies often produced different effects in different patients, medical practice appeared to be unsystematized and erratic. Moreover, the same remedy prepared by different physicians usually tasted and acted differently in various cases. This problem was compounded by a lack of consensus among physicians about appropriate practice.[15]

Much of the public accepted heroic methods, but impatience, opposition, and skepticism grew as physicians and alternative practitioners questioned the practice. By the 1830s and 1840s, physicians themselves had begun to distrust the efficacy of their medical treatments. Empirical statistical studies inspired by Pierre Louis in Paris demonstrated that heroic treatments were generally useless and sometimes harmful.[16] Medical writers began to stress the "uncertainty" of medical practice, the healing powers of nature, "self-limiting" diseases, and the merits of "conservative" treatments.[17] Still, physicians' gradual abandonment of heroic therapy did not improve their image significantly. Instead, intraprofessional resistance to the regime helped undermine the legitimacy of the medical community in general. The public distrusted and was increasingly unwilling to support a profession that first endorsed harsh heroic therapies and then began to abandon them within three decades.[18]

These therapeutic fluctuations were relevant to the malpractice phenomenon in two respects. On the one hand, the absence of widespread agreement on the diagnosis and treatment of most maladies precluded the establishment of an "ordinary standard of care." Even when physicians agreed on a remedy, they followed the dictum of *specificity*, a theory that held that medicines acted differently on different patients.[19] Therefore, malpractice suits for purely medical, as opposed to surgical, treatments were rare and usually unsupportable. On the other hand, therapeutic inconsistencies subverted physicians' general status as competent public servants and left them more vulnerable to malpractice charges for treatments in which they did claim proficiency, like orthopedics. In 1854 a Kentucky Medical Society committee on the causes of malpractice suits noted: "During the last half century, the relative position of our profession to the public has undergone a marked change. Implicit confidence, amounting in some instances to blind credulity, has given place to widespread skepticism as to the powers and capabilities of the healing art."[20]

Other professional activities contributed to public fear and distrust. Physicians' and medical students' quests for cadavers for anatomical study helped to brand members of the profession as unfeeling ghouls. The public was repelled by the use of cadavers for instruction. Some early medical schools obtained their dissection subjects from other states or countries, but many merely retrieved recently buried corpses from the local cemetery or relied on professional grave robbers. Attempts to introduce dissection into early anatomy classes often met with violent opposition. Thus, for example, rioters, believing that William Shippen had robbed graves to acquire teaching aids, attacked his Philadelphia School of Anatomy in 1765. By the mid–nineteenth century, similar riots had occurred in Maryland, New York, Vermont, Massachusetts, Ohio, Illinois, and Connecticut. Three rioters were killed in a Baltimore disturbance and seven in a New York uprising.[21]

Violent opposition to "body-snatching" and dissection continued far into the nineteenth century and encouraged state legislatures to establish penalties for grave-robbing and to criminalize the use of human cadavers for instruction. The dissection controversies colored the public's perception of the medical profession at large. A group of enraged Ohioans in 1845 passed a resolution "That we most solemnly believe that those who have no regard for the dead, can have but little respect for the living, and those who respect neither the dead nor the living, should never receive the confidence of the public."[22]

The reaction to the study of anatomy both damaged the medical community's status and hindered the acquisition of anatomical knowledge. Medical societies and contemporary observers argued that physicians would be subject to malpractice suits if they did not understand the workings of the human body and yet were being denied the primary source of that knowledge.[23] In one of the rare nineteenth-century malpractice cases decided by arbitrators, a panel of Michigan physicians refused to award damages to a plaintiff because they found that the injury resulted from defective medical knowledge, and declared that it was unfair to hold physicians responsible for insufficient training when "the study of anatomy essential to the proper treatment of such cases, is by the laws of the state of Michigan a penitentiary offense."[24]

Although judges never appeared to consider the lack of access to proper training as a mitigating factor in malpractice cases, physicians often complained. Josiah Trowbridge, a Buffalo, New York, physician, reported in 1848 that he abandoned his twenty-five-year medical practice in protest because the state legislature criminalized human dissection as a method of teaching anatomy and surgery. Since physicians would be "mulcted with ruinous damages" if they did not possess this knowledge, Trowbridge resolved "not to serve the public on such conditions."[25] John Elwell, in his 1860 treatise, stressed that a physician "may be a good theorist without it [dissection of cadavers], but he cannot be a ready, practical practitioner; and he will be very liable, at some stage of his life, to be awakened to his defective education, by having to respond, in damages, for Malpractice." Elwell contended that it was wrong to punish ignorant physicians if it was impossible to attain proper training. "The court should either permit the student of medicine and surgery to obtain all the subjects they may require . . . or it should cease to punish those who are guilty of Malpractice, by reason of the great difficulty in obtaining subjects for dissection."[26] Although several state legislatures passed laws allowing dissections under certain circumstances, most soon repealed these statutes. By 1860 only two states allowed the use of human cadavers.[27]

Physicians in the late eighteenth century had hoped that they could use improved medical education to increase the ability and the status of their profession. Before 1765 most aspiring American physicians trained as apprentices to established practitioners. These preceptorships varied in quality and length. Some physicians required their trainees to read the important medical texts, but others merely used them as a source of cheap menial labor. Relying on the many self-help medical books or on experience, still other physicians were entirely self-trained. A few wealthy medical students were able to study in the universities of Britain and Europe.[28]

Earlier reformers had believed that Americans could improve the quality of medical care as well as physicians' social standing by introducing the London guild system to the colonies. Medical practice in London was theoretically regulated through three royally chartered corporations: the Royal College of Physicians of London, the United Company of Barber Surgeons, and the Guild of Apothecaries. Under this scheme, the rights and duties of physicians, surgeons, and apothecaries within a seven-mile radius of London were strictly defined.[29]

In this system the physician was an aloof and gentlemanly advisor who did not sully his hands with the task of manually dealing with patients. In fact, physicians were not allowed to do anything but diagnose, prognose, and prescribe. Surgeons, however, were not permitted to carry out any of these responsibilities, and were limited to manual treatments. Apothecaries, who were formerly associated with the grocer's guild, mixed and sold pharmaceuticals and potions. Both surgeons and apothecaries were forbidden to act without a physician's direction.[30]

When any member of a group performed a function reserved for another, he could be prosecuted. While each of the three required specialized training, only physicians were required to possess a university education. Physicians could not charge or sue for fees, but had to accept the payment that was offered. This hierarchical arrangement applied only to the London area, but even in this setting it was theoretical rather than actual. Nevertheless, this arrangement was important because it supported the image of the physician as an elite, gentlemanly public servant who was uninterested in financial gain.[31]

This system was not transplanted to the American colonies. The majority of the immigrants to New England did not come from London, where at least the ideal of the elite physician existed. Instead, colonists came from rural farming communities like East Anglia, where the highest percentage of practitioners was comprised of physicians who diagnosed, prescribed, performed surgery, and mixed drugs. In addition, many of the practitioners in these areas also served as cobblers, wheelwrights, ministers, and innkeepers. Most emigrants had no experience with and saw no reason for the specialized, educated, full-time physicians of London.

Virtually all colonial physicians were generalists. They eschewed the distinctions of London because of the type of practitioner common in rural England, because of the scarcity of university-educated physicians in the colonies, and because they could make more money by prescribing and preparing medications than by prescribing alone. It was this image of the physician as generalist practitioner that would influence American attitudes toward medicine.[32]

The prevailing attitudes toward physicians in the mid-1700s did not stop physicians from attempting to raise the standards and change the image of the profession. John Morgan, born of an upper-class Philadelphia family in 1735, served a medical apprenticeship in America and studied medicine in London and Edinburgh. When he returned to America in 1765, he attempted to organize the medical profession into the hierarchical guilds he had seen in London. More importantly, he met with the board of trustees of the College of Philadelphia (now the University of Pennsylvania) and convinced them to establish the first medical school in America. The school adopted formidable entrance requirements and demanded four years of study for a doctorate. Morgan also called for strict licensure and separation of medicine from surgery and pharmacy.[33]

Despite Morgan's stature, his proposals did not have the desired impact. Some colonies passed licensure laws in the last half of the eighteenth century, but these laws did not effectively limit or proscribe practice.[34] Although Morgan promised to forgo all surgery and pharmacy, most physicians could not afford to make that sacrifice and continued to practice in all three roles.[35]

Morgan's campaign to transform medical education also failed. In fact, the effort to improve medical education succeeded only in institutionalizing poor training. Several schools copied the College of Philadelphia model, but the institutions were unable to maintain its high standards. By 1789 even the Philadelphia medical school had lowered its entrance requirements and reduced the length of study to one year. Other schools followed suit. Morgan and his supporters introduced medical schools into America to enhance the status of the profession. Other American physicians had the same idea, and by the early nineteenth century, medical schools began to proliferate. In 1834 there were over twenty. By 1850 forty-two schools, as well as many diploma mills, had been established in the United States.[36] Many of these institutions were proprietary schools, and in their competition for students they had low entrance requirements and graduation standards. Even earnest medical administrators were forced to forgo enhanced standards. Admission was open to any student who could pay the fees. By 1850 the typical program at American medical schools was comprised of two identical, four-month terms of lectures. At Harvard, one of the better schools in the country, students were required to pass only five of nine five-minute oral examinations. As late as 1870, perhaps one-half of Harvard's medical students could not write.[37]

Alfred Stillé, a professor of pathology at the University of Pennsyl-

vania, admitted in 1847 that the medical profession had become
"[d]egraded in its position and authority" and forfeited "public confidence" as a result of the state of medical education.

> By an extraordinary multiplication of medical schools a vulgar rivalry has
> arisen in spirit and conduct similar to that displayed in the competitions of
> steamboats, and railroads, with the same means resorted to for reaching suc-
> cess. Education is cheapened, the period of study abridged, or lightened—no
> irksome examinations are to be endured, and degrees acquired easily and
> assuredly.[38]

The proliferation of medical schools and diplomas, and the accompanying deterioration of educational standards in the first half of the
nineteenth century affected physicians' status and their vulnerability
to malpractice suits in two ways. First, the mediocre education offered
at most schools left graduates ill prepared to deal with the complexities
of the human body. Physicians' resulting deficiencies often led to
bungled diagnoses and treatments, which in turn generated law suits.
An editorialist for the *Medical Examiner* admitted in 1841 that while
"malignity and sordid calculation are no infrequent instigators of prosecutions for malpractice, it is quite possible for medical men, in these
days of easy graduation and multiplied professorships, to be guilty of
culpable neglect or—in the existing condition of many medical schools
—scarcely blamable neglect."[39] Alden March, a nationally known
specialist in surgery and a professor at Albany Medical School, agreed.
Although he condemned the wave of malpractice suits that threatened
even "respectable surgeons," he confessed that "too many ignorant and
careless men get into the ranks of our profession, who are liable to
commit errors, for the consequences of which, the law holds them
responsible. This would seem to indicate the necessity of higher attainments in our profession."[40] Individual doctors who were the product
of cursory medical educations that were devoid of clinical experience
and anatomical instruction were more likely to make mistakes and
become defendants in malpractice suits.

Second, the farcical educational process debased the status of the
medical profession as a whole. Physicians had hoped to use education
to establish professional credibility and overcome the multitude of
home practitioners, folk healers, midwives, and irregular practitioners
who practiced in the early nineteenth century.[41] Indignation with this

attempt arose from contradictory sentiments. The popular democracy of the Jacksonian period was accompanied by an anti-intellectualism that elevated native intelligence over education and common sense over expertise. This feeling informed attitudes toward politics, law, religion, and medicine. Andrew Jackson personified the unschooled, uncorrupted, unassuming wisdom that captured the imagination and hearts of the country.[42]

Jacksonian Democrats resented the pretension of physicians who endeavored to place themselves above other practitioners and the common people. Worthington Hooker, a Connecticut doctor who wrote in the 1840s, lamented that "education in the science of medicine is practically despised by quite a large portion of the community.' According to Hooker, many people demonstrated a "readiness to put the quack on a level with the thoroughly-educated physician, or even above him," because they felt that "[m]any a man has arisen to eminence in other professions by his own exertions, without any great amount of education, and why should this not be the case in the practice of medicine?"[43] Jacksonian antipathy toward educated elites was undoubtedly compounded by the fact that even properly trained physicians could cure only a few maladies with any consistency.

A Pennsylvania physician, William Wood, commented on the phenomenon in 1849 and linked it to the profession's malpractice woes. He explained that physicians had customarily defended medical education despite the facility with which diplomas were granted "on the ground that it is better to provide the people with imperfectly educated physicians, than with those not educated at all." However, the experience of "some few years" had led Wood to change his position. He now believed that in light of many of the malpractice suits: "It is better to be without a diploma; for then besides having the sympathies of the community, the practitioner can say, 'I make no pretensions, I offer no certificate of ability, and only gave my neighbor in his sufferings such aid as I could.' "[44] It is unlikely that the abolition of medical degrees would have immunized the profession from accusations of malpractice, but Wood's assertion underscored the public's attitude toward education and the profession: The physician was at greater legal peril because he had undemocratically claimed expertise through education.

Ironically, physicians could be maligned for possessing both a medical education and a defective medical education. Although Jacksonians resented the ostentation of the medical degree, they were appalled by the insufficient education of most physicians. As Alfred Stillé reported in 1847, the "diploma [M.D.] has lost its value. Everyone knows of its prostitution, and has ceased to regard it as in itself deserving attention."[45]

Stillé cited another important product of the burgeoning number of American medical schools: a burgeoning number of doctors. He speculated that "the annual number of graduates, in medicine, is at present probably larger in the United States, than in the whole of the residue of the civilized world."[46] Other physicians shared Stillé's concern over the flood of physicians entering practice in the first half of the nineteenth century. One writer reported in 1858 that "[e]very little hamlet has now two or three physicians, where one physician, forty years ago did the entire practice of half a dozen such hamlets."[47] Between 1765 and 1800 the five existing American medical schools produced less than 250 physicians. Many communities subsisted without the benefit of a formally educated practitioner.[48] But most figures suggest that the supply of physicians between 1790 and 1850 grew from scarcity to surfeit.

With the medical school "mania" of the early 1800s, the number of graduates increased dramatically. During the 1830s medical schools granted approximately 6,800 degrees. In the 1850s almost 18,000 physicians received their M.D.'s. Although most early estimates are imprecise, the total number of practicing physicians grew from between 3,500 and 4,900 in 1790, to 40,564 in 1850.[49] Some of this increase reflected the medical needs of the growing population. However, the ratio of physicians to inhabitants increased between 1790 and 1850 from between 1:800 and 1:1,100, to about 1:570.[50] In some areas of the country the density of physicians was greater. In 1846 a speaker before a graduating medical class bemoaned the crowded state of the profession and argued that the country did not need more than 1 physician for every 2,500–3,000 inhabitants.[51] It was said that in 1845 there was 1 doctor for every 400 persons in Buffalo; in St. Louis, the proportion reached 1 to 274.[52]

Despite these figures, the "surplus" of physicians was regional and not national and may have represented a maldistribution, rather than an overall excess of practitioners.[53] For example, communities on the western frontier continued without adequate numbers of trained physicians. Still, physicians in the areas with an oversupply of medical practitioners suffered in several ways. The over abundance of physicians had played a major role in diminishing the respectability and status of the profession since 1800. One physician who had practiced for forty-seven years complained in 1858 that the medical profession was "greatly overstocked; and it is a natural consequence, that where there is an excess of a commodity in the market, its value should be proportionally diminished."[54]

F. Cambell Stewart, a midcentury physician, offered an additional interpretation of the relationship between an increase in numbers and the decline in status. He explained that, despite the generally low status of the physicians as a group, many individual doctors were held in high esteem by their respective communities. The elevated social status of these physicians could "excite the ambition of many of the thousand applicants for admission to our ranks, some of them thus see a road opened for access to a society which it might be much more difficult for them to reach by other more laborious and circuitous routes."[55] As unworthy social climbers crowded the profession, the overall image of the profession deteriorated further. The decline of public trust and confidence emboldened patients and made it easier for them to accuse their physicians of mistreatment.

"Want of Union and Harmony"

The rise in the number of medical practitioners created another pitfall for potential malpractice defendants. In the 1824 *Lowell* malpractice case, the defense attorney asked the jury to weigh the patient's injury against the two defendants' importance to their communities. "What is the consequence of a limb like Lowell's," the lawyer demanded, "compared with the usefulness of such a physician as Dr. Hawks, entirely lost to the present scene from his practice?"[56] Hawks and his codefendant, Faxon, were the only doctors in their respective towns. The jury could not decide on a verdict, and the trial judge issued a nonsuit ruling.[57] The prospect of losing the sole practitioner in the village may have intimidated the judge and jury and influenced their decision.

If other late eighteenth- and early nineteenth-century juries were influenced by physicians' value to their communities, as suggested by the *Lowell* case, they were probably less likely to charge and convict physicians and risk denying their villages medical aid. The alteration of legal rules regarding contract, tort, property, and corporations between 1780 and 1820 encouraged the expansion of commercial enterprises that would presumably serve the public interest.[58] Similarly, the attitudes of juries and judges in medical cases may have represented the socially "instrumental function" of law by protecting and allowing the development of another resource vital to the welfare of the public: medical care. But by 1850 the number of physicians in some areas had increased to the point of a glut. If a malpractice suit destroyed a physician's career, there was always another doctor, or more, ready to take his place. In this situation, juries and judges were less likely to shelter physicians from unhappy, litigious patients.

The surplus of physicians in many parts of the country also subverted the medical profession's status and gave rise to malpractice suits by engendering and exacerbating competition among regular practitioners. Competition, however, did not arise merely from the excess of doctors. Physicians often fought bitterly over control of local medical societies and against rival organizations. Other intraprofessional disputes centered on issues such as fee bills and consultations. Local medical societies set price guidelines for physicians to follow. When practitioners undercut or overpriced, quarrels ensued.[59] Physician-owned and operated medical schools were also the source of open economic conflict.[60] One physician, writing in 1846, admonished his colleagues that they "too often pursued a course in furtherance of their own individual interests which was calculated to impair that of the body [medical profession] generally." If the profession did not stem the tide of dissension, the writer warned, conflict would "lessen the estimation in which [the profession] should be held by the public at large."[61]

The founders of the American Medical Association recognized that the lack of internal cohesion and low education standards damaged public confidence in the profession. Representatives from various state medical societies met in 1846 to attack the problems of the national medical community. A second convention in 1847 finalized the form of the organization and devised a code of ethics that reflected the concerns of elite physicians. The code enumerated the reciprocal obligations of doctor and patient and condemned fraternization with irregular practitioners and quacks. It also devoted considerable attention to relations among regular physicians and their impact on public confidence and respect. It advised that since

the feelings of medical men may be painfully assailed in their intercourse with each other, and which cannot be understood or appreciated by the general society, neither the subject matter of such differences nor the adjudication of the arbitrators should be made public, as publicity in a case of this nature may be personally injurious to the individuals concerned, and can hardly fail to bring discredit on the faculty.[62]

The authors hoped both to encourage internal peace and to portray a harmonious front for the public. The AMA, however, wielded little or no coercive power. It was comprised of only a small number of physicians and a multitude of local and state societies that jealously retained their sovereignty. Consequently, the warnings in the code failed to restrain the competition and strife that were seemingly endemic to the profession.

Large numbers of physicians streaming out of medical schools in search of patients added to the discord. The competition for patients became so vigorous that a young student was advised in 1836 that the "only way to get practice would be to underbid those already practicing."[63] Conversely, established practitioners considered new physicians trespassers. As one writer confirmed, "[A]ny new comer is looked upon as an intruder upon vested rights."[64] Many doctors believed that conflict indirectly encouraged malpractice suits by marring the physician's public image. But they also contended that competition, born of the physician surplus, directly incited suits.

The burgeoning number of regular physicians was joined by a wide range of medical sects, or irregular practitioners. Thomsonians formed a self-taught sect that used only botanic remedies. Samuel Thomson, the founder, was a New Hampshire farmer who claimed that all illness was caused by an imbalance of the four bodily elements of antiquity: earth, air, fire, and water. Specifically, he believed that illness was synonymous with loss of bodily heat. Thomson remedied this imbalance with large doses of botanic concoctions of cayenne pepper and other sweat-producing herbs. He frequently used steam baths or hot bricks and blankets to produce the same effect. He also employed powerful "natural" vomiting and laxative agents, specifically lobelia, to purge patients. Thomson patented and sold the rights to his medical regime, making it widely available. Despite the severity of his cures, Thomson and his followers viciously attacked regular physicians for their use of harsh, "heroic" treatments. They were able to take this seemingly hypocritical stance by successfully branding regular physicians enemies of the common man and democratic, egalitarian ideals. Thomsonian writers condemned regular physicians for their supposed aristocratic pretensions and supported popular political movements of the Jacksonian era. Thomson claimed that his medical theories were the most democratic because they made each American his or her own physician. Although there were certainly many regular physicians who also held some of these cultural and political beliefs, the Thomsonians were able to create the impression that they were the exception rather than the rule.[65]

Regular physicians also faced threats from homeopathic practitioners. Homeopathy was based on the doctrine that "like cures like." Samuel Hahnemann, the founder of the movement, cataloged substances that would produce effects similar to various maladies. The homeopathic practitioner then provided patients with the designated substance in minute doses. According to the theory of *infinitesimals*, concoctions would be diluted sometimes as much as one part to a billion or even one to a trillion. The sect believed that these virtually microscopic amounts of medication could be fortified by *dynamization*, or the vigorous shaking of the preparation, an enormous but well-defined number of times. Homeopaths were generally educated and sincere practitioners. Their treatment regime was extremely benign and harmless—a major advantage over regular physicians and Thomsonians. In addition to orthodox physicians, homeopaths, and Thomsonians,[66] Americans could choose from a medical potpourri of alternative practitioners including hydropaths, who stressed the therapeutic virtues of water in all its forms, as well as natural bonesetters, mesmerists, root doctors, and phrenologists.

Irregular physicians, especially Thomsonians and homeopaths, became enormously popular in the first half of the nineteenth century and created significant competition for regular physicians. They battled orthodox practitioners not only for patients but also for the mantle of medical legitimacy. Regular, orthodox physicians could only tenuously claim therapeutic superiority and tried to overcome their irregular rivals by mocking their techniques and lobbying state legislatures for restrictive licensure. The multitude of irregular, alternative practitioners abounding in the period may have indirectly aggravated the malpractice problem. By offering several reasonable, and in some cases viable, alternatives to orthodox treatment, irregulars helped envelop the regular medical community in a cloud of doubt and distrust.

Thomsonians and homeopaths occasionally encouraged patients to sue regular physicians for malpractice and testified against them in court.[67] Most physicians agreed, however, that irregular practitioners stimulated few suits and played only a small role in the patient's decision to bring charges. The real enemy was inside the orthodox medical community. In fact, between 1835 and 1865, doctors identified intraprofessional competition among regular physicians as the primary source of the malpractice affliction more often than any other cause. In 1847 Alden March claimed, "In most of the prosecutions of physicians and surgeons for malpractice, it is fair to presume, from a pretty extended observation, that they originate in, or grow out of an unwarrantable rivalry, or perhaps jealousy, between two neighboring practitioners."[68] The 1853 Massachusetts Medical Society committee on malpractice concluded that "the jealous eyes of rivals" were the "most important" cause of the prevalent suits.[69] Similarly, in 1854 a writer decried, "We too often find the viper within our own ranks; those who from envy or rivalry seek to destroy the hard earned fame of one in every way their superior."[70] One of the patriarchs of mid- and late–nineteenth-century medicine, Stephen Smith, concurred in 1860 that his "own experience in suits for alleged malpractice has led to the conclusion that both the source of the evil and the remedy lie within the pale of the profession itself. The secret history of the vast majority of these cases reveals the humiliating fact that they were instigated by medical men."[71]

Some physicians inadvertently generated suits with offhand remarks while examining patients. Samuel Parkman, a frequent commentator on malpractice, reported that sometimes "a medical man is entrapped into the examination of a case which he afterwards discovers involves a legal investigation." Parkman explained that a patient who believed he had been mistreated by a physician would consult a second practitioner in hope of securing evidence. "The second surgeon soon discovers that he is summoned as a witness in a trial in which the first surgeon is the defendant and the patient is the plaintiff."[72] In one such case a New York man broke his leg when he was pinned under a falling tree. A local physician set the leg, but since it was planting time, the man hobbled about in the field trying to work. About six months later he visited a second doctor who examined the limb and remarked that "the attending physician ought to be ashamed of it; and that he ought to pay him for a year's work." The farmer sued the first physician for malpractice.[73]

When physicians testified as expert witnesses in court, they attempted to display their medical superiority to the audience, often to the detriment of the defendant. In their endeavor to appear knowledgeable and competent, they often claimed or intimated that their methods of treatment were safer, more advanced, or more effective than the defendant's. As one observer noted, when physicians were "called into court, one is pitted against another, like two roosters in a cock pit."[74] Other physicians genuinely attempted to protect the defendant when they testified in malpractice trials. But under the rigorous cross-examination of the prosecuting attorney medical witnesses often found themselves giving more damaging evidence than they had intended.[75]

Some physicians, however, deliberately used malpractice suits against competitors. When Dr. Sargent was sued by a New Hampshire man in 1852 for the treatment of a broken leg, the medical witnesses separated into two camps according to their place of practice. The two expert witnesses for the prosecution were local physicians who undoubtedly competed with Dr. Sargent for patients. All the physicians who testified for Sargent came from surrounding communities. Sargent lost two trials relating to the case, won on appeal, and finally settled out of court.[76] Physicians sometimes urged patients to sue their professional antagonists in order to ruin their reputations and destroy their practices. Often the accuser served as an expert witness for the prosecution. Covetous, aspiring physicians used suits to discredit established practitioners. Established practitioners used them to discourage new competitors. Occasionally, these suits inspired retaliatory litigation.

The Crosby case is once again illustrative. In 1847 a Vermont man sued his two physicians for malpractice. They had treated the patient for a broken tibia, the smaller bone in the lower leg, which healed in a twisted position. Dixi Crosby, a local medical man, served as the key witness for the prosecution. He argued that the defendant physicians should have visited the patient more frequently, perhaps even daily. He questioned the defendants' treatment and declared that they had failed to diagnose an accompanying fracture of the fibula. The jury ruled against the defendants and charged them $500. In reporting the case for the *Boston Medical and Surgical Journal* an editorialist noted that the defendants were Crosby's competitors and that the plaintiff had previously been a patient of the star witness. The editorialist, carefully avoiding libel, remarked that "Dr. Crosby, no doubt, intended to do justice to all parties, although his testimony was strongly for the plaintiff, as evidently were his feelings." While all the other medical physicians in the case "expressed no doubt" as to the propriety and quality of the defendants' conduct, Crosby's "testimony upon the main points, method of treatment, and attendance, was at variance with the testimony of the other witnesses."[77]

While the reporter tempered his analysis of Crosby's motives, the message remained plain. Crosby had used his position as expert witness to undercut his competitors. A Vermont appellate court overturned the conviction of the physicians, and in May 1851 a subsequent jury found them innocent of any malpractice.[78] The same month, Crosby found himself the target of a malpractice accusation for an injury and treatment that had occurred six years earlier. When a jury convicted and fined Crosby $800, medical editorialists rushed to his defense and speculated that a "scheme is imagined to have been devised for breaking down the professor [Crosby] . . . in other words, by driving off an old surgeon, there is a chance of dropping into his place."[79] The coincidental timing of the suit against Crosby also suggests that it may have been a reprisal for his role in the previous malpractice trial.

A young physician in the 1840s complained that he was plagued by accusations and suits for malpractice as soon as he arrived in Erie, Pennsylvania. The suits, he said, were instigated by local practitioners "who regarded his advent with a jealous eye." The same practitioners who encouraged patients to sue the newcomer served as expert witnesses for the prosecution. The strategy worked. After being sued for two smallpox vaccinations and one fracture treatment, the doctor "wearied of vexation . . . [and] left his suits, his property, and his family, to seek a more generous home and better rewards, in the golden valleys of California." The physician eventually returned to Erie County to face trial. He was acquitted on two charges, but fined $1,450 in the third trial.[80]

Even powerful and famous physicians were vulnerable to suits incited by professional enemies. William Beaumont became world renowned in the 1830s for his historic studies on digestion gained by observations through the chronically unhealed wound in Alexis St. Martin's stomach.[81] In 1844 Beaumont, practicing in St. Louis, Missouri, took a public position in a dispute between two rival medical schools. The opposing faction convinced two patients to sue Beaumont for malpractice. In one case he was charged, along with a codefendant, with an incompetent hernia operation that left the young woman patient with a small, open incision. Beaumont neither assisted in the surgery nor advised the attending physician. Although he was only one of several physicians to view the patient during her long convalescence, his name was added to the $10,000 suit. A local physician claimed that some doctors "resolve to attain practice at any cost, whether of professional principles or of a brother's character." They were willing to use "unholy means" and "calculated success by others' downfall, and by means of detraction will sap the reputation of a professional brother, with the hope of building up a practice in his ruin." Beaumont was ultimately exonerated, but a vicious pamphlet debate continued for many months.[82]

Medical literature counseled physicians against playing either an accidental or a malicious role in inciting litigation. An editorialist in 1847 gently advised that a "difference of opinion between two or more physicians, where the spirit of kindness and courtesy controls the intemperate expressions of vanity and malevolence, may often lead to the best results."[83] Another writer, commenting on malpractice cases for fractures, observed, "These cases should lead members of our profession to be kind, generous, liberal to one another, and not to impute to ignorance or inattention, that which is the result of a generally incurable accident."[84] Other writers encouraged harsh reprisals against physicians who purposefully instigated litigation. As one physician declared in 1854, "Those puny strife engenderers, who stir up these unnatural suits, deserve the execrations of all classes and conditions." He recommended that "they should be shunned and left to wallow in their own filthiness."[85]

"Radical and Progressive Proclivities"

The medical profession's open competition within itself, combined with its lack of a respected and distinct social status, reflected the social and political environment of Jacksonian America. The roots of the crisis are somewhat earlier. Although the stratified nature of society had been under attack since the early eighteenth century, the republican rhetoric of 1776 hastened the process. Between the American Revolution and 1800, the traditional ranks of society rapidly blurred, and social hierarchies weakened. Plain, unlettered men started to believe that they were the equals of men of any rank and began to resent and hate any emblem of hierarchical privilege or status.

Professional monopolies reeked of aristocratic privilege and were inconsistent with the growing notion of equality and democracy because they interfered with free and open competition. The late eighteenth-century attempts of elite physicians to organize the profession failed because they could not provide efficacious care and because their reorganization plans mirrored the hierarchical, tripartite arrangement of the London medical profession. Consequently, when physicians lobbied early state legislatures to pass licensure laws, they met with limited success. Virtually every state had passed some type of licensure statute by the late eighteenth century but the laws were inclusive rather than exclusive. Many of the statutes did not forbid unlicensed practice but merely provided certificates of legitimacy to "qualified" doctors. In some states unlicensed physicians were only prohibited from suing in court for unpaid fees. Unlicensed physicians in these jurisdictions could mitigate this handicap by requiring payment in advance.[86] Even in states where licensure laws provided penalties for unsanctioned practice, juries generally would not convict violators. For much of the public, physicians' education and results did not justify the establishment of a medical monopoly. Many Americans, especially in the working classes, believed that a physician's status should be determined by his performance and not by legislation.[87]

This trend of decreasing respect for traditional authority and status accelerated after 1800. Physicians were continually frustrated in their attempts to retain their social status and to establish a market monopoly by licensure. They lost ground as democratic, antistatus feelings grew. Alexis de Tocqueville, one of the most eloquent and opinionated observers of Jacksonian culture, concluded that democratic revolutions were generally followed by an attack on symbols of social aristocracy and an increase in individualism.[88] The old order was changing rapidly. These new sentiments glorified the image of a society of common, hard-working individuals operating without legal or institutional restraints. This philosophy had no room for aristocratic, intellectual, or economic privilege and was accompanied by widespread attacks on various forms of authority. Jacksonian Democrats praised free trade and competition and condemned monopolies and chartered corporations. They attacked professional licensure as an injustice as odious as the monster U.S. Bank.[89]

Critics of the profession argued that physicians were no different from merchants or craftsmen. Medical sects such as Thomsonians, homeopaths, and hydropaths claimed to embody the free-market, common-man mentality of the Jacksonians and joined in the attack on the desires of regular physicians for a privileged legal position. An antebellum Ohio journalist exemplified the mood of much of the working class when he declared that "[w]e go for free-trade in doctoring."[90]

State legislatures responded. Beginning in 1838, jurisdiction after jurisdiction abolished already weak licensure laws. By 1850, only New Jersey and the District of Columbia retained any effective controls over medical practice.[91] There was "free trade in doctoring." These were the "radical and progressive proclivities" that Alexander Garnett believed "induce[d] every street urchin or illiterate mechanic, to entertain the belief that he has not only the unquestionable right to fill, but that he is eminently fitted for any station or position in society."[92]

Physicians saw an intimate connection between Jacksonian rhetoric, their decline in status, the abolition of licensure, and the increase in malpractice suits. William Wood noted in 1849 that "the general influences leading to these perversions of justice [malpractice cases] can be readily perceived by all." According to Wood, the efforts to limit the practice of medicine to those who "have the abilities and acquirements essential to its proper understanding" had failed. The public, Wood held, considered the limitation of medical practice to those with "scientific attainments" as an attempt to "monopolize rights and infringe on the greatest liberty." As a result, "ignorant and impudent pretenders, under a great variety of humbugging titles, come before the public with equal rights and a better chance for public favour, than the regular practitioners." Meanwhile, the medical doctor was forced to pursue his profession "under risks and hazards no prudent man could encounter."[93]

Stephen Smith saw a direct correlation between the lack of medical licensure in the United States and climbing malpractice rates. Smith pointed out that Britain, France, and Germany had enacted stringent licensure laws that were designed "to develop, foster, and advance true scientific medicine." The physicians in these countries, Smith noted, suffered fewer malpractice suits than their American counterparts.[94] In the absence of any limitation on medical practice, malpractice became the only way to protect the public from incompetence. Thus, in 1847 one writer recognized that the lack of effective licensure in most states left "to the common law the task of guarding their citizens by suits for malpractice."[95]

The use of market forces and individual malpractice cases to oversee the medical profession was a characteristically Jacksonian approach to regulation. Licensure, in the Jacksonian mind, represented regulation from the top down and appeared to benefit the physician by creating an unfair monopoly and relying on artificial measures of merit. Malpractice suits, however, represented regulation from the bottom up. Individual patients could choose which practitioner to patronize, and individual juries could decide if the medical treatment had been competent. This arrangement was consistent with regulating patterns in other areas of early nineteenth-century life. Most regulation was "local and self-sustaining." States made few overarching efforts to enforce existing regulations, and if an individual did not initiate a lawsuit, the statutes were not enforced.[96] Indeed, one of the hallmarks of the Jacksonian movement was the desire to make the courts and the law more accessible and responsive to the common person.[97]

While patients increasingly accused regular physicians of malpractice, Thomsonians and homeopaths, who espoused the social and political equalitarianism of the working classes, were seldom sued. The Pennsylvania medical society committee investigating malpractice found that irregular physicians, who are "gross and ignorant pretenders, [and] whose whole existence is a continued system of mal-practice, pass unnoticed and unharmed." A judge interviewed during the investigation confirmed that although he had seen many suits against regular physicians, he knew of only one malpractice charge against a "quack doctor." The committee concluded that irregular physicians avoided law suits because "they act on popular prejudices." The regular physician "is hunted as the victim of popular prejudice, while the quack who has complied with that prejudice goes free."[98] Other writers agreed. In 1853 the *Western Medical and Surgical Journal* reported "that the chances are all together better for the acquittal of an ignorant, uneducated pretender to medical knowledge, who is really guilty, than that of an intelligent, well-educated surgeon to whom no fault can justly be charged."[99]

Physicians recognized that they were at greater risk from the poorer segments of society and blamed political and class antipathy for many of the suits and subsequent convictions. Malpractice suits offered injured farmers and laborers an outlet for antistatus, antiprofessional sentiment. A writer alleged in 1847 that "the people, or, at least that class of persons who are most exposed to accidents, and the least responsible, either for the surgeon's bill for professional attendance, or for the costs of a suit for mal-practice seem to require high surgical attainments."[100] And, as a physician claimed in 1849, "the interests and prejudices of the whole class are against the acts and doings of the regular practitioner."[101]

Prosecuting attorneys sometimes exploited this prejudice in their arguments to juries. In an 1848 New York case the patient's attorney condemned the medical profession as an "oppressive and aristocratic monopoly." While the trial court judge cautioned the jury to disregard the remarks, and while they returned a verdict for the physician, other physicians were not so lucky.[102] One layman observed that

[a] jury of laboring men . . . go into the jury box with feelings excited against the surgeon, because they think his business should produce no better pecuniary returns than his own; the surgeon's bill is always deemed exorbitant by them; and he is generally looked upon as almost a swindler, and living luxuriously upon their hard earnings; therefore they are always inclined to render a verdict against your profession, and in favor of one of their own class.[103]

The lay observer also described the reaction of a working-class jury to expert witness testimony. According to the narrator, "after a few questions are answered, they sneer and laugh at you [physicians], and make up their minds long before they leave the box." A medical editorialist verified the characterization and confirmed that a "great number of these trials in various parts of the Union, but especially amongst farmers, are terminated in this way."[104] A writer in 1856 concluded, "The trial of a professional man for an alleged malpractice by a jury of laborers is a farce and a disgrace to our country."[105] All malpractice juries, however, were not composed solely of doctor-hating laborers and farmers. Otherwise physicians would not have won as many cases as they did.

Corporations and physicians shared working-class resentment and distrust. The Massachusetts Medical Society committee on malpractice concluded that patients "from whom the least remuneration is to be obtained" were responsible for most of the suits. The committee believed that the sympathy of the jury was generally with the plaintiff. According to the study, "this sympathy for the seemingly oppressed and misused has influence in all cases where a corporation, civic or otherwise is the defendant; and it cannot be denied that it is an important element in the patient's decision to bring a suit against his physician."[106] Corporations, specifically railroads, were also suffering through their first wave of lawsuits in the early 1840s and 1850s. In personal injury cases against corporations, plaintiffs' attorneys often described the cases as battles between oppressive, powerful corporations and virtuous, hard-working laborers.[107]

Declining social status of physicians, "defective medical acquirements," the "want of union and harmony," and "radical and progressive proclivities" were central elements in the increase of malpractice suits between 1835 and 1865. These factors clearly helped to generate, directly and indirectly, many of the suits in the period. However, they do not provide the fundamental explanation for the malpractice phenomenon. Poor medical training and therapy, intraprofessional competition, and Jacksonian sentiments were immediate causes of the dramatic increase in litigation and help to explain why these three decades contrasted so starkly with the pre-1835 years. Yet, as important as these elements were in 1835–1865, their gradual disappearance did not retard the rate of malpractice prosecutions.

Appellate malpractice decisions multiplied at a rate faster than the population through the early twentieth century. During this time the therapeutic, educational, professional, and social trends that played an important role in promoting suits during the 1835–1865 period faded and in some cases reversed. The malpractice epidemic did not.

In the 1870s, medical education started its long trek toward excellence and respectability. The new medical school produced more competent physicians and slowly raised respect toward the profession.[108] Much of the competitiveness and divisiveness that had afflicted the profession in the Jacksonian period dissipated by the first decades of the twentieth century. Statistical revelations and scientific discoveries of the last half of the nineteenth century helped standardize and unify medical beliefs and treatments, as did the standardization of medical education. Medical societies, which were weak and contentious in the 1840s, settled their differences, increased their membership, and successfully promoted professional harmony by 1900. Likewise, a reorganized AMA had a unifying and pacifying effect on the profession.[109] Finally, the Jacksonian antipathy for corporations, monopolies, and professions declined. In the 1880s and 1890s states instituted effective medical licensure laws that helped limit access to the profession. By 1900 the public still distrusted the intellectual, but recognized and often deferred to the authority of experts. These developments, the improvements in therapy in many areas of medicine, and the promise of the future significantly raised the status of the medical profession by 1920.[110]

Malpractice suits continued to rise in spite of the general improvement in the status of the profession and the disappearance of many elements that had incited litigants between 1835 and 1865. Contemporary observers were correct in blaming these factors for the wave of malpractice suits. However, litigiousness persisted because these factors were only the immediate and topical causes of suits in a specific historic period. The presence of these elements alone did not automatically lead to runaway litigation.

Despite the existence of many of the same elements that encouraged litigation in the rest of the country, medical malpractice suits in the South were rare. Antebellum southern physicians were also poorly organized and educated. Irregular practitioners, especially Thomsonians, were prevalent and popular there. Southern state legislatures abolished licensure about the same time as their northern counterparts. But, southern society had not yet undergone the cultural transformations that provided the fundamental preconditions for widespread malpractice prosecution. Therefore, even though many of the immediate factors that inspired suits in the North existed, they did not produce the same results.[111]

Suits continued to proliferate in the rest of the country long after the immediate causes of the Jacksonian period dissipated because the social and cultural foundations for the litigation continued to evolve unabated. Immediate factors such as low status, antiprofessionalism, and competition were responsible for provoking the first malpractice crisis of the 1840s. Without these elements, medical malpractice rates may have risen more gradually, but they cannot completely explain the flood of suits in the years 1835–1865 nor the unremitting litigation since.

CHAPTER 4

"The Expression of a Wellmade Man"

The expression of a wellmade man appears not only in his face,
It is in his limbs and joints also. . . . it is curiously in the joints of
  his hips and wrists,
It is in his walk . . . the carriage of his neck . . . the flex of his waist
  and
knees. . . .

—Walt Whitman, "I Sing the Body Electric"[1]

Malpractice suits arising from the treatment of fractures and disloca-tions constituted most of the increased litigation after 1835, and contin-ued to be the major complaint through the early decades of the twen-tieth century.[2] Lay and professional attitudes toward orthopedic practice and the development of fracture treatment, like physicians' low status, intraprofessional rivalry, and Jacksonian sentiment, represented one of the immediate causes of the first dramatic leap in malpractice rates. But at the same time the impact of technological developments illus-trates an underlying cultural attitude that helped cause suits into the twentieth century. Malpractice suits were, in part, an expression of a transformed view of the human body and an unprecedented concern for physical well-being.

"The Mechanic's Hand"

Before 1835 fractures accounted for a small percentage of the total malpractice cases unless they resulted in a severe deformity or amputation. Malpractice suits were neither a common nor an entirely acceptable practice in the first third of the century, and patients generally refrained from bringing charges for milder injuries. As the practice of suing physicians became more acceptable and prevalent, patients freely sued on the basis of more moderate physical damage. Fractures and dislocations were the type of injuries most likely to have permanent but not grievous physical results such as shortened or deformed limbs, frozen joints, and long periods of convalescence. These injuries left the prospective plaintiff with a physical manifestation of the defendant/physician's supposed incompetence to display to sympathetic jurors. The long recovery period usually required for orthopedic injuries provoked potential plaintiffs by keeping them out of work and causing them long-term discomfort.

In spite of the protracted healing process, however, patients sometimes left their beds and went to work before doing so was safe or sensible. Occasionally, patients would loosen or remove painful or restrictive splints and bandages. Premature activity and interference with the physician's treatment could hamper the healing process, distort the results, or even worsen the patient's injury. In these instances physicians could ostensibly protect themselves in court with the doctrine of *contributory negligence* by arguing that the patient was responsible for the bad results of treatment.

In one such case in 1856 an Ohio man was thrown from a sleigh near his home. He severely fractured both bones in his lower leg. A year later, when his leg healed with some shortening and deformity, he sued his physician for malpractice. The defense attorney introduced a parade of witnesses who affirmed that the patient had been careless and did not follow the physician's instructions. One witness testified that he had accompanied the patient, still on crutches, on an all-night, whiskey-drinking raccoon hunt. Another witness had drunk with the patient until he became "pretty well sprung." Then the injured man "said he could walk as good as me; jumped over a manure pile by aid of his cane; [and] tried to walk curb stone without [his] cane." According to one witness, the plaintiff admitted that "the leg had been set straight and he had hurt it running about." The jury returned a verdict of not guilty after only three minutes of deliberation.[3]

Patient complicity was not always so obvious. Contributory negligence was a "complete defense" and a potentially powerful weapon for defendants. If the defendant/physician could demonstrate that the patient was in any way responsible for the failure of the treatment, the injured party would receive no award. However, contributory negligence was not always easy to prove and could be ignored by juries. Additionally, juries may have been hesitant to accept contributory negligence as a defense because it so thoroughly absolved the physician of liability. Therefore, it is difficult to determine the impact of the doctrine in the early nineteenth century.

When malpractice suits for all types of injuries increased after 1835, it was not surprising that fracture cases became the predominant subject of litigation. Fractures and dislocations were common in a society dominated by manual labor.[4] They yielded less severe, but often permanent injuries, which, in a culture increasingly sympathetic to malpractice charges, were considered legitimate subjects for litigation. Moreover, orthopedic injuries were occurring at an increasing rate in the first half of the century because of the newly mechanized and dangerous workplace. By 1860 arms and legs were being torn, crushed, and mutilated at an unprecedented rate on railways, in textile mills and mines, and by powerful steam engines.

Fracture and dislocation suits multiplied after 1835 not only because of burgeoning injuries and the general increase of malpractice cases of all types. The relationship between orthopedic treatment and contemporary malpractice rates was interactive. Before 1835 suits fell into two categories: severe injuries and mechanical treatments. By 1800 and through the first two decades of the nineteenth century, physicians could offer several moderately successful medical procedures. They were able to administer smallpox vaccinations, amputate limbs, set simple fractures and dislocations, excise superficial growths, and remove foreign objects.[5] Blood-letting was considered a relatively standardized procedure. By the third decade of the nineteenth century, male physicians had displaced many midwives by touting their scientific and technical expertise. Early obstetricians championed the advantages of superior physiological knowledge, drugs such as opium and ergot, and instruments like forceps and the crochet to ease painful and dangerous births. This new, but still primitive technology gave physicians a competitive advantage over the traditional midwife.[6]

Even though their successes were tenuous, physicians asserted technical expertise in these treatments, and patients began to expect mechanical, predictable results. As an 1827 judge explained, the physicians often exercised a profession "beset by great difficulties, [but] the employment of a man midwife and surgeon, for the most part, is merely mechanical."[7] These areas, especially vaccination, amputations, and obstetrics accounted for most of the scattered malpractice cases before 1835.

Even though orthopedics was in some respects considered a mechanical enterprise, fractures and dislocations generated very few cases in the early part of the nineteenth century. Physicians were moderately adept at restoring simple fractures, and even when they failed, the resulting deformity was usually too minor to warrant a suit in an atmosphere that was generally not conducive to malpractice charges. Severe compound fractures and dislocations, on the other hand, usually required amputation. Benjamin Bell's *System of Surgery*, a widely used textbook in the early part of the century, advised that "[f]rom the difficult treatment and uncertain event of compound fractures practitioners have been very universally disposed to consider the amputation of the fractured limb as necessary."[8] In his 1819 treatise on compound fractures Percival Pott noted that a surgeon often "showed much more rashness in attempting to save a limb, than he would have done in the amputation of it: The amputation would have been the more justifiable practice."[9] Similarly, Samuel Cooper, author of an 1813 handbook on surgery, warned that although "apparently desperate cases [of compound fracture] are sometimes cured, . . . every man also knows, that such escapes are very rare to admit of being made precedents and the majority of such attempts fail."[10] The standard of good practice before the 1820s demanded that physicians amputate badly broken limbs early instead of risking losing the patient to subsequent complications in an ill-advised attempt to save an arm or leg.

Amputations did not generate a large number of suits. By its nature,

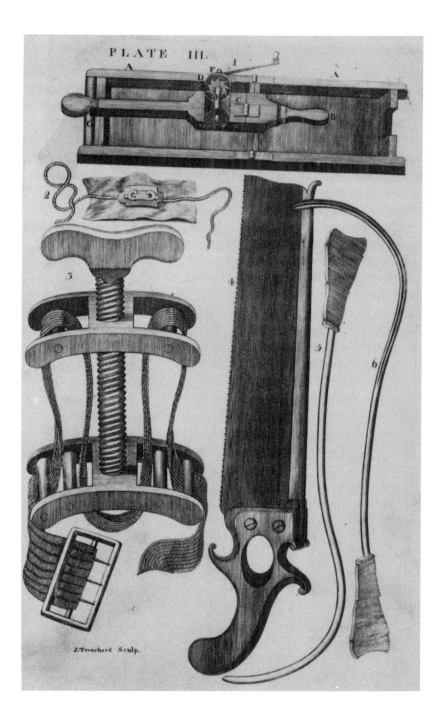

PLATE III.

J. Trenchard Sculp.

amputation complicated the prosecution of a physician. Often, medical experts, juries, and judges could not examine the excised limb to determine if it truly required the operation. Even if the patient died during the procedure, as many did, there were limited legal remedies before the 1850s, when state legislatures enacted wrongful death statutes.[11] Even compound and complicated fractures in which patients kept their limbs yielded very few cases before 1835. Although the profession and the public were beginning to view procedures such as childbirth, vaccination, and amputation as mechanical and expected mechanical predictability, the treatment of complicated fracture injuries did not inspire the same confidence, and hence, the same demands.

Physicians were making dramatic improvements in the treatment of compound fractures and dislocations between 1820 and 1840, and these would change the basis of prognosis for fractures and dislocations, transform professional and lay attitudes, and provide the raw material for malpractice suits. During this period evidence rapidly accumulated against the desirability of frequent and perfunctory amputation. Astley Cooper, a surgical pioneer, declared in 1835:

Formerly, and with my recollection, it was thought expedient for the preservation of life, by many of our best surgeons to amputate the limb in these cases, but from our experience of late years, such advice would in a great majority of instances be now deemed highly injudicious.[12]

Physicians had developed new techniques, such as excising jagged pieces of exposed bone with saws and roughing the exposed ends of bones to facilitate union. They developed new bandaging and splinting procedures that allowed them to save both limbs and lives. Although antiseptic practices were not popular until the 1870s and 1880s, antebellum physicians also devised methods to counter the deadly infections that often followed compound fractures. For instance, innovative packing procedures ensured that wounds healed from the inside to the outside and diminished the number of severe internal infections. Consequently, during the 1830s and 1840s medical journals reported case

Machine for adjusting dislocations; screw tourniquet for amputations; seventeen-inch amputating saw; and grooved staffs for lithotomies. From Benjamin Bell, A System of Surgery *(1806). (Courtesy of the Historical Research Center, Houston Academy of Medicine, Texas Medical Center Library, Houston, Texas.)*

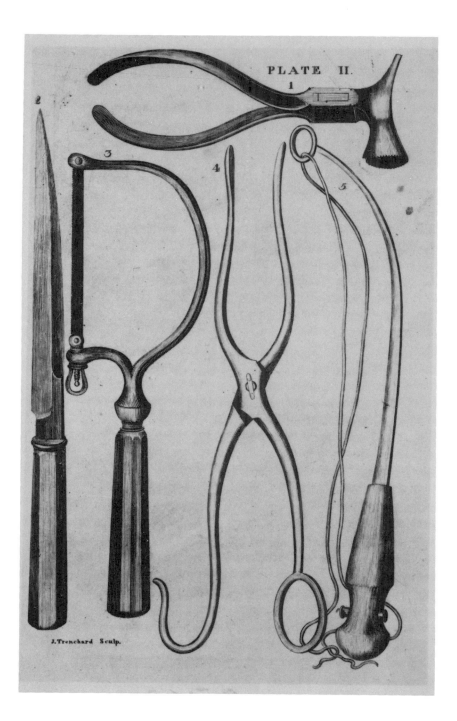

PLATE II.

J. Trenchard Sculp.

after case where compound fractures healed with the only bad effect being some shortening or deformity of the patient's limb.[13] William Walker presented a lengthy paper to the Massachusetts Medical Society in 1845 celebrating the advancements made in the treatment of compound and complicated fractures.[14] Finally, with the advent of anesthesia and painless surgery in the late 1840s, physicians could work longer and more carefully on patients and save rather than amputate limbs.[15]

Concurrently, a strong revulsion developed against amputations on other grounds. American physicians, under the influence of foreign clinicians such as Pierre Louis, scrutinized the treatment's efficacy statistically and discovered that the procedure was dreadfully dangerous.[16] In 1838 George Norris published a statistical appraisal of amputations, reporting that "[t]he endeavors that have been made for many years past, to save limbs under almost desperate circumstances . . . ha[ve] almost imperceivably produced a great unwillingness with us as to the performance of amputations." Moreover, Norris noted that amputations were hazardous. An 1833 survey of a St. Louis hospital found 13 fatalities out of 21 amputations. Norris conducted a survey at the Pennsylvania Hospital between 1831 and 1838 and discovered that 21 of 55 amputees died.[17]

Finally, physicians who embraced the move toward the "conservative medicine" of the late antebellum period were abandoning heroic medical and surgical procedures and placing a greater trust in the healing powers of nature. Austin Flint, a prominent surgeon, wrote in 1862 that the history of surgery in the first third of the century was characterized by the "introduction and frequent performance of numerous formidable operations." But, Flint remarked, "The change that has taken place is marked. We hear now comparatively little of the terrible operations of that sort which is associated with bloody deeds. What would have once been considered as a degree of courage to be admired is now stigmatized as rashness."[18] As William Walker recom-

Forceps for removing skull bone in trepanning; twelve-inch amputating knife; small spring saw for amputating fingers and toes; forceps for removing nasal polyps; and ligatures for removing uterine polyps. From Benjamin Bell, A System of Surgery *(1806). (Courtesy of the Historical Research Center, Houston Academy of Medicine, Texas Medical Center Library, Houston, Texas.)*

mended, physicians began to "estimate the powers of nature and of art in resisting and surmounting injuries."[19]

Not surprisingly, wholesale amputations had become less acceptable by the 1850s. As John Elwell declared in his 1860 work on malpractice, "An amputation that would have been justified by the rules of surgery and the operator protected in court, twenty years ago or even less time than that, would now be repudiated by the best authority and the operator justly chargeable with malpractice."[20] Physicians were caught in a double bind. The treatment of fractures had improved dramatically over the first half of the century, and they were more often able to save, rather than amputate limbs. However, badly injured limbs, even if spared, usually healed with some shortening or deformity. By the late 1830s patients were willing to sue physicians for treatment that saved profoundly injured limbs, albeit with some accompanying imperfection. The less than perfect results following compound fractures and dislocations were the single most common source of malpractice suits in the nineteenth century.

Physicians who exercised the most up-to-date techniques and preserved badly injured limbs often found themselves in greater legal danger than those practitioners who followed the archaic practice of perfunctory amputation. For example, in 1853 a New Hampshire man who had suffered a compound fracture-dislocation of his ankle and lower leg sued his physician after the joint became frozen in an awkward position. Despite testimony from expert witnesses that this type of an injury would have previously required amputation and that the patient should have been "glad to get off with any foot that would do to walk on," the jury found the physician guilty of malpractice.[21]

Though unnecessary or incompetent amputations were seldom penalized, physicians who saved limbs with compound or complex fractures were regularly sued. In 1856 the *Medical News* reported a typical case in an article titled "Legal Robbery of a Physician." A man had crushed his leg so badly that "the first question was as to the propriety of primary amputation." A doctor saved the man's leg, but as in other cases, some deformity resulted. The patient sued for malpractice and won a substantial award.[22]

The irony of physicians being placed at greater risk because of medical advancements and successes in saving limbs was noted by

Abraham Lincoln during his legal career. In 1856 Lincoln, a successful lawyer, represented two physicians against a charge of malpractice. An elderly man had badly broken his leg, which had shortened as it healed. Lincoln searched out physicians to coach him on fracture treatment and used a chicken bone at the trial to demonstrate the comparative brittleness of young and old bones. During his closing address Lincoln chastised the plaintiff: "Well! What I would advise *you* to do is get down on your *knees* and thank your heavenly Father, and also these two Doctors that you have any legs to stand on at all." Lincoln declared that the injury might have easily warranted amputation but that the physicians had exercised their skill and saved the leg. He reasoned that "[t]he slight defect that finally resulted, through Nature's methods of aiding the work of surgeons, is nothing compared to the loss of the limb altogether." The jury ruled in favor of the physicians and charged the trial costs to the plaintiff.[23]

Although physicians continued to practice the new fracture and dislocation procedures, the vagaries of malpractice litigation could have diminished the quality of medical care in individual cases by making it more attractive to condone amputation than to follow the safer and more effective procedure of saving limbs. Often, then, the best treatment for the patient was not necessarily the safest treatment for the surgeon. In fact, physicians were left more vulnerable by medical progress that frequently provided patients with visible, bodily evidence for malpractice lawsuits.

After the introduction of ether in 1846, amputations became less horrible and encouraged some physicians to operate indiscriminately. As a physician in 1851 noted, "anesthesia has its drawbacks and evils." Patients were too easily persuaded to submit to the knife of "what are called promising young men who carve their way into practice."[24] This small, but not insignificant, problem arose at the same time that methods for saving mangled limbs were improving and malpractice suits were increasing. Irresponsible practitioners had sufficient motivation to avoid the chance of a suit and enhance their image as heroic physicians with a few strokes of an amputating saw. Faced with a difficult fracture, an unethical or unscrupulous doctor might recommend a dramatic amputation to portray himself as a courageous surgeon and, at the same time, sidestep the prospect of an imperfect result and possible malpractice charge. As one writer suggested after observing a dispute between two physicians over treatment in the late 1830s, "In the absence of every other motive, one might almost suppose that amputation was desired to get rid of a troublesome case, and the more effectively to conceal a bad piece of surgery."[25] In this case, as in other scattered instances, the fear of prosecution may have encouraged the physician to ignore improvements in medical practice while more responsible surgeons saved limbs and left themselves open to attacks in ways that would not have been possible before the 1830s.

The prominence of fracture malpractice suits highlights an additional reason why regular physicians were more susceptible to malpractice charges than alternative practitioners. Thomsonians, homeopaths, and hydropaths were more likely to espouse the cultural, equalitarian sentiment that much of the public found lacking in the regular physician. They portrayed themselves as anti-elitist friends of the common people. Irregulars were also often less likely to treat the orthopedic injuries that generated the bulk of suits. Many focused their attention on medical therapeutics rather than surgery. Consequently, regular physicians treated more of the legally hazardous medical problems. This factor, however, only aggravated the regular physician's already vulnerable position. Irregulars did not completely eschew fracture treatment. Indeed, some irregulars specialized in orthopedic injuries. "Natural bonesetters" claimed to possess divinely-endowed, innate skill to manipulate and cure fractures and dislocations and actively competed with regular physicians. Bonesetters were competent, but not unerring practitioners.[26] Their failures, however, seldom resulted in lawsuits.

Worthington Hooker, a regular physician, repeatedly attempted to discredit the bonesetters by recounting episodes of the practitioners' ineptitude and mismanagement. In one case, a bonesetter had violently rebroken a man's nearly healed, fractured wrist. Complications from the treatment rendered the entire arm useless for life. Hooker noted, "If this man had been treated by an educated surgeon instead of an infallible bonesetter, he could undoubtedly have recovered large damages for such mal-practice."[27] Hooker explained that while bonesetters were quite willing to accuse regular physicians of malpractice, they rarely suffered the same fate themselves. Patients and juries treated bonesetters' shortcomings more gingerly than those of regular practitioners. According to Hooker, in some parts of the country "no jury could be found sufficiently unprejudiced to inflict any just penalty upon a bone-setter for mal-practice; though they would inflict it to the full if the same facts were proved to them in regard to any educated surgeon."[28]

The state of fracture treatment played a major role in the multiplication of suits, but it did not affect regular and irregular practitioners equally. While regular physicians' disproportionate share of the orthopedic cases may have increased their chances of being sued, it did not completely explain their near monopoly over malpractice suits. The various sources of cultural antipathy and intraprofessional rivalry were equally important in making regular physicians the prime target for malpractice accusations.

The dramatic advancements in fracture treatment technology of the first third of the nineteenth century contributed to the leap in malpractice rates in another way. Through much of this period physicians and the public recognized the uncertainty in the treatment of complex orthopedic injuries and refrained from characterizing the procedures as "mechanical." Regular physicians began to use the image of a machine to counter the claims of irregular physician competitors. Worthington Hooker, who usually stressed that medicine was a mixture of art and science and inherently uncertain, abandoned this view when discussing orthopedics. Hooker wrote that the public should realize that "the joints of the body are constructed upon *mechanical* principles, and that they are to be understood just like any other *machine*."[29] After the improvements in treatments proliferated, physicians and the public alike began to conceive of orthopedic practice in mechanistic terms. Many physicians were dazzled by recent advancements and seduced into unrealistic expectations.

Physicians and medical writers began to believe that mechanical, standardized treatment yielded consistent, faultless cures. An Ohio medical society committee studying malpractice concluded that the absence of a realistic and accurate standard of success was responsible for the outbreak of fracture-related suits. "There is little in our textbooks, or courses of instruction, from which the beginning practitioner would be led to expect anything but perfect results." The committee explained that doctors called to examine possible instances of malpractice were often misled by unrealistic expectations of cures. If their colleagues did not attain their ideal standard, they could "by the honest convictions of right" be "drawn into the service of the prosecution."[30] An antebellum surgery text introduced into evidence in an 1850 suit advised that "in such cases [compound fractures], . . . where shortening [of a limb] took place, it was owing to the carelessness of the surgeon, or the use of improper apparatus, and need not be so in these days, with the modern improvements."[31]

As the public began to perceive the physician as a technician in specific areas of medicine, the range of injuries open to lawsuits widened. A New Yorker wrote in 1848 that "there is but one method of setting a limb, of taking up an artery, or of extracting a bullet, and upon this method all well-educated surgeons are agreed."[32] In the same year, a plaintiff's attorney confidently told a malpractice jury that a "fracture is a simple thing to cure . . . there are no arbitrary rules on the subject."[33] Vaccination, obstetrics, and amputation were considered mechanical practices in the first third of the century and therefore dominated the small number of cases before 1835. After, the dramatic improvements in severe fracture and dislocation treatment contributed to the development of the image of the physician as a technician. Accordingly, the expectation of standard treatment and predictable, near perfect results intensified. Technological advancement and the accompanying expectations of complete proficiency have always helped fuel significant increases in malpractice rates. The malpractice rate between 1835 and 1865 was particularly sensitive to the improvements in fracture treatment because they occurred at the same time that factors such as competition and antiprofessional sentiment were also driving the litigation rates up.

Despite the growing view of both the public and the profession, it is clear that fracture treatment at midcentury was neither standard nor predictable. No one approach or device dominated practice. The point

Method for setting thigh fracture with adjustable tension. From Samuel Cooper, First Lines of the Practice of Surgery, *vol. 2 (1830). (Courtesy of the Historical Research Center, Houston Academy of Medicine, Texas Medical Center Library, Houston, Texas.)*

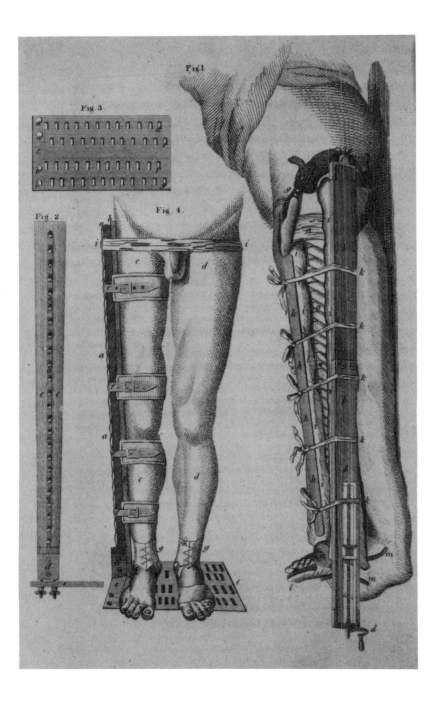

was not lost on perceptive observers. Frank Hamilton, a Buffalo, New York, physician, served as an expert witness in dozens of malpractice trials. Hamilton believed that the misunderstanding surrounding the results of fracture treatments was the principal cause of the sudden increase in malpractice suits. He lamented that "surgeons themselves have believed, and taught, and testified, that in a large majority of cases, broken limbs may be made perfect, while the fact is not so!" [34] He reasoned that lower expectations from both physicians and patients would curb the seemingly rampant litigation. Using statistical methods he had learned in France in the 1840s, he compiled data on the treatment and results of hundreds of fracture and dislocation cases. Hamilton carefully measured and recorded imperfect alignment, shortening, or other deformations and matched the results with the treatment each patient had received. [35] He discovered that despite the claims of many practitioners, perfect restorations were uncommon. For example, one study revealed that forty of fifty fractures of the lower extremities healed with either deformity or shortening. [36] Hamilton began publishing his results in pamphlets, medical journals, and books in the late 1840s and by 1860 had reached a wide audience. [37]

Medical writers exclaimed that Hamilton's study had "revolutionized the opinion of surgeons the world over" and would "influence courts and juries, and constitute an imperishable defence and refuge, making his name and his fame immortal." [38] Defense attorneys and expert witnesses relied on Hamilton's findings. In an 1857 Ohio case in which the plaintiff had broken both bones in his lower leg, Hamilton's figures demonstrated that out of seventy-two similar cases, only thirty-two yielded perfect results. [39] The jury refused to award damages to the patient. Other defendants successfully used the fracture tables. Occasionally Hamilton himself would appear at trials to present and explain his findings. [40]

Hamilton's approach implicitly suggested that the bulk of malpractice suits represented a technological problem that could be cured with a technological solution. He was partially correct. Reasonable expectations of cure might have prepared patients for imperfect results. Physicians could consult statistical studies and choose the most effective treatment for the particular class of fractures. One reviewer hoped that Hamilton's work would "erect something like a standard which

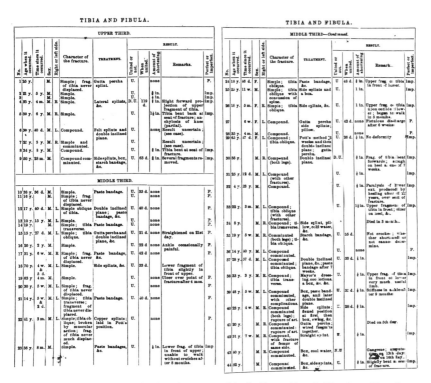

Plates from Frank Hamilton's "fracture tables." From Frank Hastings Hamilton, "Report on Deformities after Fractures," TAMA 10 (1857): 239–453. (Courtesy of the Historical Research Center, Houston Academy of Medicine, Texas Medical Center Library, Houston, Texas.)

may be generally agreed upon for the protection and satisfaction of all parties who may hereafter be involved . . . in the miseries of a prosecution for 'malpractice.' "[41]

However, Hamilton's statistics were not conclusive, and his preferred treatments were not unanimously supported. No approach regularly produced either cures or failures. Even the reviewer who anticipated that the studies would establish a medical "standard" disagreed with several of Hamilton's surgical procedures. Quantification of several hundred cases helped guide physicians, but practitioners still had to treat each fracture individually, and uncertainty remained. In addition, fracture treatment was still in flux, with physicians continually developing new approaches. Reliance solely on the procedures enum-erated in the statistical studies would have slowed medical progress and blunted beneficial innovation by encouraging doctors to use only familiar procedures.

Some physicians contended that the vast number of imperfect cures in statistical studies demonstrated the need for more effective treatments. These practitioners hoped that a technological breakthrough would limit the litigation. In 1851 a writer declared that "[t]he statistics of dislocations and fractures, display the limping gate of modern surgery, and we are solicitous to do all in our power to remedy the evil." He believed that "if surgeons used the proper means, in the reunion of fractured bones, no justifiable claim for mal-practice would live long before a jury." The physician commended the Jarvis adjuster, a mechanical device with gears that stretched, then compressed, fractured limbs, into their proper position. He claimed that "a correct understanding of its merits, and the use of its powers, would do much toward stopping those suits for malpractice."[42]

The writer's hopes were in vain. Within five years the Jarvis adjuster was generating suits instead of preventing them. The AMA condemned the mechanism, and Massachusetts General Hospital forbade its use. In 1856 a man sued a physician for breaking his wife's arm when the woman had dislocated her shoulder and the physician had used a Jarvis adjuster to relocate it. An expert medical witness claimed that the injury was caused by the machine: "The power of this adjuster is very great. We have considered it, in the Hospital [Massachusetts General], as a dangerous instrument, and it has not been used with us for four or five years."[43]

Confidence in technological solutions, such as Hamilton's tables or Jarvis' adjuster, was unfounded because technology could not stand still. Progress and advancement heightened expectations. Physicians' optimism for finding a technological cure for the profession's malpractice woes was illusory because the roots of the phenomenon were more complex than the development of fracture treatment. The new proclivity to sue physicians between 1835 and 1865 reflected, in part, the new way that Americans had come to look at their bodies.

"Song of Myself"

A committee on malpractice in 1850 argued that the principal source of malpractice suits was the popular misunderstanding of the nature of medical practice.

From this prevailing ignorance and misconception, the medical practitioner is expected to be the bold controller of nature instead of her vigilant observer, faithful follower and intelligent assistant . . . The jury is, perhaps told that the work of a mechanic is rejected, unless it comes up to a standard of perfection, so the work of the physician and surgeon must come to a like perfection; and such illustrations are received as parallel and analogical. By such reasoning, the mysteries of vitality, of that machine fearfully and wonderfully made in the image of its Maker, and living by the breath of the Deity, is reduced to a level with inanimate wood, stone, and iron, obedient to the mechanic's hand.[44]

These sentiments were the result of the mechanistic mentality that pervaded the first half of the nineteenth century. In 1800 the United States was still relatively untouched by the technological advances already transforming England. Within fifty years, however, profound changes had altered the landscape of the countryside and the contours of the American mind. From 1800 to 1830 entrepreneurs dug dozens of canals covering thousands of miles and built hundreds of roads in every part of the country. After 1840 railroad construction accelerated at a tremendous rate, fanning west from the business centers of the East Coast. A long series of inventions, including improved seed-drills, plows, reapers, and threshers, engendered unprecedented agricultural productivity. Similarly, water turbines, steam engines, mechanical drills, saws, pumps, and sewing machines sparked an accompanying boom in manufacturing.[45]

The tremendous advances in the physical sciences, industry, and transportation transformed the relation between humans and nature. As mechanization and transportation transcended the previous limits of the environment, humans felt a new power over nature and their destiny. By the 1840s many Americans felt that these material achievements made their society greater than any in the past, and they saw no reason why advancements would stop or even slow. Social commentary in every circle was filled with the enthusiastic expectation of perpetual material progress.[46] Some contemporary observers even believed that the democratic society accentuated and directed these attitudes.[47]

During the first half of the century society shifted much of its esteem from the divine wonders of nature to a fascination with the marvels of technological innovation.[48] The feeling was inspired by humans' growing ability to manipulate the natural environment in which they lived and their enhanced confidence that nature conformed to mechanistic laws. Similarly Americans gradually gained the ability to look at the human body as if it were a thing that could be manipulated and fixed, like any other machine and like other aspects of the natural world. Mechanistic mentality had its roots at least as early as the work of Issac Newton and René Descartes but began to reach its full expression in the early nineteenth century when it yielded widespread applications in a variety of fields.[49]

Some observers noticed that this newfound mechanistic mentality was accompanied by unfortunate side effects. Since "[m]en have grown mechanical in head and in heart, as well as in hand," Thomas Carlyle, the English social critic, warned "it is no longer the moral, religious, spiritual condition of the people that is our concern, but their physical, practical, [and] economic condition."[50] De Tocqueville confirmed that Americans were increasingly concerned with the material world. "Everyone," he noted, "is preoccupied caring for the slightest needs of the body and the trivial conveniences of life." He concluded that "[d]emocracy favors the taste for physical pleasures. This taste, if it becomes excessive, soon disposes men to believe that nothing but matter exists."[51] De Tocqueville speculated that "[i]n aristocratic ages the chief function of science is to give pleasure to the mind, but in democratic ages to the body."[52]

In the first half of the nineteenth century nearly every segment of Anglo-American culture expressed this unprecedented preoccupation with physical well-being. Concern with the body intensified to the point where many people were willing to believe that all health—intellectual, spiritual, and moral—began with bodily health.[53] Fitness promoters warned that Americans were suffering from widespread physical degeneracy.[54] In 1830 one observer suggested that the society was becoming a "weakened" one characterized by the "puny arm and shrinking sensibility of dyspepsy."[55] Even writers who concentrated on spiritual and intellectual matters exhibited a heightened concern over the state of the body and physical well-being. William Channing, a leading Unitarian minister in the 1830s, warned that the "puny, half-healthy, half-diseased state of body is too common among us," and he counseled that "nothing can be gained by sacrificing the body to the mind." Transcendentalists, who might have been expected to empha-size the spiritual above the material, were affected by similar senti-ments. Ralph Waldo Emerson declared that "bodily vigor becomes mental and moral vigor." Other Transcendentalists concurred that a strong, healthy body was an important prerequisite to higher con-sciousness.[56]

Popular writers agreed. In an 1858 article in the *Atlantic Monthly* titled "Saints and their Bodies," Thomas Higginson explained that "the mediæval type of sanctity was a strong soul in a weak body." Saints in previous eras had emaciated bodies. "But happily," he wrote, "times change, and saints with them." The new American image of the saint, he continued, now included a vigorous and well-developed physique. Higginson declared, "We distrust the achievements of every saint without a body."[57] Similarly, Walt Whitman filled his 1855 *Leaves of Grass* with dozens of paeans to flesh and blood. Lines such as "If life and the soul are sacred the human body is sacred," and "Who degrades or defiles the human body is cursed" expressed the poet's regard for the physical nature of humankind.[58]

While none of these writers spoke for the entire population, they represented a broad spectrum of cultural and intellectual life in ante-bellum America in which materialistic sentiments were becoming in-creasingly common. Colonial Calvinists would have considered regu-lar, organized play frivolous and unproductive. But by the 1830s and 1840s, Americans had initiated for the first time formalized physical fitness programs.[59] The antebellum physical education movement was only one expression of the new materialism and the changing view of the body.

Although de Tocqueville chronicled Americans' growing material-ism and concern with bodily worries and pleasure, he simplified, if not mistook, the basic cause of the transformation. Democracy may have encouraged materialistic attitudes, but it did not create them. Origins of a transformed vision of physical well-being can be found as early as the eighteenth century, but two interwoven developments between 1820 and 1860 heightened awareness of and concern with the body. The mechanization of the body encouraged physicians and laymen to believe that physical ills were understandable and remediable. Mechanical successes in manufacturing and transportation generated an atmosphere of optimism and a faith in material progress. Optimism was fortified by evolving religious beliefs in the 1830s and 1840s that supported the idea of a benevolent God. Many northern evangelicals began to believe in both social and individual perfectionism. Individuals felt that they had access to spiritual and bodily salvation.[60]

A variety of health reformers reflected this trend and exhorted Americans to revere and care for their bodies. They argued that good general health was within reach of all Americans. Sylvester Graham, one of the most prominent representatives of this movement, contended that the human body conformed to a set of rational yet divinely endowed rules. With proper diet, exercise, and temperance, Americans could preserve and improve their health. Bodily improvement was theoretically possible because reformers believed that the natural laws of health had been uncovered and because God wished humans to work toward both physical and spiritual perfection.[61]

It was clear that the mechanical workings of the body had not been completely explained. Many Americans, however, came to expect health and physical vitality in those areas in which science and medicine appeared to have unraveled the laws of the physical world. In preventative health, physical education, and some areas of surgery, physical problems and solutions seemed simplest and most mechanical. Grahamites explained that if individuals lived life according to human nature—practicing temperance and following a diet of whole grains, fruits, vegetables, and little meat—health would inevitably result. Fitness enthusiasts introduced a series of exercises carefully designed to benefit specific parts of the body. In medicine the process developed more slowly. Obstetric and vaccination treatments were widely, although wrongly, considered mechanical, predictable procedures by the early nineteenth century. During the next forty years fracture treatment sparked widespread optimism. In other areas of medicine, however, progress and the accompanying expectations did not come until the late nineteenth century or later.

Heightened public concern for physical well-being, combined with real progress in fracture treatments, created unrealistic expectations and demands. Suits for fracture treatments were uncommon before the late 1830s for three reasons. First, the general unacceptability of malpractice accusations discouraged many prospective plaintiffs. Second, fracture treatment was not developed enough to engender high expectations in either physicians or patients. Finally, America's preoccupation with material well-being was not sufficiently developed to provoke public comment, inspire health and fitness movements, or generate anger over minor bodily deformities. Before then, suits for treatments that resulted in only minor deformities were unsupportable.

The social and cultural factors that focused individuals' attention on their bodies did not disappear. Instead, they matured. Secularization, affluence, and the nascent consumer culture continued to evolve, and individuals became even more concerned about their health, comfort, and appearance.[62] As other medical treatments became mechanical and routinized, expectations grew, patient tolerance for imperfection decreased, and physicians were sued for a wider variety of medical treatments.

CHAPTER 5

Community, Providence, and the Social Construction of Legal Action

Malpractice litigation flourished for the first time in the Jacksonian period because the social and medical environments were conducive to the frequent prosecution of physicians. The contributing causes in the first malpractice "crisis" were intraprofessional rivalry, and the decline of the professional and social status of the physician. Additionally, dramatic technological advancements blurred previous conceptions of standards of care and created unrealistic expectations in both patients and physicians. These immediate causes increased the impact of Americans' long-term growing concern for physical well-being. But these factors alone still do not account for the sudden and unprecedented appearance of large numbers of malpractice suits.

In an 1824 malpractice trial a defense attorney castigated the plaintiff in front of the jury. The lawyer declared that "it is not a very commendable sight anymore than a very customary sight to see a patient prosecuting his physician." "[P]ublic judgment," he argued, was the "proper tribunal to regulate this species of responsibility," and it was doubtful that a lawsuit would increase the "intensity of moral obligation."[1]

The lawyer's comments illustrate that potential litigants are often constrained by more than just legal rules. Cultural and community attitudes, habits, and customs define socially acceptable ways to respond to grievances and disputes. As modern legal anthropologist Carol Greenhouse observes, "Before a person can sue, he must have not only a legally justiciable issue and a legal forum, but also a personal conceptualization of conflict that is adversarial in structure and remedial in orientation."[2] Individual action is shaped by community beliefs and informal moral codes about the type of wrongs that warrant legal action. Changing cultural beliefs can make recourse to courts either more or less acceptable.

The initial burst of suits in the late 1830s and the subsequent "crisis" of the 1840s and 1850s would not have been possible without complex psychological and cultural developments. The two essential preconditions for the rise of malpractice suits were the dissolution of community stigmatization of certain types of litigation and the decline in belief in the concept of providence that held misfortune to be an expression of divine will. Without these two underlying, long-term developments, the widespread prosecution of physicians would have been inconceivable.

The Role of the Community and the Decision to Sue

The nature of the community an individual belongs to and the notion of community he or she holds determine the amount of influence that custom will have on that individual's behavior.[3] Throughout much of America's early history, community custom relegated many types of disputes to extralegal forums, but by the mid–nineteenth century, communities' coercive power had weakened. As a result, disputants were able to bring previously unlitigated forms of conflict into court, among them an expansion of medical malpractice claims. This change in legal culture did not cause malpractice suits. Without this development, however, and its subsequent expansion, widespread prosecution of physicians could not have occurred.

Although there is no effective or accurate way to measure the existence of community, seventeenth-century New England towns provide a convenient model.[4] A *community* may be defined as a group of people living in a defined geographic area who share the same basic values and view of the world. The early settlements were Christian, closed, corporate communities.[5] The demands of economic survival and old-world farming patterns encouraged cooperation. The citizens of the town were bound tightly by economic interest and also by family ties and religious beliefs. Indeed, part of the function of the social unit was to glorify God on earth. In the quest to create a "city upon a hill," colonists created integrated, organic, social systems. Individualism was both socially and religiously condemned.

Social relations in these settlements were dominated by face-to-face, personal relationships with a limited number of neighbors. Dissension was rare because the interests of the colonists were relatively homogeneous. They did similar work and worshipped the same God in the same way. In an effort to maintain social and spiritual peace, community members discouraged conflict in general and litigation specifically.[6] Scholars have suggested that the "relational distance" between members of a community influences their willingness to rely on legal remedies: When the "distance" is great, law will be relied on more frequently; when people live in tightly knit, kinship-based, corporate communities, the social costs of disrupting the order are greater, and litigation is relied on less frequently.[7] In early colonial America individuals were tied to one another in an interlocking network of family, church congregation, and community relationships.

Colonists were remarkably successful in discouraging disruptive litigation in the first half of the seventeenth century. Disputes were settled more often through arbitration, mediation, and mutual agreements. Often the entire church congregation judged conflicting claims of disputants. The inhabitants of Dedham, Massachusetts, for example, were largely able to avoid the use of courts in disputes through the 1680s. After that point, land hunger, population increases, generational conflict, and economic diversification had begun to undermine the homogeneous nature of colonial existence. Consensus weakened, disputes multiplied, and colonists more frequently resorted to courts. Community opinion and collective self-interest were no longer strong enough to keep public quarrels out of courts completely. Internal dissension was never eliminated, but the use of alternative means of settlement—arbitration, for example—had helped resolve quarrels without litigation.[8]

Despite the incipient breakup of communal structures, many patterns remained, and colonists were able to retain a relative degree of uniformity of thought through much of the eighteenth century. Although litigation was increasingly common, many communities were able to control access to their towns through "warning out" unwanted outsiders. Religious attitudes were changing, but they still stressed selflessness and restraint, compromise instead of conflict, and encouraged conformity to prevailing social standards. This ethos was reinforced by everyday relations, which were still dominated by face-to-face communications.[9] Uniformity and consensus were undermined significantly by the religious tumult and factionalism of the Great Awakening in the early eighteenth century, increased economic growth and political activity, and ever-growing geographic mobility.[10] Even though it was not static, in many cases community life in the eighteenth century remained stable, relatively insular, and maintained many of the customary prohibitions against the use of courts.

A study of fourteen Massachusetts towns suggests that shared ethical values and a respect for consensus retarded widespread litigation into the early nineteenth century. William Nelson discovered that the people in towns still "shared assumptions about how 'good people' lived . . . These assumptions were prescribed at the level of moral ideal by church doctrine and confirmed at the level of practice by geographic, demographic, and technological realities that precluded most people from adopting styles radically different from the one they knew." In these towns, it was not until 1790–1825 that the seventeenth-century methods of accommodation and consensual dispute settlement broke down significantly and yielded increased litigation.[11]

Although the first signs of the breakup of communal consensus were visible as early as the mid–seventeenth century, the most profound shocks to old ways of thinking occurred in the late eighteenth and early nineteenth centuries. The change took place at different rates in different communities and regions, but there is a clear overall movement from the communalism of colonial America to Jacksonian individualism and pluralism.

The crucial break with colonial communal habits was especially evident after the first third of the nineteenth century. As Michael Frisch notes, in the early nineteenth century "the fading of this homogeneity in fact had not yet disturbed the dominance of older patterns of social leadership and socialization—the accepted articulation, rather than the importation, of community standards, values, and practices by the social establishment."[12] But the massive geographic dislocation from westward expansion, the growth of a national economy, and advances in transportation severely undercut the insularity of community life. In addition, the democratizing effects of the American Revolution and the impact of economic competition helped both to nurture the growth of and to transform individualism. The expansion of the village economy increased the number of contacts with the outside world and led to specialist production. People no longer did the same kind of work and were more likely to form interest groups. Increasing religious diversity and a decline in piety also undercut the consensus that had characterized early America. De Tocqueville recognized the increasing fragmentation of community life, the accompanying weakening of personal ties, and the decline in the influence of custom over the individual in the 1830s.[13]

Community was not destroyed, nor was individualism created in the first third of the century, but the nature of both changed. Recent studies have suggested that the nature of community and individualism can influence the type and rate of litigation. According to David Engel, in communities more completely dominated by face-to-face relationships and economically self-sufficient farmers and merchants, such as those of eighteenth-century America, "it was considered inappropriate for injured persons to transform their misfortune into a demand for compensation or to view it as an occasion for interpersonal conflict."[14] Contract or defamation of character cases, for example, would have been more acceptable than personal injury suits; slander suits reflected the importance of reputation in communities dominated by face-to-face relations.[15]

However, in this form of cooperative, communal, individualism, it would have been inappropriate to sue for personal injury for three reasons: such suits disturbed the peace of the community; they contradicted notions of self-sufficiency by demanding compensation; and they violated other religious-based community strictures against suing for misfortune. Prohibitions against conflicts and certain types of suits were reinforced by the influence and coercive power of living in a closely knit community. The opinion of the community could not stop litigation, but it could discourage it by viewing those persons who initiated unacceptable types of suits with suspicion.

By the Jacksonian period much of America had moved toward a different world and a different vision of individualism. On the one hand, individuals were less self-sufficient than their predecessors. Farmers and merchants were connected to larger markets, and the economy was becoming more integrated. On the other, migration and social mobility had made individuals less integrated into the traditional organic and hierarchical society and less bound by ever-weakening public mandates. In this form of society, a "rights-oriented individualism," in Engels' term, "is consistent with an aggressive demand for compensation (or other remedies) when important interests are perceived to have been violated."[16] "Rights-oriented individualism" is illustrated, for example, in Jacksonian Democratic demands for more access to the benefits of law. Self-sufficiency was slowly fading into the realities of market economy. Individuals felt freer to sue for personal misfortune because recourse to law did not contradict their feelings of self-sufficiency. Although community proscriptions against suing remained, albeit in attenuated form, the power of community opinion lost influence as towns became increasingly heterogeneous and anonymous. This gradual transformation became especially evident in the first third of the century and was a prerequisite for the growth of personal injury suits. The shift from cooperative, self-sufficient individualism to competitive, rights-oriented individualism continued and allowed a wider scope of litigation as the decades passed.

Rod in the Hand of God?

Communal discouragement of certain types of litigation was based partially on religious grounds. Personal moral codes, formed largely from fundamental religious beliefs, however, may have kept potential litigants out of courts even in the absence of those community pressures.

The relationship between religious change and increased litigation during this period was subtle, not overt. The gradual secularization of

American society, combined with a growing confidence in material progress and a glorification of individual will, led to a search for the temporal, human agents of misfortune. When God no longer ordained specific social or physical ills, it became acceptable to search for human culprits, assign responsibility, and demand reform or restitution through the courts.

In the seventeenth and eighteenth centuries doctrines of direct, divine providence were common among America Protestants. The most powerful churches and the majority of the public subscribed to the Calvinist 1647 Westminister Confession, which proclaimed that "God the great creator of all things, doth uphold, direct, and dispose, and govern all creatures, actions and things from the greatest even to the least by his most wise and holy Providence."[17]

Providence theory reflected the prevalent belief that God both created the world and sustained it from moment to moment. Nothing in heaven or earth occurred by chance.[18] Puritan objections to card games, dice, and lotteries were based on the premise that they trivially abused divine providence.[19] God might manipulate events to punish sinners and reward saints, or he might rain misfortune on the holy to test or teach them. This intervention was known as *special*, or *specific*, *providence*. God's will brought lightning, bad crops, earthquakes, epidemics, a sick horse, or the death of a child.[20] John Winthrop, who helped found and govern early seventeenth-century Massachusetts, filled his journals with examples of colonists punished or rewarded by "a special providence of God." Individuals suffered or were spared the effects of fire, drowning, smallpox, Indian attacks, birth defects, and accidental injury because of the "righteous hand of God."[21]

In this setting the proper response to God's will was submissive acceptance. Human resignation to providential misfortune was defended on the grounds that human beings could not possibly hope to understand God's plan, and faith demanded that they believe that the Lord ultimately worked toward only good ends. More importantly, suffering and misfortune on earth were often rewarded in heaven.[22]

After the American Revolution many northerners began perceptibly to shift their view of the impact of providence on human affairs and moved gradually away from their fatalistically minded predecessors. Colonial engineered lotteries in the eighteenth century were one "symptom" of the gradual waning of conventional piety. Concurrently, the growth of insurance companies which reimbursed losses for such events as fires and storms reflected the gradual move away from the notion of "acts of God." Potential victims now sought protection, as well as strength and patience, when faced with misfortune.[23] By the beginning of the nineteenth century the belief in direct providential intervention was attacked overtly by Unitarians, deists, and liberal clergymen from various Protestant denominations.[24]

Still, fatalistic sentiments and the submissive acceptance of misfortune as God's will remained common throughout the first three decades of the nineteenth century. In 1823 a writer for the orthodox Presbyterian magazine *Christian Spectator* claimed that providence "extends to all beings that have existed, or ever will exist;—to all events that have occurred or ever will occur." "The impious scoffer will tell us that all is the result of accident; and he will misname the signal interpositions of heaven by the epithets of 'good fortune' and 'good luck' but the humble Christian will discern in them all the hand of a wise and holy God."[25] Another writer in the same magazine declared that "without [God's] permission, no power can harm, no ill can befall us; and every afflicting stroke is meant for our good."[26]

A belief in providence affected potential malpractice claimants. A "humble Christian" patient who discerned the wise hand of God in his broken leg would be unlikely to sue his physician if the leg healed with a deformity; to do so would be to question God's wisdom. The doctrine of providence according to the writer in the *Christian Spectator* turned "tears into gratitude."[27] Similarly, "humble Christian" juries would not be willing to hold physicians responsible for bad results that were most likely ordained by God either as a punishment or as a test. During the first three and a half decades of the nineteenth century, when a belief in specific providence was still strong, medical journals and state supreme courts reported only a handful of malpractice cases, and writers commented on the rarity of the litigation.

The apparent contradiction between human free will and God's providential control fueled theological debates in the 1820s and 1830s. Many groups who attacked the notion of direct providence claimed that it undermined the responsibility of the individual. Other writers argued that providential ideas left the status quo untouched by encouraging the acceptance of remediable ills. During the first half of the nineteenth century those theologians who saw God's direct intervention in every event lost ground to more liberal thinkers. A growing segment of the population believed that God operated only through universal, natural laws and influenced world events on the grand, historical level.[28] Instead of causing each particular event, God created an overall scheme, the environment for the unfolding of his will. The trend away from a belief in direct or special providence varied from person to person, denomination to denomination, and region to region. But through the course of the nineteenth century, progressively fewer Americans accepted social and physical ills as purely God's will.

Malpractice and God's Will

Malpractice suits were rare in the transition period of the 1820s and 1830s, before a large proportion of the population began to hold human agents responsible for human misfortune. When patients did sue their physicians, the cases generally involved only severe injuries or death.

One of the few cases before 1835 illustrates the relationship of providential belief to medical malpractice of the period. In 1824 the city dispensary of New York hired Dr. Gerald Bancker to vaccinate for smallpox all the citizens within an assigned urban district. For a $100 fee, Bancker vaccinated 870 patients without incident. In April 1824 the physician vaccinated the four-year-old son of Michael O'Neil. Eight days after the visit, the boy became dreadfully ill. When the symptoms worsened, O'Neil called in another physician who diagnosed the case as smallpox. The child's health deteriorated. He went blind, a brown crust covered him, and he began to lose his hair and skin. The boy's lower jaw disintegrated and fell out of his mouth, and he developed an ulcerous hole through his neck and into his throat. Finally, after four months of profound suffering, the child died. O'Neil sued Dr. Bancker for malpractice and demanded $5,000 in damages.[29]

O'Neil's lawyer and several medical witnesses claimed that Bancker had infected the child with smallpox by inoculating instead of vaccinating him. In a *vaccination* a physician took material from a cowpox sore and inserted it into a patient's arm. This process effectively immunized the patient against smallpox. For an inoculation, an already obsolete practice, material was extracted from a smallpox sore and inserted into the subject's arm. Inoculation was often effective, but patients contracted a form (usually mild) of the disease from the procedure. O'Neil's lawyers argued that Bancker had carelessly and negligently drawn material from a smallpox, instead of a cowpox, sore and had infected the boy with the dread disease.[30]

The doctor's lawyers argued that the O'Neil boy's disease was nothing short of miraculous. The physician had vaccinated scores of patients, and none had contracted this seemingly virulent form of the disease. Medical witnesses for Bancker testified that while some of the symptoms resembled smallpox, they knew of no instance from experience or literature in which such ravages followed an inoculation. The disease, though occasionally fatal, did not exhibit features such as the loss of the jaw or the frightful ulcer in the patient's neck. Therefore, the defense attorney claimed, providence, not the vaccination was responsible for this tragedy. "In a word," Bancker's attorney explained, "we expect to prove the child died of smallpox, proceeding from the visitation of God, and not from any negligence or any want of skill on the part of the defendant." The jury retired after the testimony and found the physician not guilty.[31]

The defense attorney's use of a divine explanation for the disease to defend his client suggests that much of society accepted the notion of a specific or direct providence. The apparent success of the lawyer's strategy helps to confirm this view. Moreover, O'Neil likely had to overcome personal reservations concerning God's will and misfortune before he sued Bancker. Where other victims of medical accident or incompetence may have been less willing to question God's visitations and considered malpractice litigation an improper, or irreligious. remedy, perhaps the horrific nature of the affliction wiped away O'Neil's misgivings. Indeed, the majority of the scattered suits before 1835 involved severe injuries or death.

Charles Lowell, who sued his physician in 1823, having suffered a severe, permanent hip deformity after an accident, felt uncomfortable enough with blaming the physician for his injury to justify his action to his community.[32] In a pamphlet describing the trial Lowell explained that "I am aware of the necessity of kissing the rod and him who hath appointed it; and were it purely an act of God, I could submit to it without a murmur." But since he had suffered this "calamity" only through the "ignorance and unprecedented fraud of the physicians," he claimed that he could force himself to sue. Even after losing his case in civil court, Lowell comforted himself that the physicians would "be brought to a higher tribunal than that of their country" in the afterlife.[33] Lowell's comments suggest that although he had abandoned a strict definition of direct providence, he, like much of society, still felt its influence enough to defend his legal action against religious questions. Over the next two decades many more Americans were able to shake off their nagging doubts and hold other people responsible for their misfortune.

Judges rarely openly revealed their beliefs about divine providence and malpractice. However, in explaining why physicians did not implicitly guarantee the results of their work, one judge noted, "The event is in the hands of *Him* who giveth life and not within the physical control of the most skilful *[sic]* of the profession." Even these types of statements were absent from judges' decisions after the 1830s.[34]

Few contemporary observers grasped the underlying theological changes that were making the litigation acceptable. The 1850 Pennsylvania Medical Society committee on malpractice argued that while medical science had advanced rapidly in the previous fifty years, the public and physicians had to acknowledge that there was a "mysterious agency of vital laws which are hidden by providence from the scrutiny of man." God still occasionally played an active role in the affairs of humans. Despite the medical community's progress in discovering physical laws, "occasionally all the arrangements and protections of science and philosophy vanish before the Deity . . . It is an ignorance of, or want of reflection upon these principles which forms the foundation for the prevalence of quackery, and of the unjust persecutions which pursue the regular practitioner, and display themselves in groundless suits."[35] The committee's insightful comment on the impact of attitudes toward providence on malpractice rates was unique in nineteenth-century medical literature. Most writers concentrated their attention on more immediate, concrete, and presumably remediable causes, such as low status or the strife created by intraprofessional competition.

The precise moment of the decisive shift in the notion of direct providence, which opened the door to widespread prosecution of physicians, is impossible to pinpoint. Several factors suggest that a critical transformation occurred in the decade and a half between 1835 and 1850—the same period that bore America's first malpractice "crisis."

This shift resulted from a variety of changes during the Enlightenment and the scientific revolution of the eighteenth and nineteenth centuries.[36] American intellectuals and theologians, especially Unitarians, were influenced by European philosophers of the 1830s and 1840s, including John Stuart Mill and Auguste Comte. These writers' conception of God, as Charles Cashdollar notes, "forced man away from the pietistic or providential to a naturalistic view of social problems, from prayer to human action."[37] The providential view of earthly events was inherently conservative; the naturalistic view was unreservedly reformist. The new perspective made it more difficult to claim that poverty, for instance, was a punishment for a sinful life.[38] What before had been divinely ordained burdens or punishments for sin became remediable ills. A Romantic belief in perfectionism, the ability to improve the individual and society, swept much of the country.[39] During this period a vast number of broadly humanitarian movements flourished for the first time in history, movements that were eager to address human suffering with human intervention. The social improvement efforts that arose included abolition, prevention of cruelty to animals, child protection, and prison reform.[40] Beginning in the late 1830s and contemporary with the outpouring of social reform and the theological debates over the nature of providence, physicians reported a massive, unprecedented attack of malpractice prosecutions.

Scientific and naturalistic explanations of specific phenomena accelerated the decline in the perception and acceptance of different varieties of misfortune as divine will. Medical researchers in the late eighteenth and early nineteenth centuries explored the mechanical aspects of the body and explained more and more functions in biological or physiological terms.[41] In addition, statistical analyses of diseases, treatments, and cures, as well as of other areas of society, began to engender the hope of scientifically predictable medicine.[42] Perceptions of scientists and physicians diverged from the views of many theologians and the general public, but the new attitudes slowly permeated much of society.[43]

Religious Reform

In the 1830s and 1840s liberal theology, embodied in ministers such as Horace Bushnell, William Channing, and Charles Grandison Finney, began to gain the upper hand in the battle against orthodox Calvinist views of providence.[44] Finney, a minister from New York, believed that God was the creator of the world and governor of natural law but contended that the Almighty did not interfere with the day-to-day life of human beings. Finney's 1835 *Lectures on Revivals of Religion,* according to one writer, "clearly marks the end of two centuries of Calvinism and the acceptance of pietistic evangelicalism as the predominant faith of the nation."[45] Finney explicitly denounced the precepts of the Westminister Confession that supported the notion of specific providence and the Christian's humble acceptance of misfortune.

The appearance of *Lectures on Revivals* in 1835, almost the exact point at which malpractice suits suddenly increased, does not suggest a direct causal connection between the work and the frequency of lawsuits. However, the success of Finney's book and career does reflect the widespread public acceptance of the religious and social beliefs that were the necessary precondition for intensified litigation. Finney glorified the individual will and expressed an optimistic belief in human progress.[46] He preached that humans, using their own free will, could achieve sanctification on earth; they could become morally perfect. This idea nourished the belief that other aspects of life on earth could and should be made perfect and fed the evangelical and health reform movements of the period. The body and the soul could be molded into almost ideal forms.[47] Moral and physical perfectionism made it much easier and more acceptable to assign human responsibility to earthly ills. These ideas were also compatible and intertwined with the individualistic tenor of Jacksonian democracy. Finney's theology appealed to the so-called working classes, whom physicians found most likely to sue, by stressing the individual's ability to make a personal peace with God and hew out his or her own place in the world.[48] These sentiments marked a further breakup of the hierarchical and communitarian attitudes that had played a role in discouraging early lawsuits.

Finney's brand of Protestantism had swept through western New York in a series of revivals in the late 1820s and early 1830s. These revivals were so frequent and did so much damage to Calvinist tradition that the region became known as the "burned-over district."[49] After an 1831 revival in the area Finney's enthusiastic perfectionism moved west into such states as Ohio and Michigan and east into the towns of New England. Within a few years much of the North accepted the importance of human action in the improvement of physical and moral life.[50] By the early 1840s observers had begun to identify this same burned-over district of western New York as the source of the malpractice "fever" that was sweeping the Northeast.

Finney's revivalism alone did not make western New York the seedbed of medical malpractice, or carry the phenomenon to other states. The political and social elements of Jacksonian democracy were particularly strong in the area, medical sectarians were popular and prevalent, and regular physicians competed and fought continually among themselves. Yet, combined with the transformation of religious attitudes, these factors undoubtedly propelled the state to an early lead in the field of malpractice suits. The revivals, however, did promote ideas that made the litigation more acceptable. As religious attitudes evolved in other areas of the country, conditions there also became conducive to the suits.

Epidemics, Providence, and the Role of Medicine

American attitudes towards epidemics serve as an important gauge of the nature and timing of religious changes in the nineteenth century. In the 1790s Philadelphia suffered a series of devastating yellow fever epidemics.[51] During the 1793 affliction one inhabitant revealed that "[m]ost, if not all [of the population] were convinced it was a judgment sent by the immediate hand of God."[52] When, in 1822, a yellow fever epidemic hit New York, public opinion had changed significantly.[53] While most of the population of the city still viewed the epidemic as moral retribution, the scientific camp had gained many converts. The yellow fever crisis of 1822 inspired an open debate over its divine or earthly origins, a debate that represented, according to one scholar, "an intellectual cameo, the miniaturized playing out of a national drama of the mind." Orthodox ministers still preached jeremiads and called for days of fasting, but other civil leaders had already begun to demand clean streets, pure water, strict shipping regulations, and proper disposal of bodies.[54]

The reaction to the 1822 New York yellow fever epidemic represents one transition point in the evolution of public attitudes toward divine providence. The majority of Americans had not yet abandoned the notion of direct intervention, but an increasing minority was willing to entertain alternate explanations for malevolent events.

Cholera, which swept through most large cities in America between 1832 and 1834, was also, according to most ministers and lay persons, "a rod in the hand of God."[55] They called for fast days to demonstrate their contrition and belief. Despite the arguments of physicians and various liberal clergymen, who rarely explained epidemics in supernatural terms, the majority of society believed that the disease, like yellow fever, was a punishment for social or individual sins. Although materialism and Enlightenment rationalism were already eroding traditional piety in 1832, they had not seeped into the consciousness of a sufficient proportion of society to affect the predominant view of misfortune. And during the 1832 epidemics the debates among theologians over special providence were still undecided.[56]

By the time cholera struck the country again in 1849, the notion of special providence had faded considerably. Orthodox clergymen, trying to hold a conservative line, warned that Americans had "lost sight of nature's divine Author and Govenor [sic]."[57] By the 1840s a significant percentage of clergymen had abandoned the idea of direct intervention and much of America had accepted a materialistic philosophy which embraced the goals of scientific, economic, and social progress. A decade later an 1857 article in *Harper's* on the "causes and prevention of epidemics" did not mention God, providence, or religion; instead it outlined the secular, scientific debate over whether contagion or infection was the cause.[58]

By the time of new epidemics in 1866 the transformation of the public's view of cholera was apparent. During the late 1850s John

Snow had demonstrated that cholera was transmitted through contaminated water and had encouraged Americans to work to remedy the scientific and physical causes of the disease.[59] Physicians and government officials used statistical surveys to determine that clean streets, ventilated housing, and pure water were more effective health measures than prayers and fasting days.[60] Secular interpretations of specific misfortunes that originated with scientists and physicians influenced other segments of society as soon as the interaction of religious views, medical interpretations, and effective cures made other explanations untenable. This process began at least as early as the eighteenth century and affected different physical events and ailments at different rates, but the scientific and religious developments in the first half of the nineteenth century contributed to a profound shift in public attitudes on a wide variety of subjects.[61]

Pain and Providence

The timing of this transformation and its relevance to malpractice suits are also supported by the concurrent shift in public attitudes toward pain and suffering. The secularization of pain was brought about by the same combination of religious, philosophical, and biomedical factors that changed the public perception of various diseases. Through the eighteenth century pain, like other forms of physical misfortune, was accepted as divine will and as such was both explicable and bearable.[62] There are numerous biblical justifications for the notion that pain was a punishment for original or earthly sins. Paracelsus experimented with ether on animals in the early sixteenth century, but fearing clerical reaction, did not use it on humans.[63] By 1818 scientists had discussed the clinical benefits of hypnotism, nitrous oxide, and ether, and yet none of these procedures gained popular acceptance until after 1830. Ether was not "discovered" until 1846.[64] Many writers have claimed that available analgesics were not employed because most individuals accepted pain as a divinely ordained fact of life. They have argued, moreover, that between 1780 and 1845 pain sensitivity may have increased as individuals began to view the phenomenon less as a message from God and more as a physiological mechanism.[65]

According to Nathan Rice, a prominent nineteenth-century physician, "[t]he curious ground of opposition to the use of ether[,] that of religious scruples—[was] based on the argument that, as man was condemned by Providence to suffer pain, it was wrong in him to endeavor to palliate the decree." Some patients consulted clergymen before accepting analgesics. Rice offered an anecdote that underlined the transitional, interrelated nature of attitudes toward providence and pain in this period.[66] In 1850 Rice was present when a messenger called on a fellow physician and explained that a local farmer had cut an artery in his hand. The physician sent the man back to tell the farmer that a minor operation would be necessary and that he would bring some ether to ease the surgery. While waiting for the physician to arrive, the farmer and his wife knelt, prayed together, and decided not to use the ether because they both considered it wrong. The farmer declared that he "would not endeavor to escape any of that punishment which had been ordained by sin."[67]

When the physician arrived, the farmer lay down on the kitchen table and his wife left the room. As soon as the physician began the operation, however, the man cried out in pain. "Doctor do you think that it would be really wrong to take it; of course you don't. You are a good man and you wouldn't do anything wrong I know; besides if you recommend it to me, the blame ought to fall on you . . . Well wicked or not I guess I'll have the ether." The farmer's wife came into the room soon after the surgery and began to chastise her husband for his weak faith while the farmer, drunk with ether, staggered around the room and vainly tried to defend himself from the woman's verbal onslaught.[68] His stream-of-consciousness justification for using ether symbolically encapsulates the more general shift in society's attitude toward pain and providence. Although this couple ostensibly retained traditional beliefs about the role of providence later than much of the population, their experience illustrates the complex religious change in the middle decades of the century. The farmer was a devout Christian. Yet, when faced with the opportunities presented by modern science, he formulated a justification for exemption from the restrictions of his beliefs. This adaptation, however, was not simply an acknowledgment and acceptance of the existence of scientific explanations and the availability of technology over and above religion. Scientific progress and theological evolution were both responsible for the decline of the role of special providence in everyday life.[69]

As with attitudes toward disease, the changing perception of pain was a product of a popularized concept of Enlightenment rationalism and scientific optimism that permeated much of Western society in the early nineteenth century. For example, social philosophers such as Jeremy Bentham and John Stuart Mill, in contrast to previous thinkers, portrayed pain as an "inherent evil." Pain was neither punishment, nor redemption.[70] In addition, significant advances in anatomy and physiology between 1800 and 1850 illuminated the physical mechanisms of pain to such a degree that physicians and lay persons began to view it as an essentially biological function that could and should be controlled by any available scientific means.[71]

Society's new sensibility regarding pain was reflected in many of the movements that had themselves been inspired by the possibility and advisability of reform. A variety of groups campaigned against cruelty to animals, flogging, capital punishment, vivisection, and blood sports such as bull-baiting, and cock- and dog-fighting.[72] When William Morton effectively publicized the clinical use of ether in 1846, the public and the medical profession were for the most part ready to accept the innovation. Still, many physicians and ministers condemned the use of ether during childbirth on the grounds that labor pains were a divinely ordained punishment for the sins of Eve.[73]

The Case of the South

The importance of the secularization of public attitudes toward misfortune as an essential precondition for the rise of the malpractice suit in the Jacksonian era is confirmed by the relationship between the two phenomena in different areas of the country. The change in the popular view of providence, pain, natural disaster, disease, and social reform did not occur throughout the entire country at the same rate; neither did malpractice litigation.

New England and western physicians, assailed by an increasing number of malpractice suits in the 1840s and 1850s, marveled at the apparent rarity of such litigation in the South. Of the 216 state supreme court malpractice decisions reported between 1790 and 1900, only eight originated from the eleven states of the Confederacy.[74] Even considering the relative populations of the North and South, there is a significant difference in the frequency of litigation. The *Boston Medical and Surgical Journal* reported that the first malpractice case in Tennessee did not occur until 1855.[75] By that time suits were a common occurrence in states such as New York, Pennsylvania, Massachusetts, and Ohio where hundreds of cases had been reported. Frank Hamilton, speaking to the Medico-Legal Society in the 1870s, observed that while "suits for malpractice were so very frequent in the Northern States—they were always less frequent in the Southern States."[76]

At an American Medical Association conference in 1873 a Pennsylvania physician noted this disparity and asked a Mississippi colleague to explain the phenomenon. The southern physician acknowledged that malpractice suits were not a problem in the South and that he had never heard of a case in his state. He suggested that strong medical societies had discouraged intraprofessional rivalry and prevented suits.[77] While his interpretation was plausible, it is not clear that southern medical societies were better organized or less contentious than their northern counterparts. Even if the explanation were valid, it alone could not account for the vast disparity in suits.

Most of the immediate factors that incited suits in the North also existed in the South. Homeopaths and especially Thomsonians enjoyed a booming business. In 1835 a Mississippi governor estimated that half the citizens of his state relied on Thomsonian therapy. Antebellum medical sectarians wooed patients away from regular practitioners in states as diverse as Virginia, South Carolina, Louisiana, and Texas.[78] Just as in the North, the practice of southern sectarians thrived as the reputation of orthodox practitioners declined. Public scorn and distrust emanated from the same sources as in the North. Although deceased slaves provided a somewhat more accessible pool of dissection subjects, southern physicians and medical students were often forced to rely on grave-robbers to acquire research and teaching cadavers.[79] The medical community's standing was undermined by highly visible incidents such as one in 1838 in which a prominent New Orleans physician was accused of using bodies of patients who had died at the charity hospital for dueling practice.[80]

Southern physicians employed different and less severe remedies than other doctors, but many people continued to associate regular practitioners with the horrors of heroic practice. J. Marion Sims, a southern physician, reported that some "[p]atients were bled, purged, administered tartar emetic, and given fever mixtures every two hours during the twenty-four . . . Those who were bled and purged the strongest died the quickest."[81] Jacksonian antiprofessional sentiment was equally strong in the South and added impetus to the delicensure movement that occurred the same time as in the North. The evils of inadequate education, defective therapies, and soaring public disdain helped inspire the many malpractice suits in the North. The existence of these factors alone, however, was not enough to produce widespread litigation in the South because the region had not undergone the cultural transformations that were the preconditions for large numbers of malpractice suits.

Southern culture grew out of and maintained the hierarchical rural communities that resembled and reinforced the old world and colonial order. Face-to-face, kinship, and community-based relationships continued to dominate social life in the South. Community opinion was much more important than legal action in settling quarrels.[82] The existence of such hierarchical, communal settlements in colonial late–eighteenth-century New England had to a certain degree discouraged extensive litigation. While the social, economic, and political turmoil of the first three decades of the nineteenth century destroyed this communal base in much of the country, southern culture retained many of its features and continued to distrust legal redress as the most appropriate solution to conflict.[83]

The relative infrequency of malpractice litigation in the South may also be explained by the absence there of the religious and cultural changes that were preconditions for the malpractice phenomenon in other parts of the country. Southerners retained traditional, eighteenth-century views of divine providence much longer than northerners, and these beliefs shaped southerners' attitudes toward misfortune, disease, pain, and reform.

The antebellum years were probably the most religious period in the history of the South. During the era of the American Revolution the intellectual leaders of the South shared Enlightenment ideas about humanity and society, but these ideas never penetrated much below the upper class. The popular evangelical churches had slowly begun to take root in the decades before the revolution, and after the Great Revival of 1800 they came to dominate the popular mind of the South. By the third decade of the nineteenth century, for example, even the aristocrats of Virginia had essentially accepted the evangelical ethos with its emphasis on human depravity and belief in the concept of direct providence.[84]

Conservative religious views that stressed providence were useful in the defense of slavery and encouraged southerners to retain traditional interpretations of providence.[85] Unitarians, Transcendentalists, and other liberal sects that assailed the notion of direct providence in the North were virtually nonexistent in the South. Southerners believed that their God supervised day-to-day life on earth to such a degree that He willed each sparrow's fall. They were resigned to the fact that a certain part of life and nature would always remain inscrutable and must be accepted as God's will.[86] In an ultimate sense God's will, not human action, determined the timing of one's fate, and neither the patient nor the doctor was finally responsible for healing or death.

The transformation of the concept of providence from a specific to general one, which encouraged society to prevent and remedy earthly ills in the North, had virtually no impact in the South. Southern evangelical fervor had a different face. While the rest of nineteenth-century America grew increasingly optimistic and confident of the prospects of human and social perfectibility, the South remained pessimistic and stoical. It did not search for cures for every evil because it did not believe they existed.[87] The region was relatively untouched by almost every reform movement of the early nineteenth century: abolitionism, feminism, humanitarianism, prevention of cruelty to animals, and prison reform.[88]

The history of the discovery of ether suggests that people living in the South may have held a considerably different view of pain and misfortune than most of their northern counterparts. In the early 1840s, before Morton's famous demonstration in 1846, Crawford Long, a Georgian physician, experimented extensively with ether. Despite his moderate successes, he failed to convince patients or other physicians of the value or propriety of his work. Long even noted that his colleagues advised him to abandon his experiments. When Morton demonstrated ether to a group of physicians in Boston just two years later, the northern medical world hailed him as a hero. Long lived and worked in a stronghold of orthodox Protestantism where an eighteenth-century view of pain was still prevalent. Morton, on the other hand, presented ether to a liberal, progressive society that believed pain was a biological function that should be remedied. While other conditions contributed to Long's failure and Morton's success, the divergent views of pain in their respective communities may have been a factor in the reactions of their colleagues.[89] A final barometer of southerners' perception of pain was their continued enjoyment of so-called blood sports such as cock- and dog-fighting, ring tournaments, and vicious man-to-man battles.[90] It may also have been expressed in their willingness to discipline their slaves physically.

The views of two physicians, one northern, one southern, reflected the sectional disparity in attitudes towards God's role in the world. Samuel Gross, one of the most revered surgeons in nineteenth-century America, lived and practiced medicine in Philadelphia. In his 1887 autobiography Gross declared that "God cannot be said ever to have killed or willfully afflicted any human being." On the contrary, Gross argued that people suffer and

die by and through natural laws, none by and through God's interposition or direct agency; and the same is true whether life is destroyed by disease or by accident, by the upsetting of a carriage, by the pistol's bullet, by a railway collision, by a boiler explosion, by a tidal wave, by a cyclone, or by an earthquake.[91]

Gross's position typified the worldview that accepted and stressed scientific rationality and perfectibility.

In contrast, Edward Warren, a physician who had been born and raised on an antebellum North Carolina plantation, held a different view of divine intervention. Warren explained in his 1885 memoirs that medicine had brought him into "daily contact with the misfortunes of humanity," and had left him with an "exalted faith." He was "compelled to attribute the harrowing scenes . . . [to] the attributes of a God having as a purpose the ultimate rectification of a work which he is compelled to do in the vindication of his governmental policy."[92] Warren, like many of his fellow southerners, believed late into the century that providential interposition sometimes guided, taught, and tested humankind.

Southern attitudes toward direct providence, natural disaster, reform, and pain suggest that they had a fundamentally different response to natural and physical misfortune than most northerners of the same period. Historians have consistently agreed that the culture of the American South "grew out of a fatalistic world view which assumed that pain and suffering were man's fate."[93] Fatalism formed an integral part of the southern worldview and encouraged individuals to accept society and their lives as they were. This resignation, born of religious conviction, may have played an important role in discouraging malpractice suits in the nineteenth-century South.

The history of a small, predominantly Baptist community in Georgia reveals that both communal and religious sanctions against legal conflict discouraged litigation into the 1970s.[94] Residents of the town maintained what they believed was a "community of Christ." Local Baptists' aversion to the adjudication of adversarial conflict in civil courts, outside the local church community, reached back into the first half of the nineteenth century and persisted through the twentieth. Their substantial rejection of the use of civil courts was based on the notion that God is the judge of humanity and that resorting to an earthly power questioned divine wisdom.[95] Consequently, as late as the mid-1970s, residents of the town considered personal injuries, accidents, automobile wrecks, and even personal violence as examples of God's will, and community members generally refused to seek legal redress. To do so would have violated both God's will and community customs that emphasized Christian and social harmony.[96] While this consensus is probably possible only in small socially and religiously homogeneous societies, it suggests a reason why malpractice suits in the American South remained relatively rare through the nineteenth century.

Jacksonian society's secularized, scientific view of general misfortune, disease, and pain was the psychological backdrop for the dramatic increase in malpractice suits in the late 1830s and early 1840s. Moreover, it was the foundation for the continued rise in suits through the twentieth century. Since the 1830s social and physical misfortune has been perceived more and more as preventable or at least remediable. While there was an array of complex causes for the initial increase in lawsuits, Americans' faith in the benefits of science and their new-found certainty that God did not intend man to suffer on earth freed them to blame physicians for incomplete cures. Widespread lawsuits would not have been possible without a fundamental shift in public attitudes about divine providence in everyday life. Although the transformation of public belief was gradual, and not complete by 1865, the threshold point had been reached as early as the 1840s.

Religious attitudes continued to evolve through the nineteenth century as the notion of providence lost its grip on the American mind. Providence was replaced by a secularized, optimistic view of the merits and promise of material and social progress.[97] Broad public confidence, however, was accompanied by higher expectations and increased demands. When these demands were not met, individuals increasingly blamed people and institutions for their personal misfortune. Although the decline in the importance of providence in the public mind paved the way for beneficial and humane reform, it also encouraged the proliferation of lawsuits by removing the possibility of divine intent and highlighting human culpability. This process, beginning in the late eighteenth century and continuing through today, helps explain the perpetual increase of malpractice suits in the face of profound and unceasing medical progress.

CHAPTER 6

"Dangerous Ground for a Surgeon"

"Western New York is becoming dangerous ground for a surgeon" a writer complained in 1844. According to the observer, qualified physicians were "constantly liable to vexatious suits, instituted by ignorant, unprincipled persons, sometimes urged on, it is presumed, by those who have a private grudge." This editorialist warned "that unless a better state of things could be brought about, the medical practitioners in that part of the country would unitedly refuse to render any assistance in cases of fractures and dislocations."[1] One physician claimed that between 1833 and 1856, "[t]here was scarcely a surgeon in the State of New York, of any respectability, who had not been prosecuted one or more times; and probably not one who had not been often threatened."[2] In 1853 Frank Hamilton estimated that nine out of every ten physicians in Western New York had been forced to defend themselves against malpractice charges.[3]

This apparent malpractice epidemic reflected the confused professional and political position of embattled doctors in Jacksonian America, especially in New York. Irregular practitioners were numerous and popular in the state, and they eroded the status and political power of regular physicians. Western New York was a stronghold of Jacksonian sentiment, which was incompatible with the type of monopoly privilege represented by medical societies and licensure laws. Competition among regular practitioners and disputes over therapeutic procedures weakened professional solidarity and sabotaged public confidence. Physicians' social status and lack of professional cohesion encouraged disgruntled patients to sue their doctors. Western New York, in the wake of Charles Finney's revivalism, was also one of the first areas of the country to feel the impact of the notion of perfectionism and the accompanying decline in the belief in special providence. Perfectionist sentiments helped create the optimism and expectations that underlay the new demands for physical well-being and were an essential precondition for widespread personal injury suits.

Once instituted, malpractice litigation exposed and exacerbated the fundamental weaknesses of contemporary medical professionalism in the Jacksonian era. Individual physicians, professional journals, and local medical societies were faced with dilemmas they could not solve. No matter how they reacted to the crisis, they contributed to either public distrust, professional competition, or physicians' incompetence. In turn, this suspicion, divisiveness, and medical ineptitude aggravated what seemed to be an ever-increasing wave of malpractice prosecutions. One New York malpractice case in the early 1840s demonstrates how destructive litigation could be and how the crisis confused professionals.

Doctors and Politics

New York physicians in the early 1840s suffered under even greater debilities than their colleagues in other states. In 1836 the *Boston Medical and Surgical Journal* reported that New York was filled with "troops of quacks [and] foreign pretenders of all grades, from pill makers to magicians."[4] John Thomson, the son of the founder of the Thomsonian sect, organized the New York opposition to the licensure laws in the state. He forged a temporary alliance between the Thomsonians, Homeopaths, and other irregular practitioners against the regular physicians and helped make the licensure struggle more intense than in any other state. Job Haskell served as the medical sects' spokesman in the New York state assembly. In 1834 he presented the legislature with a petition with forty thousand signatures that called for an end to restrictive medical legislation. Haskell claimed that licensure laws encouraged "privileged physicians" to "depend on their diplomas and legislative enactments to advance them instead of worth and merit."[5] The obvious popularity of irregular practitioners in New York indicated the public distrust of the regular practitioners.

The political atmosphere in New York also worked against the regular physicians. Thomsonians were natural allies with the Jacksonian Democratic party and its Loco Foco spin-offs. New York was a Democratic state and "served as an acknowledged Democratic tutor for the newer western states."[6] The party's anti–National Bank, antimonopoly philosophy fit well with Thomsonian goals. The Loco Focos, a radical strain of Jacksonian Democrats, were especially strong in New York. They opposed all privileged or aristocratic pretension and declared that "every profession, business, or trade not hurtful to the community, shall be equally open to the community."[7] It was not surprising that Haskell, the Thomsonians' advocate in the legislature, became a Loco Foco supporter. These forces were successful, and the New York legislature repealed the licensure statute in 1844.

Even in the face of these outside threats to the medical profession, the state's physicians failed to put aside their intraprofessional battles. In the *New York Journal of Medicine* F. Campbell Stewart wrote in 1846 that the New York medical profession was marked by "a degree of jealousy and unkind feeling which ought nowhere to exist."[8] Doctors fought each other over therapeutic doctrine, fee schedules, and the profits and prestige of controlling medical education in the state. To reduce conflict, competition, and jealousy among themselves, some New York physicians tried to strengthen the influence of medical societies and associations. For example, the state medical society adopted a code of ethics that stressed the need to avoid disputes within the profession. These active professional organizations sometimes provided an enlarged and more public forum for dispute. Historian Daniel Calhoun has characterized the unsuccessful efforts to create a united front of physicians in Jacksonian New York as "the clash between community consciousness and individual ambition." Local and state medical societies served as new bases of professional discord and were often used as weapons in the battle of physician against physician.[9]

New York physicians' tendency toward professional "suicide" as well as their declining social status and weakened political position encouraged dissatisfied patients to seek relief or revenge in court. Many observers believed that New York was the source of the malpractice "fever" in the 1840s that later spread into New Hampshire, Vermont, Pennsylvania, and Massachusetts.[10] The *Boston Medical and Surgical Journal* reported in 1847 that public sentiment in Western New York was so much in favor of "breaking down surgeons" that the most distinguished physicians "were hardly willing to give advice in surgical practice." New York physicians regularly ran the risk of "being prosecuted by some unprincipled fellow, who either expected to gain more money by it than he could get by honest industry" or sought revenge "for some supposed injury, by ruining the surgeon in purse and reputation."[11] Relatively unsensational malpractice cases of little legal doctrinal importance often disrupted professional relations, distorted standards of care, and further damaged physicians' status in society.

Smith v. Goodyear and Hyde

William Smith was fifty years old, had a "strong and robust constitution," but, by all accounts, was "addicted to intemperance." On 4 July 1839, while working on a house in Cortland, New York, Smith fell from a scaffold and injured his leg. Witnesses sent for Dr. Azariah Booth Shipman, who lived several miles away.[12] Shipman, who was thirty-six had, since his late teens "determinately g[iven] his odd leisure to studying medicine." He later spent two years working under his brother, who was a physician. Though he never studied at a medical school, the county medical society granted Shipman a license in 1826. He earned a good reputation for surgery and was called for nearly all the important operations for miles around, including such difficult procedures as the removal of tumors, tracheotomies, and lithotomies. At the time of Smith's accident, Shipman was president of the Cortland County Medical Society.[13]

Shipman examined Smith two hours after the accident and discovered that Smith had broken both bones in his lower leg about two inches above his ankle. The jagged edge of the fibula had penetrated the skin, puncturing Smith's boot and pants' leg. Despite the severity of the compound fracture, there was little damage to the nerves, blood vessels, or leg muscles. Shipman cleaned the wound, removed a small piece of bone, and was able to place the bones in their proper positions, by "extension and counter-extension," the procedures by which physicians stretched a broken limb, either manually or mechanically, to make the adjustment of broken bones easier. Smith also prescribed an anodyne of sulfate and morphine for pain. Shipman closed the gash with adhesive plaster, and put three padded splints on Smith's leg.[14] The next day, 5 July, Smith was sent to the county almshouse and put under the care of doctors Goodyear and Hyde.

Miles Goodyear had graduated with the first medical class at Yale in 1816. He moved to Cortlandville and became "a man of large influence in the city." Fredrick Hyde "read medicine" under several private physicians, attended three medical lecture courses in the early 1830s, and was granted a county license in 1833. In 1836 he received a diploma from Fairfield Medical College in New York. Two years later he married Miles Goodyear's daughter and joined the older man's established practice. In addition to their private patients, Goodyear and Hyde were responsible for the sick and injured clients of the county poorhouse.[15]

Goodyear and Hyde competed with Shipman for patients and prestige in Cortlandville. Though Goodyear and his partner advertised in the *Cortland Republican & Eagle*, they were careful not to impugn the ability of other local physicians. The partners claimed to specialize in "practical and operative surgery," but they cautiously noted that their "treatment of all surgical cases shall not be inferior to the ordinary practice of this country."[16]

By modestly professing to provide only "ordinary" care instead of claiming superior ability, Goodyear and Hyde were attempting to avoid public quarrels with other practitioners. Though competition among regular physicians was a fact of life in the 1830s and 1840s, the profession collectively faced the greater threat of a hostile public, sectarian rivals, and decreasing legal legitimation. Therefore, many physicians strove to portray a united front to the public and downplay professional dissension. Inevitably, individual doctors broke ranks and destroyed this artificial professional solidarity. Shipman was one of these physicians. Through most of the 1830s his advertisement appeared immediately adjacent to the modest claims of Goodyear and Hyde. In it Shipman confidently promised that he could provide "the best treatment which the art can afford." His willingness to proclaim his technical superiority and to compete openly for patients antagonized other physicians and set the stage for more bitter disputes.[17]

On 13 July, nine days after the accident, the superintendent of the almshouse visited Shipman at his office and asked him to help Goodyear and Hyde amputate Smith's leg. When Shipman arrived, he discovered that the splints and dressings had been removed from the limb. Smith's foot was swollen and twisted to one side and his leg was in a double-inclined plane, a device with a joint in the middle that supported the leg in a 45-degree, bent-at-the-knee position. Worst of all, the broken end of Smith's fibula was again protruding nearly two inches out of the original wound. He was in considerable pain and part of the bone had begun to decay. Smith's general health, however, was fairly good. Part of the wound had healed, there was little pus, his pulse and appetite were normal, and he was free from fever.

Goodyear and Hyde argued that Smith's age and alcoholic habits convinced them that immediate amputation was necessary. In addition, they held that the hot weather might induce a dangerous fever. Shipman disagreed. He contended that the physicians should remove the dead portion of the bone, close the wound, and replace the splints. Goodyear, who had apparently helped Shipman in his early practice, cursed the physician and warned, "[D]on't mention the villain's [Shipman's] name, I have been a father to him." Nevertheless, Shipman held to his contention that Smith's leg should be saved and declared that "a man would be a ——— fool to propose amputation in this case." Shipman explained later that the abusive language from Goodyear had prompted his strong response.[18] Three other local physicians joined the debate. Three of the six physicians opposed the amputation, one doctor believed that amputation might be "talked of," and Goodyear and Hyde supported the operation. Shipman refused to assist in the amputation and left the almshouse.[19]

The leg remained untreated for ten days until on 23 July the superintendent of the almshouse allowed Smith to choose his own doctor. Smith dismissed Goodyear and Hyde and sent for Shipman. When Shipman arrived, he found that Smith's condition had deteriorated. Following the course of treatment he had recommended ten days before, Shipman removed about an inch of the decaying end of the

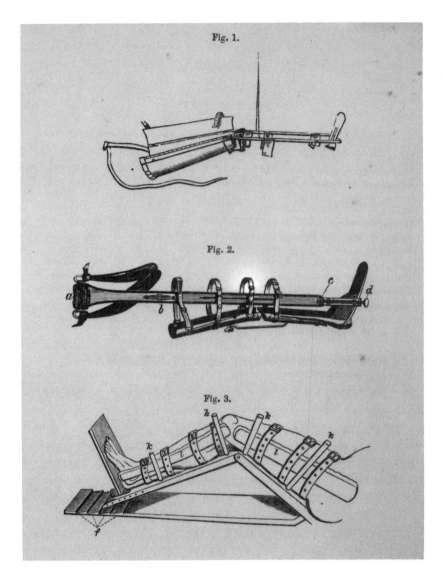

Various double-inclined planes for fractures. From Frank Hastings Hamilton, "Report on Deformities after Fractures," TAMA 10 (1857): 239–453. (Courtesy of the Historical Research Center, Houston Academy of Medicine, Texas Medical Center Library, Houston, Texas.)

protruding bone with an amputating saw and set the leg in splints. He also cleaned the wound of pus and maggots and closed it with adhesive plasters. Throughout Smith's recovery Shipman or one of his colleagues visited the almshouse daily to clean and dress the wound and keep the bone in place. Smith's leg healed slowly but steadily, and he was able to leave the poorhouse in the spring of 1840. His leg was an inch and a quarter shorter, but it was strong and "he walk[ed] without difficulty and without much lameness."[20]

During the summer of 1840 local residents collected money to help Smith hire an attorney.[21] In February 1841 Smith sued Goodyear and Hyde for malpractice. Smith asserted that they had been negligent in allowing the bone to become displaced and in failing to keep the wound clean and dressed. They were also negligent, Smith claimed, for refusing to perform the resection of the decayed bone ultimately carried out by Shipman. Shipman was Smith's strongest witness. He and three other physicians testified that Goodyear and Hyde did not regularly attend Smith and that the broken end of the bone was left untreated until Shipman reset it nearly three weeks after the accident. They also claimed that amputation would not have been the proper treatment.[22] Dr. Lewis Riggs, a member of the U.S. House of Representatives, had examined Smith in the almshouse. Imputing sinister motives to Goodyear and Hyde, Riggs declared that a physician should never "deprive a poor patient of a leg or an arm, or subject him to any other severe and cruel operation, to gain a reputation as an operative surgeon, or to rid [him]self of the trouble, care or expense of a protracted cure."[23]

Goodyear and Hyde presented a strong defense. Six local physicians, plus James Webster and Frank Hamilton, professors at the Geneva Medical College, testified on their behalf. Webster and Hamilton had long and respected careers. Hamilton was an authority on fractures whose later tabulations on the results of fractures led doctors to lower their expectations of complete cures.[24] In the Smith case, Hamilton and Webster testified that Shipman's resection of the end of the bone was improper and that an amputation would have been the correct treatment. After the witnesses for both sides testified, Smith's lawyer withdrew the complaint and agreed to drop the suit.[25]

Professional Reaction. This aborted suit from a small town eventually gained national attention. Ironically, Shipman, the star witness for the prosecution, and not the defendants, Goodyear and Hyde, suffered most from negative publicity. Local physicians, who were already antagonized by Shipman's aggressive advertising campaign, attacked him in the county newspaper both for his medical treatment and for his role in the trial. Anonymous letters published in the *Cortland County Whig* praised the character of Goodyear and Hyde, questioned Shipman's medical ability, and insinuated that he had encouraged the lawsuit. During the trial, under cross examination, Shipman had admitted that he had remarked to some of the town's residents that Goodyear and Hyde's treatment constituted malpractice.[26]

On April 20 1841, about two months after the trial, the *Whig* published a letter signed by "Justice." The writer explained that Goodyear, a twenty-year resident, had raised his family in Cortland and had distinguished his professional life by "faithful, disinterested and laborious service." These attributes gave "him a hold on the affections of the people," which grew stronger with the "lapse of time." The letter characterized Hyde as a young but thoroughly educated and talented physician with a bright future. The author recounted the events leading to the litigation and reported that the trial was a "triumphant vindication of the professional merit and private worth" of Goodyear and Hyde. The pseudonymous observer "Justice" was, however, "indignant at the foul spirit, that instigated the groundless prosecution" and warned that the "vain," "secret machinations" against the defendants would, "return 'to plague the inventor.' "[27]

One week later, a response, signed by "Truth," defended Shipman in the pages of a rival paper, the *Cortland County Democrat*. "Truth" contended that he did not have "any feelings of prejudice against either of the parties," but that the articles in the *Whig* had been "calculated to lead the public mind to erroneous conclusions, and to reflect dishonor upon the professional judgement and practice of the leading surgeons of our country." The letter-writer argued that common sense and "successful precedent" supported Shipman's treatment. If Shipman had not removed the diseased part of the bone, then the patient would have been "lying around for months with the bone projecting through the wound waiting for it to rot off before the limb could be straightened and properly adjusted." "Truth" questioned the value of the testimony of the famous medical professors Webster and Hamilton, who had spoken in defense of Goodyear and Hyde. The writer for the *Democrat* argued that the newspaper attacks on Shipman had relied on the testimony of the "learned professors" "who were summoned from a distance" and ignored the evidence presented by the intelligent, local physicians who were acquainted with the case and "therefore the most competent to decide." In sparkling Jacksonian rhetoric, "Truth" exclaimed that he was confident that

our community profess[es] too much intelligence to be awed by titles and induced to hold the mere opinions of such men ["learned professors"] paramount to the actual knowledge of men of equal talents who have lived among and in the community and proved their judgement and skill by their practice.[28]

The *Whig* and the *Democrat* continued the debate through the following year, the *Democrat* consistently supporting Shipman, the *Whig* reviling him. Shipman may have represented to the editors of the *Democrat* the prototypical democratic physician. He excelled by his superior abilities, did not rely on conspiratorial professionalism, refused to protect incompetent practitioners, and was willing to engage in "free trade in doctoring." When in April 1842 the editors of the *Whig* and the *Democrat* both received an anonymous article entitled "Medical Ethics," the editor of the *Democrat* refused to print the piece because it "was a wanton and malicious attempt to injure Dr. Shipman" written by a "vile" and "low blackguard." The *Whig*, however, printed the article even though the editor later admitted that it had been "written with an express design to cast ridicule and reproach upon him [Shipman]—to injure his reputation as a citizen, and to impair and ruin his business as a practitioner."[29] According to one medical journal, the case had "been extensively misrepresented in the neighborhood, and rumors circulated in every direction touching the professional character of [Shipman], and the gentlemen associated with him in the treatment."[30]

Shipman complained that "[t]he 'miasma' of falsehood ha[s] been permitted to go out in every direction, and as yet no antidote ha[s] been offered." He charged that the accounts of the trial and treatment in local newspapers "abound in grandiloquent and bombastic bursts of rhapsody, evidently proceeding from the brain of some conceited attorney."[31] To vindicate himself, Shipman had the *Cortland Democrat* publish a thirty-five-page pamphlet chronicling the case and his medical treatment and sent copies to major medical journals around the country.[32] In his attempt to win a local battle against rival physicians, Shipman escalated the debate to a national level and risked undermining public confidence in the profession as a whole. But Shipman's action was consistent with his willingness to engage in open competition with his local rivals.

An editorialist for the *Boston Medical and Surgical Journal* was the first to respond to Shipman's pamphlet, in November 1841. The writer attempted to maintain professional solidarity at all costs and took the opportunity to rail against litigious patients. He noted judiciously that all the witnesses were "[s]urgeons of respectability and skill" and that they had testified ably to the expediency of both modes of treatment. Shipman's pamphlet, the writer believed, presented "sufficient authority . . . for his choice of treatment to prevent any stigma attaching to his reputation as a surgeon." The editorialist was careful to add that his comments were not intended to reflect on the ability or performance of Goodyear and Hyde. He noted candidly that "[i]n all trials for mal-practice . . . our sympathies are in the first place enlisted on the side of the defendant." Continuing, he asserted:

Prosecutions for malpractice are pretty much of a piece with those for a breach of promise of marriage, and are looked upon by the discriminating public in a similar light. They are in general a pretext, and that is all, for sponging, a little money out of someone who has got more than the plaintiff . . . the public good, humanity, benevolence, philanthropy or any other praiseworthy object, is in most cases entirely out of the question.

The writer hoped that Shipman's pamphlet would "have the effect of putting surgeons on their guard against unprincipled patients and their special friends."[33] It was not clear whether "special friends" referred to lawyers, or if the term masked criticism of Shipman and the other physicians who testified against Goodyear and Hyde.

This writer's comments demonstrated the lengths to which some physicians would go to avoid criticizing other practitioners. He did not question Goodyear's and Hyde's methods, though they left Smith's wound open, pus-filled, and maggot-infested with a protruding bone for nearly three weeks. Rather, he implied that both modes of treatment were acceptable even though the respective results would have been radically different. Moreover, he ignored the growing body of medical opinion that increasingly questioned the wisdom of amputations.[34]

But while the writer endeavored to preserve the dignity and legitimacy of the profession by refusing to disparage other physicians, he was also damaging the profession's image by confirming the prevalent belief that physicians closed ranks to protect their own monopolistic interests. The writer's refusal to support one treatment over another was more suspicious in light of an article published in the same journal two months before about a man who had suffered an injury identical to Smith's. The two bones in his lower leg were broken about two inches above the ankle and the fibula protruded from a wound in the leg. The physician sawed off about an inch of the bone and set the leg. The patient recovered, as had Smith, with some minor shortening of his leg.[35]

Other observers were less blindly loyal to the profession. One, identified only as "R. C.," criticized Goodyear and Hyde in an 1841 issue of the *Medical Examiner*. He commented that, though it was proper that amputation was considered, he was "acquainted with no experienced surgeon in this section of the country who would have ventured to perform it in the then existing state of the constitution." He believed that Shipman's treatment was correct and would have "expected with some confidence to see the necessity of wearing a high-heeled shoe, the worst ultimate consequence of the avoidance of amputation" in this type of case. Though the writer held that "a difference of opinion on this subject would not be just ground for a charge of ignorance or even censure," he believed that there were "more formidable questions" about the case. He wondered why the bone was allowed to become displaced after it had been adjusted following the accident and why the wound was not dressed and cleaned. He did not condemn Goodyear and Hyde; instead, he asked probing questions and made it clear that he opposed amputation.[36]

After reading the whitewashed account of the case that had appeared in the *Boston Medical and Surgical Journal*, "R. C." of the *Medical Examiner*, composed a follow-up to his original commentary. He believed that his first report a week earlier had been written "in a spirit, perhaps, of too great mildness." While he could "sympathise" with the *Boston Medical and Surgical Journal* author's "leaning toward the profession," he could not "forget that the first professional duty is toward the patient." He said that though "malignity and sordid calculation are no infrequent instigators of prosecutions for mal-practice, it is quite possible for medical men, in these days of easy graduation and multiplied professorships, to be guilty of culpable neglect or—in the existing condition of many medical schools—scarcely blamable ignorance." On reviewing the evidence, the author concluded that "had we been the prosecuting party,—not only should we have avoided requesting the withdrawal of the case, but we would have not permitted it." Shipman's pamphlet, the writer concluded, "as painful as it must be to lovers of professional concord . . . will have the effect of 'placing surgeons on their guard', as to the necessity of keeping pace with the advance of science." [37]

This writer's response underlined physicians' and medical societies' dilemma in dealing with local quarrels and public malpractice controversies. By courageously supporting the best medical practices and condemning incompetent physicians, the author helped to publicize what constituted good practice, but he damaged professional solidarity and the profession's public image. Individual physicians, such as Shipman, retained their reputations, but the profession was exposed as a factious, sometimes dishonest, group of practitioners possessing an uneven amount of skill and knowledge.

Early in 1842 George W. Norris lamented in the *American Journal of Medical Science* that commenting

upon the doctrines and practice of members of our profession where malpractice has occurred, is one of the most unpleasant duties of the medical journalist, and would in the present instance be avoided, did we not hold it to be a duty both to our readers and the cause of truth, to raise our voice in support of sound surgical principles.

Norris stated frankly that Goodyear and Hyde's treatment had been poor. Moreover, he defended Shipman's refusal to accede to an amputation. "Is it the custom of the gentlemen, who recommended and approved such a course [amputation], to doom to amputation every limb affected with fracture and issue of the bone, which is found to be irreducible, without first resorting to other means of relief?" Norris asked. He reminded his readers that amputation was a dangerous operation and that "sound surgical principles, humanity and daily experience teach" that it should never be resorted to until other means had failed. Norris included accounts of several cases similar to Smith's dating as early as 1815 in which amputation was avoided and the patient survived with only a shortening of the leg.[38]

Despite these articles defending proper treatment in the face of blind professional loyalty, physicians in Cortland, New York, still supported Goodyear and Hyde. At their January 1842 meeting the Cortland County Medical Society, of which Shipman was still president, discussed a new bylaw. The rule would have required that before "any member shall instigate a prosecution against another member of this Society," he must submit the question to the annual meeting of the society and obtain a two-thirds vote of confidence before proceeding. In addition, he must give the accused physician thirty days notice of the charge or be expelled from the society. It was clear that "there would have been an almost unanimous vote in favor of the resolution." But no vote occurred. Shipman, president of the society, refused to put the question to a vote when it was moved and seconded and refused to leave the chair when requested to do so. Though the society tabled the bylaw, its members removed Shipman from the presidency and replaced him with Goodyear. The society then passed a resolution stating "[t]hat on review of the facts in relation to the prosecution by Wm. Smith against Drs. Goodyear and Hyde, for mal-practice, we have yet to see nothing [sic] to diminish our confidence in their skill as practical Surgeons." The society published a report of the proceedings in the *Cortland Democrat* and relayed this vote of confidence to the Philadelphia and Boston medical journals.[39]

After hearing of the activities of the Cortland Medical Society, a writer for the *Medical Examiner* noted that "although it seems a clique of his [Shipman's] professional brethren in the neighborhood are weak enough to put him down for doing his duty," Shipman deserved "great praise" for his "manly and successful efforts to save the limb." The medical society's resolutions, the commentator noted, "besides endorsing bad surgery, have another obvious ill tendency":

They create among the public an impression that physicians are disposed to screen each other from the just consequences of ignorance and incapacity, that they regard their duty to their patients as secondary, and that, as in the present instance, they deem the preservation of limb and life as of little weight in the balance with the observance of a false code of professional etiquette.[40]

The Aftermath. This editorial offered a remarkably clear perspective on the case, in which three arms of the profession—a medical journal, an expert witness, and a local medical society—had attempted to close ranks and express solidarity. In doing so, they refused to condone good practice and condemn obsolete procedures. The public, as the author noted, could believe only that members of the profession were "disposed to screen each other from the just consequences of ignorance and incapacity." However, the physicians who had attacked Goodyear and Hyde and supported modern techniques damaged the profession in other ways. When malpractice debates exposed professional discord and therapeutic uncertainty, physicians' status and legitimacy suffered. The public distrust born of these debates aggravated patients' suspicions and encouraged additional suits.

The Goodyear and Hyde case also demonstrated how malpractice litigation and the profession's reaction to it could discourage medical advancement. Amputation was considered the standard treatment for compound fractures until the 1820s. By 1835, in cases of compound fractures of the tibia and fibula near the ankle joint, the injury suffered by Smith, Astley Cooper, the leading expert on orthopedic injuries, eschewed amputation and recommended removing the broken and jagged pieces of bone with a saw.[41] Goodyear and Hyde were sued in part for refusing to do so and for advocating amputation instead. When Shipman took over the case and followed the most current authorities on fractures, Goodyear and Hyde's supporters attacked him at the trial and later in newspapers. Similarly, the members of the Cortland county medical society, two expert witnesses, local physicians, and a few medical commentators, spurned the evidence of almost a decade, condemned Shipman, and defended Goodyear and Hyde.

By ignoring these advancements in orthopedics, Goodyear and Hyde's supporters impeded the acceptance of improved forms of treatment and encouraged the discredited alternative of amputation. Indiscriminate amputation also conflicted with the general trend toward "conservative medicine" and placing a greater trust in the healing powers of nature.[42] For example, one of Shipman's supporters, a writer for a medical journal, claimed that "nature" had pointed out the correct treatment. The same observer could not find a single reason to support amputation and suggested, as had some of the witnesses, that "[i]n the absence of every other motive, one might almost suppose that amputation was desired to get rid of a troublesome case, and the more effectively to conceal a bad piece of surgery."[43] The author's suggestion was not so farfetched. The vagaries of malpractice litigation could have affected treatment decisions by making it more attractive to condone amputation than to follow the safer and more effective procedure of saving limbs.

The professional and personal animosity aggravated by Goodyear and Hyde's prosecution persisted. In the spring of 1842 Henry Brockway fractured his leg and dislocated his ankle when he jumped from a buggy pulled by a runaway horse. Shipman treated the injury until August 1842. Brockway then went to work as a millwright and told Shipman that he was pleased with the results of the treatment. Early in 1844 Brockway visited several local physicians who told him that his ankle was dislocated and advised him to sue Shipman for malpractice. The editors of the *Boston Medical and Surgical Journal* received an anonymous letter informing them of the suit and "rejoicing" over Shipman's prosecution.[44] The editors refused to print the report but warned that western New York was rife with accusations of malpractice. The writer noted that Shipman had been a witness for the prosecution in a malpractice case three years previously and acknowledged that the suit had probably been instigated by another physician with a private grudge. The following week the journal reported that a Cortland County jury voted eleven to one to dismiss the charges against Shipman.[45]

Surprisingly, these public battles did not drive Goodyear, Hyde, and Shipman out of Cortland or into professional obscurity. In 1845 Goodyear and Hyde opened a private school of anatomy and surgery. Later, in 1855, Hyde filled the chair of surgery at Geneva Medical College, in 1865 he was elected president of the state medical society, and, when Geneva Medical College joined with Syracuse University in the 1870s, Hyde became the dean of the new faculty. Shipman eventually served as a professor of surgery at Indiana University.[46]

Although the three physicians survived the ordeal, the profession suffered significant damage from the public conflict. In an 1846 article F. Campbell Stewart tried to warn New York physicians that self-aggrandizement often amounted to professional suicide. Stewart claimed that "many of our body fall into the gross error of considering that their individual success depends on decrying their professional rivals and indirectly leading patients to conclude that they alone, of all others are able and capable of rendering effectual assistance." He insisted that this "course [was] calculated both to impair the credit of the general body and lessen the estimation in which it should be held by the public at large" and advised that "all of our faults and our errors should be kept within our own bounds."[47] Despite Stewart's initial insight, malpractice litigation rendered his advice inappropriate and useless.

Local medical societies and codes of ethics failed to contain completely individual ambition in disputes over patients, education, therapy, and malpractice incidents. Some doctors were willing to use malpractice accusations as competitive tools. Their no-holds-barred, free-market competition was a significant cause and an aggravating factor in the crisis. Once a physician was accused of malpractice, the charge disrupted professional relations in a variety of ways, all of which damaged the profession.

The spectacle of one physician testifying against another itself shattered the thin veneer of professional solidarity that Stewart and other writers recommended. However, when physicians defended obviously ignorant, incompetent, or careless colleagues, suspicious lay observers could rightly accuse them of protecting quacks. As *Smith* v. *Goodyear and Hyde* demonstrated, malpractice litigation could be antagonistic to medical advancement. The medical profession's fear of the malpractice epidemic and the desperate efforts to establish a united front sometimes encouraged physicians to accept substandard performances from their colleagues and implicitly support outdated and dangerous treatments. And, especially in the case of amputations and fractures, the best treatment for the patient was not necessarily the safest treatment for the physician.

Local medical societies and medical journals that were founded in part to unify the profession sometimes served instead as public forums for personal disputes. These institutions failed to devise an objective means of responding to the flood of malpractice suits that did not harm the profession they were intending to promote and protect. The societies and journals damaged the profession by either exposing an incompetent surgeon, implying that there must be other doctors who could not be trusted, or helping to perpetuate poor or outdated treatment and confirming the claims of their many critics by sheltering substandard practitioners. Finally, malpractice suits in the 1830s and 1840s were a self-perpetuating phenomenon. Some cases, like Goodyear and Hyde's, generated retaliatory suits against physicians who testified for the prosecution. Almost all malpractice cases in the period, however, contributed to the public distrust and resentment, and the professional competitiveness and divisiveness that helped cause the suits initially.

CHAPTER 7

The Road Not Taken: Medical Malpractice and the Path of the Common Law

In 1956 a North Carolina state supreme court judge declared that a physician agreeing to accept a person as a patient "does not create a contract in the sense that the term is ordinarily used." In medical malpractice cases, the judge observed, "it is apt and perhaps more exact to say it [the doctor-patient relationship] creates a status or relation rather than a contract."[1] This observation is consistent with the modern tendency to view medical malpractice as a tort of negligence rather than a breach of contract. Twentieth-century legal theorists define *torts* broadly as private civil wrongs that violate certain duties or responsibilities within a social context that condones certain behaviors and condemns others. The modern law of *contract*, by contrast, holds that the duty owed by the respective parties is theoretically agreed upon by the individuals involved in the contract.[2]

One hundred and fifty years ago the picture was less clear. Judges and legal theorists had not yet molded the notions of tort and contract into discrete categories, and there was no need or basis upon which to classify malpractice under one abstract heading or the other. The prevailing writ system designated specific legal actions and procedures for various civil wrongs and obviated much of the need for overarching doctrinal theory.[3] When lawyers brought a suit before a court, they selected the appropriate action and cited pertinent case-law precedent.

The earliest American malpractice cases relied heavily on English common law procedures and assumptions about the nature of the doctor-patient relationship.

The political, social, and economic changes of the first half of the nineteenth century, however, transformed the American public view of the physician's role in society and threatened to alter fundamentally the grounds of the physician's personal and legal responsibility. By the 1830s a significant number of Americans were willing to treat medical practice as if it were a purely commercial enterprise. Malpractice law reflected this trend, and some judges and physicians tentatively incorporated aspects of contractual language into medical liability doctrines. Although this deviation was not directly related to the sudden increase in litigation, the two phenomena shared political and social origins. If the midcentury flirtation of malpractice law with contractual doctrine had matured, the nature of a doctor's liability would have been profoundly different. Ultimately, however, subjective feelings about medical practice, the medical community's self-image, and the inappropriate matching of commercial doctrines to the doctor-patient relationship doomed the marriage of malpractice and contract and relegated medical liability to the province of tort.

Common Law Origins

Blackstone categorized malpractice under neither contract or mercantile law, but under private wrongs. He defined *mala practice* as an injury or damage to a person's "vigor or constitution" sustained as a result of "the neglect or unskillful management of [a] physician, surgeon, or apothecary." Blackstone declared that malpractice was an offense because "it breaks the trust which the party placed in his physician." The injured patient possessed a remedy for damages with the special legal action, or writ, of "trespass on the case."[4]

According to eighteenth-century lawyers, when a defendant was charged with a civil offense, the court required the plaintiff to designate the specific writ or action that entitled him or her to recover damages. There were ten basic writs or actions, and, if the purported offense did not fall under one of the ten, then the plaintiff did not have a legal remedy.[5] The *writ of trespass* was the legal remedy for damages resulting from direct force to a person or his or her property. Broken contracts were prosecuted under the *writ of assumpsit*.[6]

When the writ system was established in the late fourteenth century, it did not initially include the action of trespass on the case, the writ Blackstone designated to prosecute malpractice cases. Since the trespass writ applied exclusively to a direct and unauthorized interference with an individual's person or property, a plaintiff could not use the trespass writ if he or she had voluntarily submitted to a physician's care. The writ was also useless in cases where injury or damage was the result of an indirect or careless action by the defendant. With no remedy available for an entire class of cases, English courts slowly accepted the notion that injured plaintiffs were entitled to remuneration even where there was no breach of contract (assumpsit) or injury by force (trespass).

In two cases in the 1370s English courts allowed a special trespass writ (which would become known as *trespass on the case*) to apply against veterinary surgeons who injured horses instead of curing them. Through the fifteenth century courts accumulated a significant body of precedents in which they allowed the application of the special trespass writ.[7] In 1553 in his *Natura Brevium* Anthony Fitzherbert declared that individuals were liable for injuries caused by negligent conduct even when there was no breach of contract or actual trespass. This new writ, which had been evolving for one and a half centuries, was called *trespass on the case*, or *action on the case*. Fitzherbert asserted that if a [black]smith prick my horse with a nail, I shall have an action upon the case against him [even] without any warranty by the smith to do it well. . . . For it is the duty of every artificer to exercise his art rightly and truly as he ought."[8] Fitzherbert's remarks were the modern foundation for action on the case. Later writers argued that his statement applied not only to smiths, but also to innkeepers, ferrymen, carpenters, barbers, and physicians.[9]

Sixty years later Edward Coke, the great English jurist, explicitly used the trespass on the case writ for damages arising out of the doctor-patient relationship. In *Everard* v. *Hopkins*, a man employed a physician who promised to cure his injured servant's leg,[10] but who instead prescribed harmful medicines and delayed the servant's recovery by a year. Coke declared that the master could sue using the writ of assumpsit because the physician had failed to fulfill his part of the contract to cure the servant. If the physician had not promised a cure, then the master could not have recovered under the writ of assumpsit. More significantly for modern malpractice law, however, Coke held that the servant, even though he had not made a contract with the physician, could bring charges against the doctor under the writ of trespass on the case. This holding was important because it supported the notion that the physician's liability and responsibility for his patient emanated not from a commercial contractual agreement but from the affirmative act of entering into the doctor-patient relationship.[11]

Writing in the late eighteenth century, Blackstone drew from this long evolution. Judges adopted this variant of the trespass writ to fill in situations where there had been no remedy. Blackstone explained that the malpractice prosecution allowed a plaintiff "to bring a special action on his own case, by a writ formed according to the particular circumstances of his own particular grievance." The plaintiff's official form of action would be trespass on the case but the whole "cause of complaint [is] set forth at length in the original writ."[12]

In 1767 the case of *Slater* v. *Baker and Stapleton* involved a man who sued a physician and an apothecary, claiming that they had rebroken his partially healed leg and caused it to heal poorly. In addition, the physician had used an experimental steel device with gears to stretch the limb. Employing a special trespass on the case action, Slater declared that he had hired the physician and his assistant to treat his broken leg but that they, "not regarding their promise and undertaking, and the duty of their business and employment, so ignorantly and unskillfully treated" him that his leg was permanently injured. Several other physicians testified that injured limbs should be rebroken only in cases of extreme deformity and that they had neither seen, nor heard of the experimental device. The court agreed with Slater and ruled that the physician had acted "ignorantly and unskillfully contrary to the known rule and usage of surgeons."[13]

The decision in *Slater* made it clear that a physician would be held liable for unskillful and negligent conduct even if the damage to the patient was unintentional. The accused physician's medical treatment would be measured against the therapeutic conventions or standards of the profession. *Slater* granted juries the important role of determining "questions of fact" such as what constituted carelessness and what were standards and practices of the medical profession at large.

Early American lawyers and trial court judges used *Slater* as a guide for the presentation of malpractice pleas in the trial courts, and appellate judges cited the case regularly in the first half of the nineteenth century. Other English cases also shaped early malpractice pleas.[14] In *Seare* v. *Prentice* (1807) Lord Ellenborough, the chief justice of the King's Bench, declared that a physician could be held responsible for either negligence or unskillfulness. Ellenborough stated:

an ordinary degree of skill is necessary for a surgeon who undertakes to perform surgical operations . . . in the same manner as it is necessary for every other man to have . . . common skill at least in his business, and that is implied in his undertaking.[15]

Ellenborough's ruling confirms that physicians and members of other occupations had special duties that arose out of their calling or role in society. The judge implicitly warned these men that their status as innkeepers, ferrymen, barbers, blacksmiths, lawyers, and physicians implied that they possessed the "ordinary degree of skill" essential for the fulfillment of their respective tasks.

Until the civil procedure reforms of the late 1840s and 1850s the trespass on the case writ remained the appropriate remedy for American malpractice prosecutions. In his plea to the court, the prosecuting attorney adopted the language of Blackstone, *Slater*, and *Seare* to justify the charge. For example, a Connecticut appellate court in *Landon* v. *Humphrey* used these precedents when it ruled that anyone who undertakes "any office, employment, duty, or trust" must "perform it with integrity, diligence and skill." If an individual was injured as a result of the want of any of these qualities, then the courts would accept an action on the case.[16] Prosecuting attorneys used this language in their initial pleas, judges incorporated it into their charges to juries, and appellate jurists measured lower court proceedings against it.

While the basic action of trespass on the case did not change, its underlying principles and the wording of the justification evolved as more appropriate precedents surfaced. *Lamphier and Wife* v. *Phipos* (1838) was the last English decision to contribute influential statements of principle to American malpractice law.[17] As a result of physician

Phipos's failure to diagnose correctly Mrs. Lamphier's broken wrist, she lost the use of her hand. In charging the jury, Judge Tyrdall explained that every person who entered into "a learned profession undertakes to bring a fair, reasonable, and competent degree of skill to his endeavor." Attorneys did not "undertake" to win every case; surgeons did not "undertake" consistently to cure. Because some practitioners would always have "higher educations and greater advantages" than others, no physician was required to use the profession's highest degree of skill or care.[18]

Tyndall's charge did not alter earlier precedents, but it did provide the clearest and most enduring elaboration of the principles of malpractice. Trial and appellate court use of Tyndall's language made it the standard charge in nineteenth-century malpractice charges.[19] The formula, like the prescriptions of Blackstone, *Slater*, and *Seare*, was consistent with the notion that medical men were accountable for their actions because of the public nature of their calling. It did not suggest that physicians incurred responsibilities because they had entered into commercial associations with their patients. By measuring accused physicians' skill and care against the "ordinary" standard set by the rest of the profession, judges demonstrated that doctor's duties arose out of their general status as medical men rather than from their particular one-on-one "contracts" with their patients. These rulings supported the idea that the medical profession could represent an independent "community of the competent" wherein a member's actions were judged against the standards of peers. The responsibility, both moral and legal, of medical professionals emanated from membership in that community. It could not be abrogated or altered by agreements with persons outside that body.[20]

American Innovations

While American courts accepted the wording of these malpractice principles, they did not completely adopt the traditional conception of professional relationships. According to English common law, the services of lawyers and physicians were considered gratuitous. Blackstone had declared that lawyers could not sue for fees, and, since

medicine was an "honorary employment," a physician could not recover compensation for his practice but had to take what was voluntarily given him.[21] This doctrine originated in Roman civil law in an era
when physicians did not practice medicine as their sole livelihood, and
the legal relation of doctor to patient was referred to as a *mandate*, an
implicit agreement to provide service for no fee.[22] English common
law gradually dropped the idea of a strict mandate, but it retained the
assumption that medical and legal services were intrinsically gratuitous
and that doctors had a legal right only to an honorarium.

American courts never accepted the concept of honorariums. As the
nineteenth-century judge and treatise writer Gulian Verplank explained, the growing demand for the services of full-time lawyers and
physicians "pointed out the injustice, as well as the absurdity, of
leaving them, as a class remediless for the value of such services as
they may render to the public."[23] His views reflected the growing
belief that physicians did not occupy a special social or legal status in
American society. He contended that it was "wholly inconsistent with
all our ideas of equality to suppose that" medicine or law, businesses
or professions "by which one earns the daily bread of himself or his
family, [are] so much more honorable than the business of other members of the community."[24] Significantly, Verplank's major contribution to general American law was his *Essay on the Doctrine of Contracts*
(1825), where he attempted to "modernize" contract law and bring it
in line with the demands of a free-market economy.[25]

John Ordronaux, who had both legal and medical training, argued
that repudiating the conception of the doctor-patient relationship as an
intrinsically gratuitous service "reduce[d] professions to the status of
artisanship" and placed them on a par with manual laborers. The
unrestricted right of professionals to sue for fees in America brought
the legal relationships and liabilities "directly within the pale of consensual agreements based upon sufficient consideration."[26] Therefore,
in suits for fees the legal relationship of doctor to patient shifted from
status-based responsibilities growing out of a physician's role as a public
servant to *contract-based* responsibilities emanating from bilateral agreements.

In his pioneering *Ancient Law* (1884) Henry Maine contended that
in "progressive societies" legal relationships tend to evolve from status-

determined duties to contract-determined duties; legal rights, duties, and liabilities derived more from explicit, conscious agreements than from a person's role, position, or status in society.[27] More recent writers have portrayed the specific development of contract law in a similar vein.[28] They argue that in earlier times legal obligations including those originating in private agreements between two parties, were often judged by the community's standards of fairness instead of the contracting parties' agreement. Implied obligations often went beyond the responsibilities the parties themselves had chosen to undertake. During the eighteenth and especially the nineteenth centuries these arrangements were replaced by the belief that legal obligations seldom went beyond what the individual parties had specifically agreed to in a contract. The specific agreement represented a so-called "meeting of the minds." The swing away from community determined standards and the acceptance of the idea that masters, employers, and vendors owed no special duty beyond the cash-based commercial agreements with their apprentices, employees, and customers, reached its apex by the mid–nineteenth century.[29]

Americans' repudiation of the notion of honorariums for physicians and lawyers and the recognition of commercial relationships in allowing suits-for-fees illustrated the evolution of status-based to contract-based liabilities. The move from status to contract in malpractice law, however, was subtle, complex, slow, and ultimately incomplete. Initially Americans accepted English malpractice precedents and the technicalities involved in the common law system of writ pleading.[30] The rationale for the writ system was that through it a simple, specific, well-defined issue could be presented whereby plaintiffs could offer only appropriate evidence for their claim and defendants could respond with suitable rejoinders. In theory juries would decide a clear, simple issue of fact. The system was intricate and technically unforgiving. Judges dismissed charges, for example, when a plaintiff's lawyer failed to state the full name of a party to the suit, misspelled the town or county where the defendant resided, or did not properly state the occupation of both the plaintiff and the defendant. Procedural rules required the plaintiff to choose the correct writ (action) under which he or she was bringing suit. If a plaintiff sued using a writ of debt when he or she should have used a writ of ejectment, the judge would dismiss the case and the plaintiff would have to start over and repeat the entire, costly, complicated pretrial process. The selection of the correct writ or charge was not simple and required extensive legal training.[31]

Popular and professional discontent with the intricate writ system led to a gradual abandonment of the technical pleading. Opponents of the system complained that the strict procedural rules often interfered with substantive justice, that specific forms of action, such as trespass and assumpsit, had outgrown their usefulness, and that the rules that defined their applicability did not fit new social circumstances. In the late eighteenth century American judges began to ignore many common law pleading technicalities. Judges became less interested in technical exactitude and more concerned with providing substantive justice.[32] Specific pleas as answers to specific writs were less important than the underlying nature of the cause of action.[33]

The writ system, in its strict form, had served as a substitute for doctrinal classification. Judges and lawyers did not have to think in terms of contract and tort because there were specific writs for specific wrongs. When pleading became more concerned with substance and less with form, the distinction among writs such as debt, covenant, and assumpsit became blurred, and judges allowed them to be applied to a broader array of breach of contract offenses. By the early 1800s lawyers and judges began to segregate informally the wrongs previously covered by specific writs into the categories of tort and contract and searched for general principles that characterized the two areas of law.[34] Many ancient writs fell readily into one category or the other. Covenant, debt, and assumpsit could be combined under the rubric of contract violations; trespass was a tort violation.

Malpractice and its common law remedy, the writ of trespass on the case, did not fall naturally into these abstract categories. Blackstone explained that when a litigant sued for damages because of a debt or a breach of personal duty, the suit belonged to the broad theoretical class of contract. When plaintiffs sued complaining of injuries to their persons or property, however, Blackstone classified the claim as a tort.[35] Malpractice exhibited characteristics of both categories. It was a breach of duty, and it resulted in personal injury. This doctrinal ambiguity probably caused few problems in ordinary law practice as

long as strict adherence to the writ system made theoretical classification irrelevant. In addition, the language of English malpractice precedents demonstrated that a physician's liability emanated from his status as a public servant and not from his contractual, commercial
relationship with his patient.[36] As formal pleading rules were more
frequently ignored and eventually abandoned, and as American society's attitude toward the medical profession changed, malpractice law
felt the strong pull of contract.

Early nineteenth-century legal handbooks reflected the blurred distinctions among specific writs. The 1812 American edition of Joseph
Chitty's *Practical Treatise on Pleading* informed lawyers that they could
sue physicians for malpractice using either a writ of assumpsit, which
provided for the recovery of damages for the nonperformance of a
simple contract, or they could use trespass on the case, which offered
a remedy for injuries resulting from a breach of duty.[37] Other legal
handbooks published before the civil procedure reforms of the late
1840s and early 1850s echoed Chitty's guidelines. In *Law of Pleading
and Evidence* (1844) John Saunders advised that physicians were "liable
in assumpsit or [trespass on the] case, for ignorance or unskillfulness,
and for negligence in the exercise of [their] profession." Citing *Slater*
and *Seare*, Saunders explained that the law implied a "duty" on the
part of the physician to exercise "due and reasonable skill." To win a
case, the plaintiff had to "prove that the defendant was a surgeon or
apothecary by profession, *or* that he was retained and paid as such by
the plaintiff, *or* that he especially engaged to cure the plaintiff for
reward" (emphasis added). The patient/plaintiff was required to present "persons of skill and experience" as expert witnesses who would
offer testimony on the suitability of the defendant's treatment. The
patient would have to prove that the physician's treatment had been
unskillful and improper and that he caused a "wound or complaint, or
increased [the] wound or complaint of the plaintiff."[38]

The malpractice references in these early nineteenth-century hand
books suggested that the law was beginning to reflect the contractual
aspects of the doctor-patient relationship as well as the traditional legal
duties associated with a common calling. Both Chitty and Saunders
declared that malpractice charges could be initiated under the writ of
assumpsit (simple contract) or under trespass on the case. None of the

eighteenth-century English precedents mentioned the use of assumpsit as a remedy for malpractice; they uniformly used trespass on the case.[39] The incorporation of assumpsit into the malpractice lawyer's armory is an example of the informal loosening of technical requirements. Under Saunders' criteria, a doctor's legal responsibility arose from his status as a medical man, or his financial contract with a particular patient, or his explicit promise to cure an illness or injury.

Drifting toward Contract

The commercial aspect of a physician's liability was consistent with American judges' abandonment of the notion of honorariums and their acceptance of physicians' suits-for-fees. The early nineteenth-century doctor-patient relationship seemed to drift equivocally between the legal categories of contract and tort, which remained vague and unqualified until at least the middle of the century.[40] As the notion of contract gained more acceptance in society and law, it played a more important role in defining the doctor-patient relationship and in influencing malpractice litigation.

The process was slow because state supreme court judges erected barriers against this growing tendency. For example, in the Connecticut supreme court case of *Grannis* v. *Branden* (1812) a man claimed that he had paid a physician "reasonable compensation" to deliver his wife's child. The infant died during delivery, and, while removing the dead fetus, the physician severely cut and injured the mother. The husband's charge implied that a physician's liability originated in the economic relationship that was established when the fee was paid. A jury found the physician guilty of malpractice. When the state supreme court reviewed the case, it let the conviction stand but emphasized that "the only point in issue between the parties, was whether the defendant had neglected to perform his professional duty." The judges ignored the service-for-pay claim of the husband.[41]

In another Connecticut case in order to meet the requirements of a new state law requiring vaccinations, the board of health of Salisbury, Connecticut, hired Dr. Asabel Humphrey and three other physicians to vaccinate all the town's uninoculated citizens against smallpox.[42]

Humphrey and his colleagues contracted to carry out their task "in a faithful manner" and "according to our best skill and judgment." The Salisbury board of health agreed to pay the four physicians together $50 for the treatment. The doctors divided the town into four districts and assigned each physician one section as his personal responsibility. The fee, split among the four physicians, averaged about $.04 for each person vaccinated in the town.[43]

Dr. Humphrey, who was ill, hired Rollin Sprague, a young medical student, to vaccinate the residents of his district. The procedure required Sprague to make a small, shallow incision on the upper part of the patient's arm and insert a quill containing the vaccine virus. Sprague apparently vaccinated several residents successfully before he visited twenty-year-old Harriet Landon. "[F]rom real or affected modesty," she refused to raise her sleeve, and Sprague made two punctures in her upper arm just above her elbow but about one inch lower than standard practice. According to witnesses, she immediately experienced great pain and was unable to use her arm for several weeks.[44]

Landon brought an action on the case against Humphrey for malpractice. The plea to the court, to justify the writ, consisted of two separate counts. Landon first claimed that Humphrey had held "himself out to the world as a skillful practitioner [and] was employed by the plaintiff . . . to inoculate her with kine pox." Humphrey had been paid, but he "unskillfully" and "unfaithfully" treated the patient and "cut a tendon, cord, ligament, and nerve of the patient's arm." Because he vaccinated Landon in "an improper, unusual, and dangerous place," she had been "deprived of the use of her arm, [and] prevented from pursuing her necessary business."[45]

Landon's complaint was noteworthy because it accepted without comment that Sprague was Humphrey's direct agent and presumed that a duty-filled relationship existed between Humphrey and Landon even though the two had never met. Humphrey, by virtue of his status as a physician and his acceptance of the responsibility of inoculating the residents of his district, entered into a relationship with Landon that rendered him liable if he did not act according to certain standards.[46] In a second count, to support the action on the case writ, Landon argued that the board of health had employed Humphrey to vaccinate the inhabitants of the town in "a skillful and safe manner."

Instead, Humphrey had acted with a "negligence and unskillfulness" that resulted in an injury to Landon. In other words, Humphrey, through his agent, failed to act with the skill and care that his status as a physician demanded.[47]

Thomas Hubbard, a professor of surgery at Yale, testified that Landon's affliction could have been caused by damage to the nerve suffered if the medical assistant made the puncture too deep. Several other physicians confirmed that the punctures were in a very unusual place. The physicians who testified for Humphrey agreed that the incisions were not in the place usually selected, but argued that it was perfectly safe to inoculate that portion of the arm and that they had not heard of a single case where this type of injury had occurred after a vaccination.[48]

The trial court judge instructed the jury that anyone who undertook "any office, employment, duty, or trust *contracts* to perform it with integrity, diligence and skill" (emphasis added). If a physician lacked any of these qualities and injured a patient, the judge continued, the injured party could claim damages by a special action on the case. The judge also charged the jury that a physician who vaccinated patients was "liable for all the consequences if he neglects the usual precautions, or fails to insert the virus in that part of the arm *usually selected* for the purpose" (original emphasis). The jury ruled in favor of Landon and awarded her $500 and costs. The total judgment against Humphrey amounted to $1,000.[49]

Humphrey appealed the verdict to the Connecticut supreme court of errors. He argued that he did not have a contract with Landon and that the written agreement to vaccinate the citizens of Salisbury should not have been accepted into evidence. He maintained that he had contracted with the board of health and that Harriet Landon "had nothing to do with it personally." Humphrey asserted that physicians should be liable for "nothing short of gross ignorance or gross negligence." Because there was "nothing like mechanical perfection in the healing art," he pleaded, "some little failure might sweep from [a physician] the whole earning of a life of toil and drudgery." According to Humphrey, even skilled physicians would not be able to avoid prosecution and fewer men would enter the profession.[50]

The language of both the trial court judge and the physician reflected the influence of contract ideas. The judge told the jury that a physician "contracts" to perform his duty with "integrity, diligence and skill." In addition, he ruled that a physician was required to vaccinate patients in the place "usually selected for the purpose" even if there were more suitable locations. He illustrated this principle by explaining that a man transporting property would be liable for all consequences if he departed from the usual route. Portraying the physician not as a healer with a special status, but as a technician for hire who had to perform in the manner expected of him, the trial judge reinforced the notion that physicians carried contractual responsibilities; as did the physician when he argued that the "contract" was with the board of health and Landon "had nothing to do with it personally."

The Connecticut supreme court refused to grant the physician a new trial. The majority opinion explained that the written contract between Humphrey and the board of health was not an important part of the evidence against the physician and that its inclusion as evidence was, at worst, unnecessary. The court ruled that there was sufficient evidence without the contract to prove that Humphrey had accepted the responsibility of inoculating the residents of his district. The contract was merely additional proof that he had undertaken the role of physician in the community. Including superfluous evidence could not be grounds for a new trial.[51]

The supreme court's comments and lack of interest in the written contract demonstrated that the origin of Humphrey's liabilities and duties was his status as a medical man and his informal relationship with his patient rather than an explicit agreement. Humphrey had argued that Landon took no part in the agreement, so the contract could not be used against him. The supreme court, however, was concerned only with establishing Humphrey's status in the community as a physician and his relationship to the patient. Explicit, contractual arrangements were irrelevant.

Although the state supreme court eschewed the notion that a physician's liability arose out of a bilateral, exchanged-based relationship, the contentions of Dr. Humphrey and the lower court judge suggested that contractual ideas had made significant inroads into American legal thought. The roots of these attitudes were intertwined with the country's political, social, and economic history. A Lockean version of the social contract had helped justify the colonists' break from the mother country and explained their subsequent reliance on a written constitution to create a new government.[52] The unforeseen social leveling effect of the new environment, the revolutionary rhetoric of equality, and the failure to translate old-world institutions in America combined to undermine traditional relationships of status. For example, apprenticeship relationships had been governed by a set of unwritten, mutual responsibilities that were shared and sanctioned by the entire community. The apprentice owed the master work and respect; the master owed his apprentice such things as room, board, training, and religious instruction. In America this status-based relationship broke down, and each party owed the other only what they had mutually agreed to exchange.[53]

Similarly, the guild system never took hold in the colonies, and access to crafts and professions was generally open.[54] In the late eighteenth century elite American physicians attempted to replicate English institutions that gave professional men a special legal and social status. However, the medical schools, professional societies, and licensure laws failed to elevate the physician's image. Professional monopolies were inconsistent with the republican rhetoric of the post-Revolution years. The schools, designed to enhance the physician's status, instead contributed to a backlash against professionalism by producing undertrained and ignorant practitioners. Licensure regulations were weak and ignored.

Laissez-faire sentiment toward medical licensure developed at the same time as reliance on status in other legal relationships declined. From his travels in early nineteenth-century America de Tocqueville concluded that democratic revolutions are followed by an attack on symbols of social aristocracy and an increase in individualism. He observed, "[E]ach citizen of an aristocratic society has his fixed station, one above another, so that there is always someone above him whose protection he needs and someone below him whose help he may require."[55] In short, many rights and duties were a result of social or professional status. During the first half of the nineteenth century this system disintegrated in America. A society filled with people who praised equality and individualism took its place. Especially between 1800 and 1860 localism was broken up by economic development, transportation improvements, and massive migration, and these forces in turn contributed to the antiprivilege, antimonopoly, antiprofessional philosophy of the Jacksonian period.

Free trade, laissez-faire ideas, individualism, and the breakdown of status relationships all served as the underpinnings of the so-called "golden age of contract." The *will theory of contract* was a model that suggested that legal responsibilities were the consequence of a "meeting of the minds" of two presumably equal bargainers. According to one writer, the "will theory of contracts carried the republican impulse to the smallest unit of society—two individuals, who in concert formed a microlegislature and made law."[56] Under this concept, which gained prominence between 1750 and 1850, the law more frequently disregarded traditional community standards of fairness and protected only the explicit expectations of the bargaining parties as expressed in their private agreements.[57] This notion of contract seeped into many areas of law and altered traditional liability.

Employers abandoned their status-based, paternalistic, hierarchical relationships with their employees and customers and relied on written agreements to define respective rights and liabilities. Just price and fair wage standards were out; caveat emptor ("let the buyer beware") was in. Employers' traditional liability for the actions of their employees under *respondeat superior* was diminished. Common carriers such as trains and steamboats frequently asked their customers to sign contractual waivers and relinquish their rights to sue for damages in case of accidents. Virtually every area of law felt the impact of this movement.[58]

The rise of contract mentality in the 1830s, 1840s, and 1850s contributed to the already declining professional status of the physician. Medical sectarians who claimed to embody free-market Jacksonian sentiment called for an end to restrictive licensing and praised open competition. By 1850 only two states retained licensure statutes, and the medical world became characterized by "free trade in doctoring." Physicians' changing legal and social status and the rise of contract mentality in other areas of law spilled over into malpractice prosecutions. Although the technical legal forms did not change, the language and implications of many malpractice cases reflected the growing predilection to treat physicians like ordinary businessmen. In *Grannis* v.

Branden (1812), *Landon* v. *Humphrey* (1832), and other cases, doctors, patients, or trial lawyers attempted to define physicians' liabilities in contractual terms. The appellate court judges, however, had refused to refer to the doctor-patient relationship as contractual. Instead, state supreme court judges, drawing on the guidance of English precedents, usually agreed that physicians' professional responsibilities emanated from their status as members of a common calling. In the 1840s and 1850s, physicians, lawyers, and judges more frequently referred to the relationship as contractual and began to apply general legal doctrines, drawn from the growing category of contract law, in malpractice cases. Malpractice law was drifting from status to contract.

The Iowa case *Bowman* v. *Woods* (1848) exhibited the impact of contract doctrine on malpractice liability. Bowman, a Thomsonian, or botanic, doctor, delivered Woods's child, but failed to remove the afterbirth. Thomsonians believed that the placenta should remain in the uterus until expelled by nature. Although Mrs. Woods survived, her husband sued Bowman for malpractice. A jury agreed and awarded Woods $50.[59]

The Iowa supreme court overturned the conviction. The majority decision explained that since Iowa had no licensure laws, no particular system of medicine was legally supported or prohibited. While the appellate court judges clearly preferred regular practitioners to medical sectarians, such as homeopaths or Thomsonians, they ruled that the standards of regular physicians were not the exclusive standard or test by which the other systems were to be judged. "A person professing to follow one system of medical treatment, cannot be expected by his *employer* to practice any other," the court noted (emphasis added). Although the law required physicians to use an "ordinary degree of care and skill," it did not require a man "to accomplish more than he undert[ook], nor in a manner different from what he profess[ed]." The wording of the majority decision implied that this doctor-patient relationship resembled a contract. There had been a "meeting of the minds" between Bowman and Woods. Bowman had been hired as a Thomsonian, so he only needed to perform as a Thomsonian.[60]

Since physicians possessed no special status in law or society, the idea of contractual responsibilities became more important. The *Bowman* v. *Woods* decision constructed a clear analogy between the doctor-patient relationship and the commercial marketplace. "If a person will knowingly employ a common mat maker to weave or embroider a fine carpet, he may impute the bad workmanship to his own folly." Therefore, the court reasoned, if a patient chose the wrong type of physician to treat him, "in all such cases, the employer ought properly to attribute loss or injury to his own negligence and mismanagement." The court recognized that the country was filled with quacks, "novices," and "empirics," but lamented that "these are evils which courts of justice possess no adequate power to remedy."[61]

According to *Bowman* v. *Woods*, the medical world was a free market where physicians and patients met to bargain. The watchword was *caveat emptor*. If patients were careless when hiring physicians, then the courts would not protect them. This doctrine could have easily been used to diminish physicians' liability, especially in a country where the elimination of licensing had denied physicians official status and eliminated official standards. Though judges in the 1840s and 1850s did not abandon basic legal forms or the common law prescription that physicians had to perform with "ordinary skill and care," the growing reliance on doctrines associated with contract signaled a significant shift in judicial emphasis.

Although many courts at the trial and appellate levels began to view the doctor-patient relationship in at least quasicontractual terms, they still recognized that much of a physician's liability arose from his status as a member of a common calling.[62] After witnessing a malpractice trial in 1860, a physician noted that "our Judiciary look upon the relation of Physician and Patient as that of a CONTRACT" (original emphasis). At the same time, however, he explained that the contract required physicians to act with the "ordinary amount of skill, care, and attention that pertains to the profession of which he is a member."[63] A quasicontractual view did not automatically alter a physician's liability.[64] But if local and appellate courts allowed defense attorneys to apply contractual doctrines such as caveat emptor and contractual waivers of liability to medical relationships, then physicians' traditional liability would be modified. The decision in *Leighton* v. *Sargent* (1853) provides one of the most frank examples of contractual language in malpractice cases and demonstrates the practical ramifications of this doctrinal drift.

Leighton v. *Sargent*

In September 1850 Joseph Leighton injured his ankle and leg when he lost his balance and fell from a moving carriage in Strafford, New Hampshire. Friends of Leighton sent for Dr. Sargent who lived in Barnstead six miles away. After examining the injury, Sargent discovered that Leighton had dislocated his ankle and fractured and partially shattered his lower leg. Sargent wrapped Leighton's inflamed and swollen limb in a starched bandage and immobilized the entire leg in a homemade fracture box.[65] Leighton's injury, a compound fracture, was profound. The starch dressings irritated Leighton's leg, and his foot became "greatly inflamed" and covered with a "mass of gathering putrid sores." During his long convalescence, Leighton suffered "feverish excitement" and coughs and "had to resort to stimulation to withstand the prostrating effects of the disease"—that is, he resorted to brandy, port, or some other alcoholic beverage. Sargent attended Leighton from September 1, 1850, until January 12, 1851. During this time, he visited and treated Leighton sixty-two times, or an average of once every two days.[66]

Though Sargent did not see his patient after January 1851, Leighton continued to suffer from his injury. Pus-filled sores periodically formed on his ankle, and slivers of bone occasionally oozed from the ulcerations. By the spring of 1852 Leighton's foot had healed, but his ankle joint was frozen in an unusual position so that the toes of his foot were permanently pointed downward and three to five inches lower than his heel. Leighton was unable to work and could not walk without the use of a cane or crutches.[67]

Leighton charged Sargent with malpractice, complaining that the physician's starch wrapping and the setting of his leg had resulted in a "greatly inflamed, virulent, corrupt and festering . . . mass of gathering and putrid sores" which caused him great bodily pain and caused the ankle to heal in a deformed position.[68] Medical witnesses from both sides immediately undermined Leighton's case. They testified that the swelling, inflammation, and sores that plagued Leighton for so many months were a "necessary and unavoidable consequence of the severe injury" he had received and would "accompany even the best possible surgical and medical treatment." Since Leighton had linked the inflammation to the fixed joint, his claim lost its credibility.[69]

Seeing his case destroyed by his own expert witnesses, Leighton changed his complaint in the middle of the trial. Ignoring the objections of Sargent's lawyer, the trial court judge allowed Leighton to enter his new claim. He now argued that he had "employed [Sargent] for a reasonable reward" to treat, set, and cure his right ankle and foot, but that Sargent had instead behaved "negligently, carelessly, and unskillfully" and allowed the foot to become deformed and useless. Leighton produced a new parade of witnesses who testified that the deformed position of his foot was identical to its position when Sargent first placed it in the fracture-box. They recalled that they had brought the unnatural position of the foot to the physician's attention on many occasions, but that Sargent had answered that the angle of the joint was correct and that the toes should be dropped "to get the spring of the foot."[70]

Only two medical men testified for the prosecution. They declared that, though Leighton's injury was severe, there was no difficulty in fixing the foot in any position desired and that they had "never seen an instance where it could not be maintained in that [the correct] position."[71] Twenty witnesses for Sargent testified that they frequently saw a three-quarter–inch book behind the footboard of the fracture box. Defense lawyers claimed that the book would have positioned the foot at nearly a right angle with the leg. They argued therefore that Leighton's foot had become deformed for some other reason than its position in the fracture-box. Other medical witnesses told the jury that compound dislocations were very severe injuries and often resulted in amputations. "The best treatment," one testified, "cannot make a good limb . . . and the patient and doctor should be glad to get off with any foot that will do to walk on."[72] In his instructions to the Strafford County jury, the trial judge stated that a physician must possess "a reasonable degree of skill, such as is ordinarily possessed by his profession," and he must "exercise that skill with reasonable care and diligence." Although the "legal gentlemen of the Strafford bar" believed that the jury would exonerate Sargent, the jury declared that the physician was guilty and awarded Leighton $1,500.

Sargent appealed the verdict to the New Hampshire supreme court in 1853. The court ruled that the trial court judge should not have allowed Leighton to change his charge in the middle of the trial, overturned the jury's decision, and granted the physician a new trial. Judge Bell, who wrote the opinion for the New Hampshire supreme court, noted, however, that the principles of malpractice were of "great consequence to all classes of professional men" and should be "settled and well understood." "At the present moment," he observed, "it is to be feared there is a tendency to impose some perilous obligations beyond the requirements of the law on some professional men."[73] Bell declared that while doctors did not implicitly guarantee the results of their work, they were required to possess a "reasonable, fair, and competent degree of skill" and exercise this skill with "ordinary care and diligence." Judge Bell's definition of professional responsibility was no different in substance from the trial court judge's charge to the jury or the common law precedents articulated in previous appellate decisions. Bell's description of the legal relationship between doctor and patient, however, while it resembled the ruling in *Bowman* v. *Woods*, did vary significantly from the opinions of his early nineteenth-century counterparts.

Bell stated that when a physician "offers his services to the community generally, or to any individual, for employment in any professional capacity, [he] *contracts* with his employer. (emphasis added)"[74] Judge Bell's use of the term *contract* in his decision was not a harmless and meaningless abstraction. The judge was concerned that medical men were suffering under "some perilous obligations," and he was going to give them a judicial remedy. Bell ruled that while physicians must exercise "ordinary good judgement," the risk from "mere errors and mistakes is upon the employer [patient] alone." The judge continued: "He [the patient] too has judgement to exercise in the selection of the physician or the lawyer whom he will employ, and if he makes a bad selection, if he fails to choose a man of the best judgement, the result is fairly attributed to his own mistake."[75]

Judge Bell's decision, like the majority ruling in *Bowman* v. *Woods*, viewed the doctor-patient relationship through the lens of contract. Two years later in *Cater* v. *Fernald* a New Hampshire trial court judge used this medical version of caveat emptor to charge a jury in a malpractice case. He reminded them that the "employer has to exercise judgment too in the employment of a professional man."[76]

The Connecticut supreme court judge in the 1832 *Landon* v. *Humphrey* ruling had dismissed the importance of a contract in adjudicating malpractice cases. In the *Bowman, Leighton,* and *Cater* decisions, however, the judges specifically referred to the doctor and his patient as *employee* and *employer*. The decisions assumed that the medical world was merely an analogue of the commercial marketplace and should operate by many of the same rules. The judges embraced contract doctrines and provided physicians with a defensive legal weapon by constructing a medical malpractice version of caveat emptor. Treating malpractice as a type of contract could affect potential financial awards to injured patients in other ways. If malpractice were considered purely under the rubric of tort law, as it eventually was, pain and suffering, as well as damages, could be used as grounds for remuneration. If malpractice was treated as a contract case, the law generally provided only that plaintiffs be placed in the same position they would be in if the contracts had been properly performed.[77]

Contractual Waivers of Liability

If the doctor-patient relationship was truly a "meeting of the minds," the doctor should have also been able to contract for less liability. Despite the efforts of some corporations, state courts of the 1830s and 1840s had refused to allow common carriers to "contract away" their common law liability. But the abstract notion of freedom of contract and a desire by state court judges to encourage economic expansion broke down old barriers. In 1850 New York judges allowed common carriers to restrict their liability by special agreement with their customers. By 1853 corporations could limit lawsuits even for gross negligence. Despite these decisions, treatise writers remained tentative in their support of contractual protection from lawsuits.[78]

Physicians began to seek the same right. They attempted to force their patients to accept liability waivers. Many doctors asked prospective patients to sign a bond agreement that stipulated a monetary penalty in event of a malpractice charge. Patients could still sue for malpractice, but they would presumably lose more than they would gain.

As early as 1847 an editorialist advised Ohio physicians to use bonds to slow the "endless vexations and pecuniary losses" of malpractice suits.[79] By the early 1850s the practice had become common. In 1851 the *Medical Examiner* advised that "[i]t would perhaps be the course of prudence for surgeons among us to keep blank bonds on hand."[80] A New York physician reported that he refused to treat the fractures and dislocations of working-class patients, perceived as the group most likely to sue, without first receiving an indemnity bond. He warned his colleagues, "Surgeons! Take an indemnity bond or never treat a poor patient."[81] In 1854 a writer for the *Boston Medical and Surgical Journal* lamented:

It is almost a wonder that any surgeon, now-a-days, can be found . . . to remedy a deformity, or treat a case of injury, without a bond from the patient or his legal guardian that he shall not be subjected to a suit for damages in case he should fail to make the patient as whole and perfect as he was when he came from the hands of the creator.[82]

The injuries generally convinced patients to sign bonds, and the penalties were usually high enough to discourage them from violating the agreements. Horace Nelson, a New York physician, recounted his use of bonds. In December 1855, when Louisa Bovee brought the physician her two-year-old child, who had fractured and dislocated his right arm, Nelson informed the woman that he would not treat the child unless she signed a bond agreement guaranteeing not to sue for malpractice. Bovee declined, and the physician refused to treat the child. After conferring with her friends, the woman returned and signed the bond agreeing to pay the physician $2,000 if she attempted to sue him for malpractice. In Nelson's words, "We are now safe, let the result be what it may."[83] Nelson published a copy of the bond as a model and promised that it was good in any state of the Union.

STATE OF NEW YORK
Clinton County

KNOW all men by these presents, that I, Louisa Bovee, the wife of Orrey Bovee, am held and firmly bound to Doctor Horace Nelson, practicing surgeon, of the town of Plattsburg, in the county of Clinton, in the sum of two thousand dollars, lawful money in the United States, to be paid to the said Doctor Horace

Nelson, his executors, administrators, or assigns: for which payment, well and truly to be made bind myself and each of my heirs, executors, and administrators, jointly and severally firmly be these presents. Sealed with my seal. Dated this 28th day of December, 1855.

Whereas the above bounden has this day applied to, and requested the said Horace Nelson, surgeon aforesaid, to set and reduce a fracture and dislocation of the right elbow joint of Charles Leonard Perry, an infant, and now child by adoption of the above bounden, the wife of Orrey Bovee, of Plattsburg.

Now therefore, the condition of this obligation is such, that if the above bounden Louisa Bovee, shall well and truly keep and bear harmless, and indemnify the said Horace Nelson, surgeon aforesaid, his executors, administrators and assigns, and every other person or persons aiding and assisting him in the premises, of and from all harm, let, trouble, damages, costs, suits, actions, judgments, and executions that shall be brought against them, or any of them, as well for the setting of said arm, as for the inconvenience and damage arising therefrom. Then this obligation to be void, else to remain in full force and virtue.

Louisa Bovee [L.S.]

Sealed and delivered in presence of F.L.C.
Sailly, Justice of the Peace[84]

The careful, legalistic exactness of Nelson's bond mocked Blackstone's notion that medical men held a position of public trust or that they were honored public servants with a special legal and social status. Instead, the written pretreatment agreement resembled, more than anything else, a carefully framed labor or commercial contract. Moreover, the bonds reinforced the Jacksonian contention that physicians were no different from mechanics or merchants, a contention that ran counter to the elite physicians' claims that medicine was a profession and not a trade.

The use of bonds was probably the surest method of discouraging litigation by contract. Physicians also experimented with contracts that completely immunized them from lawsuits. These agreements were identical to the court-supported liability waivers of common carriers. Some physicians attempted to mimic the corporations, in the shadow of the 1850s rulings, and to contract away their liability with a waiver. The legal status of these arrangements, however, was ambiguous. Apparently absolute waivers of liability were used only infrequently.

In 1861 an Ohio man caught his leg in the flywheel of a sawmill. Physician G. W. Butler examined the injured leg and discovered a compound fracture and crushed bone. The doctor warned the patient that the injury was severe and dangerous and declared, "I will not treat your case at all unless you clear me of all responsibility for results." According to witnesses, the injured man replied: "I will clear you of all responsibility. Go on and treat my case. I would rather have you than anyone else." Butler placed the leg in a bandage and splint but after eight days, the leg required amputation.[85]

The patient sued for malpractice, claiming that the physician cut off the circulation by bandaging the limb too tightly. The defense attorney argued that the physician had made a "special contract" with the patient absolving him of all liability. The patient's attorney

quoted legal decisions to show that Dr. Butler could not make a special contract with the patient, by the terms of which he obligated himself to render to the patient anything less than the ordinary amount of "skill, care and attention," [and] that such a rule would do away with all standards of comparison and prove positively injurious to the interests of society.[86]

Ignoring the arguments of the defense attorney, the trial court judge accepted the validity of the pretreatment agreement. "This contract," the judge ruled, "the defendant had the right to make." If the jury believed that an agreement existed, then Butler was not liable for the loss of the leg. The jury retired and after a "short absence" decided in favor of the physician. A jubilant editorialist declared that if other physicians and courts used contractual immunity, "damages in favor of the plaintiff could not in one case in a hundred be obtained."[87]

Despite this isolated case, there was no simple solution to the malpractice problem. The use of agreements to contract away liability was rare. No specific case ruling on special contracts and malpractice existed. However, the near consensus of both legal and medical writers suggested that absolute abrogation of medical liability never completely took hold and was in any case discredited by the 1860s. Similarly, judges' use of contractual language in defining the origin of physicians' malpractice liability declined in the late 1850s.

The Road Not Taken

Doctors generally resisted the notion of contractual relationships with patients because it conflicted with the image of the physician as a public servant with a distinct social status. Most physicians maintained this position even though some contractual doctrines, such as waivers and caveat emptor, could have mitigated verdicts in malpractice cases. Worthington Hooker warned the profession: "The relation of a physician to his employers is not shut up within the narrow limits of mere pecuniary considerations. There is a sacredness in it, which should forbid its being subjected to the changes incident to the common relations of trade and commerce among men."[88] Valentine Mott, an eminent surgeon, enjoined physicians, "Condemn with relentless severity the slightest deviation from professional honor. Find no excuse for anyone who is induced to lower our noble art to the condition of a trade."[89]

A Massachusetts medical society committee on malpractice agreed that the doctor-patient relationship was different from purely economic arrangements. "[T]he peculiar relations always existing between physician and patient and the fact of one of the parties always being more or less incapacitated by his condition, have put out of sight the idea of a bargain, as in other engagements between man and man."[90] The committee concluded, "It cannot be conducive to the interests of the patient that his relation with his physician should be reduced to a mere business transaction, to be judged as a contract, to which the employer strictly holds the employed."[91]

Medical and legal writers also attacked the use of bonds and contractual waivers. Constitutional commentator Joel Parker, at one time a Massachusetts supreme court judge and professor of medical jurisprudence at Dartmouth, deflated the hopes of those physicians who believed that bonds and contracts could protect them from malpractice suits. In an 1855 lecture he explained that while there was no specific ruling on the issue, there was "very grave doubt whether it [contractual waivers of liability] could have any legal operation to exempt the physician from any responsibility." Since waivers from liability remained a controversial practice in other areas of law, Parker felt that the best a physician could hope for was that the agreement, despite its feeble legitimacy, might discourage the disgruntled patient from instituting a suit.[92] Physicians undoubtedly recognized the legal weakness of contractual waivers, but most opposed it on other grounds.

One physician argued that while some of his colleagues required bonds or contracts before treatment, he objected on the grounds that "in the first course, such refusals would be considered *inhuman;* and in the second, it is *undignified* for a well qualified profession to resort to such expedients" (original emphasis).[93] Both John Elwell, in his *Medico-Legal Treatise on Malpractice* (1860), and John Ordronaux, in *The Jurisprudence of Medicine* (1869), agreed that physicians could not use special contracts to protect themselves. According to Ordronaux, "With or without such a bond he may still be prosecuted for malpractice. And certainly, it is a derogation of his dignity, and an attempt on his part to pervert the equitable streams of jurisprudence."[94]

Ordronaux, a physician and a lawyer, was one of the leading nineteenth-century experts on medical jurisprudence. He declared unequivocally that "the duty of professing skill and exhibiting correctness in prescribing is not created by contract, but by law." Drawing on the status of physicians in Roman law, Ordronaux explained that "the very nature of the relation between patron and client raised it [the doctor-patient relationship] above all taint of a mercenary character." Professional responsibility had its origins in "the character publicly assumed by him who undertakes to render such services."[95] Liability flowed not from the financial arrangement between doctor and patient, but from the practitioner's public assertion that he was a physician. According to Ordronaux doctor-patient associations could never be considered "purely commercial" relations. He argued that they are "far higher in their nature and consequences than any transactions relating merely to tangible materialities and have always been regarded among civilized nations as not amenable to any similar standards of value." He held that physicians owed their patients duties and responsibilities that could never be enumerated in or bound by a contract.[96]

Ordronaux shared the assumptions of the majority of judges in the late 1850s and 1860s. Although some earlier courts had referred to the doctor-patient relationship as contractual, most judges objected. A Massachusetts judge observed that medical relationships were fundamentally different from purely commercial contracts. He noted, "In ordinary cases the employer governs or directs the employed; but in surgery the case is reversed. The surgeon controls the patient."[97] In an 1854 case the plaintiff's attorney declared that the physician had agreed to treat his client "for a reasonable reward and compensation." The trial court judge, in his charge to the jury, however, stressed that this

> is not an action on a contract, although the declaration alleges what the law would make a contract . . . still the action is not for a breach of contract, it is not for the defendant's not doing what he agreed to do, but for doing what he did agree to do in a careless, unskillful and negligent manner as to injure the patient.[98]

In the void left by the decaying and abandoned writ system, lawyers and judges yearned for rationalized, general legal principles on which to base legal duties. Midcentury treatise writers segregated legal duties into the broad categories of tort and contract. Traditional, status based responsibilities were generally classified as torts.[99] Francis Hillard wrote the first American treatise on torts in 1859, dividing all legal actions into contracts, torts, and crimes. *Contracts* were based on "agreements, express or implied"; *torts* were "injuries of omission or commission, done to individuals"; and *crimes* were "injuries done to the public or the state."[100] Hillard included malpractice actions under the heading of tort because the offense was a breach of public duty.[101] Amasa Redfield and Thomas Sherman's important 1870 treatise on negligence also reflected the noncommercial basis of physicians' liability. Redfield noted: "The peculiar nature of the services which a medical man undertakes to render, often makes it his duty to continue them long after he would gladly cease to do so . . . Even if his services are gratuitous, he must continue them until reasonable time has been given to procure other attendance."[102]

Appellate court judges in the 1850s and 1860s reinforced the notion that a physician's responsibility emanated from his status as a professional instead of from the relationship created by a contract. They resurrected the contractual language of *Bowman*, *Leighton*, and *Cater* only when the suit involved a conflict over fees or an explicit promise to cure.[103]

In *Smith* v. *Overby* the Georgia supreme court sanctioned a jury charge that explained that "the profession of physician is one of the learned professions . . . as in all professions in which learning and skill are required, the rule of law is, that every person who enters into a learned profession undertakes to bring to the exercise of his profession, a reasonable degree of care and skill."[104] The Illinois supreme court in *Ritchey* v. *West* affirmed that "when a person assumes the profession of a surgeon, he must in its exercise, be held to employ a reasonable amount of care and skill."[105] Finally, the majority in *McNevins* v. *Lowe* ruled:

> If a person holds himself out to the public as a physician he must be held to ordinary care and skill in every case of which he assumes the charge, whether in the particular case he has received fees or not. But if he does not profess to be a physician nor practice as such, and is merely asked his advice as a friend or neighbor, he does not incur any professional responsibility.[106]

Overby, *Ritchey*, and *McNevins* were characteristic enunciations of malpractice case law in the mid 1860s. In contrast to some of the rulings of the late 1840s and early 1850s, they banished contractual language from the doctrine of physicians' liability. A doctor was liable for his actions not because he treated a patient for pay, but because he held a special status in society: that of the public servant, the professional.

The midcentury flirtation of malpractice law with contractual language and doctrine and the eventual abandonment of the notion reflected the paradoxical legal and social position of the American medical profession. The English precedents that informed early malpractice law were based on the assumption that physicians' liability arose from their special status as public servants. English common law prohibitions on suits for fees reinforced the noncommercial nature of the doctor-patient relationship. American courts never accepted the idea of honorarium pay for physicians, but they did initially follow the malpractice rulings that implied status-based responsibility.

But by the late 1840s the contractual view of society was strong enough in America to threaten the status-based foundations of malpractice law. The Lockean, contractual character of a written constitution and the ideals of individualism and free trade in the Jacksonian era provided a fertile environment for contractual interpretations. Jacksonian commentators condemned traditional professional groups as antidemocratic and aristocratic. Other status-based relationships were being undermined as well: master-servant doctrine, aspects of family law, and the responsibility of common carriers all increasingly reflected the influence of contract mentality. In suits for fees, the legal relationship of doctor and patient had already evolved from status-based responsibility to contract-based liability. Since Jacksonian Americans refused to grant physicians either legal status through licensure or social status through respect, it is not surprising that some judges, attorneys, and physicians began to integrate market-oriented principles into malpractice law.

Ultimately, judges and treatise writers turned away from contractual views of the doctor-patient relationship because the medical world was not analogous to the commercial world. Physicians retained remnants of the idea of the doctor as public servant and sought to raise the profession morally above the position of a mere wage earner. The contractual model of two presumably equal bargainers engaging in a "meeting of the minds" does not accurately describe medical relationships. Patients who have injuries cannot freely consent to treatment in the same way a merchant freely decides to purchase commercial goods. Lay people approach the doctor-patient relationship with less knowledge about their illness, their probability of recovery, and the various treatments and medical alternatives than the physicians with whom they deal. Therefore, notions such as caveat emptor are not appropriate or effective safeguards on the "medical market."[107] Open self-interest from both parties is an acknowledged component of contractual theory. This doctrine is inconsistent with the majority of the medical community's self-image as a benevolent profession.[108]

The banishment of the will theory of contract from mainstream malpractice law had ethical and practical consequences. It was an implicit recognition that physicians filled an extraordinary role in society that severed the doctor-patient relationship legally, ethically, and economically from the principles that usually governed the exchange of goods and services in a laissez-faire economy. In the late twentieth century medical practice, institutions, and organization have increasingly taken on the appearance of commercial enterprises.[109] A growing segment of the population and the profession have again begun to view physicians as mere businessmen, and medical ethicists debate the viability of contract as a source of professional responsibility. In addition patients and scholars have attacked paternalistic features of the medical relationship and argued in favor of a greater role for the patient in the decision-making process. Emphasis on individual rights in many areas of American life and law since the 1950s has nourished this trend and elevated the value of patient autonomy. Consequently, contract is again discussed as a potential source of professional liability.[110] Medical commentators debate the sufficiency of contract as a guide for acceptable and ethical behavior, and some of the debates surrounding twentieth-century malpractice reform have suggested the use of contract as a basis for defining physicians' liability.[111] Society, the courts, and the profession may have to decide again the way in which the doctor-patient relationship is different from a commercial contract.

CHAPTER 8

The More Things Change...: Medical Malpractice, 1865-1900

Medical malpractice suits continued to plague physicians through the last third of the nineteenth century. Although the suits and professional responses to them changed in several important respects, the trends and patterns that surfaced between 1835 and 1865 endured. The rate of suits and size of the awards climbed steadily but undramatically. The evolution of medical practice and organization generated new suits and new issues. Ceaseless development of medical innovations inspired new litigation in the same way that the improvement in fracture treatment engendered suits in the first half of the century. Physicians blamed many of the same factors they had earlier for the litigation, but changes in the legal and medical professions altered the ways in which they interpreted and dealt with the suits. Appellate courts modified traditional legal doctrines, but the central tenets of malpractice law remained unchanged. While physicians' experience with malpractice between 1865 and 1900 followed a course set earlier in the century, the suits, responses, and the law reacted to the evolving medical environment and represented a prelude to the twentieth century.

"The Malpractice Fad Is upon Us"

Physicians were relieved when malpractice rates apparently abated somewhat during the tumultuous 1860s. Editorials and reports of cases appeared less frequently in medical journals. One observer at the end of the decade remarked that the problem was "not so urgent as it was a dozen years ago, when the number of actions for malpractice brought against respectable practitioners caused a good deal of excitement in the medical profession."[1]

The respite, if it did indeed occur, did not last long. By the early 1870s, patients were suing physicians with renewed vigor. In 1872 William Wey, the president of a New York medical society, commented that while suits were "rarely found" in previous years, "of late they have become frequent. At nearly every sitting of the court one or two of such cases are on the calendar."[2] A writer in 1875 remembered that "suits were prominent between 1833 and 1861 in New York and also in the Eastern and Western states." He lamented that "[l]atterly the danger to the profession has been revived."[3] Another physician echoed that writer's concern the following year and reported that "the increase in the number of suits for malpractice has again become a topic of remark in medical circles."[4]

After suffering two suits in the 1870s, Eugene Sanger, a prominent physician in Maine, produced a detailed report of malpractice litigation in the state. Sanger's study, published in 1879, surveyed approximately six hundred regular physicians practicing in Maine and yielded the most evocative picture of the phenomenon in the nineteenth century.[5] Of the 114 doctors who responded to Sanger's query, only 58 had escaped prosecutions, threats of suits, or "the payment of smart money." The remaining 56 physicians had been threatened with legal action 55 times and actually charged with malpractice a total of 70 times. In 6 of those cases prospective defendants paid amounts ranging from $100 to $350 rather than allow a trial to commence.[6] Sanger argued that the true number of suits for the state was undoubtedly higher since many physicians "from modesty and disinclination to advertise their contributions to the patients and attorneys, who follow us as the shark does the emigrant ship, have failed to report."[7]

Through the remainder of the century physicians and other observers claimed that doctors were subjected to an ever-increasing burden of litigation. Not only did malpractice accusations continue without relief, but most writers believed that each decade was more litigious than the last. The problem was evident enough for an editorialist in

Popular Science Monthly (then a serious effort to popularize science) to complain in 1880 that "[s]o jealously does the law guard the lives and persons of the people, that every time the physician writes a prescription, or the surgeon makes an incision, he takes his purse, his liberty, or, perhaps, his life in his hand."[8] A physician in 1882 warned that "[t]he increasing frequency of the allegations of malpractice in surgery makes the subject one of great interest to nearly every physician."[9] In a paper read before the Chicago Medical Society in 1886 a local doctor declared that "[i]t is undoubtedly a fact that such suits against physicians are on the increase. The New York *Medical Record* has reported a large number in the course of the past year, and a glance over the Court-record in this city will prove the correctness of my assertion, as far as Chicago is concerned."[10] In 1889 a San Francisco physician reported that "the majority of physicians who have attained prominence and a reputation for ability to pay, have been obligated to defend suits of this character."[11] The following year, a Michigan physician informed the state medical society that "[t]here is scarcely a surgeon of any great experience in this State who has not either been prosecuted or many times threatened."[12] By the turn of the century the *Colorado Medical Journal* reported that "[t]he malpractice fad is upon us."[13]

Although appellate decisions are an uncertain measure of trial court litigation rates, they tend to confirm physicians' impressions that malpractice suits were a growing problem. State appellate courts handled a gradual but clearly increasing stream of cases as the decades passed: 1860–1870—25; 1870–1880—45; 1880–1890—47; 1890–1900—77; 1900–1910—116.[14] While figures on the absolute number of cases remain elusive, appellate rates and contemporary commentary demonstrate that frequent malpractice suits were a persistent phenomenon from the late 1830s through 1900. Malpractice rates in the last third of the century were a natural continuation of the course and patterns set in antebellum America.

Awards

While immense monetary penalties did not become popular until much later, damage awards slowly climbed between 1865 and 1900. Before

1865 the typical malpractice judgment was between $200 and $800, with a few isolated verdicts reaching $1,000 to $3,000.[15] In contrast, 38 sample malpractice awards between 1870 and 1900 averaged $2,492 (see appendix B). Of those judgments 19 were over $2,000, and only 13 were $1,000 or lower.[16] Some of the larger awards included: $3,000 to a woman who lost her nose, allegedly to cancer treatment, in 1876; $4,000 for a fracture case in 1872; $4,000 in 1882 for a man who lost the use of his legs; $7,000 for a fracture case in 1885; $12,000 for a fracture case in 1894; and $5,000 for a destroyed penis in 1895.[17] Other studies suggest a similar range in the judgments, most awards falling between $1,000 and $5,000.[18] Physicians' average income in this period probably ranged from about $1,000 to $1,500 per year when the average annual income for all nonfarm occupations averaged about $500.[19]

Appellate courts refused to overturn or reduce the gradually increasing malpractice judgments as excessive. While it is true that most malpractice defendants escaped paying any penalty, the awards, when compared to the income of physicians, were substantial. If the sample judgments averaging over $2,000 are a reliable gauge, they represent a larger portion of physicians' income than the typical award of the late twentieth century. For example, in 1971, at a time when the median income of physicians hovered around $100,000 a year, 59.9 percent of all malpractice awards were under $3,000.[20] Late nineteenth-century appellate courts deferred to the damages awarded at the trial level and generally stepped in only if the jury had "acted under some bias, prejudice, or improper influence, or [had] made some mistake of fact or law."[21] In 1882 the Indiana supreme court affirmed a judgment against a physician for rendering a patients' legs useless. The court compared the $4,000 award to other personal injury judgments against railroads, corporations, and municipalities and ruled that it was not excessive.[22] Similarly, when a physician was penalized $5,000 for carelessly tying off a newborn infant's penis instead of its umbilical cord, the Texas supreme court upheld the judgment.[23] The increases are significant but not dramatic and underscore the continuity with the first two-thirds of the century.

"Impecunious Clients of Desperate Lawyers"

Medical spokesmen reiterated many prewar assumptions. In the early 1870s and 1880s physicians continued to blame their colleagues for many of the suits. Writers complained of "traitorous" and careless physicians. In 1872 Stephen Smith declared that "the origin of nearly every trial for alleged malpractice may be traced to the reckless criti-cisms which rival practitioners pass upon the works of one another."[24] But as the profession became less contentious and more solidified, both socially and organizationally, there were progressively fewer charges of physician complicity in malpractice suits. By 1900 editorials rarely cited intraprofessional competition as a major source of the suits. The development of professional solidarity and the threat of suits encour-aged physicians to close ranks.

While doctors ceased blaming their fellow physicians for their mal-practice woes, the profession remained convinced that the poor and laboring classes were their chief tormentors.[25] The contention that base greed, and status and class resentment generated suits remained central in malpractice editorials. In the 1840s New York physicians lived in fear of malpractice juries filled with "anti-rent communists" and antiprofessional Jacksonian Democrats.[26] In the 1870s physicians still claimed that suits and convictions were generated by "an ill-feeling toward the 'class to which the defendants belong.' " This prejudice, a physician explained in 1872,

is simply the same idea which led to the robberies and murders of the [1871] Paris Commune, and which is subversive of justice everywhere. For it repre-sents simply the jealousy and hate which unsuccessful and poor men bear those who have been, through greater industry and care, more fortunate than they in amassing wealth . . . What is it but robbery to adjudge against all evidence, the equalization of property between the doctor and his patient.[27]

The Paris Commune had ballooned anxieties of American elites, and was widely considered a symbol of the evils of out-of-control democracy. The antebellum upper and professional classes feared egal-itarian farmers and workers. In the late nineteenth century, this anxi-ety metamorphized into elite alarm over social unrest, labor agitation, and Granger, Alliance, and Populist political organization. Frightened social and political elites in the late 1800s decried the common man's supposed perversion of democracy and declining respect for property and authority.[28] Physicians in the 1840s had believed that excessive democracy engendered antipathy toward regular practitioners and helped incite malpractice suits. By the 1890s doctors were even more convinced that their malpractice problems originated in one class of patients and jurors. As one writer explained, "the evil is in the imperfection and prejudices of the twelve specimens of human nature, in the jury box."[29]

Although class resentment existed against physicians, theirs was a profession whose average income still placed most of its members in the middle class. Much of the public antipathy toward doctors emanated from the physicians' quest and demands for the social status and prestige of learned professionals. Jacksonians had been repelled by the quasiaristocratic, gentlemanly ideals espoused by early nineteenth-century physicians. Many later patients also resented what they saw as the unjustified pretension and affected dignity of physicians.

Indeed, much as it had attempted to do earlier in the century, late nineteenth-century professional advice literature counseled physicians to maintain a social distance from their patients to inspire respect. D. W. Cathell, who published *The Physician Himself* in 1881, cautioned that intimacy and familiarity between doctor and patient has a "levelling effect and divests the physician of his proper prestige." Dressing or acting poorly in public, according to his professional etiquette guide, would "show weakness, diminish your prestige, detract from your dignity, and lessen public esteem, by forcing on everybody the conclusion that you are, after all, but an ordinary person."[30] Many Americans, even in this period of growing but grudging respect for experts, deeply resented the notion that one segment of society merited special deference.

But the impulse behind the hostility of some segments of the population to the profession had clearly begun to shift. In the early nineteenth century, antagonism was status-based and had arisen from antiaristocratic, democratic sentiments. Physicians had hoped to translate enhanced status into both honor and gold, but progress was slow. By the late nineteenth century, however, physicians' income had begun to rise. Status-based antagonism remained and probably continues to inspire negative feelings toward doctors to the present. But hostile attitudes toward physicians, where they existed, increasingly merged with class-based resentment. As medical incomes slowly increased, segments of the population took offense at physicians both for making more money than the average American and for believing that they were better than common people. Late nineteenth-century doctors contended that these feelings were more prevalent in working class and lower income families.

Observers continued to maintain, as they had before the Civil War, that "[p]hysicians and corporations are too often regarded as fair game by the impecunious clients of desperate lawyers." The young physician, they argued, soon had "his ardor dampened, his interest cooled, [and] his humanity chilled by the hardness of the material with which he comes in contact . . . he is gradually brought to regard a certain class of his patients as seeking to enrich themselves."[31] Sanger's study of malpractice in Maine seemed to confirm the profession's informal profile of the typical plaintiff. Out of the 70 malpractice charges he investigated, only 8 plaintiffs were able to pay the costs of the trials and allegedly "very many of them were drunken and shiftless persons."[32] Most physicians agreed that "nine times out of ten the plaintiff is a pauper who has received the gratuitous service of the man who [sic] he prosecutes."[33] Sanger warned that physicians would have to give up surgery entirely, select among reliable patients cases that promised favorable results, or "leave the afflicted poor, as barbaric tribes do, to perish by the wayside." In disgust and anger, he drafted a proposal to the Maine Medical Association: "Resolved, that with the existing laws on civil malpractice, it is unsafe to practice surgery among the poor." The medical society approved the resolution.[34]

Physicians felt that working class juries were particularly susceptible to the lawyer who "alluded to the poor laboring man and [the] rich doctor."[35] Sanger's 1878 report warned of "the dangers from jealous rivals, tricky lawyers, [and] impecunious and ignorant patients."[36] In the first half of the century physicians seldom accused lawyers of fomenting or aggravating malpractice suits. They considered lawyers a sometimes ill-informed but "noble sister profession."[37] Physicians and lawyers in the early nineteenth century were often drawn from the same social class, and both groups suffered under the antiprofessional Jacksonian sentiment of the 1830s and 1840s.[38] This social and political common ground may have bred sympathy between the professions.

But beginning in the 1870s physicians began to revile lawyers for their alliances with working-class plaintiffs. By the 1880s the composition of the bar was more socially diverse, more lawyers came from the working classes, and the two professions lost some of their natural social affinity.[39] It also appeared to many observers that lawyers were relinquishing their traditional role as protectors of social order. James Bryce, an English visitor, was one of the most perceptive commentators on American culture and public life in the late nineteenth century. He confirmed in 1889 that American lawyers had "it in their power to promote or to restrain vexatious litigation, to become accomplices in chicane, or to check the abuse of legal rights in cases where morality may require men to abstain from exacting all that the letter of the law requires."

It was evident to Bryce, however, that lawyers no longer fulfilled the function they had in the age of Jackson and de Tocqueville. Bryce reported that "taking a general survey of the facts of to-day, as compared with those of sixty years ago, it is clear that the Bar counts for less as a guiding and restraining power, tempering the crudity or haste of democracy by its attachment to rule and precedent, than it did then."[40] While law remained an essentially conservative discipline, the social attitudes of its membership had become less monolithic, and an increasing number of individual attorneys were willing to serve non-elite interests and clients.

In addition, the number of lawyers in the country increased in the last half of the century, from about 22,000 in 1850, to 60,000 in 1880, to 114,000 in 1900. Per capita estimates increased from 1 lawyer to 947 inhabitants in 1870 to 1 lawyer for every 662 inhabitants in 1990.[41] This increase put financial and competitive pressures on American lawyers and may have driven some to create business in previously objectionable ways.[42] In 1877 a physician exclaimed, "A surplus of cheap and briefless lawyers fosters the spirit of litigation, which is too common among certain classes of all large cities."[43] Another complained, "Every large city is overrun with petty lawyers, who have little or nothing to do, and are always willing to undertake any suit whether there is the least prospect of getting something out of the defendant."[44]

The abusive language physicians hurled at plaintiffs' attorneys reflected the depth of the medical profession's new fears. Physicians called malpractice lawyers "human vampires," "sharks," "jackals," "legal adventurers," "pettifogging attorneys," and "shysters."[45] An Illinois physician in 1882 claimed that unethical lawyers played the central role in inciting unwarranted suits. He warned his colleagues to beware of the "wily machinations of that most despicable of creatures (excepting only the quack doctors)—the shyster lawyer like the vulture hovering near his prey, he quietly watches for his opportunity to pounce upon the purse of the unwary surgeon."[46] Theoretically the common law offenses of *barratry* and *maintenance* prohibited lawyers from inciting suits. Many states, however, required a succession of abuses before charges could be filed, and the remedies were rarely invoked.[47]

Yet while lawyers were an important component in the prosecution of malpractice cases, they did not constitute the chief cause of increased litigation. Lawyers were, at most, a match to a fuse, taking advantage of a situation that already existed, another immediate, aggravating cause of the late century suits. The fundamental explanation remains the social and cultural factors behind the patients' proclivity to sue.

Physicians also denounced the increased use of contingency fees by lawyers representing poor patients. The no award–no fee arrangements were not unknown in the first half of the century. Contingency arrangements were probably a more informal and less visible aspect of legal practice. Antebellum physicians rarely mentioned contingency arrangements in conjunction with malpractice suits. In the last third of the century they became a common, if incompletely accepted, legal practice. Lawyers who employed them charged no initial fee and generally received 50 percent of the damage award if victorious. Defendants could not benefit from the contingency fee's new popularity, and defendant physicians felt that they were at an immediate disadvantage. Physician/defendants had to pay for their legal help and expert witnesses whether they won or not. In addition, doctors believed that contingency fees, by giving the attorney an interest in the case, tended to increase the amount of damage awards. William Wey, president of the New York State Medical Society, argued that attorneys who encouraged suits and then represented patients under contingency fee arrangements were "mischief makers" and "professional pirates" who were themselves guilty of the "most flagrant malpractice."[48] The *Medical Times* editorialized "that respectable members of the legal profession do not usually accept contingent fees from poor people."[49]

The author's comment expressed the profession's persistent belief that malpractice suits were a subtle form of class and status conflict. It also strengthened the overt and underlying connections between physicians and other personal injury defendants, especially corporations. Like physicians, railroads and other corporations became the frequent object of damage claims beginning in the late 1830s. And, like physicians, railroads and other corporations suffered an intensified rate of personal injury litigation as the century progressed.[50]

As in malpractice suits, a growing number of plaintiff's attorneys accepted contingency fees when attacking corporate defendants. Although the United States Supreme Court upheld the legitimacy of contingency arrangements, elite members of the legal profession condemned them.[51] Supreme Court Justice Joseph Bradley declared that the fee "degrad[ed]" the profession and encouraged "stale or doubtful claims, which would have never been put in suit." Bradley argued that "the peace of society is disturbed by litigation fomented by those who are not concerned with it."[52] Thomas McIntyre Cooley, one of the most influential constitutional theorists of the century, claimed that the fees produced "a feeling of antagonism between aggregated capital on the one side and the community in general on the other."[53]

Observers like Bradley and Cooley feared the social unrest and class disquiet of the late nineteenth century and believed that contingency fees gave poor, resentful plaintiffs the means to attack possibly innocent targets. According to these writers, Granger and Populist groups harassed propertied interests in state legislatures while individuals sued corporations for personal injuries. Some poor patients were able and willing to sue physicians who represented status, privilege, and gradually increasing income.

Although conservative critics overstated the threats of supposedly irresponsible democracy, it is easy to see how physicians believed that corporations and doctors were the working class' common victims. As a physician complained in 1890, "Suits against corporations, lumber companies, railroad companies, and against physicians are pursued to an alarming extent."[54] During the Jacksonian period popular feeling ran against banks and physicians. By the 1870s railroads had replaced financial corporations as the focus of popular resentment, but physicians remained villains through both periods.

Remedies

Physicians in the late nineteenth century proposed a variety of remedies and strategies to discourage malpractice suits. Antebellum doctors were concerned with the problem, but their proposed solutions were fewer, less sophisticated, and generally useless. One writer mocked an 1853 Massachusetts Medical Society pamphlet on the causes and prevention of malpractice. "After reading the ten pages, we defy anyone to determine from the directions therein contained, how to stop a lawsuit." The commentator maintained that the only sensible solution was to refuse to treat certain classes of patients and injuries.[55] Indeed, physicians at midcentury had regularly threatened to shun complex fracture cases if the danger of lawsuits did not diminish, but apparently only a few actually resorted to this tactic. Most doctors probably felt that turning away injured patients would violate the humanitarian foundation of medical practice. The large number of regular and irregular practitioners in Jacksonian America also undermined the effectiveness of this remedy. If one physician abandoned fracture treatment, a competitor was always waiting to take his business. Finally, avoiding dangerous cases was an inappropriate response to the malpractice "crisis" because only a small minority of patients sued their physicians. By refusing to treat a whole class of cases, a physician turned his back on many deserving patients and their fees.

Medical observers in the 1840s and 1850s had believed that raising educational standards and reinstituting licensure would raise the profession's status and contain the malpractice threat. By 1900 the profession was well on its way to accomplishing these goals. Almost all the states that had abandoned licensure before the 1850s had re-established it by the turn of the century. The early reenactments, coming in the 1870s, were weak and did little to control access to practice or raise standards. But by 1880 half the states enacted licensure laws, and by 1901 every state imposed punishment for unlicensed practice. The various state legislatures created boards to administer the statutes. Some jurisdictions required an examination as well as a medical diploma for certification. Other states established curriculum and content requirements for the medical schools from which license applicants would be accepted. These reforms eventually reached and surpassed the goals of antebellum medical leaders who wished to elevate the practice of medicine.[56]

Antebellum observers also felt that improved medical education would slow malpractice rates by producing better physicians and by raising the public perception of the medical community. In the last third of the century physicians could point to a virtual revolution in medical training. Beginning in the 1870s schools such as Harvard, Pennsylvania, Michigan, and Johns Hopkins pioneered a new model of medical education. While proprietary institutions and absurdly low standards remained prevalent, the outlines of the modern medical school were becoming clear. Leading schools lengthened the course of study from one to as many as four years. Basic science was integrated into the curriculum and pace-setting schools employed full-time, salaried professors. Administrators initiated higher entrance qualifications and more demanding requirements for graduation. Aspiring physicians at these select schools were required to study an expanded range of subjects including chemistry, physiology, and the young science of bacteriology. Equally important, schools such as Harvard symbolized a fundamentally different approach to medical training. Under the inspiration of university president Charles Eliot, it abandoned its slavish reliance on the traditional lecture method and dramatically expanded the role of "hands on" laboratory training and research. Led by Johns Hopkins, elite medical schools also introduced extensive programs in clinical clerkships in which students could work directly with patients in hospital wards. These reforms, originating in only a handful of institutions, had inspired imitation by less prestigious schools by the 1880s and 1890s. By the time Abraham Flexner published his 1910 report condemning the state of medical education, the scandalous schools of the antebellum years were rapidly closing their doors and were clearly destined for extinction.[57]

While the public distrust reserved for learned experts had aggravated the antebellum malpractice problem, and while physicians felt that they were popular targets often merely because they claimed expertise, by the late nineteenth century the Jacksonian hatred of the expert and the professional had virtually passed. Americans began to accept and value the role and judgment of the expert on a variety of subjects. Engineers, geologists, scientists, and agricultural specialists proliferated. Social scientists influenced all levels of government. Academics and intellectuals were expected to play a central role in shaping late-century progressive reforms. The status and influence of the expert/professional grew as an increasingly complex industrial society posed new questions and demanded innovative responses.[58]

Physicians had believed that inadequate education, the lack of effective licensure, and antiprofessional bias helped generate litigation in the first half of the century. These conditions dissipated in the 1880s and 1890s, but suits continued to thrive seemingly unabated. Universal licensure, educational reforms, and the rise of the expert appear to have had very little impact on patients' propensity to sue in the latter part of the century. These factors had indeed helped multiply the number of suits in the 1840s, but they did not constitute a fundamental cause of the litigation. They merely incited and aggravated litigation in a specific historical period. Therefore, when they weakened late in the nineteenth century and virtually disappeared in the twentieth, suits did not automatically cease. Instead, other aggravating factors arose, and the cultural presuppositions that nurtured and encouraged the phenomenon remained.

The medical community was pleased with the progress it had made in education, licensure, and status, but it searched for effective tactics to combat the continuing law suits. While it is difficult to determine how much late nineteenth-century proposals influenced litigation rates, physicians developed additional and more comprehensive remedies than their midcentury counterparts. Most solutions were designed to stem the tide of suits without undermining the profession's dignity or blunting its boldness in practice. In a bizarre 1871 anecdote a fracture patient told his physician that he was going to sue for his badly healed leg. The physician asked the man in to his office and offered to operate on the limb and repair the deformity. When the patient refused, the doctor knocked him down, chloroformed him, and operated on the unconscious man's leg. The patient recovered and dropped all charges against the physician. A medical journal praised the physician for having "the courage that many surgeons lack, to take the responsibility to act, and look up the law afterward."[59] Of course, such approaches to the malpractice problem were rare.

Some physicians believed that charging fees to all patients would discourage litigation. D. W. Cathell continued the refrain that poor patients were not to be trusted. He counseled his colleagues that "you should not induce people to let you involve yourself for their benefit without being paid for your risk and responsibility." Cathell believed that physicians should "send [their] bill promptly to dissatisfied patients who are threatening to sue for malpractice." "[S]ending your bill," he reasoned, "gives you a better position before the public, and raises an issue that checkmates theirs. *Do not fail to charge the full amount in all such cases*" (original emphasis).[60] A writer for the *New York Medical Journal* also believed that immediate payment of fees was "the best possible safeguard" against suits for malpractice.[61] Such commentators reasoned that, having paid for services, patients would be less tempted to escape the charges by a claim of malpractice. Moreover, they hoped that a paid fee implied satisfaction and would be a good defensive weapon in court. Despite the internal logic of this tactic, the realities of medical practice rendered it unfeasible. As part of their self-image and public posture, physicians were expected to perform a certain amount of charity practice and could never completely eliminate non-paying patients.

Late nineteenth-century physicians seldom blamed their colleagues for instituting suits because strengthened professional organizations were able to soften the competitive medical market of the 1840s.[62] Local and state medical societies with enhanced moral and professional authority discouraged physician complicity in malpractice suits. Stephen Smith advised that the class of physicians who incited litigation "should be stricken from the membership of every medical organization."[63] During the late 1870s medical societies condemned "ill advised" remarks against "brother practitioners" and ostracized members who willingly supported unjustified suits. The Baltimore Medical and Surgical Society encouraged its members to "be on the safe side by actively discouraging all such suits."[64]

The medical community's campaign proved increasingly successful and effective. In 1879 a medical journal celebrated that a malpractice plaintiff had been "unable to produce a single medical witness to controvert the testimony" of the defendant.[65] By 1890 attorneys and the public believed that members of the medical profession invariably supported the malpractice defendant. Physicians, however, responded that "[t]his is as it should be because we can always give the benefit of the doubt to the right side."[66]

William Mayo, patriarch of the famous Rochester, Minnesota, surgical clinic, typified the new jurisprudential posture of many American physicians. By the 1880s malpractice suits were common in Minnesota. Leaders of the state medical society pointed out that doctors' performances as expert witnesses often made physicians accomplices in the prosecutions. They warned that doctors should learn to defend their colleagues in court if they hoped to reduce the overall risk of malpractice charges. Mayo followed the society's advice. Ironically, he testified at the trial of a long time personal and professional enemy, Edwin Cross. A patient claimed that the physician had bandaged his arm too tightly, cutting off the circulation and leading to an unwarranted amputation. Mayo not only testified in behalf of Cross, but also devised the substance of the defense attorney's position. He argued that the vital arteries of the arm may have been damaged as a result of the fracture itself and not from the treatment. The jury found Cross innocent of wrongdoing. When a Rochester man asked Mayo why he so fervently defended a despised enemy, the physician responded: "I did it for the profession, not for him, damn him."[67] This variant of professional solidarity was not nearly as common in the first half of the century.

As frequent malpractice prosecutions became a permanent feature of American medical practice, advice literature became more prevalent. "It would seem," a speaker told the Medico-Legal Society of New York in 1876, "that the most efficient means of prevention (and consequently self-protection) is enlightenment—the knowledge of medical men of their legal duties and liabilities, the knowledge among courts of law and the general public of the possibilities of surgical skill."[68] Medical jurisprudence was not a standard part of medical school curricula in the 1870s, and interested physicians had to rely on handbooks and professional journals for practical guidance.[69] John Elwell's 1860 treatise on malpractice was reprinted three times before 1881, John Ordronaux published his erudite *Jurisprudence of Medicine* in 1869, and Milo McClelland added a huge compendium, *Civil Malpractice: A Treatise on Surgical Jurisprudence*, in 1877. McClelland reprinted extensive samples of Frank Hamilton's fracture tables and representative court decisions that "are inaccessible to medical and legal practitioners."[70] His commentary explained the various legal dangers of medical practice.

Physicians turned to professional periodical literature for more practical advice and strategies. One article counseled that the prospective defendant, "instead of spending the best of his time in vehement vituperation against 'ungrateful patients,' [and] 'rascally lawyers' . . . should select one or more *good* lawyers, and go to work, for a malpractice suit means business." The defendants should coach their attorneys on the medical and anatomical aspects of the case. They should also interview their expert witnesses, with their attorneys, before the trial. Juries, according to the article, "are partial to print [so] it is better to have six recorded cases similar to the one under trial, than the testimony of six experts."[71] Medical journals also instructed defendant physicians in finer points of trial tactics. Writers warned doctors to avoid continuations of trials from one term to another because valuable evidence could be lost. They also cautioned physicians "not [to] reveal to the outside world what you propose to use as evidence." Plaintiffs' depositions, a potential source of defense evidence, should be taken as early as possible.[72]

Some writers suggested that physicians could best avoid and defend suits by practicing more "ethical" medicine. According to McClelland,

To avoid the annoyance of such suits, surgeons should above all be *honest* with their patients, apprising them of the difficulties of the case and the uncertainties of perfect results . . . They should be candid in regard to their deficiencies, claiming no more than they can perform, no more knowledge than they possess.[73]

Other advisors admonished physicians to drink moderately or not at all and to "[b]e careful in profession deportment" and diligent in their studies, keeping up with every advance. Cautious physicians warned patients to be aware of "all the possible contingencies which may result from the operation—be they ever so remote." One writer claimed that the reputation of a good, safe physician "will make imputations of malpractice too improbable to be feared."[74]

Most observers doubted that ethical and careful medical practice alone could immunize physicians against malpractice charges. Physicians claimed that most suits and threats of suits were only "blackmail" ruses to extort money from reputation-conscious doctors. They argued that the majority of plaintiffs and lawyers did not intend for their cases to reach the courtroom but hoped to settle out of court. The generally low quality of the plaintiff's expert witnesses and evidence and estimates of high acquittal rates lent credibility to physicians' claims. Eugene Sanger's study of 70 prosecutions revealed that only 9 plaintiffs won judgments.[75] Estimates of acquittal sometimes reached 9 out of 10. Many physicians, according to one journal, would have been "unwilling to face the annoyance and publicity which a trial necessarily entail[s]." When John Reese, an expert on medical jurisprudence, faced a malpractice case, he "might have easily avoided [it] by listening to the base proposals of the plaintiff's counsel to pay blackmail." Instead, he decided, in his words, "fearlessly [to] meet this lawsuit."[76] Lewis Sayer and Samuel Gross, two renowned surgeons, were also sued in the early 1870s, and, when the plaintiffs' attorneys attempted to settle the cases out of court, both men declined. Gross "scornfully refused . . . deeming it but just to himself and to the profession to defy the threats of the plaintiff."[77] When Reese, Sayer, and Gross decided to face public trials, their prosecutors were left with embarrassingly weak cases and lost.[78] After the trials, the *Medical Record* entreated, "Let us hope that the manly conduct of Professors Gross and Reese . . . as well as the results of the suits . . . has convinced the most unscrupulous among the legal fraternity that members of our profession, one and all, intend to resist all attempts to levy black-mail upon them."[79]

The message was clear. Most charges were unwarranted and indefensible. The strategy and best hope of lawyers representing patients was to coerce the payment of "smart money." When the physician refused, he won his case and was congratulated in the pages of medical journals. In 1889 a Chicago attorney agreed with the medical profession's impression of the typical case. After discussing the issue with some of his colleagues, the lawyer reported that "nine-tenths of the malpractice suits were blackmailing suits."[80] Wealthy surgeons, especially, preferred to pay off plaintiffs, but editorialists argued that this was a "mistaken policy, and has a tendency to propagate an evil which in the end reacts with terrible force upon the poorer surgeon."[81] In his commentary on malpractice McClelland sternly declared that "[u]nder no circumstances should suits be compromised." After performing their duty, surgeons "owe it to their professional brethren to let the matter be tried by the letter of the law."[82]

Mutual Protection

Physicians slowly realized that profound problems were involved in fighting every case in court. Not only did they risk their reputations, but legal fees and court costs were often prohibitive. One doctor, a defendant in two trials in the 1870s, reported that he paid $1,100 to lawyers and witnesses and for other court costs.[83] Sanger's study suggested that legal expenses, even in successful cases, averaged between $800 and $1,000.

The threat of suits, financial realities, and the commitment to fight all charges of malpractice inspired the innovation of group defense organizations. Although mutual insurance groups had been suggested earlier in the century, the notion was opposed or ignored until the 1880s.[84] In 1886 a speaker before the Chicago Medical Society proposed the creation of an association of local physicians. Each physician, after screening by the society, would contribute five dollars a year to the legal defense fund. The association would hire a prominent law firm to defend any suit arising against a member physician. According to the speaker,

Let it be known that the individual physician is backed by the financial and moral support of a few hundred of the best physicians, and aided by the best legal talent available, and he will be let severely alone by the dregs of society who constitute, almost without exception, the blackmailing element in our professional life.[85]

Although some critics believed that a mutual defense association would "prejudice the jury against the defendant, just as corporations do," the notion gained many converts in the 1880s. In 1887 a writer for the *Boston Medical and Surgical Journal* agreed that physicians should combine to protect themselves from the "ever impending risk of actions for malpractice." Because the lawsuits were expensive in time, money, and anxiety, "there are few [physicians] who can afford to engage in defending a suit[;] an easy and honorable way of avoiding it is afforded."[86] By the first decade of the twentieth century legal defense associations sponsored by medical societies had become popular in many areas including Massachusetts, New York, Chicago, Cleveland, and Detroit. Local medical societies embraced the innovation with enthusiastic, but ultimately unfounded, optimism. In 1902 the *New York State Journal of Medicine* predicted that "through the publicity given to a suit or two, the blackmailing variety of malpractice suits will cease. This class constitutes 97% of all such suits brought."[87]

The medical defense leagues were closely linked with the rejuvenated professional organizations of the late nineteenth and twentieth centuries. Physicians became increasingly confident that they could slow malpractice rates by group concert. Although malpractice insurance from private companies did not become available until after 1900, group defense associations could promote medical malpractice insurance, and societies could castigate or even expel members who instigated or participated in suits. As medical societies gained control over licensure, access to hospital practice, and referrals, they could increasingly dictate individual physicians' behavior.[88]

Organized physicians were also becoming a more potent political force, and many medical societies began to investigate legislative remedies to malpractice suits. Sanger had argued that "[s]urgery is indispensable to the welfare and existence of the human race, and by saving life and utilizing labor it is a productive industry which needs the protection of general law." He reasoned that there were laws protecting other public service entities, such as towns, and contended that physicians too deserved a shield so that they could practice their "hazardous" but essential calling.[89] Similarly, a writer declared in 1882 that the "medical profession surely is entitled to, and I believe possesses, sufficient influence if we would exert it, to have framed and passed by our legislative bodies such laws as we are justly entitled to for our protection."[90] Medical societies drafted prospective legislation that would retain the jury trial but institute a system by which the court, and not the parties to the suit, would select the expert witnesses who would be paid by the county.

Sponsors believed that this provision would decrease contradictory and interested testimony and protect defendants.[91] Other proposals included recommendations that prospective plaintiffs be forced to post bonds to cover the costs of the trials. Physicians designed this alteration with the litigious poor patient in mind, but they held little hope of getting it passed in state legislatures because it clearly prevented legitimate claims from being brought by destitute patients.[92] Some proposals merely asked for the legitimation of contractual waivers, while others petitioned for the complete abolition of the jury trial. The Ohio Medical Association, for example, sent a draft to the legislature to introduce trial by arbitrators to the state. The three-man board would consist of physicians: one chosen by the plaintiff, one by the defendant, and the third by the other two arbitrators.[93] The spate of proposals in the last two decades of the century was not fruitful. State legislatures did not tamper significantly with the malpractice trial procedure, and the process remained essentially unchanged.

The Law of Malpractice

Despite the significant leap in appellate decisions between 1865 and 1900, the basic requirement that physicians "must possess and exercise that degree of skill ordinarily possessed by members of the profession" proved durable, and the doctrine governing malpractice law stable.[94] Courts reaffirmed the antebellum doctrine that physicians did not automatically guarantee cures, but were responsible only for failures if they specifically promised success. Most of the many appellate cases in the late nineteenth century dealt with important, but mechanical, procedural, pleading, or administrative issues or questions of fact relating only to individual cases.[95] State appellate judges also ruled on the proper role of expert testimony. Witnesses could offer or comment on hypothetical examples to illustrate a case, but they could not draw conclusions on the facts of the case. When witnesses crossed this indistinct line, appellate judges usually overturned the lower court decision.[96]

Appellate courts also reversed decisions in which the verdict seemed to be unjustified by the evidence. For example, in 1875 a jury ignored the overwhelming evidence that a physician had properly set a plaintiff's broken arm and awarded $4,000. The Minnesota supreme court reversed the decision and granted a new trial because "the jury did not accept and weigh as they should have done, the testimony of the experts, but must have acted independently of it."[97] Appellate judges also overturned decisions when trial judges made inappropriate conclusions on the facts when defining the legal issues for the jury.[98]

These rulings were important and occasionally significant as precedents, but they did not set a basic common law doctrine of malpractice. Courts were frequently asked to rule on the different instructions on the "ordinary standard of skill and care" requirement offered by trial judges. Appellate courts overturned convictions in cases in which trial judges required the skill of a "thoroughly educated physician." State supreme court judges also rejected trial definitions that demanded that the physician possess and exercise "full skill" or be liable for "any want of skill." These definitions set too high a standard for medical practitioners.[99] When a trial court announced that a physician must take advantage of the "most accredited sources of knowledge," the Iowa supreme court overturned the judgment because it demanded too high a standard of education.[100] An Illinois appellate court reversed a decision in which the trial judge instructed the jury that if the physician "could have learned the nature of the injury, and applied the proper remedy, and failed, he is liable."[101] And in 1873 the Indiana supreme court overturned a conviction in which the judge stated that a physician is "required to exercise care and skill proportionate to the character of the injury he treats."[102] Courts rarely held that the degree of care and skill set by the trial court was too low.

Although rulings varied slightly from state to state, courts in the late nineteenth century accepted a variety of substitutes for the term *ordinary* in the description of the physician's responsibilities. Appellate judges generally agreed that terms such as *average skill, fair knowledge and skill, adequate care,* and *reasonable skill* were legitimate synonyms for *ordinary.*[103] These modifications did not materially alter the doctrine, and judges continued to use midcentury precedents to frame the basic charge to malpractice juries. Late nineteenth-century treatises on malpractice and tort reflected this continuity. Elwell's work on malpractice remained essentially unchanged through four editions. Thomas Cooley's 1906 *Law of Torts* held that a physician must "possess ordinary skill, [and] that he will use ordinary care."[104]

The organizational structure of medical practice changed considerably between 1865 and 1900. These developments led to new forms of malpractice litigation that required adaptation to but no significant alteration of the common law. The absolute dominance of the solo practitioner began to wane, and physicians joined with other physicians, clinics, and hospitals. The increasing importance of technology and access to new techniques encouraged hospital practice.[105] As hospitals became increasingly important in the delivery of medical care, they also became targets of malpractice charges.

In the first two-thirds of the century most hospitals were charity institutions. The legal doctrine concerning charity hospitals was clear and unequivocal. Although physicians who practiced at the institutions were liable for their conduct under the standard rules of law, the hospital was virtually immune from prosecution. If the charity hospital had "exercised due care in the selection of its agents, it [was] not liable for injury to a patient caused by their negligence."[106] Group practices, like the Mayo Clinic, and for-profit hospitals also proliferated. When malpractice plaintiffs sued such an institution, judges held it responsible only for exercising the same "due diligence in securing skillful and careful medical men for the treatment of its patients."[107] Railroad companies occasionally organized hospitals or clinics to provide free care for their employees. Courts generally gave the railroad company medical facilities the benefit of the doctrine that applied to other medical institutions.[108]

The *Medical Record* applauded these rulings, rejoicing that "[f]or the first time, therefore, in our history, hospitals are protected from suits of this kind, for it is not to be conceived that any respectable hospital will not exercise due diligence in securing careful medical officers."[109] For once, medical optimism regarding a facet of malpractice was well founded. Institutional plaintiffs in the late nineteenth century appeared easily to convince courts and juries that they had carefully selected their staff physicians. Judges had effectively eliminated the doctrine of *respondeat superior* from hospital malpractice law, which held that employers were liable for the actions of their employees. This generous move allowed most medical institutions to escape payment of damages in the nineteenth century.

The last third of the century brought other notable changes to the law of malpractice. In antebellum America the physician could not be held liable for malpractice if a patient contributed in any way to his or her injury. The doctrine irregularly influenced verdicts in the first half of the century, perhaps because it was a complete defense and entirely absolved the defendant/physicians.[110] Some jurisdictions continued to accept a strict interpretation of contributory negligence in malpractice cases through the end of the century. In 1883 the Indiana supreme court ruled that "a party seeking to recover for an injury must not have contributed to it in any degree, either by his negligence or the disregard of a duty imposed upon him by his physician."[11]

Some appellate judges, however, fashioned exceptions to the strict doctrine of contributory negligence. In *Carpenter* v. *Blake* (1878) a physician's attorney asked a trial judge to instruct the jury that if the patient had contributed in any degree to his injuries, then the physician was not responsible even if he too was negligent. The judge refused, and the jury found the physician guilty of malpractice. The physician claimed that he had not received the full benefit of the contributory negligence defense. The highest court in New York, however, ruled that once the physician had negligently caused an injury, "The most that could be claimed on account of any subsequent negligence would be that it should mitigate damages."[112] Therefore, it was possible to hold a physician responsible for damages even if the patient aggravated the injury.

An *Albany Law Journal* writer explained in 1881 that while irresponsibility and complicity of patients usually absolved the physician from all liability, the doctrine could have limits if the respective responsibilities could be "separated."[113] This version of contributory negligence was especially important in cases in which patients refused to follow the instructions of their physicians. In *Dubois* v. *Decker* (1891) a physician failed to leave enough tissue to cover the protruding bone on the stump of a patient's amputated leg. Consequently, the leg took an inordinately long time to heal, and the patient was left with protruding bone. The physician argued that the patient had refused to leave the leg in the prescribed position, declined to take medicine, and eventually left the physician's care without permission. The jury found the physician guilty of malpractice, and he appealed the decision to the New York high court. Citing *Carpenter* v. *Blake*, the court ruled that even though the patient's actions may have aggravated his injury, the physician was clearly liable for the initial malpractice. Therefore, the patient's actions could only mitigate and not preclude the damage award he would receive from the physician.[114]

This modification of the contributory negligence doctrine worked against physicians/defendants, but its effect was not clear cut in malpractice cases. Each state developed variant patterns and bodies of case law, but a clear bending of the doctrine occurred in most jurisdictions. In the first half of the century, when the doctrine was in its strictest form, judges and juries may have avoided its use in malpractice cases because it completely indemnified physicians from liability. Though the softened version of contributory negligence threatened physicians because it abandoned absolute immunity, it may have indirectly helped some defendants by forcing juries and judges to reduce damage awards.[115]

Locality Rule

Another late innovation in malpractice law bestowed unambiguous advantage to the defendant/physician. Through the first two-thirds of the century physicians and scattered trial court judges contended that malpractice defendants should be measured against the "ordinary" practitioners in the locality in which they practiced. These physicians and jurists argued that because physicians' skill, education, and experience differed greatly in various geographic locations and social surroundings, it was unrealistic and unfair for a jury to require the same degree of skill from a small-town rural practitioner as from a hospital-based physician with a thriving urban practice. Notwithstanding these arguments, trial judges only irregularly instructed juries to calculate medical competence by community standards, and appellate courts never made the notion part of malpractice doctrine.[116]

Despite appellate judges' midcentury indifference toward the locality rule, physicians and treatise writers campaigned for its inclusion into case law. Although Hillard's treatise on torts did not mention the doctrine, Elwell supported community standards in 1860, as did Ordronaux in 1869 and McClelland in 1873.[117] In his important 1870 treatise on negligence Redfield cited no precedential support, but asserted that "the standard of skill may vary according to circumstances, and may be different even in the same state or country." He explained that in "country towns, and in unsettled portions of the country remote from cities, physicians, though well informed in theory, are but seldom called upon to perform difficult operations in surgery, and do not enjoy the greater opportunities of daily observation and practice which large cities afford." Therefore, he declared, it would be unreasonable to expect the same degree of skill from both classes of physicians.[118]

In the wake of these writings the idea became more widely cited both in trial and appellate courts. William Wey called for the universal use of the locality rule in 1872. He noted that "[t]his estimate of skill has undoubtedly been considered by courts in holding physicians to account for alleged malpractice, and in this way we are enabled to reconcile the otherwise conflicting character of the principles of law by which such cases have been governed."[119] Appellate judges began to discuss the community standard rule in their judicial opinions. The Kansas supreme court quoted Elwell in *Teft* v. *Wilcox* (1870) and stated that "[t]he opportunities by reason of locality, or other circumstances, of one portion [of the profession], may be many times more favorable than those of another; and the responsibilities resting upon them would be correspondingly greater."[120] The court, however, reversed the physician's conviction on other grounds. Therefore, the comments were probably obiter dictum and did not have the precedential legitimacy of an explicit ruling on the issue.

In *Smothers* v. *Hanks* (1872) the locality rule gained further ground. The Iowa supreme court overturned a malpractice conviction because the trial judge's instructions to the jury required that the defendant be a "thoroughly educated" physician. The majority opinion, citing

Redfield, noted that "[i]t is also doubtless true that the standard of ordinary skill may vary even in the same state, according to the greater or lesser opportunities afforded the locality for observation and practice."[121] Like *Teft* v. *Wilcox*, the discussion of the community standard in *Smothers* was superfluous to the central issue of the appeal, and its comments were probably not binding as precedent.

The locality rule did not yet command universal approbation. A dissenting judge in *Smothers* argued against the locality rule because "In this age [1872] of books, professional periodicals, and mails . . . [w]e may safely say that no respectable surgeon, wherever he may be, is uninformed of the progress and discoveries in his profession."[122] In 1876 the Vermont supreme court accepted a trial court charge to a jury that incorporated the rule without comment. But the following year the Indiana supreme court refused to overturn a conviction on the grounds that the trial judges did not invoke the community standard.[123]

The Massachusetts supreme court provided the definitive precedent in support of the locality rule in the 1880 case of *Small* v. *Howard*. A man living in a small country town of about 2,500 residents severely cut the inside of his wrist with a piece of glass, severing vital arteries and tendons. The local physician, a common general practitioner, possessed no extraordinary surgical skill to treat complicated and unusual injuries. When the injury healed imperfectly, the patient sued. Over the objection of the patient, the trial judge instructed the jury that the physician was "bound to possess that skill only which physicians and surgeons of ordinary ability and skill, practicing in similar localities . . . ordinarily possess." The jury found for the physician, and the patient appealed the case to the state supreme court, claiming that the community standard rule lowered the standard of care required of a physician. In *Small* v. *Howard* the Massachusetts appellate court ruled that it was a matter of common knowledge that physicians in small country towns and villages could not possess the same degree of skill as their big city counterparts, who had more opportunities to observe practice. The Massachusetts court made this decision despite the fact that an eminent physician, who could have treated or advised on the case, lived only four miles from the patient's community.[124]

The decision in *Small* v. *Howard* ushered in an almost universal, one-hundred year acceptance of the locality rule. The doctrine was a powerful defensive weapon for defendants. It explicitly lowered the standard of skill courts required of some physicians. In its strictest form, it limited the pool of expert witnesses to those physicians who practiced in the same community as the defendant. While it is not certain why appellate courts included the locality rule in the common law definition of malpractice, several reasons are possible. The burgeoning number of appellate cases allowed judges to fine-tune aspects of the law that had been previously ignored. Judges may have sympathized with the plight of the medical profession and wished to provide physicians with a defensive strategy. But the doctrine was not pure judicial creation. The locality test had been invoked by scattered trial court judges throughout the century and other areas of law recognized the relevance of local custom. Perhaps most importantly, appellate judges in the last third of the century became increasingly receptive to ideas promulgated by treatise writers who argued that a physician's standard of skill should be judged by local circumstances.

As professional opposition to malpractice suits solidified, local medical societies gained coercive power over their members. Some societies threatened prospective medical witnesses with expulsion if they gratuitously testified against other practitioners. It was sometimes difficult for plaintiffs to secure qualified expert testimony. Physicians who were the sole practitioners in their communities could likewise escape prosecution by asserting that they set the standard of care for their location or by claiming that there existed no legitimate expert witnesses to participate in the trial. Judges soon recognized the difficulties of narrow applications of the locality rule and modified the doctrine.[125] Appellate courts ruled that physicians should not be protected merely because they were the only practitioners in a particular community. They altered the locality rule so that physicians were required to exercise the skill and care of doctors in "similar" or "like" surroundings.[126] This adjustment in the doctrine made it easier to prosecute isolated practitioners and to secure expert testimony in communities where physicians had established a united front against malpractice prosecutions.

In *Pike* v. *Honsinger* (1898) the New York high court relied on traditional precedent, incorporated the changes of the previous twenty

years, and articulated the precepts that would guide malpractice litigation through much of the twentieth century. The case began when
George Pike, a middle-aged farmer, was kicked in the knee by his
horse. Pike drove his wagon to the medical office of Willis T. Honsinger. Honsinger was absent, but his physician son set Pike's leg with
adhesive plasters and splints. Pike returned home but sent for the elder
physician a week later. Honsinger examined the man's badly swollen
leg and told him that he had ruptured a ligament. The injury resisted
the physician's treatment over the next two months, but he allowed
Pike to continue working the fields. Pike repeatedly complained that
the leg was not set correctly. The following spring Pike consulted
another physician and learned that he had broken his kneecap. Honsinger admitted that he had initially misdiagnosed the injury, but told
Pike that "the leg was not worth a damn and he would have to go into
something besides farming." Pike reported that he could lift only half
as much as he could before the accident and that he was unable to walk
on plowed ground.

Pike sued Honsinger for malpractice. The physicians who testified
at the trial contended that Honsinger had not only erred in diagnosing
the injury, but also should have watched the patient more carefully
and kept him in splints and out of work for at least a year. The trial
court judge did not allow the jury to decide the case, but directed a
verdict in favor of Honsinger. Pike appealed, and in 1898 the New
York appellate court agreed that he deserved a new trial and that the
judge should have allowed the jury to decide the case.[127]

The appellate judges also restated the "well-settled" tenets of American malpractice in "simple language." The court explained that a
physician was required to possess "that reasonable degree of learning
and skill that is ordinarily possessed by physicians in the locality where
he practices." In addition, every physician must "keep abreast of his
times." If the physician departed from "approved methods, in general
use" and injured a patient, he would be liable for damages. Once
physicians began treatment, they were required to exercise their "best
judgment" and "use reasonable care and diligence."[128] Although *Pike*
did not represent a significant departure from previous decisions, it
served as a key precedent because it clearly delineated the physician's
legal responsibilities.[129] The *ordinary* standard of care remained unchal-

lenged as the central tenet of American malpractice law until the last third of the twentieth century. Then, important rulings suggested that in some instances advanced technological procedures could be required, even if accepted ordinary practice did not customarily make use of the technology.[130]

New Treatments, New Suits

Treatment for fractures and dislocations continued to generate the vast majority of malpractice suits through the beginning of the twentieth century. In 1884 a writer estimated that nine-tenths of all suits were the result of orthopedic treatment.[13] This figure was undoubtedly inflated. Fracture and dislocation cases probably constituted between two-thirds and three-quarters of the litigation.[132] Some physicians claimed that fracture cases remained common because those injuries plagued manual laborers, "the poorer and more ignorant classes . . . precisely the class to be influenced, by their necessities, to be open to the golden dreams of plenty which a crafty and unscrupulous lawyer knows how to awaken."[133] The explanation is somewhat more complicated. The first rise in suits had been fueled in part by the rapid advances in fracture treatment between 1820 and 1850 and the accompanying exaggerated expectations.[134] Frank Hamilton and his supporters had believed that his 1850s fracture tables would reduce suits for this class of treatment. They reasoned that statistical demonstrations of standard treatments and standard results would lower the expectations of both physician and patient and provide evidence of what constituted competent practice.

Despite their popularity and wide dissemination, Hamilton's tables and other similar strategies could not suppress suits. The device was ultimately ineffectual because it could not take account of perpetual and rapid medical technological advancement. For instance, the profound advances of antebellum fracture treatment had been rapidly superseded. In the 1870s plaster of Paris dressings for fractures became "the rage, and, he who neglected to employ it was an 'old fogy' or was not up in progress." The initial reports of plaster of Paris recalled the early responses to the advances of the prewar years. Enthusiasts claimed

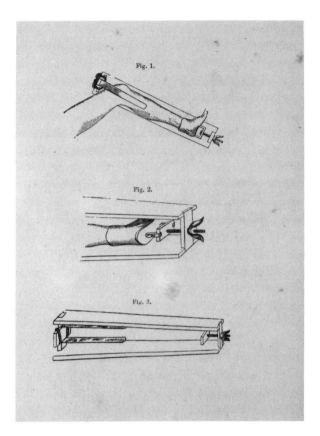

Fracture box with adjustable footboard. From Frank Hastings Hamilton, "Report on Deformities after Fractures," TAMA 10 (1857): 239–453. (Courtesy of the Historical Research Center, Houston Academy of Medicine, Texas Medical Center Library, Houston, Texas.)

perfect cures with no shortening or deformity. The innovation brought about a "revolution" in fracture treatment. Older methods were "thrown out as relic[s] of barbarianism." Results, however, did not always meet expectations, and less proficient physicians did not always achieve optimum results. Consequently, the "revolution" of plaster of Paris gave rise to suits, just as the advancements of the first half of the century had.[135]

In fractures as well as other areas of medical treatment innovation often ran through the cycle of advancement, inflated expectations, limited successes, and lawsuits. By the 1890s fracture treatment had undergone yet another "revolution," provoked in part by the advances in aseptic surgery, and physicians predicted total cures. In 1893 one writer reported, "So great and rapid have been the advances in the treatment of compound fracture within the last two decades that, when properly managed, now many lives and limbs are spared which were formerly sacrificed, distortions obviated, inflammation, necrosis, tetanus, and mortification prevented." Recent advances had brought "the treatment of compound fractures to well-nigh a state of perfection."[136] Despite the steady therapeutic advancement, suits for fractures continued.

Although fracture cases dominated malpractice litigation, new classes of suits arose out of new and improved practice. After the invention of the ophthalmaloscope (a device that allowed physicians to view the structure of the retina) in 1851, ophthalmology made rapid and dramatic advancements in the last half of the century. Accompanying this progress, suits against physicians for eye damage became more common between 1880 and 1900.[137] Obstetric and gynecological surgery also flourished in these years. Surgeons performed a variety of new and sometimes unjustified operations on women's reproductive organs, from clitoridectomies to hysterectomies.[138] Ovariotomies were especially popular. These treatments contributed to the rising and increasingly diverse body of suits. Beginning in the 1880s, women sued physicians for removing their ovaries unnecessarily or without their consent. They also accused physicians of malpractice for complications following obstetrical surgery.[139]

Malpractice suits for general surgery proliferated more slowly than those for ophthalmology, obstetrics, and gynecology. Surgical procedures were neither rational nor predictable. Few physicians attempted major operations, and patients rarely expected positive results. The specters of infection, hemorrhage, and incompletely understood shock haunted operating theaters and blocked physicians' paths into the abdomen, chest, and head. As late as 1876 Samuel Gross reported that "enlightened" American surgeons "scrupulously refrained from the employment of the knife whenever it was possible." According to

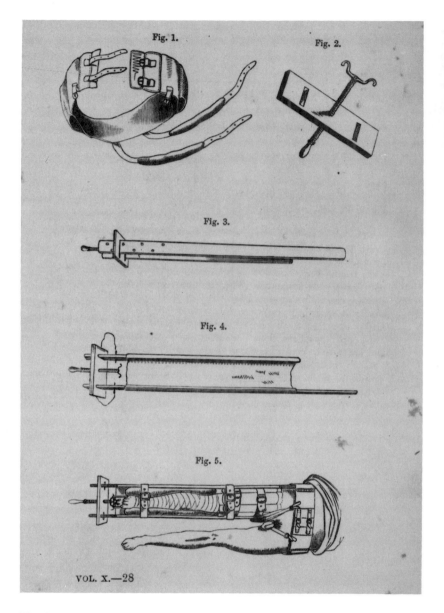

Flagg's apparatus for thigh fractures with straps and adjustable footboard. From Frank Hastings Hamilton, "Report on Deformities after Fractures," TAMA 10 (1857): 239–453. (Courtesy of the Historical Research Center, Houston Academy of Medicine, Texas Medical Center Library, Houston, Texas.)

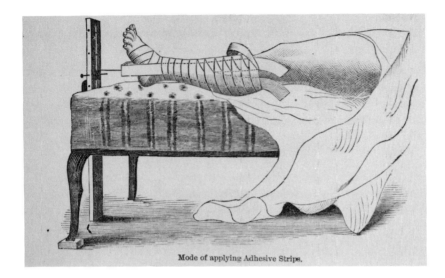

Mode of applying Adhesive Strips.

Adhesive strip with counterweight method of setting leg fractures. From Frank Hastings Hamilton, Principles and Practice of Surgery *(1886). (Courtesy of the Historical Research Center, Houston Academy of Medicine, Texas Medical Center Library, Houston, Texas.)*

Gross, surgeons limited themselves to "the great family of external diseases and accidents."[140]

Rampant postoperative infections, especially in hospitals, had severely restricted the range and frequency of surgical procedures. Joseph Lister began to popularize his theories on antiseptic surgery in the late 1860s. Using the findings of microbiologist Louis Pasteur, Lister recognized that microorganisms in the air could produce infections in compound fractures, wounds, and surgical incisions. But his ideas were not perfected, accepted, or practiced on a wide scale in America until the late 1880s. Lister had devised a cleansing system by which the wound, the instruments, and even the air in the operating room would be sprayed with a carbolic acid solution. Although the procedure had its merits, it was not always effective, and sometimes it was even harmful. In addition, many surgeons failed to appreciate the importance of the scrupulous disinfection ritual. They dropped instruments and continued surgery without resterilization. Some probed wounds with their bare hands after wiping their brows or noses. Other surgeons regularly wore operating smocks imbued with the gore of previous operations. Moreover, American physicians only gradually accepted the value of developing sterile surgery and opposed the notion of the germ theory in general. The retarded development and proliferation of sterile operating practices slowed surgical progress. With few surgical procedures attempted and muted optimism, malpractice charges were seldom associated with general surgery before the 1880s.

Eventually, however, physicians accepted the essentials of Lister's findings and developed more effective devices and procedures, such as steam and dry heat sterilization. In addition, in the late 1880s and 1890s surgeons and their staffs adopted sterile caps, gowns, masks, and rubber gloves. Medical inventors developed more efficient and sanitary stainless steel instruments. Physicians discovered that the use of finer needles and silk thread led to better results and developed new techniques and devices to control surgical bleeding. Finally, more sophisticated analgesics and anesthetics made surgery easier and safer.[141]

Consequently, by 1890, with the advent of sterile practice, innovative procedures, and new instruments, body cavity surgery slowly became a viable and attractive frontier for physicians.[142] Physicians were quicker to perform nonemergency appendectomies. Hernia operations and simple surgery on the stomach, intestines, liver, and kidneys became more feasible.[143]

These accomplishments raised the general status of physicians, but paradoxically also increased their vulnerability to dissatisfied patients. By the first decade of the twentieth century patients were suing their physicians for surgically related offenses such as leaving sponges, broken needles, or drainage tubes in closed incisions. Ignorance of deadly surgical shock, as well as other mysteries, however, blunted surgical daring and progress. Therefore, the frequency of surgical procedures and the certainty of regular success remained low. General surgery cases would not surpass orthopedics as the most common source of malpractice suits until the 1940s.[144] By then, physicians had solved some of the problems associated with operative shock and infection, advanced surgery further, and helped create the impression that many procedures were routine.

The speed of medical innovation created opportunities, dilemmas, and dangers for physicians. Advancements increased the medical community's status, but they also intensified expectations and demands. Doctors who attempted new, nonstandard procedures did so at their own peril. A physician who practiced in the late nineteenth century noted in his memoirs that "[t]he surgeon who is advancing his profession with new work stands at all times over the muzzle of a loaded gun hoping that no lawyer will come along to pull the trigger."[145] In the early 1880s one woman sued a physician after an operation, claiming that the carbolic acid solution, intended as a sterilizing agent, had complicated her injury.[146] The physician, who had apparently attempted to keep pace with enlightened practice, instead found himself in court.

At the same time new procedures surfaced and were accepted faster than many physicians could assimilate them. In 1886 a physician used chloroform to sedate a young girl on whom he was performing eye surgery. During the operation, the patient flinched, and the surgeon's knife blinded her. The girl's parents sued, claiming that standard practice demanded the use of cocaine as a local anesthetic in similar operations. The physician had consulted an 1880 treatise on eye surgery that prescribed chloroform; in 1884, however, a German surgeon, for the first time, had successfully employed cocaine anesthetic in the same procedure. By 1886, when the surgery took place, cocaine had already superseded general anesthetic as the accepted analgesic in such operations.[147] Physicians could be penalized for adopting a new practice too soon, but they were also under immense pressure, intellectually, professionally, and legally, to keep pace with rapidly evolving medical technology.

Willhelm Röentgen, a German researcher discovered the power of x-rays in November 1895. The inexpensive and simple construction of the device put it in the hands of many American physicians within weeks. Physicians as well as the public not only appreciated the invention's intrinsic interest but also immediately realized its diagnostic and jurisprudential potential.[148] One optimistic writer declared that "[t]he courts can show endless histories of grave errors committed, to the detriment of poor patients and not the less of poor practitioners; but the discovery of William Conrad Röentgen has come to do away with all of this." Another observer predicted in early 1896 that x-rays would play a leading role in "cases where surgeons are charged with having overlooked a fracture, or dislocation, where no such injury is present." Many writers, as early as 1897, recommended its use in every orthopedic case.[149] They were partially correct. Radiological evidence often convinced juries that physicians had acted properly.

X-ray technology, however, proved a mixed blessing for malpractice defendants. By 1896, less than a year after the discovery, patients were suing physicians for failing to take x-rays before fracture treatment.[150] In 1897 a writer for the *American X-Ray Journal* realized, "If it increases our diagnostic ability it also increases our responsibilities, and we are more exposed to suits for malpractice in fractures, particularly if deformity exits and we have not used it as a means of diagnosis." Other patients and their attorneys secured x-rays as evidence of a physician's incompetence. Novelty x-ray studios, which pandered to public curiosity, often provided the photographs for dissatisfied patients and their lawyers. One physician claimed in 1899, "Ever since its discovery, especially in the last year, every malicious person who can scrape up enough money for a shadow-graph [x-ray] is having one taken for the purpose of bringing a damage suit for personal injuries or malpractice."[151] The first x-rays introduced into a Maine court were supplied by the plaintiff in a malpractice case. A music teacher in Bangor claimed that her physician had failed to treat a backward dislocation of her forearm properly. After examining an x-ray, three expert witnesses agreed that the injury had not been properly treated. The jury found the physician guilty and charged him $500.[152]

X-ray results, especially from the early equipment, were often distorted, inconclusive, and vulnerable to subjective interpretation by "innovative attorneys." The reliability and objectivity of x-ray evidence depended on the angle of the photograph, the thickness of the flesh surrounding the bone, the quality of the plate, and the length of the exposure. Fractures could exist without x-rays' revealing evidence of the injury. Conversely, enterprising lawyers soon discovered that merely flexing one's muscles could severely distort results and simulate injuries.[153]

Primitive machines, rudimentary knowledge, and inexperienced operators led to burned patients and provided another source of malpractice suits. Burns could be induced by excessive electric current or duration of exposure, frequent repetition, or individual differences of sensitivity. In October 1897 a patient sued a physician after an x-ray machine produced "a severe dermatitis." The physician was attempting to locate a foreign object lodged in the patient's body. The patient's attorney claimed that the physician had been careless and that the technology was insufficiently developed to use for this purpose.[154] In less than five years after its discovery x-ray technology evolved from a promising medical and legal tool, to a source of suits when physicians failed to use it, to a cause of suits when it injured patients. X-rays and other more sophisticated technology would play a much larger role in malpractice litigation in the twentieth century.

Malpractice suits between 1865 and 1900 invoked the same legal doctrine, followed the same patterns, and provoked many of the same responses as they had in the prewar years. Appellate judges fine-tuned traditional common law doctrine to create a standard that would last into the next century. Technological advancement and professional relations had begun to change the character of the phenomenon. Physicians still blamed poor, resentful patients for their woes, but they discovered a new villain: the lawyer. More tightly organized medical societies, with the newly ratified locality rule, were able to limit the use of malpractice litigation as an intraprofessional, competitive weapon. By 1900 American medicine was on the eve of therapeutic and social respectability. As the scope of medical practice widened, the type of suits changed, hinted at the future, and provided a preview of the twentieth century.

CHAPTER 9

Conclusion

Malpractice suits became a prominent and permanent feature of American medical life in the 1840s. A combination of immediate, short-term causes and underlying, long-term developments explain the first dramatic increase in the litigation. Although the short-term, inciting factors disappeared, new technological, social, professional, and legal factors arose to take their place in generating suits. Moreover, the long-term cultural preconditions for the suits matured, allowing and even encouraging a broader segment of society to sue for a wider range of misfortunes.

Physicians' declining status in the first half of the century provided the context for the initial malpractice "crisis." Poor, uneven, and disorganized medical education left physicians ill prepared to deal with the complexities of the human body. The notoriously low quality of medical training aggravated the profession's declining status. Ironically, segments of the public in Jacksonian America distrusted physicians both for their poor education and for possessing any education at all. The prevailing spirit of the period glorified the virtues of native intelligence and common sense and derided formal education and the authority of experts. These sentiments formed the basis for the anti-professional feeling that pervaded the age. In the socially and politically increasingly egalitarian country, the public resented any quasi-aristocratic trappings of economic or social privilege. Physicians who had hoped to rely on licensure to improve the state of the profession antagonized large segments of the population who believed in the merits and morality of free and open competition.

Competition among regular physicians also played a central role in the initial increase in litigation. The weak and ultimately nonexistent medical licensure laws of the Jacksonian period swelled the ranks of physicians. Dozens of medical schools with low educational standards graduated thousands of practitioners to compete for patients and fees. Intraprofessional competition engendered suits in two ways. Individual physicians were willing to denigrate the therapeutic practices of their medical competitors to improve their own position. Open criticism sometimes encouraged patients to sue their physicians.

When physicians appeared as expert witnesses in malpractice trials, they often exaggerated their own abilities and results of their treatments while implicitly demeaning the defendant's performance. Other physicians used malpractice suits as a competitive weapon against potential competitors. They explicitly encouraged patients to sue rivals. Occasionally these attacks generated retaliatory suits. When rival practitioners testified as expert witnesses, they were in a particularly strategic position to attack their competitors. Although local, state, and national medical societies existed at midcentury, they did not have sufficient influence or coercive power to limit physician complicity effectively in malpractice prosecutions.

Dramatic technological advances also contributed to the rise in malpractice litigation. At the beginning of the nineteenth century amputation served as the standard treatment for severe fractures and dislocations. These cases generated few malpractice suits in the first third of the century. By 1840 physicians had learned to save seriously injured limbs that would have previously been amputated. These improvements inspired inflated expectations in both physicians and patients. Many professionals and laypeople characterized orthopedic practice as a mechanical task with predictable, standard results. However, badly injured limbs, though saved, seldom healed perfectly. These cases constituted the bulk of the malpractice suits in the nineteenth century.

While antiprofessional sentiment, low educational standards, intraprofessional rivalry, and technological development were central components in the increase of suits in the Jacksonian period, the mere existence of these factors would not have generated suits without the accompanying appearance of three interrelated cultural preconditions. First, although community life had been evolving for at least a century, traditional community customs inhibiting litigation weakened in many parts of the country. This change occurred in different parts of the country at different rates, but by the mid–nineteenth century it allowed a larger number of individuals to resort to courts for redress of personal injuries.

Second, Americans began to change their attitudes toward divine providence and misfortune. While many individuals retained the notion of God working through history, they abandoned the idea of special or direct providence. Progressively fewer individuals believed that God willed every event that occurred on earth. An absolute belief that God ordained every occurrence precluded a search for earthly causes and earthly culprits. By the 1840s a large number of Americans had shifted their beliefs and were free to look for remedies in reforms and in courts. General secularizing trends, perfectionist impulses of northern evangelicals, and advancements in industry, transportation, and science combined to give society a new faith in the possibility and probability of progress. Finally, an increasingly mechanistic, interventionist view of the world, along with various social changes, introduced a new view of the body. Individuals from a wide spectrum of society became conscious of their bodies as "things" and grew progressively more concerned with pursuing physical well-being. Consequently, as optimism and expectations grew, patient intolerance for imperfect results increased, and patients began to sue physicians far more frequently for less severe injuries.

Transformed attitudes toward the body, providence, and the community were the result of long-term, continuous developments and are the preconditions of modern medical malpractice. These factors allowed more frequent litigation, but they did not directly cause its dramatic increase in the early 1840s. If the immediate causes of antiprofessional sentiment, low educational standards, and intraprofessional competition had not existed in Jacksonian America, malpractice suits would have increased slowly as a result of the underlying cultural developments. The immediate causes were a match to a fuse. They account for the dramatic jump in rates, but not for the widespread acceptability of suing for personal injuries. In areas of the country such as the antebellum South, where the immediate factors existed but the cultural preconditions did not, suits remained rare.

In the last half of the century and beyond, many of the inciting agents present in the Jacksonian period disappeared. Medical education slowly improved, state legislatures reinstituted licensure, and medical societies were able to blunt the malevolent effects of intraprofessional competition. But suits continued. New aggravating factors arose to provoke litigation. As Americans lost some of their antipathy toward professionals, a class-based resentment toward physicians gradually merged with the status-based resentment that had characterized attitudes of the first half of the century. A slowly increasing population of lawyers and more frequent use of contingency fee arrangements gave a greater number of dissatisfied patients access to legal remedies.

Rapidly advancing medical technology routinized more treatments, raised expectations and demands, and provided the basis for more suits. Beginning in the early twentieth century, newly introduced medical discoveries yielded continual practical improvements in treatments. Bacteriological science contributed both preventative and curative remedies for a parade of dread diseases, including diphtheria, cholera, malaria, gonorrhea, and influenza. Nutritional advances, especially the identification of vitamins, destroyed the endemic threat of disorders such as scurvy, rickets, beri-beri, and pellegra. The field of pharmacy blossomed, and in the 1930s and 1940s scientists produced the "miracle" sulfonamide drugs and penicillin. Surgery, which was only beginning to show promise in the 1890s, became common in the first half of the twentieth century with the control of shock, hemorrhage, and greater weapons against wound infection. Since the 1940s discoveries in immunology, heredity, molecular biology, and chemistry as well as the development of a pantheon of diagnostic and therapeutic technologies have profoundly increased the capabilities of modern medicine.[1]

The tremendous advances in medical science and practice have had a paradoxical impact on the origins of malpractice suits. Therapeutic progress as well as steady improvement of the medical education system have inspired deep public respect for physicians, and their status has risen dramatically.[2] Consequently, one of the inciting causes of suits in the antebellum era—low public esteem—has been virtually eliminated. Suits, however, have continued because low status was only a secondary, aggravating cause of the litigation in a specific historical period. Other sources of resentment toward physicians have remained. Moreover, the highly visible successes of twentieth-century medicine have created higher expectations in both physicians and the public, much in the same way that improvements in antebellum fracture treatment produced inflated predictions of regular, complete cures. Higher expectations have bred higher demands and greater dissatisfaction when treatments fail.

The cultural developments that had made suits more acceptable in the Jacksonian period neither disappeared nor remained static. Instead they ripened. There is evidence that relatively homogeneous, stable, community environments continued to slow the use of law to settle conflicts, especially for personal injuries, well into the twentieth century.[3] But shared communal values and the power of public opinion over individual action only decreased as the decades passed.

It is impossible and unnecessary to identify any one period as the fundamental break with communal life. The movement from insular communities to individualism and pluralism has been a long process. This transformation has occurred in different regions at different rates. In most areas, however, a variety of factors has overwhelmed the insular community. The rise of the national corporation has tied the fates of individual communities with the outside world. Continuing developments in transportation and communication have made both people and ideas more mobile, and immigration from other countries has diversified the composition of cities and towns. Finally, increased urbanization and the growth of urban populations have made American life progressively more anonymous. As historian David Potter puts it, by the mid–twentieth century "the solidarity of communities was fractured, their cohesion was diluted, and their power over individuals was but a shadow of what it had been."[4] As a result, most cities and towns have gradually lost the consensus and structures that slowed suits in the eighteenth and early nineteenth centuries.

Similarly, American attitudes toward the role of God in the world have continued to evolve. By the late nineteenth century more Americans were replacing their acceptance of "providence" with a faith in "progress."[5] Scientific and material advancements from late in the century to the present have given Americans good reason to expect ongoing improvement both socially and personally. While the notion of providence still plays a role in the lives of many individuals, its nature has been altered and its potency profoundly diluted. People are much more likely to depend on government agencies, reformers, or scientists to cure the ills of the world than they are to expect divine rescue. Southern culture continued to espouse traditional Christian notions regarding God's actions on earth, but there too the idea has weakened.

Americans have also continued to become more materialistic and increasingly concerned with physical well-being. An attorney discussing malpractice litigation in 1889 suggested that some of the blame for the suits should be attributed to "the materialistic tendency of modern days."[6] His comment reflected the heightened late nineteenth-century preoccupation with health and the body. The 1890s brought an enthusiasm for physical culture that surpassed that of the pre–Civil War period. Even more individuals viewed the human form as a mechanical entity susceptible to manipulation and alteration. This attitude was expressed in the late-century expansion and institutionalization of exercise and sports and the new popularity of outdoor activities, bicycling, and body building.[7] Health reformers built on mechanistic antebellum conceptions of the body and worked for and promised physical soundness.

Since the late nineteenth century a variety of popular movements progressively elevating the importance of health and physical appearance in the American mind has surfaced.[8] These trends, especially in the twentieth century, have been given added impetus by the values generated by modern advertising and the abundance of consumer culture.[9] Religious transformations, scientific and material progress, and the comforts of a growing consumer society have led to what one author describes as a "therapeutic ethos—the fretful preoccupation with preserving secular well-being."[10] While most eighteenth- and early nineteenth-century Americans worried first about the soundness of their soul, a growing segment of the population has put a higher premium on physical and psychic health and pleasure. Indeed, in the twentieth century Americans' pursuit of comfort, pleasure, and physical well-being is often characterized by a quasireligious dedication. Ironically, this transformed attitude does not always inspire greater care of the body; but it has made some individuals more confident that something can be done to cure their ills and less patient when failure occurs.

One historian has argued that Americans in the twentieth century have come to expect something akin to a system of "total justice" in many areas of the law. In some respects general tort law moved from a notion of no liability without a demonstration of fault early in the nineteenth century, to a form of absolute liability represented by workers' compensation laws by 1900. A similar movement is suggested by the history of contributory negligence. The doctrine was slowly undercut by the introduction of comparative negligence, which allowed individuals to gain awards even if they were partially responsible for their own injuries. In numerous other fields, from civil rights and constitutional law to government regulation and the creation of the welfare state, legal doctrine and practice have moved toward a posture of greater access to wider remedies for personal and social misfortune and wrongs. This tendency in policy and practice has helped provide fair treatment where there used to be discrimination and relief where there used to be suffering. Like the profound advances in material culture, it has also given rise to higher expectations and greater anticipation of social success and personal health.[11]

The continuation and intensification of the cultural trends first clearly visible in the years before the Civil War help explain the persistent expansion in the range and number of malpractice suits in late nineteenth- and twentieth-century America. In addition, a legal system that provides access and availability to virtually every inhabitant and a medical system that constantly promises grander achievements and better health have influenced twentieth-century malpractice rates. While Americans may devise methods to slow or discourage suits, it is unlikely that they wish to stifle the medical advancement or legal traditions that have contributed to malpractice litigation. And no reform, no matter how ingenious, can reverse the long-term cultural trends that underlie the suits.

Abbreviations

ABFRJ	*American Bar Foundation Research Journal*
AHR	*American Historical Review*
AJLH	*American Journal of Legal History*
AJMS	*American Journal of Medical Science*
AJPH	*American Journal of Public Health*
AJS	*American Journal of Sociology*
ALJ	*Albany Law Journal*
AMM	*American Medical Monthly*
AP	*American Practitioner*
AtlM	*Atlantic Monthly*
BHM	*Bulletin of the History of Medicine*
BMSJ	*Boston Medical and Surgical Journal*
BufMJMR	*Buffalo Medical Journal and Monthly Review*
BufMSJ	*Buffalo Medical and Surgical Journal*
CH	*Church History*
CM	*Connecticut Medicine*
CS	*Christian Spectator*
DPLR	*DePaul Law Review*
DTMJ	*Daniel's Texas Medical Journal*
For	*Fortune*
Gym	*Gymnasium*
Har	*Harper's*
HCR	*Hastings Center Report*
HTR	*Harvard Theological Review*
IMH	*Indiana Magazine of History*
JAAR	*Journal of American Academy of Religion*
JAH	*Journal of American History*
JAMA	*Journal of the American Medical Society*
JHMAS	*Journal of the History of Medicine and Allied Sciences*

JISHS	*Journal of the Illinois State Historical Society*
JLH	*Journal of Legal History*
JLM	*Journal of Legal Medicine*
JLP	*Journal of Legal Pluralism*
JMCS	*Journal of Medicine and Collateral Sciences*
JPH	*Journal of Presbyterian History*
JSH	*Journal of Sports History*
JSocH	*Journal of Social History*
JSJ	*Justice System Journal*
LHR	*Law and History Review*
LSR	*Law and Society Review*
MassR	*Massachusetts Review*
MA	*Mid-America*
MCMMS	*Medical Communications of the Massachusetts Medical Society*
ME	*Medical Examiner*
MLR	*Modern Law Review*
MNL	*Medical News and Library*
MRep	*Medical Reporter*
MSR	*Medical and Surgical Reporter*
MT	*Medical Times*
MVHR	*Mississippi Valley Historical Review*
NEJM	*New England Journal of Medicine*
NEQ	*New England Quarterly*
NHJM	*New Hampshire Journal of Medicine*
NMSJ	*Northwestern Medical and Surgical Journal*
NOMSJ	*New Orleans Medical and Surgical Journal*
NYH	*New York History*
NYJM	*New York Journal of Medicine*
NYJMCS	*New York Journal of Medicine and Collateral Sciences*
NYMPJ	*New York Medical and Physical Journal*
NYSJM	*New York State Journal of Medicine*
OMSJ	*Ohio Medical and Surgical Journal*
PAAS	*Proceedings of the American Antiquarian Society*
PBM	*Perspectives in Biology and Medicine*
PSI	*Physician's and Surgeon's Investigator*
PSM	*Popular Science Monthly*
RAH	*Reviews in American History*
SA	*Scientific American*
Scal	*Scalpel*
SCLR	*South Carolina Law Review*
SLR	*Stanford Law Review*
SR	*Sewanee Review*
StLMSJ	*St. Louis Medical and Surgical Journal*
TAMA	*Transactions of the American Medical Society*

TLQ	*Temple Law Quarterly*
TM	*Texas Medicine*
TOMS	*Transactions of the Ohio Medical Society*
TRBM	*Texas Reports on Biology and Medicine*
TSMSNY	*Transactions of the State Medical Society of New York*
VLR	*Virginia Law Review*
VMHB	*Virginia Magazine of History and Biography*
WJMPS	*Western Journal of Medical and Physical Science*
WJMS	*Western Journal of Medicine and Surgery*
WL	*Western Lancet*
WMSJ	*Western Medical and Surgical Journal*

APPENDIX A

Representative Malpractice Awards, 1835-1865

Source	Awards
"Excision of Tonsils," *BMSJ* 28 (15 February 1843):29–33	$100
"Trial for Malpractice," *BMSJ* 31 (22 January 1845):43–45	$275
"Case of False Aneurism—Action for Malpractice," *BMSJ* 35 (12 August 1846):43–45	$275
Dan Brainard, "Another Prosecution for Malpractice," *JMCS* 3 (November 1846):406–7	$300
Howard v. Grover 28 Me. 97 (1847)	$2,025
Alden March, "Prosecutions for Mal-Practice," *ME* 10 (1847):502–5	$450
"Surgical Malpractice," *BMSJ* 36 (5 May 1847):283–85	$2,500
"Prosecutions for Mal-Practice in the State of N. York," *BMSJ* 36 (14 July 1847):477–80	$450
"Trial for Mal-Practice in Pennsylvania," *BMSJ* 37 (15 September 1847):141–42	$30
"Trial for Malpractice. *Francis Bugard* v. *George Gross*," *BMSJ* 37 (22 September 1847):162–64	$1,000

The figures represent the damage awards. Losing defendants were generally also charged for court costs. Some of these awards may have been increased, reduced, or overturned on retrial or on appeal. Where available, the subsequent award is included parenthetically.

"Trial for Malpractice, and One Thousand Dollars Damages," *BufMJMR* 3 (1847–1848):145–48	$1,000
Walter K. Manning, "Prosecutions for Malpractice," *BMSJ* 40 (23 May 1849):318–19	$362.5c
"Suit for Malpractice," *NWMSJ* 6 (1849–1850):227–30	$200
"Trial for Mal-Practice," *BMSJ* 41 (17 October 1849):216–19	$500
"Trial for Malpractice in Surgery," *BMSJ* 2 (January 1850): 213–22	$200
William M. Wood, "A Statement of two Suits for Malpractice, tried in November and December, 1850, in the Court of Erie County, Pa.," *AJMS* 22 (July 1851):43–50	$1,400; $500
McCandless v. McWha 22 Penn. 261 (1853)	$850 ($500)
"Prosecution for Mal-Practice," *BMSJ* 48 (4 May 1853):281–83	$1,675
Leighton v. Sargent 7 Foster 460 (N.H. 1853)	$1500
Twombly v. Leach 6 Mass. 397 (1853)	$300
"Trial for Malpractice—Dr. Crosby's Acquittal," *BMSJ* 50 (21 June 1854):424–25	$900
"A Surgical Case of Mal-Practice," *BMSJ* 51 (8 November 1854):289–97	$1,500 ($525)
"The Greenpoint Malpractice Case," *Scal* 8 (April 1856):311–25	$2,500 ($3,000)
"Report on the Difficulties Growing Out of alleged Mal-Practice in the Treatment of Fractures," *TOMS* 11 (1856):53–66.	$150; $100; $300; $1,200
"Case of a Trial for Malpractice," *BMSJ* 61 (19 March 1857):148	$1,000
"Alleged Malpractice," *BMSJ* 62 (31 May 1860):364–65	$120
Woodward v. *Hancock* 1 *Quarterly Law Review* 385 (1860–1)	$500
"Malpractice," *BMSJ* 66 (24 July 1862):524	$300

APPENDIX B

Representative Malpractice Awards, 1865–1900

Source	Awards
Teft v. Wilcox 6 Kan. 460 (1870)	$2,900
John J. Reese, "Case of Alleged Malpractice," *MT* 1 (1 December 1870):73–74	$1,359.70
W. F. Hutchinson, "A Recent suit for Malpractice," *BufMSJ* 12 (1872–1873):290–99	$4,000
Smothers v. Hanks 34 Iowa 287 (1872)	$2,000
Almond v. Nugent 34 Iowa 300 (1872)	$2,000
Kendall v. Brown 74 Ill. 232 (1874)	$1,375.17
Getchell v. Hill 21 Minn. 464 (1875)	$4,000
Weger v. Calder 78 Ill. 275 (1875)	$1,500
Musser v. Chase 29 Ohio 577 (1876)	$3,000
McKehoe v. Hall (pre-1877), McClelland, *Civil Malpractice,* 261–69	$800
Young v. Fullerton (pre-1877), McClelland, *Civil Malpractice,* 253–56	$1,000

The figures represent the damage awards. Losing defendants were generally also charged for court costs. Some of these awards may have been increased, reduced, or overturned on retrial or appeal.

Means v. Hallam & Barns (pre-1877), McClelland, *Civil Mal-practice*, 176–80	$1,000
"An Outrageous Suit for Malpractice," *BMSJ* 99 (28 November 1878):700–704	$4,916.57
Brooke v. Clarke 57 Tx. 1905 (1882)	$5,000
Kelsey v. Hey 84 Ind. 189 (1882)	$4,000
"Some Recent Malpractice Suits," *MR* 28 (19 December 1885):690–91	$7,000
Quinn v. Higgins 63 Wisc. 664 (1885)	$1,600
Hyrne v. Erwin 23 S.C. 226 (1885)	$1,000
E. J. Doering, "Mutual Protection against Blackmail," *JAMA* 6 (1886):114–17	$4,480
Gates v. Fleisher 67 Wisc. 504 (1886)	$350
Holtzman v. Hoy 118 Ill. 534 (1886)	$2,500
Reber v. Herring 115 Penn. 599 (1887)	$900
Graves v. Santway 6 N.Y. Supp. 892 (1889)	$500
Sanderson v. Holland 39 Mo. App. 233 (1889)	$1,000
F. J. Groner, "The Causes and the Remedies for Suits for Malpractice," *MR* 37 (9 August 1890) 143–44	$1,000
Langford v. Jones 18 Ore. 307 (1890)	$1,000
Stevenson v. Gelsthorpe 10 Mont. 563 (1891)	$500
Link v. Sheldon 136 N.Y. App. 1 (1892)	$4,000
Lewis v. Dwinell 84 Me. 497 (1892)	$450
Peck v. Hutchinson 88 Iowa 321 (1893)	$2,500
Carpenter v. McDavitt 53 Mo. App. 393 (1893)	$2,000
Cayford v. Wilbur 86 Me. 414 (1894)	$2,075
"Confidential Communications and Suits for Malpractice," *NYMJ* 60 (3 November 1894):576	$1,500
Jackson v. Burnham 20 Colo. 533 (1895)	$5,000
"Verdict Against a Physician," *MR* 47 (12 January 1895):64	$12,000
Hedin v. Minneapolis Medical & Surgical Inst. 62 Minn. 146 (1895)	$500
Eighmy v. Union Pacific Railway Cc. 93 Iowa 538 (1895)	$1,500
Gores v. Graff 77 Wisc. 174 (1896)	$2,500

$\mathcal{N}otes$

Preface

1. J. R. Weist, "Civil Malpractice Suits: How Can the Physician Protect Himself against Them?" *AP* 30 (1884):161.

2. Hubert Winston Smith, "Legal Responsibility for Medical Malpractice," *JAMA* 116 (1941):942–47, 2149–59, 2670–79, and *JAMA* 117 (1941):23–33.

3. Andrew Sandor, "The History of Professional Liability Suits in the United States," *JAMA* 163 (9 February 1957):459–66; Earl F. Rose, "Major Court Decisions that Have Influenced the Practice of Medicine," *TM* 72 (October 1976):90–96; Victor Gordon, "The Origin, Basis, and Nature of Medical Malpractice Liability," *CM* 35 (February 1971):73–77; Joseph C. Stetler, "The History of Reported Medical Professional Liability Cases," *TLQ* 30 (1957):366–83; E. A. Reed, "Understanding Tort Law: The Historical Basis of Medical Liability," *JLM* 5 (1977):50–53.

4. Louis B. Harrison, Melvin H. Worth, Jr., and Michael A. Carlucci, "The Development of the Principles of Medical Malpractice in the United States," *PBM* 29 (1985):41–72; Edward J. Larson, "Medicine, Physicians and Malpractice Law," Paper delivered to the American Association for the History of Medicine, Rochester, New York, 30 April–3 May 1986; and Joseph F. Sandusk, "Analysis of Professional Factors in Medical Malpractice Claims," *JAMA* 161 (2 June 1956):442–47, discuss malpractice in the twentieth century.

5. Chester Burns, "Malpractice Suits in American Medicine Before the Civil War," *BHM* 43 (1969):41–56; and Burns, "Medical Malpractice Law and the Public's Health in the United States During the Nineteenth Century," *Actes Proceedings, XXVIIIᵉ Congrès International d'Histoire de la Médecine* 1 (1982):75–77.

6. William Rothstein, *American Physicians in the Nineteenth Century* (Baltimore: Johns Hopkins University Press, 1972), 324.

7. Burns, "Malpractice Suits," 42.

8. See Gerald N. Grob, "The Social History of Medicine and Disease: Problems and Possibilities," *JSocH* 10 (1977):393–405; and Ronald L. Numbers, "The History of American Medicine: A Field in Ferment," *RAH* 10 (1982):245–52.

1. Before the Flood, 1790–1835

1. Landon v. Humphrey 9 Day 209 (Conn. 1832); "Alleged Mal-Practice," *BMSJ* 6 (21 March 1832):98–99. For an extended discussion of this case, see chapter 7.

2. Lawrence M. Friedman, *A History of American Law* (New York: Simon and Schuster, 1973), 282–83.

3. Hubert Winston Smith, "Legal Responsibility for Medical Malpractice," *JAMA* 116 (14 June 1941):2671; and Andrew A. Sandor, "The History of Professional Liability Suits in the United States," *JAMA* 163 (9 February 1957):465.

4. Even an incomplete search of antebellum medical journals uncovers a large percentage of the 243 expected suits using the 9:1 ratio and there were clearly many cases that journals did not report. See Bibliography.

5. "Prosecutions for Mal-Practice," *OMSJ* 13 (January 1861):253–60; Bliss v. Long 1 Wright 351 (Ohio 1833) and Grindle v. Rush 7 Ohio 123 (1836).

6. Drawn from Smith, "Legal Responsibility," 2672–73. A decade-by-decade tally: 1790–1800, 1 case; 1800–1810, 0 cases; 1810–1820, 1 case; 1820–1830, 0 cases; 1830–1840, 5 cases; 1840–1850, 3 cases; 1850–1860, 13 cases; 1860–1870, 25 cases; 1870–1880, 45 cases; 1880–1890, 47 cases; 1890–1900, 77 cases. For another useful pioneering study, see Chester R. Burns, "Malpractice Suits in American Medicine Before the Civil War," *BHM* 43 (1969):41–56.

7. Francis A. Walker, *A Compendium of The Ninth Census* (Washington, D.C.: GPO, 1872), 8–9, and *Abstract of the Eleventh Census: 1890* (Washington, D.C.: GPO, 1894), 3. The number of appellate decisions was calculated from Smith, "Legal Responsibility," 2672–73.

8. Figures drawn from Smith, "Legal Responsibility," 2672–73 (1790–1920 case counts); Sandor, "History of Professional Liability Suits," 461–63 (1920–1950 case counts); and Walker, *Compendium of The Ninth Census*, 8–9, for population statistics.

9. "Mal-Praxis in Midwifery," *BMSJ* 2 (9 June 1829):270 (France); "Malpraxis in Midwifery," *BMSJ* 3 (3 March 1830):50 (England); "Alleged Malpractice," *BMSJ* 6 (21 March 1832):98–9 (United States).

10. See Bibliography for citations

11. Sandra Cirincione, "The History of Medical Malpractice in New York State: A Perspective from the Publications of the Medical Society of New York," *NYSJM* 86 (July 1986):361–62.

12. While an increase in the number of medical journals may account for some of the increase in reported cases, as many as 74 journals had been founded by 1840. See James H. Cassedy, *Medicine and American Growth, 1800–1860* (Madison: University of Wisconsin Press, 1986), 66–67; and Henry Burnell Shafer, *The American Medical Profession, 1783–1850* (New York: AMS Press, 1968), 181–99, for a discussion of early nineteenth-century medical journals.

13. See Chester R. Burns, "Medical Ethics and Jurisprudence," in *The Education of American Physicians*, edited by Ronald L. Numbers (Berkeley: University of California Press, 1980), 273–89.

14. Theodoric R. Beck, *Elements of Medical Jurisprudence* (Albany: Webster and Skinner, 1823); and Joseph Chitty, *A Practical Treatise on Medical Jurisprudence* (London: Butterworth, 1834).

15. Chester R. Burns, "Medical Ethics in the United States Before the Civil War," Ph. D. dissertation (Johns Hopkins University, 1969), 140, 143. For more on antebellum writers and their neglect of the medical jurisprudence of malpractice, see the glowing testimonials to the first book-length treatise on the topic: John Elwell, *A Medico-Legal Treatise on Medical Malpractice and Medical Evidence* (New York: John S. Voorhis, 1860). The comments are printed before the preface in the first edition.

16. Timothy Walker, *Introduction to American Law, Designed as a First Book for Students* (Philadelphia: P. H. Nicklin and T. Johnson, 1837; reprint DACAPO Press, 1972), 467, 472.

17. Friedman, *History of American Law*, 88–89, 282–91. See also Charles Warren, *A History of the American Bar* (Boston: Little, Brown, 1911), 19–39, 325–41.

18. Friedman, *History of American Law*, 280.

19. William Blackstone, *Commentaries*, St. George Tucker's ed. (Philadelphia: William Birch Young and Abraham, 1803), 122–23.

20. For an extended and more detailed discussion of the legal aspects and development of malpractice law as well as its English origins, see chapter 7.

21. This quotation is from Landon v. Humphrey 9 Day 209 (Conn. 1832).

22. There was nothing unique in the jury's power to determine "questions of fact" in malpractice cases. This role was routine in other areas of Anglo-American law.

23. Burns, "Medical Ethics in the United States," 91–92.

24. Cross v. Guthery 1 Amer. Dec. 61 (Conn. 1794).

25. Idem.

26. "*Michael O'Neil v. Gerard Bancker*," *NYMPJ* 6 (1827):145–52. This case is discussed at length in chapter 5.

27. Bliss v. Long Wright 351 (Ohio 1833). A *nonsuit* results when a judge dismisses the charges after ruling that the plaintiff had no grounds for prosecution.

28. The words *guilt, conviction, defendant, plaintiff,* and *prosecutor* are now

the language of criminal law. In the nineteenth century they were also acceptable and commonly used terms in civil cases. I will use the nineteenth-century terminology throughout this work.

29. Grannis v. Branden 5 Day 260 at 261, 267 (Conn. 1812).

30. Bemus v. Howard 3 Watts 255–58 (Penn. 1834). See Grindle v. Rush 7 Ohio 123 (1836) for another pre-1835 amputation malpractice case.

31. Landon v. Humphrey 9 Day 209 (Conn. 1832).

32. Sumner v. Utley 7 Conn. 256 at 260 (1828). This was a slander case where a patient accused a physician of malpractice but did not file a formal charge.

33. James H. Cassedy, *American Medicine and Statistical Thinking, 1800–1860* (Cambridge: Harvard University Press, 1984), 9–10.

34. See chapter 4.

35. Charles Lowell, *An Authentic Report of a Trial before the Supreme Judicial Court of Maine for the county of Washington, June Term 1824, Charles Lowell v. John Faxon & Micajah Hawks Surgeons and Physicians In an Action of Trespass on the Case for Ignorant and Negligent Treatment with Observations on the Prejudices and Conduct of [Unreadable] in Regard to This Case* (Portland: Printed for the Author, 1826), 4, 9.

36. Ibid., 9–10.

37. Ibid., 4.

38. Ibid., 5, 18; James Adams, Jr., comp., *Report of a Trial of an Action, Charles Lowell Against John Faxon and Micajah Hawks Doctors of Medicine, Defendants for Malpractice in the Capacity of Physicians and Surgeons at the Superior Judicial Court of Maine Held at Machias for the County of Washington June, 1824 before the Hon. Nathan Weston* (Portland: Printed for James Adams, Jr., by David and Seth Paine, 1825), 7; John Collins Warren, *A Letter to the Hon. Isaac Parker, Chief Justice of the Supreme Court of Massachusetts, Containing Remarks on the Dislocation of the Hip Joint* (Cambridge: Hillard and Metcalf, 1826), 1, 6. For biographical information on Warren, see Howard Kelly, *A Cyclopedia of American Medical Biography: Comprising the Lives of Eminent Deceased Physicians and Surgeons, 1610–1900* (Philadelphia: W. B. Saunders, 1912), 2:478; and Henry K. Beecher and Mark D. Altschule, *Medicine at Harvard: The First Three Hundred Years* (Hanover: University Press of New England, 1977), 35–39.

39. Warren, *A Letter*, 7–9.

40. Ibid.

41. Lowell, *Authentic Report*, 5, 18; and Adams, *Report of a Trial*, 7.

42. Lowell, *Authentic Report*, 6–7; Adams, *Report of a Trial*, 5.

43. Adams, *Report of a Trial*, 10–30. For Warren's testimony, see ibid., 12–13, 15, 23–25.

44. Kelly, *American Medical Biography*, 388–89; Lowell, *Authentic Report*, 15; Adams, *Report of a Trial*, 33–36.

45. Lowell, *Authentic Report*, 18, 20; Adams, *Report of a Trial*, 110.

46. Adams, *Report of a Trial*, 49–50, 52–53, 71.

47. Ibid., 48, 74, 99.

48. Ibid., 97.

49. Ibid., 86-95, 100-101.

50. Ibid., 112-22.

51. Lowell, *Authentic Report*, 29 pp.; Adams, *Report of a Trial*, 117 pp.; and Warren, *A Letter*, 142 pp.

52. Lowell, *Authentic Report*, 7, 18.

53. Eugene F. Sanger, "Report cn Malpractice," *BMSJ* 100 (9 January 1879):41-50.

54. The newspaper article is excerpted in Warren, *A Letter*, 138.

55. Ibid., 15, 58.

56. Ibid., 1, 11, 12, 16.

57. Rowland Berthoff, *An Unsettled People: Social Order and Disorder in American History* (New York: Harper and Row, 1971), 177-295. The impact of this social transformation on law and litigation is analyzed in chapters 5 and 7.

58. Most legal writers trace the origins of the locality rule to the 1870s and 1880s, but it is clear that the doctrine was employed much earlier. For comments on the locality rule and medical malpractice, see Jon R. Waltz, "The Rise and Gradual Fall of the Locality Rule in Medical Malpractice Litigation," *DPLR* 17 (1969):408-21; David D. Armstrong, "Medical Malpractice—The 'Locality Rule' and the 'Conspiracy of Silence,'" *SCLR* 22 (1970):811-21; Carleton Chapman, *Physicians, Ethics, and the Law* (New York: New York University Press, 1984), 96. See chapters 2 and 8 for more on the locality rule.

59. Adams, *Report of a Trial*, 51.

60. Stephen Smith, "[Review of John Elwell's *A Medico-Legal Treatise on Malpractice and Medical Evidence* 1860]," *AJMS* 40 (July 1860):158-59.

61. Adams, *Report of a Trial*, 100.

62. Lowell, *Authentic Report*, 6, 7.

63. The increased supply of physicians and their impact on malpractice is discussed in chapter 3.

64. Lowell, *Authentic Report*, 18.

65. For a discussion of the transformation of attitudes toward providence and its role in the malpractice epidemic, see chapter 5.

66. Adams, *Report of a Trial*, 52.

67. James Thomas Flexner, *Doctors on Horseback: Pioneers of American Medicine* (New York: Dover, 1969), 115-18.

2. *The Deluge, 1835–1865*

1. "Accusation of Mal-Practice," *BMSJ* 31 (11 September 1844):123-24.

2. "Reviews," *WJMPS* 28 (1853):300.

3. Frank H. Hamilton, "Suits for Malpractice in Surgery: Their Causes and Their Remedies," *Papers Read before the Medico-Legal Society of New York, 1875–1878* (New York: Medico-Legal Society of New York, 1886), 98.

4. John Elwell, *A Medico-Legal Treatise on Malpractice and Medical Evidence* (New York: John S. Voorhis, 1860), 83.

5. See chapter 1.

6. [Alden March], "Case of Alledged [sic] Malpractice in Surgery," *BMSJ* 37 (4 August 1847):9–14.

7. "Prosecution for Malpractice," *ME* 14 (November 1851):728–29.

8. Worthington Hooker, *Physician and Patient: or, A Practical View of the Mutual Duties, Relations, and Interests of the Medical Profession and the Community* (New York: Baker and Scribner, 1849; facsimile reprint Arno Press, 1972), 277.

9. "Surgical Malpractice," *BMSJ* 36 (5 May 1847):283–84.

10. Hamilton quoted in Chester Burns, "Medical Ethics in the United States Before the Civil War," Ph.D. dissertation (Johns Hopkins University, 1969), 143.

11. "Accusation of Mal-Practice," *BMSJ* 31 (11 September 1844):123–24. The case, *Smith* v. *Goodyear & Hyde*, is the subject of the study in chapter 6.

12. "Report of Trial for Mal-Practice. *William Tims* v. *James P. White.* Supreme Court Erie County Circuit, June 26th, 1848," *BufMJMR* 4 (August 1848):135.

13. "Trial for Malpractice," *BufMJMR* 10 (1854–1855):569–70.

14. "Bibliographic Notices," *NYJM* (September 1853):272–75.

15. For examples of other New York cases from this period see: "Excision of the Tonsils," *BMSJ* 28 (15 February 1843):29–32; "Prosecutions for Mal-Practice in the State of New York," *ME* 10 (August 1847):502–5; "Trial for Malpractice, and One Thousand Dollars Damages," *BufMJMR* 3 (1847–1848):145–48; "Trial for Malpractice," *BufMJMR* 10 (1854–1855):568–70; "The Greenpoint Malpractice Case," *Scal* 8 (April 1856):311–15; and "Alleged Malpractice," *BMSJ* 62 (31 May 1860):364–65.

16. See chapters 3–5 for an exposition of these social and professional conditions.

17. For example, see *Gallaher* v. *Thompson* (1833) in Elwell, *Treatise on Malpractice*, 115–17; Bliss v. Long 1 Wright 351 (Ohio 1833); and Grindle v. Rush 7 Ohio 123 (1836).

18. S. P. Hildreth, "Trial for Mal-Practice in Surgery," *OMSJ* 2 (January 1850):213–22; and Arthur Merrill, "Mal-Practice in Surgery," *WL* 11 (1850):763–68.

19. "Report on Difficulties Growing Out of Alleged Mal-Practice in the Treatment of Fractures," *TOMS* 11 (1856):54. For examples of other Ohio cases in this period, see Theodore Nichols, "Trial for Mal-Practice," *OMSJ* 2 (September 1849):6–10; "Suit for Malpractice," *OMSJ* 2 (November 1849):161–63; Elwell, *Treatise on Malpractice* (four Ohio cases from the 1850s), 81–82,

146–62, 163–68; "Suit for Alleged Mal-Practice," *OMSJ* 10 (September 1857):13–24; "Important Case of Alleged Mal-Practice," *Scal* 9 (April 1857):54–57; "Suit for Alleged Mal-Practice," *OMSJ* 10 (May 1858):447–51; *"Terrence Mc Queeney v. W. W. Jones*. A Prosecution for Alledged [sic] Mal-Practice," *OMSJ* 12 (September 1859):22–24; *"Mary Ann Decrow, et al.*, v. *H. H. Little*. A Prosecution for Alleged Mal-Practice," *OMSJ* 12 (January 1860):194–98; and John Dawson, "Suit for Damages in a Case of Fracture of the Leg," *OMSJ* 14 (July 1862):283–90.

20. "Prosecutions for Mal-Practice," *OMSJ* 13 (January 1861):253–60.

21. William M. Wood, "Thoughts on Suits for Malpractice, Suggested by Certain Judicial Proceedings in Erie County, Pennsylvania," *AJMS* 18 (October 1849):398; and Wood, "A Statement of Two Suits for Malpractice, Tried in November and December 1850, in the Court of Erie County, Pa.," *AJMS* 22 (July 1851):43–50.

22. "Extracts from the Report of the Committee on the Prevalence of Suits for Mal-Practice," *MNL* 8 (March 1850):17–20. For examples of other Pennsylvania cases from this period, see Mertz v. Detweiler 8 Watts 376–8 (1845); "Trial for Mal-Practice in Pennsylvania," *BMSJ* 37 (15 September 1847):141–42; Fowler v. Sargent 1 Grant's Cases 355 (1856); Isaac Lefever, "Report of a Trial for Malpractice in the Court of Common Pleas of Perry County, Pennsylvania," *AJMS* 48 (July 1864):72–86; "Trial for Mal-Practice," *AJMS* 12 (1865):555–58, 569–73; and Stephen Smith, *Doctor in Medicine and Other Papers on Professional Subjects* (New York: William Wood, 1872), 277–82.

23. "Prosecution of Mal-Practice," *BMSJ* 50 (21 June 1854):424–25. For examples of cases from New Hampshire and Vermont in this period, see "[Suit for malpractice]," *WMSJ* 28 (1853):346–47 (N.H.); "Suit for Mal-Practice," *BMSJ* 51 (8 November 1854):289–97 (N.H.); "Trial for Mal-Practice," *BMSJ* 51 (22 November 1854):345 (N.H.); "A Case of Alleged Mal-Practice," *BMSJ* 54 (24 April 1856):229–42 (N.H.); "Prosecution for Malpractice," *MRep* 8 (November 1855):522–29 (N.H.); "Trial for Mal-Practice," *BMSJ* 41 (17 October 1849):216–19 (Vt.): "Trial for Mal-Practice," *BMSJ* 41 (23 January 1850):500–502 (Vt.); "Suit for Mal-Practice in Vermont," *BMSJ* 44 (11 June 1851):377–88 (Vt.); "Trial for Mal-Practice," *BMSJ* 54 (20 March 1856), 129–38, *BMSJ* 54 (27 March 1856):149–56 (Vt.); "Malpractice," *BMSJ* 66 (24 July 1862):524 (Vt.); and Wilmot v. Howard 39 Vt. 447 (1863).

24. "Prosecution for Malpractice," *BMSJ* 30 (29 May 1844):344–45.

25. "Surgical Malpractice," *BMSJ* 36 (5 May 1847):283–84.

26. "Prosecution for Malpractice," *BMSJ* 48 (11 May 1853):304.

27. "Mal-practice," *BMSJ* 49 (26 October 1853):270.

28. "Case of Malpractice," *BMSJ* 54 (13 March 1856):109–12. For examples of other cases from Massachusetts in this period, see McClallen v. Allen 19 Pick. 333 (Mass. 1837); Worthington Hooker, *Physician and Patient*, 160–64; Walter K. Manning, "Prosecution for Mal-Practice," *BMSJ* 40 (23 May 1849):318–19; Walter K. Manning, "Trial for Mal-Practice." *BMSJ* 42 (27

February 1850):79–80; "Prosecution for Mal-Practice," *ME* 14 (November 1851):728–29; Moody v. Sabin 63 Mass. 505 (1852); Twombly v. Leach 65 Mass. 397–406 (1853); "Prosecution for Mal-Practice," *BMSJ* 48 (4 May 1853): 281–83; "Suit for Mal-Practice," *BMSJ* 50 (19 April 1854):246; "The 'Suit for Malpractice,' " *BMSJ* 50 (3 May 1854):287; "Prosecutions for Mal-Practice," *BMSJ* 51 (8 November 1854):305; "Another Suit for Mal-Practice," *BMSJ* 51 (17 January 1855):504; "Case of Mal-Practice," *BMSJ* 54 (13 March 1856):109–13; "Trial for Malpractice," *BMSJ* 55 (22 January 1857):515; and "Trial for Malpractice," *BMSJ* 56 (5 February 1857):9–26.

29. Hamilton, "Suits for Malpractice in Surgery," 98. Chapter 5, below, contains a short comment on the absence of widespread litigation in the nineteenth-century South.

30. "A Report of the Facts and Circumstances Relating to a Case of Compound Fracture, and Prosecution for Mal-Practice . . . ," *AJMS* 3 (January 1842):181–84.

31. [Frank] Hamilton, "Prosecution for Alledged *[sic]* Mal-Practice," *BufMJMR* 4 (1848–1849):274–77.

32. "Prosecution for Mal-Practice," *BMSJ* 48 (20 July 1853):503–4.

33. See chapter 4.

34. Elwell, *Treatise on Malpractice*, 55.

35. Steven Smith, "[Review of John Elwell's *Treatise on Malpractice*]," *AJMS* 40 (July 1860):162. Unfortunately, Smith did not provide the total number of cases used in his study. However, he noted that 142 cases represented a "little over two-thirds" of his total. Therefore, his study was drawn from approximately 213 cases. I have used this total in calculating these percentages.

36. These issues will be discussed further, and more fully, in chapter 4.

37. John Ordronaux, *The Jurisprudence of Medicine* (Philadelphia: T. and J. W. Johnson, 1869), 101.

38. Ibid., 101.

39. "Heroic Surgery: Extirpation of a Malignant Tumor from the Arm, Death the Next Day," *Scal* 2 (1850):121–22.

40. "Shocking Outrage on Professional Humanity," *Scal* 7 (January 1856):253–55.

41. "Gross Malpractice," *MSR* 22 (5 February 1870):121–22.

42. One physician, whose patient died after he had dosed her with cayenne pepper, wrapped her in kerosene-soaked blankets, and put her in a steam bath for three days, was acquitted under the Thomson doctrine. The Thomson case and its legacy is chronicled in Milo A. McClelland, *Civil Malpractice: A Treatise on Surgical Jurisprudence* (New York: Hurd and Houghton, 1877), 384–92.

43. Baker v. Bolton 1 Camp. 493 (1808); Wex Malone, *Essays on Torts* (Baton Rouge: Paul M. Herbert Law Center, Louisiana State University Press, 1986), 75–117; Richard Morris, *Studies in the History of American Law* (Philadelphia: J. M. Mitchell, 1959), 247–48; and Leonard Levy, *The Law of the Com-*

monwealth and Chief Justice Shaw (Cambridge: Harvard University Press, 1957), 156.

44. For example, in the 1793 Connecticut case Cross v. Guthery 1 Amer. Dec. 61 (Conn. 1793), a woman died after an inept breast amputation. Despite the English precedents and the objections of the defendant, the Connecticut superior court awarded the husband £40.

45. Wex Malone, "The Genesis of Wrongful Death," *SLR* 17 (July 1956):1043–76.

46. Shaw's key decisions included *Farwell* v. *Boston and Worcester R.R. Corp.* (1842) and *Brown* v. *Kendall* (1850). See, Levy, *Law of the Commonwealth*, 166–82; Lawrence M. Friedman and Jack Ladinsky, "Social Change and the Law of Industrial Accidents," *Columbia Law Review* 67 (1967):151–82.

47. Carey v. Berkshire R.R. 55 Mass. 475 (1848); Levy, *Law of the Commonwealth*, 155–65; and Malone, *Essays on Torts*, 79–91.

48. "Braunberger v. Cleis," in McClellend, *Civil Malpractice*, 127–45; and "Trial for Malpractice," *MSR* 12 (1865):555–59, 569–73.

49. McClelland, *Civil Malpractice*, 139–40, 145.

50. Hyatt v. Adams 16 Mich. 179 (1867).

51. Peter Davis, "Michigan's First Malpractice Case: Its Lessons Linger," *Journal of Legal Medicine* (June 1977):49–52. Although this is a good account of the details of the case, it is not the first malpractice case in Michigan as the title suggests, but only the first case appealed to the state supreme court.

52. Ibid., 51.

53. Hyatt v. Adams, 182.

54. Idem, 174.

55. Idem, 192.

56. Idem, 198.

57. "Report on the Difficulties Growing Out of Alleged Mal-Practice in the Treatment of Fractures," *TOMS*, 11 (1856):57–58.

58. "Suit for Alleged Malpractice," *OMSJ* 10 (1857–1858):13–24. The physician eventually won the case.

59. Alden March, "Prosecutions for Mal-Practice in the State of N. York," *BMSJ* 36 (14 July 1847):477–80.

60. A. B. Shipman, *A Report of the Facts and Circumstances Relating to a Case of Compound Fracture and Prosecution for Mal-Practice* (Cortlandville, N.Y.: Cortland Democrat, 1841).

61. See two cases described in "Report on the Difficulties Growing Out of Alleged Mal-Practice in the Treatment of Fractures," *TOMS*, 11 (1856):53–66.

62. Under strict application of the eighteenth-century writ system, prospective litigants would be forced to file an entirely separate action for malpractice. For discussion of the writ system see chapter 7.

63. Piper v. Menifee 51 Ky. 465 (1851).

64. Graham v. Gautier 21 Tex. 111 (1858). For examples of other malpractice suits that originated out of suit-for-fees, see Bellinger v. Craigue 31

Barbour 534 (N.Y. 1860); Akin v. Green (N.Y. circa 1850s), in Elwell, *Treatise on Malpractice*, 102–3; and *McClallen v. Adams* 19 Pick. 33 (Mass. 1837).

65. Alden March, "Case of Alleged Mal-Practice in Surgery," *BMSJ* 37 (4 August 1847):13.

66. Eugene Sanger, "Report on Malpractice," *BMSJ* 100 (2 January 1879):14–23; and Sanger, "Report on Malpractice," *BMSJ* 100 (9 January 1879):41–50. Sanger did not provide dates but noted that the suits and threats occurred within the "remembrance of the present generation."

67. Smith, "[Review of Elwell]," 153–66.

68. "Correction," *WMSJ* 32 (1855):50.

69. Ibid.

70. "Trial for Mal-Practice," *BMSJ* 54 (27 March 1856):156.

71. Samuel Parkman, "On the Relations of the Medical Witness with the Law and the Lawyer," *AJMS* 23 (January 1852):132.

72. "Report on the Difficulties Growing Out of Alleged Mal-Practice in the Treatment of Fractures," *TOMS*, 11 (1856):56.

73. "Alleged Malpractice," *BMSJ* 62 (31 May 1860):364–65.

74. Elwell, *Treatise on Malpractice*, 2.

75. "Trial for Malpractice," *BMSJ* 56 (5 February 1857):9–23; "Trial for Malpractice," *BMSJ* 55 (22 January 1857):515.

76. T. J. W. Pray, "Suits for Mal-Practice," *BMSJ* 51 (8 November 1854):297.

77. Alexis de Tocqueville, *Democracy in America*, translated by George Lawrence, edited by J. P. Mayer (Garden City, N.Y.: Doubleday, 1969), 263, 268.

78. See, for example, Perry Miller, ed., *The Legal Mind in America: From Independence to the Civil War* (Garden City, N.Y.: Doubleday, 1962), 238–84.

79. Elwell, *Treatise on Malpractice*, 44.

80. Competition's role in generating malpractice suits will be discussed in greater length in chapter 3.

81. In one Michigan case in the late 1840s a jury had granted the plaintiff $300 in damages for injuries that supposedly resulted when a physician failed to diagnose a dislocated arm immediately. A state appellate court judge granted the physician a new trial, but removed the case from the court and referred the complaint to two physician-arbitrators. The arbitrators reported to the chief justice of the state supreme court. They decided that although the dislocation was not discovered, it was a rare injury and in many cases was untreatable even if diagnosed. They recommended no award with both parties paying their own costs. The judge accepted their recommendation. See Dan Brainard, "Another Suit for Malpractice," *JMCS* 3 (November 1846):406. For another case of the anomalous use of referees, see "Trial for Mal-Practice," *BMSJ* 51 (November 1854):345.

82. See chapters 1 and 7 for discussion of common law writs.

83. For some history and impact of the civil procedure reforms, see Joseph H. Koffler and Alison Reppy, *Handbook of Common Law Pleading* (St. Paul:

West Publishing, 1969), 15, 22–29; Robert Wyness Millar, *Civil Procedure of the Trial Court in Historical Perspective* (New York: Law Center for New York University, 1952), 52–54; Edson R. Sunderland, *Cases on Procedure Annotated, Code Pleading* (Philadelphia: Callaghan, 1913), 1–23. Compare pleading requirements for malpractice before and after reforms, see Joseph Chitty, *A Practical Treatise on Pleading* (New York: C. Wiley, 1812), 92, 137–38; John Simcoe Saunders, *The Law of Pleading and Evidence in Civil Actions* (Philadelphia: Robert Small, 1844), 89–90, 109; and Conway Robinson, *The Practice of Courts of Justice* (Richmond: A. Morris, 1855), 394–95, 398–99.

84. See chapter 7 for a discussion of legal theory and the source of malpractice liability.

85. *Bliss v. Long* 1 Wright 351 at 352.

86. *Grindle v. Rush* 7 Ohio (Charles Hammond Reports 7) part 2, 123–25.

87. Mc Candless v. Mc Wha 22 Penn. 261 (1853) at 263–64, 267. Reynold v. Graves 3 Wisc. 416 (1853) is another of the rare examples in which a trial judge allowed a defendant/physician to be held responsible for an implied contract to cure. The decision against the physician, as with all similar cases, was overturned.

88. Landon v. Humhrey 9 Day 209, 216 (Conn. 1832).

89. Howard v. Grover 28 Me. 97, 101 (1848).

90. Ritchey v. West 23 Ill. 329, 330 (1860).

91. Francis Hillard, *The Law of Torts or Private Wrongs* (Boston: Little, Brown, 1859), 1:238–40; and Thomas G. Shearman and Amasa A. Redfield, *A Treatise on the Law of Negligence* (New York: Baker, Voorhis, 1870), 504–17.

92. Chapter 7 contains a discussion of state courts' use of English precedents.

93. Elwell, "Experts—Professional Opinions," in *Treatise on Malpractice*, 273; and John Ordronaux, *The Jurisprudence of Medicine in its relations to the Law of Contracts, Torts, and Evidence* (Philadelphia: T. and J. Johnson, 1869), 8–9, 27; Simon Greenleaf, *A Treatise on the Law of Evidence* (Boston: Charles C. Little and James Brown, 1842; reprint Arno Press, 1972), 153, 376, 488–91.

94. Bowman v. Woods 1 Iowa 441.

95. Idem, 442–43. Also see Patten v. Wiggin 51 Me. 594 (1862) for a ruling that held that physicians were to be judged by the standards of their school of practice only.

96. A preliminary paper prepared by James B. Speer suggests that irregular practitioners and physicians on the outside fringes of respectability were the most common victims of malpractice charges. Speer, "Malpractice: The Historical Viewpoint," in *Proceedings of the Malpractice Conference: The Interaction of Medicine and Justice Through Public Policy*, edited by Donnie J. Self (Eastern Virginia Medical School, Old Dominion University, 1976), 1–10. But my evidence, and nineteenth-century commentary, confirms the claim that irregulars were relatively immune to charges.

97. Wood, "Thoughts on Suits," 399.

98. Chapter 3 contains more discussion on the issue of intraprofessional rivalry.

99. Elwell, *Treatise on Malpractice*, 81, 146–62.

100. Ibid., 37. See also Elisha Bartlett, *An Inquiry into the Degree of Certainty in Medicine; and into the Nature and Extent of Its Power over Disease* (Philadelphia: Lea and Blanchard, 1848), excerpted and reprinted in Gert H. Brieger, ed., *Medical America in the Nineteenth Century: Readings from the Literature* (Baltimore: Johns Hopkins University Press, 1972), 115–27; Erwin H. Ackerknect, "Elisha Bartlett and the Philosophy of the Paris Clinical School," *BHM* 24 (January–February 1950):43–60; and Worthington Hooker, "Uncertainty of Medicine," in Hooker, *Physician and Patient*, 25–49.

101. See chapter 4 for discussion of fracture treatment.

102. Isaac Lefever, "Report on a Trial for Malpractice in the Court of Common Pleas of Perry County, Pennsylvania," *AJMS* 48 (July 1864):72–86.

103. [Justice], "The Late Suit for Mal-Practice in Delaware Co., N.Y.," *BMSJ* 37 (11 August 1847):35–37.

104. "Trial for Malpractice," *BufMJMR* 10 (1854–1855):570.

105. See chapter 1.

106. Smith, "[Review of Elwell]," 159.

107. Wood, "Thoughts on Suits," 400.

108. Elwell, *Treatise on Malpractice*, 22.

109. Ibid., 162.

110. Walter K. Manning, "Prosecution for Mal-Practice," *BMSJ* 40 (23 May 1849):318–19; "Trial for Malpractice," *BMSJ* 41 (10 October 1849):206; W. K. Manning, "Trial for Mal-Practice," *BMSJ* 42 (27 February 1850):79–80.

111. Henry Steele Commager, "The Nationalism of Joseph Story," in *The Bacon Lectures on the Constitution of the United States* (Boston: Boston University Press, 1953), 33–94; and R. Kent Newmyer, *Supreme Court Justice Joseph Story: Statesman of the Old Republic* (Chapel Hill: University of North Carolina Press, 1985), 154–235.

112. Gibbons v. Ogden 9 Wheaton 1 (1824); Wilson v. Blackbird Creek Marsh Co. 2 Peters 245 (1829); and Genessee Chief v. Fitzhugh 12 Howard 443 (1851).

113. Swift v. Tyson 16 Peters 1 (1842).

114. Morton J. Horwitz, *The Transformation of American Law, 1788–1860* (Cambridge: Harvard University Press, 1977), 160–211. See also chapter 7.

115. Story quoted in Horwitz, *Transformation*, 196–97.

116. The locality rule did not surface as a defensive tool for physicians until 1880, when state appellate courts began to rule that the doctrine set limits on the skill required of doctors. Small v. Howard 128 Mass. 131 (1880) is usually cited as the first appellate decision requiring the use of the locality rule. The acceptance of the locality rule by appellate courts is discussed in chapter 8.

117. "Trial for Malpractice," *BufMJMR* 10 (1854–1855):570.

118. "Correction," *WMSJ* 32 (July 1855):50.

119. "Legal Liabilities of Physicians and Surgeons," *BufMSJ* 5 (1855–1866):353–56.

120. "Mal-Practice," *OMSJ* 12 (November 1859):166–67.

121. Andrew A. Sandor, "The History of Professional Liability Suits in the United States," *JAMA* 163 (9 February 1957):459–66.

122. The only study of cases and convictions prepared in the nineteenth century was Eugene F. Sanger's review of physicians and malpractice in Maine. Sanger, "Report on Malpractice," *BMSJ* 100 (2 January 1879):14–23 and *BMSJ* 100 (9 January 1879):41–50.

123. Elwell, *Treatise on Malpractice*, 8.

124. "Prosecution for Mal-Practice," *BMSJ* 48 (20 July 1853):503–4; "Prosecution of Mal-Practice," *BMSJ* 50 (21 June 1854):424–25; and Dixi Crosby, comp., *Report of a Trial for Malpractice* [85 pp.] (Woodstock: Printed by Lewis Pratt, Jr., 1854).

125. T. J. W. Pray, "A Surgical Case of Malpractice," *BMSJ* 51 (8 November 1854):289–97; Leighton v. Sargent 7 Foster 460 (N.H. 1853); and Leighton v. Sargent 31 N.H. 39 (1855). There is a discussion of this case in another context in chapter 7.

126. "Case of Malpractice," *BMSJ* 54 (13 March 1856):109–12.

127. See appendix A.

128. Howard v. Grover 28 Me. 97 at 101 (1848).

129. "Trial for Mal-Practice in Pennsylvania," *BMSJ* 37 (15 September 1847):141–2.

130. Henry Burnell Shafer, *The American Medical Profession, 1783 to 1850* (New York: AMS Press, 1968), 166–68; and Paul Starr, "Medicine, Economy, and Society in Nineteenth-Century America," *JSocH* 10 (Summer 1977):602.

131. See Sandra Cirincione, "The History of Medical Malpractice in New York State: A Perspective from the Publications of the Medical Society of the State of New York," *NYSJM* 86 (July 1986):363–68 for comments on early group defense and insurance plans after 1900.

132. Theodore Nichols, "Trial for Mal-Practice," *OMSJ* 2 (September 1849):10.

133. "Prosecution for Mal-Practice," *OMSJ* 13 (January 1861): 253.

134. Ibid.

3. Schools for Scandal

1. "Extracts from the Report of the Committee on the Prevalence of Suits for Mal-Practice," *MNL* 8 (March 1850):17–20; "[Proceedings of the Kentucky Medical Society, October 1854]," *WJMS* 30 (November 1854):365–67; [S]amuel Parkman and Calvin P. Fiske, "Report on the Causes and Prevention of Suits

for Mal-Practice," *MCMMS* 8 (1853):appendix, 123–32; and "Report on Difficulties Growing Out of Alleged Mal-Practice in the Treatment of Fractures," *TOMS* 11 (1856):53–66.

2. "[The Status of Physicians]," *MSR* 11 (Jan. 1858):60–63.

3. Ibid., 62.

4. Alexander Y. P. Garnett, "Professional Standing; Its Decadence; the Cause; How to Be Remedied; Radicalism; Young America," *MSR* 7 (March 1854):99–100. For other comments on the declining status of physicians in the first half of the nineteenth century, see "The Status of Our Profession," *MSR* 11 (February 1858):133–36; "The Status of Our Profession," *MSR* 11 (March 1858):194–96; and O. H. Taylor, "On the Obvious Decline in the Respect of the Public for the Medical Profession in New Jersey with an Inquiry into Some of Its Causes," *MSR* 11 (July 1858):460–69.

5. Paul Starr, *The Social Transformation of American Medicine* (New York: Basic Books, 1982), 30–32.

6. Ibid., 32–37; and Joseph Kett, *The Formation of the American Medical Profession, 1780–1860* (New Haven: Yale University Press, 1968), 30–31; James H. Cassedy, "Why Self-Help? Americans Alone with their Diseases, 1800–1850," in *Medicine Without Doctors: Home Health Care in American History*, edited by Guenter B. Risse, Ronald L. Numbers, and Judith Walzer Leavitt (New York: Science History Publications, 1977), 31–47.

7. Cassedy, "Why Self-Help?" 31–47; Charles E. Rosenberg, "Medical Text and Social Context: Explaining William Buchan's *Domestic Medicine*," *BHM* 57 (1983):22–42; John Blake, "From Buchan to Fishbein: The Literature of Domestic Medicine," in *Medicine without Doctors*, 11–48; and John Harvey Young, *The Toadstool Millionaires: A Social History of Patent Medicines in America before Federal Regulation* (Princeton: Princeton University Press, 1961), 3–43.

8. Richard Harrison Shryock, *Medicine and Society in America: 1660–1860* (Ithaca: Cornell University Press, 1960), 67–72; and James H. Cassedy, *American Medicine and Statistical Thinking, 1800–1860* (Cambridge: Harvard University Press, 1984), 50–54.

9. Quoted in Martin Kaufman, *Homeopathy in America: The Rise and Fall of a Medical Heresy* (Baltimore: Johns Hopkins University Press, 1971), 2–3.

10. George J. Monroe, quoted in William G. Rothstein, *American Physicians in the Nineteenth Century* (Baltimore: Johns Hopkins University Press, 1972), 49.

11. Quoted in Kaufman, *Homeopathy in America*, 12.

12. Ibid., 1–14; and Sarah Stage, *Female Complaints: Lydia Pinkham and the Business of Women's Medicine* (New York: Norton, 1971) provide useful sketches of heroic practice.

13. Quoted in Rothstein, *American Physicians*, 127.

14. Charles Rosenberg, "The American Medical Profession: Mid–Nineteenth Century," *MA* 44 (1962):166; Rosenberg, "The Therapeutic Revolution: Medicine, Meaning, and Social Change in Nineteenth-Century America,"

in *The Therapeutic Revolution: Medicine Meaning and Change in 19th Century America*, edited by Morris J. Vogel and Charles E. Rosenberg (Philadelphia: University of Pennsylvania Press, 1979), 3–25. John S. Haller surveys nineteenth-century *materia medica* in *American Medicine in Transition, 1840–1910* (Urbana: University of Illinois Press, 1981), 67–99.

15. Rothstein, *American Physicians*, 54; Gert H. Brieger, "Therapeutic Conflicts and the American Medical Profession in the 1860s," *BHM* 41 (1967):215–22.

16. Shryock, *Medicine and Society*, 130–32; Erwin Ackernecht, "Elisha Bartlett and the Philosophy of the Paris Clinical School," *BHM* 24 (1950):49–60; and Cassedy, *American Medicine*, passim.

17. Worthington Hooker, *Physician and Patient* (New York: Baker and Scribner, 1849; reprint, Arno Press, 1972), 25–49; Elisha Bartlett, *An Inquiry into the Degree of Certainty in Medicine; and into the Nature and Extent of Its Power over Disease* (Philadelphia: Lea and Blanchard, 1848), excerpted in *Medical America in the Nineteenth Century: Readings from the Literature*, edited by Gert H. Brieger (Baltimore: Johns Hopkins University Press, 1972), 115–27; Jacob Bigelow, "On Self-Limiting Diseases," *MCMMS* 5 (1836):319–58, excerpted in ibid., 98–106; and Austin Flint, "Conservative Medicine," *AMM* 18 (1852):1–24, reprinted in ibid., 115–26.

18. John Harley Warner, however, demonstrates that the drift away from heroic theory was slow and subtle. See *The Therapeutic Perspective: Medical Practice, Knowledge, and Professional Identity in America, 1820–1885* (Cambridge: Harvard University Press, 1986).

19. See ibid., 58–80.

20. "[Proceedings of the Kentucky Medical Society, October 1854]," 366.

21. Linden F. Edwards, "Resurrection Riots During the Heroic Age of Anatomy in America," *BHM* 25 (1951):178–84; and John B. Blake, 'Anatomy," in *The Education of American Physicians*, edited by Ronald L. Numbers (Berkeley: University of California Press, 1980), 34–38.

22. Quoted in Edwards, "Resurrection Riots," 178.

23. Blake, "Anatomy," 37.

24. "Another Prosecution for Malpractice," *JMCS* 3 (November 1846):406.

25. James Sheldon, "Report of Trial for Malpractice. *William Tims* v. *James P. White*," *BufMJMR* 4 (August 1848):135.

26. John Elwell, *A Medico-Legal Treatise on Medical Malpractice and Medical Evidence* (New York: John S. Voorhis, 1860), 53–54.

27. Blake, "Anatomy," 37–38.

28. Eric H. Christianson, "Medicine in New England," in *Medicine in the New World*, edited by Ronald L. Numbers (Knoxville: University of Tennessee Press, 1987), 117–26.

29. Ibid., 103–6.

30. Ibid.; and Starr, *Transformation*, 37–40.

31. Shryock, *Medicine*, 3–5.

32. Christianson, "Medicine," 112–15, 119–20.

33. Starr, *Transformation*, 40–47.

34. See below for more on licensure in America.

35. Shryock, *Medicine*, 7.

36. In comparison, France had three medical schools in 1850. James H. Cassedy, *Medicine and American Growth, 1800–1860* (Madison: University of Wisconsin Press, 1986), 68.

37. Ludmerer, *Learning*, 11, 47–48; and Martin Kaufman, "American Medical Education," in *Education of American Physicians*, 10–12.

38. [Alfred Stillé and R. M. Huston], "Medical Reform," *MNL* 5 (May 1847):49.

39. [R.C.], "A Report of the Facts and Circumstance Relating to a Case of Compound Fracture and Prosecution for Malpractice," *ME* 4 (1841):712–14.

40. Alden March, "Case of Alleged Mal-Practice in Surgery," *BMSJ* 37 (4 August 1847):13.

41. Peter Dobkin Hall discusses this idea in "The Social Foundations of Professional Credibility: Linking the Medical Profession to Higher Education in Connecticut and Massachusetts," in *The Authority of Experts: Studies in History and Theory*, edited by Thomas L. Haskell (Bloomington: Indiana University Press, 1984), 107–41. However, Hall does not provide a detailed picture of the profound difficulties faced by these early professionals.

42. Richard Hofstadter, *Anti-Intellectualism in American Life* (New York: Vintage, 1962), 154–59; and John William Ward, *Andrew Jackson: Symbol for an Age* (New York: Oxford University Press, 1953), 46–78.

43. Hooker, *Physician and Patient*, 223–24.

44. William M. Wood, "Thoughts on Suits for Malpractice, suggested by certain Judicial Proceedings in Erie County, Pennsylvania," *AJMS* 18 (October 1849):400.

45. [Stillé and Huston], "Medical Reform," 49.

46. Ibid., 49.

47. "To What Causes Are We to Attribute the Diminishing Respectability of the Medical Profession in the Estimation of the American Public?" *MSR* 1 n.s. (1858):141–43.

48. Cassedy, *Medicine and American Growth*, 67–68.

49. These figures include any practitioner, educated or not, who called himself a *physician*.

50. These statistics were drawn from Cassedy, *Medicine and American Growth*, 66–68, 232–33.

51. Samual Jackson, "Critical Analysis," *NYMJ* 8 (March 1847):218–22.

52. Ibid., 232–33. See also Rothstein, *American Physicians*, 344–45 for a discussion of the perceived surplus of physicians.

53. Cassedy, *Medicine and American Growth*, 70.

54. "To What Causes?" 141–43.

55. Stewart, "The Actual Condition of the Medical Profession in This

Country; with a Brief Account of Some of the Causes which Tend to Impede Its Progress, and Interfere with Its Honors and Interests," *NYJM* 6 (1846):151–71, excerpted in *Medical America*, 64.

56. James Adams, Jr., comp., *Report of a Trial of an Action, Charles Lowell against John Faxon and Micajah Hawks Doctors of Medicine, Defendants for Malpractice in the Capacity of Physicians and Surgeons at the Superior Court of Maine Held at Machias for the County of Washington, June 1824 before the Hon. Nathan Weston* (Portland: Printed for James Adams, Jr., by David and Seth Paine, 1825), 7.

57. See chapter 1 for a fuller discussion of this case.

58. Morton J. Horwitz, "The Emergence of an Instrumental Conception of American Law, 1780–1820," in *Law in American History*, edited by Donald Fleming and Bernard Bailyn (Boston: Little, Brown, 1971), 287–326. See also Horwitz, *The Transformation of American Law, 1780–1860* (Cambridge: Harvard University Press, 1977), passim.

59. The standard work on the subject is George Rosen, *Fees and Fee Bills: Some Economic Aspects of Medical Practice in Nineteenth-Century America*, supplement to the *Bulletin of the History of Medicine*, no. 6 (Baltimore: Johns Hopkins University Press, 1946).

60. Daniel H. Calhoun, *Professional Lives in America: Structure and Aspiration, 1750–1850* (Cambridge: Harvard University Press, 1965), 20–58.

61. Stewart, "The Actual Condition," passim and 69, 71. For other comments on the effect of professional quarrels on professional status, see "Review: Medical Ethics," *AJMS* 23 (January 1852):151.

62. "Code of Medical Ethics Adopted by the National Medical Convention in Philadelphia, June 1847," article VI § 1, printed in Hooker, *Physician and Patient*, appendix, 440–53. See Chester R. Burns, "Medical Ethics in the United States Before the Civil War," Ph.D. dissertation (Johns Hopkins University, 1969), 91–125, for a discussion of how other ethical codes were used to blunt the conflict among physicians.

63. Quoted in Starr, *Social Transformation*, 64.

64. S. W. Butler, "Physician's League," *MSR* 7 (March 1854):97.

65. James Harvey Young, *Toadstool Millionaires*, 44–57; Joseph Kett, *Formation of the American Medical Profession*, 96–127.

66. Martin Kaufman, *Homeopathy in America*, 23–47; Kett, *Formation of the American Medical Profession*, 132–64; and James H. Cassedy, *American Medicine and Statistical Thinking*, 124–39.

67. For example, see Wood, "Thoughts on Suits for Malpractice," 395–400.

68. Alden March, "Prosecutions for Malpractice," *BMSJ* 36 (14 July 1847):477–80.

69. Parkman and Fiske, "Report on the Causes and Prevention of Suits for Mal-Practice," 128–29.

70. "S.", "Suits for Mal-Practice," *BMSJ* 51 (13 December 1854):402–3.

71. Stephen Smith, "[Review of John Elwell's Treatise on Malpractice],"

AJMS 40 (July 1860):156. For other claims that suits were instigated by rival practitioners, see William M. Wood, "A Statement of Two Suits for Malpractice, Tried in November and December 1850, in the Court of Erie County, Pa.," *AJMS* 22 (July 1851):43–53.

72. Samuel Parkman, "On the Relations of the Medical Witness with the Law and the Lawyer," *AJMS* 23 (January 1852):128.

73. The jury could not agree on a verdict, and the patient withdrew the charges. Both parties paid their own legal fees and court costs. March, "Case of Alleged Mal-Practice," 9–10.

74. "Critical Analysis," *NYMJ* 3 (March 1847):218–22.

75. Lewis Bauer, "Surgical Contributions," *MSR* 13 (1865):270–72.

76. T. J. W. Pray, "A Surgical Case of Malpractice," *BMSJ* 51 (8 November 1854):289–97. This case is discussed in chapter 7.

77. "Trial for Mal-Practice," *BMSJ* 41 (17 October 1849):216–19.

78. "Trial for Mal-Practice," *BMSJ* 41 (23 January 1849):500–502; "Suit for Mal-Practice in Vermont," *BMSJ* 44 (11 June 1851):377–78.

79. "Prosecution for Mal-practice," *BMSJ* 48 (20 July 1853):503–4.

80. William M. Wood, "Thoughts on Suits," 395–96; Wood, "A Statement of Two Suits," 43–50.

81. Flexner, *Doctors on Horseback: Pioneers of American Medicine* (New York: Dover, 1968), 217–64.

82. "Suit for Mal-Practice," *JMCS* 3 (November 1846):407–8; and "Suit for Malpraxis," *StLMSJ* 3 (May 1846):553–54.

83. [Justice], "The Late Suit for Mal-Practice in Delaware Co., N.Y.," *BMSJ* 37 (11 August 1847):35.

84. T. J. Pray, "A Case of Alleged Mal-Practice," *BMSJ* 54 (24 April 1856):242. For another writer who counseled physicians to be circumspect in judging the work of their peers, see March, "Case of Alleged Malpractice," 9–14.

85. "Suits for Mal-Practice," *BMSJ* 51 (13 December 1854):402–3.

86. Richard Harrison Shryock, *Medical Licensing in America, 1650–1965* (Baltimore: Johns Hopkins University Press, 1967), 3–23.

87. Starr, *Transformation*, 44–45; and Charles E. Rosenberg, *The Cholera Years: The United States in 1832, 1849, and 1866* (Chicago: University of Chicago Press, 1962), 70.

88. See specifically, Alexis de Tocqueville, *Democracy in America*, edited by J. P. Mayer, translated by George Lawrence (Garden City, N.Y.: Doubleday, 1969), 506–13.

89. Arthur M. Schlesinger, Jr., *The Age of Jackson* (Boston: Little, Brown, 1945), 306–21; Marvin Meyers, *The Jacksonian Persuasion* (New York: Vintage, 1960), 185–205; and Rush Welter, *The Mind of America, 1820–1860* (New York: Columbia University Press, 1975), 72–104.

90. Rosenberg, *Cholera Years*, 151–72, quotation at 161.

91. Shryock, *Medical Licensing*, 30–31.

92. Garnett, "Professional Standing," 99–100.

93. Wood, "Thoughts on Suits for Malpractice," 395–96.

94. Smith, "[Review of Elwell]," 154.

95. [Stillé and Huston], "Medical Reform," 50.

96. Lawrence M. Friedman, *A History of American Law* (New York: Simon and Schuster, 1973), 165.

97. Schlesinger, *Age of Jackson*, 329–31.

98. "Extracts from the Report of the Committee," 17, 19. See Kett, *Formation*, 107–21, for a discussion of political rhetoric of the medical sectarians.

99. "Prosecutions of Medical Men," *WJMS* 28 (1853):346–47.

100. March, "Case of Alleged Malpractice," 13.

101. Wood, "Thoughts on Suits," 395–96.

102. [Frank] Hamilton, "Prosecution for Alledged *[sic]* Mal-Practice," *BufMJMR* 4 (1848–1849):275.

103. A "farmer," quoted in "The Greenpoint Malpractice Case," 312–13.

104. Ibid., 313.

105. Ibid.

106. Parkman and Fisk, "Report on the Causes and Prevention of Suits," 129–30.

107. Christopher L. Tomlins, "A Mysterious Power: Industrial Accidents and the Legal Construction of Employee Relations in Massachusetts, 1800–1850," *Law and History Review* 6 (Fall 1988):386, 395.

108. Kenneth Ludmerer, *Learning to Heal: The Development of American Medical Education* (New York: Basic Books, 1985), passim; and Starr, *Transformation*, 123–27.

109. Rothstein, *American Physicians*, 249–81; and Starr, *Transformation* 102–7.

110. Rothstein, *American Physicians*, 305–10; and Thomas Haskell, *The Emergence of Professional Social Science* (Urbana: University of Illinois Press, 1977).

111. See chapter 5 for a discussion of the rarity of malpractice suits in the South.

4. *"The Expression of a Wellmade Man"*

1. Walt Whitman, *Leaves of Grass: The First (1855) Edition*, edited with an introduction by Malcolm Cowley (New York: Viking Press, 1960), 116.

2. See chapter 2; and Charles J. Weigel II, "Medical Malpractice in America's Middle Years," *TRBM* 32 (Spring 1974):193–94.

3. "Suit for Mal-Practice," *OMSJ* 10 (1857–1858):21.

4. See, for example, Charles E. Rosenberg, *The Care of Strangers: The Rise of*

America's Hospital System (New York: Basic Books, 1987), 101; and James H. Cassedy, *American Medicine and Statistical Thinking, 1800–1860* (Cambridge: Harvard University Press, 1984), 85.

5. William G. Rothstein, *American Physicians in the Nineteenth Century: From Sects to Science* (Baltimore: Johns Hopkins University Press, 1972), 27.

6. For example, see Judith Walzer Leavitt, *Brought to Bed: Childbearing in America, 1750–1950* (New York: Oxford University Press, 1986), 36–63 and passim; and Cassedy, *American Medicine and Statistical Thinking*, 80–81.

7. Sumner v. Utley 7 Conn. 257, 260 (1827). Also quoted and discussed in chapter 1. Practitioners in America, unlike many of their counterparts in Britain, performed both surgical and medical procedures, so the judge was drawing a distinction between *surgical* practice and *medical* practice even though both were usually embodied in one practitioner. See Richard Harrison Shryock, *Medicine and Society in America, 1660–1860* (Ithaca: Cornell University Press, 1960), 59–60.

8. Bell quoted in William J. Walker, "On the Treatment of Compound and Complicated Fractures," *MCMMS*, 7 (1842–1848):209.

9. Percival Pott, *Treatise on Compound Fractures* (Philadelphia, 1819), 1:266.

10. Samuel Cooper, *A Dictionary of Practical Surgery* (London, 1813), 420. It is important to note that, as early as 1776, John Jones called perfunctory amputation in compound fractures into question. Jones's position, however, was not accepted. John Jones, *Plain Concise Practical Remarks on the Treatment of Wounds and Fractures* (Philadelphia: Robert Bell, 1776; reprint Arno Press, 1971), 45–46.

11. The issue of *wrongful death* actions is complicated. While there was apparently a common law action for wrongful death, many judges in the early nineteenth century held that there was not. Husbands could, however, sue for loss of consortium. In the early nineteenth century *consortium* was the husband's conjugal rights to his wife's labor and companionship. Women could not sue for loss of consortium until much later in the century. Wex Malone sheds some light on the topic in "The Genesis of Wrongful Death," *SLR* 17 (July 1965):1043–76.

12. Astley Cooper, *The Lectures of Sir Astley*, 4th American ed. (Philadelphia: E. L. Carey and A. Hart, 1835), 616; and Cooper, *A Treatise on Dislocations and on Fractures of the Joints*, 1st American ed., 3rd London ed. (Boston: Wells and Lilly, 1825), 193.

13. For example, see several dozen healed cases reported in Walker, "On the Treatments of Compound and Complicated Fractures," i–lvi; *ME* 3 (1841):207; and *ME* 5 (1843):1555.

14. See note 8, above.

15. Martin S. Pernick, *A Calculus of Suffering: Pain, Professionalism, and Anesthesia in Nineteenth-Century America* (New York: Columbia University Press, 1985), 30, 82–83.

16. Cassedy, *American Medicine and Statistical Thinking*, 85–87.

17. George W. Norris, "Statistical Account of the Cases of Amputation Performed at the Pennsylvania Hospital from Jan. 1, 1831, to Jan. 1, 1838," *AJMS* 22 (1838):356–65. See also Norris, "Statistical Account of the Cases of Amputation Performed at the Pennsylvania Hospital from Jan. 1, 1833, to Jan. 1, 1840," *AJMS* 26 (1840):35–36; Henry W. Buel, "Statistics of Amputation in the New York Hospital from Jan. 1, 1839, to Jan. 1, 1848," *AJMS* 16 (1848):33–43.

18. Austin Flint, "Conservative Medicine," *AMM* 18 (1862):1–24 reprinted in *Medical America in the Nineteenth-Century: Readings from the Literature*, edited by Gert H. Brieger (Baltimore: Johns Hopkins University Press, 1972), 135.

19. Walker, "On the Treatments of Complicated and Compound Fractures," 181.

20. John Elwell, *A Medico-Legal Treatise on Medical Malpractice and Medical Evidence* (New York: John S. Voorhis, 1860), 56, 54–58, and passim.

21. "A Surgical Case of Mal-Practice," *BMSJ* 51 (8 November 1854):292.

22. "Legal Robbery of a Physician," *MN* 14 (April 1856):61–62.

23. Harry E. Pratt, "The Famous 'Chicken Bone' Case," *JISHS* 45 (Summer 1952):166; and Clark Heath, "How Abraham Lincoln Dealt with a Malpractice Suit," *NEJM* 295:735–36.

24. "Anesthesia and Its Influence on Surgery," *MN* 9 (1851):21–22.

25. "A Report of the Facts and Circumstances relating to a case of Compound Fracture and Prosecution for Malpractice . . . ," *WMSJ* 5 (1842):145.

26. Robert T. J. Fox, "The Natural Bonesetters, with Special Reference to the Sweet Family of Rhode Island," *BHM* 28 (1954):416–41.

27. Worthington Hooker, *Physician and Patient: or, A Practical View of the Mutual Duties, Relations, and Interests of the Medical Profession and the Community* (New York: Baker and Scribner, 1849; facsimile reprint Arno Press, 1972), 156, 154–70, and passim.

28. Ibid., 160.

29. Ibid., 161; emphasis added.

30. "Report on Difficulties Growing Out of Alleged Mal-Practice in the Treatment of Fractures," *TOMS* 11 (1856):64–65.

31. S. P. Hildreth, "Trial for Malpractice in Surgery," *OMSJ* 2 (January 1850):220.

32. Quoted in Charles Rosenberg, *The Cholera Years: The United States in 1832, 1849, and 1866* (Chicago, University of Chicago Press, 1962), 157.

33. James Sheldon, "Report of [a] Trial for Mal-practice. *William Times* v. *James P. White*," *BufMJMR* 4 (August 1848):132.

34. "Prosecutions for Mal-Practice," *NHJM* 4 (January 1854):20–23.

35. James H. Cassedy, *American Medicine and Statistical Thinking*, 87–88.

36. "Reviews," *WJMPS* 28 (1853):309–12.

37. For example, see Hamilton, "Report on Deformities after Fractures," *TAMA* 8 (1855):347–93, *TAMA* 9 (1856):69–233, *TAMA* 10 (1857):239–453;

and Hamilton, *A Practical Treatise on Fractures and Dislocations* (Philadelphia: Blanchard and Lea, 1860).

38. "Legal Liability of Physicians and Surgeons," *BuffMSJ* 5 (1865–1866):353–56.

39. "Suit for Alleged Mal-Practice," *OMSJ* 10 (1857–1858):13–24. There was also strong evidence that the patient himself had contributed to the bad result. See above, this chapter.

40. "*Steele* v. *Newton*, Superior Court, Cincinnati; Nov. Term, 1856," Reprinted in Milo Adams McClelland, *Civil Malpractice: A Treatise on Surgical Jurisprudence* (New York: Hurd and Houghton, 1877), 50; "Suit for Alleged Mal-Practice," *OMSJ* 10 (May 1858): 447–51; and "*Mary Ann Decrow, et. al*, v. *H. H. Little:* A Prosecution for Malpractice," *OMSJ* 12 (January 1860):194–98.

41. "Reviews [Review of Frank Hamilton's work]," *AJMS* 39 (April 1860):422.

42. "Jarvis' Adjuster," *WJMPS* 22 (1851):272–73.

43. "A Case of Alleged Mal-Practice." *BMSJ* 54 (24 April 1856):234.

44. "Extracts from the Report of the Committee on the Prevalence of Suits for Malpractice," *MNL* 8 (March 1850):17, 19.

45. Thomas C. Cochran and William Miller, *The Age of Enterprise: A Social History of Industrial America* (New York: Harper and Row, 1961), 1–59.

46. Hugo A. Meier, "Technology and Democracy, 1800–1860," *MVHR* 43 (1956–1957):632; and Arthur Alphonse Ekirch, *The Idea of Progress in America, 1815–1860* (New York: Peter Smith, 1951), 72–143.

47. Meir, "Technology and Democracy," 624–25. Specifically, see Alexis de Tocqueville, "Why the Americans are More Concerned with the Applications than with the Theory of Science," *Democracy in America*, edited by J. P. Mayer, translated by George Lawrence (Garden City, N.Y.: Doubleday, 1969), 459–65.

48. Leo Marx, *The Machine in the Garden: Technology and the Pastoral Ideal in America* (New York: Oxford University Press, 1973), 160–61, 194–97, quotation at 197.

49. James C. Whorton, *Crusaders for Fitness: The History of American Health Reformers* (Princeton: Princeton University Press, 1982), 17–18. For background see Richard S. Westfall, *The Construction of Modern Science Mechanisms and Mechanics* (New York: John Wiley, 1971), 82–104; Siegfried Gideion, *Mechanization Takes Command: A Contribution to Anonymous History* (New York: Norton, 1978), 16–37; and Jan Broekhoff, "Physical Education and the Reification of the Human Body," *Gym* 9 (1972):4–11.

50. Thomas Carlyle, "Signs of the Times" (1829) in *Critical and Miscellaneous Essays* (London: Chapman and Hall, 1899), 2:63, 67.

51. de Tocqueville, *Democracy*, 530, 540.

52. Ibid., 462.

53. Bruce Halley, *The Healthy Body and Victorian Culture* (Cambridge: Harvard University Press, 1978), 21–22.

54. Ailene S. Lockhart and Betty Spears, eds., *Chronicle of American Physi-*

cal Education: Selected Readings, 1855–1930 (Dubuque, Iowa: William C. Brown, 1972), 3–43. See also John R. Betts, "Mind and Body in Early American Thought," *JAH* 54 (March 1968):787–805.

55. Quoted in Harvey Green, *Fit for America: Health, Fitness, Sport and American Society* (New York: Pantheon, 1986), 14.

56. Channing and Emerson quoted in Roberta J. Park, "The Attitudes of Leading New England Transcendentalists Toward Healthful Exercise, Active Recreations, and Proper Care of the Body, 1830–1860," *JSH* 4 (1977):39–41 and 46. See also Roberta J. Park, "Embodied Selves: The Rise and Development of Concern for Physical Education, Active Games and Recreation for American Women, 1776–1865," *JSH* 5 (1978):5–41.

57. Thomas Wentworth Higginson, "Saints and Their Bodies," *AtM* 1 (March 1858):582–86.

58. Whitman, *Leaves of Grass*, 122–23.

59. Betts, "Mind and Body," 788; Broekhoff, "Physical Education and the Reification of the Human Body," 4–11; and Charles W. Griffin, "Physical Fitness," in *Concise Histories of American Popular Culture*, edited by M. Thomas Inge (Westport, Conn.: Greenwood Press, 1982), 262–70.

60. The best discussion of these changes is in Martha H. Verbrugge, *Able-Bodied Womanhood: Personal Health and Social Change in Nineteenth-Century Boston* (New York: Oxford University Press, 1988), esp. 3–10. Anita Clair Fellman and Michael Fellman, *Making Sense of Self: Medical Advice Literature in Late Nineteenth Century America* (Philadelphia: University of Pennsylvania Press, 1981), 5–6; and Green, *Fit for America*, 11–14, are also excellent.

61. Ronald G. Walters, *American Reformers, 1815–1860* (New York: Hill and Wang, 1978), 145–57, quotation at 145.

62. T. J. Jackson Lears, "From Salvation to Self-Realization: Advertising and the Therapeutic Roots of Consumer Culture," in *The Culture of Consumption: Critical Essays in American History, 1880–1980*, edited by Richard Wightman Fox and T. J. Jackson Lears (New York: Pantheon, 1983), 3–38; and Philip Rieff, *The Triumph of the Therapeutic* (New York: Harper and Row, 1966).

5. Community, Providence, and the Social Construction of Legal Action

1. James Adams, Jr., *Report of an Action, Charles Lowell against John Faxon and Micajah Hawks, Doctors of Medicine, Defendants* (Portland: Printed for James Adams, Jr., by David and Seth Paine, 1825), 52. See also chapter 1.

2. Carol J. Greenhouse, "Nature is to Culture as Praying is to Suing: Legal Pluralism in an American Suburb," *JLP* 20 (1982):17.

3. Sally Engle Merry and Susan S. Sibley, "What Do Plaintiffs Want? Reexamining the Concept of Dispute," *JSJ* 9 (1984):151–78; David M. Engel,

"The Oven Bird's Song: Insiders, Outsiders, and Personal Injuries in an American Community," *LSR* 18 (1984):551–61; and Greenhouse, "Nature is to Culture," are enormously helpful in understanding the relationship between community and certain types of litigiousness.

4. Debate concerning the notion of *community* is one of the most contentious and treacherous in contemporary historiography. For the best overview of the complex issues, see Thomas Bender, *Community and Social Change in America* (New Brunswick: Rutgers University Press, 1979).

5. The term and characterization is from Kenneth A. Lockridge, *A New England Town: The First Hundred Years* (New York: Norton, 1970), 16.

6. Ibid., passim.

7. Greenhouse, "Nature is to Culture," 18.

8. Lockridge, *New England Town*, 13–14, 159–60; and Jerold S. Auerbach, *Justice Without Law?* (New York: Oxford University Press, 1983), 19–46.

9. James A. Henretta, *The Evolution of American Society, 1700–1815: An Interdisciplinary Analysis* (Lexington, Mass.: D. C. Heath, 1973), 112–16. Michael Zuckerman, *Peaceable Kingdoms: New England Towns in the Eighteenth Century* (New York: Random House, 1970), argues for the retention of community consensus through 1776 but probably makes his point too strongly.

10. See Richard Bushman, *From Puritan to Yankee: Character and the Social Order in Connecticut, 1690–1765* (Cambridge: Harvard University Press, 1967), 183–95, 258–88.

11. William E. Nelson, *Dispute and Conflict Resolution in Plymouth County, Massachusetts, 1725–1825* (Chapel Hill: University of North Carolina Press, 1981). For a vigorous critique of Nelson's position, see Robert Gordon, "Accounting for Legal Change in American Legal History," in *Law in the American Revolution and the Revolution in the Law*, edited by Hedrick Hartog (New York: New York University Press, 1981), 93–112. For a more general attack on the notion that America has become more litigious, see Marc Galanter, "Reading the Landscape of Disputes: What We Know and Don't Know (and Think We Know) about Our Allegedly Contentious and Litigious Society," *UCLA Law Review* 31 (1983):4–71.

12. Michael H. Frisch, *Town into City: Springfield, Massachusetts, and the Meaning of Community, 1840–1880* (Cambridge: Harvard University Press, 1972), 32–49, quotation at 35.

13. Rowland Berthoff, *An Unsettled People: Social Order and Disorder in American History* (New York: Harper and Row, 1971), 177–234; Richard Brown, "Modernization and the Modern Personality in Early America, 1600–1865: A Sketch of a Synthesis," *Journal of Interdisciplinary History* 11 (Winter 1972):221–22; Robert N. Bellah, et al., *Habits of the Heart: Individualism and Commitment in American Life* (Berkeley: UCLA Press, 1985), vii, viii, 37–38, 222.

14. Engel, "Oven Bird's Song," 559. I have relied heavily on Engel for this argument.

15. These suits were common in early communities. See John Demos, *A

Little Commonwealth: Family Life in Plymouth Colony (New York: Oxford Press, 1982), 49, 112, 138, 153.

16. Engel, "Oven Bird's Song," 558.

17. Henry F. May, "The Decline of Providence?" in *Ideas, Faiths, and Feelings: Essays on American Intellectual and Religious History, 1952–1982* (New York: Oxford University Press, 1983), 136 and passim.

18. Perry Miller provides an excellent discussion of early American attitudes toward divine providence in *The New England Mind: From Colony to Province* (Cambridge: Harvard University Press, 1953).

19. Perry Miller, *The New England Mind: The Seventeenth Century* (Cambridge: Harvard University Press, 1939), 14–17.

20. See, for example, Charles Edwin Clark, "Science, Reason, and an Angry God: The Literature of an Earthquake," *NEQ* 38 (1965): 340–62; Eleanor M. Tilton, "Lightning Rods and the Earthquake of 1755," *NEQ* 13 (March 1940):85–97; and Miller, *From Colony to Province*, 345–66.

21. John Winthrop, *Winthrop's Journal: History of New England, 1630–.649*, edited by James Kendall Hosmer (New York: Charles Scribner's Sons, 1908), 1:114–9, 226, 270, 291; 2: 138, 141, 153–54, 209–10, 220, 354–55.

22. Lewis O. Saum, "Providence in the Popular Mind of Pre–Civil War America," *IMH* 72 (1976):341–42.

23. Miller, *The Seventeenth Century*, 30; and Richard Brown, *Modernization: The Transformation of American Life, 1600–1865* (New York: Hill and Wang, 1976), 111.

24. Charles D. Cashdollar, "Social Implications of the Doctrine of Divine Providence: A Nineteenth-Century Debate in American Theology," *HTR* 71 (1978):268.

25. Religious, "The Doctrine of Providence Vindicated," *CS* 5 (1823):173–74.

26. "The Doctrine of a Particular Providence," *CS* 8 (1836):2.

27. Religious, "The Doctrine of Providence," 175; Cashdollar, *Social Implications*, 277–78.

28. Cashdollar, *Social Implications*, 268, 275, 279, 280–82. For a description of how Americans in the Jacksonian period came to see God's hand in broad national and historical trends, see Lewis O. Saum, *The Popular Mind of Pre–Civil War America* (Westport, Conn.: Greenwood Press, 1980), 3–26; and John William Ward, *Andrew Jackson—Symbol for an Age* (New York: Oxford University Press, 1953), 101–49.

29. "*Michael O'Neil v. Gerard Bancker*," *NYMPJ* 6 (1827):145–52.

30. Ibid.

31. Ibid., 150–51.

32. Charles Lowell, *An Authentic Report of a Trial before the Supreme Judicial Court of Maine for the County of Washington, June Term 1824, Charles Lowell v. Jon Faxon & Micajah Hawks Surgeons . . .* (Portland: Printed for the author, 1826).

33. Ibid., 8. See chapter 1 for an extended narrative on this case.

34. See Grindle, etc. v. Leo Rush et al. 7 Ohio 123–25 (1836).

35. "Extracts from the Report of the Committee on the Prevalence of Suits for Malpractice," *MNL* 8 (March 1850):18–19.

36. Cashdollar, *Social Impliations*, 280; Donald Caton, "The Secularization of Pain," *Anesthesiology* 62 (April 1985):493–501; Ronald L. Numbers and Ronald C. Sawyer, "Medicine and Christianity in the Modern World," in *Health/Medicine and the Faith Traditions: An Inquiry into Religion and Medicine*, edited by Martin E. Marty and Kenneth Vaux (Philadelphia: Fortress Press, 1982), 133–60; Miller, *The Seventeenth Century*, passim; and Albert Post, *Popular Freethought in America, 1825–1850* (New York: Columbia University Press, 1943).

37. Charles Cashdollar, "European Positivism and the American Unitarianism," *CH* 45 (1976):490–92.

38. Cashdollar, *Social Implications*, 283; and Robert Bremner, *From the Depths: The Discovery of Poverty in the United States*. (New York: New York University Press, 1956), 16–45.

39. John L. Thomas, "Romantic Reform in America, 1815–1865," *American Quarterly* 17 (Winter 1965):656–81.

40. The literature on the history of reform is both rich and vast. A small sample includes: James Turner, *Reckoning with the Beast: Animals, Pain, and Humanity in the Victorian Mind* (Baltimore: Johns Hopkins University Press, 1980); Robert Bremner, *American Philanthropy* (Chicago: University of Chicago Press, 1960), ch. 1 and 2; Arthur M. Schlesinger, *The American as Reformer* (Cambridge: Harvard University Press, 1950); and Ronald G. Walters, *American Reformers, 1815–1860* (New York: Hill and Wang, 1978).

41. Cashdollar, *Social Implications*, 280; Caton, "Secularization of Pain," 497.

42. James H. Cassedy, *American Medicine and Statistical Thinking, 1800–1860* (Cambridge: Harvard University Press, 1984); and in general Thomas M. Porter, *The Rise of Statistical Thinking, 1820–1900* (Princeton: Princeton University Press, 1986).

43. Numbers and Sawyer, "Medicine and Christianity," passim.

44. Irving H. Bartlett, *The American Mind in the Mid–Nineteenth Century* (New York: Thomas Y. Crowell Company, 1967), 5–18; and Martin E. Marty, *Righteous Empire: The Protestant Experience in America* (New York: Dial Press, 1970), 83–88.

45. William G. McLoughlin, "Introduction to Charles G. Finney, *Lectures on Revivals of Religion*," in *Essays on Jacksonian America*, edited by Frank Otto Gatell (New York: Holt, Rinehart and Winston, 1970), 242.

46. Ibid., passim. Also, for an insightful commentary on these issues, see Major L. Wilson, "Paradox Lost: Order in Evangelical Thought in Mid–Nineteenth-Century America," *CH* 44 (September 1975):352–66.

47. Walters, *American Reformers*, 145–46, 171, and 145–72 generally.

48. McLoughlin, "Introduction," 252–53; and Paul E. Johnson, *A Shopkeeper's Millennium: Society and Revivals in Rochester, New York, 1815–1837* (New York: Hill and Wang, 1978), 3–14.

49. McLoughlin, "Introduction," 252; see also Whitney R. Cross, *The Burned-Over District: The Social and Intellectual History of Enthusiastic Religion in Western New York, 1800–1850* (New York: Harper and Row, 1965).

50. Johnson, *Shopkeeper's Millennium*, 5, 109.

51. John Duffy, *Epidemics in Colonial America* (Baton Rouge: Louisiana State University, 1953); J. H. Powell, *Bring Out Your Dead* (Philadelphia: University of Pennsylvania Press, 1949).

52. Quoted in William Gribbin, "Divine Province or Miasma? The Yellow Fever Epidemic of 1822," *NYH* 53 (July 1972):287, 289.

53. Ibid., 294–97.

54. Ibid., 298.

55. Rosenberg, *The Cholera Years: The United States in 1832, 1849, and 1866* (Chicago: University of Chicago Press, 1962), 43.

56. Ibid., 40–54. See also Numbers and Sawyer, "Medicine and Christianity," 137–40.

57. Quoted in Rosenberg, *Cholera Years*, 128, 130.

58. "Causes and Prevention of Epidemics," *Har* 15 (1857):194–203.

59. Rosenberg, *Cholera Years*, 193–96.

60. See for example Cassedy, *American Medicine and Statistical Thinking*, 222–27.

61. Numbers and Sawyer, "Medicine and Christianity," 139; Rosenberg, *Cholera Years*, 5. For a helpful interpretation of the origins of this transformation see Thomas, *Religion*, 647–68.

62. For example, Keith Thomas offers a discussion of the use of supernatural explanations to ease acceptance of misfortune, *Religion and the Decline of Magic: Studies in Popular Beliefs in the Sixteenth and Seventeenth Centuries in England* (London: Weidenfeld, 1971), 5–7, 651–63. See also Ivan Illich, *Medical Nemesis: The Expropriation of Health* (New York: Pantheon, 1976), 133–54.

63. See Walter Kaufman, "Suffering and the Bible," in *The Faith of a Heretic* (Garden City, N.Y.: Doubleday, 1961), 137–69; and H. B. Gibson, *Pain and Its Conquest* (Boston: Peter Owen, 1982), 22.

64. Caton, "Secularization of Pain," 493.

65. Although he makes a slightly different argument, Daniel De Moulin, "A Historical-Phenomenological Study of Bodily Pain in Western Man," *BHM* 48 (Winter 1974):540–71, surveys some of the literature. See also Caton, "Secularization of Pain," passim.

66. Nathan P. Rice, *Trials of a Public Benefactor* (New York: Pudney and Russell, 1859), 124.

67. Ibid., 125.

68. Ibid., 126.

69. Two of the most learned discussions of these general issues are: Boyd Hilton, *The Age of Atonement: The Influence of Evangelicalism on Social and Economic Thought, 1795–1865* (Oxford: Clarendon Press, 1988); and Charles D. Cashdollar, *The Transformation of Theology, 1830–1890: Positivism and Protestant Thought in Britain and America* (Princeton: Princeton University Press, 1989).

Martin Pernick provides the most important discussion of the interrelationship of pain, anesthesia, and religious beliefs in *A Calculus of Suffering: Pain, Professionalism and Anesthesia in Nineteenth Century America* (New York: Columbia University Press, 1985), 49–57 and passim.

70. Caton, "Secularization of Pain," 496. For samples of Bentham's and Mill's comments on pain see *Utilitarianism and Other Essays*, edited by Alan Ryan (New York: Penguin, 1987), 93–97, 278–79.

71. Caton, "Secularization of Pain," 497.

72. See Turner, *Reckoning with the Beast*.

73. Pernick, *A Calculus of Suffering*, 49–57; and John Duffy, "Anglo-American Reaction to Obstetrical Anesthesia," *BHM* 38 (January–February 1964):32–44.

74. North Carolina; Alabama; Arkansas; Florida; Georgia; Louisiana; South Carolina; Mississippi; Tennessee; Texas; and Virginia — calculated from Hubert Winston Smith, "Legal Responsibility for Medical Malpractice," *JAMA* 116 (1941):2672–73; and Chester R. Burns, "Malpractice Suits in America before the Civil War," *BHM* 43 (1969):41–56.

75. "Case of a Trial for Malpractice," *BMSJ* 57 (March 19, 1857):148.

76. Hamilton, "Suits for Malpractice in Surgery," in *Papers Read Before the Medico-Legal Society of New York, 1875–1878* (New York: Medico-Legal Society of New York, 1886), 98–99.

77. "Report of the Section of Surgery and Anatomy," *TAMA* (1873):226–29.

78. For example, see John Harley Warner, "Southern Medical Reform: The Meaning of the Antebellum Argument for Southern Medical Education," *BHM* 57 (Fall 1983):367; James O. Breeden, "Thomsonianism in Virginia," *VMHB* 82 (1974):150–80; John Duffy, ed., *History of Medicine in Louisiana* (Baton Rouge: Louisiana State University Press, 1962), 2:32–42; and Alex Berman, "The Thomsonian Movement and its Relation to American Pharmacy and Medicine," *BHM* 25 (September–October 1951):407.

79. James O. Breeden, "Body Snatchers and Anatomy Professors: Medical Education in Nineteenth-Century Virginia," *VMHB* 83 (1975):321–45; and Todd L. Savitt, "The Use of Blacks for Medical Experimentation and Demonstration in the Old South," *Journal of Southern History* 48 (1982):331–48.

80. John Duffy, "American Perceptions of the Medical, Legal, and Theological Professions," *BHM* 58 (1984):7.

81. John Harley Warner, *The Therapeutic Perspective: Medical Practice, Knowledge, and Professional Identity in America, 1820–1885* (Cambridge: Harvard University Press, 1986), 71–72; Martin Kaufman, *Homeopathy in America: The Rise and Fall of a Medical Heresy* (Baltimore: Johns Hopkins University Press, 1971), 10–11; John Duffy ed., *History of Medicine in Louisiana* (Baton Rouge: Louisiana State University Press, 1950), 1:69–80; Duffy, *Medicine in Louisiana*, 2:3–42; J. Marion Sims, *The Story of My Life* (New York: Da Capo Press, 1968), 171–72, for comments on heroic practice in the antebellum South.

82. Elliot J. Gorn, " 'Gouge and Bite, Pull Hair and Scratch': The Social Significance of Fighting in the Southern Backcountry," *AHR* 90 (February, 1985):27, 29, 40. See also Bertram Wyatt-Brown, *Southern Honor: Ethics and Behavior in the Old South* (New York: Oxford University Press, 1982), passim; and Edward L. Ayers, *Vengeance and Justice, Crime and Punishment in the Nineteenth-Century American South* (New York: Oxford University Press, 1984).

83. See Brown, *Modernization*, 114, 129, 152–53, for comments on the South's retention of traditional communal structures.

84. John B. Boles, "Evangelical Protestantism in the Old South: From Religious Dissent to Cultural Dominance," in *Religion in the Old South*, edited by Charles Reagan Wilson (Jackson: University Press of Mississippi, 1985), 13–34.

85. Elizabeth Fox-Genovese and Eugene D. Genovese, "The Divine Sanction of Social Order: Religious Foundations of the Southern Slaveholders' World View," *JAAR* 55 (Summer 1987):211–33; and Anne Loveland, *Southern Evangelicals and the Social Order, 1800–1860* (Baton Rouge: Louisiana State University Press, 1980).

86. Clement Eaton, *The Mind of the Old South* (Baton Rouge: Louisiana State University Press, 1964), 159–61, 174–80; Eaton, *The Freedom of Thought Struggle in the Old South* (New York: Harper and Row, 1964), 300–305; Frank Lawrence Owsley, *Plain Folk of the Old South* (Baton Rouge: Louisiana State University Press, 1949), 96; and R. M. Weaver, "The Older Religiousness in the South," *SR* 51 (1943):237–49.

87. C. Vann Woodward, *The Burden of Southern History* (Baton Rouge: Louisiana State University Press, 1968), 21; and Winfred B. Moore, Jr., Joseph F. Tripp, and Lyon G. Tyler, Jr., eds., *Developing Dixie: Modernization in a Traditional Society* (Westport, Conn.: Greenwood Press, 1988), xvii–xxiii.

88. John B. Boles, *The Great Revival, 1787–1805* (Lexington: University Press of Kentucky, 1972), 183–203; and Tommy W. Rogers, "Dr. Fredrick Ross and the Presbyterian Defense of Slavery," *JPH* 45 (March 1967):112–24, esp. 118–19, 122–24.

89. Caton, "Secularization of Pain," 498–99.

90. For example, see Wyatt-Brown, *Southern Honor*, 165–66, 340, 341, 344–46.

91. Samuel D. Gross, *Autobiography of Samuel D. Gross* (Philadelphia: George Barrie, Publisher, 1887; reprint Arno Press, 1972), 2:44, 202–3.

92. Edward Warren, *A Doctor's Experiences in Three Continents* (Baltimore: Cushings and Bailey, 1885), 31.

93. Quotation from Gorn, "Gouge and Bite," 40. Also see W. J. Cash, *The Mind of the South* (New York: Random House, 1941), 56–57, 83–84; and Wyatt-Brown, *Southern Honor*, 25–30.

94. Carol Greenhouse, *Praying for Justice: Faith, Order, and Community in an American Town* (Ithaca: Cornell University Press, 1986); Greenhouse, "Interpreting American Litigiousness," paper presented at the Wenner-Gren Foun-

dation for Anthropological Research, Bellagio, Italy, 10–18 August 1985; and "Nature is to Culture as Praying is to Suing: Legal Pluralism in an American Suburb," *JLP* 20 (1982):17–35.

95. Residents relied on such biblical invocations as: "Pray for them which despitefully use you" (Matthew 5:44); "Be not overcome by evil, but overcome evil with good." (Romans 13:21); and "Dearly beloved, avenge not yourself" (Romans 12:19). See Greenhouse, *Praying*, 80–81.

96. Ibid., 43, 79, 107, 115, 118, 182.

97. See, for example, Martin E. Marty," "From Providence to Progress," in *Righteous Empire*, 188–98.

6. *"Dangerous Ground for a Surgeon"*

1. "Accusation of Mal-Practice," *BMSJ* 31 (11 September 1844):123–24.

2. Frank H. Hamilton, "Suits for Malpractice in Surgery," *Papers Read Before the Medico-Legal Society of New York, 1875–1878* (New York: Medico-Legal Society of New York, 1886), 99, 100.

3. "Prosecutions for Mal-Practice," *NHJM* 4 (January 1854):20–23.

4. "Medical Science in New York," *BMSJ* 15 (16 November 1836):241–42.

5. Alex Berman, "The Thomsonian Movement and Its Relation to American Pharmacy and Medicine," *BHM* 25 (September–October 1951):405–8.

6. Marvin Meyers, *The Jacksonian Persuasion: Politics and Beliefs* (New York: Vintage, 1957), 235–36.

7. Walter Hugins, *Jacksonian Democracy and the Working Class: A Study of the New York Workingman's Movement, 1829–1837* (Stanford: University of Stanford Press, 1960), 166–71; William Trimble, "The Social Philosophy of the Loco-Foco Democracy," *AJS*, 31 (May 1921):710–15; Meyers, *Jacksonian Persuasion*, 183–205.

8. Stewart, "The Actual Condition of the Medical Profession in This Country . . . ," *NYJM* 6 (1846):151–71, reprinted in Gert H. Brieger, ed., *Medical America in the Nineteenth Century: Readings from the Literature* (Baltimore: Johns Hopkins University Press, 1972), 69–70.

9. These observations on the New York medical profession before 1850 were drawn mostly from Daniel Calhoun's study of the physicians in that state. See chapter 2 of his *Professional Lives in America: Structure and Aspiration, 1750–1850* (Cambridge: Harvard University Press, 1965), especially 24–27, 34–37, 46–58.

10. See chapter 2.

11. "Surgical Malpractice," *BMSJ* 36 (5 May 1847):283–84.

12. "A Report of the Facts and Circumstances Relating to a Case of Compound Fracture, and Prosecution for Malpractice," *AJMS* 3 n.s. (January 1842):181–84; some accounts reported that the scaffolding collapsed beneath Smith.

13. D. W., "Shipman, Azariah B. (1803–1868)," *A Cyclopedia of American Medical Biography: Comprising the Lives of Eminent Deceased Physicians and Surgeons, 1610–1900*, edited by Howard Kelly (Philadelphia: W. B. Saunders, 1912), 2:366–67.

14. "A Report of the Facts," *AJMS* 3 n.s. (January 1842):181; also "A Report of the Facts and Circumstances Relating to a Case of Compound Fracture and Prosecution for Malpractice," *WMSJ* 5 (1842):141–48.

15. Howard A. Kelly and Walter L. Burrage, *Dictionary of American Medical Biography* (New York: D. Appleton, 1928), 626–27; "Hyde, Fredrick," *A Biographical Dictionary of Contemporary American Physicians and Surgeons*, 2d ed., edited by William Biddle Atkinson, (Philadelphia: Brinton, 1879), 208.

16. *Courtland Republic and Eagle*, 17 May 1836, 5.

17. Ibid.

18. A. B. Shipman, *A Report of the Facts and Circumstances Relating to a Case of Compound Fracture and Prosecution for Malpractice, in which William Smith Was Plaintiff, and Drs. Goodyear and Hyde Defendants, at Cortland Village, Cortland County, N. Y., March 1841: Comprising Statements of the Case by Several Medical Gentlemen, Together with Notes and Comments on the Testimony* (Cortlandville: Printed at the office of the *Cortland Democrat*, 1841), 8, 13, 16.

19. "A Report of the facts," *AJMS* 3 n.s. (January 1842):181–83; Shipman, *A Report of the Facts*, 4.

20. "A Report of the Facts," *AJMS* 3 n.s. (January 1842):181–84; "A Report of the Facts," *WMSJ* 5 (1842):141–48.

21. Shipman, *A Report of the Facts*, 17.

22. "A Report of the Facts," *AJMS* 3 n.s. (January 1842):181–84; "A Report of the Facts," *WMSJ* 5 (1842):141–48.

23. Shipman, *A Report of the Facts*, 7.

24. Hamilton published his famous fracture tables between 1849 and 1360. Though his study appeared too late to influence this case, his work was often cited by defense attorneys in later malpractice cases. See chapter 4.

25. "A Report of the Facts," *AJMS* 3 n.s. (January 1842):181–82. For excerpts of Webster's and Hamilton's testimony, also see "A Report of the Facts," *Western Journal of Medical and Physician Surgery* 5 (1842):145–48.

26. Shipman, *A Report of the Facts*, 16.

27. *Cortland Democrat*, 4 May 1841, 2. Reproductions of the *Cortland County Whig* for the 1840s are not existant, but the debate may be followed with some success in the *Democrat*, which reprinted several of the letters that appeared initially in the *Whig*.

28. Ibid.

29. Ibid.

30. "A Report of the Facts," *AJMS* 3 n.s. (January 1842):182.

31. Shipman, *A Report of the Facts*, 3.

32. See n. 17 above.

33. "Trial for Malpractice," *BMSJ* 25 (8 September 1841):73–75.

34. See chapter 4.

35. "Cases of Compound Fracture of the Leg," *BMSJ* 25 (8 September 1841):73–75.

36. R. C., "A Report of the Facts and Circumstance Relating to a Case of Compound Fracture and Prosecution for Malpractice," *ME* 4 (1841):712–14.

37. R. C., "The Cortlandville Trial for Malpractice," *ME* 4 (1841):766–67.

38. G. W. N. [George W. Norris], "Bibliographic Notices," *AJMS* 3 n.s. (January 1842):181–84.

39. *Cortland Democrat*, 2 February 1842, 2–3; "The Cortland Case of Malpractice," *ME* 5 (5 March 1842):149–51.

40. "The Cortland Case," *ME* 5 (5 March 1842):149–51.

41. Cooper, *The Lectures of Sir Astley Cooper*, 4th American ed. (Philadelphia: E. L. Carey and A. Hart, 1835), 628–30.

42. See chapters 3 and 4.

43. "A Report of the Facts," *WJMS* 5 (1842):145.

44. "Trial of Dr. Shipman for Mal-Practice," *BMSJ* 31 (18 September 1844):140–42.

45. "Accusation of Mal-Practice," *BMSJ* 31 (11 September 1844):123–24; "Trial of Dr. Shipman for Mal-Practice," *BMSJ* 31 (18 September 1844):140–42.

46. Kelly and Burrage, *American Medical Biography*, 626–27; and Atkinson, *Dictionary of Contemporary American Physicians*, 208.

47. Stewart, "Actual Condition of the Medical Profession," 70–71.

7. The Road Not Taken: Medical Malpractice and the Path of the Common Law

1. Kennedy v. Parrott 243 N.C. 355 (1956), quoted in Louis B. Harrison, Melvin H. Worth, Jr., and Michael A. Carlucci, "The Development of the Principles of Medical Malpractice in the United States," *PBM*, 29 (Autumn 1985):46.

2. Harrison, Worth, and Carlucci, "Principles of Medical Malpractice," 42.

3. G. Edward White, *Tort Law in America: An Intellectual History* (New York: Oxford University Press, 1980), 8–10. See also Percy H. Winfield, *The Province of The Law of Tort* (Cambridge: Cambridge University Press, 1931), 27–28; and Richard B. Morris, "Responsibility for Tortious Acts in Early American Law," in *Studies in the History of American Law* (Philadelphia: J. M. Mitchell, 1959), 207.

4. William Blackstone, *Commentaries*, St. George Tucker's ed. Vol. 3 (Philadelphia: William Birch Young and Abraham, 1803), 122, 123.

5. The ten actions included: trespass; debt; covenant; account; assumpsit; detinue; trespass on the case; trover; ejectment; and replevin. For a short and clear description of early American pleading see Mitchell G. Williams, "Plead-

ing Reform in Nineteenth-Century America: The Joinder of Actions at Common Law under the Codes," *JLH* 6 (1985):299–335; and William Nelson, *The Americanization of the Common Law: The Impact of Legal Change on Massachusetts Society, 1760–1830* (Cambridge: Harvard University Press, 1975), 21–23. 71–87.

6. C. H. S. Fifoot, *History and Sources of the Common Law* (New York: Greenwood Press, 1970), 67–78.

7. Ibid., 75–77, 156–58. Research is underway which challenges the standard historiography on the origins and development of the modern writ system. See Robert Palmer, "In Plague and Oppression: The Foundations of Anglo-American Law, 1348–1381," presented as the Harold and Margaret Rorschach Lecture in Legal History, Rice University, 15 February 1989.

8. Quoted in Hubert Winston Smith, "Legal Responsibility for Medical Malpractice," *JAMA* 116 (31 May 1941):2490.

9. Fifoot, *History and Sources*, 157.

10. Everard v. Hopkins 2 Bulst. 332; 80 E. R. 1164; quoted in Smith, "Legal Responsibility," 2491.

11. Smith, ibid., makes a similar point at 2492.

12. Blackstone, *Commentaries*, 3:123.

13. Slater v. Baker and Stapleton 2 Wils 359.

14. *Slater* is noted, for example, in Landon v. Humphrey 9 Day 209 (Conn. 1832); Howard v. Grover 15 Me. 97 (1848); and Mc Candless v. Mc Wha 22 Penn. 261 (1857).

15. Seare v. Prentice 8 East's Term Rep. 347 (1807).

16. Landon 9 Day 216.

17. Lamphier v. Phipos 8 Carr & Payne 475 (1838).

18. Decision reprinted in Martin J. Wade, *A Selection of Cases on Malpractice of Physicians, Surgeons, and Dentists* (St. Louis: Medico-Legal Pub. Co., 1909), 21–23.

19. For examples of American judges who incorporated Tyndall's language, see Patten v. Wiggin 51 Me. 549; Leighton v. Sargent 7 N. H. 460 (1853); Reynolds v. Graves 3 Wisc. 416 (1854); Graham v. Gautier 21 Tx. 111 (1858); and Richey v. West 23 Ill. 385 (1860).

20. I am indebted to Thomas L. Haskell, *The Emergence of Professional Social Science: The American Social Science Association and the Nineteenth-Century Crisis of Authority* (Urbana: University of Illinois Press, 1977), 65–75, for introducing me to these ideas.

21. Blackstone, *Commentaries*, 3:28; John Ordronaux, *The Jurisprudence of Medicine* (Philadelphia: T. and J. W. Johnson, 1869), 34–35.

22. Ordronaux, *Jurisprudence of Medicine*, 10–11.

23. Ibid., 37.

24. Adams v. Stevens & Cagger 26 Wendell 448 at 455 (N.Y. 1841).

25. Morton Horwitz, *The Transformation of American Law, 1780–1860* (Cambridge: Harvard University Press, 1977), 181–83.

26. Ordronaux, *Jurisprudence of Medicine*, 14.

27. Henry Maine, *Ancient Law* (New York: Henry Holt, 1884), 164–65. See also Bernard Schwartz, *Law in America* (New York: McGraw Hill, 1974), 117–18. This explanatory theory can easily be carried too far. For a sober analysis of its utility, see R. H. Graveson, "The Movement from Status to Contract," 4 *MLR* (April 1941):261–67.

28. Grant Gilmore, *The Death of Contract* (Columbus: Ohio State University Press, 1974); Horwitz, *Transformation*, 160–210; Lawrence Friedman, *Contract Law in America: A Social and Economic Case Study* (Madison: University of Wisconsin Press, 1965); and P. S Atiyah, *The Rise and Fall of Freedom of Contract* (Oxford: Clarendon Press, 1979), esp. 167–68.

29. Horwitz, *Transformation*, 160–201.

30. Nelson, *Americanization*, deals with early American practice in detail. Also, though some of the conclusions are questionable, Herbert A. Johnson, "Civil Procedure in John Jay's New York," *AJLH* 11 (January 1967):69–80, discusses early legal practice.

31. Nelson, *Americanization*, 21–23, 71–76; Joseph H. Koffler and Alison Reppy, *Handbook of Common Law Pleading* (St. Paul: West Publishing, 1969), 10–17, 37–45.

32. Edson R. Sunderland, *Cases on Procedure Code Pleading* (Chicago: Callaghan and Company, 1923), 6; Nelson, *Americanization*, 77.

33. Nelson, *Americanization*, 83.

34. White, *Tort Law in America*, 9–12; Nelson, *Americanization*, 81; and Percy H. Winfield, *The Province of the Law of Tort*, 27–30, for the imprecise distinction between the various categories of law in the late eighteenth and early nineteenth centuries.

35. Koffler and Reppy, *Common Law Pleading*, 47.

36. See chapter 1.

37. Joseph Chitty, *A Practical Treatise on Pleading and on Parties to Actions and Forms of Actions* (New York: C. Wiley, 1812), 1:92, 134, 137.

38. John Simcoe Saunders, *The Law of Pleading and Evidence in Civil Actions* (Philadelphia: Robert H. Small, 1844), 1:90.

39. See above, chapter 1.

40. White, *Tort Law in America*, chs. 1 and 2.

41. Grannis et ux v. Branden 5 Conn. 260 at 269.

42. Charles Lee, "Medical Jurisprudence," *NYJMCS* 1 (November 1843):352.

43. For more on the case, see Landon v. Humphrey 5 Conn. 209 (1832); and "Alleged Malpractice," *BMSJ* 6 (21 March 1832):98–99.

44. Lee, "Medical Jurisprudence," 354–56.

45 Landon v. Humphrey 5 Conn. 209, 210 (1832).

46. The prosecution was allowed as many counts of wrongdoing as they wished, but all the counts had to support the one writ. In this first count, Landon's attorney accused Humphrey of what amounted to misfeasance. *Misfeasance* was grounds for an action on the case and was the doing of an act in an injurious manner, or the improper performance of an act that might other-

wise have been lawfully done. In this instance, Humphrey, acting through his agent, had improperly performed the otherwise legal act of vaccination.

47. In this count Humphrey was being accused of nonfeasance. *Nonfeasance* occurred when a person failed to perform a duty that was required of him.

48. Lee, "Medical Jurisprudence," 354–59.

49. Ibid., 360–61; Landon v. Humphrey 5 Conn. 209, 212–13 (1832).

50. Landon v. Humphrey 5 Conn. 209, 213–14 (1832).

51. Idem, 209.

52. Gordon Wood, *The Creation of the American Republic, 1776–1787* (New York: Norton, 1969), 295–305; and Carl L. Becker, *The Declaration of Independence: A Study in the History of Political Ideas* (New York: Random House, 1921), 30–36, 68–75.

53. Bernard Bailyn, *Education in the Forming of American Society* (New York: Vintage, 1960), 29–36.

54. Magali Sarfatti Larson, *The Rise of Professionalism: A Sociological Analysis* (Berkeley: University of California Press, 1977), 105, 110.

55. Alexis de Tocqueville, *Democracy in America*, edited by J. P. Mayer, translated by George Lawrence (Garden City, N.Y.: Anchor, 1969), 507.

56. George Dargo, *Law in the New Republic: Private Law and the Public Estate* (New York: Alfred A. Knopf, 1983), 40.

57. Horwitz, *Transformation*, 173–210. Horwitz's thesis is not universally applicable and has come under considerable attack. For example, see A. W. B. Simpson, *Legal Theory and Legal History: Essays on the Common Law* (London: Hambledon Press, 1987). While much of the criticism of Horwitz is justified, he does illuminate an important trend in early nineteenth-century law and errs mostly from overstatement.

58. Horwitz, *Transformation*, 201–10.

59. Bowman v. Woods 1 G. Greene 441 at 442 (Iowa). See chapter 2 for a discussion of another aspect of this case.

60. Idem, at 442–43.

61. Idem, at 443–44.

62. For cases that exhibited similar contractual language, see Piper v. Menifee 51 Ky. 465 (1851); Alder v. Buckley 1 Swan 69 (Tenn. 1851); Moody v. Sabin 63 Mass. 505 (1852).

63. John Dawson, "Suit for Damages in a Case of Fracture of the Leg, Followed by Mortification and Amputation," *OMSJ* 14 (1 July 1862):284.

64. Ordronaux, *Jurisprudence of Medicine*, in fact refers to the doctor-patient relationship as quasicontractual.

65. T. J. W. Pray, "A Surgical Case of Malpractice," *BMSJ* 51 (8 November 1854):289–90.

66. Ibid.

67. Ibid., 289–91.

68. Leighton's lawyer used a "trespass on the case writ."

69. Leighton v. Sargent 7 Foster 460 at 460–63, 465 (N.H. 1853); *BMSJ*

51 (1854):290; Chester Burns presented a short discussion of this case in his "Medical Ethics in the United States Before the Civil War," Ph.D. dissertation (Johns Hopkins University, 1969), 147–48.

70. Leighton v. Sargent 7 Foster 460 at 465; (N.H. 1853); *BMSJ* 51:290.

71. Pray, "A Surgical Case," 290.

72. Ibid., 291.

73. Leighton v. Sargent 7 Foster 460 at 464–66 (N.H. 1853).

74. Idem, at 468, 469, 471, 472.

75. Idem, 460 at 472. After losing his award in the state supreme court, Leighton again charged Dr. Sargent with malpractice in the Strafford county court. The jury again sided with Leighton and fined Sargent $525 plus the cost of both trials. Sargent appealed to the state supreme court in 1855, claiming that three jurors at the second trial had shared a "gill" of brandy the night before they agreed on the guilty verdict. On these grounds, the supreme court set aside the verdict and called for a third trial. Finally, after five years of litigation, Leighton and Sargent agreed to an undisclosed, out-of-court settlement. Leighton v. Sargent 11 Foster 119, 130, 138 (N.H. 1855); and Milo McClelland, *Civil Malpractice* (New York: Hurd and Houghton 1877), 210.

76. "Case of Alleged Malpractice," *BMSJ* 54 (24 April 1856):239.

77. Harrison, Worth, and Carlucci, "Development of the Principles of Medical Malpractice," 42, 44, 45.

78. Horwitz, *Transformation*, 206.

79. "Surgical Malpractice," *BMSJ* 36 (5 May 1847):283–84.

80. "Prosecution for Malpractice," *ME* 14 (n.s. 8) (1851):728–29.

81. "Important Case of Alleged Malpractice," *Scal* 9 (April 1857): 56.

82. "Suit for Malpractice," *BMSJ* 50 (19 April 1854):246. For other references to the use of bonds to stifle suits, see "Prosecutions for Malpractice," *BMSJ* 51 (8 November 1854):305; "Prosecutions of Medical Men," *WMSJ* 28 (1853):346–47; "Prosecutions for Malpractice," *BMSJ* 48 (11 May 1853):304.

83. "The Greenpoint Malpractice Case," *Scal* 8 (April 1856):311–15.

84. Ibid., 315.

85. John Dawson, "Suit for Damages in a Case of Fracture of the Leg, Followed by Mortification and Amputation," *OMSJ* 14 (1 July 1862):283–84.

86. Ibid., 284–85.

87. Ibid., 287–88. For more discussion of contracting away, see Joel Parker, "Extract from a Lecture on the Rights and Liabilities of the Physician and Surgeon," *WMSJ* 31 (March 1855):217–19.

88. Worthington Hooker, *Physician and Patient*, 410.

89. "Valentine Mott on Medical Ethics; He Throws a Medical Boomerang," *Scal* 9 (July 1857):125–26.

90. Samuel Parkman and Calvin P. Fiske, "Report on the Causes and Prevention of Suits for Mal-Practice," *MCMMS* 8 (1853): appendix, 124.

91. Parkman and Fiske, "Report on the Causes and Prevention," 130.

92. Joel Parker, "Extract from a Lecture," 218.

93. "Case of Mal-Practice," *BMSJ* 54 (13 March 1856):112. See also "Trial for Malpractice—Dr. Crosby's Acquittal," *BMSJ* 50 (21 June 1854):424–25, for more medical opposition to contracting away.

94. Ordronaux, *The Jurisprudence of Medicine*, 104; and Elwell, *A Medico-Legal Treatise on Malpractice and Medical Evidence* (New York: John Voorhis, 1860). Courts accepted special contracts from common carriers until 1873, when the United States Supreme Court, in N.Y. Central R.R. v. Lockwood 84 U.S. 357, ruled against them.

95. Ordronaux, *Jurisprudence of Medicine*, 11, 71, 73, and 96.

96. Ibid., 2.

97. "Trial for Alleged Malpractice," *BMSJ* 50 (8 March 1854):120–21.

98. Dixi Crosby, comp., *Report of a Trial for Alleged Malpractice Against Dixi Crosby* (Woodstock, N.H.: Printed by Lewis Pratt, Jr., 1854) 5, 79.

99. White, *Tort Law in America*, 10–12, 40.

100. Francis Hillard, *The Law of Torts or Private Wrongs* (Boston: Little, Brown, 1859), 1–2.

101. Ibid., 238–40.

102. Thomas G. Sherman and Amasa A. Redfield, *A Treatise on the Law of Negligence* (New York: Baker, Voorhis, Publishers, 1870), 511.

103. See for example Piper v. Menifee 51 Ky. 465 (1851); and Alden v. Buckley 1 Swann R. 69 (Tenn. 1851).

104. Smith v. Overby 30 Ga. 241 (1860).

105. Ritchey v. West 23 Ill. 329, 330 (1860).

106. McNevins v. Lowe 40 Ill. 209, 210 (1866).

107. There are rich philosophical and ethical discussions of contract and the nature of the doctor-patient relationship. See Roger Masters, "Is Contract an Adequate Basis for Medical Ethics?" *HCR* 5 (December 1975):24–28; William May, *The Physician's Covenant: Images of the Healer in Medical Ethics* (Philadelphia: Westminster Press, 1983), 42–45, 116–27; and May, "Adversarialism in America and the Professions," in *Community in America: the Challenge of Habits of the Heart*, edited by Charles H. Reynolds and Ralph V. Norman (Berkeley: University of California Press, 1988), 185–201.

108. Elizabeth Heitman "Caring for the Silent Stranger: Ethical Hospital Care for Non-English Speaking Patients," Ph.D. dissertation (Rice University, 1988), 11.

109. Starr, *Transformation*, 421–49; Donald W. Light, "Corporate Medicine for Profit," *SA* 255 (December 1986):38–45; and Gwen Kinkead, "Humana's Hard-Sell Hospitals," *For* (17 November 1980):68–81.

110. There is a synthetic overview of the debate over contract, ethics, and the doctor-patient relationship in Heitman, "Caring for the Silent Stranger," 1–32.

111. Richard A. Epstein, "Medical Malpractice: The Case for Contract," *ABFRJ* (1976):87–149; and Epstein, "Market and Regulatory Approaches to

Medical Malpractice: The Virginia Obstetrical No-Fault Statute," *VLR* 74 (1988):1451–74.

8. The More Things Change . . . : Medical Malpractice, 1865–1900

1. Alexander Young, "The Law of Malpractice," *BMSJ* 5 (9 June 1870):443.

2. H. F. Montgomery, "Suits for Malpractice," *BufMSJ* 11 (July 1872):445.

3. "On the Avoidance of Causeless Suits for Malpractice," *MSR* 33 (25 September 1875):255–56.

4. "The Liability of Physicians," *MSJ* 34 (15 April 1876):315–16. See also John J. Reese, "Case of Alleged Malpractice," *MT* 1 (1 December 1870):73–74; and George M. Blake, "Suits Against Surgeons," *BufMSJ* 18 (1879–1880):309–16, for comments on renewed malpractice suits.

5. Sanger's study included suits brought against respondent physicians at any time (including the first half of the century) up to the time of the survey. Eugene F. Sanger, "Report on Malpractice," *BMSJ* 100 (2 January 1879):14–23; and Sanger, "Report on Malpractice," *BMSJ* 100 (9 January 1879):41–50. Sanger first read his report in 1878 before the Maine Medical Association.

6. Sanger, "Report on Malpractice," *BMSJ* 100 (2 January 1879):19–20.

7. Sanger quoted in "Medical Notes," *BMSJ* 100 (9 January 1878):91.

8. O. E. Lyman, "Some Notes on a Doctor's Liability," *PSM* 18 (1880–1881):770.

9. A. M. Powell, "Surgical Malpractice," *StLMSJ* 42 (March 1882):231.

10. E. J. Doering, "Mutual Protection Against Blackmail," *JAMA* 6 (1886):114.

11. "Malpractice Suits," *MSR* 61 (21 September 1889):326.

12. F. J. Groner, "The Causes and the Remedies for Suits for Malpractice," *MR* 37 (9 August 1890):143.

13. Quoted in Robert H. Shikes, *Rocky Mountain Medicine: Doctors, Drugs, and Disease in Early Colorado* (Boulder, Colo.: Johnson Books, 1986), 118–19. See also J. R. Weist, "Civil Malpractice Suits: How Can the Physician Protect Himself Against Them?" *AP* 30 (1884):160–74; and "Medical Malpractice," *MSR* 47 (23 December 1882):716–17, for more on the increase of suits.

14. Hubert Winston Smith, "Legal Responsibility for Medical Malpractice," *JAMA* 116 (14 June 1941):2672–73; and Charles J. Weigel II, "Medical Malpractice in America's Middle Years," *TRBM* 32 (Spring 1974):203.

15. See chapter 2.

16. See appendix B.

17. Musser v. Chase 29 Ohio 577 (1876) (lost nose $3,000); W. F. Hutchinson, "A Recent Suit for Malpractice," *BufMSJ* 12 (1872–1873):290–91 ($4,000, fracture); Kelsey v. Hey 84 Indiana 189 (1882) ($4,000, damage to legs); "Some Recent Malpractice Suits," *MR* 28 (19 December 1885):690–91 ($7,000, frac-

ture); "Verdict Against Physician," *MR* 47 (12 January 1895):64 ($12.000, fracture); and Jackson v. Burnham 20 Col. 533 (1895) ($5,000, lost penis). Some of these awards, as well as the judgments rendered in the 38 sample cases, were reduced on retrial.

18. Weigel's study, based on appellate decisions between 1860 and 1915, uncovered awards in 34 cases: 5 awards were less than $100; 4 awards were less than $500; 22 awards were between $1,000 and $5,000; and 3 awards were between $6,000 and $10,000. Weigel, "Medical Malpractice," 194, 195. The awards cited in Eugene Sanger's 1878 study averaged only $584, but he drew many of his cases from the first half of the century, so I did not include them in my averages. Sanger, "Report on Malpractice," *BMSJ* 100 (2 January 1879): 20.

19. Paul Starr, *The Social Transformation of American Medicine* (New York: Basic Books, 1984), 84–85.

20. Awards average from Department of Health, Education, and Welfare report quoted in David Ghitelman, "Medical Malpractice in the Last Thirty Years," *MD Magazine* (April 1987):62–73. Physician mean, real income (in 1983 dollars) from H. E. French III, ed., *Health Care in America: The Political Economy of Hospitals and Health* (San Francisco: Pacific Research Institute for Public Policy, 1988), 311.

21. Cayford v. Wilbur 86 Me. 414 (1894).

22. Kelsey v. Hay 84 Ind. 189 (1882).

23. Brooke v. Clarke 57 Tx. 1905 (1882).

24. William C. Wey, "Medical Responsibilty for Malpractice. Anniversary Address delivered before the Medical Society of the State of New York," *TSMSNY* (1872):84; and Steven Smith, *Doctor in Medicine* (New York: William Wood, 1872; reprint, Arno Press, 1972), 286.

25. See chapter 3 for a discussion of the working class and the role of the poor in malpractice litigation.

26. Wey, "Medical Responsibility," 87.

27. W. F. Hutchinson, "A Recent Suit for Malpractice," *BufMSJ* 12 (1872–1873):297.

28. See Harold M. Hyman, *A More Perfect Union: the Impact of the Civil War and Reconstruction on the Constitution* (New York: Alfred A. Knopf, 1973), 360, 347–49, 359–61, and passim; and Samuel Bernstein, "The Impact of the Paris Commune in the United States," *MassR* 12 (1971):435–45.

29. Blake, "Suits against Surgeons," 316.

30. Starr, *Transformation*, 85–88. D. W. Cathell, *Physician Himself* (1850), quoted in ibid.

31. "Civil Malpractice," *BMSJ* 96 (19 April 1877):470.

32. Sanger quoted in "Medical Notes " (summary of Sanger's study), *BMSJ* 99 (18 July 1878):91.

33. "The Animus of Suits for Malpractice," *MSR* 34 (September 1878):218.

34. Sanger, "Report on Malpractice," *BMSJ* 100 (9 January 1879):43, 50

35. "Medico-Legal Notes," *BMSJ* 100 (1879):390.

36. Sanger, "Report on Malpractice," *BMSJ* 100 (2 January 1879):18.

37. See chapter 2. John J. Elwell, *A Medico-Legal Treatise on Malpractice and Medical Evidence* (New York: John Voorhis, 1860), 44.

38. Daniel H. Calhoun, *Professional Lives in America: Structure and Aspiration, 1750–1850* (Cambridge: Harvard University Press, 1965), 2–7; and John Duffy, "American Perceptions of the Medical, Legal, and Theological Professions," *BHM* 58 (1984):8, discuss Jacksonian attitudes towards the professions.

39. For comments on the composition of the early bar, see Kermit Hall, *The Magic Mirror* (New York: Oxford University Press, 1989), 216–18.

40. James Bryce, *American Commonwealth* (London: Macmillan, 1889), 2:490–91.

41. Lawrence Friedman, *A History of American Law* (New York: Simon and Schuster, 1973), 549; and Joseph Gordon Hylton, Jr., "The Virginia Lawyer from Reconstruction to the Great Depression," Ph.D. dissertation (Harvard University, 1986), 139.

42. See Hylton, "Virginia Lawyer," 99–145 passim. The issue and significance of the "overcrowding" of the lawyers are much-debated and unresolved. See, for example, J. Willard Hurst, *The Growth of American Law: The Law Makers* (Boston: Little, Brown, 1950), 313–19; Terrance C. Halliday, "Six Score and Ten: Demographic Transitions in the American Legal Profession," *LSR* 20 (1986):53–77.

43. "Civil Malpractice," *BMSJ* 96 (19 April 1877):471.

44. Doering, "Mutual Protection," 114.

45. For example, see "*Fisher* v. *Gross*," *MR* 6 (15 May 1871):133–34; J. K. Stockwell, "Suits for Malpractice," *MR* 17 (7 February 1880):161–62; "The Animus of Suits for Malpractice," *MSR* 34 (September 1878):218; and "The Proper Steps for Physicians in Suits for Malpractice," *MSR* 27 (7 December 1872):496–97.

46. Powell, "Surgical Malpractice," 232.

47. Weist, "Civil Malpractice," 165.

48. Wey, "Medical Responsibility." 83; Simon Greenleaf, *A Treatise on the Law of Evidence* (Boston: Little, Brown, 1853), 3:63–64.

49. "The Suit Against Professor Gross," *MT* 1 (1 May 1871):281. For other attacks on contingency fees from physicians, see Weist, "Civil Malpractice Suits," 164; "*Fisher* v. *Gross*," 133; Stockwell, "Suits for Malpractice," 161; and "A Suit for Malpractice", *MR* 52 (1898):925–26.

50. Lawrence M. Friedman, *Total Justice* (Boston: Beacon Press, 1985), 25.

51. Stanton v. Embrey 93 U.S. 548 (1877). For a history of the attacks from the bar on the use of the contingency fees, see Jerold S. Auerbach, *Unequal Justice: Lawyers and Social Change in Modern America* (New York: Oxford University Press, 1976), 45–49; and F. B. MacKinnon, *Contingent Fees for Legal Services* (Chicago: Aldine, 1964), 8–15.

52. "The Contingency Fee Business," *ALJ* 24 (1881):24–25.

53. Cooley quoted in Lawrence M. Friedman, *A History of American Law*, 422–23.

54. F. J. Groner, "The Causes and the Remedies for Suits for Malpractice," *MR* 37 (9 August 1890):143–44.

55. "Causes and Prevention of Suits for Mal-Practice," *BMSJ* 48 (27 July 1853):525; the writer was referring to Samuel Parkman and Calvin P. Fiske, "Report on the Causes and Prevention of Suits for Mal-Practice," *MCMMS* appendix 8 (1853):124–32.

56. Samuel L. Baker, "Physician Licensure Laws in the United States, 1865–1915," *JHMAS* 39 (April 1984):173–97; and Richard Harrison Shyrock, *Medical Licensing in America, 1650–1965* (Baltimore: Johns Hopkins University Press, 1967), 48.

57. Kenneth Ludmerer, *Learning to Heal: The Development of American Medical Education* (New York: Basic Books, 1985), 47–101.

58. Richard Hofstadter, *Anti-Intellectualism in American Life* (New York: Vintage, 1962), 197–213; and Robert H. Wiebe, *The Search for Order, 1877–1920* (New York: Hill and Wang, 1967), 112–23.

59. W. L. Appley, "How Rip Van Winkle, Jr., M.D. Disposed of a Case of Malpractice," *MSR* 25 (25 October 1871):381–82.

60. D. W. Cathell, *The Physician Himself and What He Should Add to His Scientific Acquirements* (Baltimore: Cushings and Bailey, 1882; reprint, Arno Press, 1972), 49.

61. "Remarks on Suits for Malpractice," *NYJM* 65 (15 May 1897):676–8 at 678.

62. See Starr, *Transformation*, 99–127.

63. Smith, *Doctor in Medicine*, 156.

64. "Suits for Malpractice," *MR* 16 (20 December 1879):591; and "Suit for Malpractice," *MR* 16 (20 December 1879):599.

65. "Malpractice," *MR* 15 (24 May 1879):492.

66. "Concerning Suits for Malpractice," *MR* 36 (5 October 1889):375.

67. Quoted in Helen Clapesattle, *The Doctors Mayo* (New York: Simon and Schuster, 1970), 63–64.

68. James J. O'Dea, "Medico-Legal Science: A Sketch of its Progress, Especially in the United States," *Papers Read Before the Medico-Legal Society of New York*, 3rd series, 1875–1878 (New York: Medico-Legal Society, 1886), 305.

69. Chester R. Burns, "Medical Ethics and Medical Jurisprudence," in *The Education of American Physicians*, edited by Ronald L. Numbers (Berkeley: University of California Press, 1980), 273–89.

70. Elwell, *Treatise on Malpractice* (1860, 1866, 1871, 1881); John Ordronaux, *The Jurisprudence of Medicine* (Philadelphia: T. and J. W. Johnson, 1869; reprint, Arno Press, 1973); and Milo A. McClelland, *Civil Malpractice: A Treatise on Surgical Jurisprudence* (New York: Hurd and Houghton, 1877), v.

71. Brewer Mattocks, "Malpractice," *NMSJ* 3 (August 1872):51–52.

72. "Actions for Malpractice," *NYMJ* 68 (24 December 1898):940.

73. McClelland, *Civil Malpractice*, 528.

74. "Effect of Malpractice Charges and How to Avoid Them," *MR* 44 (30 December 1893):847–48; and Mattocks, "Malpractice," 46.

75. Sanger, "Report on Malpractice," *BMSJ* 100 (2 January 1879):20.

76. John J. Reese, "A Case of Alleged Malpractice," *MT* 1 (1 December 1870):73–74. For comments on success rates of suits, see Mordecai Price, "Remarks on Suits for Malpractice," *NYMJ* 65 (15 May 1897):676–78.

77. "*Fisher* v. *Gross*," *MR* 6 (15 May 1871):133–34.

78. "A Case of Alleged Malpractice," *MR* 5 (16 January 1871):517–18; "A Case of Alleged Malpractice," *NYMJ* 13 (January 1871):124–28; "Judge Thayer's Charge in the Case of *Haire* v. *Reese*," *MT* 1 (15 December 1870):99–101; and "[Suit against Dr. Sayer]," *MR* 5 (1 November 1870):398–99.

79. "The Suit against Professor Gross," *MT* 1 (May 1871):281.

80. Lucius Weinschenk, "Malpractice," *DTMJ* 5 (1889):219.

81. "Blackmailing of Surgeons and Malpractice Suits," *MR* 13 (20 April 1878):315–16. See also "The Proper Steps in Suits for Malpractice," *MSJ* 27 (7 December 1872):496–97.

82. McClelland, *Civil Malpractice*, 528.

83. E. J. Doering, "Mutual Protection Against Blackmail," *JAMA* 6 (1886):116; and Sanger, "Report on Malpractice," *BMSJ* 100 (2 January 1879):21 and passim.

84. See Parkman and Fiske, "Report on the Causes and Prevention of Suits for Mal-Practice," 131.

85. Doering, "Mutual Protection," 114.

86. "*Stogdale* v. *Baker*," *BMSJ* 117 (1887):610.

87. "Organized Medical Defence," *JAMA* 38 (4 January 1902):37; "Organized Medical Defence," *JAMA* 38 (4 January 1902):43; "The Varied Functions Possible in the County Medical Society," *JAMA* 44 (18 March 1905):881–82; Starr, *Transformation*, 111; and Sandra Cirincione, "The History of Medical Malpractice in New York State: A Perspective from the Publications of the Medical Society of New York," *NYSJM* 86 (July 1986):363–64.

88. Starr, *Transformation*, 111–12; William G. Rothstein, *American Physicians in the Nineteenth Century* (Baltimore: Johns Hopkins University Press, 1972), 324–25. See, Cirincione, "History of Medical Malpractice," 364–65.

89. Sanger, "Report on Malpractice," *BMSJ* 100 (9 January 1879):46.

90. Powell, "Surgical Malpractice," 236.

91. Weist, "Civil Malpractice Suits," 173; and "Medical Expert Testimony," *BMSJ* 116 (31 February 1887):119–20.

92. Weist, "Civil Malpractice Suits," 169; "On Suits for Malpractice," *NYMJ* 49 (9 February 1889):158; and "Malpractice Suits and their Prevention," *MR* 29 (13 February 1886):188.

93. "Malpractice—Proposed Law," *MR* 9 (1 October 1874):527; and "Law of Malpractice," *MSR* 30 (28 February 1874):2.

94. Ritchey v. West 23 Ill. 329 (1860).

95. Weigel, "Medical Malpractice in America's Middle Years," 198.

96. Hoener v. Koch 84 Ill. 408 (1877); and Weigel, "Medical Malpractice," 199.

97. Gerchell v. Hill 21 Minn. 464 (1875). See also Fisher v. Niccolls 2 Ill. App. 484 (1877); Gores v. Graff 77 Wisc. 174 (1890); Stevenson v. Gelsthorpe 10 Mont. 563 (1891); Feeney v. Spalding 89 Me. 111 (1896); and Richards v. Willard 176 Penn. 181 (1896) for samples of cases overturned for verdicts rendered against the weight of the evidence.

98. Spalding v. Bliss 83 Mich. 31 (1890).

99. Weigel, "Medical Malpractice," 195–96; McNevins v. Lowe 40 Ill. 209 (1866); and Smothers v. Hanks 34 Iowa 286 (1872).

100. Almond v. Nugent 34 Iowa 300 (1872).

101. Quinn v. Donovan 85 Ill. 194 (1877).

102. Utley v. Burns 700 Ill. 162 (1873).

103. Kendall v. Brown 74 Ill. 232 (1874); Jones v. Angell 95 Ind. 376 (1883); and Carpenter v. Blake 60 N.Y. 12 (1878). See also David McAdam, *Malpractice with Reference to the Legal and Medical Professions* (1893), 13.

104. Thomas M. Cooley, *A Treatise on the Law of Torts*, 3rd ed., (Chicago: Callaghan, 1906), 2:1391. For another example of the essential stability of basic malpractice doctrine, see Marshall D. Ewell, *A Manual of Medical Jurisprudence for the Use of Students at Law and of Medicine* (Boston: Little, Brown, 1887), 282–83.

105. In general, see Charles E. Rosenberg, *The Care of Strangers: The Rise of America's Hospital System* (New York: Basic Books, 1987); Stanley Joel Reiser, *Medicine and the Reign of Technology* (New York: Cambridge University Press, 1978), 153–56; and Starr, *Transformation*, 209–15.

106. McDonald v. Massachusetts General Hospital 120 Mass 432 (1876). See also Downes v. Harper Hospital 101 Mich. 555 (1894); and Hearns v. Waterbury Hospital 66 Conn. 93 (1895).

107. "Malpractice," *MR* 15 (24 May 1879):492. See also "Noteworthy Malpractice Decisions," *NYMJ* 33 (April 1881):731; "Malpractice," *MR* 15 (17 May 1879):468–69; "Malpractice Suits Against Hospital Surgeons," *NYMJ* 54 (26 December 1891):718; Hedin v. Minneapolis Medical & Surgical Institute 62 Minn. 146 (1895); and Beck v. German Klinik 78 Iowa 696 (1889).

108. Union Pacific Ry Co. v. Artist 60 Fed. Rep. 365 (1894); and Eighmy v. Union Pacific Railway Co. 93 Iowa 538 (1895).

109. "Malpractice," *MR* 15 (24 May 1879):492.

110. See chapter 2.

111. Jones v. Angell 95 Ind. 376 (1883). See also Hibbard v. Thomson 109 Mass. 286 (1872); and Potter v. Warner 91 Penn. 362 (1879).

112. Carpenter v. Blake 75 N.Y. 12 (1878). For the medical profession's view of the softening of the contributory negligence doctrine, see T. C. Becker, "*Carpenter v. Blake*: An Important Decision by the Highest Court of

New York State for an Action for Malpractice," *PSI* 1 (1880):119–25, 142–44, 174–76.

113. "Contributory Negligence in Malpractice," *ALJ* 24 (1881):403–6.

114. Dubois v. Decker 130 N.Y. 331 (1891). For a similar example, see Sanderson v. Holland 39 Mo. App. 233 (1889).

115. The full history of the doctrine and application of contributory negligence has yet to be written. The best introduction is Wex S. Malone, "The Formative Era of Contributory Negligence," in *Essays on Torts* (Baton Rouge: Paul M. Herbert, 1986), 116–45. After the turn of the century, various state legislatures played a role in limiting contributory negligence by statute. G. Edward White, *Tort Law in America: An Intellectual History* (New York: Oxford University Press, 1980), 164–68.

116. See chapter 2.

117. Elwell, *Treatise on Malpractice*, 22; and McClelland, *Civil Malpractice*, 17–18.

118. Amasa A. Redfield and Thomas G. Shearman, *A Treatise on the Law of Negligence* (New York: Baker, Voorhis, 1870), 508.

119. Wey, "Medical Responsibility," 72, 73.

120. Teft v. Wilcox 6 Kan. 46 (1870), at 63, 64.

121. Smothers v. Hanks 34 Iowa 286 (1872).

122. Dissent quoted in David D. Armstrong, "Medical Malpractice—The 'Locality Rule' and the 'Conspiracy of Silence,' " *SCLR* 22 (1970):812.

123. Hawthorn v. Richmond 48 Vt. 557 (1876); and Gramm v. Boener 56 Ind. 497 (1877).

124. Small v. Howard 128 Mass. 131 at 131, 136 (1880); and "Measure of Skill Required by the Law," *NYMJ* 33 (April 1881):731–32.

125. Starr, *Transformation*, 111; Armstrong, *Medical Malpractice*, 813; and John R. Waitz, "The Rise and Gradual Fall of the Locality Rule," *DPLR* 18 (1969):410–11.

126. Pelky v. Palmer 109 Mich. 561 (1896); and Whitesell v. Hill 101 Iowa 630 (1897). Progressively more exceptions were made to the locality rule until 1968, when states began to eliminate it outright. See, Waitz, "The Rise and Gradual Fall," passim.

127. Pike v. Honsinger 151 N.Y. 201 at 204–8 (1898).

128. Idem, 209–10.

129. Louis B. Harrison, Melvin H. Worth, Jr., and Michael A. Carlucci, "The Development of the Principles of Medical Malpractice in the United States," *Perspectives in Biology and Medicine* 29 (Autumn 1985):41–72, discusses *Pike* and the fundamentals of twentieth-century malpractice law.

130. See, for example, William J. Curren, "The Unwanted Suitor: Law and the Use of Health Care Technology," in *Machine at the Bedside: Strategies for Using Technology in Patient Care*, edited by Stanley Joel Reiser and Michael Anbar (New York: Cambridge University Press, 1984), 119–33.

131. E. F. Hodges, "Malpractice," *AP* 3 (1884):152.

132. Weigel, "Medical Malpractice," 193.

133. Hodges, "Malpractice," 155.

134. See chapter 4.

135. Thomas Manley, "The Medico-Legal Aspects of Fractures of the Bones of the Extremities, and Others," *NYMJ* 58 (9 September 1893):283–89; and "Heavy Damages in a Malpractice Suit," *MR* 41 (30 January 1892):121.

136. Manley, "Medico-Legal Aspects," 290.

137. Fielding H. Garrison, *An Introduction to the History of Medicine* (Philadelphia: W. B. Saunders, 1914), 548–55. For examples of suits, see "Malpractice," *MR* 15 (17 May 1879):468–69; Pettigrew v. Willard 46 Kan. 79 (1891); Jones v. Vroom 8 Col. 143 (1896); "Some Recent Malpractice Suits," *MR* 28 (19 December 1885):690–91; Feeney v. Spalding 89 Me. 111 (1896); and Peck v. Hutchinson 88 Iowa 320 (1893). If a physician portrayed himself as a "specialist," such as an ophthalmologist, the ordinary skill and care test was modified to "the degree of skill and diligence which other physicians in the same general neighborhood and in the same general line of practice ordinarily have and practice." See Force v. Gregory 63 Conn. 167 (1893).

138. Rothstein, *American Physicians*, 251–59; Laurence D. Longo, "The Rise and Fall of Batty's Operation: A Fashion in Surgery," *BHM* 53 (1979):244–67; and G. J. Barker-Benfield, *Horrors of a Half Known Life* (New York: Harper and Row, 1976), 120–32.

139. "Some Recent Malpractice Suits," *MR* 28 (19 December 1885):590–91; Langford v. Jones 18 Ore. 307 (1890); Kansas v. Reynolds 42 Kan 320 (1889); and Lewis v. Dwinell 84 Me. 497 (1892).

140. Samuel D. Gross, "A Century of American Medicine, 1776–1876," *AJMS* 71 (1876):484; and Gross, quoted in Peter C. English, *Shock, Physiological Surgery, and George Washington Crile: Medical Innovation in the Progressive Era* (Westport, Conn.: Greenwood Press, 1980), 25.

141. For a survey of developments leading to improvement of surgery, see Rothstein, *American Physicians*, 249–56; and Gert H. Brieger, "American Surgery and the Germ Theory of Disease," *BHM* 40 (1966):135–45.

142. Rothstein, *American Physicians*, 249–56; and English, *Shock, Physiological Surgery*, 20–29.

143. For a good survey of surgical milestones in the late nineteenth century, see Morris J. Fogelman and Elinor Reinmiller, "1880–1890: A Creative Decade in World Surgery," *American Journal of Surgery* 115 (1968):812–24; and English, *Shock, Physiological Surgery*, 30–33.

144. Andrew A. Sandor, "The History of Professional Liability Suits in the United States," *JAMA* 163 (9 February 1957):464.

145. Robert T. Morris, *Fifty Years a Surgeon* (New York: E. P. Dutton, 1935), 66.

146. "Judge Aldrich's Decision in a Suit for Malpractice," *BMSJ* 106 (4 May 1882):425–26.

147. Peck v. Hutchinson 88 Iowa 320 (1893); and Fogelman and Reinmiller, "A Creative Decade," 819.

148. Reiser, *Medicine and the Reign of Technology*, 58–67.

149. "Report of the Committee of the American Surgical Association on the Medico-Legal Relation of the X-Rays," *AJMS* 120 n.s. (1900):13, 32; and physician quoted in David Walsh, *The Röentgen Rays in Medical Work* (New York: William Wood, 1898), 125–26.

150. Shikes, *Rocky Mountain Medicine,* 118–19; and "Report of the Committee on X-Rays," passim.

151. Quoted in "Report of the Committee on X-Rays" 8, 16, 32.

152. Ibid., 12.

153. Ibid., 21, 25, 26.

154. F. Boyd, "X-Ray Dermatitis; Suit for Damages," *JAMA* 30 (12 February 1898):381; and Ruth and Edward Brecher, *The Rays: A History of Radiology in America* (Baltimore: William and Wilkens, 1969), 106.

9. Conclusion

1. Leighton E. Cluff, "America's Romance with Medicine and Medical Science," *Daedalus* 115 (Spring 1986):137–59.

2. John Duffy, "American Perceptions of the Medical, Legal, and Theological Professions," *BHM* 58 (1984):1–15.

3. David Engel, "Oven Bird's Song: Insiders, Outsiders, and Personal Injuries in an American Community," *LSR* 18 (1984):551–61; and Carol Greenhouse, *Praying for Justice: Faith, Order and Community in an American Town* (Ithaca: Cornell University Press, 1986).

4. David M. Potter, "Social Cohesion and the Crisis of Law," in *American Law and the Constitutional Order, Historical Perspectives,* edited by Lawrence M. Friedman and Harry M. Scheiber (Cambridge: Harvard University Press, 1978), 432; and Robert H. Wiebe, *The Search for Order, 1877–1920* (New York: Hill and Wang, 1967), 1–10, 44–75.

5. Martin Marty, "From Providence to Progress: A New Theology," in *The Righteous Empire: The Protestant Experience in America* (New York: Dial Press, 1970), 188–89.

6. Lucius Weinschenk, "Malpractice," *DTMJ* 5 (1889):208.

7. John Higham, "The Reorientation of American Culture in the 1890s," in *Writing American History: Essays in Modern Scholarship* (Bloomington: Indiana University Press, 1970), 73–102; and Donald J. Mrozek, "Toward a New Image of the Body," in *Sport and the American Mentality, 1880–1910* (Knoxville: University of Tennessee Press, 1983), 189–222.

8. John C. Burnham, "Change in Popularization of Health in the United States," *BHM* 58 (1984):185–97.

9. Mike Featherstone, "The Body in Consumer Culture," *Theory, Culture, and Society* 1 (1982):18–33.

10. T. J. Jackson Lears, "From Salvation to Self-Realization: Advertising and the Therapeutic Roots of Consumer Culture, 1880–1930" in *The Culture of*

Consumption: Essays in American History, 1880–1980, edited by Richard Wightman Fox and T. J. Jackson Lears (New York: Pantheon, 1983), 4; Lears, *No Place of Grace: Antimodernism and the Transformation of American Culture 1880–1920* (New York: Pantheon, 1981), 54–56, 221–22, 296–97, 303–5; and Philip Rieff, *The Triumph of the Therapeutic* (New York: Harper and Row, 1966).

11. This is Lawrence M. Friedman's thesis. See his *Total Justice* (Boston: Beacon Press, 1985), 43–51, 63–67, 147. See also Charles O. Gregory, "Tresspass to Negligence to Absolute Liability," *Virginia Law Review* 37 (April 1951):359–97.

Bibliography

Primary Sources

JOURNAL ARTICLES AND BOOKS

These articles do not constitute all the accounts of malpractice prosecutions and editorials on the topic published in the nineteenth century. Instead they are the sources that I cited and consulted in preparation of this essay. Elwell, McClelland, and Wade (see below) contain dozens of accounts not noted in the bibliography. A fuller survey of nineteenth-century medical journals would undoubtedly yield a considerable number of additional cases.

A list of unattributed articles precedes works whose authors are given.

"The Accountability of Medical Men. *Commonwealth* v. *Franklin Pierce*." *BMSJ* 3 (1884):545–46.
"Accusation of Mal-Practice." *BMSJ* 31 (11 September 1844):123–24
"Action for Mal-Treatment in a Case of Dislocation." *BMSJ* 32 (28 May 1845):346–47.
"Action for Malpractice." *MSR* 20 (20 January 1868):18–19.
"Actions for Malpractice." *NYMJ* 68 (24 December 1898):940.
"Alleged Mal-Practice." *BMSJ* 6 (21 March 1832):98–99.
"Alleged Malpractice." *BMSJ* 62 (31 May 1860):364–65.
"Alleged Malpractice." *MT* 1(1 June 1871):327–28.
"Alleged Malpractice—Case of *Russel* v. *Warden*." *MSR* 24 (1871):410–11.
"American Intelligence [suit]." *MNL* 6 (May 1848):60.
"Anesthesia and Its Influence on Surgery." *MN* 9 (1851):21–22.

"Animus of Suits for Malpractice." *MSR* 34 (September 1878):218.

"Another Malpractice Suit." *NOMSJ* 10 (1882):470–71.

"Another Prosecution for Malpractice." *JMCS* 3 (November 1846):406.

"Another Suit for Mal-Practice." *BMSJ* 51 (17 January 1855):504.

"A Bar to an Action for Malpractice." *NYMJ* 37 (3 February 1883):139.

"A Bar to Malpractice Suits." *MSR* 50 (31 May 1884):703.

"Bibliographic Notices." *NYJM* (September 1853):272–75.

"Bibliographic Notices." *BMSJ* 89 (24 July 1873):85–86.

"Blackmailing of Surgeons and Malpractice Suits." *MR* 13 (20 April 1878): 315–16.

"Case of Alleged Mal-Practice." *BMSJ* 54 (24 April 1856):229–42.

"A Case of Alleged Malpractice." *NYMJ* 13 (January 1871):124–28.

"A Case of Alleged Malpractice." *MR* 5 (16 January 1871):517–18.

"A Case of Alleged Malpractice." *NYMJ* 38 (25 August 1883):212–13.

"Case of False Anneurism—Action for Malpractice." *BMSJ* 35 (12 August 1846):43–45.

"Case of Mal-Practice." *BMSJ* 34 (8 July 1846):449–51.

"Case of Mal-Practice." *BMSJ* 54 (13 March 1856):109–13.

"A Case of Malpractice." *BMSJ* 9 (28 March 1872):201.

"A Case of Malpractice." *MR* 45 (23 June 1894):793–94.

"Case of Trial for Malpractice." *BMSJ* 56 (19 March 1857):148.

"Cases of Compound Fracture of the Leg." *BMSJ* 25 (8 September 1841): 73–75.

"Causes and Prevention of Epidemics." *Har* 15 (1857):194–203.

"Causes and Prevention of Suits for Mal-Practice." *BMSJ* 48 (27 July 1853):525.

"Civil Malpractice." *BMSJ* 84 (24 July 1873):85–86.

"Civil Malpractice." *BMSJ* 96 (19 April 1877):470–73.

"Concerning Suits for Malpractice." 36 *MR* (5 October 1889):375–76.

"Confidential Communications and Suits for Malpractice." *NYMJ* 60 (3 November 1894):576.

"Contributory Negligence in Malpractice." *ALJ* 24 (1881):403–6.

"Correction." *WMSJ* 32 (July 1855):49–50.

"The Cortland Case of Malpractice." *ME* 5 (5 March 1842):149–51.

"The Cortlandville Trial for Malpractice." *ME* 4 (1841):766–67.

"Critical Analysis" (address of Samuel Jackson to the medical class of University of Pennsylvania, 1846). *NYMJ* 8 (March 1847):218–22.

"A Curious Malpractice Suit." *NYMJ* 67 (12 March 1898):373.

"Damages for Fracture." *BMSJ* 101 (11 September 1879):390.

"Death by Supposed Mal-Practice." *BMSJ* 44 (28 May 1851):345.

"Discouragement of Suits for Malpractice." *MSR* 42 n.s.(1880):37.

"The Doctrine of Particular Providence." *CS* 8 (1836):1–12.

"The Doctrine of Providence Vindicated." *CS* 5 (1823):169–75.

"Dr. Riggs of Cortland County." *MSR* 6 (July 1861):81.

"Effect of Malpractice Charges and How to Avoid Them." *MR* 44 (30 December 1893):847–48.

"The End of a Curious Malpractice suit." *MR* 31 (8 January 1887):54.

"The End of a Malpractice Suit." *MR* 42 (2 July 1892):16.

"Estimation of Damages in Actions for Malpractice." *NYMJ* 72 (18 August 1900):308.

"Excision of Tonsils." *BMSJ* 28 (15 February 1843):29–33.

"Extracts from the Report of the Committee on the Prevalence of Suits for Mal-Practice." *MNL* 8 (March 1850):17–20.

"Fisher v. *Gross."* *MR* 6 (15 May 1871):133–34.

"Fracture of the Thigh Bone—The Late Suit Against Dr. Colby." *BMSJ* 30 (31 July 1844):509–14.

"The Greenpoint Malpractice Case." *Scal* 8 (April 1856):311–15.

"George Chase v. *Calvin Sweeny."* *MSR* 19 (28 May 1868):449.

"Gross Malpractice." *MSR* 22 (5 February 1870):121–22.

"Heavy Damages in a Malpractice Suit." *MR* 41 (30 January 1892):131.

"Heroic Malpractice." *MT* 1 (1 October 1870):16.

"Heroic Surgery: Extirpation of a Malignant Tumor from the Arm, Death the Next Day." *Scal* 2 (1850):121–22.

"Important Case of Alleged Mal-Practice." *Scal* 9 (April 1857):54–57.

"An Interesting Malpractice Suit." *MR* 32 (16 July 1887):81.

"An Interesting Question in a Charge of Malpractice." *MR* 25 (16 February 1884):186.

"Jarvis' Adjuster." *WJMPS* 22 (1851):272–73.

"Judge Aldrich's Decision in a Suit for Malpractice." *BMSJ* 106 (4 May 1882):425–26.

"Judge Thayer's Charge in the Case of *Haire* v. *Reese."* *MT* 1 (15 December 1870):99–101.

"The Late Suit for Mal-Practice in Delaware Co., N.Y.." *BMSJ* 37 (11 August 1847):35–37.

"Law of Malpractice." *MSR* 30 (28 February 1874):2.

"Legal Liabilities of Physicians and Surgeons." *BufMSJ* 5 (1865–1866):353–56.

"The Legal Responsibilities of Physicians." *MSR* 46 n.s. (1882):298–99.

"Legal Responsibility." *BMSJ* 54 (24 April 1856):228.

"Legal Robbery of a Physician." *MN* 14 (April 1856):61–62.

"Legal Robbery of a Surgeon." *MSR* 10 (April 1857):217.

"Liability of Physicians." *MSR* 34 (15 April 1876):315–16.

"Mal-practice." *BMSJ* 49 (26 October 1853):270.

"Malpractice." *OMSJ* 6 (November 1853):182.

"Mal-practice." *OMSJ* 12 (November 1859):166–67.

"Malpractice." *BMSJ* 66 (24 July 1862):524.

"Malpractice." *MR* 15 (17 May 1879):468–69.

"Malpractice." *MR* 15 (24 May 1879):492.

"The Malpractice Case in Brooklyn." *MR* 12 (27 October 1877):688.

"Malpractice Case Settled." *MSR* 24 (20 May 1871):428.

"Malpractice Decisions." *NYMJ* 33 (April 1881):731.

"Malpractice in a Case of Midwifery." *BMSJ* 32 (30 April 1845):266.

"Malpractice in a Case of Midwifery." *BMSJ* 32 (28 May 1845):346.

"Malpractice in Its Legal Relations." *MSR* 15 n.s. (1866):444–45.

"Malpractice Insurance." *MR* 44 (1892):401.

"Mal-Practice in Midwifery." *BMSJ* 2 (3 March 1830):50.

"Malpractice in Surgery." *BMSJ* 25 (26 January 1842):404.

"Malpractice—Proposed Law." *MR* 9 (1 October 1874):527.

"A Malpractice Suit Triumphantly Defended." *MR* 17 (17 January 1880): 67–68.

"Malpractice Suits." *MR* 14 (6 July 1878):13.

"Malpractice Suits." *MSR* 61 (21 September 1889):326.

"Malpractice Suits against Hospital Surgeons." *NYMJ* 54 (26 December 1891):718.

"Malpractice Suits and Their Prevention." *MR* 29 (13 February 1886):188.

"Malpractice, with Reference to the Legal and Medical Professions." *MR* 45 (3 February 1894):145.

"Malpraxis." *BMSJ* (3 July 1873):22.

"Malpraxis in Midwifery." *BMSJ* 2 (9 June 1829):270.

"*Mary Ann Decrow, et al.* v. *H. H. Little:* A Prosecution for Alleged Malpractice." *OMSJ* 12 (January 1860):194–98.

"Measure of Skill Required By the Law." *NYMJ* 33 (April 1881):731–32.

"Medical Expert Testimony." *BMSJ* 116 (3 February 1887):119–20.

"Medical Malpractice." *MSR* 47 n.s. (23 December 1882):716–17.

"Medical Notes" (comments on Eugene Sanger's malpractice study). *BMSJ* 99 (18 July 1878):91.

"Medical Reform." *MNL* 5 (May 1847):49–54.

"Medical Science in New York." *BMSJ* 15 (16 November 1836):241–42.

"Medical Testimony in Malpractice Cases." *MSR* 28 (1 February 1873): 122–23.

"*Michael O'Neil* v. *Gerard Bancker.*" *NYMPJ* 6 (1827):145–52.

"New York Supreme Court Decision of Justice Laurence in the Case of Mary Ann Proctor against the Manhattan Eye and Ear Hospital." *MR* 15 (1879):599.

"Noteworthy Malpractice." *NYMJ* 33 (April 1881):731–32.

"The Old Excuse for Cheating the Doctor." *MR* 45 (6 January 1894):19.

"On the Avoidance of Causeless Suits for Malpractice." *MSR* 33 (25 September 1875):255–56.

"On Suits for Malpractice." *NYMJ* 49 (9 February 1889):158.

"Outrageous Suit for Malpractice." *BMSJ* 99 (28 November 1878):700–704.

"Organized Medical Defence." *JAMA* 38 (4 January 1902):37.

"Organized Medical Defence." *JAMA* 38 (4 January 1902):43.

"A Physician Sued for Malpractice and Acquitted." *MSJ* 27 (2 November 1872):415.

"Plans for Restraining Groundless Suits for Malpractice." *MSR* 34 (24 August 1878):171–72.

"[Proceedings of the Kentucky Medical Society, October 1854, discussed malpractice]." *WJMS* 30 (November 1854):365–67.

"Proper Steps for Physicians in Suits for Malpractice." *MSR* 27 (7 December 1872):496–97.

"Prosecution for Alledged Mal-Practice." *BufMJMR* 4 (1848–1849):274–77.

"Prosecution for Malpractice." *BMSJ* 30 (29 May 1844):344–45.

"Prosecution for Malpractice." *BMSJ* 32 (2 April 1845):185.

"Prosecution for Mal-Practice." *BMSJ* 48 (4 May 1853):281–83.

"Prosecution for Mal-Practice." *BMSJ* 48 (11 May 1853):304.

"Prosecution for Mal-Practice." *BMSJ* 48 (20 July 1853):503–4.

"Prosecutions for Mal-Practice." *ME* 14 (November 1851):728–29.

"Prosecutions for Mal-Practice." *NHJM* 4 (January 1854):20–23.

"Prosecutions for Mal-Practice." *BMSJ* 51 (8 November 1854):305.

"Prosecutions for Mal-Practice." *OMSJ* 13 (January 1861):253–60.

"Prosecutions of Medical Men." *WMSJ* 28 (1853):346–47.

"The Recent Malpractice Suit." *MR* 19 (4 June 1881):630–31.

"Report of the Committee of the American Surgical Association on the Medico-Legal Relations of the X-Rays." *AJMS* 120 n.s. (1900):7–35.

"Report of the Facts and Circumstances Relating to a Case of Compound Fracture and Prosecution for Malpractice . . ." *ME* 4 (1841):712–14.

"Report of the Facts and Circumstances Relating to a Case of Compound Fracture, and Prosecution for Malpractice . . ." *AJMS* 3 n.s. (January 1842):181–84.

"Report of the Facts and Circumstances Relating to a Case of Compound Fracture, and Prosecution for Malpractice . . ." *WMSJ* 5 (1842):141–48.

"Report on Difficulties Growing Out of Alleged Mal-Practice in the Treatment of Fractures." *TOMS* 11 (1856):53–66.

"Review: Medical Ethics." *AJMS* 23 (January 1852):149–178.

"Reviews" (review of Frank H. Hamilton's 1853 *Fracture Tables*). *WJMPS* 28 (1853):309–12.

"Reviews" (review of Frank Hamilton's 1860 work). *AJMS* 39 (April 1860):419–39.

"Shocking Outrage on Professional Humanity." *Scal* 7 (January 1856):253–55.

"Singular Suit for Spiritualistic Surgery Malpractice." *MSR* 28 (15 April 1873):290.

"Some Recent Malpractice Suits." *MR* 28 (19 December 1885):690–91.

"Status of Our Profession." *MSR* 11 (February 1858):133–36.

"Status of Our Profession." *MSR* 11 (March 1858):194–96.

"[The Status of Physicians]." *MSR* 11 (January 1858):60–63.

"*Stogdale* v. *Baker*." *BMSJ* 117 (1887):610.

"*Stogdale* v. *Baker*." *Annals of Gynaecology* 1 (1887–1888):150–51.

"Stover-Catlin: The Malpractice Suit." *MR* 17 (1880):573–74.

"Strictures on Professor Parker's Surgical Evidence in the Suit for Malpractice at Green Point: The Value of Title and Consultations." *Scal* 5 (August 1853):230–36.

"Suit against a Physician for Neglect of Vaccination." *MSR* 28 (1 March 1873):202.

"The Suit against Professor Gross." *MT* 1 (1 May 1871):280–81.

"Suit for Alleged Mal-Practice." *OMSJ* 10 (1857–1858):13–24.

"Suit for Alleged Malpractice." *OMSJ* 10 (May 1858):447–51.

"A Suit for Alleged Malpractice. *Gallagher* v. *Herrick*," *CMG* 2 (1886–1887):117–32.

"Suit for Damages . . ." *BMSJ* 66 (31 July 1862):544.

"Suit for Mal-Practice." *JMCS* 3 (November 1846):407–8.

"Suit for Malpractice." *OMSJ* 2 (November 1849):161–63.

"Suit for Mal-Practice." *BMSJ* 50 (19 April 1854):246.

"The 'Suit for Malpractice.' " *BMSJ* 50 (3 May 1854):287.

"Suit for Malpractice." *NMSJ* 6 (1849–1850):227–30.

"Suit for Mal-Practice." *BMSJ* 66 (27 February 1862):95.

"[Suit for Malpractice]." *BMSJ* 6 n.s. (27 October 1870):276.

"[Suit for Malpractice]." *MR* 5 (1 November 1870):398–99.

"Suit for Malpractice." *MSR* 32 (22 May 1875):419.

"Suit for Malpractice." *MR* 19 (28 May 1881):616.

"A Suit for Malpractice." *NYMJ* 46 (24 December 1887):718.

"Suit for Malpractice." *MR* 44 (18 November 1893):658.

"A Suit for Malpractice Decided against the Surgeon." *MR* 39 (14 March 1891): 322.

"A Suit for Malpractice." *MR* 52 (18 June 1898):925–26.

"Suit for Malpractice: Prof. Spencer on Mercury in Dysentery." *WJMPS* 24 (1851):168–70.

"Suit for Malpractice Decided." *MSR* 7 (1 March 1862):525–26.

"Suit for Malpractice Withdrawn." *MSR* (6 January 1866):19.

"Suits for Mal-Practice." *BMSJ* 51 (13 December 1854):402–3.

"Suits for Malpractice." *MR* 16 (20 December 1879):599.

"Suits for Malpractice." *MSR* 40 n.s. (1879):197.

"Suits for Malpractice." *MR* 17 (7 February 1880):161–62.

"Suits for Malpractice." *BMSJ* 96 (17 May 1887):598–99.

"Suits of Malpractice." *MR* 16 (20 December 1879):591.

"A Surgical Case of Mal-Practice." *BMSJ* 51 (8 November 1854):289–97.

"Surgical Malpractice." *BMSJ* 36 (5 May 1847):283–84.

"To What Causes Are We To Attribute the Diminishing Respectability of the Medical Profession in the Estimation of the American Public?" *MSR* 1 (1858):141–43.

"*Travers* v. *Boardman*: An Action of Tort, and What It Teaches." *BMSJ* 104 (17 February 1881):160–61.

"Trial for Alleged Malpractice." *BMSJ* 50 (8 March 1854):120–21.

"Trial for Mal-Practice." *BMSJ* 25 (10 November 1841):226–27.

"Trial for Malpractice." *BMSJ* 37 (22 September 1847):162–64.

"Trial for Malpractice." *NMSJ* 5 (1848–1849):536–46.

"Trial for Malpractice." *BMSJ* 41 (10 October 1849):206.

"Trial for Malpractice." *BMSJ* 51 (22 November 1854):345.

"Trial for Malpractice." *BufMJMR* 10 (1854–1855):568–70.
"Trial for Mal-Practice." *BMSJ* 54 (20 March 1856):129–38.
"Trial for Mal-Practice." *BMSJ* 54 (27 March 1856):149–56.
"Trial for Malpractice." *BMSJ* 55 (22 January 1857):515.
"Trial for Malpractice." *BMSJ* 56 (5 February 1857):9–23.
"Trial for Malpractice." *BMSJ* 56 (5 February 1857):25–26.
"Trial for Mal-Practice." *MSR* 12 (1865):555–58.
"Trial for Mal-Practice." *MSR* 12 (1865):569–73.
"Trial for Malpractice." *MSR* 28 (24 May 1873):399–401.
"Trial for Malpractice, and One Thousand Dollars Damages." *BufMJMR* 3 (1847–1848):145–48.
"Trial for Malpractice—Dr. Crosby's Acquittal." *BMSJ* 50 (21 June 1854):424–25.
"Trial for Mal-Practice in Pennsylvania." *BMSJ* 37 (15 September 1847):141–42.
"Trial for Malpraxis." *StLMSJ* 3 (May 1846):529–62.
"Trial of Dr. Shipman for Mal-Practice." *BMSJ* 31 (18 September 1844):140–42.
"Trial of Dr. Spencer for Mal-Practice." *BMSJ* 44 (11 June 1851):384.
"An Undefended Suit for Malpractice." *NYMJ* 69 (29 April 1899):616.
"An Unfounded Charge of Malpractice." *NYMJ* 38 (22 September 1883):324.
"An Unsuccessful Malpractice Suit." *MR* 47 (25 May 1895):669.
"Valentine Mott on Medical Ethics." *Scal* 9 (July 1857):125–26.
"The Varied Functions Possible in the County Medical Society." *JAMA* 44 (18 March 1905):881–82.
"Verdict Against a Physician." *MR* 47 (12 January 1895):64.
"The Whitney Case Again." *OMSJ* 12 (November 1859):167.
"X-Ray Dermatitis. Suit for Damages." *BMSJ* 38 (17 February 1898):166; and *JAMA* 30 (1898):397.
Adams, James, Jr. *Report of an Action, Charles Lowell against John Faxon and Micajah Hawks, Doctors of Medicine, Defendants*. Portland: Printed for James Adams, Jr., by David and Seth Paine, 1825.
Appley, W. L. "How Rip Van Winkle, Jr., M.D. Disposed of a Case of Malpractice." *MSR* 25 (28 October 1871):381–82.
Barnett, Clement B. "Trial for Malpractice." *BMSJ* 30 (19 June 1844):405–6.
Bauer, Lewis, "Surgical Contributions." *MSR* 13 (1865):270–72.
Beck, Theodoric R. *Elements of Medical Jurisprudence*. Albany: Webster and Skinner, 1823.
Becker, T. C. "*Carpenter* v. *Blake*: An Important Decision by the Highest Court of New York State for an Action for Malpractice." *PSI* 1 (1880):119–25, 144–47, 174–76.
Bentham, Jeremy, and John Stuart Mill. *Utilitarianism and Other Essays*. Edited by Alan Ryan. New York: Penguin, 1987.
Blackstone, William. *Commentaries*. St. George Tucker's edition. Philadelphia:

William Birch Young and Abraham, 1803; reprint, Augustus M. Kelly, Publishers, 1969.

Blake, G. M. "Suits Against Surgeons." *BufMSJ* 18 (1879–1880):309–16.

Brainard, D. "Trial for Malpractice." *BMSJ* 31 (22 January 1845):501–2.

Brown, William A. *"Mary Ann Decrow et al.*, v. *H. H. Little*: A Prosecution for Alleged Mal-Practice." *OMSJ* 12 (January 1860):194–98.

Bryce, James. *The American Commonwealth*. London and New York: Macmillan, 1889.

Buel, Henry W. "Statistics of Amputation in the New York Hospital from Jan. 1, 1839, to Jan. 1, 1848." *AJMS* 16 (1848):33–43.

Burnham, Walter. "The Dangers and Responsibilities of a Surgeon." *BMSJ* 5 (3 February 1870):77–78.

Carlyle, Thomas. "Signs of the Times" (1829). In *Critical and Miscellaneous Essays*, vol. 2. London: Chapman and Hall, 1899.

Cathell, D. W. *The Physician Himself and What He Should Add to His Scientific Acquirements*. Baltimore: Cushings and Bailey, 1882; reprint, Arno Press, 1972.

Chitty, Joseph. *A Practical Treatise on Medical Jurisprudence*. London: Butterworth, 1834.

Clinton, G. W. "Malpractice." *BufMSJ* 19 (1879–1880):229–40.

Cooley, Thomas M. *A Treatise on the Law of Torts*. Chicago: Callaghan, 1880, 1906.

Cooper, Astley. *A Treatise on Dislocations and on Fractures of the Joints*. 1st American ed., 3rd London ed. Boston: Wells and Lilly, 1825.

———. *The Lectures of Sir Astley Cooper*. 4th American ed. Philadelphia: E. L. Carey and A. Hart, 1835.

Cooper, Samuel. *A Dictionary of Practical Surgery*. London, 1813.

Crosby, Dixi, comp. *Report of a Trial for Alleged Mal-Practice*. Woodstock: Printed by Lewis Pratt, Jr., 1854.

Cunningham, H. S. "Fracture with Treatment and Suit for Malpraxis." *MSR* 54 (8 May 1886):579–80.

D. W. C. "Suits for Malpractice." *BMSJ* 40 (2 May 1869):287.

———. "Civil Malpractice." *BMSJ* 96 (19 April 1877):470–73.

Dawson, John. "Suit for Damages in a Case of Fracture of the Leg, Followed by Mortification and Amputation." *OMSJ* 14 (1 July 1862):283–90.

de Tocqueville, Alexis. *Democracy in America*. Translated by George Lawrence. Edited by J. P. Mayer. Garden City, N.Y.: Doubleday, 1969.

Detwiler, B. H. "Malpractice Suits and Their Remedy." *Pennsylvania Medical Journal* 1 (1897):295–98.

Doering, E. J. "Mutual Protection against Blackmail." *JAMA* 6 (30 January 1886):114–17.

Elwell, John. *A Medico-Legal Treatise on Medical Malpractice and Medical Evidence*. New York: John S. Voorhis, 1860.

Ewell, Marshall D. *A Manual of Medical Jurisprudence for the Use of Students at Law and of Medicine*. Boston: Little, Brown, 1887.

Garnett, Alexander Y. P. "Professional Standing; Its Decadence; the Cause; How to Be Remedied; Radicalism; Young America." *MSR* 7 (March 1854): 98–103.

Greenleaf, Simon. *A Treatise on the Law of Evidence*. Boston: Charles C. Little and James Brown, 1853; reprint, Arno Press, 1972.

Groner, F. J. "The Causes and the Remedies for Suits for Malpractice." *MR* 37 (1890):143–46.

Gross, Samuel D. "A Century of American Medicine, 1776–1876." *AJMS* 71 (1876):431–84.

———. *Autobiography of Samuel D. Gross*, vol. 2. Philadelphia: George Barrie, 1887; reprint, Arno Press, 1972.

Hadden, A. "Ohio Statutes and Decisions Relating to Malpractice." *Cleveland Medical Gazette* 13 (1897–1898):687–700.

Hamilton, Frank H. *Fracture Tables*. Buffalo: Jewett, Thomas, 1853.

———. "Deformities after Fractures." *TAMA* 8 (1855):349–54.

———. "Report on Deformities after Fractures." *TAMA* 8 (1855):347–93; *TAMA* 9 (1856):69–233; and *TAMA* 10 (1857):239–453.

———. *A Practical Treatise on Fractures and Dislocations*. Philadelphia: Lea and Blanchard, 1860.

———. "Suits for Malpractice in Surgery: Their Cause and Their Remedies." In *Papers Read before the Medico-Legal Society of New York*. 3rd Ser. New York: Medico-Legal Society of New York, 1886.

Hildreth, S. P. "Trial for Mal-Practice in Surgery." *OMSJ* 2 (January 1850): 213–22.

Hillard, Francis. *The Law of Torts or Private Wrongs*. 2 vols. Boston: Little, Brown, 1859.

Higginson, Thomas Wentworth. "Saints and Their Bodies." *AtlM* 1 (March 1858):582–95.

Hodges, E. F. "Malpractice." *AP* 30 (1884):152–60; *Transactions of the Indiana Medical Society* 34 (1884):147–58; and *Fort Wayne Journal of Medical Science* 4 (1884–1885):146–54.

Holt, A. F. "Medical Expert Testimony, as Given in the Courts at Present," *BMSJ* 105 (25 November 1886):493–96.

Hooker, Worthington. *Physician and Patient: or, A Practical View of the Mutual Duties, Relations and Interests of the Medical Profession and the Community*. New York: Baker and Scribner, 1849; facsimile reprint, Arno Press, 1972.

Hunt, W. "Inequality in Length of the Lower Limbs, with a Report of an Important Suit for Malpractice, and also a Claim for Priority." *AJMS* 77 (1879):102–7.

Hutchinson, W. F. "A Recent Suit for Malpractice." *BufMSJ* 12 (1872–1873):290–98.

Jones, John. *Plain Concise Practical Remarks on the Treatment of Wounds and Fractures*. Philadelphia: Robert Bell, 1776; reprint, Arno Press, 1971.

[Jones, W. W.] "*Terrence Mc Queeney v. W. W. Jones*." *OMSJ* 12 (September 1859):22–24.

Ledergeber, Fred. "Suggestions in Relation to Questions of Law that May Be of Service to the Medical Practitioner." *StLMSJ* 43 (1882):494–504.

Lee, Charles A. "Medical Jurisprudence, — Being Notes of a Trial for Mal-Practice." *NYJMCS* 1 (November 1843):352–62.

Lefever, Isaac. "Report of a Trial for Malpractice in the Court of Common Pleas of Perry County, Pennsylvania." *AJMS* 48 (July 1864):72–86.

Lowell, Charles. *Authentic Report of a Trial before the Supreme Judicial Court of Maine for the County of Washington, June Term 1824.* Portland: Printed for the Author, 1826.

Lyman, Oliver E. "Some Notes on a Doctor's Liability." *PSM* 18 (1880–1881):769–76.

McAdam, David. *Malpractice with Reference to the Legal and Medical Professions.* 1893.

McClelland, Milo. *Civil Malpractice.* New York: Hurd and Houghton, 1877.

Manley, T. H. "The Medico-Legal Aspects of Fractures of the Extremities, and Others, from a Consideration of Their Aetiology, Diagnosis, Prognosis, and Treatment." *NYMJ* 58 (1893):281–90.

Manning, Walter K. "Prosecution for Mal-Practice." *BMSJ* 40 (23 May 1849):318–19.

———. "Trial for Mal-Practice." *BMSJ* 42 (27 February 1850):79–80.

March, Alden. "Prosecutions for Malpractice in the State of N. York." *BMSJ* 36 (14 July 1847):477–80.

———. "Prosecutions for Mal-Practice in the State of New York." *ME* 10 (August 1847):502–5.

———. "Case of Alleged Mal-Practice in Surgery." *BMSJ* 37 (4 August 1847):9–14.

Mattocks, B. "Malpractice." *NMSJ* 3 (1872–1873):45–52.

Medora, E. "*White* v. *Hiram L. Chase.*" *BMSJ* 99 (1878):700–704.

Merrill, Arthur. "Court of Common Pleas, Meigs County, Ohio, September Term, 1850: Hon. A. G. Brown, Presiding. *Holt* v. *Rathburn.* Mal-Practice in Surgery." *WL* 11 (1850):763–68.

Miller, Perry, ed. *The Legal Mind in America: From Independence to the Civil War.* Garden City, N.Y.: Doubleday, 1962.

Montgomery, H. F. "Suits for Malpractice." *BufMSJ* 11 (1871–1872):445–60.

Moore, A. "Prosecution for Malpractice, in a Case of Imperfect Recovery from a Dislocation of the Elbow." *MR* 8 (November 1855):552–59.

Morris, Robert T. "Circumstances Alter Malpractice Case." *MR* 38 (20 December 1890):718.

———. *Fifty Years a Surgeon.* New York: E. P. Dutton, 1935.

Nichols, Theodore. "Trial for Mal-Practice." *OMSJ* 2 (September 1849):6–10.

[Norris, George W.] "Bibliographic Notices." *AJMS* 3 n.s. (January 1842):181–84.

Norris, George W. "Statistical Account of the Cases of Amputation performed at the Pennsylvania Hospital from Jan. 1, 1831, to Jan. 1, 1838." *AJMS* 22 (1838):356–65.

———. "Statistical Account of the Cases of Amputation performed at the Pennsylvania Hospital from Jan. 1, 1838, to Jan. 1. 1840." *AJMS* 26 (1840):35–36.

Noyes, Henry D. "Tucker against Noyes." *MR* 19 (1881):25–26.

O'Dea, James J. "Duties of a Medical Witness in Cases of Malpractice." *MR* 2 (1867–1868):474.

———. "Medico-Legal Science A Sketch of its Progress, Especially in the United States." In *Papers Read Before the Medico-Legal Society of New York*, 3rd ser. New York: Medico-Legal Society, 1886.

Ordronaux, John. *The Jurisprudence of Medicine*. Philadelphia: T. and J. W. Johnson, 1869; reprint, Arno Press, 1973.

Ormsby, O. B. "Fracture of the Humerous, with Injury of the Musculo-Spiral Nerve: Suit for Malpractice." *MSR* 38 (1877):447–48.

Parker, Joel. "Extract from a Lecture on the Rights and Liabilities of the Physician and Surgeon." *WMSJ* 31 (March 1855):217–19.

Parkman, Samuel. "On the Relations of the Medical Witness with the Law and the Lawyer." *AJMS* 23 (January 1852):126–34.

———, and Calvin P. Fiske. "Report on the Causes and Prevention of Suits for Mal-Practice." *MCMMS* (appendix) 8 (1853):123–32.

Perkins, N. R. "A Suit for Malpractice Resulting from a Case of Fracture of the Femur, with a Verdict of Judgment for Defendants." *New England Medical Gazette* 32 (1897):116–21.

Pillsbury, A. E. "Ignorance as a Legal Excuse for Malpractice." *Transactions of the Massachusetts Medico-Legal Society* 1 (1878–1884):191–95.

Pott, Percival. *Treatise on Compound Fractures*, vol. 1. Philadelphia, 1819.

Powell, A. M. "Surgical Malpractice." *Saint Louis Medical and Surgical Journal* 42 (March 1882):231–36.

Price, Mordecai. "Remarks on Suits for Malpractice." *NYMJ* 65 (15 May 1897):676–78.

R. M. K. O. "Trial for Mal-Practice." *BMSJ* 41 (17 October 1849):216–19.

———. "Trial for Mal-Practice." *BMSJ* 41 (23 January 1850):500–502.

———. "Suit for Mal-Practice in Vermont." *BMSJ* 44 (11 June 1851):377–78.

Reamy, Thaddeus A. "Suit for Alleged Mal-Practice." *OMSJ* 10 (1857–1858):13–24.

Redfield, Amasa A., and Thomas G. Shearman. *A Treatise on the Law of Negligence*. Baker, Voorhis, 1870.

Reese, John J. "Case of Alleged Malpractice." *MT* 1 (1 December 1870):73–74.

Rice, Nathan P. *Trials of a Public Benefactor*. New York: Pudney and Russell, 1859.

Robinson, Conway. *The Practice of Courts of Justice*. Richmond: A. Morris, 1855.

Sanger, E. F. "Report on Malpractice." *BMSJ* 100 (2 January 1879):14–23.
————. "Report on Malpractice." *BMSJ* 100 (9 January 1879):41–50.
Saunders, John Simcoe. *The Law of Pleading and Evidence in Civil Actions.* Philadelphia: Robert Small, 1844.
Sheldon, James. "Report of Trial for Malpractice." *BufMJMR* 4 (August 1848):131–54.
Shipman, Azaiah Booth, *A Report of the Circumstances Relating to a Case of Compound Fracture and Prosecution for Mal-Practice.* Cortlandville, N.Y.: Cortland Democrat, 1841.
Shrady, J. "The Civil and Criminal Responsibility of Physicians for Malpractice." *Bulletin of the Medico-Legal Society of New York* 1 (1878–1879):65–84.
Sims, J. Marion. *The Story of My Life.* New York: Da Capo Press, 1968.
Smith, Stephen. "[Review of John Elwell's *Treatise on Malpractice*]." *AJMS* 40 (July 1860):153–66.
————. *Doctor in Medicine and Other Papers on Professional Subjects.* New York: William Wood, 1872; reprint, Arno Press, 1972.
————. "On the Legal Responsibilities of Medical Men." *OMSJ* 1 n.s. (1876):46–50, 148–52; *OMSJ* 2 n.s. (1877):63–67.
Souwers, G. F. "The Laws of Malpractice." *MSR* 4 (1 October 1881):386–88, 414–16.
Stockwell, J. K. "Suits for Malpractice." *MR* 17 (1880):161–62.
Taylor, O. H. "On the Obvious Decline in the Respectability of Public for the Medical Profession . . ." *MSR* 11 (July 1858):460–69.
Vinnedge, W. W. "*Groenendyke v. Thos. W. Fry, M.D.*" *Transactions of the Indiana Medical Society* 26 (1874):107–12.
Wade, Martin J. *A Selection of Cases on Malpractice of Physicians, Surgeons, and Dentists.* St. Louis: Medico-Legal, 1909.
Waggoner, F. R. "Alleged Malpractice—Case of *Russel v. Wardner.*" *MSR* 24 (20 May 1871):410–11.
Walker, Timothy. *Introduction to American Law, Designed as a First Book for Students.* Philadelphia: P. H. Nicklin and T. Johnson, 1837; reprint, DaCapo Press, 1972.
Walker, William J. "On the Treatment of Compound and Complicated Fractures." *MCMMS* 7 (1842–1848):171–215.
Walsh, David. *The Röentgen Rays in Medical Work.* New York: William Wood, 1898.
Warren, Edward. *A Doctor's Experiences in Three Continents.* Baltimore: Cushings and Bailey, 1885.
Warren, John Collins. *A Letter to the Hon. Isaac Parker, Chief Justice of the Supreme Court of Massachusetts, Containing Remarks on the Dislocation of the Hip Joint . . .* Cambridge: Hillard and Metcalf, 1826.
Weinschenk, L. "Malpractice." *DTJM* 5 (1889–1890):208–22.
Weist, J. R. "Civil Malpractice Suits. How can the physician protect himself against them?" *AP* 30 (1884):160–74; *Transactions of the Indiana Medical*

Society 34 (1884):132–46; *Fort Wayne Journal of Medical Science* 4 (1884–1885):154–66; and *Indiana Medical Journal* 3 (1884):1–11.

Wey, C. William. "Medical Responsibility and Malpractice. Anniversary Address Delivered before the Medical Society." *TSMSNY* (1872):65–89.

Whitman, Walt. *Leaves of Grass: The First (1855) Edition*. Edited, with an introduction by Malcolm Cowley. New York: Viking Press, 1960.

Wilding, R. J. "The Necessity of an Amendment in the Law Governing Medical Evidence in Malpractice Suits." *Transactions of the Medical Society of the State of New York* (1891):390–94.

Winthrop, John. *Winthrop's Journal: History of New England, 1630–1649*. 2 vols. Edited by James Kendall Hosmer. New York: Charles Scribner's Sons, 1908.

Wood, William M. "Thoughts on Suits for Malpractice, Suggested by Certain Judicial Proceedings in Erie County, Pennsylvania." *AJMS* 18 (October 1849):395–400.

———. "A Statement of Two Suits for Malpractice, Tried in November and December 1850, in the Court of Erie County, Pa." *AJMS* 22 (July 1851): 43–50.

Young, Alexander. "The Law of Malpractice." *BMSJ* 5 (9 June 1870):425–43.

———. "Criminal Malpractice." *BMSJ* 7 n.s. (5 January 1871):1–12.

AMERICAN MALPRACTICE APELLATE CASES

These cases constitute only a portion of the 216 appellate malpractice decisions in the nineteenth century.

Cross v. Guthery 1 Amer. Dec. 61 (Conn. 1794)
Grannis v. Branden 5 Day 260 (Conn. 1812)
Landon v. Humphrey 9 Day 209 (Conn. 1832)
Bliss v. Long 1 Wright 351 (Ohio 1833)
Gallaher v. Thompson 1 Wright 466 (Ohio 1833)
Bemus v. Howard 3 Watts 255 (Penn. 1834)
Grindle v. Rush 7 Ohio 123 (1836)
McClallen v. Adams 19 Pick. 333 (Mass. 1837)
Mertz v. Detweiler 8 Watts & Sargent 376 (Penn. 1845)
Bowman v. Woods 1 Green 441 (Iowa 1848)
Howard v. Grover 28 Me. 97 (1848)
Piper v. Menifee 51 Ky. 465 (1851)
Ballard v. Russell 33 Me. 196 (1851)
Adler v. Buckley 1 Swan. 69 (Tenn. 1851)
Moody v. Sabin 63 Mass. 505 (1852)
Twombly v. Leach 65 Mass. 397 (1853)
McCandless v. McWha 22 Penn. 261 (1853)

Leighton v. Sargent 7 Foster 460 (N.H. 1853)
Moor v. Teed 3 Cal. 190 (1853)
Reynolds v. Graves 3 Wisc. 416 (1854)
Leighton V. Sargent 31 N.H. 119 (1855)
Fowler v. Sergent 1 Grant 355 (Penn. 1856)
Clapp v. Wood 4 Sneed 65 (Tenn. 1856)
Graham v. Gautier 21 Tx. 111 (1858)
Ritchey v. West 23 Ill. 385 (1860)
Smith v. Overby 30 Ga. 241 (1860)
Piles v. Hughes 10 Iowa 579 (1860)
Belinger v. Craig 31 Bar. 534 (N.Y. 1860)
McCrory v. Skinner 2 Ohio 268 (1860)
Woodward v. Hancock 1 Quarterly Law Review 385 (N.C. 1860)
West v. Martin 31 Mo. 375 (1861)
Cochran v. Miller 13 Iowa 128 (1862)
Patten v. Wiggin 51 Me. 594 (1862)
Wilmot v. Howard 39 Vt. 447 (1863)
Chamberlain v. Porter 9 Minn. 260 (1864)
McNevins v. Lowe 40 Ill. 209 (1866)
Craig v. Chambers 17 Ohio 254 (1867)
Hyatt v. Adams 16 Mich. 174 (1867)
Teft v. Wilcox 6 Kan. 46 (1870)
Chamberlin v. Morgan 68 Penn. 168 (1871)
Hibbard v. Thompson 109 Mass. 286 (1872)
Smothers v. Hanks 34 Iowa 287 (1872)
Almond v. Nugent 34 Iowa 300 (1872)
Branner v. Stormont 9 Kan. 51 (1872)
Scudder et al. v. Crossan 43 Ind. 343 (1873)
Kendall v. Brown 74 Ill. 232 (1874)
Ballou v. Prescott 64 Me. 305 (1874)
Getchell v. Hill et al. 21 Minn. 464 (1875)
Wenger v. Calder 78 Ill. 275 (1875)
Hathorn v. Richmond 48 Vt. 557 (1876)
Musser v. Chase 29 Ohio 577 (1876)
McDonald v. Mass. General Hospital 120 Mass. 432 (1876)
Gramm v. Boener 56 Ind. 497 (1877)
Hoener v. Koch 84 Ill. 408 (1877)
Fisher et al. v. Niccolls 2 Ill. App. 484 (1877)
Quinn v. Donovan 85 Ill. 194 (1877)
Carpenter v. Blake 75 N.Y. 12 (1878)
Higgins v. McCabe 126 Mass. 13 (1878)
Hitchcock v. Burgett 38 Mich. 501 (1878)
Potter v. Warner 91 Penn. 362 (1879)
Small v. Howard 128 Mass. 131 (1880)

De May v. Roberts 46 Mich. 160 (1881)
Ressequie v. Byers 52 Wisc. 651 (1881)
Gobel v. Dillon 86 Ind. 327 (1882)
Mallen v. Boynton 132 Mass. 443 (1882)
Kesle v. Hay 84 Ind. 189 (1882)
Brooke v. Clarke 57 Tx. 1905 (1882)
Jones v. Angell 95 Ind. 376 (1883)
O'Hara v. Wells 14 Neb. 403 (1883)
Secord v. St. Paul, M. & M. RY. Co. 18 Fed. Rep. 221 (1883)
Hyrne v. Erwin 23 S.C. 226 (1885)
Whittaker v. Collins 34 Minn. 299 (1885)
Quinn v. Higgins 63 Wisc. 664 (1885)
Holtzman v. Hoy 118 Ill. 534 (1886)
Mayo v. Wright 63 Mich. 32 (1886)
Gates v. Fleischer 67 Wisc. 504 (1886)
Vanhoover v. Berghoff 90 Mo. 488 (1887)
Reber v. Herring 115 Penn. 599 (1887)
Davis v. Spencer 27 Mo. App. 279 (1887)
Lower v. Franks 115 Ind. 334 (1888)
Bute v. Potts 76 Cal. 304 (1888)
Nelson v. Harrington 72 Wisc. 592 (1888)
Ayers v. Russell 3 N.Y. Supp. 338 (1888)
Graves v. Santway 6 N.Y. Supp. 892 (1889)
Sanderson v. Holland 39 Mo. App. 233 (1889)
Beck v. German Klinik 78 Iowa 696 (1889)
Hess v. Lowery 122 Ind. 225 (1889)
Spaulding v. Bliss 83 Mich. 311 (1890)
Gores v. Graff 77 Wisc. 174 (1890)
Langford v. Jones 18 Ore. 307 (1890)
DuBois v. Decker 130 N.Y. 325 (1891)
Pettigrew v. Lewis 46 Kan. 78 (1891)
Stevenson v. Gelsthorpe 10 Mont. 563 (1891)
Sims v. Parker 41 Ill. App. 284 (1891)
Link v. Sheldon. 136 N.Y. 1 (1892)
Lawson v. Conaway 37 W.Vir. 159 (1892)
Lewis v. Dwinell 84 Me. 497 (1892)
Hewitt v. Eisenbart 36 Neb. 794 (1893)
Mitchell v. Hindman 47 Ill. App. 431 (1893)
Carpenter v. McDavitt 53 Mo. App. 393 (1893)
Peck v. Hutchinson 88 Iowa 320 (1893)
Force v. Gregory 63 Conn. 167 (1893)
Cayford v. Wilbur 86 Me. 414 (1894)
Mucci v. Houghton 89 Iowa 608 (1894)
Downes v. Harper Hospital 101 Mich. 555 (1894)

Styles v. Tyler 64 Conn. 433 (1894)
Swanson v. French 92 Iowa 695 (1894)
Union Pacific Ry. Co. v. Artist 60 Fed. Rep. 365 (1894)
Yunker v. Marshall & Daly 65 Ill. App. 667 (1895)
Jackson v. Burnham 20 Col. 533 (1895)
Hedin v. Minn. Med. & Sur. Inst. 62 Minn. 146 (1895)
Eighmy v. Union Pacific Ry. Co. 93 Iowa 538 (1895)
Hearns v. Waterbury Hospital 66 Conn. 93 (1895)
Moratzky v. Wirth 67 Minn. 46 (1896)
Dashiell v. Grifith 84 Md. 363 (1896)
Harriott v. Plimpton 166 Mass. (1896)
Feeney v. Spalding 89 Me. 111 (1896)
Jones v. Vroom 8 Col. App. 143 (1896)
Wurdemann v. Barnes 92 Wisc. 206 (1896)
Richards v. Willard 176 Penn. 181 (1896)
Griswold v. Hutchinson 47 Neb. 727 (1896)
Pelky v. Palmer 109 Mich. 561 (1896)
Whitesell v. Hill 101 Iowa 630 (1897)
Pike v. Honsiger 49 NE 760 (N.Y. 1898)

Secondary Sources

Ackernecht, Erwin. "Elisha Bartlett and the Philosophy of the Paris Clinical School." *BHM* 24 (1950):49–60.
Armstrong, David D. "Medical Malpractice — The 'Locality Rule' and the 'Conspiracy of Silence.' " *SCLR* 22 (1970):811–21.
Atiyah, P. S. *The Rise and Fall of Freedom of Contract.* Oxford: Clarendon Press, 1979.
Auerbach, Jerold S. *Unequal Justice: Lawyers and Social Change in America.* New York: Oxford University Press, 1976.
———. *Justice Without Law?* New York: Oxford University Press, 1983.
Ayers, Edward L. *Vengeance and Justice, Crime and Punishment in the Nineteenth-Century American South.* New York: Oxford University Press, 1984.
Bailyn, Bernard. *Education and the Forming of American Society.* New York: Vintage, 1960.
Barker-Benfield, G. *Horrors of a Half-Known Life.* New York: Harper and Row, 1976.
Becker, Carl L. *The Declaration of Independence: A Study in the History of Political Ideas.* New York: Random House, 1921.
Beecher, Henry K., and Mark D. Altschule. *Medicine at Harvard: The First Three Hundred Years.* Hanover: University Press of New England, 1977.
Bellah, Robert N., Richard Madsen, William M. Sullivan, Ann Swindler, and Steven M. Tipton. *Habits of the Heart: Individualism and Commitment in American Life.* Berkeley: University of California Press, 1985.

Bender, Thomas. *Community and Social Change in America*. New Brunswick: Rutgers University Press, 1979.

Berman, Alex. "The Thomsonian Movement and Its Relation to American Pharmacy and Medicine." *BHM* 25 (September–October 1951):405–28.

Bernstein, Samuel. "The Impact of the Paris Commune in the United States." *MassR* 12 (1971):435–45.

Berthoff, Rowland. *An Unsettled People: Social Order and Disorder in American History*. New York: Harper and Row, 1971.

Betts, John R. "Mind and Body in Early American Thought." *JAH* 54 (March 1968):787–805.

Black, Henry Campbell. *Black's Law Dictionary*. 5th ed. St. Paul: West Publishing, 1979.

Blake, John. "From Buchan to Fishbein: The Literature of Domestic Medicine." In *Medicine Without Doctors*, edited by Guenter B. Risse, Ronald L. Numbers, and Judith Walzer Leavitt. New York: Science History Publications, 1977.

———. "Anatomy." In *The Education of American Physicians*, edited by Ronald L. Numbers. Berkeley: University of California Press, 1980.

Boles, John B. *The Great Revival, 1787–1805*. Lexington: University Press of Kentucky, 1972.

———. "Evangelical Protestantism in the Old South: From Religious Dissent to Cultural Dominance." In *Religion in the Old South*, edited by Charles Reagan Wilson. Jackson: University Press of Mississippi, 1985.

Brecher, Edward and Ruth. *The Rays: A History of Radiology in America*. Baltimore: William and Wilkins, 1969.

Breeden, James Otis. "Thomsonianism in Virginia." *VMHB* 82 (1974):150–8.

———. "Body Snatchers and Anatomy Professors: Medical Education in Nineteenth-Century Virginia." *VMHB* 83 (1975):321–45.

Bremner, Robert. *American Philanthropy*. Chicago: University of Chicago Press, 1960.

———. *From the Depths: The Discovery of Poverty in the United States*. New York: New York University Press, 1956.

Brieger, Gert H. "American Surgery and the Germ Theory of Disease." *BHM* 40 (1966):135–45.

Brieger, Gert H. "Therapeutic Conflicts and the American Medical Profession in the 1860s." *BHM* 41 (1967):215–22.

———, ed. *Medical America in the Nineteenth Century: Readings from the Literature*. Baltimore: Johns Hopkins University Press, 1972.

Broekhoff, Jan. "Physical Education and the Reification of the Human Body." *Gym* 9 (1972):4–11.

Brown, Richard. "Modernization and the Modern Personality in Early America, 1600–1865: A Sketch of a Sythesis." *Journal of Interdisciplinary History* 11 (Winter 1972):201–28.

———. *Modernization: The Transformation of American Life, 1600–1865*. New York: Hill and Wang, 1976.

Burnham, John C. "Change in Popularization of Health in the United States." *BHM* 58 (1984):185–97.

Burns: Chester R. "Malpractice Suits in American Medicine Before the Civil War." *BHM* 43 (1969):41–56.

———. "Medical Ethics in the United States Before the Civil War." Ph.D. dissertation. Johns Hopkins University, 1969.

———. "Medical Ethics and Jurisprudence." In *Education of American Physicians*, edited by Ronald L. Numbers. Berkeley: University of California Press, 1980.

———. "Medical Malpractice Law and the Public's Health in the United States During the Nineteenth Century." *Actes Proceedings, XXVIIIe Congrès International d'Histoire de la Médecine* 1 (1982):75–77.

Bushman, Richard. *From Puritan to Yankee: Character and the Social Order in Connecticut, 1690–1765.* Cambridge: Harvard University Press, 1967.

Cash, Wilber J. *The Mind of the South.* New York: Random House, 1941.

Cashdollar, Charles D. "European Positivism and the American Unitarianism." *CH* 45 (1976):490–97.

———. "Social Implications of the Doctrine of Divine Providence: A Nineteenth-Century Debate in American Theology." *HTR* 71 (1978):265–84.

———. *The Transformation of Theology, 1830–1890: Positivism and Protestant Thought in Britain and America.* Princeton University Press, 1989.

Cassedy, James H. "Why Self-Help? Americans Alone with Their Diseases, 1800–1850." In *Medicine Without Doctors: Home Health Care in American History.* Edited by Guenter B. Risse, Ronald L. Numbers, and Judith Walzer Leavitt. New York: Science History Publications, 1977.

———. *American Medicine and Statistical Thinking, 1800–1860.* Cambridge: Harvard University Press, 1984.

———. *Medicine and American Growth, 1800–1860* Madison: University of Wisconsin Press, 1986.

Caton, Donald. "The Secularization of Pain." *Anesthesiology* 62 (1985):493–501.

Chapman, Carlton. *Physicians, Ethics, and the Law.* New York: New York University Press, 1984.

Christianson, Eric H. "Medicine in New England." In *Medicine in the New World*, edited by Ronald L. Numbers. Knoxville: University of Tennessee Press, 1987.

Cirincione, Sandra. "The History of Medical Malpractice in New York State: A Perspective from the Publications of the Medical Society of New York." *NYSJM* 86 (1986):361–69.

Clapesattle, Helen. *The Doctors Mayo.* New York: Simon and Schuster, 1970.

Clark, Charles Edwin. "Science, Reason, and an Angry God: The Literature of an Earthquake." *NEQ* 38 (1965):340–62.

Cluff, Leighton E. "America's Romance with Medicine and Medical Science." *Daedalus* 115 (Spring 1986):137–59.

Cochran, Thomas C., and William Miller. *The Age of Enterprise: A Social History of Industrial America*. New York: Harper and Row, 1961.

Commager, Henry Steele. "The Nationalism of Joseph Story." In *The Bacon Lectures on the Constitution of the United States*. Boston: Boston University Press, 1953.

Cross, Whitney R. *The Burned Over District: The Social and Intellectual History of Enthusiastic Religion in Western New York, 1800–1850*. New York: Harper and Row, 1965.

Curren, William J. "The Unwanted Suitor: Law and the Use of Health Care Technology." In *Machine at the Bedside: Strategies for Using Technology in Patient Care*, edited by Stanley Joel Reiser and Michael Anbar. Cambridge: Cambridge University Press, 1984.

Dargo, George. *Law in the New Republic: Private Law and Public Estate*. New York: Alfred A. Knopf, 1983.

Demos, John. *A Little Commonwealth: Family Life in Plymouth Colony*. New York: Oxford University Press, 1982.

De Moulin, Daniel. "A Historical-Phenomenonological Study of Bodily Pain in Western Man." *BHM* 48 (1974):540–71.

Duffy, John. *Epidemics in Colonial America*. Baton Rouge: Lousiania State University, 1953.

———. "Anglo-American Reaction to Obstetrical Anesthesia." *BHM* 38 (1964):32–44.

———. "American Perceptions of the Medical, Legal, and Theological Professions." *BHM* 58 (1984):1–15.

———, ed. *History of Medicine in Louisiana*. 2 vols. Baton Rouge: Louisiana State University Press, 1950, 1962.

Eaton, Clement. *The Freedom of Thought Struggle in the Old South*. New York: Harper and Row, 1964.

———. *The Mind of the Old South*. Baton Rouge: Louisiana State University Press, 1964.

Edwards, Linden F. "Resurrection Riots During the Heroic Age of Anatomy in America." *BHM* 25 (1951):178–84.

Ekirch, Arthur Alphonse. *The Idea of Progress in America, 1815–1860*. New York: Peter Smith, 1951.

Engel, David. "Oven Bird's Song: Insiders, Outsiders, and Personal Injuries in an American Community." *LSR* 18 (1984):551–61.

English, Peter C. *Shock, Physiological Surgery, and George Washington Creel: Medical Innovation in the Progressive Era*. Westport, Conn.: Greenwood Press, 1980.

Epstein, Richard A. "Medical Malpractice: The Case for Contract." *ABFRJ* (1976):87–149.

———. "Market and Regulatory Approaches to Medical Malpractice: The Virginia Obstetrical No-Fault Statute." *VLR* 74 (1988):1451–74.

Featherstone, Mike. "The Body in Consumer Culture." *Theory, Culture, and Society* 1 (1982):18–33.

Fellman, Anita Clair, and Michael Fellman. *Making Sense of Self: Medical Advice Literature in Late Nineteenth-Century America*. Philadelphia: University of Pennsylvania Press, 1981.

Fifoot, C. H. S. *History and Sources of the Common Law*. New York: Greenwood Press, 1970.

Flexner, James Thomas. *Doctors on Horseback: Pioneers of American Medicine*. New York: Dover 1968.

Folgelman, Morris J., and Elinor Reinmiller. "1880–1890: A Creative Decade in World Surgery." *American Journal of Surgery* 115 (1968):812–24.

Friedman, Lawrence M. *Contract Law in America: A Social and Economic Case Study*. Madison: University of Wisconsin Press, 1965.

———. *A History of American Law*. New York: Simon and Schuster, 1973.

———. *Total Justice*. New York: Russell Sage, 1985.

———, and Jack Ladinsky. "Social Change and the Law of Industrial Accidents." *Columbia Law Review* 67 (1967):151–82.

Frisch, Michael H. *Town into City: Springfield, Massachusetts, and the Meaning of Community, 1840–1880*. Cambridge: Harvard University Press, 1972.

Galanter, Marc. "Reading the Landscape of Disputes: What We Know and Don't Know (and Think We Know) About Our Allegedly Contentious and Litigious Society." *UCLA Law Review* 31 (1983):4–71.

Garrison, Fielding H. *An Introduction to the History of Medicine*. Philadelphia: W. B. Saunders, 1914.

Genovese, Elizabeth Fox, and Eugene Genovese. "The Divine Sanction of Social Order: Religious Foundations of the Southern Slaveholder's World." *JAAR* 55 (Summer 1987):211–33.

Gibson, H. B. *Pain and its Conquest*. London: Peter Owen, 1982.

Gideion, Siegfried. *Mechanization Takes Command: A Contribution to Anonymous History*. New York: Norton 1978.

Gilmore, Grant. *The Death of Contract*. Columbus: Ohio State University Press, 1974.

Gordon, Robert. "Accounting for Legal Change in American Legal History." In *Law in the American Revolution and the Revolution in Law*, edited by Hedrick Hartog. New York: New York University Press, 1981.

Gorn, Elliot J. " 'Gouge and Bite, Pull Hair and Scratch': The Social Significance of Fighting in the Southern Backcountry." *AHR* 90 (1985):18–43.

Graveson, R. H. "The Movement from Status to Contract." *MLR* 4 (1941):261–67.

Green, Harvey. *Fit for America: Health, Fitness, Sport, and American Society*. New York: Pantheon, 1986.

Greenhouse, Carol. "Nature is to Culture as Praying is to Suing: Legal Pluralism in an American Suburb." *JLP* 20 (1982):17–35.

———. "Interpreting American Litigiousness." Paper presented at the Wenner-Gren Foundation for Anthropological Research, Bellagio, Italy, 10–18 August 1985.

———. *Praying for Justice: Faith, Order, and Community in an American Town.* Ithaca: Cornell University Press, 1986.

Gregory, Charles O. "Trespass to Negligence to Absolute Liability." *VLR* 37 (1951):359–98.

Gribbin, William. "Divine Providence or Miasma? The Yellow Fever Epidemic of 1822." *NYH* 53 (1972):283–98.

Griffin, Charles W. "Physical Fitness." In *Concise Histories of American Popular Culture,* edited by M. Thomas Inge. Westport, Conn.: Greenwood Press, 1982.

Grob, Gerald N. "The Social History of Medicine and Disease: Problems and Possibilities." *JSocH* 10 (1977):393–405.

Hall, Kermit. *The Magic Mirror.* New York: Oxford University Press, 1989.

Hall, Peter Dobkin. "The Social Foundations of Professional Credibility: Linking the Medical Profession to Higher Education in Connecticut and Massachusetts." In *The Authority of Experts: Studies in History and Theory,* edited by Thomas L. Haskell. Bloomington: Indiana University Press, 1984.

Haller, John S. *American Medicine in Transition, 1840–1910.* Urbana: University of Illinois Press, 1981.

Halley, Bruce. *The Healthy Body and Victorian Culture.* Cambridge: Harvard University Press, 1978.

Halliday, Terrance C. "Six Score and Ten: Demographic Transitions in the American Legal Profession." *LSR* 20 (1986):53–77.

Harrison, Louis B., Melvin H. Worth, Jr., and Michael A. Carlucci. "The Development of the Principles of Medical Malpractice in the United States." *PBM* 29 (Autumn 1985):41–72.

Haskell, Thomas. *The Emergence of Professional Social Science.* Urbana: University of Illinois Press, 1977.

Heath, Clark. "How Abraham Lincoln Dealt with a Malpractice Suit." *NEJM* 295:735–36.

Heitman, Elizabeth. "Caring for the Silent Stranger: Ethical Hospital Care for Non-English Speaking Patients." Ph.D. dissertation, Rice University, 1983.

Henretta, James A. *The Evolution of American Society, 1700–1815: An Interdisciplinary Analysis.* Lexington, Mass.: D. C. Heath, 1973.

Higham, John. "The Reorientation of American Culture in the 1890s." In *Writing American History: Essays in Modern Scholarship.* Bloomington: Indiana University Press, 1970.

Hilton, Boyd. *The Age of Atonement: The Influence of Evangelicalism on Social and Economic Thought, 1795–1865.* Oxford: Clarendon Press, 1988.

Hofstadter, Richard. *Anti-Intellectualism in American Life.* New York: Vintage Books, 1962.

Horwitz, Morton J. "The Emergence of an Instrumental Conception of American Law, 1780–1820." In *Law and American History,* edited by Bernard Bailyn and Donald Fleming. (Boston: Little, Brown, 1971).

Horwitz, Morton J. *The Transformation of American Law, 1780–1860.* Cambridge: Harvard University Press, 1977.

Hurst, J. Willard. *The Growth of American Law: The Law Makers.* Boston: Little, Brown, 1950.

Hylton, Joseph Gordon. "The Virginia Lawyer from Reconstruction to the Great Depression." Ph.D. dissertation. Harvard University, 1986.

Hyman, Harold M. *A More Perfect Union: The Impact of the Civil War and Reconstruction on the Constitution.* New York: Alfred A. Knopf, 1973.

Illich, Ivan. *Medical Nemesis: The Expropriation of Health.* New York: Pantheon, 1976.

Johnson, Herbert A. "Civil Procedure in John Jay's New York." *AJLH* 11 (1967):69–80.

Johnson, Paul E. *A Shopkeeper's Millennium: Society and Revivals in Rochester, New York, 1815–1837.* New York: Hill and Wang, 1978.

Joy, Robert T. J. "The Natural Bonesetters with Special Reference to the Sweet Family of Rhode Island." *BHM* 28 (1954):416–41.

Kaufman, Martin. *Homeopathy in America: The Rise and Fall of a Medical Heresy.* Baltimore: Johns Hopkins University Press, 1971.

———. "American Medical Education." In *The Education of American Physicians* edited by Ronald L. Numbers. Berkeley: University of California Press, 1980.

Kaufman, Walter. "Suffering and the Bible." In *The Faith of a Heretic.* Garden City, N.Y.: Doubleday, 1961.

Kelly, Howard. *A Cyclopedia of American Medical Biography: Comprising the Lives of Eminent Deceased Physicians and Surgeons 1610–1900*, vol. 2. Philadelphia: W. B. Saunders, 1912.

Kett, Joseph. *The Formation of the American Medical Profession, 1780–1860.* New Haven: Yale University Press, 1968.

Kinkead, Gwen. "Humana's Hard Sell Hospitals." *For* (17 November 1980):68–81.

Koffler, Joseph H., and Alison Reppy. *Handbook of Common Law Pleading.* St. Paul: West Publishing, 1969.

Larson, Magali Sarfatti. *The Rise of Professionalism: A Sociological Analysis.* Berkeley: University of California Press, 1977.

Lears, T. J. Jackson. *No Place of Grace: Antimodernism and the Transformation of America, 1880–1920.* New York: Pantheon, 1981.

———. "From Salvation to Self-Realization: Advertising and the Therapeutic Roots of Consumer Culture." In *The Culture of Consumption: Critical Essays in American History, 1880–1980*, edited by Richard Wightman Fox and T. J. Jackson Lears. New York: Pantheon, 1983.

Leavitt, Judith. *Brought to Bed: Childbearing in America, 1750–1950.* New York: Oxford University Press, 1986.

Levy, Leonard. *The Law of the Commonwealth and Chief Justice Shaw.* Cambridge: Harvard University Press, 1957.

Light, Donald W. "Corporate Medicine for Profit." *SA* 255 (December 1986):38–45.

Lockhart, Ailene S., and Betty Spears, eds. *Chronicle of American Physical Education: Selected Readings, 1855–1930.* Dubuque, Iowa: William C. Brown, 1972.

Lockridge, Kenneth A. *A New England Town: The First Hundred Years.* New York: Norton, 1970.

Longo, Laurence D. "The Rise and Fall of Batty's Operation: A Fashion in Surgery." *BHM* 53 (1979):244–67.

Loveland, Anne C. *Southern Evangelicals and the Social Order, 1800–1860.* Baton Rouge: Louisiana State University Press, 1980.

Ludmerer, Kenneth. *Learning to Heal: The Development of American Medical Education.* New York: Basic Books, 1985.

Maine, Henry. *Ancient Law.* New York: Henry Holt, 1884.

MacKinnon, F. B. *Contingent Fees for Legal Services.* Chicago: Aldine, 1964.

McLoughlin, William G. "Introduction to Charles G. Finney, *Lectures on Revivals of Religion.*" In *Essays on Jacksonian America.* Edited by Frank Otto Gatell. New York: Holt, Rinehart and Winston, 1970.

Malone, Wex. "The Genesis of Wrongful Death." *SLR* 17 (1965):1043–76.

———. *Essays on Torts.* Baton Rouge: Paul M. Herbert, 1986.

Marty, Martin E. *Righteous Empire: The Protestant Experience in America.* New York: Dial Press, 1970.

Marx, Leo. *The Machine in the Garden: Technology and the Pastoral Ideal in America.* New York: Oxford University Press, 1973.

May, Henry F. "The Decline of Providence?" In *Ideas, Faiths, and Feelings: Essays on American Intellectual and Religious History, 1952–1982.* New York: Oxford University Press, 1983.

May, William. *The Physician's Covenant: Images of the Healer in Medical Ethics.* Philadelphia: Westminister Press, 1983.

———. "Adversarialism in America and the Professions." In *Community in America: The Challenge of Habits of the Heart,* edited by Charles H. Reynolds and Ralph V. Norman. Berkeley: University of California Press, 1988.

Meier, Hugo A. "Technology and Democracy, 1800–1860." *MVHR* 43 (1956–1957):618–40.

Merry, Sally Engle, and Susan S. Sibley. "What Do Plaintiffs Want? Reexamining the Concept of Dispute." *JSJ* 9 (1984):151–78.

Meyers, Marvin. *The Jacksonian Persuasion: Politics and Belief.* New York: Vintage, 1960.

Millar, Robert Wyness. *Civil Procedure of the Trial Court in Historical Perspective.* New York: Law Center for New York University, 1952.

Miller, Perry. *The New England Mind: The Seventeenth Century.* Cambridge: Harvard University Press, 1939.

———. *The New England Mind: From Colony to Province.* Cambridge: Harvard University Press, 1953.

Miller, Perry, ed. *The Legal Mind in America: From Independence to the Civil War*. Garden City, N.Y.: Doubleday, 1962.

Moore, Winfred B., Joseph F. Tripp, and Lyon G. Tyler, eds. *Developing Dixie: Modernization in a Traditional Society*. Wesport, Conn.: Greenwood Press, 1988.

Morris, Richard B. "Responsibility for Tortious Acts in Early American Law." In *Studies in the History of American Law* Philadelphia: J. M. Mitchell, 1959.

Morris, Richard B. "Responsibility for Tortious Acts in Early American Law." In *Studies in the History of American Law*. Philadelphia: J. M. Mitchell, 1959.

Nelson, William E. *The Americanization of the Common Law: The Impact of Legal Change on Massachusetts Society, 1760–1830*. Cambridge: Harvard University Press, 1975.

———. *Dispute and Conflict Resolution in Plymouth County, Massachusetts, 1723–1825*. Chapel Hill: University of North Carolina Press, 1981.

Newmyer, R. Kent. *Supreme Court Justice Joseph Story: Statesman of the Old Republic*. Chapel Hill: University of North Carolina Press, 1985.

Numbers, Ronald L. "The History of American Medicine: A Field in Ferment." *RAH* 10 (1982):245–52.

———, ed. *The Education of American Physicians*. Berkeley: University of California Press, 1980.

———, and Ronald C. Sawyer. "Medicine and Christianity in the Modern World." In *Health/Medicine and the Faith Traditions: An Inquiry into Religion and Medicine*, edited by Martin E. Marty and Kenneth Vaux. Philadelphia: Fortress Press, 1982.

Nye, Russel Blaine. *Society and Culture in America, 1830–1860*. New York: Harper and Row, 1974.

Owsley, Frank Lawrence. *Plain Folk of the Old South*. Baton Rouge: Louisiana State University Press, 1960.

Park, Roberta J. "The Attitudes of Leading New England Transcendentalists Toward Healthful Exercise, Active Recreations, and Proper Care of the Body, 1830–1860." *JSH* 4 (1977):34–50.

———. " 'Embodied Selves': The Rise and Development of Concern for Physical Education, Active Games, and Recreation for American Women, 1776–1865." *JSH* 5 (Summer 1978):34–50.

Pernick, Martin. *A Calculus of Suffering: Pain, Professionalism, and Anesthesia in Nineteenth-Century America*. New York: Columbia University Press, 1985.

Porter, Thomas M. *The Rise of Statistical Thinking, 1820–1900*. Princeton: Princeton University Press, 1986.

Post, Albert. *Popular Freethought in America, 1825–1850*. New York: Columbia University Press, 1943.

Potter, David M. "Social Cohesion and the Crisis of Law." In *American Law and the Constitutional Order: Historical Perspectives*, edited by Lawrence M.

Friedman and Harry M. Scheiber. Cambridge: Harvard University Press, 1978.

Powell, John Harvey. *Bring Out Your Dead*. Philadelphia: University of Pennsylvania Press, 1949.

Pratt, Harry E. "The Famous 'Chicken Bone' Case." *JISHS* 45 (Summer 1952):164–67.

Reed, E. A. "Understanding Tort Law: The Historical Basis of Medical Liability." *JLM* 5 (1977):50–53.

Reiser, Stanley Joel. *Medicine and the Reign of Technology*. New York: Cambridge University Press, 1978.

Rieff, Philip. *The Triumph of the Therapeutic*. New York: Harper and Row, 1966.

Risse, Guenter B., Ronald L. Numbers, and Judith Walzer Leavitt, eds. *Medicine Without Doctors: Home Health Care in American History*. New York: Science History Publications, 1977.

Rogers, Tommy W. "Dr. Fredrick Ross and the Presbyterian Defense of Slavery." *JPH* 45 (1967):112–24.

Rosen, George. *Fees and Fee Bills: Some Economic Aspects of Medical Practice in Nineteenth Century America*. Supplement to the *Bulletin of the History of Medicine*, no. 6. Baltimore: Johns Hopkins University Press, 1946.

Rosenberg, Charles E. "The American Medical Profession: Mid–Nineteenth Century." *MA* 44 (1962):163–71.

———. *The Cholera Years: The United States in 1832, 1849, and 1866*. Chicago: University of Chicago Press, 1962.

———. "The Therapeutic Revolution: Medicine, Meaning, and Social Change in Nineteenth-Century America." In *The Therapeutic Revolution: Medicine, Meaning, and Change in Nineteenth-Century America*, edited by Morris J. Vogel and Charles E. Rosenberg. Philadelphia: University of Pennsylvania Press, 1979.

———. "Medical Text and Social Context: Explaining William Buchan's *Domestic Medicine*." *BHM* 57 (1983):22–42.

———. *The Care of Strangers: The Rise of America's Hospital System*. New York: Basic Books, 1987.

Rothstein, William G. *American Physicians in the Nineteenth Century*. Baltimore: Johns Hopkins University Press, 1972.

Sandor, Andrew A. "The History of Professional Liability Suits in the United States." *JAMA* 163 (1957):459–66.

Sandusk, Joseph F. "Analysis of Profesional Factors in Medical Malpractice Claims." *JAMA* 161 (2 June 1956):442–47.

Saum, Lewis O. "Providence in the Popular Mind of Pre–Civil War America." *IMH* 72 (1976):315–46.

———. *The Popular Mind of Pre–Civil War America*. Westport, Conn.: Greenwood Press, 1980.

Savitt, Todd L. "The Use of Blacks for Medical Experimentation and

Demonstration in the Old South," *Journal of Southern History* 48 (1982): 331–48.

Schlesinger, Arthur M. *The Age of Jackson*. Boston: Little, Brown, 1945.

Shafer, Henry Burnell. *The American Medical Profession, 1783–1850*. New York: AMS Press, 1968.

Shikes, Robert H. *Rocky Mountain Medicine: Doctors, Drugs, and Disease in Early Colorado*. Boulder, Colo.: Johnson Books, 1986.

Shryock, Richard Harrison. *Medicine and Society in America, 1660–1860*. Ithaca: Cornell University Press, 1960.

———. *Medical Licensing in America, 1650–1965*. Baltimore: Johns Hopkins University Press, 1967.

Simpson, A. W. B. *Legal Theory and Legal History: Essays on the Common Law*. London: Hambledon Press, 1987.

Smith, Hubert Winston. "Legal Responsibility for Medical Malpractice." *JAMA* 116 (1941):942–47, 2149–59; 2670–79; and *JAMA* 117 (1941):23–33.

Speer, James B. "Malpractice: The Historical Viewpoint." In *Proceedings of the Malpractice Conference: The Interaction of Medicine and Justice Through Public Policy*. Edited by Donnie J. Self. N.P.: East Virginia Medical School, Old Dominion University, 1976.

Stage, Sarah. *Female Complaints: Lydia Pinkham and the Business of Women's Medicine*. New York: Norton, 1971.

Starr, Paul. "Medicine, Economy, and Society in Nineteenth-Century America." *JSocH* 10 (1977):588–607.

———. *The Social Transformation of American Medicine*. New York: Basic Books, 1982.

Stetler, Joseph C. "The History of Reported Medical Professional Liability Cases." *TLQ* 30 (1957):366–83.

Sunderland, Edson R. *Cases on Procedure Annotated, Code Pleading*. Philadelphia: Callaghan, 1913.

———. *Cases on Procedure Code Pleading*. Chicago: Callaghan, 1923.

Schwartz, Bernard. *Law in America*. New York: McGraw-Hill, 1974.

Thomas, John L. "Romantic Reform in America, 1815–1865." *American Quarterly* 17 (Winter 1965):656–81.

Thomas, Keith. *Religion and the Decline of Magic: Studies in Popular Beliefs in the Sixteenth and Seventeenth Centuries in England*. London: Weidenfeld, 1971.

Tilton, Eleanor M. "Lightning Rods and the Earthquake of 1755." *NEQ* 13 (1940):85–97.

Tomlins, Christopher L. "A Mysterious Power: Industrial Accidents and the Legal Construction of Employee Relations in Massachusetts, 1800–1850." *LHR* 6 (Fall 1988):375–438.

Turner, James. *Reckoning with the Beast: Animals, Pain, and Humanity in the Victorian Mind*. Baltimore: Johns Hopkins University Press, 1980.

Verbrugge, Martha J. *Able-Bodied Womanhood: Personal Health and Social Change in Nineteenth-Century Boston*. New York: Oxford University Press, 1988.

Waiz, Jon R. "The Rise and Gradual Fall of the Locality Rule in Medical Malpractice Litigation." *DPLR* 17 (1969):408–21.

Walters, Ronald G. *American Reformers, 1815–1860.* New York: Hill and Wang, 1978.

Ward, John William. *Andrew Jackson—Symbol for an Age.* New York: Oxford University Press, 1953.

Waring, Joseph I. "Charleston Medicine, 1800–1860." *JHMAS* 31 (July 1976):320–342.

Warner, John Harley. "Southern Medical Reform: The Meaning of the Antebellum Argument for Southern Medical Education." *BHM* 57 (Fall 1983): 364–81.

———. *The Therapeutic Perspective: Medical Practice, Knowledge, and Professional Identity in America, 1820–1885.* Cambridge: Harvard University Press, 1986.

Warren, Charles. *A History of the American Bar.* Boston: Little, Brown, 1911.

Weaver, R. M. "The Older Religiousness in the South." *SR* 51 (1943):237–45.

Weigel, Charles J. "Medical Malpractice in America's Middle Years." *TRBM* 32 (1974):191–205.

Welter, Rush. *The Mind of America, 1820–1860.* New York: Columbia University Press, 1975.

Westfall, Richard S. *The Construction of Modern Science Mechanisms and Mechanics.* New York: John Wiley, 1971.

White, G. Edward. *Tort Law in America: An Intellectual History.* New York: Oxford University Press, 1980.

Whorton, James C. *Crusaders for Fitness: The History of American Health Reformers.* Princeton: Princeton University Press, 1982.

Wiebe, Robert H. *The Search for Order, 1877–1920.* New York: Hill and Wang, 1967.

Williams, Mitchell G. "Pleading Reform in Nineteenth-Century America: The Joinder of Actions at Common Law Under the Codes." *JLH* 6 (1985): 299–335.

Wilson, Major L. "Paradox Lost: Order in Evangelical Thought of Mid–Nineteenth-Century America." *CH* 44 (1975):352–66.

Winfield, Percy H. *The Province of Tort.* Cambridge: Cambridge University Press, 1931.

Wood, Gordon. *The Creation of the American Republic, 1776–1787.* New York: Norton, 1969.

Woodward, C. Vann. *The Burden of Southern History.* Baton Rouge: Louisiana State University Press, 1968.

Wyatt-Brown, Bertram. *Southern Honor: Ethics and Behavior in the Old South.* New York: Oxford University Press, 1982.

Young, James Harvey. *The Toadstool Millionaires: A Social History of Patent Medicines in America before Federal Regulation.* Princeton: Princeton University Press, 1961.

Zuckerman, Michael. *Peaceable Kingdoms: New England Towns in the Eighteenth Century.* New York: Random House, 1970.

Index